THE OYSTER

Volumes One, Two and Three

The Oyster Omnibus

Anonymous

NEW ENGLISH LIBRARY
Hodder & Stoughton

The Oyster Copyright © 1985 by New English Library Ltd
The Oyster 2 Copyright © 1986 by Glenthorne Historical Associates
The Oyster 3 Copyright © 2001 by Glenthorne Historical Research

This collected volume published in paperback in 2001
by Hodder and Stoughton

A NEL Paperback

10 9 8 7 6 5 4 3

A CIP catalogue record for this title
is available from the British Library.

ISBN 0 340 62333 0

Printed and bound in Great Britain by
Mackays of Chatham plc, Chatham, Kent

Hodder and Stoughton
A division of Hodder Headline
338 Euston Road
London NW1 3BH

BOOK ONE

PUBLISHER'S FOREWORD

THE PEARL was perhaps the most famous of all underground magazines which flourished in Britain throughout the mid-Victorian years. The first issue was published in London in July, 1879 and eighteen editions were printed until its sudden closure in December, 1880.

Although this monthly 'journal of facetiae and voluptuous reading' was given a brazen *imprimatur* of 'Oxford: at the University Press', in actual fact the magazine was brought out privately by a mysterious individual named Lazenby who—according to G. Legman, that indefatigable researcher and writer on erotica—published and indeed wrote much of the contents under the pseudonym of D. Cameron. Another contributor, says Legman, was the noted journalist and war correspondent George Augustus Sala but the identities of the other correspondents will probably never be revealed.

After the sudden disappearance of *The Pearl*, other similar magazines were quickly produced to take its place in the highly efficient subterranean marketing system that existed throughout the 1880s and 90s for the distribution of forbidden literature. Lazenby/Cameron offered *The Cremorne* whilst others of the same ilk that flourished during this period included *The Boudoir* and *The Oyster*.

And it is from *The Oyster*, one of the successors to the much imitated *Pearl*, that the novel in this volume is taken. Sir Andrew Scott began his reminiscences of his schooldays in an earlier issue (reprinted in *The Pearl, Volume Three*, New English Library) and this longer extract is very much in the

5

same vein. Although prurient, it is well worth noting that like all the other material from *The Oyster* the novelette eschews sado-masochistic behaviour, flagellation and the even grosser sexual perversions such as pederasty and incest that cropped up regularly in many other such publications.

Whilst little attempt is made by our unknown author to write in any serious depth, and although the characters are at best two-dimensional, there is yet a pungent, lively spirit and a bawdy vitality in the writing which is rarely found in collections of popular erotica from this rather stuffy period of British history.

Certainly there can be little doubt that Sir Andrew Scott thoroughly enjoyed penning his memoir of youthful sexual frolics even if the apparent ease of finding ready and willing partners somewhat stretches our credulity. Perhaps we should heed the words of a more famous scribe of the time, Oscar Wilde, who once commented that: 'Memory is the diary we all carry about with us, even if it chronicles events that never happened and could not possibly have happened.' Yet it may be wrong to dismiss the narrative totally as mere boastful fantasising, despite the extraordinary ease of conquest displayed. Whilst a far stronger taboo on sex before marriage then existed, coupled of course with a very real fear of unwanted pregnancy, we know full well that many Victorian ladies were far less strait-laced than usually depicted either then or now. Amongst the upper crust, to take a well-documented example, there was often much flitting between bedrooms at country house weekend parties. Conversely, in all large British cities throughout the mid to late nineteenth century there were a shameful number of prostitutes (including a high number of under-age girls and boys driven to the brothels by abject hunger and often appalling poverty) to quench the sexual appetites of the lonely and the repressed.

So there may well be more than a kernel of truth in the narrative even if Sir Andrew has doubtless embellished his personal account of sexual discovery! He writes, it should be remembered, not as a social historian but primarily for his own enjoyment, and perhaps his account of how he came to

6

write his memoir is quite true, and he did indeed compose the story sitting at a writing desk in the sumptuous library of his friend, Sir Lionel T——(whose name, incidentally, crops up in previous issues of *The Oyster*). One can only hazard a guess as to the identity of this gentleman, but he could well be Sir Lionel Trapes (1826-1908), a high-ranking Treasury official and patron of the arts who was a member of the circle that included '*Pisanus Fraxi*', alias H. Spencer Ashbee, the doyen of all collectors of erotic and gallant literature.

Scott, then, writes to titillate and amuse and not to instruct, and it must be admitted that he writes with some genuine style, keeping the simple story moving as briskly as he can between the frequent bouts of sexual grappling. He appears to have been a man of straightforward sexual taste although, somewhat unusually for this age, he regards oral sex quite equitably and takes no joy whatsoever from the idea of giving or receiving corporal 'punishment' in the bedroom.

The Oyster continued to thrive until 1889. The last recorded issue just preceded the first public news about the notorious Cleveland Street scandal, a *cause célèbre* that involved the exposure of a high-class homosexual brothel where Post Office messenger boys were encouraged to participate in sexual acts with some extremely well-known personages. Indeed, it has been suggested that the demise of the magazine was not unconnected with the hasty flight to France of Lord Arthur Somerset, a close friend and equerry to the Prince of Wales, who was heavily implicated in the Cleveland Street affair. Lord Arthur and Lord Euston were just two of a raffish group of men-about-town who were well known for their varied and robust sexual proclivities.

Other magazines appeared at regular intervals and these along with *The Pearl* and *The Oyster* provided a platform of resistance to the suffocating, guilt-ridden climate in which they appeared. They set themselves firmly against the notion that sexuality was an area over which the Establishment should exercise a stringent, rigid control and this led to a more sceptical, questioning attitude which in turn brought

7

about the more relaxed and understanding liberal philosophy that by and large exists today.

The writers in these 'underground' magazines of our great-grandparents show that even during the stern days of Bowdlerism, when even piano legs were covered for the sake of a false and imaginary 'decency', there was still a fierce questioning of taboos, and there existed a simple desire to explore frankly the actual mechanics of sexuality.

There may be some who question the need to produce and to receive explicit works, but the modern acceptance of the view that adults must in general be allowed to read whatever they desire has its origins in such material as is produced in this jolly little book.

The identity of Sir Andrew Scott and others of his ilk will remain unknown. Although they should not, perhaps, be regarded as pioneers of freedom of expression, it is none-theless most probable that they wrote purely for pleasure, and not merely for financial gain. Even so, it would be naive to suppose that the question of payment never crossed their minds. It should be pointed out, however, that whilst *The Pearl, The Oyster*, and other similar magazines were strictly illegal, there is little evidence of a rich black market for pornography, although there were doubtless several printers who would gladly have risked prosecution to print saucy material on an undercover basis. Lazenby and Cameron certainly made money out of publishing *The Pearl*, but what of the writers such as Scott? He writes with some erudition and is by no means averse to slipping in the occasional French, Italian or even Latin phrase, or regaling the reader with bouts of philosophising in between the more robust pieces of action. Some readers will recognise in his opening paragraphs the Platonic argument taken from the prologue of *The Republic* about the advantages and disadvantages of old age.

Without any genuine hard evidence to back up one's supposition, only mere conjecture can be made as to Scott's true identity. In the manner of the born gossip, he tan-talisingly gives only the Christian names of his friends, most of whom appear to be titled. Indeed, he himself may well have been one of the idle, wealthy young men who took morning rides down Rotten Row, enjoyed huge lunches and lazy afternoons at their clubs and spent their evenings either at formal dinner parties or at the already popular music halls and theatres where hordes of ladies of pleasure awaited these sybaritic young drones.

My own view is that Scott was probably a writer. Not necessarily a professional hack on one of the fledgling popular newspapers that were surfacing throughout this era, but an occasional contributor to one of the many magazines and reviews that flourished during the 1880s. His apparent lack of interest in bondage and flagellation would appear to rule out George Augustus Sala, but he was most certainly a member of a similar semi-leisured circle willing and eager to spin out a tale for the amusement of his friends.

Copies of these and other works have fortunately survived to delight and amuse us as well as to provide an unusual and unconventional insight into the manners and mores of a vanished world, the reverse side to the coin of iron-clad respectability which appeared to characterise British society some hundred years ago.

Antoinette Hillman-Strauss
March, 1985

PREFACE TO THE FIRST EDITION

What it is that causes my lord to smack his chops in that wanton, lecherous manner, as he is sauntering up and down Bond Street, with his glass in hand, to watch the ladies getting in and out of their carriages? And what is it that draws together such vast crowds of the holiday gentry at Easter and Whitsuntide to see the merry rose-faced lassies running down the hill in Greenwich Park? What is it causes such a roar of laughter when a merry girl happens to overset in her career and kick her heels in the air? Lastly, as the parsons all say, what is it that makes the theatrical ballet so popular?

There is a magic in the sight of a female leg, which is hardly in the power of mere language to describe, for to be conceived it must be felt.

Most of my readers will be acquainted from experience with that magic which emanates from the sight of a pretty leg, a delicate ankle and a well-proportioned calf.

Your editor never sees a pretty leg but feels certain unutterable emotions within him, which as the poet puts it:

Should some fair youth, the charming sight explore,
In rapture he'll gaze, and wish for something more!

The Editor of The Oyster

Thus in the zenith of my lust I reign;
I eat to swive, and swive to eat again;
Let other monarchs, who their sceptres bear
To keep their subjects less in love than fear
Be salves to crowns, my nation shall be free;
My pintle only shall my sceptre be,
My laws shall act more pleasure than command,
And with my prick I'll govern all the land.

Bolloxinion, King of Sodom or The Quintessence of Debauchery
The Earl of Rochester (1647-1680)

CHAPTER ONE

A FOND RECOLLECTION OF YOUTHFUL DAYS—
BY SIR ANDREW SCOTT

WHEN EVEN now I awaken in the still darkness of the night with a sudden start that appears to possess no apparent physical origin, when I am driven mad with passion and feel my hands stealing down to caress my ramrod-hard pego, then I know that the sweet dreams fast vanishing, alas, into the shelter of oblivion must have contained at least a fragment of fantasy about my darling Lucy, or one of the other young ladies who helped make my formative years so pleasurable during those dear days almost beyond recall.

I refer, my friendly reader, to the times spent as a schoolboy at the Nottsgrove Academy for Young Gentlemen situated near the pleasant hamlet of Arkley, deep in the wilds of rural Hertfordshire. Perhaps my first essay upon the delights of studying at that most progressive academy, penned for a previous issue of our esteemed journal, is not unknown to you. [See *The Pearl, Volume 3.*] Though the years have passed by, the pictures of Lucy will never vanish from my brain: her dear face next to mine, close enough for me to see her lips parting with desire; her ripe body touching mine, setting me on fire with carnal yearnings, clasping me with pleading urgency.

Ah, sweet recollections of lying naked on crushed and rumpled sheets, watching the early morning sunlight caress my sated, sleeping lover, listening to the muted sounds beyond the boudoir as the countryside wakes to another morn. Alas, often when old men meet together, many are full of woes. They hanker still for the joys of youth, remembering how in their spring years they would besport themselves with wine, women and song all hours of the day and night. Now, in the autumn of their time upon this planet, they think it is a great deprivation that those times are way behind them. Life was good then, they moan, whereas now they feel that they hardly live at all. I do not agree with this pessimistic outlook, for old age has the advantage of offering more time for contemplation and relaxation. I look back with much enjoyment upon my memories of a boisterous youth, and utterly refuse to allow my old age to be crabbed, for my recollections are to me as a fine summer's day of much sunshine and few clouds.

One further word before I open my store of the times that have passed. Hopefully we shall see the day when science and not theology will become the arbiter of personal morality; when pure reason, unfettered by the bumbling antics of well-meaning but ignorant clergymen, bound and limited by the dogmas of preconception, will seek and find sane and sensible standards of civilised conduct between the sexes.

For I hold that there is no distinction to be found between the sexual needs of the married and unmarried, as a young man's passion does not suddenly awaken at the moment of his betrothal. Nor are the desires of a widow permanently extinguished upon the death of her spouse. The number of predatory widows in London Society is proof enough, and the names of such ladies may be omitted here as they are well-known to all the many gentlemen who frequent the salons of Belgravia and Mayfair. So Lady Cecilia A—— and Mrs Hester S—— may with others of their ilk rest easy, as I do not propose revealing their secret lives in this manuscript.

Fortunately our century has produced an abundance of publications proclaiming the delights of the body in all its forms. And now I offer my own journey down the lane of memory as a humble addition to those other memoirs penned by that group of lusty scribes who have built up such a fine stock of gallant literature.

16

Finally, I would add only this—no apology will be forthcoming from me for putting into print this highly charged erotic narrative, as I feel assured that every devotee of voluptuous reading will derive as much, or hopefully even more, pleasure than that afforded your humble author in the writing of this epistle. I would like to thank my old friend and mentor Sir Lionel T——, himself an Old Nottsgrovian, for allowing me the use of his fine library to compose this work, and I end this prologue with the wise words of Boccaccio:

If in my tales there are a few words rather freer than suits the prudes, who weigh words more than deeds and take more pains to appear than to be good, I say I should no more be reproved for having written them than other folk are daily reproved for saying 'hole', 'peg', 'mortar', 'sausage' and like things.

No corrupt mind ever understands words healthily. And just as such people do not enjoy virtuous words, so the well-disposed cannot be harmed by words somewhat less virtuous, any more than mud can sully sunlight or earthly filth the beauty of the skies.

Those of us fortunate enough to have studied under the wise and caring guidance of Doctor Simon White will always salute the achievements of this remarkable scholar whose main educational aim was to break the shackles that bind us to a false morality. He showed his pupils that in his learned opinion, throughout man's past, throughout all known civilisations of both East and West, there have always been conflicts between the desires of some and the imposed wills of others. Sometimes, one class has been in a minority, sometimes it has been the other; but the rule holds good and indeed, it seems but only yesterday that I was back in my favourite chair in the prefects' room at Nottsgrove Academy, listening with the other senior boys to our dear old headmaster espousing his theories of philosophy with that characteristic passion and lucidity that were hallmarks of his delivery of a lecture to us. I should say that he encouraged argument and never attempted to indoctrinate us against our.

wills. But I digress, so I shall take up again the strands of memory to a day of excitement at Nottsgrove.

It was a lazy summer afternoon during my last term at Nottsgrove. The day's classes had ended and I was busily engaged in deciding what news to pen in my obligatory letter home (no excuses for the absence of such an epistle were ever allowed), when Doctor White entered the hallowed portals of the prefects' common room to pin up a notice of forth-coming sports fixtures upon the wall board.

After a moment or two my old friend Pelham Forbes-Mackenzie asked the good doctor some trifling question about a paper on modern philosophy that he was preparing for the summer examination—and of course this was more than enough to set our much loved and respected old pedagogue on course for yet another lecture about the faults of present-day civilisation.

'My dear old chap,' he boomed, 'never forget how we are unchained in body yet still shackled mentally to grossly outdated ideas that make our lives unnecessarily worrisome. But soon, Forbes-Mackenzie, very soon we shall face a climax in this continual struggle between, upon one hand, estab-lished authority with its clutch of beliefs and rituals and, upon the other, the soon-to-be-awakened intelligence of the until now uninformed, ignorant masses!'

All conversation in the room ceased, as we knew that the Doctor always enjoyed as large an audience as possible for his little speeches, and I sat back to hear him continue.

'To deflect the attack on these taboos which will be made when the general education of the common people is completed,' he announced, 'I believe that our so-called masters and betters will attempt to reinforce all those rules and regulations (which they themselves often ignore!) in an attempt to hold back the natural flow of self-understanding and enlightenment that mass education will surely bring.

'It is up to you all, the new leaders of the Empire, to resist these oppressive inroads before they are firmly established as the laws of the land, as unchangeable as those of the Medes and Persians!' he thundered.

'Above all, it is in your interests to fight the good fight! I know that you boys think of little else in your hours of free time except the desirability of fucking a pretty girl. Well, if the new barbarians achieve their ends, all you will ever be able to do is think about it until the time that you may marry!'

When our headmaster was firmly mounted upon his hobbyhorse, it took a great deal of energy to persuade him to dismount! Of course, those readers who have perused my previous recollections of life at Nottsgrove will recall that we fortunate boys who studied under his care were given a most pleasing row across the sexual Rubicon by the doctor's young niece, Lucy, and by other young ladies of her acquaintance all, of course, to further Doctor White's belief in freedom in all social and personal relationships.

However, to return to that particular afternoon, Pelham turned to me after the Doctor had finally swept out of the room after finishing his oration and said: 'Andrew, my old chap, I believe that in your case, our headmaster has translated principle into practice as far as relations with the fair sex are concerned?'

'This is so,' I replied carefully. 'I received my first lesson from Lucy some ten days ago.'

'That's damned unfair,' complained my friend. 'I have yet to fuck my first girl and I am only three months younger than you.'

'Well, that is something you should perhaps speak about to a higher authority than I, for it is up to Doctor White to decide when a fellow is ready to lose his virginity,' I said, trying very hard to keep any note of gloating or superiority from my voice. Pelham was a hot-tempered chap and easily angered, but his temper was short and not malignant. His name, of course, may not be totally unfamiliar to readers of this chronicle as he later made a great name for himself in the 13th Hussars in India and later in Canada. A very striking and commanding figure, even as a youth, he possessed a strong, determined face—and as we will later find out, an equally determined pego! But while he had a fierce exterior, there lay behind it a warm and kindly heart, and I never knew

19

a better friend, so I had no desire to upset his injured sensibilities any further as he furrowed his brow in anger.

'I do think it is time for my turn now!' he said crossly.

I urged him to speak to Doctor White whose administration, it must be admitted, could be a little slipshod if truth be told, as his memory was cluttered with so many matters to which he had to give his fullest attention. Thankfully, he accepted my advice and marched off directly to tackle the headmaster directly as to why he was still waiting for his first encounter in *l'art de faire l'amour.*

Later that evening, only half an hour or so before lights-out, one of the doctor's house-servants knocked upon the door of my study and announced that the headmaster wished to see me immediately. It was a warm July night and I was dressed only in a shirt and trousers and, as the matter seemed of such prime urgency, I slipped on a jacket and followed the man to the door of Dr White's private domain. I knew he would forgive my omission of a waistcoat and tie, as punctuality was a virtue he prized highly.

It occurred to me that in all probability my call was in connection with the truly heartfelt plea Pelham had made to Doctor White to be allowed to cross the Rubicon—and indeed, my premonition was soon to be proved absolutely correct. For when I knocked smartly on the door of the headmaster's private chambers, instead of a deep, somewhat gruff voice commanding me to enter, there was a soft sound of a muffled little giggle. Instantly I knew that the little minx Lucy was behind the door waiting for me—possibly alone but more probably with Pelham, as she had used my services before to demonstrate the art of fucking to newcomers to the sport.

Without further ado I opened the door and, as I had expected, there was the pretty little filly attired simply in a light blue cotton robe that she was very fond of wearing, especially as it had been a birthday gift from Doctor White. It was a wide, sweeping garment with ruffles, held together only by a blue sash of the same material. From underneath, the intoxicating aroma of her luscious young body poured out, mingling subtly with the French perfume I knew that she had dabbed between her bare breasts. And there, standing forlornly, without a stitch of clothing to his name, was poor Pelham looking a trifle shamefacedly down at the floor.

'My dear Andrew,' smiled Lucy. 'As you can see from the droop of his little pego, your friend is rather nervous. Perhaps he is a little frightened of me. Will you help me put him at his ease?'

'We can easily cure this malady, my sweet Lucy, by showing him how to fuck like a gentleman!' I said, already fired by the stunning beauty of this delicious girl.

'Those are my sentiments exactly,' she agreed, and as if by a prearranged mutual signal, we both stepped forward and engaged in a hearty embrace. As we kissed and our mouths opened to receive each other's tongues, Lucy tugged at the sash of her gown to untie the simple knot. The sash fell to the ground, the gown opened and she stepped out in all her naked glory. She stood before me like a statue crafted by a master sculptor come magically to life. Below the roots of her golden blonde hair, her creamy white skin was of an incredible softness. Her beautiful full breasts were as firm and round as two globes; her well-rounded shoulders tapered down into a small waist; her small feet, with delicate ankles, expanded upwards into fine calves, her thighs were full and proportionately made, whilst hanging down between them, forming a perfect veil over the pouting little slit, was a mass of silky blonde hair that contrasted so well with the snowy whiteness of her belly. As we writhed about in each other's arms, I managed to disengage myself of my clothes and my prick began to leap and prance about between her thighs, seeking an entrance into the hospitable retreat that awaited him. Her breasts rose and fell with the quickening pace of her breathing but I realised that I had to instruct Pelham in the full range of lovemaking. I therefore disengaged my mouth from her burning kiss and sank down to my knees, pushing her down onto the carpet. I squeezed those gorgeous orbs and ran my fingers over the stiff, engorged nipples that stood out like taps waiting to be drawn upon, then, as I heard her gasp with

21

pleasure, I buried my face in the thick brush of fluffy pubic hair. I grasped her lovely bottom cheeks as I flashed my tongue round the damp motte. She whimpered as her pussy opened wide and I slipped my probing tongue between the pinky sex lips. I felt myself flicking against her stiffening clitty as I licked and licked in long thrusting strokes. Her cunny was now gushing love-juice and as you may well imagine, my young pego was straining at the leash.

Lucy moaned with desire and I knew that such a sound heralded her wish to receive me fully. I raised my head and Lucy lay flat on her back on the lush green carpet with her legs spread wide to await the arrival of Mr Pego. She reached out and grasped my swollen rod, which was now in its prime state of erection. She caressed the throbbing shaft and I knew the time had come to conclude the overture and begin the performance in earnest.

I knelt between her sturdy white legs as she handled my prick so gently that I was concerned that I might come in her hands before I had tasted the full delights of her juicy quim.

'Come now, Andrew,' she murmured. 'Let's show Pelham how to do this exercise properly.'

As she guided my throbbing cock into her moist crack I noticed that Pelham's thick prick was now swollen upwards as he watched Lucy guide my cock into her warm, moist love channel. To hold her creamy buttocks was sheer delight and to suck her stiff little pink nipples was just too much for me. As soon as Lucy began to massage the underside of my balls I pumped wildly into her eager cunt and she groaned with delight as the gush of my juices sent wave upon wave of erotic energy passing through our bodies.

I knew that the delicious girl needed more fucking and that I had to be unselfish and let Pelham have his way with her. I heaved myself off Lucy and, after a questioning glance, Pelham gently lowered himself upon her, his body quivering with anticipation of the joys to come. There was a brief moment before his tight little arse was lowered and Lucy moaned when he finally managed to guide his excited cock into her. Although this was his first fuck, Pelham had a

And also naked was his companion who was lying on the bed slowly frigging his standing prick as if keeping it in a state ready for use. I peered forward and saw that it was Gilbert Bell, a third-form boy who was supposedly ill with a severe cold. He too was fourteen or fifteen years of age, a tall slender boy whose girlish features had caused him to bear the brunt of much teasing by his classmates.

Jack lay down on the bed and began to rub his own prick up and down until it too was in a fine state of erection. He slipped the skin of the shaft down from the red mushroomed head and said to Gilbert, 'Well, shall we see who can come quicker, you or me? Mind you, it would not be a fair contest as you've been frigging your prick for at least five minutes already.'

'Alright, Jack, on the count of three. One, two, three, go!' And to my surprise they began fondling each other's cocks (fortunately Gilbert was left-handed) and, sure enough, within moments they both began to spend with the first spurtings of white juice shooting out of their pricks like miniature fountains.

Pelham was about to speak and no doubt halt the proceedings, but I put my finger to my mouth and motioned him towards the door. When we were back in the corridor and I had shut the sanitarium door, he exclaimed: 'Why didn't you let me stop those two dirty beasts?'

'Look, we've had a jolly time and those two will forget the pleasures of solitary vice once Doctor White introduces them to nice girls like Lucy!' I said, feeling generous to one and all in anticipation of frolics the next night.

'Well, I don't know about that,' said Pelham with a dubious note to his voice.

'Live and let live!' I said cheerily as we strolled back to our studies.

'Plato believed that punishment brought wisdom,' remarked Pelham somewhat pompously.

'Ah yes, and Aristotle viewed it as a kind of medicine,' I replied gaily.

'But then Oscar Wilde has written that punishment is often

25

more brutalising than the crime—which I find difficult to believe,' said Pelham.

'I'm not so sure,' I said thoughtfully. 'Would it have made any difference if you had swished young Bell! I have grave doubts about that and you remember what Doctor White is always telling us. Mankind's efforts to enforce conformity in social morality has had a truly disastrous record of failure.'

'I suppose so, for it is true that no-one has yet devised a system of punishment that immunises society from evil or revolt.'

'So there you are. Good night, Pelham. I've just remembered that there's only a morning's lessons to be slept through tomorrow, as in the afternoon we are playing cricket against the Savages from High Barnet.'

'Good night, Andrew. Yes, we can sit and snooze whilst our team thrashes those yokels and then there is the evening to look forward to. My, I have only one regret.'

'What's that?' I asked.

'That Doctor White did not let Lucy initiate me into the arts of love last term!' he laughed. I joined in his merriment and we both undressed quickly and prepared for bed. Tomorrow would be a day worth waiting for!

I will pass over much of the happenings of that day, though I recall well how we eyed the clock frequently, waiting for the tedious hours to pass till the time appointed to meet our partners for the evening's frolics. Suffice it to say that somehow we managed to pay sufficient attention to our lessons in the morning to escape detention or extra evening preparation. We spent most of the afternoon lolling in the grass watching, as I had forecast, Nottsgrove's senior cricketers easily vanquish the team of gentlemen farmers from neighbouring High Barnet.

After a light meal, Pelham and I decided to take a short stroll through nearby Arkley Woods.

'We should have some fun tonight, old boy,' I said to Pelham, who looked somewhat thoughtful as we walked towards the quiet of Oaklands Lane.

'Yes, Andrew, I am looking forward to it tremendously,' he replied. 'I am just a little worried that Mr Priapus will fail me as he did with Lucy.'

I laughed and reassured him that he had little about which to worry. 'My dear old chap,' I said, 'The first time or two you will naturally be nervous, but once you become accomplished all will be well.' I could see by the bulge in his breeches that he was already thinking about the joys to come that evening, and I laid my hand on the pulsating swelling. 'My goodness, Pelham,' I said. 'I am sure that your prick is even bigger than mine. Let us compare and see who has the larger.'

Without ado I opened his trousers and let out his naked red-headed cock which stood in all its manly glory, stiff and hard as marble with the hot blood looking ready to burst from his distended veins. He then pulled out my own not inconsiderable affair which was, as it happened, fractionally shorter in length, which must have given Pelham further confidence for the evening's entertainment. We handled each other's tools in an orgy of delight during which I spunked creamy jets of froth onto his hand. I then dropped to my knees and played and sucked his delicious prick till he spent in my mouth with an exclamation of rapture, as I eagerly swallowed every last drop of his copious emission.

When we had recovered our serenity we walked back to the school, still pulsating with unsatisfied desire, to await with scarcely concealed impatience the appointed time of half past eight o'clock. And who could find it in his heart to blame us for wanting to speed the passage of time as the hands of the clock seemed to move so slowly! Ah, the fire of passion that coursed through our youthful bodies is now but an ember, though my torch is still capable of lighting a fire or two! Many a good tune is played upon an old fiddle!

CHAPTER TWO

IN MY experience, most pretty girls are not friendly towards one another, thinking perhaps that an equally attractive companion may turn some of the attention of the gentlemen present in the company. In fact, Lucy was not one of this flighty breed, and she chose her friends of the fair sex for their true qualities rather than any other. And indeed, this was well shown that marvellous summer evening.

The sultry day had ended with one of those wonderful sunset skies—with such gold as Cuyp himself never painted—though if truth be told both Pelham and myself were far too agitated to enjoy fully the beauties of nature. I cautioned my friend not to eat too hearty a meal. Somehow, we contained our impatience until the time came for us to wander through the cool of the old schoolrooms to our arranged meeting place. As we reached the bedroom door I could see Pelham trembling with excitement.

'Look, old man,' I said to him, 'Don't worry if you have, ah, starting problems again. Just relax and let yourself be swept along with the tide, so to speak.'

'Yes, Andrew, thank you for the advice,' he said. 'I suppose you can see that I am nervous.'

'Well, just don't fret yourself,' I said firmly. 'Fucking is as natural as swimming. All you have to learn is to do what comes naturally and all will be well.'

'I hope she's a pretty girl, this friend of Lucy's,' he muttered. 'Would you like to be a good chap and pair off with her and leave Lucy for me?'

I smiled as I guessed that Lucy would not be satisfied until we had tried every known sexual permutation but I judged it best to leave Pelham in ignorance of the full joys awaiting him behind the door which stood before us.

'Don't worry, Pelham,' I promised. 'I'll stay with Amelia whilst you and Lucy do whatever takes your fancy.'

I knocked lightly upon the door and I heard a little giggle and then Lucy called out for us to enter. I opened the door and ushered Pelham in. The room was dark as the girls had closed the curtains and only two lamps lit the large room. I closed the door and locked it behind me. Although the girls were obviously there, we could not see them. Then we heard another muffled giggle from the far side of the large bed and I grinned—so that was where the two hussies were hiding!

'I can hear you though I cannot see you!' I called out, 'you are discovered, my pretties!' At this Lucy rose from her hiding place and to my amazement the delicious girl was quite naked! Although I had seen her in a state of nudity before, I gasped with admiration at her uptilted breasts, her flat stomach and the thick blonde mass of hair at the base of her belly. In a trice I rid myself of my shirt, trousers, socks and boots, and I moved purposefully towards her. We embraced and now it was my turn to tremble with delight as I felt the touch of her lips and the soft probing of her tongue in my mouth. My cock was now as stiff as a poker and ready for action. Though I could hardly wait to plunge Priapus into her waiting love bush, I knew what Lucy preferred me to do beforehand. So with a gentle effort I reclined her backwards upon the bed and moved my head down between her splendid white legs where the luscious, pouting lips of her cunny, quite vermilion in colour and slightly gaping open, invited my attention as she drew her legs further apart.

I was down on my knees in a moment and I glued my lips to that lovely little crack, sucking and kissing furiously to the infinite delight of the delicious girl who sighed and groaned with pleasure. It was now impossible to hold back, and getting up on my knees I brought my straining shaft to the charge and, to Lucy's high squeal of delight, fairly ran it right through into the depths of her throbbing pussy until my balls banged hard against her bottom. We lay still for a few moments whilst Lucy's pulsating pussy squeezed my cock so beautifully that I almost swooned away with pleasure. She then heaved up her bottom and I responded to this move with a shove of my own and we commenced a most exciting struggle. My manly staff fairly glistened with love-juice as it worked in and out of her sheath, whilst the lips of her cunny seemed to cling to it at each time of withdrawal as if afraid of losing such a delightful sugar stick; but this did not last long as our movements got more and more furious; and then suddenly she was transformed into a wild animal, screeching as she bucked and jerked uncontrollably beneath me. Then, with a little wail she slumped backwards, her buttocks and thighs clenched as she shook all over in a rapid drawn-out series of tiny spasms. Her cunt squeezed my prick even tighter, and the continuous pressure was now too much for me to bear. I could feel the boiling sperm rising and then it surged out of me, spurting from my prick deep inside her secret parts in an orgasm that seemed to last and last as I pumped my creamy white froth into her juicy, dark warmth.

We lay there panting with exhaustion from our labours and to my surprise I could see young Pelham and Amelia standing stock still watching us in some kind of awe at our performance. Like Lucy, Amelia was quite naked. She was a tall girl blessed with long tresses of light auburn hair, slightly golden in tint, deep brown eyes set off by dark eyebrows and long dark eyelashes, a full mouth, richly-pouting cherry lips and a brilliant set of pearly white teeth. And what magnificent swelling young breasts she possessed, round and firm with a lovely whiteness of belly which was set off below by a bushy Mons Veneris, itself covered lightly with silken, reddish hair through which I could just perceive the outline of her slit. Her breathing had quickened with excitement brought about by the passion that she had just seen displayed in front of her, her eyes were unduly bright and her nostrils flared out like those of a stallion coming upon a mare in heat.

'Come on, you two slowcoaches,' called out Lucy. 'Why, Pelham, you still have your clothes on. That is almost an insult to Amelia. Don't you want to fuck her?'

'Oh, of course I do!' Pelham stammered out.

'I think he is just a little bit shy,' said Amelia gaily, as she stroked the huge bulge between Pelham's legs which showed well that his equipment was now in the finest working order. She gave the bulge an encouraging rub up and down with her hand and this had the desired effect of setting a match to the tinder.

This was indeed all the encouragement he needed and in a veritable flash he was undressed and I noticed his thick cock with its enormous red head was bolt upright. Amelia and Pelham rolled beside us in the huge bed and now it was our turn to take the part of spectators at the match.

Amelia was experienced enough to see that her partner was fast approaching the climax of delight so she climbed onto his lap facing him and squeezed her knees alongside his muscular thighs. She put one arm round his neck and felt for his cock with her other hand, adjusting her position as she slipped his rock-hard tool between them, fitting it snugly into her quim. When she was sure that the few inches were safely inside, she hugged him tightly, kissing the corners of his mouth, and whispered: 'Push your prick into me darling—harder, that's right, you won't hurt me, keep pushing!' She worked her hips up and down, riding slowly but firmly on the throbbing shaft, letting it sink all the way into her juicy snatch, holding it there completely engulfed.

Pelham was in his own private heaven now—too excited to remember that he was performing in front of an audience and, within a minute, I saw him shudder as the spunk began to gather for the finale. Amelia began to grind her bottom round and bounced up and down on his mighty cock. Pelham thrust upwards as his prick began to spurt, giving complete and utter satisfaction for them both. But Amelia was now a-fire and, to my astonishment, she shot out her right hand and grabbed my cock which immediately responded by standing smartly to attention as she rubbed it up to its peak condition.

'I hope you don't mind, Lucy, if I get Andrew to fuck me,' said the little minx with a great show of politeness.

'Not at all, my dear friend,' replied Lucy. 'Please feel free

31

to do so whilst I suck that lovely young prick of Pelham's which looks as if it still has some life in it.' And so saying, Lucy moved across me to kiss the end of Pelham's rod which was still oozing tiny drops of semen. Her tongue encircled his knob, savouring the juices and she drew him in between her rich, generous lips, sucking lustily as Pelham instinctively pushed upwards as her warm hands played with his heavy, hanging balls.

I was now more than ready for a further fray and I lifted myself onto my knees between Amelia's legs and quickly hooked them over my shoulders so that her bottom lifted entirely from the eiderdown and was immediately cupped in my hands. A low gurgle of anticipation escaped her and my tongue protruded, licking gently up between the lips of her slit whilst she bucked and writhed with pleasure. Heady as the salty musk taste of her was in those shell-like folds, I savoured too the lingering cream of her libation which had oiled her cunny as much as Pelham's pego had done just minutes before. 'Ahhh! Aaaah!' she cried as I found the pink bud of her clitoris which had erected itself like a miniature penis. My searching tongue made smaller and smaller circles till it probed that very centre of sensual enjoyment. Her rounded bottom began to move in rhythm with my explorations as I lashed juicily around the pearly flesh and gently nibbled at the swollen clitty, causing ripples of cum to spill over my tongue which I greedily slurped up.

Her heels drummed against my shoulders, her torso twisting, the silky cheeks of her plump bottom squirming in my palms whilst the tip of my tongue flicked remorselessly back and forth over her bud, diverting now and again to the sopping aperture of her cunny itself. Her quim literally mashed itself to my mouth bringing a fine salty sprinkling of her pleasure whilst I held the peach of her bottom cheeks drawn apart. 'Are you ready?' I whispered. 'Oh, yes, yes, put it in, dear Andrew without delay,' she gasped as raising my head, I slithered across her lovely body as her legs came crashing down on the bed. She opened them wide then curled them round my hips as she raised herself to meet my hungry pego. So willing and so ready was she that she clung to me as if she would draw the very last breath out as I thrust harder and harder, plunging again and again as she pulled me even deeper inside her. She reached climax after climax as my throbbing cock slid in and out of her now dripping pussy. Oh! the joy as she rotated those lovely buttocks, getting my prick to penetrate her to the very extremity! My body grew moist with perspiration yet still she held on with her legs as her cunt wildly received my boiling spurts of sperm as it jetted spasm after spasm of spunk into her writhing love-box. She squeezed my balls gently as I withdrew and the last creamy drops trickled down my thighs. I rolled back exhausted but Amelia pointed my head to the left where, holding the thick shaft at its base in both hands, Lucy was still sucking Pelham's cock! It was obvious that they too had reached the crossing of the Rubicon as his prick jerked up and down and Lucy sucked as much as she could of the gushing cum as she gobbled the ruby head and her hands jerked up and down the shaft of his thick prick. Once he had shot his load we all lay back quite exhausted.

'Let's all snuggle up under the eiderdown,' said Lucy sensibly, as we would be foolish to catch cold after our fun. Pelham lay on the outside next to Lucy whilst I was sandwiched between the two beautiful girls.

'Oh, I love sucking cocks,' said Lucy smacking her lips. 'I would like to suck and suck but even Pelham here, who is one of the best, squirts off too quickly.'

'Yes, that can happen,' agreed Amelia. 'But I also enjoy it very much stroking a cock gently, playing around until it is really stiff. Then I like to suck it, but I don't really enjoy the spunk coming in my mouth.'

'But that's almost the best part,' said Lucy. 'I just adore a man who can shoot cream again and again. I find it so satisfying swallowing spunk as it squirts into my mouth. Nothing tastes as clean and fine as fresh sperm. You really should persevere, my dear, if for no other reason than that way you will never become pregnant!'

Amelia sighed and nodded agreement. 'I suppose I must

try harder,' she said. 'Mind, I can say that I have never had any complaints. You enjoyed fucking me just as much as being sucked off by Lucy, didn't you, Pelham?'

'Oh, indeed,' said Pelham gallantly. 'Both of you are absolutely top-hole, aren't they, Andrew?'

'Absolutely so!' I said heartily, reaching out to rub Lucy's mound with my right hand whilst my left hand strayed towards Amelia's hairy cunny and I gently inserted a finger and began slipping it in and out of her juicy snatch. She wriggled slightly and laid her hands on my semi-tumescent organ, but continued her conversation.

'I like to hold a stiff prick,' Amelia said. 'I like to put it in my cunt and to hold his balls while we are fucking. I think many girls lose much pleasure by not letting themselves relax.'

'That's just what I told Pelham to do—to relax completely,' I chimed in.

'I think I need to do that right now. I feel quite shattered,' groaned Pelham.

'I think Andrew still has something left over,' laughed Amelia as she rubbed my foreskin up and down leaving the ruby-domed head uncovered.

I thought it best not to show Pelham I could still fuck again so quickly so I moved Amelia's hand away.

'Let's rest for a little while,' I suggested.

'Oh, very well,' said Amelia. 'I think that shows that we are not really the weaker sex, are we, Lucy?'

'Certainly not, my dear Amelia, far from it,' smiled Lucy.

Now I remembered how arousing it could be for Lucy to recount one of her erotic encounters and I suggested that she told us a story from her past.

'Oh, very well,' she said. 'You two might feel jealous but one of the most satisfying sexual affairs I ever took part in concerned another girl.'

'This should be worth hearing,' I replied. 'We'll all listen quietly to you.'

Lucy sat up and began her tale. She was a born storyteller and we listened in silence as she began:

'Only recently a clever girl said to me that if you want to

understand something you must face it naked. She was expressing herself in philosophical terms as the role of philosophy might well be said to extend and deepen our own self-awareness. This is true also in the field of sexual relations. We must experience everything in the conceptual framework to truly aid our understanding, and it is proper for intellectual groups to make this particular sort of effort at self-comprehension. Until recently, if I may now recall my own personal experience, I had never enjoyed the experience of an amatory affair with one of my own sex, for at my school I always had a bedroom to myself. However, at a reception given by my uncle, Doctor White, some months ago, I found myself deep in conversation with a jolly girl named Kate Wilson. I don't think any of you have had the pleasure of meeting her, though her papa is an old acquaintance of Doctor White from their days at Cambridge University. He is now a diplomat and Kate travels with him often in Europe. Last year they were away nearly three months in Central America. However, I digress, and must return to the point of this tale.

'Kate was an extremely pretty girl with lovely firm and rounded breasts, a narrow waist but with a generous posterior and long shapely legs. Her complexion was somewhat darker than mine due perhaps to the considerable amount of travel she had undertaken, but it was set off well by silken hair almost as blonde as mine. She had large sensuous eyes and her flesh was as firm and smooth as ivory. We were the only females present and I soon gained the permission of Doctor White to escort my new friend to my rooms as the conversation was not of interest to us. I showed her around and as she inspected my bedroom she pounced on a copy of *The Pearl* which I had inadvertently left on my bedside table.

' ''Heavens, how did you come by this book?'' she asked. I began to stammer a reply but she chuckled and said: ''Please do not be alarmed. I am neither shocked nor am I against people reading what they will. But the trouble with these smutty books is that they are all about men and women poking. Am I not correct?''

' "Yes, I suppose this is true," I answered. "Ah, but have you read about the joys of loving between women?" she continued. "I am sure that you have never read anything about that, let alone experienced such pleasure." I had to confess the truth of her observation though I had heard Doctor White mention this phenomenon in a lecture.

' "I am somewhat ignorant," I said. "Although my uncle tells me that there is a famous German professor who calls love between girls moral insanity because of its essential contrariness. And Professor Mantagazza classes it 'an error of nature'," I continued glibly. 'Such conduct is called a sickness by doctors though I am more tolerant, even if I still believe that there is nothing to beat the gorgeous feeling of pleasure occasioned by a thick tool entering one's damp cunt."

' "How do you know?" said Kate hotly. "In the women's club I belong to (the Holly and the Ivy Circle just off Regent Street), most of us feel that there *is* something better." And before I knew it she kissed and hugged me so lovingly that at first I felt slightly confused and, although we were all alone and no-one was in the least likely to disturb us, I felt my face burn with pink blushes as her hot kisses on my lips made me all atremble. Her touches fired my blood and the way she sucked my tongue seemed truly delicious.

'Suddenly we were locked together on my bed and her hot moist lips pressed down on my mouth as I responded as our tongues licked deeply inside each other's mouths. We rocked to and fro until she suddenly pulled away, stood up and undressed. I must tell you that the sight of her beautiful naked body sent shivers of desire up and down my spine. Her full breasts stood firm and her brown teats and rock-hard nipples contrasted excitingly with her smooth golden skin and large amount of crinkly hair covering her love mound that bulged between her long slim legs. I threw off my own clothes and in a flash she was on top of me, rubbing my titties to full erection between her fingers. She then gently eased her hands down between my legs to allow access to my own yearning cunny that was already moist, even before she began to stroke

36

my clitoris until my little button protruded stiffly. I lifted myself up and buried my face between her breasts making her titties shake with desire. I then lay back and massaged her deep breasts, stroking her titties to new peaks of hardness.

'Our pussies ground together as she sucked one of my own hard nipples making me squeal with excitement. I rubbed my pussy even harder against her until we were both practically on the brink of the ultimate pleasure. Kate gurgled with pleasure and she lowered her head towards my sopping quim and slipped her warm, wicked tongue through my cleft, prodding my little clitty, tonguing me to a little series of pleasure peaks. Our hands were everywhere, grabbing and squeezing and writhing together as our bodies locked, demanding release. "Lucy, my darling, where's your hand? Here, put it there, rub your finger on my crack, just there," she whispered. I frigged her passionately until I ducked my head between her splayed thighs and buried my mouth in the moist and succulent padding of curls in which nestled her cunny. I had a glorious view of the paraphernalia of love. A splendid mount covered with curly black hair; the serrated vermilion lips of her cunt slightly parted from which projected quite three inches a stiff fleshy clitty as big as a man's thumb. I opened the lips with my fingers, passed my tongue lasciviously over the most sensitive parts, took that glorious clitoris in my mouth, rolling my tongue around it, and playfully biting it with my teeth. It was too much for Kate and with a cry of, "Oh! Oh! You make me come, darling Lucy!" she spent profusely all over my mouth and chin.

'I continued to move my tongue along the velvety grooves of her cunt, licking and sucking the delicious juices that ran down like a stream, mixing with my own saliva. With each stroke of my tongue, Kate arched her body in ecstacy, pressing her fully erect clitty up against my flickering tongue. "Oh, Lucy!" she gasped, wrenching my mouth from her trembling slit. "Heavens! Pull my clit! Hard! You won't hurt me!" Gripping it in my fingers I tugged vigorously as she

37

writhed her hips wildly beneath me. After a brief rest she rolled me over onto my back.

' "Now it's my turn to repay the delicious pleasure I owe you," she sighed, kissing me rapturously, and sucking my tongue into her mouth so that I could scarcely catch my breath. With her fingers she opened my crack as wide as possible, then directing her fingers to the passage she probed into my most sensitive regions as only a woman would have known. Her fingers tickled round the hood of my clitty and when the little red love-bean broke from its pod, I at last had the courage to caress her own sweet body. Gladly she let her heavy breasts rest in my keen hands. I squeezed her tawny nips and then I came before I really wanted to, soaking her fingers with my pent-up juices. I sighed with utter bliss as my hands ran over her delicious body with frantic ecstasy. I cupped her breasts and stroked her buttocks and my fingers ran up the groove in between them and round and round . . . and then she pushed her head deep down between my legs and she was tonguing me to new peaks. She drove her wicked tongue right into the ring of my cunt and tossed it round the quivering walls, withdrew it, then plunged it in again deeply, rapidly in and out, in and out.

'Frantically she attacked my engorged clitty—a short, thick point of pulsating lust—as I groaned with sensual desire. She pulled away momentarily and then in a trice our bodies were locked together as she directed her own stiff clitty to the juicy passage she had opened up and she seemed to stuff it all in, lips and all, closing my cunt lips upon it and holding them together tightly with her hand. I can hardly express to you how novel and delightful this new conjunction was to me. We were both so heated as our spendings mingled together that we reached new heights of erotic fury. Without separating for a moment she rubbed and pushed about inside me, the lips and hair of her darling cunny titillating the sensitive parts in the most thrilling fashion. We swam in a veritable sea of lubricity until at last, sated with pleasure we lay panting together, almost swooning from the frenzy of our emissions.

'It was a warm evening and we recovered our strength

while we lay naked on the bed. "Was not that perfect bliss, my dear Lucy?" asked Kate.

' "It was certainly a most pleasing experience," I rejoined. "However, I still maintain that a really good fuck with a boy is even nicer."

' "I have enjoyed ordinary fucking," said Kate, "and it is true that it is certainly more pleasurable than most other activities."

'Then, to my horror, there was a knock on the door, and I remembered that I had asked one of the fifth form boys whom I tutor in French to give me the exercise I had prepared for him earlier that day. "Who can that be?" asked Kate with a note of worry in her voice. "It is Charlie Watkins, a fifth form boy who has an exercise to give me," I whispered. "Well, let's use him to see if you prefer boys to girls after all," she said.

'My blood was still up so I padded across to the door, still quite nude, and opened it wide. There stood sturdy young Master Watkins, a regular Adonis of a boy, rather slim, tall and dark, with a beautifully plump rosy face, dark hair and dark fiery eyes.

' "Come in, Charlie, don't be afraid," I said gaily. "I would like you to meet Kate, a dear friend of mine who would like you to fuck her. I'm sure that you will be a good sport and join in the fun."

'His eyes sparkled as I had never seen before. I should have guessed that he had yet to prove his manhood, and before I could close and lock the door, the bold boy had slipped out of his clothes and was on the bed with Kate.

'She reached down and encircled his fast-swelling young cock. I watched as she massaged it until it grew stiff and erect. She was now completely engrossed and unaware of my presence as she leaned over and took the ruby-headed knob between her lips, jamming down his foreskin and lashing her tongue round the rigid shaft. Then she sucked hard, taking at least half his tool into her mouth while her hands played with his rather small balls. She opened her mouth further and took the dome and stem further into the depths of her mouth, extending her tongue down to lick the soft underfolds of skin along the base of the shaft. She sucked with a firm motion as she slid her lips up and down the rock-hard cockshaft, gulping noisily as the head of his grand tool slid along the roof of her mouth to the back of her throat.

' "That is exquisite," groaned my fine young man, and from the manner of his fast breathing and twitching cock, I knew that he could not last too long and was fast approaching his climax. Kate had surmised this as well and she pulled her head up and whispered urgently: "I want your cock inside me. Lie down on your back, I want to ride you."

'He did not wait to be asked twice. He lay on the bed with his cock poking straight up. Kate quickly straddled him with her now ravenous pussy engulfing his prick, sliding down the not inconsiderable length of it until it was buried to the hilt. As soon it was lodged deep inside, she became frantic, sliding up and down, swaying back and forth with her hips as he arched up to meet her wild thrusts. This was too much for poor Charlie who began pumping faster and faster and his face reddened as his breathing quickened even further. My own juices had just begun dribbling down my legs for as you can imagine, this was most exciting to view, when Charlie came with great spurts of spunk that shot out of his prick all over Kate's lovely flat belly.

'This was too much for me to bear and I jumped on the bed and took hold of the sperm-coated cock, grasping hold of the now semi-erect monster. But after only a few quick rubs up and down, Charlie's cock was up to its full majestic height again and I lay back and opened my legs to receive him. He lowered himself gently on top of me and his lovely rod slipped into my hungry cunt. He began pumping up and down in a steady rhythm and my body surged upwards to meet his as every pounding jab struck home. I managed to slow him down, making sure that on each stroke the whole of his marvellous cock slid in and out of me like a piston. His eyes were closed and he had a dreamy look on his pretty face as his hands fondled my breasts. I whimpered with joy at every thrust and the climax came, shooting through the whole of my body, taking away every other sense as I tossed and turned in delight. My hands thrust into his back, my cunt thrusting upwards in a mad effort to cram even more of that magic hardness further inside me as his balls banged against my bottom. I tensed to drain every last drop until, as my clitty throbbed from its explosion of fulfilment, his tool jerked wildly inside me and he shot a superb load of creamy jism into me as our juices mingled happily and our hairy mottes crashed together as we reached that fabulous plateau of pleasure.

'He rolled back exhausted but I thought that the young fellow-me-lad could perform at least one service. My hands ran around the cluster of thick black hair around his tool and I let my mouth travel along that lovely blue vein that ran along the shaft to the uncovered dome at the end of his glorious knob. Even though Charlie's prick was limp, it still looked capable and as you know, I love to fondle a prick and feel it throb and swell as my hand grasps the shaft and begins rubbing it up and down. Very soon, Charlie's cock had swelled up and I gently kissed the purple dome as I eased his foreskin up and down until his strong young weapon stood smartly to attention.

'His prick was throbbing furiously now in my mouth and I greedily gobbled the pulsating tool as I looked up to Charlie with twinkling eyes. He lifted himself to cup my breasts with his hands, deftly flicking my nipples with his nails. I began to give him sharp little licks on his swollen rod followed by a series of quick kisses up and down the stem, encompassing his hairy balls and running to that amazingly sensitive zone between his prick and arsehole. I thrust his cock in and out of my mouth in a quickening rhythm—deep into my throat and out again with my little pink tongue licking at the tip at the end of each stroke, lapping up the drops of creamy white fluid that were beginning to ooze out of the tiny eye at the top of his lovely knob.

'As soon as I felt that he was on the verge of coming I made ready to swallow his love juice. Charlie thrust upwards and his cock shuddered violently between my lips—and then in one long spasm he released his spunk, first a few early shoots and then crash! My mouth was filled with juicy, gushing foam as his cock bucked uncontrollably as I held it lightly between my teeth. I let it flow sweetly down my throat, gently worrying his now spongy knob with my tongue to stimulate it as much as possible and then, very gradually, I allowed the wet shaft to slide free.

'The three of us continued to suck and fuck until sheer exhaustion compelled us to separate. I discovered that Kate had already arranged to sleep in one of our guest-rooms whilst it was not difficult to smuggle Charlie back to his dormitory. In this short narrative it would be impossible to describe everything we did at great length, but I can assure you that our worship of Venus and Priapus led the three of us to hours in Paradise!'

This voluptuous narrative had stirred my blood and Amelia, whose appetite for *l'amour* was the equal of my own, quickly perceived that I was aroused. She stroked my now rampant prick, admiring its smoothness, its large uncapped head red and glowing with the heat that was raging inside it. So, gently laying her down and placing a pillow under the half-moons of her firm bum cheeks, with my hands I gently pushed her legs as wide apart as they would go, exhibiting to my gaze the gaping lips of her cunt, ready and open to receive my throbbing cock, which by now had raised its foaming head erect against my belly. Laying myself down upon Amelia, I made her take hold of my prick and put it in, but so firm and erect was it that she could barely bend its head down to the entrance of her dripping cunny. So magnificent was the erection that I had difficulty in entering the dear girl despite the stretching her pussy had previously received from our exertions. Drawing myself back to wet the head of my charger with some spittle, I slowly shoved away until my balls banged against her bottom hole. I moved slowly in and out at first, building up to such a speed that we soon both melted away, giving us both the maximum enjoyment of a joint spend.

Watching our couplings stirred both Pelham and Lucy and I sensed that both were now ready for one last joust of a splendid evening's entertainment. Lucy lay face down and buried her pretty face well into the pillows. Immediately Pelham raised himself to kneel behind the delicious girl, clasping his arms around her waist and manoeuvring his glowing, iron-hard prick between the cheeks of her lovely bottom.

'What an adorable bottom,' he exclaimed. 'May I have the pleasure of inserting my rod *au derrière*?'

'Of course you may,' smiled Lucy. 'But do be careful as you poke me as we have no cold cream readily available.'

He made no answer but thrust his cock towards the wrinkled little bum-hole that beckoned his throbbing tool. Lucy whispered to me to aid my friend who was totally inexperienced at bottom fucking.

'Ease into her slowly but firmly, old boy,' I murmured. 'Here, let me assist you.' I took hold of his pulsating shaft and eased the glowing dome of his noble weapon between Lucy's superb cheeks which were waiting to be split. He pushed forward but found difficulty in penetrating, so with my fingers I moistened the gleaming, rubicund dome with spittle and again placed it aright. This ministration achieved the desired effect and his prick quickly enveloped itself between the in-rolling cheeks of that mouth-watering bum. A little fearful at first in case he injured the darling girl, Pelham pushed slowly at first but then realised that he was now absorbed well enough in her tight little orifice and began to work himself with vigour, pushing his whole body forwards and backwards, making her bottom cheeks slap loudly against his belly as she moaned deeply with delight. His prick was now fully ensconced in her warm, tight arsehole and he screwed up his eyes in sheer bliss.

'My love, my desire!' he cried out as he bent over Lucy to fondle and weigh her lush breasts and erect titties. As she waggled her arse provocatively she lifted her head from the pillow and we could all see that there was no doubt of her total enjoyment of Pelham's thick rod pounding in and out of her gorgeous bum.

'Now, Pelham, now!' she gasped, and he needed little effort to obey as he flooded her bum-hole with such vibrant shoots that one could almost view the ripples of orgasmic joy that ran down Lucy's spine as she shuddered to her climax. As she artfully wriggled her bottom, spout after spout of creamy spunk filled her juicy hole as with a succulent *plop*, Pelham withdrew his glistening shaft and sank back upon his haunches as the exquisite spendings melted away to a tiny blob of white spunk on the tip of his cock.

We continued to fuck, suck and gamahuche until almost half past eleven and the lustful orgy drew to a close. Our passions were sated and we were all more than ready to fall into the arms of Morpheus. Pelham and I wished the girls a loving goodnight and made our way back to our rooms. We both slept extremely well until the rising-bell awoke us from our slumbers. A new day had dawned and this day too had its charms which I will now recount.

CHAPTER THREE

IT WAS a glorious summer day and, as good fortune would
have it, my day was free of scholastic work as Doctor White
had decreed that on such a beautiful morn, his senior charges
would be best occupied in activities of a physical nature.
Although his progressive ideas were shared by few of the
parents, they all agreed that the good Doctor was always
mindful of his boys' physical as well as mental well-being.

Ah, yes, *mens sana in corpore sano* (a healthy mind in a
healthy body) was a maxim dear to his heart—and this is why
that fine July morning saw me stride out through the fields,
my rucksack on my back filled with my luncheon sandwiches
and a jacket to slip on in case the weather changed, which at
first seemed unlikely.

It was just after ten o'clock when I left Nottsgrove to walk
to a favourite spot of mine, Lapping's Meadow, some two
miles north of High Barnet. As I walked briskly along
Oaklands Lane I became aware of what I believed to be a
figure behind me that seemed to be keeping pace for pace
with me. The sensation of being followed is a disagreeable
one and I began to wonder if I were to be attacked by a
footpad, though such crimes were virtually unknown in that
sparsely populated area.

I quickened my steps and at once was conscious that the
figure behind me was doing the same. Soon the path was clear
of trees and I became ashamed of my first apprehensions.
After all, the Queen's Highway was free for one and all to
use. The steps dogged me as I walked on enjoying my

exercise. But though it had been bright and clear when I left the school, as I crossed the main Barnet road the air began to smell of rain. It was still warm when I sat down on a mossy bank between the road and the fields of a jolly local farmer, Mr Morrison, whose sixteen-year-old daughter, Louella, was a young lady much admired by all at Nottsgrove. She was one of Tennyson's rosebud garden of girls, a miniature of conventional English beauty with gold-dusted light-brown hair and soulfully expressive dark brown eyes, a most exquisite and charming girl who had attended the occasional cricket match between Nottsgrove and the local club of which her brother Harry was a noted member.

I allowed my rucksack to rest against the slope of the hillock and the skin of my back exhaled warm moisture. I stretched my arms above my head and yawned, at peace with the world. But then the first drops of a summer shower blew against my face and I stood up reluctantly and readjusted my pack. I was about to walk across the field to take shelter in a barn only some two hundred yards away when I stopped abruptly as I saw the figure that had been following me for the previous mile or so. It was none other than Louella Morrison and I blushed to think that this lovely girl had frightened me into thinking that I was in some kind of danger.

'Good morning, Miss Morrison,' I called out. 'Have you been following me? I thought I heard someone behind as I was walking.'

'Indeed I have, Andrew,' she replied shyly. 'I would have called out to you but you looked deep in thought and I had no wish to disturb your meditations.'

'That was most thoughtful of you but, indeed, my mind was engaged upon nothing more than admiring the scenery. Now, alas, the rain has interrupted any such thoughts I might have had. Let us walk briskly to your father's barn and shelter ourselves from this unfortunate shower,' I said.

'Yes, let us do so,' she replied with a little smile. We stepped out smartly, when Louella stumbled and, with a grimace of pain, hobbled along as quickly as she could.

46

'Miss Morrison, I am so sorry, let me help you,' I said and took hold of her arm and placed her hand on my shoulder. 'Is that better? Come, let us see if you can walk.'

'Thank you, Andrew,' she said, but I could see that she was in pain.

'Permit me,' I said and taking hold of her with my left arm behind her back, lifted her off her feet and carried her to the barn door which was slightly ajar. Once inside, I gently let her down by a pile of newly-mown hay. 'Are you alright?' I enquired.

'Well, yes, I think I am. Let me take a few paces. Ah, that is better, I think it was nothing more than a slight strain and I am fully recovered. Thank you so much for helping me.' And to my astonishment and delight she gave me a full kiss on my cheek.

'Why, Miss Morrison—' I stammered.

'Oh, please, call me Louella,' she said. 'After all, I call you Andrew and you do not take offence at the familiarity, I trust?'

'Not at all, no, of course not, Miss, er, Louella.'

I shrugged off my rucksack and sat down next to the girl on the huge pile of hay that performed sterling service as a couch. We were both somewhat weary from our walk and we refreshed ourselves with a drink of bottled water that I had placed in my rucksack. The shower had now ceased and the barn was warm so I removed my jacket and sat in shirtsleeves and trousers. We sat together then in silence and I could not but admire the heavenly creature next to me. Her dark hair was drawn back in a bun and, as she loosened it, I noticed that her skin appeared faintly olive-tinted but otherwise of such clarity that it seemed illumined from within. She was wearing a blue jacket which, being fashioned tightly to her torso and waist, allowed me to see the perfect development of her breasts, while her lower limbs were clad in a long, pleated skirt. Her features were finely shaped and her full rich mouth beckoned mine. Our mouths joined and in a trice we were kissing and cuddling with the greatest passion.

She pulled away from me suddenly and said: 'Andrew, I

know it is your birthday next week. I have a present. Would you like it now?'

Puzzled, I replied: 'Yes, Louella, I would, but where is it?'

She undid her jacket and threw it to the ground, then putting her hands underneath her dress, she pulled down her drawers. 'Help me off with my skirt and petticoats!' she breathed, and I needed no second bidding as my cock now reared up hard against my trousers as the skirt dropped to the ground, swiftly followed by the rest of her clothes, until she stood completely naked in front of me. I could at first only stare with wonder and then with unabashed lust at her small but exquisitely formed uptilted breasts and smooth white-skinned belly, below which twinkled a dark, rounded mass of curly black hair.

Without further words, we sank back into the hay, entwined in each other's arms, exchanging the most ardent of kisses as the clever girl began to unbutton my trousers, releasing my straining cock which sprang up like a flagpole between my thighs. She lay me down on my back and then bent forward, rubbing my rigid member against her breasts, squeezing along its length, moving to straddle across me so that her pert young bum cheeks were but inches from my face as she lowered her head, parting her full lips to take my cock into her deliciously wet mouth, sucking slowly, deeply, softly. She manoeuvred until her lips completely covered my engorged member, sucking lustily as she slurped down to the very base. The cheeks of her bare bum so close to my face fired me to even new heights of passion. The moist lips of her quim parted to my groping fingers and her bottom cheeks began a merry dance. Without delay I forced my head upwards and slipped my tongue between those pouting cunt lips which caused the lovely girl to moan with delight as she sucked steadily on my pulsating prick. She wriggled her hips anew and the curled point of my tongue found the wrinkled little bum hole into which I inserted it a trifle, as a fond murmur of pleasure escaped from the owner of the altar of love to which I was attending. My hands moved over her body in tantalising strokes and her clitty throbbed against my fingers as they slipped in and out of her pussy with ease, coated in the love juice which trickled from her in a stream.

I knew that I could not keep this position without exploding and I gently eased her off me until she lay on her back. I eased her legs apart and knelt down between them. She pulled down my head to her sweet cunny and my tongue searched out her fine stiff little clitty which projected quite an inch and a half from the pouting lips of her vagina. I sucked it in ecstasy and titillated her sensitive parts so well that she spent profusely in a moment or two, holding my head with her hands to make me go on. It was perhaps the most exciting gamahuche ever as my tongue revelled in her creamy emission till she begged me to stop and instead insert my now bursting prick.

I grasped her thrilling young body and guided my rampant cock into the soft, clinging pussy and she grasped my bottom cheeks to pull me inside her. Soon we were locked in hard, sweeping strokes as my long stiff prick slid in and out of her sopping cunt. I sank myself into her warmth, glorying in the smooth unfaltering motion of her hips, in the strong confident lifting of her body as she joined me in a wild bout of passion. I felt myself swell further within her as she kept driving up against the power of my punching hips, bouncing back from each drive, over and over again as she met every onslaught with complete delight. She bucked beneath me as I felt the juices boil up inside my throbbing tool and with one mighty *wham!* I plunged yet again into her juicy pit and the darling Louella arched her back to receive the thick squirts of frothy white cum that spurted out of my pulsating prick.

My climax rocketed through me with such force that I was totally unable to fight against the current as the hot gobs of jism continued to pour from my cock. I could only whimper as the spunk dribbled down from the tip of my glistening knob which I slowly withdrew from its enclosing sheath. 'I regret that I came too quickly for you!' I panted.

49

'Oh no, you dear boy, I have spent copiously too, but I am sure that we can repeat the game, can we not?' She smiled back at me, sweetly, with a slight nod of her head. 'This is really marvellous. I want you to fuck me again and never stop!'

'I'm sure they never taught you such words at school,' I said. 'I am most surprised.'

'Oh, every girl knows the word. Now come on, Andrew, fuck me hard! Fuck me in the mouth and fuck my cunt!'

And in a moment our lips were glued, our tongues caressing. The hairs on my chest had brushed her nipples to erection and my fingers found their way to tickle her bum-cheeks. She pushed me down onto my back and tongue-teased my prick erect. The sight of her pretty face, her mouth bulging with my rock-hard cock, prepared me soon enough. But before I could move, it was Louella who swung a leg over her mount and lowered herself upon the phallic saddle.

'Now, Andrew, now!' she cried. 'Oh, my dear love, fill me!'

Smoothing out every little wrinkle inside her cunt, it seemed to me, my prick drove upwards to her soft depths as she rode gracefully and easily, leaving me little employment. My hands roved around her slender shoulder blades and found the light contours of her spine. Following these down, I came to the cleavage of her bottom and fiddled between her cheeks to excite her doubly. She drew my hands from there, in protest, as I thought. But it was only in order that she might lead my right hand in a light smacking rhythm upon her rump. My frisky filly wanted the double pleasure of riding whilst at the same time feeling that there was a jockey upon her to spur her on! Gently and rhythmically I spanked her backside as she rode. The effect was such that I could feel warm, pearly droplets of love juice bedewing my prick as it drove into the very depths of her pussy.

Suddenly she released a muffled scream of ecstasy into my mouth and the crisis was precipitated for us both. From the swollen knob of my cock great gusts of jism jetted into her dripping cunt. Indeed, it must have felt as powerful to her as to me—a rare event if we are to believe Doctor Featherstone-haugh—for Louella had her second orgasm within seconds of the sensation of my sperm squirting into her.

We lay there quite exhausted at last though my cock still threaded her and gently we turned on our sides, remaining entwined. Presently we drew apart and hastily dressed as we had no wish to be compromised by discovery. Louella whispered to me that the house just half a mile along the road was empty but that she possessed the keys and that we could continue our pleasures there. I eagerly assented, remembering that the cottage belonged to a Mr Greenhalgh, a writer, who spent a considerable amount of time in France.

Indeed, the little cottage was quite empty when we arrived at the front door. Flowering myrtle crept up the sides and wild roses perfumed the air about it. The flowers smelled of love and excitement, an incredibly sweet and moving odour.

Louella bent down and extracted the key from under the doormat. 'That is a most unsuitable place to leave a key,' I exclaimed. 'Any robber would look for it there after ascertaining that the cottage lay empty.'

'Ah, yes,' replied Louella. 'But in fact Mr Greenhalgh gave the key to me and I left it under the mat only earlier this morning.'

Oh, sweet girl, *la bella donna della mia mente*! We kissed with burning passion as we entered the hall. I looked around as Louella led me into the drawing room. As Mr Greenhalgh used the cottage infrequently, he furnished the rooms quite sparsely. The furniture, all very old, consisted only of a large sofa with a huge bent wooden back, an oval table in front of the sofa, chairs along the walls and two or three cheap prints in yellow frames, representing girls with birds in their hands —that was all.

But the room sufficed for our needs. The sun was now shining fiercely and its rays burned through the wide windows heating the room so that we stayed warm, even as we tore off our clothes to stand before each other absolutely naked. My truncheon was already standing to attention as stiff as any guardsman, its bulbous dome bursting through the foreskin to pulsate, exposed, as the lovely girl gently clasped the shaft of my hot prick as I took her in my arms. I swept her off her feet and, with her lips still glued to mine and now fiercely rubbing my cock up and down, she put her other arm round my neck as I carried her over to the waiting sofa. I laid her down on her back and, still refusing to relinquish her hold on my throbbing rod, she continued to tongue my mouth so vehemently that I felt the boiling juices already collecting in my balls.

Somehow she sensed that my climax was nearing and she quickly withdrew from my mouth and pulled me on top of her. She motioned me to put my prick near her lush red lips and she eagerly sucked upon the red knob, noisily and uninhibitedly lashing her naughty tongue all around my rampant pole, slowly but surely encompassing inch after inch until I could hold back no longer and I began to fuck her mouth in long, slow strokes until at the downstroke, every piece of that delicious morsel was in her mouth and throat and my balls banged against her juicy lips. Such delight could not continue indefinitely and soon, all too soon, I felt the gush of sperm that was not to be denied and I spunked gob after gob of thick white foam into her throat. Louella greedily slurped every drop of love-juice from me, licking every blob from the tip of my knob until my fine prick lay limp on my thigh.

The sofa was wide enough for us to lie closely beside each other, so I rolled off her and we lay motionless in each other's arms.

'Did you enjoy that sucking-off?' enquired the delightful Louella.

'Oh, my darling, the joy was almost more than I could bear,' I replied truthfully.

'I am so glad. My dear friend Sophia taught me how to suck a stiff prick but I feared that she was more expert than I.'

'Sophia? Do you mean Sophia Lyttelton, your cousin, who came with you to Nottsgrove last April when we invited local ladies and gentlemen to see our school amateur dramatics?'

'Yes, that is the girl, Andrew. Do you remember her? She is prettier than me, is she not?'

I looked at my new love with indignation. 'Certainly not,' I said heatedly. 'She is by no means as lovely a creature as you.' This was certainly the truth although I did recall Sophia as being a most uncommon beauty. She was a tall, slim girl, not yet sixteen with wavy golden brown hair, a high complexion and intensely blue eyes, a pretty little nose and a fine bow mouth. So that little minx had instructed my Louella in the art of sucking a penis! I was quite flabbergasted, and told Louella of my surprise.

'It may shock you, dear Andrew, but Sophia has been sucking for almost a year now. In fact her first *amour* was with my brother Harry.'

'With Harry? He is only a year older than you is he not, my precious? This is indeed a surprising conversation for me.'

'Well, that may be so but Harry is quite a handsome boy and, despite your denial that Sophia is prettier than me, I know how attractive she is to men. Since Harry's cock has been able to stand, I have noticed that his breeches bulge whenever he is near my cousin!'

'Good heavens! Are you sure that they have actually—'

'Most certainly. Why, I saw them together only last month. You remember one Sunday the temperature rose to what must have been record heights. My parents were out for a walk and the three of us were left alone. Shall I continue, Andrew, as I have no desire to bore you with an uninteresting story?'

'No, no, go on, go on.'

'As I said, then, we were alone and the sun was beating down with all its might. Sophia suggested we take a short walk down to the river where it would be cooler. Our way to the river bank was by a path through a plantation of tapering firs which had been planted some years earlier and which sheltered the path in winter from the elements. By reason of the density of the interwoven foliage, it was a mite gloomy there, even during a hot, cloudless afternoon. To describe the place fully it would be best to call it a vast, low, naturally-formed hall, the plumy ceiling of which was supported by slender pillars of living wood, the floor being covered by a soft, dun carpet of needles, mildewed cones and tufts of grass.

'We all stripped off our clothes as Sophia and Harry wanted to bathe in the river and she had brought some towels with her. Nothing loath, I laid my clothes neatly in a pile but when I looked up I could see Harry and Sophia were already walking hand in hand towards the river bank and his cock was already in a state of some excitement.

'I pretended not to notice and stepped off the river bank into the cool water, which was more invigorating. But to my amazement, Sophia and Harry had set down a towel on the bank and were sitting on it, embracing passionately. Harry was squeezing her titties in between running his hands licentiously all over her naked body, whilst she had hold of his rampant cock which stood staunchly up with its bulbous dome unhooded as she rubbed his shaft to iron-hard stiffness. Then, shaking a fringe of hair clear from her eyes, she bent down and took the stiffened tool in her mouth. I could see that she sucked slowly, with every refinement of tongue, tickling and working round the little "eye" on the dome. Then, afraid that Harry would spend too soon, she left off her lubrication with a butterfly kiss and turned over on her belly, pushing out her firm young rump towards Harry's glowing face.

'By now I, too, was excited and my hand went down between my legs and I began to rub my own pussy which was already deliciously damp as I was standing in water up to my belly button. My excitement increased when Harry wet the head of his prick with spittle and, as he drove it down between Sophia's bottom cheeks, I heard her gasp with fright. She knew, however, that she should not tense herself against the knob and she relaxed her cheeks as Harry drove forward again, this time reaching her puckered little bum-hole, and he grunted with delight as he pushed in at least two or three inches of his prick, which fortunately was not too thick.

'Sophia obviously possessed an exquisitely tight rear-dimple and his cock rode in and out of the tight sheath of her bottom as at the same time he twiddled her nipples and kissed the back of her neck. Delightedly I watched his lusty young tool plunge in and out of the now widened rim of her bum-hole, pumping and sucking like the thrust of an engine. She reached back and spread her cheeks even further as the pace quickened and the movements of her rump became more hurried until Harry shot his jets of spunk deep inside her bottom.

'All the while my fingers were working in and out of my pussy as my thighs squeezed together, but though some love juice dribbled out, it was not nearly as satisfying as a good honest fuck and Sophia had obviously reached the peaks of delight. They now lay silent except for their long-drawn breaths as the call of birds and the smell of mown grass came from the sunlit world around us.

'Then Harry sat up and, with a frown, told us that he had just remembered that he was already late for an appointment with Mr Atkins, the farm manager. The matter of business would detain him only a half-hour at most but he had to make his excuses. We said we would wait for him to return and he dressed quickly and ran as fast as he could after his exertions towards the farmhouse. Meanwhile, I decided to return to the bank and I picked up a fresh towel and dried myself as Sophia lay back, exposing her firm young body to the sun.'

Listening to this sensual tale had made my cock rock-hard and the telling had stimulated Louella who responded eagerly to my advances. She wriggled herself on her belly and twitched her rounded bottom cheeks provocatively at me. I immediately positioned myself for the charge and Louella took hold of my swollen prick and lasciviously placed it at the entrance to her puckered rosette. I pushed hard and she cried out in surprise more than discomfort. 'Go on, go on, Andrew. I want a nice thick pressing of juice up my bum.'

So I went to work with a will and her bottom responded gaily to every shove as I drove home, my balls bouncing against her smooth rounded bottom. I worked my sturdy prick in as far as it would go and it tingled deliciously in her velvety depths as her nether cheeks were drawn irresistably tight against my flat belly. I had corked her to the very limit. She squeezed to eject me from the constrictions of her bottom-hole but only served to heighten my pleasure. I moved in and out in a slow shunting movement as I snaked my right hand round her waist and, diving into her curly motte, I massaged her little erect clitty, with much luscious kissing as she turned her dear head towards me. I could feel her love juices flowing as she worked her bum to bring me off in a flood of gushing come which both warmed and lubricated her superb backside. As I spurted into her I continued to work my prick back and forth so that it remained stiffly hard and, with a 'pop', I uncorked it from her well lubricated arsehole. We lay exhausted, recovering our senses as the warm sunshine bathed the room in a rosy glow. My, my, the tenderness of those hours will ever remain with me—*me tamen urit amor; quis enim adsit amori.**

By now we were hungry and we eagerly devoured the sandwiches and consumed the lemonade I had luckily packed in my rucksack. I asked Louella if she could come to the school that evening as I had no preparation before me and I wanted to fuck Louella again as soon as possible. We agreed to meet that evening at the entrance to the school and, after a fond farewell kiss, I dressed and began my walk back to Nottsgrove. At first I walked brightly with a gay demeanour, but the nearer I got to the school, the more my conscience pricked me—for how would Lucy take to the idea of my introducing a fresh girl into our sport? I knew that Lucy preferred me to fuck her above all others and she would be hurt if I showed that my heart was bound up with another. This was a delicate problem which would have to be solved and I

* Love consumes me yet—for what bound may be set to love? *Virgil.*

wondered how I could do so without hurting anyone's feelings. Never do tomorrow that which can be done well this day—this was a maxim that Doctor White was fond of repeating to us. There was much to be said for grasping this nettle at the first opportunity and I resolved to do so. Perhaps a mutual friend could come to my assistance, I mused, and by the time I reached the gates of my dear old *alma mater*, a plan of action had formed in my brain.

CHAPTER FOUR

I MAY have mentioned in a previous epistle to this esteemed journal that Doctor Simon White was a keen horticulturalist and was often to be found during his few hours of leisure preparing learned papers upon the delights of flora and fauna. And it was just such a paper that he was working on when I called upon him in his private study. It was typical of the man that, although deeply engrossed in the preparation of his thesis (those readers interested in his works may read them in the quarterly magazine produced by the Royal Horticultural Society), he looked up and greeted me in his usual affable fashion. Every boy at Nottsgrove knew that the headmaster's sanctum was somewhere they could go to at any time to discuss a personal matter of any description.

'Andrew, my dear old chap, come in,' boomed the good doctor. 'I haven't had a chance to speak to you for some days, and I wanted to know how Forbes-Mackenzie behaved himself during his recent initiation?'

'Oh, very well, sir, very well indeed. He played his part to the full, showing every kindness and consideration to his partner.'

'That is good to hear, Andrew, I am well pleased. Far too many young men partake of the joys of fucking but forget to ensure that the lady who is providing such exquisite delight is also entitled to some happiness, especially as she may be running the risk of an unwanted swollen belly! I hope that we won't have any problems on that score.'

'I don't think so, sir, as Lucy and Amelia were both experienced enough to—'

'Amelia?' interrupted my old mentor. 'Surely you don't mean that the lovely young wench Amelia Fenland partook of the delicacies of the feasts of love?'

'Well, yes, sir. I must apologise for mentioning a lady's name in such a context,' I stammered.

'Yes, to be sure, you must hold your tongue about such affairs,' said Doctor White. 'However, no damage is done as I shall not repeat your indiscretion. I am a little shocked to think that she would enjoy sharing with Lucy. Indeed, I did not know that she had even crossed the Rubicon, so to speak. I hope this was not the first time she was threaded?'

'Oh, no, sir,' I replied, somewhat relieved that I had not compromised an extremely pleasant girl. 'She was well versed in the arts of fucking, sucking and every facet of the noble sport.'

He nodded, pleased with the information as he had no wish to proselytise any young person to his own liberated philosophy—nor did he wish a breath of scandal to mar the glorious reputation of the old school.

I sighed with relief as the conversation had taken a turn in exactly the path I needed to bring up the ticklish problem that was bothering me.

'Sir, there is a problem bearing some relation to such matters which brings me here,' I said.

'Nothing too serious, I hope?' said my old mentor. 'Sit down, my boy, sit down. You know as do all my scholars that you may talk to me in complete confidence about any problem, great or small.' He motioned me to take a pew and he settled himself in the deep French armchair that the Old Nottsgrovian Society had presented to him some six years back upon the occasion of his fortieth birthday.

'Well, Andrew,' he said encouragingly. 'Spit it out and let me hear what is troubling you. As you know, I take a special interest in you and other boys whose parents are often abroad, acting *in loco parentis* especially in personal and private matters.'

Reassured, I blurted out my thoughts—how I thought so highly of Lucy yet only that morning I had banished her from my mind when the beautiful Louella offered me her delicious body and I had totally succumbed to her blandishments.

'When I am with Lucy,' I said earnestly, 'we enjoy each other's company tremendously. We talk, we laugh and when we are locked together in times of passion, we cling together in a stillness, lost in each other's presence, speaking few words, scarcely moving.'

'And yet you felt similar feelings when you were with Louella?' prompted the headmaster.

'Yes, sir, I must admit that I did,' I said somewhat shame-facedly. 'I feel that Lucy will be most hurt if she knows that I am showing favour to other girls.'

'Your worry does you credit,' said Doctor White gravely, although I could not help but perceive that he had a slight twinkle in his eye. 'But have no fear, Andrew. Lucy thinks highly of you and indeed of all her lovers. She will not fuck lightly, Andrew, and there are many students and I suppose members of staff who would give their all to have their pricks inside my niece—and I don't really blame them either! But Lucy takes her pick of the pricks that are offered to her and she has yet to find the right man to marry. When she does, I am afraid that you and all the others will have to find another mistress as she will then transfer all her favours to the lucky man who will stand beside her at the altar. But rest assured, Lucy has no thought of marriage for some time and you may enjoy your romps with a clear conscience. However, in all fairness, I think you should ask her permission before you bring another girl into your, ah, activities. She may not know the girl which could cause embarrassment or, even worse, she might not like her which could cause problems all round, not least for yourself.'

'I believe the two girls are not unacquainted, sir,' I said.

'Make sure, make sure—that is my advice, Andrew,' said Doctor White with a grin. 'And here is some final advice. Let the two of them get together first with you in a relaxed and comfortable environment. Louella is coming to Nottsgrove tonight? You know that guests must leave by ten o'clock, you randy young puppy? I expect you to obey the rules, you

60

know! However, if I were you I would entertain them first with refreshments in your room. Then, perhaps you could read to them. Oh, yes, that would be an excellent plan, and I have a splendid volume of classical literature you may borrow. I suggest you read a portion of the work of Mr Cleland which you will find on page three hundred and five.'

'I should read to them, sir?' I said, rather puzzled by this somewhat strange advice.

'Certainly, Andrew,' said the Doctor, rising from his chair. 'Most certainly you should do just what I tell you. After all, think on the words of the great Virgil:

Tale tuum carmen nobis, diuine poeta,
quale sopor fessis in gramine, quale per aestum
dulcis aquae saliente sitim restinguere riuo.'*

And with these words ringing in my ears, he sent me packing, clutching his book under my arm. I pondered yet again as to whether Doctor White had taken my problem seriously for there was, I was sure, the hint of a smile playing around his lips as he wished me good afternoon. But was there really any alternative, I asked myself with resignation? In truth, there was none and I knew that I should have to screw up my courage to the sticking point and face my beloved Lucy. I would tell her quite straightforwardly and with as much candour as I could muster that I had chanced upon meeting a very pleasant young lady that morning and that I had invited her to spend the evening with us. There was no way to avoid adding that I had enjoyed a marvellous fuck with the lady, Louella Morrison, who perhaps Lucy had met before. If Lucy chose to be annoyed by the idea, I would have to inform her that I could not now break my word to Louella and that if she, Lucy, thought I was a cad, so be it. I would accept her strictures in silence and beg her forgiveness. Of course, what

---

* For us your song, inspired poet, is like sleep on meadow grass for the fatigued, or in the heat quenching one's thirst from a leaping stream of sweet water.
Virgil, Eclogue V.

61

really concerned me was the selfish fear that Lucy might be so angry with me that she would never again enter my study at night for a mutual spending of love juices and that our liaison would terminate for ever—but this was a risk I was forced to take and there was now nothing for it but to face the music!

I was so engrossed in turning over these thoughts in my mind that I can scarce recall how I spent the next hours until I was free to meet Lucy in a favourite place of ours, behind the cricket pavilion after tea-time. This was a most handsome structure paid for by Alderman Sir Michael F——, Lord Graham G—— and a wealthy group of sporting Old Notts-grovians.

I kissed Lucy and without delay told her that something was bothering me and that we had to talk.

'Is this a matter of importance?' she enquired.

'It most certainly is,' I said heavily. How was I going to tell her?

'Does this weighty matter concern me?' she twinkled lightly. 'Oh, Andrew, what can it be?'

'Well, my dear,' I struggled out. 'The matter of concern, ah, it is, er, a very, how shall I say this, a most personal, ah, affair—'

'Concerning the fact that Louella Morrison had hold of your darling prick this morning!' she finished triumphantly with a little giggle.

Good heavens! I thought with horror. Surely Doctor White of all people would never break a confidence!

'Oh, Andrew, you are a chump!' she continued. 'Why, you silly goose, did it never cross your mind just how fortunate a coincidence it was that Louella was able to follow you? That she knew that you would be taking a walk this morning? Did you never think how ready she was for that glorious fuck in the hay? Was it by mere chance that Mr Greenhalgh's cottage was so invitingly near and empty, too? My, how convenient all the pieces in the puzzle fall so neatly into place, don't they, my dear boy!'

I stared in shocked amazement at my darling girl. Why, she

had known all the time and from her words it appeared that she had even connived in the whole affair! What a thoughtful, sweet girl she was, I thought, as she looked at me merrily with a roguish smile upon her pretty little countenance. Of course, she realised that I would enjoy nothing better than a nice fresh fuck from out of the sky, so to speak, and I swept the lovely girl into my arms and we embraced heartily, lost in that strange stillness that only lovers enjoy. Readers, I shall always remember the smell of the green grass, slightly damp still after the morning's showers, the smell of the fresh summer air and the softness of Lucy's firm young breasts crushed against my chest. My lips found that little hollow in her neck, my arms went right round her to hold her tightly against me. Ah, what joy, what bliss! My hands roved across her and her flesh quivered beneath the journeying hands and it was as if the earth itself came alive as at the touch of a gale or a storm of rain.

The scent of sweet Lucy was like that of the earth, the sighing of her breath like that of the wind in the trees. As I fastened my mouth upon hers and laid my hand on her breasts, I was under an enchantment, her spell and the earth's spell. For a moment I clung to her still more closely, and then we sank to the ground and my hands went under her skirt where, to my amazement, I found that she was quite naked underneath. As we continued to kiss passionately, I threw up the skirt to expose the naked charms of her pussy to the world. My hands pressed against the inside of her thighs and she allowed me to spread them wider and she covered my face with her own hands as she felt my breath between her thighs. My mouth touched the love-lips and my hands slid under her adorable bum cheeks, lifting her to my waiting mouth. I carefully examined the soft lips of her cunny, covered with downy golden hair and then I began to lick her and I trembled with excitement as my naughty tongue sought out and found the secrets of her quim. Her juices dribbled like honey from her parted labia and her clitty turned from pale pink to deep red as I flicked it gently with my wet, darting tongue. I delighted in the taste of her flesh as I licked and sucked at the stiffening little clitty and the juices began to flow over my face as I sniffed that erotic female odour, my nose buried in her damp motte. As I sucked and sucked bringing Lucy to new peaks of delight, I moved my own body to the side so that her eager hands could unbutton my now bursting fly. My cock shot up, rampant, as she plucked it out of its covering and pulled me across her as she reached across and sucked the tip of my red-capped cock which waved in front of her. She grasped it with both hands and took it firmly in her mouth, slurping lustily on the shaft as my body went into paroxysms of delight. I could not contain my orgasm and I shot my seed right into her mouth. Lucy's mouth was like a suction pump and she swallowed every drop of my copious emission but still my prick was ramrod stiff and then I heard her whisper: 'Andrew, my dear, I am ready for you now.'

She held me as I lowered myself on top of her and our bodies were joined from mouths to groins as her nipples brushed against my chest and I could feel their rough hardness, even through the material of her frock. I pumped again in time with her jerking hips as she clutched my own heaving bottom, inserting her finger into my bottom hole to spur me on to push my pulsating prick even further inside her sopping wet cunny. As I drove again and again she bucked her hips urgently to meet every thrust of my jabbing pelvis and she lifted her bottom to work it round and round, her hips rotating to achieve the maximum contact.

Desperately she clutched at me as I felt the boiling sperm gather in my shaft as my balls banged against her rounded bottom. She threw back her head in abandon and then a primordial sound came from deep within her as her climax spilled and coursed through her body. Her clitty rubbed against my own thatch and I groaned as I could hold back no longer and, with a crash, I pumped spurt after spurt of hot jism into her womb as wave upon wave of ecstasy thrilled through every fibre of my being. I pulled out my soaking tool, which was glistening with its coat of love-juice and was still dribbling out spunk, as Lucy swooped down and sucked the very last morsels of come from me as my cock slipped down into its natural state and the red-capped dome slithered back inside its covering of foreskin.

'Oh, I would love another fuck, Andrew, but make haste, button your fly as some people might be walking by,' she giggled.

'I would love to fuck you again, my love,' I replied gallantly, 'but you are right. However, you could suck me off if we go inside the pavilion.'

'No, my darling boy, I want you in peak condition for tonight's little frolic. Tell me, will Pelham be joining us?'

'I think not, unless you want him to be there.'

'Oh, no, although a good thick cock like his is always welcome. But let tonight be just for us alone.'

'And Louella,' I added. 'We must not forget her.'

'No, I won't forget her,' sighed Lucy. 'I suppose I must share your gorgeous prick with her but as they say, half a loaf is better than no bread.' And after a final little kiss of farewell we parted, as she had to correct some French papers for Doctor White and I had to bone up on some German verse that I was to be tested on in a lesson the next day.

I tried very hard to force the lewd images of the two girls from my mind as I studied, holding the book with both hands, and ignored as best I could the continual pressure of the erection that pushed up from between my legs. But after an hour I could bear it no longer and sat down on my bed, opened my trousers and let my stiff cock spring out from my trousers. I grasped the throbbing shaft, rubbing it furiously as the red-capped dome slipped its bulbous head out of the top as I played with myself until my seed shot forth in a fountain of frothy sperm. It was not an unpleasant sensation but what a difference there was between tossing myself off and enjoying a glorious fuck!

After a light meal of cold roast meats and salad (thanks to Doctor White's interest in horticulture we grew much of our fruit and vegetables in the school grounds and everyone will know how delicious home-grown produce can be), I decided to take a short walk around the quadrangle before retiring to my study for a short rest. After all, I would shortly have the honour of pleasuring two lovely, lusty girls and I would need all my vital health and strength if I were to give full satisfaction, especially as I had been hard at work during the day!

But as I was about to open the door to my study I heard my name being called. I turned round and saw a good friend and fellow sixth former, Paul Hill-Wallace, striding towards me. Paul was spending his last days at Nottsgrove as he had already gained a place at B—— College, Oxford, to study philosophy. He was a brilliant chap and was still working hard at his studies when most ordinary mortals like myself would have used the spare time purely for leisure pursuits.

'I say, Andrew,' he said. 'Could you spare me a minute or two?'

'What is it, Paul?' I enquired somewhat crossly. 'I am rather busy just now.'

'This won't take long and I would appreciate five minutes, old boy. Doctor White has set me a fascinating paper to prepare for next Thursday and I would like to hear your views upon the subject.'

'I am honoured,' I said rather sarcastically. 'What can I say about any matter of substance to such a distinguished scholar as yourself?'

This was a most unkind and unwarranted remark and Paul looked a trifle hurt.

'Don't be a rotter, Andrew,' he said. 'This will take only a few minutes. Come, let me in and we'll jaw about it and then I will promise to leave you alone.'

He was such a charming fellow and I felt so ashamed at my lapse of manners that I nodded and welcomed him into my room. Paul was my age, just seventeen and a half, and he was blessed with a lean yet powerful frame. His lustrous brown hair was set upon a fresh and handsome face—I am no expert in such matters but Lucy's cool judgement may be safely relied upon here—and he was of a generous spirit. Paul was always top of the class in all subjects yet he would willingly share his store of knowledge with his friends when it came to homework and he helped make our studies far less of a chore through his good nature. I must confess that I was flattered to be asked my opinion upon a matter of scholarship by so able and clever a chap!

'Please excuse my rudeness,' I said as we settled into our chairs. 'May I offer you some refreshment? No? Well, then now, I am delighted that you should ask me to assist you. How may I help?'

'Well, the essay I must prepare deals with the role of the novelist in society. I must discuss the importance of the novelist and of fiction in the continual changing pattern of the politics of the modern nation state.'

I gulped and quickly decided upon a course of action. 'What is your opinion?' I asked, throwing back the question to him.

'I am somewhat undecided which is why I would welcome another opinion. I am sure that you will agree that it is hardly surprising for a philosopher to use the novel as one of his modes of expression. However, we must of course distinguish the novel proper, such as the works of Jane Austen or of Proust, from the novel of ideas such as *Candide* or the plain tale such as *Moll Flanders* and the modern metaphysical tale of which there are innumerable examples. The novelist proper is in his way a kind of phenomenologist for he has always implicitly understood, what the philosopher has grasped perhaps less clearly, that human reason is not a single, unitary tool, the nature of which could be discovered once and for all. The novelist has had his eye fixed upon what we do and not upon what we ought to do or must be presumed to do. He has the natural gift of a precious freedom from rationalism which the academic thinker achieves, if at all, only by a precarious discipline. The writer of fiction has always been a describer rather than an explainer. Would you not agree, Andrew, with such a hypothesis?'

I struggled for words for, truthfully, the only word I fully understood was 'tool' and in his context I knew that Paul was not using the word in its vulgar form. 'I'm sure you are right, old fellow. Do continue,' I said, settling myself down in my chair for a nap. Even during the early years of my life I had learned a simple yet important rule which was that when people asked you for advice they desired not your true opinion but, in reality, a confirmation of their own views and dear old Paul (who is now, incidentally, a distinguished don with several learned tomes to his credit which to my shame I have never perused) carried on and on until I felt my eyes drooping and within a short time I was deep in the arms of Morpheus.

I awoke when I felt my shoulder being gently shaken and a voice coming through the mists of semi-consciousness saying: 'Andrew, Andrew, wake up. Oh my, oh my!' Then I heard giggling and I woke up with a start. There in front of me were Lucy and Louella, both heartily laughing, and Paul was also standing there with a smile upon his face.

'Ladies, you must forgive me,' I blurted out. 'Paul was giving me a dissertation upon the role of the novelist when I, er, I—'

'Went to sleep on me!' Paul grinned and it was typical of the fellow that he had not taken offence at my rudeness. 'Now, don't worry, Andrew, Lucy has introduced me to this charming young lady and indeed has invited me to take tea with her guest. You too of course are invited and I can continue my argument if you so wish.'

I smiled weakly and stood up. I saw the volumes that Doctor White had loaned me on the table and I took hold of it. 'Lead the way,' I said. 'And it will be my turn to entertain the company with a reading from a great novelist.'

'That sounds extremely interesting,' said Lucy and I thought I detected a note of irony in her voice but I refrained from comment as we walked towards her rooms which were on the other side of the building.

After we had made ourselves comfortable, Lucy said: 'Did you really mean what you said about giving us a reading?'

'I always mean what I say,' I replied loftily and picked up the book I had taken with me.

'Who is the author?' asked Louella.

'His name is John Cleland,' I said, looking at the cover. 'He was the composer of an erotic novel called *Fanny Hill* but this extract is from a piece extremely appropriate for Paul as he will soon be an undergraduate at Oxford University and this is entitled *Memoirs of an Oxford Scholar*!'

Lucy, Louella and Paul settled down whilst I began to read:

'*I released her, kissing her again, allowing my hungry lips to travel down to the warm spot in her throat where the twin pulses race in uneven tempo.*

'*My impatience to possess the one who had occupied my dreams impelled me to lift the dear girl, my lips still pressed upon hers, to the waiting bed. Gently, so as not to distress the tender sentiments I saw reflected in her eyes, I unloosed my Chloe's gown and, her passions keeping pace with my own, she unfastened the stays and lay back, her lovely body but barely concealed by the near-transparent shift. I made haste to remove my own shirt and breeches, and seeing Chloe's hand move towards the fastening at the bodice of her shift, I helped her to undo them—and to remove the last hindrance to my first sight of that body for which I had so long suffered in denial.*

'*Her bosom, now bare, was rising in the warmest throbs and presented to my eyes the firm swell of young breasts, such as must be imagined on the most beautiful of goddesses. Their whiteness, their delicate fashioning, were all that man had ever dreamed of in his most fantastical imaginings. Their rosy nipples, surmounting the pale mounds of taut flesh, added to the final ravishment to my eye and the most exquisite of pleasures to my roaming hands. She lay there, silent, unresisting of the examination of her body by my love-filled eyes and my pleasure-ravished hands. Her tender acquiescence to my probings encouraged me to pursue to completion my long-held goal. Taking her small hand in mine, I guided it down to my rod which had by now stretched himself to a fair tallness. The head was extended and blushed a fiery crimson showing the hot rush of blood to its tip. Chloe gasped, pulled away for an instant, then sighed as I placed her sweet hand firmly around the erect shaft, then springing up straight from the wreath of curls that lay at its base. She held her hand still, then by my tender encouragement began to stroke the member softly. Anon, with great fearfulness, she reached her hand down to its base, lingered there in the curly thicket and thence strayed between my thighs. I knew the softness of her fingers as she felt with wonder that globe of wrinkled flesh that held the honey of passion's flowering. Her hand clung to the root of my first instrument, that part in which Nature contained the stores of pleasure and I made her feel distinctly, through the soft outer cover, the pair of round balls that seemed to float within.*

'The visit of her warm hands to those impassionable parts had raised my desires to a boiling heat and I, near to over-flowing with ungovernable passions, set upon the attainment of my goal.

'Her thighs were already open to my love assaults in obedience to the irreversible laws of Nature. I lowered myself between them, and for the first time did the hard bone of my instrument feel the wiry curls that hid Chloe's full-pouted lips. Pressing on, that instrument drove at her breech, conformed to the dictates of Nature, yet shielded over with Nature's own device. I pushed vigorously, yet came against a wall which would not open to admit me.

'I begged my Chloe to bear with patience as I reached for a pillow to put beneath her buttocks, thus to make a point-blank aim at the most favourable elevation. Again, I lowered myself between Chloe's spread thighs, and rested the tip of my machine against that tiny cleft. So small was the slit that I could scarcely count upon the accuracy of my aim. But assuring myself, I stroked forward with violent energy. My rod's immense stiffness surged forth with implacable fury, wedged against, then rent, the seal that had denied me access. This furious stroke gained me entrance to the tip alone but following well the initial insertion I at once stroked again vigorously and aggressively, increasing the advantage just gained. Inch by inch, achieved with violent thrusts, I was at last in possession of that treasured prize.

'At last freed from the demands of my own throbbing loins, I looked into my Chloe's face and saw that she had pushed the sheet into her mouth to prevent her disturbing the house

with her cries of pain. I gently removed the cloth from her hands and kissed her lips. Now deep inside her, the fury of my passion drove me to complete the journey on which I had started forth with such difficulty. I thrust and stroked heedless of the pain it caused the darling virgin. With an immense shudder, my liquids burst forth from me. As I withdrew my slackening member, I saw that the love-froth was tinged with blood and that Chloe had fainted with the anguish of the tremendous onslaught.

'When she returned to her senses, she caressed and kissed me tenderly, explaining that I need not regret the pain that I had caused her.

'Immediately my member, responding to impulses deep within me, begins to transform himself into the stiff gristle of amour. I kiss Chloe again, she responding the more ardently. She wraps her arms around my neck, thus allowing me the freedom to undo the laces that close my shirt and, at length, to remove my breeches.

'I slip into the bed, already warmed by her pulsing body. Slowly I begin to make advances toward my adored wife, when she takes me by surprise—moving abruptly and lowering herself upon my member, by now extended to his fullest proportion. Following her impulse, she runs the slit of her Venus-mound directly upon the flaming point of my sword, thus piercing herself through the centre and infixing herself upon it to the very extremest degree. Thus, she sets upon me, straddling me with her open thighs.

'I, in delight, pulled her down to receive the token of my kisses, at the same time increasing the rising sting of pleasure. I toyed with her pert breasts thus arousing her to a sweet storm of wriggles which apace aroused my own sensations.

'Up and down she moved, in the inverted position of mortar and pestle. And then she swayed herself from side to side thus extending even further the arena of our mutual enjoyments. The volleys of heaves and counterthrusts increased to a violent rhythm over which neither of us had any more control. In anticipation of the ultimate moment, I pulled my Chloe down over me with a fevered emotion and, in an instant, we both discharged, flowing mightily from within, the one on the other.

'I lay back, so overcome was I with the ecstasy of the moment, and Chloe, inflamed to an intolerable point, lifted herself off my still semi-erect weapon and sank down on to the bed, stretching her love-moist body against my own, also wet with the exudations of passion.

'We remained thus, silent, for some time.

'Chloe's thighs, by now obedient to the inclinations of both Nature and passion, happily opened again and with now a glad submission, offered up that tender, ruby gateway to the portal of pleasure. The velvet tip of my aroused organ met the deliciousness of her secret haven. I entered her, inch by inch, to the utmost of my length and, for some sweet moments, remained there, my sword impaling her.

'She embraced love's arrow in eager, dear suction around it, compressing it inwardly. Every fibre of her love-bowl strained too to be conjoined with my weapon of love. We gave pause, the better to delight in the sweetness afforded in that most intimate point of union. But the impatience inevitable to such a position soon made itself felt—and drove us to the mightiest action.

'I drove into her with a fierce tumult and she responded with the most violent rejoinders. The more insistent, the more furious became my action, the more heartfelt and frenzied her reactions.

'Oh happiest of mortals! We were joined in that most intimate of all positions. The rhythm increased to a super-human intensity; and my body, suffused with the boiling blood of passion, convulsed with the agitation of my ultimate rapture. My discharge, which I thought would be diminished by the previous exertions, seemed only to be redoubled. And Chloe's discharge similarly seemed to be amplified by such previous encounter and we were near drowned in the waves of liquid sweets which emanated with the immensest force from our bliss-parts.

'We lay back, she in a pallor of faint and I, almost beyond the reaches of my mind in delight.'

72

It is not a false modesty but a true regard to the fact of the matter when I say that it was not my rendition but the beauty of Mr Cleland's imagery that thrilled my listeners. I noticed that Lucy and Paul were sitting closely together and that Paul's right arm was around Lucy's bosoms and his hand was squeezing her left breast passionately while she had her right hand placed strategically upon the bulge between his thighs which she was almost abstractedly rubbing gently as she said: 'That was quite wonderful, Andrew. Why, this has made me feel quite randy.'

'I would rather like a fuck too, Andy,' chimed Louella, climbing to her feet to nuzzle against me.

'I am sure we would all enjoy some relief,' said Paul. 'Did you notice that he stirred our sexual emotions so greatly without once using an improper word?'

'He is, or rather was, quite a special novelist,' I said, smiling, as Louella began to unbutton my shirt. I turned to kiss her passionately and she slipped her hand inside my open shirt to run her hand deliciously up and down my chest and stomach. Our mouths were glued to each other as we staggered across to the bed, still engaged in the most passionate of embraces and then, almost before I knew what was happening, Louella was unbuttoning my trousers and taking my rigid prick in her hands. 'Take off your clothes!' she whispered urgently and she undressed even more quickly than me. We lay naked on the bed and my cock was now ramrod-stiff as the darling girl knelt in front of me. When her tongue touched its end and her fingers toyed with my heavy balls I knew that already she was accepting the taste of semen. She could hardly get her mouth over the uncapped redheaded dome but she licked ecstatically until I could bear it no longer. Gently I pushed Louella's head away from my cock and lustfully grasped her to me, smothering her throbbing lips with burning kisses. As her tongue darted in and out of my mouth, a thrill of lust came over me and I pulled my face away to bury it in the silky brown motte that covered her juicy Mons Veneris. It was delicious, divine. My heartbeat quickened with erotic excitement as my tongue raked her

73

clitty then slipped down to probe deep into her cunt. Almost of their own volition, her legs splayed wider, bent at the knees, as she sought to open herself still more to me. I slurped lustily as I drew the lips of her cunny into my mouth, delighting in the taste of her flesh, licking eagerly to suck more and more of the thin fluid that was flowing from the depths of her cunt. I was in the seventh heaven of delight as I sniffed the unique female odour, my nose buried in her cunt hair. She gasped, jerking her hips upward as her stiff little clitoris was drawn further and further forward between my lips and her hands went down to clasp my head, holding my mouth tightly against her. Her legs, folded across my shoulders, twitched convulsively with joy.

'Andrew,' she gasped. 'I . . . I . . . I'm ready for you now.'

My head jerked up from between her thighs, my eyes alight with eagerness and love for this tender young creature, and gently I stretched myself on top of her. She reached down between our bodies to guide my raging prick to the slippery entrance that was to welcome it. My whole being tingled with excitement as the swollen head of my tool teased the love-lips of her juicy, wet love furrow. Slowly I edged my prick deeper and deeper into the pubic mound as wave upon wave of exquisite pleasure enveloped us both. I let my hands rove across her heavy breasts, arousing the nipples until they too stood proudly erect as I began to fuck Louella, first slowly but then increasing the speed until my prick was hammering like a piston, my balls beating a tattoo against her bottom. All too soon I felt myself approaching the ultimate pleasure stroke and, though I tried to postpone the ultimate moment, my body was being wound up tighter and tighter until finally it exploded into one climactic release as I shot my hot, sticky juice deep into the sweet girl who was writhing beneath me as she rotated her hips wildly, lifting her generous bottom to obtain the maximum contact. I groaned as I felt her finger-nails digging into my back and the tiny throbs in her cunny as my seed spurted jet after jet of love juice inside her. Desperately she clutched at me, her mouth seeking mine, arching her body towards me and somehow her clitoris rubbed against

74

my own luxuriant growth of pubic hair. 'Ooooooh, oooooooh, Andrew, my love that was the best fuck ever!' she cried, her eyes closed in her own private ecstasy.

My lusty cock had fired the sweet girl's sensuality to such an extent that she wanted me in her again. She took hold of my now shrunken prick but it would only spring to a semi-erection in her hand. 'Give me a minute to recover, my dear!' I panted.

'You may have half that time,' she teased, tweaking her nipples until they stood up like little soldiers ready to do battle. She then slid her hand down to her pussy and began rubbing herself gently as I watched with fascination. She parted the lips of her cunt with two fingers and massaged her clitty with the middle finger, her head thrown back and the other hand massaging her magnificent breasts. Shortly, her bottom started to wriggle in rhythm, her eyes closed and she was in her own private world. Her head started to roll from side to side and she moaned with bliss as she began to come to climax. Her rubbing went in jerks, her bottom cheeks tightened and slackened and by now my prick had perked up and Louella fondled my now rampant cock as we kissed passionately. She pulled my shaft beautifully as my forefinger tickled the crisp pubic hair of the lovely girl, tenderly moulding the soft, yielding lips, and then my finger slid into the dainty quim that was already moistened to a delicious wetness. Her hands roamed all over my torso as I frigged her with now one, two then with three fingers as she clutched my bum cheeks to bring me across her. Our bodies touched from head to toe as she guided the huge purple head of my tool to her dripping love hole and the silky stiff prick eased inside its natural home. Her teeth sank into my shoulder as my first strokes jerked her body to new peaks of ecstasy. I pounded home the strokes faster and faster as we rocked together, climbing to unbearable heights as our spendings mingled, and again and again my raging cock slid uncontrollably in and out of that juicy cunt. Our orgasms crashed through almost simultaneously as she milked my cock of spurt after spurt of hot, sticky spunk.

Yet my rod was still hard and the shaft throbbed with energy as Louella squeezed it gently. She lowered her pouting mouth and slid her lips across the dome, with one hand massaging the inside of my thighs and the other cupping my hairy balls. My cock was again rock hard and slowly she sucked on her sugar-sweet until her mouth was full and I began to move slowly forwards and backwards with my hips as she noisily slurped on the huge rod that engorged her mouth. I screamed inwardly as she engulfed me, taking almost all my length sheathed deep in her throat, sucking so sweetly that I was soon forced to whisper that I could no longer hold back. Faster and faster I pumped my prick until she gently squeezed my balls and I exploded inside her mouth, filling it with salty white cream which she licked greedily before swallowing, lapping up my juices, wallowing in the sweet taste of sperm as I moaned out my ecstasy, bathed in that wonderful glow of release that flowed all over every fibre of my body.

This was the most wonderful fucking session but after coming three times in a very short space of time I was quite ready for other players to take the stage! Paul and Lucy had already stripped for action and Lucy was bending over the bed, thrusting her superbly rounded bum cheeks upwards and parting her legs so that we had a marvellous view of her vermilion cunny through which dribblings of love juice were already coursing down her thighs. Paul stood behind her and paused only to give a gentle rub to his long prick which, although not of the thickness of Pelham's or mine, was perhaps an inch or even two longer and it stood stiff as steel with its uncapped red dome reaching his belly-button.

Now he began in earnest. With one hand Paul manipulated Lucy's sensitive cunt lips and clitoris and with the other he moved his long stiff pronger in a gentle in-and-out movement in the little wrinkled arse-hole that beckoned him so invitingly. He increased the tempo and pushed deeper so that soon he was driving full in and Louella and I watched with great enjoyment the long shaft of Paul's tool whizz in and out of Lucy's wriggling bum. She responded with wild, rising cries of joy and it occurred to me that a girl who is well and frequently fucked may be seen by her bright complexion and general merriness to be so.

Paul's cock pistoned in and out and the long thick shaft of my own prick began to swell yet again and Louella rubbed the great rod fervently as at last Lucy reached the zenith of her pleasure and the bubble of passion burst. Paul shot powerful jets of jism into Lucy's bottom-hole as he worked that long prick all round its tight little sheath. His strong young prick spurted with such vigour that Lucy's thighs palpitated like moth wings as she reached the crest of a tremendous orgasm, her bum cheeks rhythmically swelling and tensing.

This had roused Louella to such a state that she could not bear to be bereft of the comfort of a prick in her cunt. She lay back and I moved on top of her and inserted my cock deep into the cunny that wetly enclosed its entire length. Louella gurgled with delight and her heels drummed upon the small of my back as her legs scissored round me.

'Get your cunt right on the shaft, Louella!' I cried, oblivious to the fact that Paul and Lucy were watching with renewed interest and—of even more import—the door of the room had opened and a young servant girl, Elaine, had entered. What a surprise for that sixteen-year-old beauty who had come merely to turn down the sheets of Lucy's bed! The pretty girl stood transfixed as she watched me fuck Louella who writhed around on the floor as I shafted her with long, hard driving strokes of my thick stiff prick.

'Now, Andrew, now!' Louella cried. 'Oh, my sweet love, fill me!'

My teeth were set with the coming of a lust that I could not restrain. I would not have cared if fifty young servant girls had been viewing us. I gripped Louella's hips like a maniac, forcing her even closer to me. Smoothing out every little wrinkle inside her sopping cunny, my cock drove to her soft depths and the great gusts of love pulsed and shot deep into her womb and she too climaxed in a glorious mutual spend. How we panted and threshed around as I pumped spunk into her with Louella's own effusion drenching my pubic hairs.

My cock drained to the last drop of spunk, I then fell full upon her, heaving with passion and exhaustion with my face pressed between her large titties. We looked up at Elaine who must have been astonished to see four naked young people cavorting around Miss Lucy's bedroom! She was an appealing girl of just sixteen with straight brown hair cut just short of her shoulders. Her lively brown eyes illuminated a fair-skinned face with clear, strong lines in nose and chin. The brown hair ended in a short, slanting fringe on her forehead. In her long skirt and blouse she gave a strong hint of having a firm and luscious figure with the contours of womanhood taking shape, especially in her breasts and hips.

'Go away, Elaine!' commanded Lucy. But still the girl stood stock still, saying nothing, but looking at the four of us with wide-open eyes.

'Go away, I said, you naughty girl. How dare you come into my room without first knocking,' said Lucy, her voice rising. 'Now go before I tell the housekeeper, Miss Carlton, who will dismiss you if I complain about your work!'

The girl recovered her senses. 'Oh, don't do that, Miss Lucy,' she said somewhat breathlessly. 'I did knock but you cannot have heard me. Goodness, what a fat prick you have Master Scott, it's even thicker than Fred's!'

I wondered who Fred might be and the girl must have read my thoughts. She said: 'Fred is the gardener's boy, Master Scott, and he loves me to rub his prick up and down until he spurts his white jets of fluid all over my hand. But although I've played with myself and let Fred frig me I still have not experienced that great joy of having a lovely stiff cock throb in my pussy. I don't suppose you would do me the honour, Master Scott?'

'Well, I don't know about that,' I said slowly. 'After all, I don't want to take your virginity.'

'Oh but I'm only a virgin in that I have never had a prick inside me, sir,' she said pleadingly. 'My hymen has gone with all the frigging and all I need now is a stiff prick. Please, please fuck me, I've always thought you the handsomest fellow of all at Nottsgrove!'

I looked around for advice. Paul shrugged his shoulders for this was one question that the scholar did not wish to answer. But the two girls nodded their heads and begged me to oblige the girl who was already unbuttoning her blouse, and even before I could give my assent she pulled off her camisole and unbuttoned her skirt so that she stood only in her stockings. The young minx went about her work without wearing any knickers! She later explained to me that she only did so on hot summer days when she was feeling roused and would go to the gardener's shed for a quick frig with young Fred. She stepped out of her shoes and unrolled her stockings so that she stood absolutely naked in front of me.

I was truly enthralled by the prospect of becoming the possessor of those gorgeous limbs for Elaine was a healthy, well-exercised girl. Her thighs were taut and lightly muscled. From the front I eyed her critically yet could find little fault. I viewed the narrow triangle of bushy brown hair above her cunt which was soon to be at my disposal. Her young belly was still firm and quite flat whilst she was also well-made in the seat. The cheeks of her bottom were nicely filled but without a pinch of surplus fat. I passed my hand round her waist, drawing her close to me, caressing the *rondeurs* of her fleshy bottom. My prick now began to rise majestically upwards, stiffening and swelling against my belly as I raised her chin with my free hand and passed my lips across hers. She quivered with delight and straining upwards rose on tiptoe with my hand now firmly on her bottom crack. I passed my forefinger under her bottom cheeks and instantly felt for the soft warm lips of her delicate little quim which moistened at the touch. The impress of our mouths grew stronger as her lips parted and she received my tongue, as she slipped her hand down to grasp my throbbing cock, gently frigging the shaft as her cunny began to grow damper and damper from her juices that were beginning to flow. Our tongues flashed together in such utter yearning that the moment clearly could no longer be delayed.

'You are sure, really sure that you want to be fucked, Elaine?' I asked anxiously.

'Yes, oh, yes, very, very much—and now!' she assented and we fell together on the floor, though I took care to lay her gently upon her back, so that she would not hurt herself. I knelt before her and firmly thrust her legs apart, raising myself above her whilst I placed my lips against her soft white breasts, washing my tongue over a tiny little titty and settling full down to a lick-flick mouthing until both stood hard and erect as she arched her torso up as if to offer them for further urgent attention. My tongue licked and licked eagerly and moved in swathes over the resilient youthfulness of her breasts. No girl's bosom was ever so thoroughly or lovingly licked and her nipples were now as hard as unripe berries to the touch. My cock was now bursting and I guided the huge uncovered knob to the pouting cunny lips that were ready to receive it. For a split second our hot eyes locked together and then, with an ineffable groan, I inserted some two inches of the meaty shaft and was full on top of her. Our lips collided and meshed together. She wriggled and worked her bottom to obtain a further length of cock inside her and this enabled me to embed more of my throbbing shaft as her cunny magically expanded to receive it. With a passionate jolt of my loins my prick was fully inserted and she cried out in glee as our bottoms began to work together in unison. How tightly her cunt enclasped and sucked upon my prick! We gloried in each giant thrust as her spendings dripped onto my balls as they banged against her arse. She implored me to drive deeper by twirling her tongue in my mouth, and cupped now in my broad palms, her tight bottom-cheeks rotated almost savagely as my tool rammed in and out lustily and she withdrew her mouth from mine, gasping and panting for air. Her kisses now rained upon my neck and I felt the throbbing of her pussy increase apace as she cried out aloud with joy at the stinging excitement of my thick prick driving furiously into her soft depths.

I plunged my face between her breasts and began to suck furiously at her left nipple whilst the friction in her cunt reached new heights as my prick began to move even faster, making us breathless with excitement. All the time she wriggled lasciviously and my tongue now lifted itself from the erect titty and shot into her mouth as she automatically flexed her vaginal muscles to milk the full length of my pulsating cock that was pumping in and out as my balls swished down, banging gently against her bum. Elaine was really finding out what the pleasures of a good fucking could be as her fingers now dug into the flesh of my back and her bucking torso wildly sought more and more of my prick as our pubic hairs crashed together. Alas, I could not contain myself much longer and she screamed with joy as, arching my body upwards, I plunged down hard, crushing her soft body beneath me as her legs flexed and she gurgled with pleasure as my frothy seed poured into her with a spurting gush. Elaine too had spent copiously and I hoped that our love juices would not stain the carpet. I said as much but Elaine quickly reassured me that she could remove any stains with a patent medicine!

'A patent medicine? That is very odd,' said Lucy. 'What on earth is it called?'

'Doctor Hopkins' cough medicine, Miss Lucy,' said Elaine, sitting herself down on the bed and showing no inclination to cover up her naked charms. 'Why, we buy it especially to take the stains out of the sheets in the dormitories when the boys soil them after playing with themselves.'

'Good heavens! I must remember not to buy the mixture for any other reason,' said Paul.

'Doctor White uses it too,' laughed Elaine. 'He says it makes his roses grow!'

We all laughed merrily and cuddled up to one another on Lucy's large bed. 'There is just one matter bothering me,' I said to Elaine. 'I really should have shot my load over your tummy, for the last thing we want is to put you in the family way. This was most thoughtless of me and I do hope that all will be well.'

'Oh, yes, Master Andrew,' she replied gaily. 'I have only just finished my curse days and I am certain that no harm will come to me.'

'We are not foolish,' chimed in Louella. 'We have to take

the risks so we are always as careful as possible, aren't we, ladies? I personally sponge myself afterwards with vinegar and lemon juice, but choosing the safe days is perhaps the best way.'

'I wish there was a medicine we could take to make us completely certain that no harm will come to us,' said Lucy thoughtfully. 'Whoever discovers such a potion will make his fortune.'

'Or perhaps *her* fortune!' corrected Louella. 'I believe there should be female doctors. We are quite capable of learning the art of medicine.'

'I agree with you,' said Paul. 'But don't let us begin a discussion on the rights of women just now. Instead, who knows what Samuel Pepys said about a course of action to take if a man got a swollen belly up.' None of us knew the answer. 'Why,' said Paul triumphantly, 'he said, and I quote: "He that do get a wench with child and marry her afterwards is as if a man should shit in his hat and then clap it on his head!" '

'That's all very well,' said Lucy. 'But hopefully there will be easy, cheap ways made available soon so that society can adopt a more responsible attitude about bringing unwanted children into the world. It is a grave problem and most unfair as women take all the blame and shame of such a situation as Pepys describes, whereas it takes two to make a belly swell.'

We all agreed with her observation but were in no mood for serious talking and soon we were entangled in one heap of bodies rolling around on the bed. Unfortunately, Paul and I have only one prick each so whilst we lay on our backs with Lucy on top of Paul and Louella wriggling her pert bum in front of my face as she lowered her dripping wet pussy on my rampant pole, poor Elaine had to be content with the role of spectator. However, I placed her down between Paul and myself and frigged her hairy little slit with two fingers whilst Paul diddled her titties to an upright stance.

Now Paul professed to be a Socialist and I was (and still am) a staunch Liberal but we agreed upon the unfairness of the distribution of the good things in life. Why should Elaine be deprived of a good fuck whilst Lucy and Louella had almost as many pricks as they could comfortably manage? So to make up for this unhealthy situation, Paul and I spread the lovely sixteen-year-old on the bed and I lay down on her right, lying on my left side, and moved her firm young body to face my own.

'I am now going to fuck you, Elaine,' I declared. 'And at the same time Paul will prod your tight little bum-hole with his prick, thus enabling you to enjoy a double dose of sheer bliss.'

'Will it hurt?' she enquired anxiously. 'I have never had a cock stuffed up my backside before.'

'Not at all, Elaine,' I reassured the trembling girl. 'Just relax completely and Paul will first wet his instrument to allow it free passage.'

'I will help him,' chimed in Lucy, and taking his great tool in her mouth, liberally coated it with spittle.

Without further ado, I reached for Elaine's shoulders and glued my lips to hers, holding my hands firmly upon her shoulders. She reached for my rock-hard cock and I pushed my knob inside those juicy portals, feeling myself buried to the hilt in her throbbing sheath. We began the old heaving and shoving motions and as she thrust her luscious bum cheeks backwards as I plunged into her, I grasped them and opened wide the crack in between, parting the rounded globes so that the tiny, wrinkled little brown bum-hole was fully exposed to the attack of Paul's long cock. Fortunately, the spittle and the fact that his tool was long rather than thick enabled him to push hard from the start. With only a short cry of discomfort he was well placed as Elaine began to wriggle and twist as we jointly rammed in and out. At one stage we both pushed in together so that I could feel my own prick rubbing against Paul's with only the thin divisional membrane running between us. This was simply too much for me to bear and I pumped jet after jet of frothy white jism as Elaine and Paul continued to writhe in new paroxysms of pleasure until, screaming with excitement, they reached the summit of the mountain of love and we three sank back quite sated from this novel experience.

Lucy and Louella were so fired up by our little threesome that they frigged themselves throughout the proceedings. But what a surprise was in store as, calmly as you please, young Elaine suddenly dived down and buried her head in Lucy's blonde muff, licking frantically all over the golden forest until she came to the lovely wet crack, revelling in the depths of Lucy's pussy and licking lasciviously inside her cunny-lips as far as her tongue would go, whilst one of her hands slipped under Lucy's bum and her forefinger invaded her bottom-hole, working in and out in a most exciting way.

Elaine's own bottom wriggled up and down and I jumped behind her and, passing my hand round her narrow waist, handled her luxuriously covered mount quite freely, slipping two fingers inside her juicy quim. Her bottom cheeks wriggled again, so with my free hand, I guided my already stiff cock between them. Paul's spendings had lubricated her arse-hole so my rigid prick slipped in quite easily, deeper and deeper as she rolled around, still keeping her head firmly between Lucy's legs, nibbling away at the swollen clitty as, with a series of sighs, Lucy tried desperately to rub herself off against Elaine's mouth. I had spent so much that day that it was several minutes before the hot squirts of cream shot off into Elaine's bum-hole, in such quantities that I felt completely drained as I withdrew my still extended prick, now red and a tiny bit raw from the little wrinkled home it had found. A final spatter of love juice dribbled down from my dome onto the floor. I adjusted my foreskin and Louella giggled. 'We'll need an extra bottle of Doctor Hopkins' medicine to clean the carpet!' she gasped, and we all burst out laughing merrily.

I was now too exhausted for even one more cockstand, but Louella managed to suck Paul up to a final full erection and Lucy and Elaine took turns to have his long cock in their bum-holes until he shot a full load of sperm into Louella's furry little cunt.

We exchanged our good-nights and crept back to our

beds—Louella having arranged to stay the night with Lucy—
and we none of us needed any potion to drug our senses. As
soon as my head touched the pillow I knew nothing more
until the morning alarm bell awakened me.

All that fucking must have been refreshing for my brain,
even though physically I was quite exhausted, for I remember
distinctly that an essay I composed that next morning on the
foreign policy of Pitt the Younger was awarded an alpha
minus by Doctor White—a rare honour rarely bestowed!

CHAPTER FIVE

DO YOU ever wonder, dear reader, who you are? Do you ever think that Mr Gladstone or the dear Queen ever wonder about who they think they really are? Or the Pope? Or even the editor of this esteemed journal of quality? Obviously they know who they really are but where, I would like to know, do their minds go to during those lazy daydreaming hours?

So far as I am able to ascertain from the study of science, man is the sole animal with this extraordinary ability to while away the time in daydreaming. Occasionally, when on a journey (for my work sometimes takes me to the provinces) I look around at the silent people in my railway carriage and ponder as to where their meditations are taking them, what private thoughts are coursing through their minds and what ideas are really behind those bland, expressionless faces, what lovers both imaginary and real are being wooed, what triumphs and failures are being lived and relived.

We are none of us quite what we appear to be. Running parallel with our physical existence, with our mundane chores and daily habits, is another secret, ghostly character, a private companion forever commenting upon what we see and do, rewriting the manuscript record of our lives in a manner more satisfying to us.

It is this gap between reality and fantasy, between what is and what might be or might have been which I find truly a source of endless fascination.

Will the fucking of a particular girl be an anticlimax, I wonder? Will reality be but a pale imitation of the adventures of the mind? We accept these dreams with hardly any consideration, never questioning for a moment our right to be able to leave our bodies for a while whenever the mood takes us but for some reason, as we progress from childhood to adult life, we become peculiarly embarrassed to admit to this. For the older we become, the less likely we are to admit to the more expansive fantasies, as grown-up, responsible citizens are supposed to have put away this childish habit. This is an impossible task for surely in all of us there are two beings that ride through life as if on a tandem bicycle, steered by the chap in front but commented upon endlessly by the man in the back seat.

I do not discourage daydreaming for it represents perhaps the only time in life when you can be sure of playing the lead role—and in that sense dreams are great levellers. In the vivid play that is acted out in the daydream all manner of wrongs are put right, all kinds of witty ripostes are applauded and the most beautiful of women conquered totally and without resistance.

Throughout my life I have daydreamed. As a child my fantasies were glorious, unblocked by considerations of reality, but adults dream, increasingly as the years slip away, about what might have been had their lives taken other turnings.

I must immediately confess to this kind of post-mortem, especially over the critical decisions which affect us until our dying days. We are all faced with a series of crossroads that are unique to us and we can continually look back and examine the routes that we chose, for better or for worse, that have brought us to the present time.

By and large this is a fruitless and indeed even a totally futile exercise, but then since when was mere futility the servant of common sense?

What brings these musings to mind? I suppose, reader, that were I to be fully truthful, my brain is taking a much needed respite from the hard labours of recall. Oh, do not misunderstand me—I have enjoyed penning these sexual exploits, which are all totally verifiable. If any person wishes to see proof furnished, simply write to me care of the Post Office, Sudbury, Suffolk and I will personally reply to all letters. How pleasant it is to recall that free and easy life we enjoyed as schoolboys at the Nottsgrove Academy for the Sons of Gentlefolk and what wonderful memories I have of that giant amongst mortals, dear old Doctor White, whose wise leadership has since influenced me and all other students to such good effect. What a man! His immense learning and erudition were matched only by his cheery manner and true kindness of heart which was shown to one and all, regardless of their station in life. He was a man who won the respect of both peer and pauper. And it seems that it is but yesterday that I was sitting in his book-lined study, sipping a glass of port and discussing with the old headmaster pertinent questions of social and political affairs which had been brought up in that day's edition of *The Times*.

You will see, then, how my mind has been straying far, far away on a merry trip to the lands of yesteryear whilst my body has been locked here in the admittedly splendidly comfortable present: the warm armchair in the library of my fine old friend Sir Lionel T——, himself of course a scholar and artist of great distinction.

So I have skeltered through this brief period of my adolescent life with great joy; which leads me to suggest that if we sometimes feel prisoners of our present circumstances, this may simply be because we are blocking the escape valves of our imagination. If all adults could play the innocent game of make-believe as do our children, we would, I dare suspect, live out our lives in a fuller, more contented fashion.

Let us now return to the main theme of this narrative, and I crave again the indulgence of the reader for my digression.

I awoke that next morning quite bleary-eyed and indeed I was so tired that I even forwent my usual morning ritual of shrinking my stiff prick by a vigorous tossing off. Today, however, I performed my ablutions as if in a trance and what I consumed at breakfast will forever remain a mystery as I have no recollection whatsoever of even sitting down in the dining hall that morning! Luckily, I could enjoy a free period after breakfast, which I spent taking a refreshing sleep in the library until the mid-morning break bell shattered my slumbers.

After the interval I joined the rest of my sixth form colleagues in the Art Room where Doctor White was due to give his weekly lecture upon matters of culture. I sat down next to Pelham who whispered to me: 'I say, old chap, are you quite well? You look rather tired.'

'I am somewhat sleepy,' I confessed. 'I just could not get to sleep last night.'

'Well, you are not the only one. Look at Paul sitting slumped over his desk. He also looks as pale as a ghost,' said Pelham.

I was pleased that at this point Doctor White swept in and began his dissertation immediately, thus saving me the problem of explaining to Pelham just why Paul and I were so exhausted at a quarter past eleven in the morning!

'My subject today is women in the arts,' rumbled the Doctor. 'Let us look at the status of women in society, and of the current agitation by many females to be freed from the ties of home and hearth.

'Of course, both men and women have always needed a great deal of determination to succeed in their various professions. But historically women have needed more determination and more talent merely to keep in the race for the glittering prizes even though both sexes alike suffer from inequalities of brainpower. Let us take art and politics. This latter subject is perhaps so controversial that we will keep discussion of it until next week's lecture. So let us today look solely at the world of art, a field in which practitioners have often been forced to suffer varying degrees of injustice.

'Every artist suffers in this way, but for women the injustice has always been greater, which goes much of the way to explain why relatively few women artists have surfaced and why so many have failed, or why so many women have made initial headway against male prejudices only to sink back later into obscurity.

'Even an ardent espouser of women's rights such as my niece Lucy will admit that no significant art movement has ever been started by a woman. But, gentlemen, we must ask ourselves why this is so. And the answer is very simple: historically there has always been a lack of educational facilities for girls and, even when they have matured, there has been a taboo against women at meeting places for artists such as bars, clubs or, heavens alive!, a genuine artist's studio! So there has been no real chance availed to them and the female artist has been left in painful solitude.

'There are still far too many obstacles in their path and I propose that we at Nottsgrove here and now symbolically show the way forward.'

On this stirring note he strode to the door and motioned into the room a most attractive young girl of about nineteen or twenty years old. She was slightly taller than the average with a mop of bright auburn curls that set off a cheeky little face, the best features of which were a *retroussé* nose and large grey eyes that sparkled with promise. Her slim, athletic frame was delightfully shown off by a close-fitting dark green costume in the modern style. My tiredness vanished in a trice at the sight of this lovely girl and my eyes gazed longingly at her small but perfectly-formed breasts that jutted out like two firm apples ripe for my mouth . . .

'Gentlemen, I would like to introduce Miss Agnes Carter to you. Miss Carter is a close friend of mine and . . . ' Doctor White looked balefully around the room as some of the fellows tittered at the thought of the headmaster having such a beautiful young female friend. I saw no reason for untoward merriment as Doctor White was certainly no mysogynist. If he was fortunate enough to find such a voluptuous companion, jolly good luck to them both!

'Good morning, boys!' said the young minx with a saucy smile. 'As you heard your headmaster tell you, it is now time for women to be given their fair chance at showing their artistic prowess. Over there you will see that on the raised platform in front of the blackboard I have set up my easel. On the floor lie my pencils and brushes. With your help we shall today show the world that it is the picture that matters and that the sex of the artist is immaterial.'

'I don't think that sex is ever immaterial!' whispered Pelham Forbes-Mackenzie and there was another murmur of laughter.

Doctor White stepped forward with a frown on his face and said: 'Who said that? Was that you, Forbes-Mackenzie? Yes? I thought so. Very well, you have just volunteered to be Miss Carter's model for this morning's lesson. As for you others, I want your words of honour that you will each remain absolutely silent for the rest of this lesson which will not end until luncheon at one o'clock. Have I your words, gentlemen?'

We were abashed and readily volunteered our promise to stay silent.

'Very well,' grunted our dear old pedagogue. 'Pelham, come up here on the dais. The rest of you, stay where you are. I must finish some administrative work this morning so I leave you in the very capable hands of Miss Carter. Boys! I rely on you all not to dishonour me, yourselves and the good old school.' And with that short speech he turned on his heel and left us to the tender mercies of our new young teacher.

'Your name is Pelham?' she enquired. 'Well, I will call you Pelham and you will call me Agnes. Is that satisfactory? Good. Now, Pelham, please remove your clothes and take up the position of—'

'What did you say, Miss Carter?' interrupted Pelham in astonishment.

'You may call me Agnes,' she replied patiently. 'I said take off your clothes and then I will show you in what position I should like you to pose before I begin my work.'

We tried hard not to laugh out loud at poor Pelham's predicament as we had given our sworn word not to break silence and all that could be heard was a muffled, choking laugh from fourteen lusty young throats.

'Come on, Pelham, don't be shy. Look, if it makes you feel any easier, I shall take off my jacket so all I shall be wearing is this blouse and skirt. I am kicking off these rather uncomfortable shoes—do not tell Doctor White, boys, as they were a present from him some few weeks ago on my nineteenth birthday. Now, Pelham, please do as I ask,' pleaded Agnes. Pelham was a ripping sport and he was not that shy, especially since Lucy and I had initiated him into *l'arte de faire l'amour*. So he sat down and removed his shoes and socks, slipped off his jacket and unbuttoned his trousers. He wriggled out of his trousers and under-drawers and stood up, covered just by a flapping white shirt which he pulled off over his head. His thick prick was dangling down but I could see the tip of his foreskin rise just a little and the head of his dome rose up too to give air, so to speak, to the little 'eye' in the centre though the dome itself remained capped by the skin of the shaft. He flexed his muscles and I saw that Agnes was very taken with the handsome young specimen who paraded his naked charms in front of her.

'Yes, that's fine, Pelham. Stand with your back to the blackboard at a slight angle to the class but facing me full on. Oh, yes, that is absolutely perfect, can you hold that position, please? Are you comfortable? Lay your hands on your thighs—good, now please keep completely still.'

Pelham complied with this gentle request and I must say that I admired his fine, manly torso. His muscular chest and flat, white belly were excellently proportioned, but of course the *pièce de résistance* was his thick rod which dangled down with its ruby-coloured head semi-covered; though it was clear that Nature, as ever, could not bear to be denied and that his massive prick was stiffening perceptibly even though his hands remained firmly in place on his thighs.

This fact had not escaped the attention of Agnes, who licked her lips voraciously but said nothing as that massive tool rose higher and higher, uncapping the red-topped dome and swelling up to a full nine inches, standing smartly to attention against his belly.

'My goodness, what a truly magnificent body and such a marvellously proportioned cock. It looks so powerful yet sweet enough to eat. May I be permitted to make a closer inspection?'

92

She moved across the dais and slipped her little hand round the monstrous shaft. Her long fingers, working as though they possessed a will of their own, began to frig the giant cock slowly, rubbing it up to an even greater height.

'Ah! I really am naughty to do this to you. How silly I am to let myself be excited by this handsome creature and his enormous prick. But oh! oh! I cannot help it! I must! I must!' she muttered as she drew back the skin, making its red head swell and bound in her hand. Pelham, nothing loath, remained silent as instructed by our mentor, but this did not prevent his massaging the firm little breasts that jutted out so provocatively in front of him. With her free hand Agnes unbuttoned her thin blouse to allow Pelham to pull off the offending garment from her and on this fine July day she wore nothing underneath, which gave all the boys the horn as those bouncy breasts with exquisitely swollen nipples were exposed to our view. Still holding on to the fat lollipop of a prick, she managed to unfasten her skirt and step out of it, and Pelham assisted the completion by pulling down her short cotton drawers. We feasted our gaze upon the delicious little triangle of auburn hair into which Pelham plunged his hand as their bodies crushed together in a fierce embrace. I could see his hand working inside her hairy mound, opening the large cunny lips and inserting first one and then two digits inside the moist vaginal entrance. Agnes groaned with passion. 'Stop, Pelham, dear, you must stop. I too made a promise to Doctor White which was that I would not let myself be fucked this morning by any boy in this class.'

She sighed as her frigging hand increased the pace of its motion and Pelham's face was now flushed, yet the stalwart fellow kept his word and not a sound passed his lips even when the sensual rubbing brought him quickly to the inevitable result and he spent copiously, the froth shooting out of his prick all over her hand and sprinkling her mossy mount and belly with spunk. But Pelham was a lively chap and his prick remained firmly upright and the hot, soft head was forcing its way between the love-lips of the naked beauty in his arms.

'Oh, Pelham,' she whispered. 'I must taste that luscious sweetmeat that feels too good merely to hold in my hand.'

She knelt in front of him and slowly nibbled away at the fiery swollen dome and then she opened her mouth and sucked away noisily, massaging her breasts with one hand and plunging her other hand deep inside her own quim.

Pelham's legs became as weak as jelly and luckily there was a chair behind him as he sank backwards. Some of the other chaps could no longer contain themselves and I saw Simon Allingham and John Mitchell free their bursting tools from the confines of their trousers and were busy frigging away. Meanwhile, poor Pelham could no longer hold back and his body racked with convulsions as he shot a series of pulsating emissions straight into Agnes's mouth which was like a suction pump, milking his cock of every last drop of sperm. Still the fiery girl would not release the juicy morsel that lay between her lips and within a trice she had sucked up that thick knob to almost a full erection.

'Now I am going to explain something to you all,' she said to the class, who by some superhuman dint of strength had managed to remain true to the vow of silence sworn to Doctor White. 'I want to be fucked but precious Pelham has already spunked copiously. His sperm tastes very well, too, with just the right salty tang that I crave. But as he must be somewhat tired I shall adapt the sexual position with the female on top so that he does not have to work so hard. You may wish to watch carefully for future reference if your wife or lady partner wants a fuck but you feel too tired to perform as well as you would like to do.'

She motioned to Pelham to lie down on the floor which he did with his noble prick waving like a flagpole, and then she sat astride him, pressing down the lips of her aching slit to the glowing head. She spread her cunny lips apart and directed the tip of his cock to the entrance and slowly sat down, letting Pelham feel the juices of her warm cunny clasp his raging prick. His hands slid across to her bare bottom and Agnes wriggled around to work the hard shaft of prick inside her as far up within her as possible. Agnes bounced merrily away on

94

Pelham's iron-hard rod and though my own prick was straining unbearably against the material of my trousers I successfully fought to retain my composure—unlike Allingham and Mitchell who were both jetting creamy spurts of white foam all over their hands and trousers (Elaine would need extra bottles of that famous stain-remover that afternoon!).

'Notice how well this so-called female superior position works,' gasped out Agnes. 'I can certainly advocate it for a change in one's regular fucking pattern although I do not recommend it as a steady diet. It is quite exhausting and leaves the girl to do most of the work! Unless she has excellent control of her vaginal muscles, she has to lift herself up and down with her legs in a rather cramped position and this may occasionally—ooh, Pelham, what a superb thick prick you have—this may set up harmonic motions which can spoil the fuck in a most exasperating way.

'Also, too much fucking in this position gives my cunt walls a hard pounding, especially if the boy is as well made as young thick-pricked Pelham. Oooooh, that's good. I think this method works best for me especially when I can sit down like this and grind my arse around whilst I work my cunny muscles—this gives my clitty a good rub as well!'

She worked her bottom from side to side as Pelham jerked his hips up and down, and then she caught his rhythm and lifted herself up and down to meet his upward thrusts with downward pushes of her own.

'You see, boys,' she gasped. 'Oh, Pelham, harder, harder. Ooooh! Oooooh! A man normally enjoys this kind of fuck immensely for all he has to do is lie back and watch although dear Pelham here is a considerate sort of chap who wants to give pleasure—oooh!—as well as simply receive it. There are lazy and self-indulgent types who like this method best, but this means that the girl becomes little more than a frigging post. So this is a good, convenient variant but as a regular way of fucking perhaps—ooh! Pelham, I'm coming, I'm coming!'

And as if by magic I saw the first gush of cream spurt out

of the top of his sinewy cock as they crashed together in a glorious mutual spend. Now Doctor White had commanded silence but surely a round of applause would not be considered amiss and I began to clap heartily which was immediately taken up by the other boys, even the sticky-fingered Allingham and Mitchell, and Agnes and Pelham stood up before us and bowed.

Agnes held up her hand for silence and said: 'Boys, I hope that you have learned an important lesson which perhaps Doctor White has already given the more advanced of you lusty young men. Making love is a partnership. You may eat and drink alone. You may listen to music in solitude or read a book all by yourself. But for a proper fuck you need two people and to make it perfect there must be no holding back. Know what your partner prefers or what he or she dislikes. And you too must be frank and state what are your own preferences. Is that fully understood? Good. Now, Pelham we must return to the original purpose of this lesson. Stand as we agreed and I will draw your body. Class, you are dismissed. Please leave quietly. I am going to finish my work and then we will dress and leave. There will be no more fucking to look at so you may all rest easy!'

At luncheon I sat next to Pelham and he confirmed that Agnes had told the truth. They had not even embraced until the lesson had ended and they said a fond *au revoir*. She was leaving Nottsgrove for London that afternoon but was returning after a duty visit to a sick aunt within a week.

'Jolly good,' I said. 'You will have a marvellous fuck when she comes back.'

'Won't I just!' said Pelham. 'All this exercise has made me ravenous. I'm going for seconds. See you after lunch!'

In fact I would not see Pelham until later in the day, as along with some five other fellows I was due to spend the rest of the afternoon in our music-room. I stopped to have a quick chat with one of the chaps about some later appoint-ment for cricket practice, and then hurried along to the music room where indeed I was the last man to arrive. However Professor Marchiano had not yet arrived (which was strange,

96

as unlike most Italians he was an extremely punctual person) and I sat down with relief.

'I say, Allingham,' said Peter Hodgson, who was captain of cricket. 'I saw you and Mitchell masturbating during the last lesson. You are two dirty beasts.'

'Nonsense!' said Allingham crisply. 'You just could not free your chopper before you came!'

'That's right!' said Mitchell robustly. 'I saw you and Dixon fondling each other's bulges.'

'Come on chaps, lay off!' I cried. 'Professor Marchiano will be here any moment. Indeed, I cannot think what has detained him as he is usually the first here.'

As I spoke the door opened and to my utter amazement in came Agnes Carter! What on earth was she doing here? As if she had read my thoughts she held up her hand to quell the buzz of noise that had erupted and said: 'I know I said goodbye before luncheon but regrettably Professor Marchiano is indisposed. He has a severe cold and Doctor White has asked me to take this lesson as my train does not leave until this evening and my cases are already packed.'

'Welcome again,' I blurted out. 'I am sure that this lesson will be just as stimulating.'

'I hope so, Scott—that is your name is it not? Very well, gentlemen, I believe that Professor Marchiano was about to deliver a lecture upon the great contemporary composer Bedrich Smetana. Would you please make yourselves comfortable and I will deliver his dissertation from the notes he would have used had he been well enough to be here.'

Life is a strange thing, is it not? A drunkard is forever being offered a glass, and for a fervent fucker like myself it seemed that temptation was again being thrown in my way. Still, I settled myself as comfortably as I could with a familiar swelling beginning in my cock as Agnes began her lecture.

'Smetana was born in March, 1824 and he enjoyed a calm and happy childhood in the charming little town of Litomsyl in Eastern Bohemia. He began his studies seriously in Prague but this period was marked by poverty and hardship which was only partially alleviated by giving music lessons to the sons and daughters of noble families. From dance pieces he wrote at this time he proceeded to the responsible and purposeful work of a serious composer. In 1856, to solve his difficult financial problems, he left for the Swedish seaport of Gothenburg where he gave successful concerts and worked as a teacher.

'He returned home although he visited Sweden several times afterwards. His first opera was well received, but his second opera 'The Bartered Bride' won international acclaim, and in 1866 he was appointed Kappelmeister of the Czech Opera, which at least allowed him to eke out a modest subsistence. In the course of the years he created several more operas but his extensive works were curtailed in 1874 when, at the age of fifty, he was suddenly struck by deafness. Nevertheless he continued his music writing despite this tremendous handicap, and soon afterwards composed his symphonic poems which were to be the first parts of his planned six-part cycle 'My Country'. Other operas followed of which my favourite is 'The Kiss' and another opera, 'Viola' sadly remained unfinished at his death three years ago. I am convinced that his work will survive his death and that he will be ranked as one of the most memorable composers of the century.'

We were all most disappointed as she droned on—then suddenly I had a most brilliant idea, and I raised my hand.

'The influence of Smetana upon his country's culture is certain to be—yes, Scott, why do you wish to interrupt me?'

'I do apologise, Miss Carter, only it is most devilishly warm in here. As you know, Doctor White does not allow the windows to be opened in case the sound of music or singing disturbs others. But this means that the room becomes uncomfortably warm. May I have your permission to remove my jacket?'

'Certainly, Scott, please feel free—and this applies to anyone else who wishes to take off a jacket. I myself will take off this cardigan,' she said.

Of course this was a signal for all six chaps to take off their jackets. I remember the scene as if it were only an hour ago.

There were Allingham, Mitchell, Pearce, Foster-Jeffries, Wilkinson and myself, and I must confess that I was the leader in the sport that quickly followed.

'I think I would prefer to loosen my tie,' I said carefully.

'Oh, very well, anyone who wishes to loosen their cravats, please do so now and perhaps we can return to our study of Smetana,' said Agnes rather crossly.

We all took off our ties and as I decided that I could not find an excuse for removing any other garment, I simply proceeded to take off my shoes and socks and began to unbuckle my trouser belt.

'Scott! What on earth do you think you are doing? Stop it, my goodness, stop it immediately or I shall call for assistance,' Agnes cried out in horror as I stepped out of my trousers and pulled off my vest, standing before her in my underdrawers with the knob of my prick clearly visible through the front vent. The other chaps realised that here was a lark indeed and quickly they all threw off all their clothes except for their drawers and we stood in a line facing the shocked girl who blushed furiously as Allingham's large circumcised prick (the poor fellow had suffered from a tight foreskin and had been forced to undergo a painful operation) suddenly stuck out of his white cotton briefs.

'I think you boys would prefer to fuck rather than to hear me talk about Smetana,' she said softly. 'Mind, you are all taking advantage of the fact that I am a new and inexperienced teacher, so I think I will show you that I can give as good as I can take! All right, just let's all get into the mood!'

She was as good as her word. She immediately unbuttoned her blouse and skirt and pulled down her drawers to expose her gorgeous nude body to our view. Five pricks shot up into the air in salute and she responded by rapidly pulling down all our drawers so that we too were all naked. She first went over to Mitchell who possessed a fleshy, medium-sized chopper and she kissed him violently, exploring his mouth with her tongue and putting his hands on her heaving breasts. Nothing loath, he cupped them, squeezed them and rubbed the nipples up to a fine erection. She traced a delicate pattern on his chest with her long fingers and then she swooped down to grasp his straining cock which she began to frig expertly, stroking the shaft and capping and uncapping the swollen knob which bulged quite alarmingly from her fist. Mitchell was obviously raw at this game so I moved over and began to kiss Agnes's large erect titties, and then bent my head down to suck them as I inserted a finger into her wet cunny which was already nicely juicy and ready for a good stiff prick.

'Let me show you how to fuck properly like a gentleman,' I said to Mitchell who stepped aside to let me face Agnes. She slid down onto the floor on her back and I sat forward on my knees, and she rubbed my prick to perfection. I moved forward to tease her outer cunt lips with my swollen knob before forcefully plunging it deep inside her sopping pussy as she instinctively opened her legs to receive me. She drew her legs up either side of my body as I began to fuck her slowly with long, powerful strokes. She gyrated wildly beneath me as if her vagina had never held a cock so big before, and what with the sensation of the fucking, her nipples grazing against my chest and the hot sun beating through the closed windows, I was almost fainting away with pleasure. So to maintain our momentum I quickened my stroke as she wrapped her legs across my back so that I could fuck her even more deeply; and then I was fucking her faster and we were kissing and biting each other in a sexual frenzy as the most indescribable pleasure built up in my balls and then in my shaft, which suddenly exploded into a blistering orgasm that attacked every nerve-end in my body as I spurted jet after jet of white spunk inside the delicious slit.

We spent a couple of seconds getting our breath back and then Agnes whispered: 'Oh, darling, that was marvellous. I came at least twice before you spunked. Now roll off and let someone else have his turn!'

Obediently I disengaged myself and Mitchell got down to join us on the rug. Agnes needed a moment or two to recover so she spent a minute kissing and fondling the handsome boy. I must admit that I was fascinated by the exposed glans of his large circumcised tool and I could see that he too became worked up by pulling her cunt lips apart and watching my sperm trickle down her thighs. He then positioned himself on top of her and slid his prick into her soaking slit, and the mix of Agnes's own love-juices and my coating of spunk enabled his sinewy weapon to slide in and out extremely easily. Agnes lay blissfully with her legs stretched wide and Mitchell's huge glistening cock shafting in and out; but then she whispered something that I could not hear and he withdrew his gleaming cock as Agnes rolled over onto her belly and then lifted herself on all fours so as to present her wrinkled little arse-hole to Mitchell's fat prick. He hesitated only a moment before pushing his cock into the tight, puckered little hole and Agnes drew in her breath. 'Hold on a moment,' I cautioned him. 'First wet your prick with spittle, for you surely have no wish to hurt your partner.'

He did as I advised and pushed ahead gamely whilst I called upon Wilkinson to kneel down in front of Agnes who immediately grabbed his huge, rock-hard cock in a delirious excitement. My work as master of ceremonies was not yet over and I motioned over Pearce to place himself next to Wilkinson. Agnes took hold of his meaty prick in her other hand and began to rub it up and down. She toyed with both the cocks for a moment and then began to rub them hard as Foster-Jeffries obeyed my murmured instruction to put his finely-formed prick, which was not too large but beautifully proportioned, by Agnes's mouth. My reading of Agnes's desires proved to be correct as she opened her mouth and sucked mightily on his lovely cock, a sucking that was accompanied by a delicious squelching noise. I rightly believed her cunt was a little sore from the pounding I had given it, so I took hold of poor Allingham's tool myself and frigged him to emission as there was no other way that he could be satisfied. Almost at once miniature jets of foam spurted out from her fast-moving hands as Wilkinson and Pearce climaxed in a deluge of spunk which left Agnes's hands coated with cream. Young Foster-Jeffries came too in torrents of sperm, most of which she was able to swallow. Mitchell was still valiantly fucking her bottom, and how they panted and threshed as he slewed up and down while her bottom cheeks rose and fell. All was soon over and he pumped his spunk into her, draining his cock of the last drop until he withdrew his shrinking member out of her arse.

We all collapsed in an exhausted heap, lying awhile in the sun regaining our strength and composure, as Agnes licked the last drops of spunk from Foster-Jeffries' prick and with a handkerchief dabbed the dribbles of juice that trickled down her glistening thighs, which were drenched with perspiration.

Soon we all dressed hurriedly, and I made the other chaps promise never to reveal a word as to what had taken place that afternoon.

'You must all appreciate what a jolly sport Agnes has been and she is going to suck off Allingham before she leaves us tonight as he didn't have a fuck or suck himself. Now we have all enjoyed ourselves, haven't we, so we must all protect Agnes's reputation amongst the more prudish members of society. There are many who would, *sub rosa*, have thoroughly enjoyed our delightful afternoon but would look askance at Agnes if what we all did ever came to their attention. Gentlemen, I am sure that Doctor White would want us to swear a vow of secrecy.'

They all readily agreed upon their honour as Nottsgrove scholars, when to our horror Doctor White entered the room.

'Well, boys, how was your lecture on Smetana?' he boomed out, and I noticed a jolly twinkle in his eye.

'I'm afraid we didn't get much further than a brief biographical sketch,' laughed Agnes, and I looked puzzled— surely I had not misjudged the situation?

'They behaved exquisitely,' she went on. 'Young Andrew Scott here was everything you said—a born leader who showed every courtesy to me as well as ensuring that as many boys as possible enjoyed my favours.'

'Excellent,' said Doctor White, stroking his curly beard. 'Boys, I think you deserve an explanation. May I present to you not Miss Agnes Carter but Miss Agnes Wilson, currently of the Alhambra Theatre, Holborn. She enjoys fucking young men and I well knew that none of you would mind helping to satisfy her needs. I further took this opportunity to devise my own test of initiative and I must congratulate you, Andrew, for your performance. Forbes-Mackenzie also deserves credit for his sterling work this morning. Agnes, my dear friend, I hope you are satisfied with our labours?'

'Oh, indeed I am, Doctor. How can I ever thank you? My cunny is rather sore just now but it was well worth the ache to have those iron-hard young rods inside my orifices. To mark this auspicious occasion I have asked my patron, Lord Paddington to donate two hundred guineas for the establishment of a scholarship that will allow boys from poorer homes with the necessary academic qualifications to study here at your wonderful establishment.'

'How very kind of you,' replied the good Doctor.

'Merciful heavens, Doctor White, I do assure you most wholeheartedly that the pleasure was quite a mutual affair. Now I must thank all your wonderful pupils again for a glorious bout of fucking that has afforded me much enjoyment.'

'Is there no way by which we can repay you?'

'Oh, I suppose there is perhaps one favour you may do for me. I would be most grateful if Allingham could be excused from his studies this afternoon as I have promised to suck him off—he has never enjoyed the sensation before now and I have no wish to break my promise, particularly to such a strapping young fellow who has such a fine, upstanding prick!'

Doctor White laughed and said: 'But of course you must not break your word. Allingham, you lucky young pup, you are excused for the rest of this afternoon. Everyone else, back to your labours immediately, please, as we have much work to get through before the end of this term and I don't want anyone falling behind. Agnes, my dear, once again, *au revoir*, and do come back to visit us again as soon as you can.'

I led the chaps in a rousing chorus of 'For She's A Jolly Good Fellow' and we trudged back to the classroom to complete the day's studies—which for us all was a most disappointing anti-climax! Indeed, I can hardly recall what we were studying, but as my mind fetches forth these happy memories from the store of my recollections, I am put in mind of those famous words of the Bard of Avon as so wittily changed by Lord Byron who wrote:

'There is a tide in the affairs of women
Which, when taken at the flood, lead on to God knows
  where!'
How true, how very true!

CHAPTER SIX

THE NEXT day we were assembled in the classroom listening to Doctor White comment upon the news of the day. The good doctor was always a strong proponent of women's rights, and on that particular day he snorted with fury at a letter written to *The Times* by some 'old fool of a retired colonel' about the proposal for women's suffrage.

'Listen to this idiot,' he snorted, 'I will read you what this misguided misogynist who probably prefers to have boys in his bed has written: "Quite as disagreeable as the bearded chin, the bass voice, flat chest and lean hips of a woman who has failed physically in her rightful development, the unfeminine ways of the wild women of politics and morals are even worse for the world in which they live. Their disdain is for the duties and limitations imposed upon them by nature, their desire as impossible as that of the moth for the star. Marriage, in its old-fashioned aspect as the union of two lives, they repudiate as a one-sided tyranny; and maternity for which, after all, women primarily exist, they regard as degradation.

"Their idea of freedom is their own preponderance, so that they shall do all they wish to do without let or hindrance from outside regulations or the restraints of self-discipline; their idea of morality, that men shall do nothing, they choose to disallow. Their grand aim is to directly influence imperial policies, while they, and those men who uphold them, desire to shake off their own peculiar responsibilities.

"This clamour for political rights is woman's confession of

105

sexual enmity. Gloss over it as we may, it comes to this in the end. No woman who loves her husband would wish to usurp his province. Unless we are prepared to make of marriage a mere civil partnership, dissoluble at will, it is certain that the normal relationship between husband and wife must be one of control and decision on the husband's side and deference and submission on the wife's. For when two ride on a horse, one must ride behind.

"It is only those whose instincts are inverted or whose anti-sexual vanity is insatiable, who would wish to take the reins from the strong masculine hands which have always held them to give to others—weaker, less capable and wholly unaccustomed.

"To women who love, their 'desire is to their husbands'; and the feeling remains as an echo in the soul when even the master's voice is silent. Amongst our most renowned women are some who say with their whole heart: 'I would rather have been the wife of a great man or the mother of a hero than what I am—famous in my own person.' A woman's own fame is barren. It begins and ends with herself whilst when reflected from her husband or her son, it has in it the glory of immortality—of continuance. Sex is in circumstance as well as in body and in mind. We date from our fathers, not our mothers; and the shield they won for valour counts to us still for honour." '

'Please, Sir,' interrupted Paul. 'Surely the great houses are mostly descended from the whores who pleasured King Charles II who gave his ladies titles of nobility?'

'Of course, my boy,' beamed Doctor White, 'but let me finish this pompous idiot's nonsense. He finishes thus: "The miserable little mannikin who creeps to obscurity, over-shadowed by his wife's glory is as pitiful in history as contemptible in fact. 'The husband of his wife' is no title to honour and the best and sweetest of our famous women take care that this shall not be said of them and theirs.

"My earnest hope is that the political franchise will not be given to women. To give it may be termed 'progress' but this will be progress in the wrong direction," ' he concluded, laying down the newspaper and adding: 'Now who will be the first to comment on this piece?'

Paul Hill-Wallace, by far the brainiest chap at Nottsgrove, was naturally the first to raise his hand and Doctor White nodded at him to begin his speech.

Paul cleared his throat, stood up and began: 'Gentlemen, a woman may never be fitted intellectually to be a Minister of the Crown, an ambassador or even—and this takes an enormous flight of imagination—to become Prime Minister; but with her present rate of progress he would be a rash man who would attempt to predict just how far she will go. But, I submit, this does not affect one way or another her right to vote or the right of the nation to have her opinion recorded. Why should she sit on a School Board, for example, and in that capacity make recommendations to Parliament on the Education Code only to be denied a voice in that august assembly to support its provisions or secure its rejection? It is all quite absurd.

'We cannot afford as a great nation to allow such a potent force for good as that of our women to lie fallow. With our new, vast cities and the ever-increasing complication of interests and industry, our lives are becoming more and more impersonal, and the combination of a strong moral influence of both sexes is vital. Men are going forward so fast, gentlemen, that the rift between the sexes will grow even wider if women are to continue to be stuck in the same rigid pattern and never be allowed to take a step in advance. The choice, then, is not between standing still and going on, it is between retreating and advancing.

'There is no sadder sight in the world than that of a wasted life, yet how wanton is the huge waste continually going on in the lives of thousands of intelligent young women, whose powers, by a long course of trivialities and mental stagnation, are being slowly diminished.'

Pearce rose to question the previous speaker. 'This is all very fine,' he said, 'but I am still not convinced of the necessity for female suffrage.'

There were immediate shouts of 'Boo', 'Shame' and even

107

'Go suck your cock' from around him, and Doctor White raised his arms in the air for quiet. 'Free speech!' he thundered, and the noise died down immediately. 'Carry on, my boy, we will all listen to you, however misguided your views appear to be.'

'Thank you, sir. My contention is simply that the great danger in giving voting power to women is that those best qualified would hold aloof from those whose distorted views of their social duties would lead them to seek public office, and women's views would be represented by the noisiest and least feminine of their sex.'

'Well argued, Pearce,' said Doctor White. 'Scott, can you speak against him?'

I slowly rose to my feet, thinking how best to phrase my words. 'The fact of the matter is thus,' I said slowly, marshalling my thoughts carefully. 'When women's suffrage does come, as it assuredly must, it will not come as an isolated phenomenon but as a necessary corollary of other radical changes which have been gradually introduced during this century. It will be a political change of relatively little significance alongside the great social, economic and educational changes that will have already taken place. It will have the effect of adjusting the political machinery of the country to the altered social conditions of its inhabitants.

'So the political change will not be a revolution but a public recognition by the State that the lot of women in England is not what it was, say, at the beginning of this century.'

I will not be falsely immodest, and will record that my words were cheered to the echo, not least by Lucy who had entered the room unseen to me as I was speaking. She exchanged a few words with Doctor White who beamed broadly and said to me: 'Scott, would you be so kind as to help my niece with some corrections to the French essays handed in by the fourth form? You are excused the rest of this lesson.'

I needed no second invitation and strode down the corridor with Lucy.

'What essays do you need me to correct, sweetheart? My

108

French is not nearly up to the standard you have achieved,' I said.

'Now, now, Andrew, you need not be so unforthcoming. We are not discussing equality of the sexes!' she laughed. 'Mind, your French is not as good as mine.'

'My French kissing is top-hole!' I said, grabbing the delectable girl and forcing my lips to hers, inserting my tongue between her rich cherry adornments.

'Not here, Andrew,' she giggled. 'At least wait till we reach my study.'

'Look, we're nearer my room, let's have a quick fuck there!' I begged. 'Why, here we are already, do step inside!'

She giggled again but did not refuse my invitation. I locked the door behind her as I wanted no interruptions and quickly we threw off our clothes. When we were both naked Lucy began to stroke my skin with her fingertips. My cock was already hard but the touch of her warm hands made it even more erect. She kissed me lightly on my cheek and then her lips travelled down onto my neck and shoulders and down my body, until she was on her knees and her hands were encircling my giant prick which stood high in the air flat against my belly. Her tongue flicked out and teased the end of my knob which was oozing a drop of semen. Instinctively I reached out and pulled her head towards me and she opened her mouth wide to swallow as much of the shaft that I pushed into her.

Her mouth was like a cave of fire which warmed but did not burn as her tongue circled my knob, savouring the juices which were dribbling from the end. Her teeth scraped the sensitive dome of my glans as she drew me in between those luscious lips, sucking hard, as though she wanted to suck me right off.

I let myself gently to the ground, and without loosening her mouth's grip upon my throbbing cock, she edged round until her cunt was above my head and the delicate slit opened and closed as she moved her thighs. Drops of love-juice pattered upon my face and I pulled her down until that lovely crack was upon my mouth. My tongue now was put to good use as it slid up and down the warm slit, savouring the taste and aroma. I heard Lucy gasp with delight as I probed between her love-lips and thrust deep into her vagina. Then I found her erect little clitty and began to roll it between my lips and suck it into my mouth as she moaned with pleasure and tried to excite herself even more by rubbing herself off against my mouth. I could feel her bite on my prick, but as I pushed in and out of her sopping mouth I felt only pure ecstasy as I felt my balls hardening, and I shouted that I was going to come.

'Pump into me, darling,' she cried, letting my cock out of her mouth. We quickly changed positions so my staff rammed into her velvety cunny and its spongy gripping was accentuated by Lucy waggling her bottom. I knew that my spunking could not be held back much longer. There was nothing I could now do but let go, and the semen boiled up in my shaft to squirt thickly out of my prick as I pushed hard to ram my tool full inside her sopping pussy, which was now awash with her own juices. She screamed with happiness as the hot, creamy sperm flooded into her and at once I felt her shuddering through a tremendous orgasm as she drained the last drops of spunk from my pulsating prick. We kept glued together until my cock, which had exercised itself quite magnificently that day, fell out from the juicy folds of its nest.

I covered my darling with burning kisses and we rolled about on my bed until my cock swelled up again and, as the poet Dryden has it:

'Thus every creature, and of every kind,
  The sweet joys of sweet coition find.'

Reader, you will know that first love can be idyllic or it can be unmitigated disaster. How fortunate was I to have Lucy as my loving tutor, to find a girl who took trouble to understand and cater for my every need, so making the act of sexual union so superb an experience for us both.

I kissed her large titties and her nips stood up like twin rosebuds; below, her white belly was set off at the bottom by the golden haired pubic mound. My hand still tweaking the nipple of her right breast, I slid my other arm further down and two of my questing fingers glissaded down into the inviting wetness of her cleft. She quivered all over and softly moaned as she opened her legs and took hold of my straining cock. Still playing inside her cunny lips I sucked on her rosy nipple until she begged me to insert my rod inside her. She guided my prick with her hands and I buried my cock in her sopping slit. Oh, ye Gods! how tight did her cunny clasp my prick, and what luscious suction was created by the juicy folds of her cunt as my piston shoved in and out of its sheath. How gloriously she met all my thrusts by the most energetic heaves and oh! how her fiery kisses were lavished upon my cheeks and lips as I pressed her to my bosom. To fully enjoy the pleasures of love, it is necessary to cast away all mental restraints, for man was made for woman and woman for man —and we revelled in our voluptuous delights with the utmost vigour.

Lucy was expert in the use of her vaginal muscles to contract and relax her cunny, and she made the passage tight as I slowly drew out my cock until only the dome remained inside, causing so great a suction that it sent a thrill of pleasure through my whole body. We played at this three or four times; I would slowly draw my prick out and then dart it in again to stretch and engorge the deliciously tight cunt that held me like a soft, moist hand. I worked away for as long as I could hold back and she spent twice more until the sensitive contractions of her clever little cunt milked my cock of a flood of boiling spunk that lubricated her innermost passages.

We sank back exhausted and fell to sleep, quite forgetting that we had Doctor White's work still hanging over our heads. I woke first after about an hour and watched my love who was still deep in the arms of Morpheus. Lucy goes to sleep the way you would close the door of a cupboard. So many times have I seen her lovely body squirm a moment as though she were fitting herself into a cocoon. She sighs once and at the end of it her eyes close and her lips, untroubled, fall into that wise and remote smile of the ancient Greek gods.

She smiles in her sleep, her breath purrs in her throat, not a snore but a kitten's purr. She insists that she does not dream yet she must, of course—simply, her dreams do not trouble her so she forgets them before awakening from her slumbers. Lucy loves to sleep and sleep welcomes her.

I gently shook her shoulder and she smiled sweetly at me. 'Don't worry, Andrew,' she said. 'In fact, I have finished all the marking by myself. I only wanted to drag you out of your class because I wanted you to fuck me.'

Her candid and truthful manner warmed my heart even more towards my beloved girl. I kissed her lovely lips and she responded by waggling her little tongue in my mouth, but then pulled away.

'We will fuck a little later, darling boy,' she said. 'Let us talk awhile. I rarely have the opportunity of speaking with you. We never engage in serious conversation but as soon as we come together my blood is so fired all I want to do is possess your lovely prick!'

I laughed aloud and replied: 'Very well, my dearest Lucy. Let us not coop ourselves up here in the study, for it is a perfectly lovely afternoon. The air is exquisite so let us get dressed and go out for a walk on Arkley Common. Then we can lie on the grass and discuss Irish Home Rule!'

'For the first part, yes my dear, but let us simply take our walk and forgo lying in the grass. Nature has good intentions but, as Aristotle once said, she cannot carry them out. Grass is hard and lumpy and damp and is often full of dreadful black insects.'

I laughed again and agreed to her demand, so we soon dressed ourselves and set out for the pleasant little green. I remembered that Rosalie, the girl who cleaned my study, was eighteen years old later in the week, and I resolved to buy her some trifle. I purchased some ribbons from the village shop, which was kept by a grumpy old curmudgeon by the name of Corney who lived with his wife and pretty young daughter, Danielle, who assisted him there.

'You know, dearest,' said Lucy, after I had made my purchase, 'old Mr Corney puts himself forward as the champion of respectability in conduct, of puritanism in life, and of morality in art.'

'Is he one of the killjoys?' I said absently. 'They can be very silly sometimes.'

'I think, indeed, that such people are sinister,' replied Lucy. 'It is their very certainty that disturbs me. They are so sure of their righteousness that they can never see even a morsel of justice in the argument put forward by an opponent. For me, *voila ou mènent les mauvais chemins . . .*'

'The paths of evil lead here,' I translated, to show Lucy that my French was up to the mark.

'Precisely, Andrew,' she added. 'I am always cautious of people who are so certain of the correctness of all their actions, for it can often lead to an opposite effect to that which was originally desired.'

'Are you thinking of something specific, my love?' I enquired.

'I am, dearest, but if I confide in you, may I have your assurance that what I say will be kept in the strictest confidence?'

'I give you my word as a Nottsgrovian,' I said and this oath was of course good enough for Lucy to share her secret with me.

'Very well, then, I shall entrust my secret with you. Some few weeks back you may recall that Doctor White was suffering with a summer chill. I decided to buy him some more handkerchiefs and I walked down to the village shop where I was served by Danielle, Mr Corney's daughter, who is only sixteen years of age.

'I could not fail to observe that she walked rather ungainly and I thought that I detected a strange bulge in the front of her dress. I asked her if she was well and to my horror she burst out crying and told me that her father had taken it into his head that she had been free with her sexual favours with the local youth. The truth is, Andrew, that she is *a virgo intact* and she has only been kissed by Arthur Greystokes, that fair-haired boy who runs errands and works as an apprentice to his father, the cobbler. I made so bold as to ask her if she had

113

ever been threaded and she swore to me that the furthest she had allowed Arthur to travel was to fondle her breasts through her clothing and she had rubbed his prick through the cloth of his trousers. But be that as it may, old Corney decided to make his daughter a chastity belt!'

'A chastity belt! In this enlightened day and age?' I cried out.

'I assure you that he has done so. She called me upstairs into her room as her parents were out and stripped to the skin. She has a lovely body, I must tell you, with firm young breasts and a very pattable bottom. But around her hips is a tight but flexible wire to which is attached a loincloth of leather which runs between her legs and is pulled up snugly between her bottom cheeks so that any attempts to reach her bum-hole will also be foiled. A wire mesh covers her cunny so that she can relieve herself but each morning her loving father locks his daughter up and unlocks it at night . . . .

'Now chastity belts date back to medieval times and perhaps were a result of the Crusades. When the knights knew that they would be away from their castles for many months, or even years, they did not trust their wives to remain cockless. I shudder to think what wearing this belt will do to this poor girl in these modern times.'

'Can you not talk to her mother?' I put in with some anxiety.

'Alas, she is completely dominated by her husband. I promised Danielle that I would not mention this to a soul but I have broken my word as I feel that someone should help the poor girl. Unfortunately, they have no close friends or relations to whom she can turn, which is why she told me about this dreadful garment.'

'How about the Vicar?' I suggested. 'The Reverend Ferningham is a most liberal gentleman who surely would not countenance such a barbarity?'

'Well, he has some goodness, I suppose,' said Lucy stiffly. 'But I cannot very well speak to him just now as we had a furious argument over dinner when he came over to the school last week. He was pontificating about the dignity of manual labour and I said that there was nothing necessarily dignified about manual labour at all and that most of it was absolutely degrading. He argued that men would become demoralised if they had no work and I countered by saying that many forms of labour are quite pleasureless activities and must be regarded as such. To sweep a slushy crossing, for example, for eight hours, especially when the wind is blowing, is a particularly disgusting occupation, and to sweep it with dignity or joy is impossible.'

I had no mind to argue the point but attempted to put Lucy back in a good humour by reciting a verse I had heard the village layabouts recite after a pint or two of ale.

'*There was an old vicar named Ferningham*
Who assaulted young girls whilst confirming 'em
Midst thunderous applause
He pulled down their drawers
And injected episcopal sperm in 'em!

'Rather a jolly poem, don't you think?' I said lightly.

'If you like limericks,' said Lucy. 'At least the filthy ones are funnier than those of Lear which I find extremely tedious.'

'Why, I know some jolly ones,' I said. 'Shall I tell you another one?'

'If you must,' she smiled.

'Alright; there's just time because we are almost at the Vicarage. Here goes:—

There once was a jolly old bloke
Who took a girl to his rooms for a poke
But she said that his prong
Was too thick and too long
So he shit in her shoes for a joke!'

Despite her attempting to put on a cross face, Lucy could not help giving a little giggle.

'Hush now, Andrew, no more poetry in front of the Vicar!' she admonished me, tapping me lightly on the nose with her forefinger.

I rang the bell of the front door of the vicarage but there was no reply. The Vicarage was surrounded by a quarter acre

115

of what could best be called mature garden, as the previous incumbent, Reverend Guy, had not bothered himself with keeping the lawns and flowerbeds in a tidy state. Reverend Ferningham, though, was a younger man, some thirty-five years old. Though of a slim build, he was strong and wiry and he liked nothing better than to amuse himself in his garden. Doctor White, as you will recall my mentioning very early in this narrative, was also a keen horticulturalist, and they spent many a pleasant afternoon in the Vicarage grounds.

To go behind the house required only the opening of a wooden gate and I suggested to Lucy that perhaps our quarry was busying himself there, so we went round the back. But again there was no sign of the vicar.

'He must be out,' said Lucy.

'Hold on a moment,' I said, looking towards the uncurtained windows of the drawing room. 'I do believe that I saw some movement inside the house. Let us take a closer look.'

Well, we did take a closer-look—and what a shock we had as we gazed through the open windows. For there on the couch, stark naked, was the Reverend Colin Ferningham and next to him, also stark naked, was Rosalie, the girl who cleaned my study and for whose eighteenth birthday I had purchased a present in the village shop. She was a pretty girl, a fact I had genuinely not noticed before now, full bodied and yet not run to fat, but firm and curvaceous everywhere, and she presented in her nudity, as tasty a sight of feminine pulchritude as ever I had seen.

Now they were kissing, and as his hand cupped one large breast I saw that his thick prick was standing stiff between his thighs and that Rosalie had taken the shaft of his tool between her long fingers. Her own nipples seemed to grow before my eyes and they stabbed at his palm as he fondled each lovely large breast in turn. Then, suddenly rising, he caught her in his arms, pulled her straight up and then placed her down on her back on the rich, red carpet which set off her white skin most fetchingly. He knelt between her parted legs and she pulled his head to her bosom and he turned his lips from side to side, kissing each bubbie as he encountered its warm, rounded sides and whilst doing so his right arm reached down so that his hand was set between her legs and his fingers played with the thick brush of dark hair that covered her mound. He parted the rolled lips of her cunny, pale pink as they were, protruding enchantingly through the nest of black curls and she twisted with desire, rolling her belly silkily on his stiff cock.

As he continued to suck hard on those raised-up little nipples, she threw back her head and moaned with joy. Ever so lightly, his fingertips traced the open, wet slit of her cunny, flicking the erect little clitty that was peeping out. Then the cunny lips were forced apart as he took hold of his own rigid pole and thrust the red crown between the pouting lips of the juicy pussy, and Rosalie moaned again with delight as he propelled in inch after inch until their pubic hair was matted together. The Vicar pulled right back, and then drove the powerful length of his shaft full depth inside the lovely girl again and again as she urged him on, closing her feet together at the small of his back to try and force even more of that throbbing tool inside her. Then he gave a series of little jerks and withdrew his glistening cock and pumped spurts of white spunk onto her belly.

'No, don't say a word. I know, my dear, that you haven't come,' said the Vicar. 'So let us continue.'

'I have, Vicar, honestly, I've come,' said Rosalie earnestly.

'That is very kind of you, my sweet girl, but a man can sense when his partner has achieved full satisfaction. Now you just go over to the settee and open up for me, there's a good girl.'

She did as she was told, sitting, however, with her legs dangling wide apart over the side of the settee. He clambered up and then sank down again, gazing at the open vagina and giving Lucy and I full view of the pink inner lips.

'It is so lovely, I must suck and kiss it and pay homage to that unique womanly scent,' said the Vicar, kissing her open cunt with his tongue running the full length of its parted lips. Rosalie shuddered as his tongue found her hardened clitty that I saw sticking out like a miniature cock and he gave it his full attention. Side to side, up and down, she began to jerk wildly. 'Oh, Vicar, more, more, I'm coming, I'm coming.' His hands gripped her hips as she moaned and writhed around making it difficult for him to keep his mouth on her clit. He took his face away from between her legs and began rubbing and pinching her clitty with his thumb and forefinger.

Now Rosalie was twisting from side to side as her love-juices began to flow again and her hands went to her breasts as she played with her own titties, roughly massaging those elongated nips.

'Rub it, oh, rub it, harder, please. Ooooh, Oooooh!' she cried as her gyrations increased as she twisted and writhed, heaved and humped; until with a shriek she achieved a full climax and imprisoned the hand between her legs, wrapping it tightly between her jerking thighs as she slowly subsided. The Vicar stood before her, the red knob of his prick still visible as it stood semi-erect in front of her.

'I have been naughty,' said Rosalie softly. 'I'm such a naughty girl.'

'Yes, you were naughty, weren't you?' said the Vicar, sitting down beside her. 'And you know what happens to naughty girls, don't you?'

There was a slight pause.

'You do know, don't you?' he said again.

'They get their bottoms slapped,' said Rosalie.

'Well then?' he queried and she rose and draped herself over his knees.

'Open your legs wider, that's right, you naughty girl, for I want to ensure that your cunny feels the edge of my slaps too.'

She was now fully bent over his knees and his left hand reached under to fondle her hanging breasts and his right hand ran gently over her fat, slack bottom cheeks. Then he brought both hands up to explore the intricacies of her bum, opening the cheeks then pushing them tightly together again. Then he started, lightly at first, a few rapid slaps which made her wriggle.

'Your bum cheeks are beginning to change colour now, Rosalie,' he said, delighted with his handiwork as he quickened the pace and increased the force of the slaps, which really must have stung Rosalie's bum as she jerked and winced under her 'punishment'.

'Now then, Rosalie, you have been naughty and you must get slapped like all naughty girls. Besides, I like to see your fat bum cheeks change colour for they should always be a little red just as they are now. Also, I like the way your cheeks jiggle when I slap them!'

He must have slapped her thirty times on the rump before she got up and stood with her back to him so that he could survey his handiwork. His cock was now standing stiffly upwards, slightly curving, but the skin was pulled back to show an almost purple knob, which twitched away as she turned back and sank to her knees in front of it.

'Would you like me to suck you?' she enquired.

'Oh yes, yes, I would love that very much if you would be so kind,' said the Vicar as she kissed the purple dome and licked her way round the rim.

'You do that magnificently, Rosalie. But I do not want to force you to do this. It is of your own free choice?' he said.

She nodded as she opened her wide mouth and slipped in the knob, enclosing her lips around it as tightly as she could and working on the tip with her tongue. She eased her lips forward, taking in a little more as her hands circled the base of his cock. She worked the loose skin up and down the shaft at the same time as she began to bob her head up and down, and his hands went to the back of her head, pushing her further down on his swollen prick. Somehow she managed to swallow even more of the shaft, and soon I saw that the Vicar could contain himself no longer as he thrust his hips upward and the sperm spurted into her mouth in powerful jets. She tried hard to swallow all the creamy emission but some of the flood dripped from her lips onto the carpet, a fact that was immediately noticed by Lucy, who whispered to me: 'This means another job for Doctor Hopkins' cough mixture which Elaine told us removes any stains.'

I could not contain my mirth at her merry jest and burst out laughing noisily. Naturally, I was heard by the lovers inside the lounge and they looked up, startled, towards the window.

'Do not concern yourselves,' Lucy called out. 'It is only Lucy Essex and Andrew Scott. We must apologise for disturbing you and for not making our presence known earlier.' We stepped through the French doors as the Vicar and Rosalie hastily pulled on their clothes.

'Master Andrew, you won't shop me, will you?' said Rosalie anxiously.

'Of course not, Rosalie! I hope you enjoyed yourself. Just don't get yourself in the family way!' I said, looking hard towards Reverend Ferningham.

'No I won't do that, sir. The Vicar never comes inside me except near my bleeding times and I always give myself a douche afterwards,' said Rosalie.

'That is very sensible,' said Lucy. 'I am all for enjoying a good fucking but it is us poor ladies who have to pay for any mistakes.'

'There we are in total agreement, Miss Essex,' said the Vicar, buttoning his shirt. 'Ah, I hope that our rather unnecessarily heated words of a few days ago will not lead to any unfortunate consequences regarding what you have just seen.'

'Oh, no, I am no sneak. But I must say that I am curious, to say the least, how a man of the cloth can fornicate like this even though it is true that neither of you are married persons,' said Lucy, somewhat stiffly.

'That is not an unfair observation,' I added as the Vicar looked a little worried.

'No, it is not unfair and I think you deserve an explanation. Will you wait a moment, however, whilst I say goodbye to Rosalie?'

'Of course we will,' I replied, and at his invitation we sat down whilst he whispered a few words to Rosalie, who wished us good-day as she left to go back to Nottsgrove.

The Vicar came back and offered us some refreshment. We

accepted a glass of wine and he settled himself back in his chair to explain the unusual happenings we had witnessed.

'Perhaps you do not know that before I entered the Church I studied medicine with some of the most learned professors in Europe,' he said. 'Indeed, after my graduation I spent two years in Paris with Doctor Kleiman and Doctor Bagell who are the foremost specialists in female nervous disorders.'

'Doctor Kleiman has developed a simple, though highly original, method of curing these disorders. I won't bother you with his theories on the origin of what he calls latent neuroses except to say that all women possess a sexual feeling which either develops or vanishes to frigidity in abnormal cases.

'As might be expected, these disorders develop most easily in young women who have been brought up extremely strictly and become virtual prisoners of their own education. They cannot bring themselves to express their sexual needs by taking lovers, and even inside bonds of marriage they cannot achieve any sexual pleasure or release. Yes, indeed, as the French writer, Dumas, has said, the bonds of wedlock are so heavy that it takes two to carry them—or even three.

'Now Doctor Kleiman has dared to suggest a cure which will rid the patient of her inhibitions and enable her to enjoy sexual intercourse, and thus enable her body to achieve the satisfaction it needs in order to maintain good health—and one must remember that this is all a question of health rather than strict morality in the conventional sense of the phrase.

'To begin with, the girl who is being helped is sent to a strange house, preferably away from her own home. Usually, she stays alone with her servants although occasionally two patients go together so that they may enjoy each other's company. Then after a few days, a gentleman comes along and takes the patient out for walks during the day, on rambles, on picnics or what have you. He then arrives for dinner on one day, and sees even more of the girl until—well, I think you understand the picture, don't you?'

Lucy was fascinated by his little lecture. 'That is very interesting, Vicar, but surely you are not saying that the male

121

visitor has to have sexual relations with the patient for a cure to be effected?' she asked.

'Oh, yes, very often this follows naturally; and it is precisely because the girls meet men of experience, vigour and, dare I say, wisdom and discretion which forms the basis of the cure. The doctor cannot place his patient in weak or clumsy hands. What may surprise you is that the majority of women go back to their husbands refreshed and invigorated, and both partners will thus have benefited from this treatment. It is true that unfortunately some women, a very few, have wished to divorce their husbands and marry their instructors. This has actually happened, but more usually a patient simply continues to use the services of her, ah, lover after she goes home. This liaison is not encouraged and usually this affair terminates of its own accord within a few months and again the woman and her husband are fully reconciled and fully enjoying life.'

'This is quite extraordinary,' I said. 'But surely, Rosalie is not married and needs no help in freeing herself from the confines of a nervous disorder.'

'That is not entirely true,' replied the Vicar. 'She is unmarried, as you rightly say, but she does suffer from a sexual disorder that I believe required treatment. I do not think that either of you will repeat what I say so I will tell you of her problem.'

'Just a moment,' Lucy interrupted. 'Are you still a doctor?'

'In the sense that I am a qualified practitioner, although after a disturbing personal experience that I do not wish to relate, I left medicine and entered the Church. My father, as perhaps you know, was Rector of Grantham in Lincolnshire and so I have followed his footsteps into the ministry. I do still keep up with the world of medicine and subscribe to all the learned journals. Some day, perhaps, I shall return to it but this work keeps me occupied and thanks to my aunt, who left me a most generous annuity, I have no financial cares and so I may freely choose to do with my life whatever may take my fancy.'

'Nevertheless, it surely is a most heavy responsibility,' I said.

'It most certainly is, and is not one to be undertaken lightly or immorally. This is why instructors have to be chosen with great discretion. I am afraid that you, for example, would be considered too young for such onerous work.'

'That may be,' said Lucy. 'Certainly, I would not want to act as a female teacher for any man who had such difficulties, although I do agree with what you are trying to do. However, you said that Rosalie had been suffering from a disorder.'

'That is correct,' he said. 'Would you like me to relate the full story? You would? Let me first pour you another glass of wine, perhaps. There, now I will tell you how all this came about.

'It began earlier this summer when Rosalie came to me in some distress. She had been walking out with young Arthur Greystokes, the youngest son of old Greystokes the cobbler, and he had asked her to marry him. I would have counselled against the nuptials as she is far too young, though that is not strictly relevant here.'

'I would have counselled against it too,' I said grimly, remembering what Danielle Corney had told Lucy about young Master Greystokes.

'Anyhow, like all courting couples they had indulged in some cuddling and kissing, and indeed they had progressed right up to the point of sexual union but then Rosalie's mind would not obey the dictates of her body and she could not enjoy herself further than the gates of the mansion, so to speak.

'Perhaps you know that she is an educated girl who comes from a most respectable family. Her father was a chief clerk at a City Office until he was tragically injured by a gang of hooligans as he was walking home one night after work. He never fully recovered, and died not long after, leaving the family almost destitute. Fortunately, a wealthy relative in America now knows of their plight and has offered to bring them all out to his home in New York. They will leave in

October. Until then Rosalie, her brother, and her two sisters are working even at menial jobs to scrape together enough money to enable her eldest brother to continue his studies at medical school in London. This is how I knew Rosalie, as one of her brother's lecturers is a friend of mine.

'Of course, when she first mentioned her problem to me, I counselled against partaking of forbidden fruits, as sexual intercourse should take place inside the bounds of holy matrimony; although this narrow interpretation of the Scriptures is now being challenged by many people.

'I was firm about this until I was completely convinced that she was going to have sexual intercourse regardless of what I said, and of course that she knew when to abstain from the activity to avoid an unwanted parturient condition.

'She assured me that she was fully aware of everything I had said and to prove her point she handed me her diary out of which I will now read a relevant passage. This is what happened to Rosalie a few months ago on her day off . . .

Rosalie's Diary

It was a gloriously hot morning and the sun was high overhead, sending down great shafts of golden light, warming the earth and sparkling in the still dew-wet grass.

I was walking barefoot in the lush green meadow, my long thin dress hanging loosely on my otherwise naked body, my hair falling on my shoulders and moving slightly in the gentle breeze, filling me with a sense of freedom and carelessness that urged me to throw off my dress and run totally naked and uninhibited until I reached some distant land of erotic pleasure. I sat down on a hummock of earth which pressed into my cunny and sent an exciting, shivering sensation right through me. I leaned back against a huge tree trunk which stood behind me, opening my legs wide so that the sun struck warmly on my pussy, making its curly dark hair shine and glisten in the light. I closed my eyes, allowing the warmth to seep through me, filling me with an acute and sensuous awareness of my own physical being. I moved my hand lazily to my thigh and ran my fingertips along its smooth surface.

My hand moved down and began to fondle the lips of my cunt, rubbing up and down until I could feel the moisture beginning to form and dampen my fingertips. It filled me with an intense feeling of wholeness, and with a realisation that I could so easily fulfil my own physical needs.

Suddenly, I heard a crackling of dry leaves behind me and I didn't turn round or cease rubbing my moist pussy although I was aware that someone could be watching me from a close distance. I heard nothing more for a moment, and then who should it be but dear Arthur who walked out from behind a clump of bushes. He came towards me and stopped not a foot from where I was propped up against the tree. How tall he looked, and how I loved the mass of fair curling hair which fell forward over his face. He had a strong body, and the lump which protruded forward from his trousers looked as firm as ever. His acute blue eyes roamed all over my body but stopped at my open pussy and he smiled as he sat down, facing me but still not speaking.

'Were you looking for me?' I asked.

'Might have been, might have been looking for someone else!' he replied laconically.

'I came out here to feel sensual,' I said, 'but as you are now here—'

'Let's fuck, then,' he said quickly.

'Oh, Arthur, you cannot just undress, jump on and fuck and then simply go away leaving me wondering what on earth has happened. You must seduce me like the sun and breeze do.'

'You are over-romantic, Rosalie, and anyway the sun and the breeze cannot fuck you like my prick can,' he retorted.

'But the sun can make me feel sexual and I can do the rest by myself,' I said.

'That is not nearly so satisfying, especially when you know that you care for me,' he said. 'I will show you how good fucking can really be.'

'Oh, Arthur, will you really?'

Without replying he slid down so that he was lying beside me. I stretched my legs out in front of me leaving them wide

125

apart. My dress was lying in a cotton pile just above my pussy and his hand came to rest on my neck and he twisted his fingers through my hair. His face moved closer to mine and his moist lips touched my neck and gently moved up so that I could hear and feel his soft breathing in my ear. He took my dress in both hands and lifted it up and over my head so that now I lay totally naked before him. His fingers brushed my breasts lightly and my nipples immediately jumped to attention.

'You have really fantastic bubbies,' he muttered softly. 'Let me suck you.'

His mouth came down to meet the soft flesh, his hands gently pushing my titties together as his tongue came forward and circled round my roused nipples. Then his mouth opened and drew in the soft flesh, his tongue constantly moving, sending wild vibrations through my whole body. Then he let go my breasts and ran his hand down and over my belly until his fingers were caressing my pubic bush. My cunt throbbed, pulsing my juice from me in a hot sticky wetness. His mouth was now on my titties again, his tongue reaching out to slide around my nipples. His hand moved in and out of my now thoroughly wet cunny until he was sliding his wicked fingers around my pulsating clitty, pressing it and releasing it in a throbbing movement and my juices were now flowing freely as he inserted first one, then two and then three fingers up and into me. I moved my own hand to the bulge in front of his trousers, which he had unbuttoned, and I pushed my fingers down to feel the proud stiffness of his thick cock. He helped me pull down his trousers and drawers and his naked prick stood out hard before me. I moved forward and brought my lips down onto it. My tongue ran the length of the shaft and ran back to the dome to catch a hot sticky drip of spend that had formed at the 'eye' of the knob. I ran my lips around the tip of his noble cock and then I opened my mouth to accept its entrance. In one single movement he forced at least three inches into my mouth and my body jerked violently from the utter force of it. He retracted slightly so that it lay motionless, though throbbing on my

126

tongue. I closed my lips around the monster sweetmeat and moved my tongue across its width. I sucked greedily on his prick as Arthur twisted himself down so that his face was pushed into my love pit, and my head almost swam with delight as his tongue began to circle around my dripping crack.

Arthur's mouth closed in on my cunt as I continued to suck his throbbing cock. His own soft tongue ran along my slit in moist, teasing strokes and I moved my cunt up and down as Arthur rolled his hips to move his cock in and out of my yearning mouth. I squeezed his balls gently, and then like liquid fire he shot jets of hot, creamy spunk which poured down my throat in a frenzy of salty froth, and I swallowed it to the last burning drops.

Meanwhile, his tongue continued to quiver across my frantic clitty as I swayed my body in harmony with his hard-working tongue. At last I felt my body rocket to the heights of ecstatic madness and I moaned and tossed my head from side to side with the sheer unashamed glory of my long-awaited climax. I fell silent, shuddering quietly as each exhausted throb of relief echoed within my numbed clitty.

Arthur lifted his head from my sopping bush and he twisted back again so that his body was on top of mine and I could feel his prick stiffening up again against my cunt. Now my own body stiffened and for no reason I can give, I sat up and stared at him, all the time feeling the heat of my passion draining from me.

'What is the matter?' Arthur said, looking up at me.

'I don't know,' I said truthfully, although I somehow knew that he would not really understand.

'You've frozen up again just when I was going to fuck you,' he shouted. 'You told me to seduce you and I did but it's always the same story. Anyone would think that you were offering me Aladdin's Lamp! I am tired of all this nonsense!'

Then he pushed me down again and threw himself on top of me. His hands roamed all over my body in hurried clumsy movements. Suddenly he relaxed and leaning himself up on his elbows, he looked down into my face.

'Oh come on, Rosalie,' he said. 'You know that I cannot fuck you if you just freeze up like a block of ice. Come on, relax.'

But try as I would, I just could not let him fuck me and he stormed off in a rage saying that he wanted to break the arrangement we had and that he could find plenty of other girls who would happily let him fuck them all day and all night if he wanted.

The Vicar concluded this extract from Rosalie's diary and sipped at his glass of wine.

'That is most interesting,' said Lucy. 'But the question now of course is what caused her to be so frightened of letting Arthur fuck her. Was she a virgin, may I ask?'

'No, she had some limited experience in *l'art de faire l'amour*,' he replied, 'but only with one boy, and she had not enjoyed the experience as much as she might.'

'And because she did not enjoy the experience she was frightened to try again,' I said triumphantly.

'This is partly true. But another part of the cause was young Arthur himself who was a selfish brute and concerned only with his own pleasure. A few gentle words coupled with understanding patience might have solved the problem. If he had known better he could have purchased some cold cream although a favourite remedy for many couples is to slip a pillow in between the buttocks. This helps enormously to open out the cunny lips and make insertion easier.'

'Perhaps she was afraid of the size of his weapon,' suggested Lucy.

'I don't think so, although I am sure you will agree, my dear, that some foolish men seem to expect their girls to swoon with pleasure at the very sight of an outsize prick.'

'Yes, they do and they are very silly,' said Lucy warmly. 'Some men are sufficiently conceited to believe that a huge prick will immediately reduce the recipient to quivering ecstasy. Now I have sampled men of surprising variance of size, and neither of the two ten-inch partners I have had seemed to care a button about the finer points of the game.

On each occasion with both these men, their assurances that they would be careful were forgotten during their final throes, resulting in my experiencing in a severe, stabbing pain which led to the complete inability on my part to reach orgasm.

'The average or even smaller-than-average man, on the other hand, is more aware that he cannot rely solely on sheer dimension to bring pleasure and is generally more careful to make the act more interesting by bringing a sense of variety and purpose to his love-making.'

'I do so agree with you,' said the Vicar. 'Unusual length and girth may look quite splendid, but although they might afford an initial advantage, occasionally an oversized member can be a hazard to enjoyable sport and indeed in general size is totally unimportant. What a man needs most of all is the ability to exercise his imagination, consideration and patience.'

'I could not express these sentiments better,' cried Lucy. 'Why, I must confess to you that while Andrew's prick is of good size and he has the ability to use it well, I have been transported out of this world by the manipulation of two skilfully wielded fingers! It is a man's attitude that makes him a good lover, like Andrew here, rather than the size or shape of his equipment.'

'Thank you very much,' I said rather indignantly. 'Are you saying that my cock is too small for you?'

'Oh no, my dearest,' she laughed. 'It is just the right size and it possesses the best owner in all the world. All the Vicar and I are saying is that even the smallest tool can be like a paintbrush in the hands of an artist and that an overgrown prick can never even match a smaller one if the possessor of the large instrument does not know how to play the right melody!'

'Indeed this is so,' said the Vicar. 'Anyhow, I was telling you about Rosalie. She came to me for advice about how to solve this problem and I concluded that Arthur was far too immature a youth for her. And as we talked I must allow that I became somewhat infatuated with this pretty young girl.

'One fine day we were walking hand in hand across that

very same meadow where she had experienced her problem with Arthur and we nestled down by that very same tree trunk. I knelt down by her side and took her right hand and placed it on my cheek. Slowly her fingertips moved across my face, exploring my cheeks, my nose and my mouth and I then took hold of her hand and imprisoned it gently in my own. "I am ready now," she whispered but I hesitated—for surely she did not want me to complete the union she once desired with Arthur. "Please, please take me," she murmured, "I do so want you to make love to me." I resolved to see whether she really wanted me as opposed to the wretched boy, so I silenced her pleadings with a kiss which startled her, although she did not try to draw away. And then, as I gently forced open her lips with my tongue, she responded and clasped me round the neck. My hands held her shoulders lightly and then slid down, delving into her dress, breaking open the tiny buttons until her wriggling pulled her full firm young breasts out into the open air. I kissed her passionately again with my hand cupping those gorgeous breasts, and to my astonishment the sweet young girl moved her hand downwards to grasp my swollen tool and rubbed the shaft through the material of my trousers with her palm.

'Then to my astonishment and delight she moved away, and pulled up her frock over her head and cast it off, her raised arms momentarily muffled by it. Then her alabaster white nudity was there in front of me, her slender legs, her uptilted, pointed breasts, her flat belly below which her curly-haired love mound seemed to glint in the warm sunshine. I took her in my arms, and with my mouth on hers started to caress her thighs, and then my mouth slid down her perfect pulsating body, planting kisses on each raised nipple, then her navel until, now using both hands, I prised apart her legs and buried my face between her unresisting thighs. I licked the juice round her cunt lips and she lifted her bottom as my hands clasped her bum cheeks to lift them nearer to me. Her pussy seemed to open wide as I slipped my tongue through the pink lips and licked away between the inner grooves in long thrusting strokes. Her cunny was now gushing love-juice, and each time I tongued her the little clitty stiffened even more eagerly. I tasted her sweetness, rousing her to new peaks of delight, and her hands began to caress my hair and my cheeks, pressing on my temples as if to direct my onslaught. She exploded once, twice and yet still was not satisfied as I continued my caresses and her hips and her bottom moved in synchronised rhythm with my mouth. Her body was jerking away and my face rubbed against her thick curly bush as she screamed again with delight, and I worked my tongue until my jaw ached. Heaving violently the lovely girl managed to achieve the heights of bliss again as she gently pushed my face away from her juicy slit. "Fuck me, oh, you must fuck me now!" she gasped, and I could not deny either her or my body as chills of lust ran up and down my spine.

'My eyes were on the full flow of breasts, waist, hips and thighs as I quickly peeled off my garments and my tool sprang up fierce and free as the sweet girl kissed the uncapped red dome. She clutched at my cock and brought it to her mouth as I lay over her. She rolled her tongue round the swollen knob, and I could feel the loving playful bite of her pearly teeth. She sucked hard on my shaft and I felt my prick swell even nearer to bursting point, and I spurted a creamy emission into her tight yet luscious little mouth which was engorged with my swollen prick. She eagerly sucked every drop of my sperm and despite my copious spend, my prick was still ramrod stiff as I slowly withdrew it from her pouting lips. First wetting my finger in her juicy crack, I easily inserted it in her beautifully wrinkled brown bum-hole and I worked her up to such a state of desire that she grabbed my prick and pushed the head just slightly between the outer lips of her cunny.

'Then, throwing her arms around my neck, she drew my lips to hers, as she thrust her tongue into my mouth with all the wild abandon of love, and shoved up her bottom to meet my charge. I had placed one hand under her buttocks, while with the other I kept my cock straight to the mark and plunged into her, stretching the resilient opening of her young cunny. She spread her legs and bent her knees so that her

131

heels rested lightly on the small of my back. I pressed in and out gently and slowly, and the sensations produced on my swollen cock by her tight little cunt were almost unendurable. I knew that soon I would have to come, but I wanted to make this last for both our sakes. Unbelievably, I found the control I sought so desperately, and began to move a little more quickly. Rosalie was immediately responsive and twining her legs now about my waist she asked me to put my hands under her hips and lift her. I did as instructed and then thrust my full length inside her. As I kept my prick deep inside she began to rub her clitty hard against my rigid shaft, and I began to pump wildly feeling my balls slapping against her bottom as her sighs turned to moans and then a shriek as she reached the heights of ecstasy; and I flooded her cunny with jets of hot sperm so powerful that the love juices oozed out of her luscious nest to trickle slowly down her thighs. A few frenetic quiverings more and I slowly took out my now turgid cock and we lay in each other's arms, while over us the summer sky stretched like a giant blue tent and the smell of the crushed grasses beneath us mingled with our perspiration. The dance of butterflies, disturbed by our advent, reformed its fluttering patterns above our heads.'

We sat silently for a moment or two as the Vicar concluded his moving tale of love and passion.

'You obviously feel much love for this sweet girl,' commented Lucy. 'Do you wish to make your liaison a permanent one or do you plan to love and leave her?'

'Oh no, if she will do me the honour of becoming my wife I would be the happiest man in the world, but I fear that she will not have me because the difference in our ages is too great,' he said.

'Has she told you this?'

'No, she is the dearest soul and would not dream of hurting my feelings but I am sure that she feels this way.'

'I will speak to her and advise her not to be so silly—if indeed she does believe such foolishness,' said Lucy. 'I know that there is a gap of some eighteen years between you but this is not such a high barrier that it cannot be surmounted. As soon as I know what Rosalie really feels I will communicate those feelings to you.'

'You are most kind, my dear Lucy, how can I ever repay you?'

'There is a matter upon which I would welcome your aid,' she said, remembering the original purpose of our visit. 'I have come about poor Danielle Corney.'

The Vicar held up his hands. 'Say no more, I am sure that I know what you are going to ask. Is this about that dreadful belt that she wears? Am I correct? Yes, I thought so. Well, I can assure you that I have tried very hard to persuade old Corney to take off the stupid contraption but he will not listen to reason. What makes him so adamant is that ignoble fear that his daughter will take after his wife's example. As you may know, Mrs Corney is half French and she has a most passionate nature. It has come to my ears that she is, shall we say, somewhat free with her favours as her husband suffers somewhat from drinking too much ale and cannot always satisfy his wife in the marital pleasures.'

'So he takes out his worries on his poor daughter,' I said.

'Yes, I am afraid so, but there is nothing you or I can do about it as she is still under his care. By all means try and reason with him but I think you will find him to be a most stubborn old man. But having said that I have just remembered that my old mentor Doctor Kleiman of Vienna is coming to stay with me for a few days and is arriving in the morning. If you can persuade Mr Corney to come and see the doctor I am sure we can sort this whole sorry business out once and for all.'

'That seems a marvellous suggestion, Vicar,' beamed Lucy. 'Andrew and I will go and see Mr Corney now.'

'You will find him in Oaklands Lane,' called out the Vicar as we turned to leave. 'I know that he makes his deliveries there this afternoon to the big houses with his pony and cart.'

It was only a matter of a few minutes walk to Oaklands Lane, where we soon spotted the old red cart that Mr Corney used for making deliveries to the neighbourhood 'swells'. The pony was munching his way through a nosebag that Mr Corney had thoughtfully placed round the animal's neck.

'That is a little strange,' I said quietly to Lucy. 'I would have thought that Mr Corney only spent a minute or two in each house. Surely it would have made more sense to give the pony his meal after his deliveries had been made.'

'Well, let us wait here for him to come out of that fine new mansion on the corner,' said Lucy.

We sat down on a bank of dry grass for about ten minutes but there was still no sign of the missing shopkeeper.

'He must be inside that new house,' said Lucy firmly. 'Let us go round the back as we did at the Vicarage and see what he is up to.'

So we walked round the side to the tradesmen's entrance which was barred only by an unlatched door, and I was about to ring the back doorbell when Lucy pulled urgently at my sleeve.

'Andrew,' she whispered softly. 'I can hardly believe my eyes. Look there, in the garden. Is there something in the well water here in Arkley which makes people behave like this?'

Reader, I know well that you will hardly credit what we saw but for the second time in the space of an hour or two at the most, we saw yet another couple both quite naked, heaving merrily away on a large towel that had been draped on the back lawn! At first I could not make out who the two participants in this frenzied bout of fucking might be, but as we noiselessly approached it was clear that the owner of the fat bottom which wobbled up and down as he plunged his prick into the squelchy cunny below was none other than old Mr Corney himself! We took cover behind a huge clump of bushes, as with a final great shudder Corney discharged his seed over the belly of the well-proportioned girl underneath him. With a cry, she too finished her spending and he rolled off her, panting like a great whale for he must have weighed at least fifteen stone. He was a large man, over six feet tall and well-proportioned except for a large belly which flopped around with folds of fat as he went on his knees to wipe his wet prick with the edge of the towel. I stared at the extremely attractive girl who was dabbing at her cunt with a large handkerchief.

'Her name is Angela Anglethorpe,' whispered Lucy. 'She is the daughter of Sir Graeme and Lady Vera Anglethorpe whose residence this is, and she is only nineteen years old.'

My eyes took in more of this beautiful creature. Her hair was of a deep brown colour and she wore it long and loose so that as she sat up it hung down behind her back almost to her bottom. Her cheeks were rosy-red and her full lips were like ripe cherries while her teeth, as white as the snow of winter, were even and firm. I noted her graceful neck, her small but superbly formed uptilted young breasts each crowned with a tiny button of a pink nipple, the slender waist and there at the base of her belly was perhaps the most exquisite cunt I have ever been privileged to see.

Her splendid mount was covered with glossy brown hair, and the serrated lips of her cunny were slightly parted. From them there projected quite three inches a stiff fleshy clitoris as big as a man's thumb. She idly parted the lips with her long tapering fingers and my prick sprang to attention as I imagined passing my tongue lasciviously about those most sensitive parts, taking that glorious clitty in my mouth, rolling my tongue around it and playfully biting it with my teeth; and from Lucy's heavy breathing I knew full well that similar thoughts were passing through her mind.

Before I could say anything, Lucy stepped boldly out and approached Angela who gave a little gasp of surprise. 'Lucy,' she squawked, 'what on earth brings you here?' As for Mr Corney, he looked on dumbfounded.

'Never mind that now,' said Lucy sweetly. 'Is this a game for only two players or may a third party join in?'

'I have no objection,' said Angela. 'I don't know about my friend here.'

'You must forgive me. I am too tired to play any more, ma'am,' said the shopkeeper regretfully.

'Never mind,' said Angela. 'You may stay there and watch us!'

In a flash Lucy had pulled off her clothes and her fair,

golden hair pleasantly contrasted with the dark brown of her companion. The two girls were now entwined in each other's arms and were kissing each other, fastening their open mouths together and running their hands over each other's luscious curves. Then Angela rolled Lucy over on her back and leaning over her first kissed her face and throat. She then progressed downwards kissing her erect little titties and mouthing the little darlings as Lucy wriggled with sensuous joy.

'Lie still my precious and I will give you the most delightful thrills with my tongue,' cried Angela.

Lucy did as she was bidden, and Angela slid her hand up and down her back, gently patting the firm flesh of her bottom. She glued her lips back to Lucy's and her left hand slipped between Lucy's firm buttocks and began to frig her wrinkled little bottom-hole, while her head moved down to nestle in that glossy bush of brown curls as she kissed and tongued the mount of love in a frenzy of delight. Circling Lucy's hips now with her free right arm, she fastened her mouth to Lucy's slit, and as the darling girl's thighs fell loosely apart Lucy grasped her head between her hands as she drove her tongue deep into the juicy crack.

'Oh, that is heavenly,' gasped Lucy. 'More, more, you are making me come, darling!' And with a cry she gave a huge shudder and I could see the love-juice trickle down her thighs as Angela sucked furiously until Lucy pulled her head back and gently forced her away.

'Now it is my turn,' said Lucy as she pushed Angela's head back and cupped her partner's bottom-cheeks. Angela was nothing loath and wriggled up so that she was sitting astride Lucy with her thickly-haired slit just an inch or so away from Lucy's upturned face, and she began to rub against and between her hungry lips. Lucy's tongue revelled in slipping in and out of her partner's sopping muff, out of which that superb three inch clitty was already projecting between the pouting lips.

'Oh, I must have some cock to fully satisfy me!' shouted Angela but Mr Corney was still unable to urge his flaccid tool

136

into a state of erection. I, of course, needed not to be asked twice when such sport was at hand and it took only seconds to pull off my clothes. I ran across with my prick in my hand as I caressed it to its full height, and the swollen purple dome rammed up against my belly-button. I sank down behind Angela and carefully pointed my rod at the wrinkled brown bum-hole that wriggled so deliciously before me. There was no cold cream handy, of course, but I wet the head of my thick prick well with spittle and drove into her bottom with fury. She nipped and squeezed my stiff cock so thoroughly that I spent almost at once but my rod stayed ramrod stiff and our mutual spend made my movements blissfully pleasurable. A perfect frenzy of lust racked my body as I withdrew from the narrowest gate of Paradise to attack Lucy's gaping cunt which was well primed for the head of my tool. I moved Angela's body slightly to the side so that I could insert my full nine inches of iron-hard rammer into the womb of my only true love. She made her cunny nip and contract as I engorged her crack to repletion as she spent, sighing with delight before I could make a move, continuing throughout to greedily gobble at Angela's soaking clitty as the girl wriggled around lasciviously. Lucy heaved up her bottom to meet my manly thrusts and then raised her legs so that her feet met together behind my calves.

I stretched forward putting my face on the inside of Angela's thighs as I endeavoured to push the last fraction of my length into my lovely girl's heated cunny. We all three tried hard to keep still to enjoy the mutual sensations of repletion and possession so delightful to the participators, but I could feel my love juice gathering in my shaft, and I commenced working my cock in and out of its juicy sheath. These soul-stirring movements worked our heated desires to that state of frenzied madness which can only be allayed by the divinely beneficient ecstasy of spending, and I shot a tremendous warm flood of creamy white seed into her belly.

Do not ask me, reader, from where I summoned the strength but my cock would still not relax into flaccidity, but remained stiff in the folds of Lucy's cunny as I gently pulled away and pushed back, pulled away and pushed back, my tool almost swimming in a sea of spend. Angela moved off to sit on one side as, after lying over my girl for a few moments, I began to heave my bottom again to give Lucy the benefit of a second fucking without taking out my prick.

'My, my, my, you are so strong, Andrew!' smiled Lucy lovingly as Mr Corney stooped over us and said: 'Oh, what it is to be so powerful! I wish I could fuck as well as you two.' Lucy smiled and stretching out her hand took hold of his prick which was still soft and hanging down. I decided to carry on and slowly drove my own hard rod in and out of the delicious crack.

Now Mr Corney's prick began to stand and he pushed it towards her face as she stroked back the foreskin to uncap the fiery red dome, and she opened her mouth wide and sucked lustily away as he heaved his great heavy bum and worked his prick in and out of her mouth. With increasing vigour I drove my cock in and out of her cunt. She heaved up and down with excitement, while the sight of his tool darting in and out of her slurping lips soon made my balls harden and I gushed a creamy libation of sperm into her cunt as she drained me of every last drop of love juice, pumping my fluids out into her dark, secret warmth.

I was now as exhausted as Mr Corney, but who dares say that the female is the weaker of the sexes? As we two men lay panting from our labours, Angela jumped down between Lucy's thighs, and pushing her face down into the golden moss of blonde hair she kissed and sucked at that delicious slit, still damp with my frothy emission, as her tongue sought out the love cleft and without hesitation she drove the point of her tongue between those luscious lips and wriggled it.

'Oh, how lovely! Do it more! More!' gasped Lucy, and her bottom jerked and wriggled as Angela's tongue began to work back and forth. Lifting her legs by instinct, she placed them on Lucy's shoulders and so hid nothing of her charms. Her cunny lips became even damper as Angela's tongue prodded through to nip her clitty, licking and sucking her juices, moving quickly along the velvety grooves of her pussy as with each stroke Lucy arched her body in ecstasy, pressing her fully erect clitty against her flickering tongue.

'Aaaaahhhh!' moaned Lucy and then let out a little scream of happiness as the flames of passion crackled along her nerve fibres. By this time Angela's mouth was soaked in love juice and from the thrilling movements of her rounded bottom, she herself would have loved nothing better than to be receiving a good, stiff prick up her crack at the same time. But not only were we mere males *hors de combat*, the time was passing and though I felt some slight growth in my somewhat sore cock, I let the moment pass.

'Lucy, we must both be back at Nottsgrove shortly,' I said.

'Yes, you are right, Andrew, we had better get dressed quickly.'

'But we must speak to Mr Corney about his daughter.'

'Your daughter?' said Angela accusingly to her paramour. 'Surely you have not been guilty of the heinous crime of—'

'Certainly not,' said Mr Corney indignantly. 'Far from that, I have fixed upon her a device that will stop her playing around with the frisky lads of Arkley.'

'Yes, quite so,' said Lucy. 'But whilst I do not question your right to instruct your daughter, I most certainly do doubt your wisdom in fitting her with a barbaric device from the Middle Ages!'

'Good heavens!' said Angela. 'What on earth are you talking about, Lucy? Surely you cannot mean a chastity belt?'

'I most certainly do,' said Lucy. 'Can you actually credit such a foolishness?'

There was a short period of quiet whilst we finished dressing. Then Mr Corney, who no doubt felt abashed by our complete condemnation, said: 'Perhaps I have gone too far, but Danielle is a headstrong girl and I know that she has been seen with that rascal Arthur Greystokes, who has boasted he has poked every girl between fifteen and twenty-five in this village. You know that my wife is half-French and I am afraid that Danielle has more than her share of hot blood and I don't want to see her shamed by a villain such as young

139

Arthur! I shudder to think about what might become of her if she is left to run wild without my guidance!'

'You must trust your daughter,' said Angela sternly. 'You must also warn her of the consequences of her actions, and if she is determined to have a lover she must know all about the ways to prevent an unwanted conception.'

'That's all very well, but women must not be allowed such freedom!'

Oh, merciful heavens! I just prayed that Lucy would not strike this foolish man!

'My dear,' Lucy said sweetly to me, 'I hope you are not in too much of a hurry?'

'No, no,' I replied with resignation. 'Do say your piece, my dearest. I hope Mr Corney will listen willingly to your instruction and maybe gain the rudiments of wisdom.'

Lucy said: 'Just sit down a moment, Mr Corney. You think perhaps that women enjoy an easy time? That it is easier to be a daughter than a son?

'Let us just look at the life of the average daughter. She must arrange the flowers, help with the housework, pay the family calls, entertain the family visitors, always be at hand, well-dressed, cheerful and smiling, like household angels—which they are often called—without any personal preferences or pursuits, ready to meet every call and to contribute to everyone's pleasures except their own.

'All this is true, and an essential part of the duty belonging to an unmarried daughter at home; but it is only a part. The tyranny of it comes when it is considered to be all. It is the fact that she must always be "on tap", if I may use the expression, that makes life so hard and dull for her.

'Under such circumstances the girl can never sit down to read or write without fear of being disturbed; she can never undertake any definite pursuit however harmless lest it might interfere with some of these unceasing claims. She has, in truth, never an hour that she can call absolutely her own, free from the dangers of interruption.

'There is always something wanted by somebody, and a girl of average conscientiousness would feel very selfish

140

indeed should she refuse to meet these unceasing claims, even though many of them may be trivial and though she herself may have on hand at that moment some quite important work of her own.

'If she has a brother, who perhaps is reading at home during his vacation from school or college, he of course must never be disturbed. That is because he is reading for some examinations which will later affect his career—but the girl, who is so often refused leave to study and never expected to do any great things, she has no need to be allowed some definite time for study and improvement except for some outside philanthropic work, perhaps either in our home slums or for some benighted heathen folks overseas!

'The suffering endured by many a young woman under these circumstances has never really been fully told, perhaps because men do not wish to hear it, or know of it!'

'Hear, hear!' cried Angela. 'No one could have described our plight better, Lucy, my dear friend. Let us face the fact, that in the usual case, possessing no money in her own right and obliged to beg, too often from an unwilling father (though I must admit that this is not an adjective I would use with regard to my own Papa), a girl of character as she grows into maturity, living as a woman in her father's house, suffers a bitter, frustrating sense of sheer humiliation that no-one who has not experienced it can fully understand.

'Many young women under these circumstances would gladly engage in honourable labour, however menial, that would enable them to be independent and to own themselves. But this of course is a notion "not to be thought about for a moment" by the fathers.'

'Such an idea frightens the fathers,' chipped in Lucy. 'Could the parents of these girls, who have been instructed not to think of themselves as independent beings but only as mere appendages of their parents, created for the sole purpose of ministering to their pleasures, and waiting upon their fancies—could these parents for one single moment get a glimpse into the hearts of their quiet, uncomplaining daughters, they would be astonished and even, I would hope, horrified. They might ask what their daughters want now? They have a good home and if money is in abundance, every known comfort and the society of their parents' friends and relations; perhaps even in the upper regions of Society a carriage to drive in and a horse to ride. What more can they possibly desire?'

'I know what I would reply,' said Angela. 'To such parents I would say, your daughter wants only herself. She belongs to you now and can only walk in your paths, enjoy your pleasures and live your life. She only wants now to belong to herself. She has paths of her own she longs to walk in, and purposes of her own she is eager to carry out, for she is an independent being created by God for the development of her own talent and capabilities and for the use of her own time.

'Her capacities were not given to her parents but to herself; her life is not their possession, but her own; and to herself she must make a full account of the use she makes of it. Put yourself in her place, Nicholas Corney, and ask yourself how *you* would like to have no true independence of your own, but be obliged always to live someone else's life and carry out only someone else's purpose. You have had aims and purposes in your life and have been free, in part, to carry them out bound only by your financial position and the vagaries of fortune. Can you dare, then, to lay hands upon the life of your daughter and say that she must live not as she pleases to do but solely as you please? There can be no objection to laying down guidelines of sensible reason and exercising the wise judgement of mature parental control, and no-one is suggesting that parents should not guide and lay down rules for their children, both sons and daughters alike.

'But if the daughters yield to your demands it can only be at the expense of a truly grievous waste of energies and capabilities. Alas, this is an aspect of the question that far too few realise—though Andrew, through the sagacious teaching of Doctor White, is an exception to the rule.'

Lucy concluded the lesson by saying: 'There is no sadder sight in the world than that of a wasted life. And when this waste is the result of carelessness or selfishness on the part of the strong towards the weak, it becomes no less a tragedy even though it may be done in the name of parental love. Such tragedies are not fiction as may be read in the three-volume novel, but the very occurrence of everyday life around us. How wanton is the waste continually going on in the lives of thousands of women, whose powers, by a long course of trivialities and mental starvation, deteriorate year after year until they themselves and all their friends suffer incalculable loss!'

The strictures of the two girls evidently made a real impression on Mr Corney who heaved a sigh and said that he supposed that they had made a good point of debate.

'I will take off the belt but I would remind both of you that Danielle is still only sixteen years old and I maintain that this is still somewhat too young an age to be prick'd!'

'Perhaps it is,' said Lucy firmly, 'but she is of an age to be allowed, if she so wishes, to at least taste the fruits even if she does not at this early stage take part in the fullest expression of sexual passion. Certainly, Mr Corney, by forbidding her totally you are encouraging the very thing you do not want! I have a fine idea. Suppose this situation if you please. If you promise to release Danielle from her hideous belt, I will speak with her sensibly about country matters and advise her to keep her hymen until she is older and certain in her mind that she wishes to lose her virginity. Is this not a good plan?'

He looked doubtful for a moment and then said: 'I hope you know what you are doing. But her mother is just not capable of advising her and I suppose it would be a great weight off my mind.'

'Very well then. Send Danielle round to Nottsgrove at noon tomorrow and I will see to it.'

We took our goodbyes and Lucy and I strolled back to the old *alma mater*, and I smiled as I realised that Lucy was in danger of becoming a nurse, so to speak, for all the girls in the village.

'What is so funny?' she asked as we strode back briskly.

'You will soon be qualified as a professor of intimate affairs,' I replied. 'You have sworn to tell Rosalie about not

143

worrying overmuch about the age difference between her and the Vicar and now you have promised to instruct young Danielle Corney in *l'art de faire l'amour.'*

'Rosalie's dilemma is an easy problem to solve, but I must give great care to the words which I shall say to Danielle. After all, I don't want to put her off the sweet joys of fucking for life! Anyhow, shall we meet for lunch tomorrow? It is a half day and I could pack a picnic box and we could eat *al fresco* in Morrison's meadow if the weather is kind. You know where I mean, just where you and Louella . . .'

'Yes, yes, I know well enough,' I interrupted irritably. 'Shall we say one o'clock or just a few moments after in case Doctor White detains us for a little extra tuition?' I was somewhat short-tempered as I was not a little embarrassed about Lucy bringing up an incident that I would have preferred to keep secret from her.

I looked forward to the picnic with relish, though that evening I was pleasantly surprised to be invited to dinner with the headmaster along with some other members of the sixth form. Other guests dining that night were the Vicar and Doctor Kleiman of Vienna, and a splendid meal was enjoyed by all, especially as the headmaster opened six bottles of his Mouton Rothschild, '75.

Well, dear readers, I have excited myself so much by this recitation of times past that I must now put down my pen and repair to Leicester Square and seek a companion for this evening who may be able to rekindle my ardour. I have no apology to make in putting this to paper as my own dear wife passed on some three and a half years ago, and though I no longer possess the enormous procreative powers of my youth, I can still manage a stand once a week after a cup of refreshing beef-tea!

CHAPTER SEVEN

WE DINED that evening with the headmaster and his select party, and a most pleasant evening was enjoyed by all fourteen persons who sat down at the superb Georgian mahogany table that graced the large dining room. I must confess that my knowledge of the German language is at best rudimentary, and I was most relieved to find out that Doctor Kleiman spoke almost perfect English with only the slightest trace of a foreign accent. He was a middle-aged man of just under average height who had lost most of his hair, yet who still effused a spirit of youthfulness and a touch of devilment by his twinkling blue eyes and general agreeable manner. He still retained his vital manly functions, I was sure, for although he complained to me how he had damaged his ankle while climbing some stairs to give a lecture at the Sorbonne in Paris, it appeared to me that his injured foot sneaked out towards Lucy's legs, and more than once I thought I detected a look of surprise on her pretty face before she retired with the other ladies to leave us with the port and cigars.

Be that as it may, the next day Lucy and I made our way to the agreed location for our outdoor feast. We each carried a basket of comestibles prepared by Mrs Harris, our school cook, who was not averse to earning the odd ten shillings by preparing special repasts for the sixth formers. Again we were most fortunate as regards the weather, as the heatwave showed little sign of abatement and the sun shone down as brightly as ever—though, pleasingly, the heat was tempered

145

by a light southerly breeze as we walked slowly down to Morrison's meadow.

We struck across a half-made road, and tussocks of feathery grass covered the rough surface of the ground and out of these the larks soared into the haze of sunshine. On the far horizon over a countless succession of fields and hedges rose a line of downs, and in a silver streak to the right of us could be seen the line of the stream. Almost from our feet stretched the tall, thick grass that dipped into a small copse beyond, and I suggested that the copse would be the ideal place to partake of our repast. Lucy nodded her head and I perceived that there was a matter that was troubling her, for she had been very quiet since we had met and had hardly uttered a word to me.

I asked her if there was anything amiss and she blushed, turned to me and said: 'You are as perceptive as ever, Andrew. I can never hope to deceive you even if I were of the inclination to attempt such an unkind commission.'

'I know, Lucy, that you are the very essence of honesty,' I said gallantly. 'Lighten your heart and tell me what is of concern. You know the old saying, a trouble shared is a trouble halved.'

'You are so kind to me,' she said, her lips trembling. 'I am so ashamed about my behaviour but I can see that I must tell you all. Andrew, the fact of the matter is that I let Doctor Kleiman fuck me last night!'

I was stunned by this revelation. 'I see,' I said slowly. 'Well, I am rather surprised to hear such a confession, though I am unable to condemn you for your actions. After all, look what happened between me and Louella a few days ago.'

'You are the dearest, dearest boy to be so understanding. Later, after we have eaten, I will show my appreciation by sucking you off and then when you have recovered I will ride a St George upon your marvellous prick.'

'I would like to know exactly what happened last night,' I said as we put down the baskets and sat down on the warm earth.

'Do you really want to know? Then I will confess all to

146

you. As I think you noticed, Alfred, Doctor Kleiman that is, was spooning with me throughout dinner. He kept rubbing his leg against mine and once or twice caught hold of my hand and stroked it gently.

'After the party broke up, you had to retire at once to your study but Alfred offered to escort me back to my rooms. My blood had been fired by the rich food and the deliciously cool wine and I was feeling somewhat light-headed and gay. When we reached my door I asked him whether he wished to have a glass of brandy as a nightcap and he accepted with no little alacrity. I can remember very little after that except that I found myself lying on the bed with Alfred who was busily unbuttoning my dress and unhooking the catches. With a quick movement he pulled down the frock and my breasts burst forth from their confines. His hasty hands pulled off my shoes and stockings and in a trice my drawers were off and I was lying totally naked. He tore off his own clothes and lay down beside me. We kissed and I could feel his throbbing tool banging against me. He began squeezing my breasts, and my titties hardened up to his touch to two little pink peaks of perfection.

'I reached down for that rock-hard cock and began rubbing my hand up and down his bulging tentpole. I must tell you, my dear, that Alfred has the most delightful prick. Like many Continentals he was circumcised when he was an infant, and I really enjoyed rubbing that purple shaft up and down to the bulbous, swollen head with no foreskin to get in the way. My little cunny was sopping wet as Alfred eased his hand between my unprotesting legs and ruffled the soft down of my silky muff. His wicked fingers gradually opened my juicy slit and he slipped one and then two fingers in and out of my cunt, thrilling me with his gentle yet firm touch, and electrifying my whole body with a most delicious sensation. His pulsating tentpole of a prick was standing high and mighty above a bush of black hair and I grasped the monster just underneath its swollen rosy head and gently moved my hand up and down. "Faster, faster!" he cried, and I worked my fingers up and down as his own hand slid in and out of my sopping cunny which was pumping love juices that already were dribbling down my thighs. I jerked my hand up and down even quicker along his smooth prick until all too soon the white froth gushed out of the top of the purple-domed head like a miniature fountain. At almost the same instant I found myself climaxing beautifully as a shuddering spasm of pleasure ran through every inch of my body.

'We lay back, temporarily exhausted, with Alfred's fingers still entwined around my love nest and my hand still resting on his still hard prick. I moved over and kneeling beside him I began gently to lift his velvety tool to my lips. I kissed the top and tickled his hairy balls and I felt his prick swell on my lips as I licked all round the glans as he groaned with delight. I swung over and pushed my firm young bum cheeks almost in his face and drew up my legs so that Alfred could see the outline of my hairy crack.

'His shaft was now swollen to bursting point and the head felt even harder in my mouth. I began to suck at this great lollipop and my tongue travelled slowly from the base to the top again and again. My movement became faster and faster, and judging from Alfred's expression and his uncontrollable twitching, his first sucking off by an English girl would be an experience he would remember all his life. His eyes remained closed but he grunted away with the pure pleasure of it. His prick tightened and he began to push upwards as if he wanted to fuck my throat. I had to resist him or I would have choked and ruined everything.

'He bucked wildly as his massive prick slurped in and out of my hungry mouth. Any moment now and he will spunk, I thought, and I began to swallow in anticipation. I was soon to be proved right—a few early shoots of salty spunk and crash! My mouth was filled with lovely gushing foam as his cock throbbed wildly as I held it lightly between my teeth. My own supreme pleasure flowed from my own cunny as I sucked and sucked the spurts pouring out of his magnificent prick.

'Then I felt that gorgeous spongy tool soften as I rolled my lips around the dome. Alfred's movements ceased and he lay spent as I nibbled away at that funny round bulb with its tiny hole until at last he struggled to rise to a sitting position. 'My dear Lucy,' he said. 'You are the best lover I have had the pleasure of fucking for many a long month. I wonder if I could interest you in work as a helper at my clinic?' I thanked him for his kind offer, but of course I had no interest in accepting the work even though it was very well paid indeed. For as you know, although I enjoy a good fuck, it must always be on my terms, when and where and with whom I desire it and not just on a cold, formal basis.

'Anyhow, I have told you all, Andrew. Alfred left my room shortly afterwards and I slept alone. I do hope all this has not distressed you too much.'

Had I not played the goat with Louella I might have been more upset, but in truth her story had fired my blood and my prick was bursting within the confines of my trousers. Lucy could see the uncomfortable way I was wriggling around, and with a deft movement of her hands she unbuttoned my trousers and took out my naked prick and ran her pink little tongue up and down the shaft. Her moist tonguing and her nibbling at the tip with her pearly teeth coupled with the exciting adventure I had just heard was all far too much for me to bear and in a trice I was pumping all my cock in and out of her mouth, jetting a gush of spunk that spurted almost straight into her throat. She sucked greedily on my tool, milking every lingering drop of sperm.

'Ah, Andrew, I do enjoy sucking a good thick prick. I know that some other girls do not enjoy it but I could happily suck your prick for hours. It never lasts that long, of course, and like all men you squirt off in just a few minutes. I think swallowing the froth is just as nice for nothing tastes so clean and fine. And there is the additional benefit of knowing that I can enjoy myself without any fear of getting in the family way!'

'Whatever activity you try in bed, the essential core of enjoyment lies in choosing an understanding and tender partner,' I said, stroking her fine locks of golden hair.

Lucy did not wish to fuck until later that evening so I buttoned myself up and we began to spread out our delicacies

149

on the tablecloth that Mrs Harris had thoughtfully provided. To our surprise we saw a girl coming across the meadow to our little copse and we wondered who this could be as we had told no-one where we were going to partake of our outdoor meal. The stranger turned out to be Louella and we bid her a cheery good-day and she asked us what we were doing here. We explained and she said: 'How jolly! May I join you?'

'Of course you may,' I said gallantly. 'There is more than enough food and drink here and we would be pleased to enjoy the pleasure of your company.'

'Thank you, Andrew. You are a true gentleman which is more than can be said for one of your headmaster's guests!'

'My goodness, I had forgotten that you and your father dined with us last night. Pray who has offended you?'

'I see no reason why I should not confide in you. The wretch I refer to is that horrid Doctor Kleiman of Vienna!'

'Doctor Kleiman?' exclaimed Lucy. 'I thought he was a very interesting gentleman.'

'Yes, so did I! So much so that I invited him to visit me in my bedroom after we broke up the dinner party. But he arrived in my room so late and so tired that he could only fuck me once and then he fell fast asleep. Is that right?' cried Louella.

'What exactly happened?' I asked trying hard not to smile.

'Well, he did arrive where I was waiting at our back door, though far later than I expected. I had performed my ablutions and was more than ready when he finally came and tapped at the window. We undressed quickly and I must say that I did admire his physique. He may not be in the prime of youth but he has kept himself in trim, and what a fine looking prick swung between his legs. His foreskin has been cut away and I do not mind admitting that the thought of this rod, once swollen, surging into me heightened my appetite.

'In a matter of seconds we were on the bed and we kissed each other with tender, deep thrusts of our tongues in each other's mouths. I felt his prick swell against my pussy mound and the smell of his manliness aroused me even further. My fingers travelled down his back whilst I opened my legs even

150

further to feel his large balls against my thighs. I reached down and rubbed his cock up to a full hardness, and he slightly raised himself on to his hands and then thrust his flagpole of a prick firmly into my juicy pussy. The lunge and thrust was nigh perfect and my cunt seemed to burst open like a water lily as the fiery red head plunged into me, and our hairy triangles mingled as he pumped that great thick cock in and out of my soaking pussy. The lips of my cunny parted before his tool, wet and willing as I rocked beneath him awaiting the peak of pleasure which we were both climbing rapidly. His rampant cock pumped up and down at a steady pace until he sensed by my shuddering that I was ready to achieve the highest point of excitement. He then increased the tempo of his jerking prick until I was frantic with desire. "Now!" I whispered fiercely, as I could not scream for fear of waking others in the house. "Now!" and Alfred shot a heavy load of creamy white spunk into me as our pubic mounds crashed together; and we writhed happily on my bed as my hips gyrated forwards and backwards to enclose every piece of that darling pole that had driven me to such heights of ecstasy.'

'I cannot see why you have cause for complaint,' I said, 'Doctor Kleiman seems to have performed well enough according to this account.'

'That may be, but immediately afterwards I wanted to fuck again as my breasts were still tingling and my cunny was aching for another bout of good stiff prick pushing in and out of it. But even though I took the head of his cock in my mouth and rolled my tongue all around it, Doctor Kleiman just groaned and fell asleep and I could not rouse him until dawn. Luckily he managed to escape from the house without anyone seeing him and no doubt he is making up some strange story to tell his friend, Reverend Bernard Ferningham, as to why his bed was not slept in last night,' said Louella with some annoyance.

'I am sure that your secret is safe with Doctor Kleiman,' said Lucy in a small voice.

'How can you be so sure?' Louella demanded.

'I just know that he would not divulge details of his sexual encounters to another man. Andrew, will you bear me out here?'

'Most certainly, my dear Lucy, I am quite sure that you are correct.'

Louella still looked grim and said she hoped that we were not being too optimistic, as her opinion of Doctor Kleiman had been lowered enormously by what she considered to be extremely rude behaviour. Of course, neither Lucy nor I could enlighten her as to why Doctor Kleiman had been so weary, and indeed I made a mental note to congratulate him upon his strength; for at his age to fuck two girls after a heavy dinner was no mean feat. But Lucy was clearly embarrassed by the whole business and began to change the subject of our conversation; and at the risk of relating a somewhat tedious narrative I shall record her thoughts. Naturally, being connected with Nottsgrove Academy she enthusiastically espoused the Liberal and even Socialist ideas whilst Louella, being a farmer's daughter, was much more inclined to the philosophy of Conservatism. Lucy argued for radical changes in society and Louella argued passionately with her while I lay down and drank a glass of refreshing lemonade.

'I am as distressed as you at the condition of the poor,' said Louella, 'but I maintain that the position of the working man with regard to his own condition is pretty much that suggested by Sydney Smith. He is perfectly contented to go without things which he has never used. The working man may read about the richer man's luxurious dinners and fine cigars. Yet the humble smoker of the pipe and the diner off roast mutton is not in the least discontented, for these are unrealities which the instant needs of work and sleep and his own amusements give him very little time to bother about. The working classes are only unhappy with their lot when they are egged on by foolish agitators such as the Socialists and the Anarchists.'

'So you would deny, perhaps, that the lower classes deserve the franchise?' said Lucy in some anger.

'I am certain that those hard-working men in the rural

152

villages such as ours at best have little desire above working, eating, drinking and sleeping, and are content to let their more favoured superiors think for them, make laws for them, and administer those laws. What are your views on the question, Andrew?'

This put me on the spot, as although I agreed wholeheartedly with Lucy, I had no desire to offend Louella, especially as I had designs upon her large, heaving breasts which I longed to cup and squeeze until her little nipples stood up like two hard little bullets.

'I think we must look at this matter dispassionately,' I said carefully. 'I do not really believe that the farm labourers, for example, are such animal-like clods as you describe them, Louella. For years they have campaigned against their unenfranchised state and their position in life during past years has been such as has to a very great extent prevented them from making their grievances known beyond themselves.

'A public meeting in a rural village ten years ago would have caused considerable alarm among well-to-do people. The vicar and the maiden ladies would have wondered at the audacity of the rustics who would dare disturb the stagnant pool of social life. But all is *not* well with our peasantry. As Doctor White remarked over dinner last night, the depopulation of the countryside is a serious matter. If the men are happy here why do they run away in shoals from homes in the peaceful tranquillity of an English country village? The answer is simply that they run away from the odious thought of living and dying in a squalid hovel with a clay floor and two dark cabins under the rafters, reached by a rickety ladder. Yes! People do run away from a life like that, leaving it behind them as a dreadful past which they remember solely with indignation, or rebelling against the prospect of it as a future too hideous to be entertained except with scorn. And I, for one, do not blame them!' I concluded.

'I do not contradict you when you speak of some areas where there is abject poverty which is worse in the big cities. I only wish there were a way in which we could show sympathy with those deserving poor who have been brought to misfortune and to relieve their distress in a manner that will give no encouragement to idleness and vice,' said Louella.

'Oh, heavens alive!' exclaimed Lucy. 'Surely, you are not one of those foolish people who in detestation of possible roguery forget that by a wholesale condemnation of charity, they risk driving the honest man to despair, and threaten to turn him into the very rogue of whom they desire so ardently to be quit.'

'I must agree with you here,' I said. 'Such hesitation to show charity only plays into the hands of the Socialists, Louella. Distress among the working classes has been very general and very severe, and many have been thrown upon their own inadequate resources and not infrequently reduced to destitution by no fault of their own.'

'Quite so, Andrew. Rich people with tender hearts have been having a hard time of it lately in many ways as well,' said Lucy sarcastically. 'Never, surely, never before were so many harrowing appeals made every day to their delicate feelings on behalf of sufferers of every description. The sufferings of the poor in sickness and in poverty-stricken old age, our neglected half-starved children, hard times, strikes, workhouses, crowded alleys, fever-nests, polluted water supplies, smallpox, pauperism, all haunt our thoughts by day if not our dreams by night. Schemes for alleviations and reforms meet us at every turn. But in our fevered minds we always have this fearful concern that by helping those in need we may inadvertently demoralise the recipients. This is almost as hard a load to bear as that distress which we seek to ameliorate!'

'There is no need to speak with such heavy irony, Lucy,' said Louella stiffly. 'I am just as concerned as you that our social problems be solved.'

'I do not doubt this for an instant,' cried Lucy. 'I just wish that you would ignore the cold economic dictates of your head and let the warm, loving impulses of your heart take precedence. I know you to be a true and loving friend. Come, let us not quarrel!'

'Quite right, Lucy. I would like to see you two girls kiss

and make up your disagreements. Let us all be the very best of friends now and forever!' I said warmly.

The girls agreed, and to put them in a mood to kiss and be friends with each other I decided to read them another passage from the master of seventeenth-century gallant literature, Mr John Cleland. It also crossed my mind that the reading would quicken their pulses and lead to some fun and games! I sat them down next to each other, leaning on each other's shoulders and I began my recitation from the book that I had thoughtfully brought with me with the avowed intention of putting Lucy in a frisky mood—but there was no reason why three should not play the game that I had envisaged for just two players! I began to read:

'The girl who fell to my share either had not thrown off all, or else prudently affected some sense of modesty. Leaving the liquorish band to their rowdy devices, Jenny (for that was her name) and I stole to a small chamber furnished with a large bed and the French cabinet named an armoire.

'Jenny began to draw her pins and as she had no stays to unloose, was swiftly naked of all but her shift. For my part, my breeches were as swiftly off, my shirt collar unfastened, when Jenny, reclining amongst the soft pillows, let out a gasp. I followed the direction of her eyes with my own and saw that my rod, long absent from the pleasures of the flesh, had swollen to a fearful size. It sprang from the thicket of hairs that nestled at its root; its head was too much for the breadth of one hand; Jenny had need to encircle the demon with both hands extended to their fullest reach. As I stepped forward towards the pleasure pallet, Jenny spread her fulsome thighs to their utmost, and I discovered there with my bold eyes the erect mark of her sex, the crimson-centred cleft of flesh whose lips, blushing ever more red, led inward to the waiting pleasure channel.

'My passion, long pent, could not wait a moment more. I lay down beside the wench, kissing her moistly, making free with my hands, playing over her plump breasts with their hardened nipples, licking them furiously, arousing her to ever-higher fevers of excitation.

'*Wasting no time in the niceties of the preliminaries, I thrust my throbbing member roughly into the delicate channel. So large had my engine distended that she gasped again at the ferocity of my thrust. But I gave the girl no surcease from the vigorous onslaughts effected by my fearful member. I reached my hands beneath her luscious bottom, thus positioning her more advantageously for the thrusts of my rod. I reached down within the sweet cleft and felt with my hands the strength of my shaft as I coupled with her wide-spread nether-lips. Our hairs mingled; our most sensitive parts were entirely conjoined.*

'*Oh, What adorable bliss! What heavenly rapture! What sweetness sublime! So long had I been without the soothment of her sex that the honey liquid burst from my vessel in a tidal wave of boiling fury. It washed down her thighs and its colour was tinged pinkish by the blood my huge machine had torn from the miniature entrance of the poor girl.*

'*I lay back for the moment, drained of all strength. But the minx's fires burned high still and her little tongue slipped its humid way through the tufts of hair round my own nipples. It followed its route down towards my birth knot and ever down towards my listless member. But rogue that he was! In no time he stood up again, as firm and as strong and as large and as monstrous as if he had never been tall before.*

'*Jenny held him by the shaft with both her firm hands and circled the vermilion head of that impish demon with her pointed, slightly rough tongue. I had to clench my jaw to stop from spraying her again with the juices of passion. At length she left her lubricious tonguing of my private parts and stretched herself out on the bed. This time resolved not to be so hot in my quest, I tongued her mouth, exploring the warm, dark wetness of it with growing languor and heat.*

'*I moved next to her ripe, full breasts, first licking at the erect, long nipples then biting them ever and ever more fiercely so that the poor girl cried out despite her pleasure. I sucked their sweetness, leaving bruises around the nipples where the pressure of my mouth had drawn blood to the surface. My attention next was placed on that very summit of pleasure and I spread her knees with my hands, kissing her inner thighs so that the dear creature squealed time and time again with delight. I next mouthed the golden soft curls that sheltered the central joys of her sex. My spittle wetted and matted that fine moss and I soon found my tongue wandering round the outer portion of that pink shell. The resistant texture of the hair, that smooth resilience of the pearly flesh—such were delights to offer kings. I circled smaller and smaller with my searching tongue till it probed that very centre of sensual enjoyment.*

'Her secret orifice opened to the probing of my ardent tongue. Her rounded bottom began to move in rhythm with the explorations of my own. Sensing that it was time to leave off this occupation, pleasurable though it was, I retraced my steps, kissing again the delicate outer lips, the still-wet moss, the bluish-white skin of her inner thighs, and concentrated myself upon the main enjoyments. Inch by inch, I impaled her with my sturdy rod, now grown to even greater dimensions by preceding excitations. This time with her mount of pleasure fully receptive to the aggressions of my member, she did not gasp with pain but moaned with pleasure.

'I thrust; she answers; I stroke, she heaves; our rhythms join and our passions grew. I push so deep into her that I think I must rend the wench in twain but her sole response is yet another moan, this low in the throat as our breathing deepens to a growl, then, in unison, to a roar. The bed shudders with the weight and fury of our entwined violence. Then with a shriek she adds her juices to my own and I discharge in an enormity of passion, my juices boiling over, searing her deepest vitals.

'When we had recovered ourselves, I asked if I might call again upon her. Oh, indeed, Sir, she replied. She promised then to show me the Italian delight of which I had so oft heard but which in truth, I had not ever experienced.'

I ended my reading and sipped slowly at my glass of cool lemonade. The passionate words of Mr Cleland had certainly achieved the desired effect. Louella and Lucy were entwined in a passionate embrace and their mouths met as Lucy's hands examined the large breasts of the dark-haired Louella who unbuttoned her blouse to let Lucy enjoy free play with her plump bubbies. She continued to play with those magnificent breasts while Louella's hands were under Lucy's skirts doing all kinds of things to her clitty. Louella eased down her partner's underdrawers and Lucy's rounded bottom cheeks were naked to my eyes, which feasted upon them as Louella's hands probed the cleft between them, making the blonde girl gasp with joy.

Without further ado, they pulled off their clothes and lay naked together until Lucy stood up and Louella sank to her knees between her strong thighs and began to lick and kiss her tribade who guided her head with her long, tapering fingers. Louella pushed those long white legs apart and nuzzled her full lips around that curly bush of blonde hair, clasping Lucy's bottom cheeks as the pussy lips opened wide and Louella's tongue flashed around the damp hair as Lucy pushed her head further down and she slipped her tongue through the pink lips, licking between the inner grooves of Lucy's cunny in long, thrusting strokes. Lucy's pussy was now gushing love juice, and I stole behind Louella and tore off my clothes. I first slipped a hand round to her hairy dark mound and slipped a finger into her now sopping pussy and rubbed harder and harder until her little clitty turned as hard as my own cock to my touch.

Lucy now lay down and spread her legs wide and as Louella bent forward to suck noisily at the soaking bush in front of her, I positioned my iron-hard tool at the base of her bottom cheeks. I opened the lips wide with my fingers, and as Louella's tongue lashed juicily around Lucy's bush and in and out of her crack, my trusty prick thrust from behind into Louella's dripping slit. I banged my cock in and out as I threw my hands around her, squeezing and pinching those gorgeous, heavy breasts, tickling the nipples up to their fullest erection. I soon exploded fierce jets of hot sperm, coating Louella's cunt with love juice as her frenzied sucking brought Lucy off to a tremendous climax.

Now fair is fair, and I knew that Lucy harboured egalitarian sentiments so I whispered to Louella: 'Would you like to sit and watch while I fuck Lucy?' She assented readily and Lucy, who guessed at my intent, lay there on the ground stretching her arms out to me as I gently eased myself on top of her, my prick already standing up to my belly like a rod of iron. I slid the head of my cock into the crimson gap between her thighs which was already soaking wet from Louella's tonguing and Lucy's own copious emission of love-juices. Her head rolled from side to side in an ecstasy of delight, little moans escaped from her lips, and her hips began working as I drove my proud cock deep into the glistening slit; while her legs came up and wrapped themselves around my back and her arms encircled my neck as we swayed backwards and forwards. I fucked her with long, powerful strokes and Lucy stretched and squeezed beautifully, nipping and tickling my prick in her firm clasp. She twisted and squirmed as we went off together, our mutual spends filling her cunny, and for some moments neither of us moved as we just lay there soaking in bliss.

I rolled off her but as I lay on my back there was Louella, still quite naked, stooping over me, her heavy breasts dangling down as she kissed and sucked my prick. My eyes feasted upon those full, red lips and those rosy nipples, so firm and erect looking for all the world like two tiny strawberries.

'How handsome your prick looks, Andrew,' said Louella softly. 'Dear Lucy won't mind if I have just one suck at this delicious sweetmeat as we are such close friends!'

She worked her hand up and down the now erect shaft, kissing and sucking until with a downwards lunge with her open lips she plunged my shaft far into her mouth, sucking away with all her might. Her mass of dark hair bobbed up and down as she sucked mightily away and I slipped my hand round to her bum and frigged her bottom as I felt the sperm build up inside me. With my other hand I clutched her head and pulled it down so that my shaft was fully in her mouth and throat and I thought that she would attempt to swallow my balls as well! I shot my load of froth into her eager mouth and she greedily swallowed every drop of my boiling seed.

Ah, reader! Such joys did we experience that truly, as the poet writes:

What peaceful hours I once enjoyed!
How sweet their memory still!
But they have left an aching void,
The world can never fill.

However, let us return to the story. Into view now came the figure of the man who had been at the epicentre of our previous discussion, the one and only Doctor Alfred Kleiman. He had not spotted our party, so we hastily dressed ourselves and the girls began to lay a cloth down on the grass. Sure enough, he walked briskly towards us until we caught his eye and he waved a greeting. It was only politeness and a sense of duty that made me return his salute, which I did with a grudging heart, and the girls were somewhat displeased when he evidently decided to join our party.

'Good morning, everybody! What an extremely pleasant day. We are most fortunate to enjoy such sunshine. I declare that this reminds me of Southern France. Ladies, take care not to let the sun burn too brightly upon your faces or your beautiful white complexions may be spoiled.'

We acknowledged his greeting and Lucy politely asked if he wished to share our repast.

'I would be glad of a glass of wine,' he said. 'I am quite exhausted from my walk—but I must be frank and say that the three of you must also have walked at a brisk pace to be here. You all look quite worn out!'

I could not forbear a smile and Louella and Lucy giggled as they laid out the knives and forks.

'Oh dear! Have I said something wrong? What is so amusing?' said Doctor Kleiman good-naturedly.

'Actually, Alfred, we are all tired from having a marvellous mutual fuck,' said Louella impudently. 'Such a shame that you did not arrive some twenty minutes ago for then you could have participated.'

'Most certainly,' said Lucy, catching on to Louella's little game of teasing our visitor.

'How wonderful it would have been to suck your great cock whilst Andrew was pumping his trusty tool in and out of my crack and I was slipping my fingers in and out of Louella's hairy muff.'

'I would have then wanted to ride a St George upon your prick,' said Louella.

'And I would have made love to your bum-hole, Louella,' I chipped in, noticing that Doctor Kleiman had turned quite pale. 'Still, I am sure that after your nocturnal exertions, this would have been far too onerous a chore for you to undertake.'

To be fair, he took the jest in good part and said little as we continued to regale him with lurid accounts of what delights he might have sampled if only he had arrived just a short time before.

He drank his lemonade and indeed joined us for a light meal afterwards. As we lay back, reclining on the warm earth, Louella suddenly said: 'Alfred, I have a question concerning intimate matters. You are a noted specialist in these areas and I wonder if you would be kind enough to answer my question frankly, even though it is a query born out of an idle curiosity.'

'Of course, my dear girl, it would give me the greatest of pleasure—and this also applies to any query you other two may wish to put to me!'

'Very well, Alfred, my question is simply this,' said Louella. 'What do you say of the old country saying that a girl can gauge the size of a man's prick from the size of his nose and that a girl's mouth size will give a fair estimate of the size of her cunny?'

'I have heard that said too,' added Lucy. 'And is it true that the dome is the most sensitive part of the prick?'

'Yes, this is true,' said Doctor Kleiman. 'The head of the penis, the soft and sensitive dome, is known as the glans, and it remains soft and sponge-like even when the penis is erect, acting as a buffer to the hard, rigid shaft. The very thin outer tissue layer is crowded with highly sensitive nerve endings called genital corpuscles so that friction of any kind during sexual arousal produces exquisite pleasure, a pleasure which if prolonged culminates in the throwing-out of sperm.

'The natural principle is paradoxical in that pain and pleasure can be mixed—insomuch as any pressure on the glans for some moments after spunking can be most discomforting. It is considered by some people that the glans is more sensitive when the prick has been circumcised and the covering foreskin has been removed. Certainly, the removal means that it is easier to keep the area clean, but I do not think that the case has been proved either one way or the other.

'As to your query on sizes, I must tell you that this is pure poppycock! You may always have a private laugh about how large or small a man's prick might be, but the fact of the matter is simply that total size, height or bone-structure can never be any indication whatsoever of the dimensions of a cock or a cunt.

'A huge man may well possess a small prick while a small woman can often accommodate a very big prick in her vagina; whereas the same prick might prove to fit in very snugly in the cunny of a big woman. I hope this answers your question satisfactorily.'

'It does, Alfred, most certainly, and thank you. Now tell me, is there any truth in the potency of this mixture known as Spanish Fly?' asked Louella.

Doctor Kleiman cleared his throat and said: 'First of all, Louella, I want to tell you and your friends that there is no known chemical or substance of any kind that could be considered to be a *bona fide* aphrodisiac.

'On the other hand, there is a noxious poison known by the name of Spanish Fly which, although it might promote the sexual urge temporarily, is more likely to cause severe medical complications that often lead to a most painful death.

'My advice to anyone is to stay away from all potions and simply try to relax with a glass of wine, loose clothing and above all, a willing and patient partner. There are some men

162

who for one reason or another fear that their potency may be lost. It can occur occasionally that just when the head of the prick enters the vagina it loses its hardness.

'The most important concern here is to realise that constantly worrying about this temporary problem will make matters one thousand times worse! There can be many reasons for the loss of power—too much to drink, too much to eat or straightforward old-fashioned weariness. Or perhaps the man needs some new stimulation in his loveplay. Of this I am sure, once he has cleared his mind about this naturally disturbing phenomenon, the problem will disappear as if by magic!'

'It will just disappear?' I said, as I had expected a technical medical discourse.

'Absolutely, my boy, the problem will simply vanish,' affirmed Doctor Kleiman.

Lucy giggled and said: 'That reminds me of a joke Doctor White told me a few weeks ago.'

'Well, do tell us,' we chorused.

'Very well, if you want me to. It seems that during the age of chivalry a powerful baron rode off to the Crusades leaving only a handful of knights to guard his wife, his castle and his lands.

'His wife was a most attractive lady of only twenty years, so as a precautionary measure he called in the village smithy and arranged for his wife to have fitted a special chastity belt with a secret little mini-guillotine fitted within the mechanism.

'Six months later he returned home, weary and war-stained from his labours, but as he entered the castle the very first command he gave was for his trusty knights to line up in front of him. He ordered them to remove their clothes and, as he had feared, all but one had suffered the pain of having the knobs of their pricks cut off. "Hang them all high from the old oak tree!" he bellowed, and turning to the one remaining knight he said: "Sir Lancelot, at least I still have one true knight who served me faithfully. How did you manage to stay pure?" Sir Lancelot said nothing. "Well, tell me," urged the baron, but Sir Lancelot remained silent. "Come

163

now, there is nothing to be ashamed of; indeed, you should be proud of yourself. What do you have to say about all this?'' Sir Lancelot still said nothing and looked extremely nervous as his squire interrupted to say: "My Lord, I regret that my master is unable to speak. Somehow, he has lost his tongue!" '

We laughed heartily at this jest, and as the ladies did not seem at all offended by this rather ribald tale I ventured to tell the company another merry one.

'There was once a most religious gentleman of the Romish persuasion, who in the prime of life was stricken down by a severe attack of influenza. Happily he made a full recovery but the experience made him think upon the after-life and what might happen to his soul after it finally departed his mortal body.

'So he contacted his parish priest and informed him that he wished to do penance to ensure that he would not descend into the fiery depths. So what should he do? The priest thought for a moment and said: "My son, you must ensure entrance to the gates of St Peter by total abstinence from the pleasures of the flesh for six months. Not a drop of intoxicating liquor must pass your lips, nor a morsel of anything but the plainest of foods; and you must sleep apart from your good lady and refrain from any sort of marital relationship for the period of penance.'' The gentleman looked staggered, but he thanked the priest and resolved to undertake his punishment; for when all is said and done, what is six months set beside eternity? So he returned home and gave away the contents of his well-stocked cellar, instructed the domestic staff to prepare only the plainest of meals and informed his wife of the words of their religious mentor. As the wife, too, was a deeply religious person, she fully understood and uttered no word of reproof.

'After three months, however, there was a knock on the priest's door and the gentleman stood before him. The priest invited him in and asked if there was any matter that was troubling his mind. "Indeed there is,'' said the man. "I have tried to do as you instructed me so that I may go to heaven when I pass on, and I have not touched a single thimbleful of any liquid except water, milk or tea. I have only eaten the simplest of meals and have not faltered from the path." The priest smiled and said: "This is marvellous,' your soul is heaven-bound." But the man looked agitated and said: "Oh, Father, I must confess the truth to you. While I tried to abstain fully from relations with my wife and indeed any merriment with members of the opposite sex, every time I saw my wife in her tight riding trousers, my penis shot up to a great stiffness, and if she leaned over to pick up anything, I just could not refrain from unbuttoning my trousers and practising the sin of Onan!" At this the priest looked shocked. "My son, my son," he exclaimed. "You must desist this or you will be barred from the gates of heaven."

'And to the priest's horror, the man smiled wanly and said: "Perhaps I will, Father, and meanwhile it has also barred me from the gates of Captain Jorrocks' Riding Academy!" '

My audience roared with mirth and Doctor Kleiman said: 'I was told a story which at first I did not find amusing as I did not fully understand your English idioms and collo-quialisms, but I think you will enjoy it.

'This story concerns two gentlemen drinking an afternoon glass of wine at their club when one turns to the other and says: "Dash it all, Archie, old fellow, I quite forgot to tell you but I am going to marry Lady F——; she is a widow with nine children."

'His companion looked astounded, but being a gentleman of breeding he had no wish to offend so he simply murmured: "Douglas, old chap, I hope you have not put your foot in it!" And to this his friend retorted: "Oh no, old boy. But I could if I wanted to!" To which his friend gave no reply but simply puffed on his cigar and stared out of the window!'

'May we be serious again for a moment?' asked Lucy. 'While you are here, Alfred, perhaps there are some other problems that you could solve for us and our friends. This would be of great service. We have no money but Louella and I could find a way to repay you for your time and trouble, I am sure.'

'My dear young ladies, the pleasure is all mine,' said Doctor Kleiman gallantly. 'I would never be averse to feeling a delicious young girl's breasts or fondling the cheeks of her rounded bottom, but never would I expect to be given these or even greater liberties just for my expounding some medical theories to a few young friends.'

'Well, we shall see,' I said. 'Tell me now, why is it that many girls of our age, in their late adolescence and early adult years, prefer older men? I do not mean this in any personal manner, of course.'

'This question has been asked many times. My own belief is that the answer is simple. Many young girls prefer older men because these men are more patient, understanding, experienced, sexually skilled—or frankly, because they have more money to spend upon their companions. On the other hand, many older women prefer younger men for their sexual vigour and more direct and powerful performances in the bedroom.

'I always say to young men who put this question as to how they can compete—once you have found a girl you like, work at developing traits that she finds attractive. In other words, woo her! If this does not succeed, forget her and concentrate upon girls who like you just as you are, which is probably an even more sensible attitude to take.'

'May I ask you to treat this in confidence?' said Louella quietly. 'I will name no names but a group of boys from Nottsgrove have taken to spending their Wednesday after-noon half-holiday in a field on my father's land. They sit down on the grass and each then unbuttons his trousers and they play with themselves. They watch each other and see who can either be first to jet out his sperm or who can rub his prick for the longest without coming. Should this practice be stopped?'

Doctor Kleiman stroked his chin. 'I do not think that they should be stopped except that a way might be found to tell them that their antics have been noticed by strangers. I do not think this is too worrisome, though there are some English colleagues who would disagree violently with me. I am sure that these boys will grow out of this childish behaviour, but there is, I suppose, a problem. This group is perhaps basically shy about girls and hesitant about joining the chase for them. It would be tragic if this led to a lifelong habit of sexual withdrawal which might lead to unnatural desires.

'My speculation would be that they will tire of all this, especially when a member is fortunate enough to find a girl who would show him that instead of being alone on the grass, it is far more fun for two to roll in the hay! This is the correct expression is it not, Andrew?'

'One last query, Alfred,' said Lucy, who like us all had been greatly impressed by Doctor Kleiman's wise words. 'I know that old Walker, the gardener, is no longer enjoying relations with his wife since she gave birth to their fourth child. Although his tool is only of average dimensions, her cunny is far too loose at the moment for either of them to obtain very much joy out of having a good fuck. Now, is there anything you can suggest that might help them out of this awkward predicament?'

He pursed his lips thoughtfully and then replied: 'H'mm, in such a case I think I would recommend a regular programme of tightening of the vaginal muscles. As you know, dear friends, the major lips of the vagina are really muscles and they are quite capable of gripping a prick quite firmly without any problem.'

Louella nodded her pretty little head. 'Oh yes, this is very true. I sometimes use a dildo to keep my cunny in trim for the fray. One has to insert it gently, squeeze and relax, squeeze and relax and then after a while one finds it very easy to grip a cock as one will want to do.

'For instance, when Andrew here was fucking me, as soon as he inserted his lovely dome, I gripped him just under the rim of his prick-head and we had some marvellous fun. A kind of tug-of-war ensued with Andrew trying to get his cock out whilst I tried to stop him. Of course, with my legs closed, it was even easier and felt nicer.'

'I like to grip a cock at the base,' said Lucy. 'Then I can feel it swell up inside me.'

'Yes, I think you have proved that my suggestion is on the correct course,' said Doctor Kleiman. 'I suggest that the lady in question should try to exercise herself some ten times every day, and in a month or so I would think that there will be some genuine improvement in her condition.

'On the other hand, of course, it may be that during child-birth she suffered a small vaginal tear and a simple operation can right this very effectively,' he added.

The girls had a few further questions to put to our guest from overseas but I will not bore my readers with these delicate affairs. Suffice it to say that all this talk about *les affaires d'amour* made us all feel rather active; but my role, alas, was to be only that of a spectator as the attention of both girls was focused solely on Doctor Kleiman who, aided and abetted by Louella, quickly slipped off his clothes and he lay on his back with his large prick as stiff and ready as possible.

Lucy was first to attack that red-headed monster, and whispered something I could not make out to Louella, who was now herself quite naked and was carefully rolling her clothes into a neat pile. Lucy swung herself over his face so that her luscious pussy was directly over his mouth and as the good doctor frigged her moist hairy crack with his tongue, Louella jumped over his stiff prick and began riding up and down upon that huge weapon.

After this, each of them sucked his cock and balls by turn till he mounted Lucy and plunged his prick deep inside her whilst Louella fondled his lárge balls and worked a finger in his bum-hole to excite him to the very utmost.

I must admit that Doctor Kleiman was in a fine physical state, for even this did not exhaust him for he gamahuched them in turn and buried his great bursting cock one more time in Louella's bottom-hole and jetted a profuse emission inside her.

All this raised my own lustful feelings to an unbearable degree and in a fever of lust I hastily unbuttoned my trousers and brought out my raging prick, which was standing ramrod stiff and fairly bursting as I slipped my hand round the shaft.

And within a moment of rubbing the monster, a huge emission of white froth spurted out of the knob. Such was the force of the jet of sperm that most of the liquid splattered over the bald pate of Doctor Kleiman who was still finishing off plugging Louella's tight little arse-hole. His prick drove in and out and I admired Louella's loins which were moving in spasmodic little jerks. How they rotated! How the cheeks of her well-formed bottom opened and closed! My own cock swelled up again and Lucy sidled across to raise her cherry-red lips to mine and now our tongues mingled and we twined our bodies together as her hand stole down to cap and uncap the ruby head of my cock. For my part, I slipped my hand into her fully exposed thatch of curly hair and rubbed between the lips that opened at my touch.

We sank down to the soft earth and I rolled on top of the lovely girl who took hold of my prick, and ensuring that the foreskin was fully drawn back, inserted the uncapped dome between the lips of her aching cunny. Lucy possessed this extraordinary gift of contracting her pussy so that it took hold of my cock like a delicately soft hand making a frigging motion, and she wriggled and met my energetic thrusts as I grasped and moulded her firm breasts with both hands, inclining my neck to kiss and suck at the erect little titties. Meanwhile, Louella was busy sucking her beloved Alfred Kleiman's tool to a fine stiffness; while he concerned himself with frigging her bum-hole, which made her sigh with delight. Our lustful propensities were engaged to the utmost and we fucked with ever-increasing vigour. Lucy's legs came up and about my back while her arms circled my neck, and with a firm, forward thrust I drove my hard prick deep inside my lover, lifting her thighs to my shoulders, wrapping my arms about her hips. She was moaning with pleasure now as she stiffened, gave a startled little cry: 'Oh, oh, oh, now, Andrew, now!' as my cock explored the inner cavities of her cunt, driving deeper and deeper into the glistening crack until my balls banged against her bum. We tried hard to hold back the peak of pleasure for as long as we could but all too soon the old familiar tingling came upon me and I crashed great shoots of love-cream into my lovely girl's pulsating cunny.

What more is there to tell of this encounter? She sucked me back to erection and then sucked and swallowed my copious emission until we were sated. We dressed ourselves after an hour or so as the sun suddenly hid behind a bank of white cloud and the temperature dropped quite sharply. But as Ovid reminds us, *tempus edax rerum*. Mention of the poet reminds me that as Doctor Kleiman and I walked back to Nottsgrove together (the girls deciding to take a trip together to the village), I asked him whether we had been right to behave as we had.

'Well, my boy,' said Doctor Kleiman thoughtfully, 'you learn Latin at your college do you not? You may well recall the words of Publius Ovidus Naso who commented, *Quae dant, quaeque negant, gaudent tamen esse rogatœ!*'

I should have been able to construe but the physical exertions had tired my brain and my new friend translated for me: 'Whether they give or refuse, women are glad to have been asked!' I have kept in contact with Doctor Kleiman who is now, alas, retired from his noble profession and indeed from the equally noble sport of fucking since he has not achieved a stand for the last three years.

Eh bien, j'y suis, j'y reste!

CHAPTER EIGHT

WHEN ONCE the itch of literature comes over a man, nothing can cure it but the scratching of a pen. So let us now, dear readers, switch the scene from the gentle, rural life at Nottsgrove to the hustle and bustle of metropolitan existence.

I may have neglected to mention in this narrative that Doctor White's brother Edmund was a noted artist whose landscape scenes had attracted much critical comment—so favourable, indeed, that his work was eagerly sought by discerning collectors even while he lived! Most unfortunately Edmund was seriously injured in a railway accident in 1871, and though he still lives in quiet retirement with his wife, Lady Victoria (the third daughter of Lord W——), he was never able to paint again as his hands were both crushed when his carriage overturned. Many of you may remember the dreadful business which occurred that day when a fast train from Euston left the rails just before the approach to Wembley Station, and ploughed into a goods train that was stationary on an adjoining track. Several passengers were fatally injured and many more were hurt, including Edmund White who was never able to hold a paintbrush in his hands again after otherwise making a full recovery from his ordeal.

However, to return to a happier time before this event, Edmund had submitted some works to the Royal Academy and Doctor White, Lucy and I were invited by our great artist to the annual dinner at the Academy in London. As you will know, this is a great event and we were all terribly excited and looked forward to the event with much joy. We arranged to take a train from Barnet into London, and as usual the little country locomotive came hissing and spluttering into Barnet

Station exactly on time. The first-class compartments were empty and we sat down in comfort as the train pulled slowly away.

'You know, my children,' said Doctor White, 'in such a universe as this it is a great gain to lay hold of some one thing that has permanence—something that we can confidently count on reappearing as the years come round, something to which to cling amid the whirl and confusion of continual change.

'And in one particular world we find this blessing in the dinner of the Royal Academy! Were we to judge only by the pictures that hang upon the walls, we might sometimes be tempted to despair of English art. Exhibition after exhibition is unfolded before our eyes, and we look continually in vain for evidence of new genius coming to the front or of established genius holding its own.

'But the younger men become more mannered and the older men show more plainly that once a man enters the Academy, he becomes too contented with himself to care to do anything that he has not done before. My dear brother, I hope, will be an exception to this rule when he is elected to membership of that august assembly.

'If we let the ear rather than the eye guide us, we shall feel no uneasiness on this score. For the language of Art may vary—it may have been expressive yesterday and be mere commonplace today; but the language of compliment never varies. As each summer comes round, speaker after speaker rises to congratulate the President on the splendid works which look down on the guests as they consume their excellent dinners—and long habit has taught even the Hanging Committee to feign total belief in the words they hear!'

We laughed politely at this rather ironic observation as Doctor White brought out his battered old cigar case.

'Uncle Simon,' said Lucy. 'Would you mind very much smoking your cigar in another compartment, or indeed if you so prefer, I will move but I am suffering from a slight sore throat and the aroma from your cigar will make me ill.'

'Oh, I am so sorry,' said Doctor White genially. 'I will go to another compartment—in any case I have yet to finish my copy of *The Times* so I will leave you two young people to your own devices.'

He got up and strode down the corridor. I turned to Lucy and said: 'I am distressed that you are not feeling up to the mark. I do hope that you will be able to go to the dinner this evening.'

'Oh, yes,' she replied. 'It is only but a very minor ailment. The truth is that I don't really like the smell of any tobacco but as my uncle enjoys his cigars so much I did not wish him to forgo the pleasure on my account.'

'That is most thoughtful of you, dear Lucy,' I said. 'It is just like you always to be thinking of the happiness of others. Now to make my day, how about sucking my prick until we arrive in London?'

'Don't be silly,' said Lucy crossly. 'Someone else might come into the carriage and then where shall we be?'

'Very well, then, I surrender. Tell me, though, I have never met Edmund before. Is he a charming man?'

'An extremely charming and gifted gentleman,' said Lucy. 'I first met him some eighteen months ago when he visited my parents' home in London. You remember the house we rented in Green Street? We were there for four months before Papa was made chief of staff or whatever the position is called at our Embassy in Greece.

'Anyhow, Edmund's wife was unwell and he called upon us unexpectedly for tea. My parents and the rest of the family were out and I received him in our sitting room. I must admit to you, Andrew, that I was rather attracted to him.

'We began talking in a more familiar fashion after a time, for we were hardly strangers as he is my uncle, and he began telling me of the figure studies he had made of pretty girls. I asked him where he found the girls and he said that often they were friends, girls he met at parties and receptions, ordinary, attractive girls like me, and even though his fame was that of a landscape painter, he often preferred to make figure studies for his own pleasure. I guessed that he required his models to

173

pose in the nude but this did not worry me as I was vain enough to want Edmund to sketch me, and even if this meant letting him fuck me, well I had not enjoyed a good fuck for at least four weeks so I was feeling somewhat deprived! I crossed and uncrossed my legs, and as I stood up Edmund said: "I would love to see you quite naked as nature intended." I moved towards him and he unbuttoned my blouse, quite slowly and deliberately. He peeled the back off my shoulders and pulled down my undergarments and my breasts just tumbled into his hands. He cupped them in his palms and my nipples popped up like bullets so I could hardly pretend a false modesty. Then he helped me unbutton my skirt and in a flash I was naked except for my stockings, which he pulled off as I lay on the floor. I opened my legs with a feeling of almost total abandonment as he sat back, a movement which emphasised the huge bulge that had risen between his legs.

'A few moments later I had his stiff naked cock in my hand and I began rubbing it slowly back and forth as he slipped his fingers between my legs and started gently stroking my pussy lips. I gasped with excitement as he knelt down and began nuzzling me, running his tongue very lightly along the edge of my slit which made my insides turn to liquid. He was marvellous with his tongue and I wriggled madly as his tongue darted in and out of me so fast that I thought he was actually fucking me properly! As he increased the speed of his tongue, I started to rub his cock faster too, and soon afterwards I felt the thick cream spill out over my hand as he spent his load and his tongue worked even more furiously, making me weak with excitement as he brought me off.

'Then he raised himself to tear off his clothes and for one dreadful moment I thought he had gone but he slipped back on top of me and I felt his warm body crush me down. I reached down to guide his slick red prick and wrapped my fingers round the base of his cock. I eased him onto his back and brought my mouth down to kiss the purple uncovered dome. I opened my lips wide and then my mouth closed over the swollen head. With my other hand massaging his balls, I

174

slid my lips up and down his shaft, taking as much as I could into my mouth and sucking juicily until he began to thrust upwards in and out in time with my own movements.

'Soon I felt his balls pulsate in my hand and I knew that he was about to come. In a moment a stream of warm spunk spurted into my mouth and his prick bucked uncontrollably as I held it lightly between my teeth. My own supreme pleasure flowed over me as I sucked and sucked the jets of sperm that poured out of his magnificent cock. Then all too soon they drained away and I felt that gorgeous spongy-textured tool soften as I rolled my lips around it. Edmund's movements ceased as he lay sated and I nibbled away at that funny little round bulb with the tiny hole until he struggled to rise into a sitting position. We kissed but although I desperately wanted a good fuck, Edmund was just not up to it so we dressed and he made his farewells. I still felt frustrated and by now my cunny was on fire.'

'You should have made him fuck you first before sucking him off,' I said coldly.

'Quite right,' sighed Lucy. 'I should have taken that stiff prick straightaway. *Carpe diem, quam minimum credula postero!*'

'Seize the present day, trusting the morrow as little as you can,' I construed rather sourly, for it gave me little joy to hear of Lucy's adventures whilst my own prick was stiff as a board and in urgent need of female ministrations!

'I do believe that you are jealous, Andrew,' said Lucy, smiling at me, 'but Edmund never had his wicked way with me, you know, not then nor indeed has he ever done so since that time.'

I still looked miserable but Lucy kissed my lips and whispered that we would be able to have a long uninterrupted fucking session that night after dinner so I should not indulge myself too much at table.

We were almost at the end of our journey and Doctor White came back to our compartment.

'Come along now, you two,' said Doctor White as he came in. 'We must find a porter and then look out for the carriage that Alfred Kleiman has sent to the station to take us back to his house.'

'We are staying with Alfred Kleiman?' I asked, noting that Lucy too was surprised. On the rare occasions that we stayed in London we always took accommodation in a small private hotel in Shepherd's Market.

'Did I forget to tell you? Yes, Alfred and Edmund are great friends. Alfred is a noted connoisseur especially in that field in which Edmund specialises.'

'In sucking pussies!' I said quietly.

'In landscape pictures!' said Lucy firmly, trying hard to suppress a giggle.

In fact, Alfred himself had come to meet us, and was on the platform to greet our party. His coachman helped the porter unload our luggage, and soon we were off to his house in Golden Square which, although enjoying a most central location, was becoming far too noisy for his liking.

'The social life of the city has been revolutionised by the gas lamps and now by electricity,' said Doctor White. 'People are going out far more often at night and staying out later. This new underground railway system will also bring more and more people into town.'

'Yes, I believe you are right there,' said Alfred. 'Fortunately I have sold my house, as I am going to live in America for the next few years. Lucy, is your father still with the British Embassy in Washington?'

'No, he has moved on to Greece. I think my parents will make a permanent home in Athens as they are terribly fond of life there,' said Lucy, smiling at our host.

'I can quite believe it,' said Alfred. 'Athens is a most beautiful city and I am hardly surprised at your parents' decision. However, Greece is the country of the ancient past, and the United States of America is the country of the immediate future, do you not agree, my dear Simon?'

'Absolutely so,' boomed Doctor White. 'Our imperial power is now at its peak but I expect it to decline gradually as the colonial countries loosen the bonds that at present tie us so tightly together. Much of our wealth comes from South

Africa, India, and Australasia but I would not be surprised if at least one, if not two, of these countries leaves the Empire in the next twenty years or so.'

'You cannot mean India,' said Lucy. 'How could the natives govern themselves?'

'Pretty well, Lucy,' said Doctor White. 'They may lack our technological prowess but the Indians have their own Eastern style of life to which they can easily return if we leave. The Mutiny was but a taste, alas, of what awaits us. For however benign a rule of one people over another may be, in the end, the oppressed people will rise up and throw off the yoke of occupation.'

We continued this interesting topic until the carriage reached Golden Square. Alfred Kleiman had obviously either inherited a great fortune or made a great deal of money from his medical expertise for it was a fine house in the very heart of the Metropolis. We each had separate bedrooms and a full staff of servants was on hand to wait upon us hand and foot.

After we had unpacked, we sat down for some light refreshments, but the two doctors soon retired to Alfred Kleiman's small but extremely well-stocked library. Lucy and I were left alone, but soon she too begged to be excused.

'Have you a previous engagement?' I inquired for our Academy dinner was set for eight o'clock.

'Not exactly an engagement, but I must leave you for an hour, Andrew. I will be ready at half past seven so perhaps you would be kind enough to knock on the door of my room at that time and escort me to the festivities this evening,' she replied.

I thought nothing of her request at the time but I dressed carefully, and exactly at the time requested knocked smartly on Lucy's door. She opened it herself, her maid having left the room by then, and she looked absolutely enchanting. Her dress was an exquisite Paris creation by Messrs Axelrod, a low-cut gown in light blue satin which set off her blonde colouring quite beautifully. She added to the effect by her own appearance, for she looked the very picture of health despite a complaint earlier in the day of feeling somewhat out of sorts, and this effect had not been procured by the liberal use of any artificial aids.

'My goodness, you look stunning, my darling,' I said.

'That is very good of you, Andrew. You look quite marvellous yourself,' she replied and leaned forward to kiss me on the lips.

'I am glad that your earlier indisposition has now cleared,' I said. 'You look now as if you are on top of the world.'

Lucy smiled and I thought that I detected a slightly wicked look to her grin.

'Hold on a moment,' I said sternly. 'I believe that there may be another factor to all this. Where were you earlier this evening? And do not attempt to deceive me with a falsehood, for you know that I can always tell when you are not telling me the truth!'

Lucy sighed and shook her pretty head. 'Oh dear, I suppose I must tell all. But are you sure you want to know, Andrew?'

I nodded and motioned her to sit down on the bed whilst I drew up a chair to listen to her explanations.

She smiled again and said: 'Well, if you must know, Doctor Kleiman, Alfred that is, asked me to help cure one of his patients. I wasn't interested at first but when he told me that the young gentleman concerned was none other than Lord W—— I just had to agree.

'You may have seen Lord W——'s photograph, but I can assure you that he is a most handsome young man of nineteen. He has suffered for some years, however, from a condition known to medical science as premature ejaculation. It seems that as soon as his prick swells up he cannot prevent himself from coming so that neither he nor his partner can achieve a satisfactory pleasure. As he is soon to be engaged to Lady Helen L——, this frightful condition must be cured as soon as possible. Do think on it, what a scandal if this caused a problem after he was married!

'Anyhow, Alfred asked me to help, so he arranged for me to meet Lord W——, or Alan as I now know him, this evening to see if I could be of any assistance. I went up to my room after I left you at tea-time, and changed into a pair of tight riding trousers. Alan was waiting for me in Doctor Kleiman's bedroom and as instructed he was wearing only a bathrobe and was totally naked underneath. He knew that I was a lady and rose to greet me as I entered. We chatted away for a few minutes about mutual friends then I pretended to see a coin on the floor and leaving him sitting on the bed, I bent down to pick it up, and my bottom, encased in its tight riding trousers, was revealed in its glory to his interested gaze. I laughed and said that I must have been mistaken but then affected to trip and fell across him on the bed.

'I then took his hand and pressed it to my breasts. After a brief period during which he looked very startled, he began to respond and we were soon engaged in the most delicious kiss, our tongues flicking away in each other's mouths and his hands running all over me. I grasped his naked cock which was sticking up between the folds of his robe and though not of a great size, it was very hard when I took the knob in my mouth and sucked on it as I ran my fingernails gently up and down the shaft.

'But straightaway I felt his prick twitch, and before we could begin to really enjoy ourselves, he shot a wad of spunk into my mouth. I swallowed his come and moved over on the bed. I removed his robe leaving his slim, handsome body quite naked. I then slid off the bed and slowly removed my clothes. When I too was absolutely nude, I stood in front of him, opened my legs wide and began to stroke my cunny through my bushy growth of pubic hair. I slipped a finger inside my moist slit and began to rub myself off. Alan looked on with delight and soon his prick began to stiffen. I stopped the show and went over to lie beside him, kissing his nipples and then working my way down to his rising cock. With one sudden gulp I had his balls in my mouth and I massaged his cock up to full attention while I licked and sucked on his heavy balls.

'We moved round again so that my cunt was above his head, and as I lowered myself down he wiggled his tongue all

179

around my crack. Before long I was moaning with genuine pleasure and Alan moved round and over on top of me. I took his throbbing cock in my hands and guided him into my longing pussy.

'This time he did not come so quickly and we fucked very nicely for at least three minutes until we shuddered to a marvellous climax together and he shot a mighty spurt of spunk deep into my moist, eager crack. Oh, Andrew, it was blissful helping him over his hurdle. I am sure that he will be perfectly alright now.

'Mind, he cannot fuck as well as you,' she added hastily for she could see that I was a little miffed by hearing about this adventure. Mind, my prick was not offended by all this and was bulging out uncomfortably at the front of my trousers. Lucy saw my discomfort and slowly undid my buttons until my bursting cock was freed from its confines. She massaged the shaft slowly, capping and uncapping the purple dome and then she went down on her knees, and opening her pretty mouth as wide as possible, swallowed as much of the thick shaft as she could and began to suck noisily on my delighted tool. I pushed in and out as she held my cock in her hands as she sucked firmly, sliding her lips up and down the iron-hard shaft. Normally I would have attempted to delay the grand *finale* but time was pressing and I did not wish us to be disturbed. So I let my mind relax and very soon I gushed a creamy jet of white love-juice into her mouth, as she eagerly milked my prick of every last drop of spunk.

I would have preferred to miss the food and have some fucking instead but we could hardly excuse ourselves at this late stage. We walked slowly downstairs in absolute decorum even though we were somewhat flushed of face, as would be expected of two people who had just indulged themselves in the partaking of the most delicious pleasure known to our species. Alfred Kleiman, our genial host, and Doctor White were ready and waiting and we were ushered out into the warm evening air where Alfred's carriage awaited us.

There was a great deal of traffic in the area and we were obliged to wait until our coachman could force a way through

—though fortunately we had left sufficient time, so we were not late for the great occasion.

'London needs a Haussmann to plan a new centre for the great city,' I said, as we sat in the mêlée of coaches, hansoms and other vehicles that made up Piccadilly's highway.

'Perhaps so,' riposted my headmaster. 'But it needs to be a careful reconstruction unlike a number which have ruined so many places.'

'Certainly,' said Lucy. 'And there should be a plan that benefits all classes of the population. So often we have heard of people being driven out of their homes in the name of hygiene or of progress, but they have left their long-familiar surroundings usually for the enrichment of contractors, town councillors and speculators of every kind.'

'I agree with you,' said Alfred. 'It is most definitely the case that in an old street say in Paris or in Rome, you will almost certainly find a delight for the eye in archway and ogive, in lintel and casement, in the wallflowers rooted in the steps, in the capsicum which has seeded itself between the stones. But the modern street with its monotony, the high and long blank spaces, the even surfaces where not a seed can cling or a bird can build, what does this street say to the eyes and the heart?'

Before any of us could respond to his question, the coach slowed to a stationary position and we alighted. Dear reader, I must excuse myself from recounting the full details of the grand affair for seeing Edmund there, being fêted by the most distinguished folk, made me so angry that my appetite both for food and drink as well as for convivial company was quite taken away. Suffice it to say that I pleaded tiredness and a most uncomfortable headache, hoping of course that Lucy would accompany me back to Golden Square. Alas, though she later explained that she would have dearly loved to do so, she felt it would be too impolite to leave with me, so I took a hansom cab back to the house on my own.

Alfred had instructed his butler, Mr Newman, to wait up for the return of our party so he was on hand to open the front door for me.

'Are you well, sir? I did not expect you back so soon,' he enquired.

'I left early as I feel somewhat unwell. I shall go to bed now as I have a terrible headache,' I replied.

'One of the young house parlourmaids, Clara, could bring you up a hot drink, if you would like one, sir,' he said.

'I think I would rather have a whisky and soda to ensure that I have a good night's sleep,' I replied.

'Very good, sir. I will instruct Clara to bring up your night-cap in about ten minutes.'

I bade him goodnight and retired to my room and undressed myself, as unlike my headmaster and Doctor Kleiman, I did not have the services of a valet. I put on a soft purple bathrobe that had been thoughtfully provided for me and I debated as to whether I should in fact change into some casual evening clothes and wait up downstairs for Lucy and the rest of the party (for truth to tell, the trifling headache that had bothered me somewhat earlier on had by now disappeared), or whether I should simply go straight to bed.

A knock on the door disturbed my thoughts upon the matter and I called out for the person concerned to enter. As I expected, it was the maid with my nightcap—but I was staggered to behold not a mumping old Betty but the most ravishing beauty, who came into my room bearing whisky and soda on a silver tray. She could have been no more than twenty, a most beautiful creature, rather above medium height, with dark auburn hair, fresh colour and sparkling blue eyes that were set off by a merry smile and the most exquisite pearly white little teeth. Furthermore, this apparition wore not the severe black and white of a maid but a low-cut dark blue silk dress that revealed much of the splendours of her full-rounded breasts. I could hardly keep the surprise out of my voice as I said: 'Pardon me, but I was expected to believe that Clara, the house-parlourmaid, was going to bring me a nightcap.'

She giggled deliciously and said: 'I am Clara, sir. Please forgive my attire but I have been out this evening with my gentleman friend without Mr Newman, the butler's knowledge and I slipped in without his seeing me. Cook gave me the message to bring this tray to your room. I do hope you will keep my secret.'

'Of course I will, Clara,' I said. 'But you really did surprise me. You look far more like the ladies I have just seen at the Royal Academy dinner than a servant.'

She giggled again and said: 'Well, it is amusing that you should say that, sir, for indeed that is just where I have come from. You see, my gentleman friend is an artist who indeed may be known to you. Like yourself I left early so as not to embarrass my friend.'

'Good heavens, don't tell me that your friend is Edmund White?'

'Yes, that is his name. He is a very kind man, and as you can see he buys me the most exquisite clothes so that no-one knows that I am but a mere servant. He introduces me to his friends as Lady Clara Cuthbertson! That is my full name, after all.'

'My goodness gracious. This is quite fascinating. Tell me, is Edmund a decent sort of chap? I ask this as although I am barely acquainted with him, his brother is my headmaster and we do have a mutual friend.'

She looked at me and smiled, her blue eyes dancing as she said: 'I don't know, Andrew—I may call you Andrew, may I not? Do you really want me to stay?'

'I most certainly do!' I said warmly and jumped up and closed the door that had been left very slightly ajar.

'H'mm. Well, Andrew, after the most careful consideration, I have decided that I will stay just a little if you like.'

I poured out two large whisky and sodas and we toasted each other. We sat down on my bed and I said: 'Let us make ourselves more comfortable.'

I gently unbuttoned the top of her gown, freeing her large breasts which swelled enticingly. I let my fingers flick gently across them, feeling the hard nipples, and Clara swallowed as if her throat had suddenly gone dry. She finished her whisky, set down the glass on the carpet and went into my arms without further preamble.

Our bodies fastened against one another. Clara kept one hand curled around the back of my head whilst the other investigated the front of my robe as she slipped her hand inside, encountering my stiff cock. She squeezed my prick and gave a little sigh as I fussed with her buttons. But I was clumsy and she stepped back.

'Damn bloomers and the man who invented them!' I said, as I tore off my robe and noticed her eyes gleam with pleasure at the sight of my naked cock standing stiffly to attention against my belly. She was naked now and I moved forward and embraced her. I manoeuvred her towards the bed until the back of her legs touched the edge, and she went over backwards with a squeal of delight. I was now on top of her and our lips crushed together as she ran her hand slowly down my belly, rubbing her fingers through my pubic hair until they closed round the throbbing shaft of my prick. I cupped her superb breasts and sucked on a hard little nipple as she fondled my knob, making the foreskin slide slowly up and down. She kissed my ear and darted her tongue wetly inside, then slid her mouth gradually back towards my lips. The sensation of her palm closing over my prick-head was very exciting and my cock swelled and throbbed, giving off a little trickle of juice which seeped onto her hand. This seemed to please her for she continued to squeeze and fondle my knob, making sensual, squelching noises as she did so.

'Licence my roving hands, and let them go
Behind, before, above, between, below.'

I took John Donne's words to heart as I buried three fingers into her juicy pussy. I then rubbed the lips with my other hand until they opened up and soon I was able to reach her clitty which was standing up like a little soldier. She heaved her body backwards and forwards on my fingers and soon I felt sure that I could insert my whole hand inside her crack if I felt so inclined. Her clitty was incredibly hard and running with juice as I continued to tease it. Suddenly she arched her back and shuddered to a powerful climax. Keeping my fingers buried inside her cunt, I could feel the vibrating heat and the sticky goo of her honey as, thrusting

184

her hips upwards, she willed me to jab my fingers as far as I could get them inside her slit.

Clara's hands were still pushing my foreskin up and down over my prick at an even faster rate and before I could stop myself I spurted a stream of warm spunk over her hand. This excited her more as she moaned with pleasure, twisting and jerking as she reached a peak of shuddering release. Oddly enough, despite the alcohol I had consumed that night, I did not completely lose my stiffness. Although we both calmed down, we never stopped fondling one another and she refused to release my prick and seemed to enjoy smearing my white love-juice all over her belly. 'Oh, yes,' she murmured. 'Oh, yes, oh, yes. Very good.' Her hand moved and she started to rub my wilted prick, squeezing and kneading it gently and rhythmically between her long fingers.

I felt my tool harden and the exquisite sensations began once again until very shortly it was fully erect and raring to go to its resting place in Clara's juicy cunny. I felt myself being pushed down upon my back as Clara climbed on top of me, bending forward so as to kiss my lips as I grasped those luscious breasts which I rolled around my hands, feeling the rock-hard little nipples against my palms. Her soft, oily pussy was just touching the tip of my throbbing prick, and she moved her hips so that her cunny lips slid over it, thrilling me with the sensation of their juicy wetness. Then she lowered herself gently so that the tip of my bursting rod was just inside her inner lips, poking at the entrance to her vagina.

'There, that is nice, isn't it?' cooed the little minx.

'Perfectly splendid, Clara!' I gasped as she lowered herself firmly downwards, pushing hard on my throbbing tool. I felt my cock slip into her, pushing against the slight resistance of her vaginal muscles. Then suddenly I was deep inside her, surrounded by warm, wet flesh—the sensations were so delicious that my head swam with delight as she positioned herself for the forthcoming action.

She groaned as she started to move her strong young body up and down, using her thighs to ride me, bobbing up and down so that my prick was thrusting in and out of her. She began to move faster, panting heavily with the exertion, and her interior muscles began to milk my prick exquisitely as it slid in and out, her buttocks slapping against my thighs with every descent. She heaved herself up and down upon my throbbing length, taking every last inch of the shaft deep into her cunt, and the continuous nipping and contractions of her pussy soon brought me to the climax. I tried at first to hold back but I could feel my hot sperm boiling up inside me, and I crashed powerful jets of love-juice up into her cunt as she moved her hips faster and faster. The feel of her beautifully-formed young body rocking to and fro kept my cock hard even though I jetted spurt after spurt of spunk, filling her pussy with my cream.

Despite her urgings, I could not perform again at once, and I rolled Clara over onto her back—for not even in those days, when I was at the very height of my physical powers, could I fuck three times after a heavy meal and after partaking of alcoholic refreshment. Wine has always affected my prowess, unlike some men such as Sir Lionel T——, who I have known to down a bottle of champagne and then proceed to fuck three girls one after another. Mind, this was when this gentleman was in his prime.

I lay exhausted for some twenty minutes until Clara sucked my prick up to a new fine state of erection and I could see that she was eager for a repetition of the pleasure. She again climbed up to ride a St George upon me and had just commenced to bounce up and down when to my horror the door opened and who should be standing there but my host for the duration, Alfred Kleiman, who looked amazed and somewhat pale as Clara turned her pretty head round and said: 'Oh come in, sir, if you are staying. I know full well that you have wanted to fuck me since I took up service with you. Oooh, that's good, Andrew, push your bottom up as I push down, that's better. Do join us if you've a mind to or please withdraw and close the door behind you.'

She was certainly a cool little miss, but Alfred needed no second invitation. He tore off his clothes with an amazing rapidity and in an instant he was on the bed with us, his cock as hard as iron and eager to get in somewhere. So kneeling up behind Clara he tried to insert his prick in her cunt alongside mine but found this impossible to achieve. Then the charming wrinkled orifice of her bum-hole caught his attention and wetting the knob of his great cock, he inserted himself between the cheeks of her buttocks. Soon his cock was wet with our spendings and his vigorous shoves quickly gained an entrance as Clara wriggled deliciously. We all three rested a moment and enjoyed the sensation of feeling where we were, our two pricks throbbing against each other in a most delicious manner, with only the thin membrane of the anal canal between them. We both spent almost immediately to Clara's huge delight as she at once pleaded with us to go on.

The smooth round dome of Alfred's huge knob was now burrowed well inside Clara's bottom. Clamping his knees on either side of her waist, Alfred held her firmly until some seven inches of his thick shaft were sheathed. Clara moaned with delight and wriggled her *derrière* to each in-and-out motion of Alfred's prick. I too began to jerk my frame up and down until we ran our course, uttering the most abandoned cries. I came first, injecting the gorgeous girl with jets of bubbling spunk, and moments after Alfred pumped his prick forwards and backwards until he too discharged gushes of juice into Clara's bum. She then allowed him to withdraw his cock slowly to the sound of a faint plop! as the gleaming cock emerged and Alfred sank down beside us.

I gently moved Clara between us and asked my guests if they would like a drink, as there was still at least half a bottle of whisky on the tray Clara had brought in. I smiled as I spoke, as the thought crossed my mind that the whisky after all belonged to our kind host, so here I was offering Alfred his own drink! They declined, and not wishing to drink alone I came back to the bed.

'Tell me, Clara,' said Alfred. 'You are obviously experienced in the noble arts of *l'amour*. I wish I had known this before but Mrs Shirley the housekeeper led me to believe that you were not very keen on men.'

'Not keen on men?' laughed Clara. 'That is far from true.

However, I think this is because Mrs Shirley knows that I have visited the Lady Mumford club in Soho which is a haunt of well-known ladies who prefer the company of their own sex.'

'There is no need to mince matters,' said Alfred. 'The inhabitants of that club keep the dildo-makers in business, is this not so?'

'I suppose you could say so,' said Clara seriously. 'Other girls I know have never tried it, but I must say that while females have never formed the main part of my bedroom affairs, truth to tell they have always been in the background.

'Their bodies attract me by their soft smoothness and I enjoy turning to a girl after having a good fuck like tonight's. I was at the club only last night, where I met my good friend Patricia whose preference is definitely for the gentle sex. She asked me how I could go to bed with a man and I replied that I enjoyed tremendously the ecstasy experienced as when you, Andrew, shoved your iron-hard young cock up my pussy.

'Patricia moved closer to me on the settee and asked me if I were really sure about this. We were in her private room at the club and I looked at her pretty face and told her that I enjoyed the bodies of both men and women.

'She began kissing my face very tenderly and I could feel her other hand hovering over my breasts as she felt for the buttons of my dress. Then her fingers slipped inside the opening and her warm hands began to caress my breasts. At first I was too tensed-up to be fully aware, but gradually I felt my tenseness flow away. Patricia turned her face towards mine as she gently tweaked one of my nipples between her fingers. The delicate touch of her lips and fingers is so different from those of a man. She started slipping her tongue into my mouth and I met it halfway with my own, stroking it softly against hers and then licking around the outside of her mouth and tasting the sweet flavour of her light make-up.

'I undid the buttons on her blouse and pressed my hands cautiously onto the smooth firm flesh of her small but beautifully-proportioned breasts. I felt her nipples stiffen as I stroked across them, which was just as exciting a sensation as

188

having my own fondled. She rested her other hand on my tummy, slowly moving it further down till she was stroking my mound through the material of my dress. I could feel a warm wetness gathering between my thighs, and I raised my bottom slightly so that Patricia could pull my dress up as she rubbed me. Then she took her hand away from my breasts and putting them both underneath my dress, began to pull down my drawers.

'It took only a minute before we had pulled off all our clothes, and we both lay naked on the settee entwined in each other's arms. Patricia was like a sleek, pampered kitten, stretching out her legs and arching her back as she silently urged me to explore between her legs. I proceeded to rub the flat of her belly then let my fingers stray to the neat little triangle of mossy black hair. I tingled all over as the warm, ripe lips of her cunt opened magically under my probing fingertips. The skin of her pussy was marvellously soft and wet—I was amazed at how easily my forefinger slid into the slit and how smoothly it could work in and out.

'Still frigging slowly into her, I began to kiss passionately at the firm curve of her pubis, slithering my lips gradually downwards until they were directly over her quim. I could taste the rich juices and I could see the glistening dew on my fingers as they plunged in and out of her soaking cunny.

'Patricia was now so aroused that it was no surprise to find the tips of her fingers starting to stroke lightly round the rim of my own pussy, and with one hand around her waist and the other fondling her titties, I kissed her more urgently, sliding my tongue deep into her mouth, as at the same moment I felt one of her fingers begin to sink in between my cunt lips. Patricia rubbed her knuckles into my crotch as she penetrated further inside my crack. I soon began to get so breathless with excitement that I was forced to stop kissing her. When I took my mouth away from hers, she bent her head and pressed her soft lips against my engorged titties.

'My nipples were already aroused but when she began to lick and suck them she made my titties feel even more sensitive and excited. My whole body ached with passion as her fingers plunged deeper into my slit and her tongue stretched one of my nipples as she sucked it into her mouth. She moved her fingers so expertly in my cunny, rubbing in, out and around with simply fabulous pleasure and speed.

'Then her other hand pressed upon my mound as she slid one of her fingers through my pussy hair and into the crease that covered my clitty, I felt my excitement reach new peaks.

'She found my little button and began to stroke it gently, and it took very little time before she brought me to the most delicious orgasm—and it somehow felt different to any other I had ever experienced.

'Afterwards, I did feel a little bit guilty. Not because of what Patricia had done, you must understand, but because I had acted selfishly—like so many men, if you will forgive my saying so, Andrew. Oh, how often does a man discharge his squirts of juice and then simply lie back, exhausted to the world and unable to offer his eager partner any further delights. And now here was I guilty of such thoughtlessness, for I had neglected to ensure that my delightful partner enjoyed the very fullness of pleasures afforded by our actions.

'I began to fondle and caress her naked body and she moved herself across me so that her hairy motte brushed against my lips. I now knew what she had in mind and I started to kiss the insides of her thighs and moved my lips up until her hairy mound stroked again at my mouth.'

'*De gustibus non est disputandum*,' I muttered softly.

'No, there is no accounting for tastes,' she continued sweetly. 'Then I felt Patricia's mouth flick across the wet grooves of my own cunt, setting off a lovely tingling glow throughout my body. I then pressed my lips firmly against her pussy, feeling a new thrill as I kissed and licked the wet fleshy cunny lips. I eased my tongue into the raw centre of her red, slippery cunt, lapping swiftly against her clitoris and pressing my titties urgently down on the curves of her belly.

'I was itching wildly now, forcing my cunt against her mouth and jerking my hips, I pushed forward until she was comfortably sucking away at my cunny. My own hands went to her thighs, my fingers sinking fiercely into the soft underside of her legs while my lips worked quite feverishly on her pussy and my tongue kept darting across her ultra-sensitive little clitty. She was now enjoying the highest pleasures, as I could tell by the spasms that racked her beautiful young body as she writhed beneath me; but she would not neglect my pleasures even at the climax of her own delights. All the time her mouth continued to suck greedily at my cunny lips, her tongue lapping non-stop inside my crack until I was brought shuddering to new, previously unscaled peaks of joy.

'But yet more was to come as she continued to writhe against my mouth for I could feel her clitty pulsing with excitement as I probed in and out of her juicy quim. While I sank my tongue in as far as I could I heard Patricia mumble something about her handbag, but I was too far involved to pay much attention. I was briefly aware of Patricia fiddling about with her bag until the next thing I knew there was something nudging against my cunt lips, and it was more substantial than a girl's tongue!

'Yes, it was a superbly fashioned wooden dildo. Made from the finest rosewood, it was even thicker than Alfred's cock, which by the by is the thickest I have ever seen—and I will give it a good sucking once I have finished telling my story. It was at least seven or eight inches long. This was the very first time I had ever experienced such an instrument and I had always dismissed them as mere substitutes for the real thing. However, used by an expert, a dildo can be great fun; although in my experience it has stimulated rather than diminished my needs for a regular dosage of strong, hot cock!

'As she inserted the dildo into my receptive cunny my excitement accelerated faster to a pace almost unbearable and very soon I was again coming copiously, discharging love-juice down my thighs. The joys of it made me tremble with delight and I tongued Patricia's pussy really frantically as this wonderful little instrument brought me off time and time again. Even when she finally removed it I could still seem to

191

feel those wonderful sensations pulsing through me like a series of tiny echoes.

'Afterwards I used the dildo on Patricia and in spite of my previous exertions I was still able to thoroughly enjoy watching her squirm with excitement just as I had done.'

By now both our pricks were standing stiffly and smartly to attention and Clara inspected them critically. She was a quite delightful girl but goodness how she loved to chatter away. She commenced again to talk when all Alfred and I wanted, so help us, was some relief from our bursting pricks!

'M'mm, two fine cocks, I must admit. Yours is not so big, Andrew, but nevertheless size is not at all important as I am sure Doctor Kleiman must have told you. So many men consider the size of their cocks to be inadequate but really the problem is purely of their own making. Five inches is probably the average size prick and in my experience and the experience of my friends, a nine-inch cock is about the biggest we have ever come across.

'You are just as capable of fully satisfying a girl, for it is not mere size but the ability to pleasure a girl through sheer technique that makes all the difference. Sex is, after all, an art and if the sexual act is carried out in an artistic manner, thinking not so much of how many inches of prick you can shove into a crack but rather how you can use the whole of your mind and body to satisfy your girl, well, that is everything.'

And with a smile she swooped down, clamping her luscious lips round the dome of my prick whilst she grasped Alfred's throbbing shaft at its rigid base and began to rub the massive rod as she sucked and nibbled away at my uncapped vermilion dome. I moaned and pressed her pretty head downwards until her lips enclosed almost all my stiff shaft, and she rose and fell with a regular steady motion that sent me into realms of ecstasy. As she continued to rub Alfred's tool, I saw his hand snake out and reach for her damp pussy, and Clara gasped as he nudged his fingers against her cunny lips, parting them slowly and gently. He pushed first one and then two long fingers deeper inside her cunt as she raised her hips up, panting breathlessly as he began to move in rhythm. Her head continued to bob up and down over my prick until I felt a shudder of pleasure run through me and I shot a stream of sperm into her receptive mouth, and Clara milked my prick expertly, sucking every drain of juice out of me while Alfred continued to play with her juicy cunny as she gripped his hand between her thighs and squeezed it hard against her motte.

She must have realised from the throbbing of his prick that his time would soon come if she did not resist rubbing his tool, so she let go the throbbing shaft and he raised up his body, and Clara parted her thighs enabling him to press his knob against her cunt lips.

I took hold of his giant cock and guided it home between her aching cunny lips, and he sank into her with a grateful sigh. I was now unnecessary to the performance so I leaned back to watch them fuck.

Directly every inch of his huge prick was snugly inside her quim she closed her thighs, making Alfred open his own legs and lie astride her with his tool well and truly trapped inside Clara's pussy. She loved to do this, she told me later, as the sensation is most pleasing to both partners. Alfred could scarcely fuck in and out as the muscles of her cunt were gripping him so tightly, but then Clara began to grind her hips round, massaging his cock as it throbbed powerfully inside her juicy cunny, which was dribbling love juice down her thighs. He sank his fingers into the cheeks of her arse, inserting a finger into her bottom-hole which made her squeal and wriggle with delight. She shifted her thighs now and as the pressure around his prick eased, he began to drive wildly in and out, fucking at such an intense speed that I could not see how he could hold back the jets of spunk.

Meanwhile Clara was being brought off all the time, building herself to a magnificent climax as the fierce momentum made her pussy fairly run with love juice. She brought her legs up against the small of his back, humping the lower half of her body upwards to meet the violent strokes of his raging cock.

He bore down on her yet again, his body now soaked with perspiration, fucking harder and harder, the rippling movement of his cock playing lustily against the velvety skin of her cunt. Suddenly I saw him tense his frame and then he crashed down upon the girl, his cock jetting spasms of spunk inside her as Clara quickly squeezed her thighs together again, milking every last drop from his spurting length, not releasing him until she was sure that he had completely finished. Alfred climaxed beautifully reminding me of the words of one Mr Emerson, one of my favourite poets: 'A friend may well be reckoned to be the masterpiece of Nature.'

'Oh, Alfred,' gasped Clara. 'You certainly know how to make love to a girl. So few males know how to attack the clitoris properly.'

'Oh my, surely not,' said Alfred, who seemed to be winding himself up for a lecture—I was familiar with the symptoms from learning English with dear Doctor White—and he cleared his throat and spake forth. I will repeat his words *verbatim* as far as I can remember as I hope they may be of interest to gallant young chaps not as experienced as us old fogies in *l'art de faire l'amour*.

He began: 'Now every girl possesses one and any girl can show you exactly where it is—and far the best idea is simply to ask advice rather than pore over the pages of an anatomy book for medical students. I would hope that the girl you ask would be impressed that you care and that she would also realise that no part of her body is more sensitive than her little clitty.

'The clitoris is located between the labia near the opening of the vagina. As you begin to rub your hand over her cunny lips after massaging her breasts, you will always find that she will quite jump with pleasure when you touch this tiny nub of erectile tissue.

'To become expert at caressing the clitty requires the same attention and concentration as one would focus on the titties.

'The clitoris is far more elusive and difficult to handle, for probably before you even reach it your girl will be juicing so that everything at the vaginal entrance will be extremely slippery with her lubricants. You may not be able to see what you are doing and will be operating entirely by feel and touch, and strict attention must be paid to the response of the girl.'

'You are so wise, Alfred,' cooed Clara, 'my own clitty is my balancing point. When a man puts his finger on it he puts me into perfect suspension. Time and place simply disappear and I am in an entranced state of ecstasy,' she murmured, putting out her hand to caress my prick, which was now beginning to rise again after all its heroic labours.

'Thank you,' said Alfred, and he continued: 'So by her reaction, one can tell when the clitty has been stimulated, for she will stiffen or moan beneath your touch. When this happens, the best thing to do is to keep your hand exactly where it is and then tentatively move your finger—yes, just a single finger—around the clitoral area. When she reacts again with an expression of pleasure you will know that the slippery target has been found. Extreme gentleness and tender care are now needed. The digital movements should be continued to maximise her pleasure.

'She may have an orgasm beneath your fingertips as she is being caressed. This is nothing to occasion any alarm. If she does achieve a climax, I would suggest immediately suspending any massage of the clitty, for during orgasm and immediately afterwards the stimulation is often not pleasurable just as direct stimulation after ejaculation for a man does very little to please him. It does not matter if the girl reaches a peak, for in my experience girls possess a far greater capability for multiple orgasmic activity than men, so she can reach for the ultimate again during actual intercourse.

'One final point—some girls can become over-excited during clitoral stimulation, or there may be times when she does not require so much massage. The result is that she is put into a frenzy to reach orgasm but cannot except by immediate full intercourse, and that is time to proceed without any further foreplay. It is essential, after all, not to torture a girl by caressing and touching a clitty to a point that no longer provides pleasure.'

All this talking about clitties had fired both Clara and

myself and by the time Alfred had concluded his fascinating little lecture, Clara had grasped my prick and was busy frigging away at my swollen shaft which had now stiffened into full erectness. I reached out for Clara's beautiful breasts which, although not the largest I have ever had the pleasure to fondle, were incredibly firm, each jutting cone capped with a swollen pink aureole the size of a ripe strawberry. We eschewed any preliminaries despite Alfred's wise words and, positioning a pillow under her firm young bum and spreading her legs high and wide, Clara held her cunny lips open whilst I eased the purple dome of my bursting prick into her juicy wet slit. I pressed in and she writhed; I caught her knees in my hands and leaned my full weight into her, ramming the engorged barrel of my cock forward until it was firmly wedged right up to the tight pouch of my balls. Clara spent at once, raking my back with her fingernails whilst I rocked back and forth between her spread white thighs. I then varied my thrusts, pushing into her with short, sharp jerks, savouring the voluptuous sensation of her tight love-tube gripping my bulging prick. I was unable to hold on for very much longer and soon I felt wild sensations darting through me, and with a heartfelt sigh of joy I spurted my load deep inside her.

Clara was truly the most insatiable girl I have ever had the privilege to fuck, for although I was now *hors de combat*, Alfred was ready and willing to take my place. She turned over and lay on her belly, thrusting her firm white bottom cheeks bulging up to our delighted view. Alfred positioned himself behind her, moving his hand up and down his magnificently domed cock.

'I love your arse, Clara,' he breathed. 'It is a woman's arse, not one of those *petite derrières* which are not so good for fucking.'

He pulled her buttocks apart—and lodged that huge dome not up her bum-hole as I thought he was going to do but firmly into her cunt, moving forward, back, then further forward into her voracious crack. He pushed and rammed until the whole of his thick shaft was enclosed in her sheath, then he rested for a few moments, making his prick throb in its tight receptacle until the natural lubricity asserted itself once more and Clara answered with a wanton heave of her bottom to every thrust of her partner. Alfred clasped his arms around the delicious girl, taking one globe of her bosom in each hand, moulding them delightfully with his fingers and tweaking those upright little nipples to perfection. Soon I could see his face contort as the sperm began boiling up inside his thick shaft and he crashed a torrent of love juice inside her as she heaved up her bottom to receive his manly action with the most athletic abandon.

I heard a noise downstairs and whispered to my two friends that Lucy and Doctor White had returned. None of us thought that, however broad-minded they might be, these two would appreciate what we had been up to whilst they had been out. So Clara and Alfred scampered to their rooms whilst I jumped into bed and turned off the light, so that to all intent and purposes I was deep in the arms of Morpheus when Lucy tiptoed into my room. You may recall, dear reader, that she had promised me a good fucking before we left for the Academy dinner but now here was I, fast asleep and seemingly in no mood for night exercises! I opened my eyes narrowly and saw a look of disappointment upon her sweet face and I felt thoroughly ashamed of myself. I almost smiled as I thought of John Gay's lines that we had studied so assiduously at Nottsgrove:

How happy I could be with either
Were t'other dear chamer away!

But truth will out, and I must confess that at the time, as now, I felt that I had acted like a cad and resolved to make things up to Lucy at the very first opportunity. I was now genuinely sleepy, and in fact there was no way by which I could perform again that night after my previous exertions. So Lucy had to retire unsatisfied and I slept, sated of course with the pleasures that Clara had lavished upon me.

CHAPTER NINE

Tirez le rideau, la farce est joueé—Rabelais

I AWOKE at nine o'clock in the morning and after a good hot bath, I dressed myself and went downstairs where Doctor White was already tucking into his breakfast. I helped myself to some coffee, just a couple of eggs and some toast, and joined him. We had some time to kill before we left but Doctor White was busy reading *The Times*, so making my excuses I went back upstairs to see if my sweet Lucy had woken up, for Mr Newman had informed me that she had not yet taken any breakfast.

I was outside her door when I thought I heard a gasp from inside, and the creaking of bedsprings. I frowned—for surely Lucy would not have wanted to fuck Alfred again; and in any case, he was surely as sated as I had felt after the previous night's fun and frolics. I noticed that there was no key in the keyhole and I will admit that I bent down and peered through the orifice. And what a surprise was in store—though goodness knows I surely deserved it, and as many people say, eavesdroppers rarely hear any good of themselves. Perhaps, dear reader, you may guess at what I beheld—on the bed, absolutely naked lay Clara and Lucy, face to face lying almost motionless, their arousal stimulated by the gentle brush of nipples and the mingled warmth of loins not yet joined. Then as Lucy's hands went round her waist, Clara groaned: 'Oh, darling, take me!'

Cupping Clara's lovely buttocks, Lucy pulled her firmly against her own receptive flesh. Their lips met, parted and their heads twisted and turned in a mashing of lips. Clara's hands came up and fastened upon Lucy's soft breasts, squeezing, caressing and tweaking the stiffened nipples between finger and thumb. Clara's face was clenched up as she swung her head from side to side, and low whimpering sounds burst from her as Lucy's attentive lips stole across her cheeks, down the side of her neck, moist on her throat's little cavity before moving to enclose each turgid nipple in turn. Then her attention progressed downwards across her quivering belly until her shoulders were between her raised, spread legs. Lucy nuzzled her full lips around the curly dark bush of Clara's cunt and Clara's own hands clasped Lucy's head pulling it down as she flashed her tongue round the damp bush of pubic hair.

I opened the door quietly so as to better see this exhibition and crept into the room, closing the door very quietly behind me. The girls did not see or hear me and Clara moaned as her pussy seemed to open wide and she lifted her bottom to help Lucy slip her tongue through the pink lips as she licked between the inner grooves of the velvety cunny in long thrusting strokes. Clara's pussy was by now gushing love juice and Lucy slipped first one, then two and three fingers into her crack. Clara began to thrash about the bed in a wild ecstasy until the eruption inside her subsided and Lucy ceased her ministrations for a moment. Clara gasped out: 'Oh, Lucy, heavens, pull my clitty, hard!'

Lucy attacked her clitty, driving her tongue right into the ring of her cunny and then as the little love-bean broke from its pod, she gripped it in her fingers and tugged it quite vigorously. Then she lowered her mouth again and sucked and nibbled at it, her tongue now driving fast round the juicy crack from which dribbled a steady flow of love juice as Clara writhed her hips wildly beneath her.

The girls were so engrossed in their love-making that I was forced to cough to attract their attention. They were somewhat surprised to see me but neither of them betrayed more than a hint of embarrassment at being caught together acting as tribades.

'Goodness me, I never heard you come in, Andrew,' said Lucy, with a hint of a flush on her face.

'I hope you locked the door behind you,' said Clara coolly.

'I most certainly did,' I replied.

Clara smiled and jumped out of bed and went to the sideboard upon which rested a bottle of champagne and some glasses.

'Who will join me?' she asked, popping the cork expertly. We all three drank a toast to each other's health and as you can imagine, I quickly undressed to keep my two girls company in bed. Barely had I finished my glass of Mumm '83 (Alfred kept a fine cellar) when Lucy was on her knees in front of me, forcing apart my legs and saying: 'I don't want you to think that Clara has supplanted you in my affections, my dear. We have enjoyed some fun together but Clara will agree, I am sure, that in the final analysis there is no real substitute for a rock-hard thick cock!'

She swooped her pretty blonde-haired head down and began to slurp greedily at my swelling prick, which throbbed furiously in her sweet mouth. She sucked deeper and deeper, letting it slide thickly against her tongue whilst her lips savoured the juicy lollipop with noisy, uninhibited pleasure. I kissed her head as it bobbed up and down in front of me, but then Clara leaned over and kissed me furiously on the lips, and then taking one of her spanking breasts, pushed it towards me, gently easing the tawny nipple into my mouth. I stroked her thighs and then worked my finger in and out of her juicy cunt whilst at the same time taking my prick out of Lucy's mouth and squeezing it firmly into her wet pussy. I thrust faster and faster, pushing my prick in as hard as I could so that my balls banged against her lovely bottom while my tricky fingers slid in and out of Clara's sopping muff. I grunted with delight as I shot a marvellous load of creamy sperm into Lucy. Our juices mingled happily and our hairy pubes crashed together and rubbed against each other as she milked my cock. But poor Clara was not satisfied with the mere fingering of her quimmy so I heaved myself off Lucy (who quite understood that Clara deserved more) and Clara pulled my head between her legs, licking and sucking the swollen labia. My tongue lashed juicily around her hairy bush and in and out of her slit. My lips nibbled at her clitty and Clara's hips jerked backwards and forwards, gyrating wildly as my tongue tickled round her hole till she could stand it no longer.

'Fuck me,' she screamed. 'Please fuck me, now, quickly.'

Fortunately, my cock was now rampant, aided by some furious sucking by Lucy, and I thrust it deep into her dripping cunny. I pumped my raging tool in and out of the sodden bush but I came very quickly; though it was enough, for we climaxed together as I heaved my glutinous cum through her cunny lips for a full fifteen seconds. I sank back exhausted and try as they may, the girls could not raise Priapus again, so they were forced to play by themselves with a five inch dildo. Lucy ran it up and down the cleavage of Clara's bottom whilst playing with her cunny lips with her hand. Then she switched hands and, frigging Clara's bum, she slipped the dildo between the slightly open lips of the luscious-looking vermilion gap. This seemed to electrify Clara who reached up to fondle Lucy's succulent brown nipples which were as firm as little bullets to the grasp. They ran a delightful course, filled with voluptuous excitement, finishing in a mutual spend but of course, even an expertly handled dildo is not as good as a true cock and I was called again to partake of the feat of love.

Thus we passed a most delicious morning, refreshing ourselves from time to time with champagne and ices, for the worship of Venus and Priapus requires the continual stimulation of the most invigorating viands and liquids.

As the time came for our departure, Lucy and I dressed quickly and went downstairs to say farewell to Alfred Kleiman and to thank him once again for his generous hospitality. He was unable to travel with us back to King's Cross but insisted that we use his carriage as he had only to walk down Regent Street to meet Professor Bagell, his colleague from Vienna, who was in London for a few days to address a learned gathering. Mr Newman, the quiet butler who I suspect may have had an inkling of the high goings-on in the bedrooms, supervised the loading of our baggage and then Lucy, Doctor White and I stepped up into the fine carriage and we were off back to the railway station.

'Did you read that interesting piece in today's newspaper?' said Doctor White to us.

'Oh dear, I am afraid that I have not seen today's *Times*,' said Lucy gravely.

'Neither have I,' I added somewhat guiltily, as our good old head insisted that we took a keen interest in current affairs.

'You really should have read the article,' said Doctor White but luckily he did not sound too angry. 'Every day you are supposed to read the newspaper. However, as we are out of school I suppose you must be excused. Wait a moment, though, you can purchase a copy at the station.'

'Of course we can. That is indeed fortunate,' I said, trying as hard as I could to sound enthusiastic.

'You can read it on the train,' said Lucy with a cheeky grin.

'And when I have finished, I will pass the paper to you,' I retorted, grinning back.

'Yes, that's right, although I cannot understand why you are both smiling,' said Doctor White. 'Nevertheless, I have my copy here and I must say that it is real progress when an article like this appears in our most respected newspaper. It is all about the need for further education for women, Lucy, a subject near and dear to your heart, is it not, my dear? Listen and I will read it to you. It says, "*While we may hope that social opinion may ever continue opposed to the women's movement in its most extravagant forms—those forms which endeavour to set up an unnatural, and therefore an impossible rivalry with men in the struggles of practical life—we may also hope that social opinion will soon become unanimous in its encouragement of the high education of women. Of the distinctively feminine qualities of mind which are admired as such by all, ignorance is certainly not one.*" '

'That is quite encouraging,' I said to Lucy.

'Yes, that is good as far as it goes,but I hope that society will go further than that. We will not be satisfied by having just one or two female doctors or one or two female lawyers or scientists, novelists or teachers. My fear is that we will be outnumbered by the men who are already entrenched in all the powerful positions.'

'This is a danger,' said Doctor White genially. 'But take journalism as an example of a profession that has opened up somewhat to allow women into its ranks. How many women till lately, however talented and well educated they were, ever dreamed of openly writing in reviews and newspapers? You will agree that to do so would probably have been considered a breach of etiquette a few years back, whereas in the army of modern scribblers for the hosts of ever-multiplying popular papers the petticoats are fairly thronging the ranks. And again, when in the history of the past can one recall the spectacle of women standing upon a public platform and addressing a public assembly and haranguing the crowds? But this is happening now, and the women justly claim an equal right to be there. I think that some progress has been made.'

'You see a happy future?' I asked.

'I most certainly hope so. Yet while I do not pretend to be a prophet, it seems to me that looming through the mists of the future, there are some ugly shapes that seem to be frowning upon us.'

'Do you mean the desperate condition of the masses?' I asked.

'Yes, this is a great problem which the building of a park here and there or putting up a People's Palace or two will simply not suffice to cure. I was speaking about this to Alfred last night, and he was shocked when I told him of how many people lived in destitution in our great city. Why, only last night I went on a short tour of London after we had dropped Lucy back in Golden Square. We passed through a low slum just east of Holborn and we were both sickened by the sight of drunken women reeling about with babies in their arms. We saw girls in petticoats and with scarcely any clothing over their breasts sparring about with great hulking boys. What else have they to do and what else can they know? No wonder there are so many illegitimate births and so many unfortunates on our streets. Little tiny children were wandering abroad late at night from public house to public house looking for their parents.'

'What is the answer?' said Lucy.

'Education, my dear. Education and an interest not only in the worst slums, which I agree of course must be pulled down as soon as possible. But in addition there must be a way of helping those thrifty working people who show no apparent evidence of dire want. At present it would appear that worthy working people who by thrift and industry have raised themselves above the brink of pauperism can have no further help to lift the veil of greater want. In addition of course we also have the sad fact that people quickly forget that more than sympathy is needed to relieve those who have been brought to misfortune often by no fault of their own. There are those who in their detestation of roguery, supposed or real, forget that by a wholesale condemnation of charity and so-called demoralisation, they are running the risk of driving the honest to despair and the peaceful to violence. I sometimes wonder whether these fine rich people are in fact secret supporters of the Anarchists, for it is only in such an interest that misery and hunger should increase.'

With this declaration ringing in our ears we approached King's Cross, and with the aid of Graham, the coachman, and two porters we made our way to the train. We had timed our arrival well and in only some seven or eight minutes we were on our way back to Arkley.

We secured an empty first-class compartment (we always travelled first-class, for however egalitarian his sentiments may have been, Doctor White had an abiding fear of catching a disease from persons less fastidious than he over matters of personal cleanliness), and soon he was deeply engrossed in the newspaper.

'Aren't you going to read what is happening in the great wide world?' he asked us.

'I think Andrew and I are both rather tired, Uncle, and we

shall, you recall, have another late night tonight so we ~hall take this opportunity to rest.'

'Tonight? What is happening tonight? Oh, bless my soul, I had forgotten about Sir Terence Austin. Isn't he dining with us tonight? Lucy, how fortunate you have jogged my memory. Have you met Sir Terence, Andrew? He is chairman of the Old Nottsgrovian Association and is of course the Member of Parliament for West Bucks.'

'No, sir, I have never met him, but I know the name,' I said. 'Isn't he a rather reactionary sort of chap for a graduate of your academy?'

'Yes, he is very much an old-fashioned man. He calls himself a Liberal Unionist but he is far more resistant to change than most of the Tories. I shall take this opportunity of telling him of my opposition to his stand on the Representation of the People bill currently being discussed.'

'He is against widening the franchise?' asked Lucy, with some surprise.

'Of course he is, though strong opposition won't help his cause, for progress cannot be denied. The strong resistance is due to a dread of the people themselves being able to choose their rulers, allied to the mortification of the aristocrats and rich landlords who rightly anticipate their own deposition from power. They are making a bitter fight of it, it is true. They are especially represented in Parliament just now, and of course they have no wish to lose this exceptional position and power. They confidently predict the ruin of all, but it would be far more ruinous to let the people remain so grossly unrepresented as they are, unless you really want to see a revolution in our country, which I for one do not!'

He paused for breath and then mused upon how Sir Terence came to take up such a political stand so opposite from the Nottsgrove philosophy.

'Of course, he only studied with me for three years,' mused Doctor White. 'Before then he was at Eton which explains a lot.'

'I thought Eton was a good school,' I said.

'It's better now than it used to be. In the bad old days it

was an anarchic, dreadful place. The routine fostered drunkenness, vile manners and worse food, unnatural sexual acts, bullying and every degrading philosophy of which one can think. Did you know that whilst at Eton Mr Gladstone wrote a subversive ode to Wat Tyler? At Eton in 1809 eight masters served more than five hundred boys, and birchings were the order of the day (you know my views on the vileness of giving and receiving corporal punishment), and indeed there was one headmaster whom I shall not name who presented his first flogging victim with a case of champagne! Goodness me, we will be at Barnet soon—how quickly time flies when one is enjoying a good conversation.'

'Conversation,' echoed Lucy. 'Uncle, you have talked the whole time yourself! Surely that is not conversation.'

'I don't see why not,' replied Doctor White amiably. 'A conversation always needs one person to listen, and I like to do the talking myself. It prevents arguments and keeps me in a good humour!'

We laughed heartily and prepared to disembark. We were met by old Sharp, the head gardener, who drove us back to the dear old school. We discussed the evening ahead and it was truly fortunate that Mrs Hall, the cook, had not forgotten that Sir Terence was dining with us tonight.

'I think that you, Andrew and young Paul Hill-Wallace should join us. You too, my dear Lucy will be there, will you not?' said Doctor White.

'Of course I will,' said Lucy. 'Sir Terence will be bringing his daughter Agatha, Uncle, but Lady Mabel Austin is in France staying with Lord and Lady Clare, so she will not be with us.'

'Oh, yes, I remember. Well, now, I want you looking smart and behave yourselves as I want Sir Terence to make a generous donation to our coffers. I shall suggest a Sir Terence Austin scholarship to him and I want to conclude the matter over the port.'

I went to Paul's study and told him of the arrangements. He was very pleased to be asked, but naturally he was no great lover of Sir Terence.

'He is a pompous old beggar, Andrew. However, for the sake of the old school, I shall be as polite as I know how, for it will all be for the best of causes!' said Paul.

We had no work for the remainder of the day so I was feeling quite refreshed by the time the party gathered in Doctor White's drawing-room that evening. Sir Terence might have been a somewhat ridiculous politician but though I did not agree with his opinions, I did like the man. Since then I have kept in touch and though my contact till his death some ten years ago was limited to the occasional dinner party, I do remember him now as a very likeable chap with a warm personality. He was well built, indeed he seemed to be half as broad as tall, and his distinctive face was set off by a beak of a nose, and in later years a face deeply creased with smile lines. When I knew him better I understood it to be a parchment of experience. He was a fine raconteur though I was always struck by his willingness to let people talk, and by the interest he showed in others.

Agatha, his daughter, was an extremely pretty girl of just seventeen years, lithe and lovely as a fawn, with masses of tawny brown hair and with a fine freedom in her large blue eyes. She was a marvellous amazon and as we were to find out later, possessed a wonderful amount of animal spirits.

Over the meal I recall Sir Terence talking about the agitation for the State to help build dwellings for the homeless poor. 'If the State is to be summoned not only to provide houses for the labouring classes, but also to supply such erections with merely nominal rents, it will while admittedly doing something on behalf of their physical condition, utterly destroy their moral energies. It will, in fact, be a proclamation that without any efforts of their own, certain people, or rather certain sections of the people shall enter into the enjoyment of many good things altogether at the expense of others. The mischief of all this would be very serious, it would assume many menacing forms and be of wide extent.'

'But if private bounty be insufficient,' said Doctor White, 'surely then the State must do the work, for it is necessary to improve the domiciliary conditions of the labouring classes.'

'Perhaps, perhaps, but it is a melancholy system that debases a large mass of people to the condition of a nursery, where the children look to the mother and the father and do nothing for themselves. This will come to pass if those who should know better do not refrain from giving gigantic hints in speeches and pamphlets of the depth and extent of State benevolence.'

I was bored by all this and to my delight I could see that Agatha and Lucy were equally tired of all this political talk. When Doctor White suggested that we show Agatha round the school (for it was a fine June night and dusk was only just falling) while he and Sir Terence talked about school affairs, I was delighted.

We were soon on familiar terms, and Agatha said to me: 'I think my father is mistaken. I believe that Socialism shows the way ahead, for soon the working people will possess the full power of government through elective institutions to embody in law their economic and material desires.'

I hardly listened to what she was saying but taking her hands in mine, I asked her if she would like to see my study. Fortunately, Lucy had wandered off with Paul, so we were on our own. The dear creature agreed and we walked quietly down to my room. I lit the gas lamp and looked at the beautiful young girl who stood just a foot away from me. Before now I might have been shy but *experientia docet* and I turned her face to mine. She closed those liquid blue eyes and started to kiss me, putting her tongue deep into my mouth. I gasped as to my surprise her hand wandered to the front of my trousers and pressed hard against my swelling cock. I pulled her even closer and kissed her again, my hands kneading the full softness of her buttocks and her tongue darted into my mouth, wrapping itself around mine, sucking and licking as we kissed. I unbuttoned the front of her dress and released into view the most exquisite pair of naked young breasts, lusciously rounded, white as alabaster, crowned with superbly fashioned hard little nipples. I gasped with pleasure and the adorable girl whispered: 'Kiss them, Andrew, I love having my breasts kissed!' So I obliged, kissing and gently sucking the hard nipples, biting gently as she sighed, breathless with pleasure. Somehow, we threw off our clothes in an untidy pile and lay naked on my narrow bed. I continued to lick and suck the lovely nipples, running my hands along her thighs. She turned sideways so that I could insert my hand between her legs and gently I pushed a finger inside her dripping slit. She moved across now so that her cunt was almost above my face as she lowered her head to kiss my pulsating prick. Her soft hands caressed my heavy balls as, with infinite slowness, she licked up and around the length of my shaft, taking ages to reach the uncapped crown. I was inwardly screaming for her to engulf the throbbing knob which she suddenly did, jamming down the foreskin, lashing her tongue round the huge pole that thudded away like a steamhammer. My tongue was now pressed against her cunt and I licked at her slit and moved around the outer lips, gently pushing inside the wet crack until the juice ran out into my open mouth.

I decided to change our positions and I managed to roll off the bed, but the delightful girl kept her lips clamped to my cock and she sank to her knees to continue her sucking rhythm.

'Quickly, let me fuck you now before I come in your mouth!' I said, and gently pulled her up so that she stood before me. I turned her round, somewhat to her puzzlement, but she obediently presented her back to me and I squeezed the cheeks of her curvy bum. I told her to stand with her legs wide apart and to bend over the bed. She did as she was bidden and I enjoyed a lovely view of her open bottom and her pouting quim as the lips of her cunny stretched to expose the flushed inner flesh.

I leaned over her, and she gasped as she felt the hot shaft of my prick wedged between her bum cheeks. I did not try to cork her bum-hole but pushed my cock to find the supple, glistening crack of her cunt, thrusting deeply as she whimpered with joy. Fiercely, I pushed forward, burying the shaft to the very hilt so that my hairy balls banged against her arse cheeks. I held her round the waist until the shaft was completely engulfed, and then I shifted my hands to fondle those superb breasts, rubbing the pink little rosebuds till they were as hard as my prick which was nestling in her juicy crack.

I began to thrust backwards and forwards and I felt Agatha explode into a series of little peaks of delight as I continued to fuck her. Her cunt felt incredibly tight and wet, her channel clinging to my prick, almost preventing me from driving in and out.

We were lost in time as I rode against her, filling her pussy with my rock-hard shaft, pulling back for a moment and then surging forward again and again. I could sense Agatha experiencing orgasm after orgasm but I could feel my cock quiver and my own time to come soon followed as I poured spasm after spasm of hot love juice inside her willing cunny. What a blissful fuck this was, and my cock remained hard as I withdrew and Agatha turned round.

'Oh, how marvellous! Do let's continue,' she said, grasping my prick and rubbing it to full length and strength till it rose hard as iron against my belly. We clambered back on the bed and this time Agatha took charge.

'Let me do the work this time, Andrew. Just lie back and let me fuck your darling prick,' she murmured—and who was I to disobey such a sweet command?

She sat astride me and leaned forward, trailing those magnificent breasts up and down my torso so that her nipples flicked against my skin quite exquisitely. She then lifted her hips and crouched over my thick pole, her cunny directly overhead, poised above the uncapped red dome. Then, positioning my knob, she managed to press it directly onto her clitty, and rotating her body, she edged slightly forward, allowing my rigid prick to enter her. Ever so slowly she lifted and lowered her sopping cunny, and each time my prick went higher and deeper inside her until our bodies melted away in sheer delight. Our senses were now at fever pitch as my strokes jerked her body into a further series of peaks of sensual excitement. It was impossible to hold back as she thrust down to meet my jerking upwards to cram every inch of my hardness inside her. My proud prick spurted jets of creamy spunk up her crack as waves of pleasure coursed through my entire body. We had both climbed the summit of love together and we sank back sated on the soft blankets.

The question was now whether I could rise to the occasion for a third time. Agatha lay on her back, her full, rich breasts not flattening as did the breasts of many girls but standing out full and firm, the jutting nipples erect. Her white belly was firm and flat and her mossy mound a tawny, wild temptation.

I stretched myself alongside and then directly onto her naked body, and my cock began to swell as I rubbed it against that tantalising mound. Her young breasts were springy under my chest and I moved my hips, rotating them as I felt her body quiver beneath me. I made my movements stronger, shifting my weight to my elbows and I held those surging breasts in my hands, rubbing the swollen nipples gently with my thumbs as I heard her breath catch, saw her eyes close and her teeth hold her lower lip. I caressed the nipples more firmly and they hardened even further, stood taller and I could feel the throb of her pulse in her breasts beneath the nipples, deep and thundering.

By now my cock had regained all its grand stiffness and the red uncapped knob thrust eagerly into the dripping wet crack as she threw her legs apart and taking hold of my prick, eased the knob slowly into her eager sheath. I retracted momentarily then crashed down on top of the dear girl and she bucked uncontrollably as I pumped hard, her vaginal muscles caressing my cock as we went faster and faster, and she lifted her hips off the bed and met me stroke for stroke. I could hardly hold her for she possessed a wiry strength and speed of movement that not even my own Lucy could rival. I rode her as she bucked and twisted all the time urging me to thrust deeper, deeper, squealing and gasping with the sheer ecstasy of the sensations. And all the while my cock was twitching, burning in her hot, tight yet gloriously juicy cunny but my shaft was tightening with unexploded passion, reaching for the glorious, pouring moment. As the spunk boiled up inside me, I felt her reach for her sobbing, thrashing release and in the midst of it I hurtled jets of creamy love juice flooding into her, and she shuddered with delight as she milked my prick of every last drop of love juice, pumping my white froth into her dark, secret warmth.

We lay there panting with exhaustion until I realised that we had been gone for more than an hour and that we should be missed. 'Don't worry,' smiled Agatha. 'If I know my father, he will still be engrossed in conversation, and from what Lucy told me, I am sure that she will be enjoying all the fun of a good fucking with your friend Paul.'

'I hope that you enjoyed our gay bout,' I said politely.

'I certainly have,' she replied. 'I really enjoyed sinking down on your magnificent cock. My nerves went all a-tingle as my cunny completely enveloped your darling prick. My, how I pulsed all over as you spunked all that glorious froth into me. When I felt that gorgeous cock drenching me with all that lovely cream, oh, just talking about it is almost making me come again!'

But we both knew there was no time except for a quick hug and kiss as we quickly dressed ourselves and went across to Paul's room. We were just yards away when the door opened and out came Lucy and Paul, both breathing heavily.

'Ah, we wondered where you two had got to. We waited and waited but you never showed,' said Lucy, who looked somewhat flushed.

'I suppose you just sat waiting for us. Perhaps you sat down and played bezique?' I said somewhat sarcastically, though it was in the circumstances more than a little unfair to take up such an attitude.

'Er, yes. Well, shall we rejoin Sir Terence and Doctor White?' said Paul hurriedly.

We said no more and walked briskly back. Lucy and I were fortunately some yards ahead of the other couple when Lucy threw open the door of the diningroom. She had not thought it necessary to knock, but certainly the two people in the room would have preferred us to do so. For an amazing scene met our eyes. The table had been cleared, but it was not empty. For lying across it, stark naked, flat on his back, was our noted guest Sir Terence Austin. His chest was covered with matted black hair and his corpulent belly sagged all over the place without the restriction of his clothes to keep his body in shape. But his prick stood up smartly enough, a huge truncheon of a cock as rigid as a flagpole, and who did we see with her hands rubbing this great shaft to such fine erectness but young Elaine who had joined Paul and I with Louella and Lucy for some frolics some days before! She was dressed, or rather half-dressed in her black and white maid's uniform, for Sir Terence had undone all her top buttons and her large breasts had freed themselves of any covering and stood out, naked and mouth-wateringly ripe for the touch of lips or fingers.

'Paul, why don't you take Agatha round the cloisters for a little stroll,' said Lucy wildly, saying the first words that entered her brain. 'Go on, the night is so pleasant and there is no-one in here.' I realised that she had no desire to let Agatha view her own proud Papa *in flagrante delicto* and added my approval to her suggestion. Paul dithered and I blocked his entrance to the room and hissed: 'Or take Agatha back to your room and ask her to suck your prick!'

Nevertheless, his curiosity was aroused and he peeped in, but seeing what was in view, he hastily withdrew, dragging a puzzled but agreeable Agatha back to his study.

When they had left, we entered the room and shut the door firmly behind us.

'Ahem,' said Lucy, clearing her throat. 'Pray do not let us interrupt your jollities.'

Elaine smiled and said: 'Very well, Miss Lucy. You are both very welcome to stay and watch me pleasure Sir Terence's cock.'

She proceeded to rub the great shaft up and down and Sir Terence, who had said not a word, kept silent, closing his eyes. It was rather a foolish business, to let himself be put in this silly situation but as the old saying has it, a standing prick has no sense. I wondered whether Doctor White had offered Elaine's ministrations as a reward for the funding of a

213

scholarship but immediately I mentally rebuked myself, for the dear old headmaster would never stoop so low; and indeed I was quite wrong to let such an accusation even cross my mind but I must record the thought, however base, as a matter of historical accuracy. What had actually occurred, as I later found out, was that a small pupil had complained of feeling unwell, and as was his wont, Doctor White had gone off to visit the little chap in the sanitarium. Meanwhile, Elaine had come into the room to help clear the table and had caught Sir Terence's randy eye, and the baronet had offered her a sovereign to play with his giant pole. Elaine continued her task, pulling her hand up and down the twitching shaft whilst Sir Terence reached out to fondle her naked titties.

'Oh, harder, my love, harder. Put your other hand round my balls and squeeze very gently,' he cried.

She obliged him by rubbing at a faster pace until a sudden spurt of creamy spunk shot out from the tip of his prick, drenching her hands and liberally anointing the tablecloth.

'Never mind,' said Lucy drily. 'Elaine is an expert at stains as you will remember, Andrew.' Surprisingly for a politician, Sir Terence still said nothing, but his prick spoke volumes as it was still stiff as anything as Elaine cradled it in her hands. He stopped fondling her breasts and pulling her down across him, he undid the buttons at the back of her blouse and he slipped it off her completely.

Her skirt and underdrawers soon followed and the big man stretched out the smiling girl flat on the table next to him.

'Heavens, this is more than I bargained for,' she said with a giggle.

'I will give you a bigger present later,' growled Sir Terence, kissing her breasts and belly and then pressing his lips down onto her bushy mound. I saw his tongue licking at her clitty and Elaine pushed her mound against his own beard as he licked away and began to prise open her pussy lips with his fingers, sinking them slowly into her slit which was already dribbling with juice. She reached out and held his head firmly against her cunny with one hand as she squeezed one of her erect little nipples with the other. Then slowly he moved on top of her and she moved excitedly, opening her legs wide and clamping her feet round onto his back as he guided his throbbing prick into her soaking little nook. She took up the rhythm of his thrusts and soon they were rocking together at such a rate that I became concerned that they would fall off the table! I could see Elaine's legs shake and tremble and knew that she was coming. She continued to squirm under the marvellous surging strokes of his cock and they shouted for joy as they climaxed together, with the big man pumping jet after jet of juice into her eager crack, her hands gripping his large bum cheeks, pushing him deeper and deeper inside her.

We had all been so engrossed, both participants and spectators, that none of us had seen or heard Doctor White enter the room. It would be a kindness to draw a veil over what happened, except to say that the good Doctor White was at pains not to embarrass his guest but on the other hand wished to register his disapproval of the events that had taken place. He was not, after all, averse to girls instructing their partners on the finer points of love-making—after all, Lucy had willingly taken my own virginity and Sir Terence's son, the Honourable Nicholas Austin, would similarly be so instructed if Doctor White thought this to be in his interest at the appropriate time. But Sir Terence had abused his hospitality, when all was said and done.

In the end, little was actually said, but Sir Terence knew that he was guilty of behaviour not befitting a gentleman. He made amends by endowing a scholarship for three poor scholars to study at Nottsgrove so out of it all, some real good came about.

EPILOGUE

DEAR READER, I am now somewhat weary and must perforce finish these memoirs at a later date when I shall recall further memories for your kind perusal. But this must now be the finish of this selection from my experiences at my old *alma mater*.

And now, as I close my book, subduing my desire to yet linger, these sweet faces from my past are still with me and above all one face, that of my own dearest Lucy, will never fade from view. If I close my eyes, I can imagine that she is here beside me in all her beauty. Alas, our paths of life were fated not to cross again, for despite my offer of marriage made when I left University and came into a small inheritance from my Uncle Nicholas, we never were to be intimate again.

Lucy left England many years ago and to the best of my knowledge has never returned to our shores. She set off to the New World with a handsome rogue, Lord Arthur D——, to make a new life for themselves in the wilderness of California amongst the ruffians who settled there after the great Gold Rush of '49.

My life has not been unhappy, let me hasten to add, for I enjoyed many years of happy marriage and my travels have taken me all over Europe where, I must confess, I have dallied many times in bedrooms that were not my own.

My final thanks must be to Sir Lionel T—— for his kind hospitality and use of his fine library and of course to you, my dear readers, for allowing me to recall those fine days spent in the lovely county of Hertfordshire all those years ago.

I make no apologies for my work, though I know that certain so-called friends may disapprove of my frank recollections even though they will, *sub rosa*, buy *The Oyster* eagerly to see if I have scandalised any persons they might know. I regret that they will be disappointed for *de mortuis nil nisi bonum* is my motto.

I close then with the wise words of Molière:
Le scandale du monde est ce qui fait l'offense,
*Et ce n'est pas pécher que pécher en silence.**

---

* It is a public scandal that gives offence, and it is no sin to sin in secret.

217

LETTER FROM MRS HELENE F. TO THE EDITOR

LIKE MANY genteel but poor country girls, I was simply forced into marriage at the tender age of nineteen to a far more mature gentleman who had already celebrated his fortieth birthday when we climbed into bed on our wedding night.

I know that we rural folk are thought of as mere bumpkins by the inhabitants of the great Metropolis, but I can assure you that most girls living outside the sophisticated world of the West End of London are far more knowledgeable about intimate matters than their sisters in the smart salons of Belgravia.

Suffice it to say, however, that thanks to the enormous weapon of the Vicar's sixteen-year-old son and the equally thick pego of Captain Colin S—— of the Worcestershire Light Infantry, I was by no means a stranger to the delights of a good fucking when I married my husband; but alas, try as the poor dear might, he could never satisfy my appetite in the bedroom and I was forced to resort to buying a dildo from one of the surgical appliance shops in Holywell Street.

Last week I took my afternoon constitutional in the park, but my pleasant stroll was rudely interrupted by a sudden heavy shower of rain which completely drenched my clothes before I could find shelter. I walked briskly home immediately and went into my bedroom and took off all my clothes. I must confess that my body has always been a source of pride and I was soon quite naked. After drying myself with a large towel I lay down on the bed examining my figure. I am

218

told that I am not unattractive, possessing light blue eyes that sparkle, a tiny nose but generously wide red lips. I have been told that I am well-proportioned in leg and limb, with large round globes with dark nipples which I tickled, as I lay on my bed, until they became rock hard. My body arched and spasms of pleasure rippled through me as I thought of Captain Colin S—— and his rock-hard organ, and my hands strayed down between my thighs when there was a knock at the door. It was Elspeth, my maid, who had heard me come in and being a good servant, decided to inquire as to whether there was any service she could perform for me.

I called her in, neglecting the fact that I lay absolutely naked on my bed with my legs wide apart and my hands caressing my nice thick bush. Elspeth came in and her eyes lit up when she saw me.

'Ah, madam,' she cried. 'You have been caught in the rain. I have only just come in myself. May I use your towel to dry myself?'

And the cheeky young girl promptly undressed herself and stood in her proud, naked glory in front of me. She was certainly a beauty, only some eighteen years old with dark black hair over a low forehead. Her beautiful snowy bosom was ornamented with pretty little bubbies, well separated, each looking a little away from the other, each perfectly proportioned and both tapering in lovely curves until they came to two rosebud points. Her belly, smooth, broad and dimpled in the centre with a sweet little button, was like a perfect plain of snow which appeared the more dazzling from the thick growth of dark black hair which curled in rich locks in the triangle of her motte.

Elspeth towelled herself vigorously and when she had finished I asked her if she would like to rest a while with me on the bed. Of course this was what the little minx wanted and in a flash she was cuddling up beside me with her hand roving over my legs. I did not push her away and she moved even closer, brushing her face against mine as her other hand slid round my shoulder. Kissing my cheek, she began stroking her fingers higher up my leg. I tried to tell myself that this was mere idle curiosity, for I did not wish to admit that I was actually enjoying the sensation.

But I could not pretend for long, and when her fingers began rubbing the lips of my cunny, I heard myself sighing with pleasure. After a few moments, instead of simply lying there passively I put my arms around her, holding her gorgeous soft body to me as her fingers continued to rub my quim, sending shivers of excitement right through me. Elspeth began to fondle my naked breasts as our mouths crushed together. Her lips felt smooth and warm and I found it impossible to hold back as her wet tongue slipped inside my mouth and stroked against mine. I pressed my hands to her breasts, letting my fingers sink into the firm, yielding flesh.

This was the first experience of its kind I had ever had although being a regular tribade, Elspeth knew exactly what to do and I imitated her actions as she tweaked one of my nipples between her thumb and forefinger. So I let my other hand rest on her tummy as her fingers glided softly over my damp, hairy mound. Then her mouth came away from mine and she started kissing my neck. The feel of her body and the gentle, though stimulating touch of her fingers were amazingly arousing and every stroke she gave my pussy felt more exciting than the last.

She gazed lovingly at my cunny and, pressing her face between my breasts, she eased her hand between my thighs, parting them wide as she sank her finger into my cunt. Her thumb prodded against my clitty and I squirmed with the thrill of it as her mouth closed round my nipple and her finger slid deeper into my slit.

Elspeth enjoyed a most sensitive touch and she somehow made me forget that what we were doing was frowned upon by so-called normal people. I could not forget that she was a girl, of course, but it did not seem to matter to me as I was completely lost in the pleasure she was giving me and the joy of feeling her soft body nestling against me.

So I pressed my hand upon her mound, delving my fingers down between her fleshy thighs. Now it was her turn to moan with delight as I gently stroked her cunny lips and then slid my finger between them. As I sank it slowly inside her, she pushed herself upwards, arching her back, wriggling her body as though signalling to me to penetrate deeper. With her thumb rubbing at my clitty, she began thrusting her own finger in and out of my quim faster and faster. She was thrilling me so much that I found it difficult to concentrate on what I was doing to her. Her finger may not have been anything like the size of even my husband's short prick, but the way she was using it was just superb.

Suddenly, she began moving her body down and my finger slipped out of her crack. She raised one of her legs and locked her thighs around my knee, writhing her wet crotch back and forth as she pressed her face down into my pussy. Her hands gripped my bum cheeks and she squeezed them firmly, as her lips began kissing my quim. My senses reeled and I started moaning and panting as her tongue flicked against my clitty. I clung to the back of her head, pulling her face tightly against my cunt, while her lips slid between the lips of my pussy. I came off straight away, but her warm tongue prodding through my cleft led me to a little series of tingling peaks. My male lovers had done this to me before but none could beat Elspeth at this jolly game. Elspeth was perhaps the best pussy sucker I have ever come across and I lay back, thoroughly enjoying the delicious sensations until finally she raised her pretty head and climbed down to lie beside me. She appeared to be somewhat exhausted herself, but I think she had achieved a climax.

What happened next was like a dream. Soft lips rested gently at first and then with increasing urgency upon my own. I opened my mouth beneath the persuasive pressure and the next thing of which I was conscious was a warm friction that journeyed knowingly from the base of my throat to the valley between my breasts. I moved my head downwards and Elspeth whimpered as my probing fingers played on her body with an increasingly sure touch. Our limbs entwined and plunged into delight that ebbed and flowed, ebbed and flowed . . . I pulled her long white legs apart and nuzzled my full lips around her curly bush. My own hands clamped round her firm bum cheeks as my tongue flashed unerringly around the damp pubic hair and her pussy seemed to open wide as she lifted her bottom to enable me to slip my tongue through the pink lips, licking between the grooves of her clitty in long, thrusting strokes. Her pussy gushed love juice and each time I tongued her, Elspeth's clitty stiffened, even more eager and pulsating, wanting more and more to explode into a marvellous all-embracing climax. I rubbed harder and harder until the little clitty was hard as a prick to my touch and I slid a second then a third finger down inside her juicy cunt, and spread open the lips as she squealed with delight. Her body was jerking up and down which made it all the more exciting as my face rubbed against her curly motte.

'Ohhhhh!' screamed Elspeth, as I worked my tongue until my jaw ached, but soon the lovely girl heaved violently and got off to a tremendous orgasm and she gently pushed my face away. We turned to each other, our arms sliding easily around our perspiring bodies. Our kiss was softly intimate as we pressed together. Lying on top of Elspeth, I crushed her against me, lightly licking her breasts while I pushed my knees between her legs and spread them. I glided my hips over hers and caught hold of her wrists. Her firm breasts stuck proudly upwards when I pinned her arms high above her head. The swollen nipples glistened with my saliva as I sucked hard upon each one, slowly squirming my own drenched mound against hers. She heaved under me and again her eyes closed with knowing expectation. She opened her legs around my thighs and locked her ankles inside my calves. Then she arched her back slightly as my mouth closed over one of her juicy titties. 'Don't you want a man now?' she mumbled. 'Wouldn't you like to be fucked properly with a big, fat prick?'

'No, no, no,' I squealed as she kicked her legs out straight as we jerked in a frenzy against each other, panting and biting and then screaming as our climaxes came together, first streaking through me, then jumping to Elspeth like a flash of electricity.

My appetite was now insatiable and I leaned over to kiss and nuzzle my lips against the large mound of wet curly hair that covered her love mound bulging between her long legs. Elspeth too wished to continue the fray, and in a moment she was on top of me, rubbing my nipples between her fingers and gently her hands eased open my legs to allow full access to my yearning cunny that was already dripping juice even before she began to stroke my clitty until my little button was protruding stiffly. I lifted myself up and buried my face and kissed her deep cleavage, making her titties shake with desire. I then lay back again, massaging her breasts with my hands, stroking her nipples to new peaks of hardness.

Our pussies ground together as she sucked one of my own hard nipples making me jump with pleasure. I rubbed my pussy even harder against hers until we were almost both on the brink of coming again.

Elspeth gasped and lowered her head towards my sopping crack and slipped her tongue through my aching cleft, prodding my clitty, tonguing me to new peaks. Then suddenly she was on top of me again, pressing her lovely naked body hard against me. Our hands were everywhere, grabbing and squeezing and we writhed together as our bodies locked into each other, demanding release. She jerked her own cunny hard up against mine and I gathered the lovely girl into my arms, her breasts rising and falling from the effects of her desire. I pulled her down and it was now the turn of my mouth to bury itself into the yawning pink slit. I slipped my tongue in and out as Elspeth's arm wrapped itself round me and from behind found my own dripping quim with her long tapering fingers, stabbing them in and out with a fierce intensity that caused me to cry out with delight.

I moved my tongue along the grooves of her pussy, sucking her delicious juices, and we continued to play with each other, engaging in all kinds of intimacies for another full hour. Elspeth possessed large cunny lips, which might have led her to seek friendship with other girls, though I assured her that vaginal structural variations are commonplace. She left our service soon after this blissful afternoon and I have never told my dear husband about this incident. I recount it now as he is, alas, three thousand miles away in America, and will not be returning for at least another month. And as he never reads your excellent journal, I feel certain that my secret is safe in your hands. If any lady reading this missive wishes to contact me for a similar adventure such as I have described, perhaps she could contact me through the good offices of Lady C—— who is well-known for her inclinations regarding pretty girls.

BOOK 2

Introduction

It is somewhat difficult for the modern reader to understand the anger of the noted Victorian critic Bernard Crackenthorpe who, some one hundred and ten years ago, vented his wrath on 'the charnel-house school of literature'.

For Crackenthorpe was railing not against the salacious underground magazines such as *The Pearl, The Cremorne* or *The Oyster*, but about the language and ideas propounded in a most innocuous novel published by a most respectable, old-established firm. He bitterly attacked this now long-forgotten tome (*Three Visitors At Twilight* by John Grahame) in these words:

> 'Revolting as it is that it should be possible for a girl to project herself into the mood of a man at one of his baser moments, faithfully identifying herself with a sequence of his sensations, is it less revolting than a man should be able to conceive of a woman describing her love for a husband to his young sister in these words: "My love for Henry is a purely sensual one"?'

Naturally, this suppressive attitude found a mirror image – a forthright celebration of the joys of sexual action that was reflected in the underground magazines that flourished during the mid- and late-Victorian eras. The best-known of these publications was of course *The Pearl* which flourished during the late 1870s only to disappear without warning in 1880. It was soon replaced, however, by *The Oyster*, the magazine from which the novelette in this book was first published just over one hundred years ago, in 1884.

Issues of *The Oyster* were published throughout the 1880s only for it to disappear with equal suddenness immediately after the infamous Cleveland Street scandal at the end of the decade. This affair centred around the exposure of an upper-class homosexual brothel in London's West End. Although a discreet Establishment cover-up led to the protection of several extremely highly-placed personages in Society, the personal equerry of the Prince of Wales, Lord Arthur Somerset, was forced to flee to France (a prudent course which Oscar Wilde should have followed some five years later) although some other aristocrats and public figures escaped the full consequences of their involvement. The full account of just who was compromised in the sleazy Cleveland Street house will have to wait until sensitive official papers are released at the end of this century – although in all probability the full story will never be released to the general public.

Although the demise of *The Oyster* coincided with the Cleveland Street scandal, the magazine was a firmly heterosexual publication though surprisingly modern in its toleration of 'deviancy' (e.g. oral sex) and its detestation of 'perversity' (e.g. sado-masochistic behaviour, bondage and beating and child sex) – all well-established Victorian vices. It also encouraged the idea that bedroom frolics were to be relished by both sexes – no 'lie back and think of England' advice for the girls of *The Oyster* – but the narrator is at pains to stress that gentlemen should accept, however frustrating this could be, that 'no' meant 'no' and they should not force unwanted attentions upon unwilling partners.

Despite the sudden end of *The Oyster* in 1889, uninhibited erotic magazines were produced in no little volume during this period. In his seminal work, *The Other Victorians*, Professor Steven Marcus noted:

For every cautionary statement against the harmful effects of sexual excess uttered by medical men, pornography represented copulation *in excelcis*, endless orgies, infinite daisy chains of inexhaustibility... for every effort made by the official culture to minimise the importance of sexuality, pornography cried out – or whispered – that it was the only thing in the world of any importance at all.

Such extremes could not hold, and the open exploration of sex by art and the progress of modern psychology has led to our present morality which, though questioned by some, is at least based upon a more realistic and achievable human norm. Nevertheless, it is hard to disagree with the comment of sexologist Dr Webster Newington that:

> the cost in the interim was considerable and is still being paid in terms of needless shame that has caused not only great individual misery, but suffering to other parties through unsatisfactory personal relationships such as in marriage. Thankfully there are now far fewer attempts being made to block the flow of sexual information, though in the guilt-ridden climate in which Victorian underground magazines appeared, human sexuality was an area over which the Establishment exercised the most stringent control.

It is interesting to note that present day attempts are being made seek to re-establish this control by such methods as the false equating of sex education in schools with promiscuity. However, it must also be accepted that these social reactionaries are aided by the equally extreme posturings by the fringes of the lesbian and gay fraternities.

I would not be the first to suggest that public resistance to the stifling conventional sexual mores of our Victorian forefathers came primarily in the form of such publications as *The Oyster*. As aforesaid, this particular magazine was especially interesting for its liberal philosophy and certainly eschews the aggressive and sometimes sadistic writing that appears in some of its contemporaries. In her introduction to *The Oyster I* (New English Library, 1985), Antoinette Strauss commented upon the author's obvious lack of interest in flagellation and any of the curious perversities such as the

7

triumphant ravishment of an under-age virgin which seemed to excite so many Victorians.

She speculated upon the true identity of 'Sir Andrew Scott' whose second novella makes up the content of this second selection from *The Oyster*, rightly concluding that the absence of flagellation would rule out the poet Swinburne or his friend the journalist George Augustus Sala, both known for their predelictions in this field.

Dr Terence Cooney, one of the foremost modern authorities on Victorian erotica, suggests that the present volume may well be the work of two – or more – hands. He detects distinctive stylistic differences between the language of the first four chapters and the subsequent progress of the novel. On the other hand, as he points out, 'this apparent division of style may be the result not of the work being begun by one writer and finished by another' but of the writing being effected at different periods, 'during which a writer's own style might develop or deteriorate accordingly.' From evidence of the military allusions in the latter part of the novelette, he suggests that, in order for certain details to be contemporary, this section might well have been written *some years* before the opening chapters.

Whoever 'Scott' may have been, he would certainly have been known to 'Pisanus Fraxi' (H. Spencer Ashbee), the indefatigable collector of erotic literature and to Sir Lionel Trapes, another nineteenth-century connoisseur of gallant writing who is most surely the 'Sir Lionel T——' who appears both here and in *The Oyster I*. But Sir Lionel, a highly placed Civil Servant, was probably displeased to see even a reference to himself in *The Oyster* (hence perhaps why his name is never ever fully spelt out in the magazine) and the fast, occasionally slapdash style is far removed from the rather ponderous, dense tract Trapes published at his own expense in 1892 on the long forgotten Kentish painter Lawrence Judd-Hughes.

Another guess at 'Scott's' identity might bring in the name of Oswald Holland, a printer based in the East End of London who, with the help of a pulp-fiction scribbler, Gerald Burdett, produced *The Ram*, or *Adventures in a West*

8

Country Town and other illicit novelettes. But their backgrounds are far removed from the persona claimed by 'Scott' – 'I must remain cloaked in at least a semi-anonymity for the true disclosure of my identity will embarrass some ladies and gentlemen of high rank who are today staunch pillars of Society' (*The Oyster I*) – and it is most unlikely that they would be on speaking terms with Ashbee or Trapes.

So no real evidence of our author's true identity exists, although I understand that one of Ashbee's extraordinary circle of upper-class purveyors of erotica, Professor Jonathan Halneet-Astley, lived for many years near the then tiny village of Arkley in Hertfordshire where 'Nottsgrove Academy' (a purely fictitious hall of learning, one should add, for the benefit of any budding social or educational historian) was based. But one person named in *The Oyster* most certainly did exist and this was the bookseller John Camden Hotten, who kept a very small shop in Piccadilly but who enjoyed a tremendous reputation amongst the cognoscenti as a publisher of banned books. And the photographer who appears in the tale as Harold Sailor is surely based upon the real-life Henry Hayler who conducted an extremely lucrative business in pornographic photographs. Indeed, when the police descended upon Hayler's premises (he had prudently been paying a sergeant for a forewarning) they seized no less than 130,000 photographic negatives and more than 5,000 glass lantern-slides! Hayler himself had ample time to arrange his affairs before fleeing to the Continent where, fortunately for his many clients, he destroyed his lists of customers and lived quietly off his considerable wealth first in Berlin and later in the South of France where he died in 1902.

But we will never know our author's identity, though whoever he may have been, his ribald tale of his schooldays and early adult life offers a fascinating view of society just one hundred years ago. His chronicling of his many sexual adventures (both in fact and fancy, one would imagine) is thankfully far less verbose than many of his rivals. But above all, as Dr Newington noted in his introduction to *The Pearl 3*:

9

It should be noted that the underground magazines of our great-grandfathers show that there must have been a persistent questioning of the taboos which then existed and of a desire to experiment with the mechanics of copulation such as the pleasures of oro-genital sex. This sceptical attitude was to lead to a more relaxed self-understanding and enlightenment, concomitant with the multiplicity of attitudes and positions on morality that exist today.

Oliver Alfred Pänther
London, July 1987

Preface

It is understood to be a useful and commendable practice that in bringing out a new publication before the public, the authors should say a few words of introduction and pen their apologia for its appearance.

We have little to say of ourselves or of our work except to voice our detestation of prudery, an attitude which is a mere indulgence for those who fear the consequences of their own repressed desires. Nor will we countenance hypocrisy especially as at any time there are to be found a goodly number of mealy-mouthed persons who desire above all to suppress all mention of that most satisfying of all the physical and mental pleasures that exist.

We prefer to take our motto from Dryden:

> Thus every creature, of every kind
> The sweet joys of sweet coition find.

The Editors of The Oyster.

Preface

It is understood to be a useful and commendable practice that in bringing out a new publication before the public, the authors should say a few words of introduction and pen their apologia for its appearance.

We have little to say of ourselves or of our work except to voice our detestation of prudery, an attitude which is a mere indulgence for those who fear the consequences of their own repressed desires. Nor will we countenance hypocrisy especially as at any time there are to be found a goodly number of mealy-mouthed persons who desire above all to suppress all mention of that most satisfying of all the physical and mental pleasures that exist.

We prefer to take our motto from Dryden:

> Thus every creature, of every kind
> The sweet joys of sweet coition find.

The Editors of The Oyster.

1

Little apology will be given for putting into print the following highly erotic and racy narrative. Allow me, Sir Andrew Scott, your humble scribe, to present my compliments and trust, dear reader, that you will happily browse through my memoirs with as much pleasure as the penning of this manuscript has afforded the author.

May I also confirm yet again, for the benefit of those few doubting Thomases who have questioned the veracity of my recollections, the utter candour and high standard of truthfulness that distinguish my tale from its several imitators. However, I freely admit to the alteration of names and places, and the omission of certain events. I have no desire to embarrass or to upset the sensibilities of anyone with whom I have come into contact throughout my life.

So those fellow Nottsgrovians who enjoyed such a free and easy life with me at the dear old school, and who themselves could summon fond memories of those far-off days almost beyond recall, may rest easy. I will respect their craving for anonymity as many – especially those now occupying such exalted places in Society – may not wish to be reminded in any public style of the larks and pranks which characterised our stay at Nottsgrove Academy, a seat of learning I can heartily recommend to both boys and parents alike.

For any new readers of our secret periodical who may not be able to purchase previous editions of The Oyster, I ended my last set of recollections as my stay at Nottsgrove Academy drew to its conclusion. I take up the story from *this point, but first let me sketch some details about the school. It was situated in a large country mansion quite near the little village of Arkley in Hertfordshire and the headmaster and part-owner of the establishment was the late and much lamented Dr Simon White, M.A. (Oxon), known to many of us, of course, as an enlightened pioneer of the formulation of a set of ethical principles that are based upon a saner understanding of our own natural desires.*

Such fond memories I possess of my days there; though my fondness is tinged with a hint of melancholy best expressed perhaps in the words of Mr Cowper:

What peaceful hours I once enjoy'd!
How sweet their mem'ry still!
But they have left an aching void
The world can never fill!

One final set of words to end this short prologue; I trust there will be none offended by the telling of a tale in blunt and frank detail. If there are any priggies to be found, again I make no apology but will simply ask how they came to be in possession of this august, esteemed and privately circulated booklet! Yet, reader, it would be far from surprising to find that we have such hypocrites, sub rosa, amongst our many subscribers. For as the old saying has it, one touch of indecency makes the world grin, despite the frantic mouthings of Mr Augustus P-----, the Rev. Herbert B---- and all others of their ilk who persist in pontificating upon a vast range of subjects from a superior height; an attitude that the modern mind can never endure.

The place of theology in the sphere of mankind's knowledge tempts its doctors to believe that it confers the right of speaking with a certain authority on all kinds of topics; yet, if they could but see it, this foolishly omniscient tone in the pulpit when handling questions is the very thing that stirs such fierce rebellion in cultivated hearts and minds.

Hopefully, we shall live to see the day when science and

14

pure reason, unfettered by the bumbling antics of the ignorant governing establishment, will seek and find sane and sensible standards of civilised conduct between the sexes.

And so let me take up my pen and travel down the distant path of memory, hoping, dear friend, that you thoroughly enjoy this memoir of the somewhat unusual sport I enjoyed during my formative years. I dedicate this script to the spirit of Dr Simon White, a remarkable scholar whose kindness and wise guidance enabled so many of his pupils to break the shackles that bind us to a false morality. I am convinced that the time will shortly come when his genius will be hailed not only in this country, but all over the civilised world.

It was Founders' Day, celebrated during the last week of the summer term as a finale to the school year. Dr White and members of the staff would act as hosts at a luncheon to which would be invited various luminaries such as members of the governing board, the Lord Lieutenant of the County, the Mayor of Barnet (our nearest town of any size) and other worthies from amongst the good Doctor's many acquaintances. Afterwards, those guests who so desired could inspect our school until the afternoon ceremony at which the guest of honour (who happened upon this day to be Sir Nicholas Austin, the well-known Member of Parliament) would present the annual awards for scholarship and sporting prowess.

We were indeed fortunate that the day in question was perhaps the warmest we had experienced since the previous summer. There was but the merest whiff of a breeze to complement the glorious sunshine and Dr White ordered the luncheon tables to be set-up on his immaculately tended lawn. As one of the most senior boys – I was to leave Nottsgrove as vice-captain of the Academy and captain of cricket – I was given the privilege of sitting down with our honoured guests and answering any questions they may have wished to ask about our dear old *alma mater*.

Even more fortunate for me that day was the fact that Dr White had seated me next to Fanny (now Lady B——

15

F——), the daughter of one of Nottsgrove's neighbours, General Sir Edwin Gadson-Fisher, known to some of you perhaps for his collection of early eighteenth-century chapbooks which, on his death, changed hands at such extraordinarily high prices.

Ah, but a sprightly beauty was young Fanny, just seventeen and a half years of age, well proportioned in leg and limb, possessed of a full swelling bosom and a graceful Grecian face of rosy cheek, large black eyes and lips as red as cherries, with pearl white teeth which were frequently exhibited in a succession of winning smiles that rarely left her sweet countenance.

I recall that we ate a light luncheon, beginning with trout, freshly caught from the river only that very morning by young Adrian, the son of old Hostridge our head gardener. Then came baby lamb so tender that it simply melted in the mouth. Although thanks to the efforts of Dr White, I was well past my first experience of intercourse with the opposite sex, I was still somewhat gauche in *l'arte de faire l'amour*, and Fanny could see from the stammering replies I gave to her polite attempts at conversation that my mind was elsewhere. Perhaps she could see quite clearly that I would have been far happier sucking her rosy titties than eating the plate of strawberries that had been piled upon my dessert plate.

So I must confess that my attention had wandered though I looked earnestly at Fanny as she commented upon the growing passion for lawn tennis that was sweeping Society that summer.

'Indeed,' she said, 'the possession of a tennis ground has become such an imperative social necessity that every wretched little garden-plot is pressed into service. Courts are being religiously traced out even when the available space is often little bigger than a billiard-table.'

'Really,' I murmured, 'how very interesting.'

'You think so?' smiled Fanny. 'Yet I fear that my conversation is boring you.' And she smiled so pertly as I blushed scarlet with embarrassment.

'Oh, no, far from it!' I exclaimed. 'Please forgive me if I

gave such an impression but I would be foolish not to admit that my thoughts were elsewhere.'

'Indeed they were,' she replied quietly. 'They were probably between my legs, if that bulge in your trousers is any guide to your mental condition.'

I gasped with astonishment as I realised that the little minx had noticed Mr Pego's rise to attention occasioned by her presence.

I was dumbfounded by her brazen words, but my heart began to beat faster as I realised that this beautiful day could well hold unexpectedly exquisite pleasures for me.

'Would you care to take a walk, Miss Fanny?' I asked, rising to my feet. I noticed that several guests had already left the table of our delightful al fresco meal.

'I think that is a splendid idea, Andrew,' she said with a gay laugh, 'but let us not venture too far as we must be present for the prizegiving. Let us go somewhere quiet where we can be together undisturbed.'

'What an admirable suggestion,' I said, 'and it occurs to me that you might like to rest away from this bright sunlight. We could walk to my study. It would give me great pleasure to show it to you.'

She nodded her agreement and, taking my arm, we strolled round the garden. As we passed the shrubbery and were about to go inside the house, we met Dr White who asked us if we had enjoyed the luncheon.

'Very much, sir,' said Fanny, 'and now we are taking a short stroll round the school. Andrew has graciously offered to escort me round the buildings.'

'Capital, capital,' boomed the head. 'But just before I leave you, may I have a brief private word with Andrew?'

'Of course, Dr White,' she smiled, 'but please do not keep my guide for too long.'

'A mere minute, my dear,' muttered the good Doctor, clasping my elbow and drawing a few paces away.

'What is it, sir?' I asked with as much innocence as I could muster.

'Now, now, my boy, you do not have to pretend to me. I

can guess just what is in your mind regarding young Fanny and I must confess I envy you. You do know that she has a reputation for ah, shall we say, experience in country matters?'

'No, sir, I did not, but I can scarcely say that I am sorry!'

'Quite so – as you are leaving the school next week, I thought she would make your last Founders' Day one to remember!'

'How kind of you, sir!'

'Not at all, not at all. Fanny was well-pleased when I suggested such a course of action to her. You have met before, have you not? The last time was at Colonel Welch's Easter ball, if my memory serves me well. Anyhow, be a Nottsgrovian, Andrew. The probability is that you will be required to fuck the lovely Fanny but remember it is the prerogative of a girl to say yea or nay and her wish must always be respected!'

'Of course, sir,' I replied. 'This was one of the first principles you drummed into us.'

'Good boy, I am delighted that you have absorbed my teachings. So be off with you but remember to be back in the Great Hall by five o'clock for the speeches, the prizegiving and the private concert. You recall that Sir Joshua Cohen has persuaded the great fiddler Mayerovitch to come and entertain us. He will be bringing three of his friends and has promised a performance of Schubert's Quartet in D Minor, a particularly beautiful piece of music.'

I promised with alacrity, for though fucking Fanny was by far the most important matter on my mind, I too wished to hear the great musician.

There was a mischievous smile on Fanny's face when I returned to her.

'Did Doctor White say anything of interest?' she enquired.

'Just that we must be back in the Great Hall by five o'clock.'

'I think he may have said more than that, Andrew!'

'Oh, well, all right, if you must know he told that he had spoken to you about —'

18

'Yes, I know, I know. I hope you don't mind my saying that I have wanted you to fuck me ever since we met at Colonel Welch's ball.'

'Have you really? Why, it will be my pleasure.'

And I took her hand as we strolled towards my study.

'I like Dr White,' said Fanny. 'He is a very understanding man. He is of the firm belief that young people must be fully instructed in the field of personal relationships with the opposite sex and for himself accepts only the rules of human nature.

'He does not wish his pupils to carry the burdens of shame and guilt which so often accompany the elemental expression of the desire and need for sexual union. Why, nature has made this act extremely pleasurable yet quite absurdly we are ashamed of our basic inclinations and – well, the simple truth of the matter is that we all enjoy a good fucking and Dr White is sporting enough to let his senior boys partake of this enjoyment!'

'I could not have expressed his views with more clarity,' I said, opening the door and once Fanny was inside, following her and then carefully closing and bolting the door so that we would remain undisturbed.

'How marvellous it must be to have a bed in your study,' said Fanny, 'but as I recall, you must earn this privacy by showing that you are mature enough to spend your nights unsupervised, away from the dormitories.'

'That is correct,' I mumbled, not quite knowing how to begin making love to this delicious girl. 'Anyway, we have some time before we must go back. Tell me, Fanny, are you fond of Schubert?'

'He is one of my favourite composers,' she said, 'although Papa took me last week to a concert of the music of Dvorak which I enjoyed immensely.'

'Yes, I have not had the pleasure of hearing his music but I have read that his work is distinguished by the most lovely melodies.'

'His music is quite wonderful,' she cried, 'but enough of talk. Will you not take me in your arms and kiss me? That

19

would be nicer than the sweetest melody in the world!'

I needed no further encouragement. I held Fanny in my arms and gently pressed my lips against hers, though in a mere second my tongue forced our lips apart. We thrilled to our passion and within me a fire raged, destroying any lingering traces of shyness or fear. With a burning urgency, we swiftly shed our light summer clothes and in a trice lay entwined naked on my bed. I delighted in the wondrous feel of the gorgeous girl, as her fully bared breasts rose to my roving caresses and I marvelled at the pretty bubbies as I felt the hard, pouting nipples push firmly against my palms. Meanwhile, her wicked tongue filled my mouth, probing and rousing until my thick cock was standing sharply to attention and Fanny began to stroke the swollen uncapped shaft with her long, skilful fingers.

In the meantime, my own hands had not remained inactive and Fanny gasped with pleasure and excitement as I continued to fondle her breasts and then moving gently down to the soft, silken skin of her belly. I knelt over and bending my head downwards, kissed the swell of her white thighs that so well set off the silky patch of black curly hair that nestled between her legs.

I began to kiss the soft lips of her pussey and as Fanny began to writhe in anticipation, I began to lick her cunt, trembling myself with desire as my tongue sought out and found the secrets of her delicious quim.

Now I buried my face between those warm, wet cunt-lips and pushed my eager tongue deep inside her dark, juicy cleft. Like nipples, like clitty says the wise old adage, and Fanny proved the truth of the saying for her stiff little clit gleamed long and erect like a miniature tool through the hairy tuft. I thrust my tongue even deeper to suck her clitty, rolling the erect flesh with my willing mouth as I searched the walls of her honeypot.

I was now getting short of breath, in real danger of suffocating, for such was her insistence on crowding her cunt into my face. Her hands left my prick and slipped to her bum-cheeks in an effort to ensure that I would not lose contact

20

with her clitty. I played and teased with her, licking eagerly to suck more and more of the juices that flowed freely from the depths of her gushing pussey.

'Now push in your prick!' she gasped.

Nothing loath, I slid across her and our bodies touched from head to toe as she gripped my rampant cock and guided the huge purple head to the willing lips of her lovebox. I gently eased home and her teeth sank into my shoulder as my first strokes jerked her body to new peaks of ecstacy. I pounded home the strokes faster and faster as we rocked together, climbing to almost unimaginable heights as my raging cock slid uncontrollably in and out of that juicy quim. All too soon I felt myself approaching the ultimate pleasure and try though I may to postpone the moment, my body was being wound up tighter and tighter until finally it exploded into one climactic release as I shot my hot, sticky juice deep into the sweet girl who rotated her hips wildly, lifting her bum-cheeks to obtain the maximum contact. Our orgasms crashed through almost simultaneously as she milked my cock of spurt after spurt of hot, sticky spunk that joined her own flowing juices to lubricate her innermost passages.

I rolled off Fanny and lay on my back quite exhausted from the superb if swift bout of fucking. But Fanny's blood was up and soon she was taking my love-juice coated prick in her hands, bending her pretty head down so that it rested on my thighs. She smiled at me and then pertly sticking out her tongue began to tease my cock head by running the tip of her tongue all round the edges of the springy cap, at the same time gently manipulating my balls through the soft wrinkled skin of the bags.

She suddenly opened her mouth and enveloped the dome of my prick which began to swell menacingly in her mouth. She pulled it from her lips and began to flick her tongue delicately along the shaft as my cock rose up as stiffly as before. She responded by jamming her mouth over the mushroom dome, opening her mouth wide to encircle my cock as I instinctively pushed upwards. Her mouth was like a cave of fire which warmed but did not burn; her tongue enveloped my knob, savouring the juices which oozed from it. Her teeth scraped the tender flesh as she drew me in between those luscious lips, sucking hard as though it were the most delicious sweetmeat.

She continued to suck and stroke her tongue up and down along the under-side of my cock, making it ache with excitement as it throbbed more and more urgently. Then she cupped my balls in her hand, gently rubbing them as she slowly sucked my prick even deeper inside her mouth. She squeezed her free hand around the base of my shaft sucking me harder and harder until I felt the tingling sensations of the beginning of a climax approach. My lusty young prick pulsed in her mouth as I gave a small cry and arching my back jetted wedge upon wedge of creamy white spunk full within that adorable mouth, which ceased not to draw upon it until the last pearly essence had been greedily slurped and swallowed.

A murmur of satisfaction came from Fanny as she raised her head, kissed my glistening cock which was, truth to tell, now fast losing its proud stand.

'That was very nice, Andrew,' she laughed. 'Your spunk has a lovely salty tang and I must suck you off again before we finish this afternoon's little escapade!'

'Nothing would please me more,' I said, my chest still heaving away as I fought for composure, 'but I think you must give me a few minutes to recover. I cannot come three times in a row without a pause in between.'

'Very well. Lie down and rest. Look we can cuddle up close together. It is so warm that we need not cover ourselves with any bedclothes.'

So we lay together and I asked Fanny if she thought that I had satisfied her.

'Most certainly,' she cried, 'even more so than the other two Nottsgrove boys who have enjoyed having their pricks inside me, though I have no complaint about their ability to try and afford me the greatest pleasure of spending myself!'

I was surprised to hear that Fanny had fucked two of my schoolmates and I asked her if she would relate the experiences to me.

She said: 'It would give me great pleasure to do so, although in fact we are talking about just the one experience.

'It happened early last September in Arkley Woods, through which I was sauntering to give a letter from my father to Dr White. I cannot recall the exact nature of the matter but it was of little importance. As the day was pleasant for that time of the year, I told Papa that I preferred to give Dr White the letter myself rather than have Watkins deliver it.

'The wind was not too strong and, notwithstanding the fine summer we enjoyed last year, on many trees the leaves were already changing colour, giving the woods a dappled look. A carpet of dead leaves had already spread itself on the ground but amongst the lifeless stalks of cow parsley, I noticed some thriving bunches of its autumn relative, upright hedge parsley, flourishing with many pink and white flowers.

'I was so engrossed in my reverie that though I heard light footsteps running towards me. I made no attempt to move off the narrow path and was only woken out of my dream by the sound of a collision between two bodies that had both tried to avoid bumping into me but had only succeeded in running into each other! I let out a cry of distress for the accident was clearly my fault. And you may imagine my discomfiture when I saw that both the young men sprawled on the ground were known to me. Both are classmates of yours, Andrew, so I suppose I am being naughty by telling you their names. I trust that I can rely on your discretion and that you will never reveal to them that I have told you about this little adventure.'

'You have my word, Fanny, as a gentleman!' I eagerly exclaimed.

'Very well then, I shall continue. The two boys were none other than Pelham Forbes-Mackenzie and Gilbert Davies. I know that Pelham is one of your close friends but I believe that you know little of Gilbert. He is in the science forms as he wishes to practise medicine.

'However, both boys had decided to take advantage of a half-holiday and go for a cross-country run. They were dressed solely in athletic vests and brief running shorts which scarcely covered their knees. Now as you know, Pelham is a good-looking if stocky young chap but Gilbert Davies is simply one of the most handsome youths I have ever seen – do not be cross, Andrew, but I must speak the truth even if it pains your tender feelings!

'Gilbert's mother is Swedish and he has inherited her slim body, blond hair, and intense light blue eyes. Oh, he looked a real Adonis, so well muscled with a face smooth and free from any blemish.

'"Are you two boys hurt?" I enquired anxiously, "I am so sorry, I was miles away day-dreaming and it was so gallant of you both not to crash right into me."

'Pelham was first to scramble to his feet. "Please think nothing of it, Miss Fanny," he said, catching his breath. "Are you fit enough to continue, Gilbert?"

'Gilbert attempted to rise but he grimaced with pain and I asked if I could be of assistance. "I'll be fine in a moment, Miss Fanny. I will be as right as ninepence once I have exercised this wretched ankle."

'"Steady on, old boy!" said Pelham. "I think your ankle is somewhat swollen and I think I had better give you a hand." He helped Gilbert stand up but it was obvious that Gilbert could not walk without some help. As fate would have it, the wind began to freshen appreciably and a cold gust sent the leaves scurrying away on some mad journey. I frowned as I wondered the best course of action for us to take. As if by some feat of mesmerism, Pelham read my mind and said: "I do believe that it would be best to find some shelter as it looks fearfully like a squall is brewing up." And indeed, as he spoke, the first drops of rain pattered down upon us.

'I suddenly had a flash of inspired thought. "Let us make for Jonathan's Cave, only some five minutes walk away. You must be familiar with the cave, my dear. It lies by the stream that cuts through the southern part of the woods. Perhaps cave is the wrong word, for it is more like a miniature cottage built by that eccentric ornithologist Lester Jonathan who some forty years ago made his fortune in commercial trade of some kind and then retired from business affairs to devote his days solely to his passion for bird-watching. His essay on

24

whitethroats is still used as an admired text in many seats of learning but the love of kingfishers dominated his existence. Now as you must know, dear Andrew, the kingfisher hovers above the banks of streams and the nest is constructed at the end of a tunnel which may be as long as three feet into the riverbank. It is a shy, solitary bird and to observe its habits as closely as possible, Mr Jonathan constructed a two-roomed edifice gouging out soil from a natural cave-like structure that exists just by the bend in the stream near the furthest of the school fields. The structure is occasionally used by Sir Oliver Leigh, who owns East House and who is a keen fisherman. Two years ago he put a bed and some rudimentary sticks of furniture into the 'cave' as sometimes he slept there, waking early with the dawn to enjoy a full day's piscatorial combat.

'Anyhow, we made for the 'cave' with Pelham and I supporting Gilbert so that he did not have to put any weight upon his swollen ankle. I was glad to see that although painful, the injury could not have been too serious as he retained a good deal of movement and it was almost certain that no bones had been broken. We staggered into the 'cave' and to our great good fortune a fire had been laid near the entrance. There was a small stove with some wood and coal packed inside and inside a tiny cupboard fixed on the wall of the 'cave', I discovered to my delight that Sir Oliver had left a packet of tea and a tin of biscuits. He obviously planned to spend a night there when the weather improved.

'"Look," I said happily, "we are in luck. There is a kettle here and Sir Oliver has also had the foresight to leave a box of matches. He will not mind in the slightest if we make use of these items which I shall replenish with a note of thanks later this evening. Our coachman, Waller, can come back here tonight though I very much doubt if Sir Oliver will want to stay here in such inclement weather."'

'"No, indeed," said Gilbert. "In fact I am sure that Sir Oliver and Lady Joan are away until the weekend. Dr White happened to mention this yesterday as he had asked them to attend the dramatic society's reading of *Henry V* but they replied that they were staying with Lord and Lady Webb until the weekend."

'"Even better," I said. "Now I also presume that neither of you are in a hurry to return to school as you seemed to be dressed for a serious run."

'"Oh, yes," said Pelham. "You are quite correct. We are both in training for our paper-chase next week."

'"Well, if you want to take part, I suggest that you divest yourselves of those wet clothes so that you do not catch chills!"

'"And what do we change into?" laughed Pelham.

'I laughed too but then I noticed a bed and a narrow wardrobe in the far corner. And yet again Dame Fortune smiled upon us. I opened the wardrobe and there hanging up were two pairs of roughly made trousers which Sir Oliver must have kept for use whilst sitting on the bank waiting for the fish to bite. And even better, on the floor lay a pile of good-sized towels.

'"Slip out of your wet clothes and you can change into these dry trousers. You can keep these towels on your backs when we go back to Nottsgrove after tea. Perhaps you will light the fire for me, Pelham."'

'They looked rather sheepish until I realised that they were perhaps understandably shy about undressing in front of me! "Do not concern yourselves, gentlemen, about standing naked in my presence," I assured them. "My goodness, I have not been brought up in rural England without knowing something, as the dear Bard of Avon delicately puts it, of country matters! However, to save you any untoward embarrassment, I shall turn my head away and not see you in your birthday suits although, I must freely confess, it would give me the greatest pleasure to see your magnificent bodies unclothed."

'"Good heavens above, how can you say such a thing?" gasped Gilbert. I could not help smiling as I replied "Well, this may shock you but I have enjoyed sexual relations with men before now and indeed, Gilbert, if Pelham would enter that rather primitive water-closet behind that door, perhaps I could initiate you into the pleasures of the flesh!"

'"I am a sportsman, Miss Fanny," grinned Pelham. "I shall take this book in with me as I shall have enough light coming in through the top of the door – though talking of coming, I would rather –"

'"Do not fret," I said, "You will not leave here disappointed. Just do not frig that lovely cock of yours until I am ready for you!"

'Gilbert could hardly believe his ears but Pelham, being like yourself a select member of Dr White's favoured few, had passed his first sexual lessons with flying colours and was indeed sporting enough to let Gilbert take his ex-officio chance of losing his virginity.

'"Come now, Gilbert, my dearest," I said softly, "take off your wet singlet and sit down here whilst I undo your shoes and socks". As if in a trance, the slim young man did as he was told, but after I divested him of his shoes and socks I gently tugged down his running shorts and he wriggled his darling little bottom to allow me to divest him of his last article of clothing.

'My tongue passed hungrily over my top lip as I moved my hand up to stroke his magnificent thick cock which was already in a state of half-limber. I thrilled at the sight of this most fine-looking prick which now rose majestically high and stiff as a flagpole as I gently rubbed the shaft with my hand. I marvelled at the now uncapped, head, rubicund and gleaming and at the thick veins that knotted themselves along its rigid length. The sight was simply too exciting and dropping to my knees in front of him, I kissed, frigged and sucked his delicious prick till I could feel his hairy balls tighten under my touch as with an explosion of rapture he spent in my mouth and I eagerly swallowed every last drop of his copious emission. Now my blood was up and I quickly shucked off my dress and undergarments and stood quite naked in front of him. He gazed over my uptilted breasts with the nipples now jutting out in excitement and I rubbed my quim to see if I was now juicy (which I was) as I turned to Gilbert, flaunting myself in front of his hungry eyes.

27

'"Well now, Gilbert, do you like what you see or do you wish to send it back to the manufacturer? Come down and lie on the bed with me and I shall give you your first ever fuck, an experience that I know you will never forget."

'And so I held him by that monster tool, rubbing my sperm-coated hand up and down the loose skin which soon had the desired effect of stiffening up his cock to its former manly glory as we crashed down together on the narrow bed. Gilbert was on top of me, clutching the firm cheeks of my arse as I took hold of his marvellous cock and guided it firmly towards my aching pussey which was now wet with my own juices. I let go and reached with both hands to part the gleaming lips of my slit to manoeuvre the monster prick until with an ardent gasp, Gilbert felt the head of his cock absorbed between my willing cunt-lips.

'"Gently, my dear, go gently," I murmured as for the first time his swollen prick entered the divine haven. Gilbert all but swooned with pleasure as by simple instinct he began to move his cock in and out of my juicy, wet nest. Every nerve in my body thrilled with exquisite rapture as I heaved up to meet his thrusts, winding my legs around him so that his large, hairy balls banged against my backside as he buried that delightful cock in me to the very hilt. We rolled, we screamed together as we soon reached the peak of delight. All too soon I felt the jets of frothy seed spurting inside me as his climax juddered to boiling point. I felt the rush of liquid fire inside me with every throb of that huge shaft as spasm after spasm of creamy sperm, white as liquid starch, shot into my womb and my own pleasure followed almost immediately as my saturated pussey sent shudders of delight all over my body.

'He rolled over to lie next to me but I could see to my great excitement this his enormous cock still looked capable of a third performance. So I positioned him on his knees in front of me between my legs and I opened my legs wide so he would have full view of my pouting cunt lips. I took his hand and placed it on my soaking bush. His fingers splayed my outer lips and the fingers of his other hand ran down the length of my slit. I gently pushed the finger in to penetrate me and my hips rose up to meet it. But what I wanted was another round with his delicious young prick! So I motioned him to lie down again and slipped my hand round his slippery wet length, finding to my delight that it began to swell almost immediately, poised and ready for another joyful coupling. I jammed down his foreskin and delicately fingered the bulbous knob, bending over to lap up sweet juices.

'I moved up and over so that my pussey was over his face and though this was all a delightful novelty to Gilbert, he knew what to do, burying his face in my bush, taking my cunt into his mouth, licking me in so passionate a way that my whole pussey was soon dripping with love juices!

'My own mouth was now busy, working over his rock-hard tool, running my teeth up and down the length, sucking the glistening, wet knob, flicking my wicked tongue over its slitted end whilst my hands cradled his lovely balls.

'I knew that if we stayed like this he would spend before time, so I lay back and he was on top of me again. I gave his hot prick a final rub before guiding the monster shaft down into my raging wetness. I slipped my hands down his back to clasp his bottom cheeks and young Gilbert now needed little urging as his arms went under my shoulders. As his pelvis jabbed down I eagerly lifted my hips to welcome his thrusting, thick cock that slid so beautifully in and out of my quim. Oh, such joy! Oh, such exquisite pleasure! It was to be one of the most intense orgasms I have ever experienced. The whole length and depth of my pussey throbbed and throbbed again as his gorgeous thick tool pushed deeper and deeper to my very womb.

'He began a long slow thrusting motion and gradually I felt the tingle that accompanies the spend build up in me. As he began to heave and buck with increasing rapidity I took off once more on that journey to paradise. "Now, Gilbert, fuck me! Fuck me hard!" I screamed without restraint and my darling boy obliged as with short stabbing strokes he shot stream after stream of creamy jism deep into my willing body. Almost simultaneously, my own juices flowed out as I reached the glorious peak of pleasure...

29

'We lay with our bodies entwined, gasping for breath when I heard the sound of Pelham flushing the water-closet and he walked over to us with a huge smile on his face.

'"I am just going to bathe," said Pelham, "Perhaps I may join you when I return in about ten minutes. I hope that will give you enough time to rest from your labours!"

'This highly enjoyable bout of fucking had exhausted poor Gilbert. I do believe, incidentally, that we women should realise just how violent an exercise sexual intercourse can be for a man. Even though liberated ladies such as myself no longer simply lie back to receive our spunky libations, we still do not heave around so much as our partners.

'But I digress. Gilbert was almost asleep by the time Pelham returned. "It has stopped raining and now the sun is shining!" he said cheerily. Gilbert sat up and I said to the dear lad: "Gilbert, why not dress and exercise your injured ankle? It will probably do you good."

'I think he knew what was in my mind for he agreed immediately and told us that he would be back in about half an hour which perhaps he knew would give Pelham and I a chance to enjoy each other's bodies!

'"I presume you would like to fuck me?" I asked Pelham.

'"Of course I would, Miss Fanny," said the handsome youth, his eyes glistening with anticipation.

'"Well then, as you have been such a gentleman and let Gilbert enjoy his first fuck in peace, and because I've always rather liked you, you may. Take off your clothes and lie here next to me."

'"He obeyed my command with alacrity. I smoothed my hand over his flat stomach and into his mass of pubic hair. I licked my lips when I looked at his thick cock which was not erect but had that lovely full, heavy look. I gently squeezed the shaft and almost immediately, his gorgeous tool sprung up into full erection, uncapping the delicious-looking purple head. I felt the length of his shaft again, so thick that my hand could barely go round it and my head swooped down as I began to suck greedily on the magnificent head, dwelling around the ridge, up the underside until closing my eyes I

30

took him completely in my mouth in long, rolling sv`ks, coaxing the spunk from him that began to spend, grunting and heaving inside my mouth. I sucked furiously until I felt the juices boil up inside that velvet-hard shaft and then I knew he was about to spend which he did in long, powerful squirts that I swallowed eagerly.

'I lay back, gasping with pleasure and noted that my nipples were standing up like little bullets. I pulled Pelham's head down onto my bosom and he began to suck my left tittie as I played gently with his magical cock which soon rose high to its giant stiffness. Oh, what a physique Pelham possessed! He rolled over on top of me and I guided his monster tool into my juicy love-nest. I was so wet that his hard shaft slipped immediately into my dripping wetness and I experienced that great joy of an eager young cock stretching my pussey, filling it, pumping in it as we drove each other into a frenzy as the first jet of hot spunk came jetting into my womb. I clapped my hands over his lean buttocks and kept him deep in my cunt, heaving my body up and down his slowly deflating shaft until I reached the climax my body demanded.'

Fanny sighed at the recollection. She looked at me longingly. Her fingers gently turned around her hairy bush.

'Have we time for a very quick fuck?' she enquired.

Naturally the tale of these lusty encounters sent my blood boiling and my trusty tool was already in a state of rampant excitement when Fanny giggled and gave it a few vigorous rubs.

'I think so,' I replied, 'but we will have to be smartish, for Dr White expects us back in the Great Hall for five o'clock sharp.'

Without ado, she grasped my bursting prick and climbed on top of me to ride an exquisite St George. We both reached the haven of our desires and after quickly towelling off the perspiration our love-making had caused to form, we dressed as rapidly as we could and made our way back to the Great Hall.

We were in good time and we took our turn to file past Dr White at the main entrance. He was engaged in heated conversation with the noted writer Miss Danielle Clive (Mrs Arthur MacGillerty) but as we passed him he put a restraining hand on my arm.

'Now, Madam,' he was saying, 'you must not believe in blind fate. But I do grant you that all philosophical inquiry, and all that practical knowledge which guides our conduct in life presupposes an established order in the succession of events that enables us to form conjectures concerning the future from the observation of the past.'

'Well, I quite agree, Dr White,' said his adversary with some spirit for she well knew that in the cut and thrust of debate with our dear old Headmaster, no quarter must be expected or given. 'But you will doubtless acknowledge that the religious eccentric always will lean towards the extra-ordinary in the salvation of mankind.

'He means well from first to last; yet he is however, a fanatic on whatever doctrine or theory he advances. And it requires but unfavourable circumstances such as indifference or worse rejection by the public to push him past the mark of eccentricity towards a state of complete lunacy!

'You must have met the type of person who earnestly states that only he possesses the keys to the gates of the kingdom of heaven. All others are fools, charlatans or the very Devil, all others are lost save he!

'Yet he does not wish to enter heaven alone – far from it. It is his feverish anxiety for others that makes him exceptional. He denies himself all enjoyments in the terrible haste to accomplish his desire, hastening a further unbalancing of his mental condition.

'Today he may be a mere nuisance but in years gone by such men were able to kill others in order to save their souls. Christians and Musselmen alike have been guilty in this respect, not only towards those such as the Hebrews who are infidels in their bigoted eyes, but even towards others of their own ilk who they believe have strayed from the true paths of belief!'

I had a little idea of the subject under discussion which was probably one of Miss Clive's latest articles that had recently appeared in one of the smart journals such as *The Nineteenth*

Century to which she was a frequent contributor, and Dr White a regular subscriber. I must confess that I silently cheered for our distinguished guest as Nottsgrove always taught its pupils respect and tolerance for the religious beliefs of others, a teaching sadly lacking, I fear, in many other private educational establishments.

Dr White muttered his agreement and retired worsted from the fray. Miss Clive swept into the Hall. Her two sons, Frederick and Humphrey were pupils at Nottsgrove although both were younger than I and I cannot claim but a passing acquaintance with Frederick, now of course Sir Frederick, who is a noted mathematical scholar at the University of London.

'Ah, Andrew,' said the good Doctor genially, 'I am sorry to detain you and your charming guest, but I have a favour to ask of you. I know that Fanny has an appointment to dine with the father at the Fergusons tonight. Have you met Mr Sean Ferguson who is our new neighbour? Well, you will when I invite the family over to Nottsgrove.

'However, one of the members of Mayerovitch's quartet, Professor Beigel, has brought his niece Esther over with him from Vienna. I would like you to escort her at dinner tonight. Very well, off you go.'

I was sorry to hear that Fanny had to leave as I envisaged more larks that evening but I little guessed what fate had in store later that night!

However, we took our seats reserved in the second row and settled down to thrill to the music of Schubert, especially when played so brilliantly by Mayerovitch and his friends. Though only the maestro was a professional musician, I have always felt that the fine thing about many string quartets is that they can be mastered by gifted amateurs.

After all, most chamber music was composed for the amateur to be played at home rather than in the concert hall. Only when Count Rasumovski hired four professionals did composers write difficult pieces for professional performers.

I love the D Minor Quartet, although when first performed it was not well received. Today we know better and the exciting, sheer beauty of the piece will ensure that it will be played and loved forever.

Fanny and I sat through the concert and heartily applauded the musicians off the stage. Afterwards we attended a short reception at which Fanny and I made our farewells.

I was deep in conversation with Kenneth Latkins, a fellow pupil whose musical talents are now well known to many members of Society as his performances on the flute are in demand by hostesses throughout the London season. Few people know that his musical tuition began as a young student at Nottsgrove under the tutelage of Dr White, himself no mean exponent of both flute and oboe.

'My dear chap,' exclaimed Latkins, 'As far as music is concerned, Ludwig von Beethoven almost single-handedly created the Romantic Revolution, taking music along paths from which there was no turning back. And what an extraordinary life which knew no such triumphs and such tragedies, suffering as well as joy and afflictions that would have caused lesser men to retreat. Why, as Herr Bulka has said —'

I never found out what that distinguished gentleman of German extraction did say, for at that moment Dr White came ambling over and interrupted the lecture.

'My dear boys, just who I wanted to see. Andrew, I would like you to meet Esther Beigel, the Professor's daughter. Kenneth, perhaps you would like to meet her too. She is extremely knowledgeable about music so you two will certainly have something in common.'

He swept us along to another knot of people which parted before us and there stood the most exquisite of girls. My eyes drank in the superb beauty of a young girl, not more than eighteen years, a short, slight pretty figure, a quantity of golden hair, a pair of blue eyes that met mine with a polite, friendly look.

'Ah, my dear,' boomed Dr White, 'These are the young gentlemen I would like to present to you. Mr Andrew Scott, Mr Kenneth Latkins, this is Miss Esther Beigel from Prague. Like all good Europeans, she speaks English with distinction which she wishes to practise so you will be able to hide your

34

typically English inability to speak in a foreign tongue!'

He strode off leaving us together – there was never any thoughts of chaperones at Nottsgrove Academy!

'It is most pleasant to meet you, Miss Beigel,' I said, 'I am sure you enjoyed the concert as much as we did.'

'Yes, it was delightful,' she rejoined, in a very clear and charming young voice, only a little foreign in its accent.

'Your father is a most talented musician,' said Latkins warmly. 'Do you too play a musical instrument?'

'I play the piano purely for my own pleasure,' smiled this most delicious damsel. 'But Dr White tells me that you are the most talented musical pupil he has ever taught.'

'His performances on both oboe and flute are quite superb,' I chipped in. 'Last month we invited three musicians to accompany Kenneth in the Mozart Oboe Quartet at a reception for our Old Boys...'

'Old Boys?' queried Esther, a puzzled frown creasing her high forehead.

'A colloquiallism for former pupils of a school.' I explained. 'The violin was played by Sir Louis Segal, the clothing magnate who gave generously to the foundation appeal when Nottsgrove was but an idea in Dr White's brain. The names of the cellist and viola player would mean nothing to you. But the performance was up to a professional standard.'

'How interesting,' she smiled at us. 'I suppose it would not be possible to hear you play, Mr Latkins?'

'We have some time before we dine,' I said heartily. 'Why don't you get out your oboe and we will join you in your rooms in ten minutes or so. We may then enjoy the pleasure of seeing you play upon your noble instrument!'

Of course I immediately realised the unplanned *double entendre*, although Kenneth simply gave a slight bow and said that he would be honoured to oblige.

But to my amazement the little minx was trying extremely hard to prevent a broad smile breaking out over her pretty little face. As Latkins turned away she could restrain herself no longer and burst out into a fit of giggles.

'I might not understand the meaning of "Old Boys" but I

think I understood the meaning of "playing with his noble instrument" well enough,' she gasped through her chuckles.

'Oh, you must forgive me,' I cried. 'It was a terrible slip of the tongue.'

'There you go again,' she laughed. 'I know all about your slips of the tongue from my friend Fanny Gadson-Fisher. She tells me that although you cannot play an instrument, the way you tongue out her cunt is as blissful as a Beethoven sonata!'

I looked at her in astonishment. Goodness gracious, I could never have believed that two girls would confide intimate experiences of such a sensual nature to each other. This well shows how the daily occurences of life are continually furnishing us with matter for thought and reflection. I am apt to flatter myself that in the course of these recollections I have laid down instances and thoughts which my readers were either wholly ignorant of before, or which at least those few who were acquainted with them, looked upon as so many secrets they have found out for their own knowledge, but were resolved never to make public.

We sauntered slowly towards Latkins' rooms which were situated in the East Wing. I felt that I had to make polite conversation even though my mind was racing ahead to the delicious probability that my trusty truncheon would soon be in action again. After at least six weeks forced abstinence (except for the occasional toss) I was making up for lost time with a vengeance!

'You live in Prague, Miss Esther?' I enquired.

'My family comes from there,' she replied. 'But our home is now in the little town of Nachod near the northern frontier of Bohemia. Do you know the area? It is most charming and Nachod Château is well worth a visit.

'It was founded some four hundred years ago and is situated in the valley of the Metuje river, a major trade route in past days. A hundred years ago an Italian nobelman, Piccolomini, settled there and made extensive renovations as well as constructing a new Spanish hall decorated with a fresco ceiling. All the walls and ceilings were redecorated in the roccoco style.'

'It sounds quite perfect,' I murmured.

'You must come to see me there,' she added, as we entered the East Wing. 'But for now, do you want to hear more music?'

'I am in your hands,' I said gallantly.

'Well, we cannot disappoint our friend,' she said, squeezing my arm. 'Perhaps an opportunity for something else may arise.'

Kenneth welcomed us to his rooms with a hearty greeting. His study was one of the most luxurious in the school, consisting of a large living-room and a separate bedroom. He had managed to smuggle in a bottle of very decent claret (strictly against the rules, of course) which stood along with three glasses on a small table.

Kenneth poured us some wine and naturally the discussion turned immediately to music. The conversation was frankly beginning to bore as Kenneth and Esther discussed the merits of Herr Von Weber's Concerto for Clarinet, No. Two.

'Yes, my grandfather was a member of the Munich Opera orchestra which first played the concerto in 1811 with Weber's favourite clarinettist, Heinrich Barmann, taking the solo role,' said Esther.

'How fascinating,' said Kenneth. 'The work is a most superior piece of music, is it not? Barmann's technique allowed him to play across the full range of the instrument and in the first movement particularly, Weber, one might say, seizes the opportunity to exploit the contrast between the top register of the instrument and its darker, more mysterious tones.

'The concerto makes use of the clarinet's ability to play brilliant and beautiful scale passages,' he droned on.

I decided to interrupt this musical appreciation lecture. 'I thought you were going to play for us,' I said perhaps somewhat too forcefully as Esther looked at me with a smile upon her pretty face.

'Ah, yes, I was forgetting. Well, what would you like me to play for you?'

I was at a loss to reply but Esther had a ready answer that pleased me greatly.

'I think it wrong that we should impose on you, Kenneth,

especially as there is not even a piano upon which I could accompany you.

'Perhaps we could come together and play some pieces at one of your charming school concerts?'

I think Kenneth was also somewhat relieved as he eagerly agreed with this suggestion. 'What shall we do instead?' he asked.

'Why don't we all three just relax and drink this very acceptable claret?' I advised.

'What a splendid idea!' said Esther warmly. 'And let us talk of other matters aside from music. After all, there are other important things in life.'

'Such as what?' enquired Kenneth.

'Oh, I am not sure,' she replied. 'Everybody has a goal, a secret dream about something they have always wanted to accomplish. I sometimes wonder what fun it would be if we could live out our most outrageous fantasies.

'Many of us are afraid to dream,' she continued. 'We are frightened perhaps of never even coming close to achieving our ideals. What we should realise is that true fulfilment comes through the attempt itself and not necessarily in any final victory.

'As the Chinese proverb puts it "It is better to travel hopefully than to arrive". It is our pursuit of perhaps the unattainable that is really at the core of the matter.'

'I see what you mean,' said Kenneth. 'If we give up even before the race has begun, then life will become dull. It is better to take the risk of disappointment, for what one stands to lose by avoiding the chance to participate, so to speak, is far worse than never to have taken part.'

'I agree too,' said Esther. 'There is an English saying, is there not, that it is better to have loved and lost than never to have loved at all.'

We nodded our agreement and the room fell silent. 'Well, why do you not take up your own argument?' said Esther. And to my astonishment, after a brief pause, Kenneth suddenly blurted out: 'Very well, then, Esther, I would be in the very heaven of delight if I may be allowed to make love to you.'

38

Esther nodded solemnly and slowly smiled. 'I admire your blunt honesty,' she said, unpinning her hair so that her golden locks billowed free down almost over her shoulders.

'But in all truth I was thinking about Andrew's prick this evening. On the other hand, it has already seen sterling service this afternoon with my friend Fanny so I think I will accept your kind invitation with pleasure, Kenneth. However, I do not think that Andrew should be totally excluded from participation so with your permission, I suggest that he be allowed to watch.'

'My goodness, does not that show the worth of daring to ask?' murmured Kenneth, unbuttoning his shirt.

'You are not complaining, I hope?' said Esther with a smile.

He shook his head. 'Certainly not, my dear.' He sat down to tug off his shoes and socks as Esther slipped out of her clothes, bending to one side and the other and lastly, forward. When she straightened up her naked body glowed in the subdued light, shadowed in mystery and toned to excite. She stepped towards Kenneth and the movement left her in profile, leaving me to drink in the proud thrust of her full, uptilted breasts crowned by the pink titties that were already pointing out their firmness, the sweep of the thighs moulding into gorgeous legs and the fluffy, crisp thatching over her love box nestling at the top of those lovely limbs.

Kenneth too was now nude, and I saw his slim yet muscular chest heave as he took the delicious girl into his arms. He held her to him gently and pressed his lips against hers. I saw his tongue dart between her unresisting lips as she slipped her hand down to grasp his swollen cock. As if in a trance, I heard myself say: 'It would be far more comfortable inside the bedroom.' I never realised before how strong Kenneth was for he stooped, gathered her in his arms and lifted her. Quickly then, he carried her into the next room. I followed, hastily discarding my own clothes as he deposited her carefully upon the bed. I could see the delight in Esther's face as Kenneth's roaming hands made her gasp with pleasure as he fondled those plump breasts and ran his palms across the upturned nipples. His eyes smouldered with passion as he moved on to the soft, silken skin of her belly and then his fingers moved between her thighs and she writhed in response.

He lifted himself over her as their mouths glued together in a passionate kiss and as I saw Esther shudder with delight, he broke off the embrace to caress moistly with attentive lips first her throat and then moving from side to side to suck in turn on each nipple that proudly jutted out. When he reached her quivering tummy, Kenneth slid his hands beneath her – fondling those curvacious buttocks, caressing the pliable flesh and lifting her lower torso until his shoulders were between those strong thighs. Now his hands changed course as his fingers teased the upper thighs, caressing the sleek columns as he pressed his mouth to that wonderfully soft body, kissing, licking, gradually easing his lips down to the fluffy bush of golden down that covered her cunt lips.

Kenneth buried his head between her thighs as she clasped his head between her legs. I could hear his tongue slurping and licking around her labia as she slid her hands into his hair, urging him to lick her harder as he tasted her sweetness, exploring her very essence with his lips and tongue. Her hips and bottom were now moving in synchronised rhythm with his mouth as she cried out with joy as she reached the summit of pleasure.

He straightened up and knelt in front of her. His thick cock stood out very large and hard, nudging between her legs. She reached out and rubbed the shaft up and down and then she pulled it forward as she sat up and opening her mouth, eased his cock between her lips. With one hand she grabbed his bum cheek and with the other she gently massaged his hairy balls as she sucked firmly on the red, throbbing prick that was jammed in her mouth. Alas, he could not contain his ardour for long and when I saw his body contract violently, I knew that he would spend too soon. And sure enough, his body bucked to and fro as hot streams of spunk spurted into Esther's sweet mouth and she sucked and sucked every last drop as she swallowed his copious emission.

Fortunately, his young prick was still hard as Esther licked the last of his spend off his purple domed shaft. She pushed him down so that he was now lying on his back and Esther hauled herself up till she was in a sitting position on top of his thighs. She held Kenneth's cock in her hand and rubbed the knob lightly over her superb pubic bush. The moist end of his penis massaged her cunt lips as she pulled herself over his upraised flagstaff of a prick and sat down suddenly so that all of his cock was embedded in her.

'Oh, that is delightful!' she squealed. She leaned forward and brushed her breasts against his chest as they kissed with renewed passion.

'Now, Kenneth, I want as much of your darling cock as possible for as long as you can hold that marvellous stiffness inside my juicy wet cunt!' And she began to bounce up and down upon him with a look of bright-eyed delight. Her cheeks were flushed, her nipples were standing out like little rocks as her breasts bounced and her long golden hair danced around his face as her bum cheeks rhythmically smacked against the top of his legs.

She whimpered with excitement as she held her hips hard down upon him, rubbing from side to side, clenching her cunt as a series of exquisite spasms rocked her lithe body as she threw back her head and spent just as his juices came boiling up to soak her love channel with a second libation of thick, creamy sperm.

Esther rolled off him, gasping for breath. Her legs remained parted and I could see juices from her vagina dripping gently on to the sheet.

Now my cock was fairly bursting at the sight of this frenetic activity and instinctively I jammed down my foreskin to fully release the red-headed knob. But before I had rubbed my prick for more than a second or two, Esther said to me: 'Come now, Andrew, don't let that fine looking cock spend any time in your own hand. Would it not prefer plunging into a juicy, wet pussey?'

I needed no further word and I too first paid my devotions at the shrine of love by burying my face in her golden fluff of cunt-hair, licking and sucking her quim until her legs locked themselves around my face as I lapped up her juices, sucking and playfully nipping her hard little clitty, rolling it between my lips as she called on me to do it again and again, frantically rubbing her quim over my mouth. I felt her climax as she shuddered to the ultimate joy and the juices fairly flowed all over my lips.

'Oh, my dear,' she said with mock seriousness. 'You have not yet reached satisfaction, have you? Let me first take you in my mouth.'

And with those words the little minx pushed me down on my back and suddenly her now tousled blonde hair was between my legs as her mouth jammed round my rampant cock. Her magic tongue circled my knob, savouring the juices, and her teeth scraped my shaft as she drew me in between those luscious lips, sucking slowly from top to base again and again sending shock waves of pleasure throughout my entire body. She continued to suck my delighted prick, handled and kissed my balls until I cried out that ecstacy was near.

But before I could spend, Esther desisted from this delicious pursuit and lay back, opening her arms to encourage me to come forward and throw myself upon her in the most ardent manner. She threw her legs over my back and heaved up and down to meet my thrusts as commenced a most excellent bout of fucking. Despite the libations of her own and Kenneth's love juices, her cunt was exquisitely tight, holding me in the dearest vice conceivable, in fact so tight that I could feel my foreskin drawn backwards and forwards at every shove.

But by now her own juices were flowing, oiling the love channel so my further thrusts were made somewhat easier as my eager cock buried itself within the soft, luscious folds of her juicy crack.

'Andrew, Andrew!' she screamed. 'Now, my dear boy, push in, push in, ahhh, ahhh! How marvellous, how delightful, how you do make me come.'

Making one last lunge forward, my balls fairly banging against her bum-cheeks, I felt myself about to spend and with a hoarse cry, sent streams of creamy white spunk hurtling into her eager pussey. I pushed in and wriggled my cock around inside her as the sperm gushed out of my prick in great jets as we writhed around together, enjoying the sublime bliss that only a really good fucking can produce.

The exertions of the afternoon had made me incapable of any further performance but in an inspired mood, Kenneth was on top of us, firmly pushing me to one side, and rolled Esther over onto her tummy.

'On your knees, my darling girl!' he commanded, and Esther obediently pushed up her lovely bum towards him. He forced her legs open a little further with his knees and then slipped round his hand to play with her horned-up titties, squeezing and nipping them as she stooped down with her head on the pillow. Kenneth's thick prick was swollen to its full erectness as he pushed his uncapped shaft between the lovely girl's bum cheeks. 'No, no, not in my arse!' she called out.

No Nottsgrovian would ever disregard the wishes of a lady so I took hold of Kenneth's throbbing cock and guided it slowly towards her warm crack, just touching her cunt-lips. 'That's it, that's it,' she cried. 'Now, push in hard and let me feel you inside me.' Nothing loath, Kenneth plunged his weapon into her warm crack and his balls bounced against her bottom. 'What a lovely cock you have, Kenneth! Push harder now, further in, further in!'

Her bottom responded to every shove as he drove home, until, excited to such raging peaks, the contractions of that deliciously tight cunt sucked the seed from his tool as the sweet friction of her cunney lips against the head of his cock sent his love juice pumping through in great dollops of frothy spunk as he thrust his delighted prick in and out with all his youthful vigour.

Naturally this fired my senses and seeing my cock standing up stiff in all its sturdy glory, Esther rubbed my shaft up and down, playing with my prick (for her cunt was now somewhat sore) until I could no longer restrain a copious spend of sperm all over her hand. We continued our own little menage á trois and later she changed her mind about receiving a cock *au derrière*.

As she kneeled down with her lovely bum cheeks before

me, lustily sucking Kenneth's silky erect cock, I wet my finger in her dripping crack, and easily inserted into her beautifully wrinkled brown bum-hole, and keeping my other hand busy in titillating the stiff little clitoris, I worked her up into such a furious state of desire that she begged me to insert the head of my uncapped bursting tool. She squirmed and wriggled with pleasure as I put my left hand under her thighs and inserted my fingers between her cunt lips, holding them stiff whilst I worked in her arse-hole.

The motions of her bottom, caused by the fall of my thighs against her backside, made her frig herself on my fingers, thus enjoying a double pleasure as I squirted a jet of boiling sperm into her very vitals, as at the same time Kenneth spurted great globules of white love liquid into her willing mouth which she eagerly swallowed as she milked his superb prick of every last drop.

We lay exhausted on the bed until I remembered that Dr White expected us to dine at his table that evening. How we managed to get dressed and maintain our composure that evening is perhaps a story in itself about the amazing strength of will-power one possesses in one's subconscious. However, that will have to wait for another time.

For now, suffice it to say that for the rest of that last summer at Nottsgrove were given up to those joys of *l'art de faire l'amour*.

I must confess that few women since those oft-remembered bygone days have been more beautiful than Fanny or Esther and certainly none since have proved themselves more devoted to my capricious carnal desires.

My adventures at Nottsgrove ended with this dalliance and these my memoirs of a sated scholar, may be found (as may be the recollections of myself and Sir Lionel T—— at the fair University of Oxford) in other editions of our naughty publication.

I pass on now to the days spent after leaving B——College when for a short time I lived in the great Metropolis, being articled as a clerk to the well-known society solicitors Webb, Clarke, Stockman and Tony.

2

My first days spent in the teeming sprawl of our gigantic Metropolis were as a prelude, so to speak, to my life's work as a lawyer. My dear parents were resolved that I should take up the appointment as an articled clerk after I had obtained my degree (alas, the jolly prick-wearing escapades enjoyed with the younger daughter of Rev E—— N—— were much responsible for my failure to obtain first-class honours).

But before I started work, it was necessary to find suitable lodgings near our establishment which was situated in Grafton Street, in the epicentre of the smartest area of London's West End.

As some of you know, our family seat is deep in the heart of rural Sussex, a nice country residence, standing in large grounds of its own and surrounded by small fields of arable and pasture land, interspersed by footpaths and shady walks where you are not likely to meet anyone in a week. I shall refrain from placing the locality more exactly or it may embarrass certain parties, as I have fucked more than a few willing wives in my time and I have no desire to reopen old wounds long since healed.

At this time, we were rarely in London for any length of time – even for the Season – as my parents were so often abroad. So instead of renting a house, we would stay with my mother's widowed sister, Lady Carola E—— whose liberality was buttressed by the three hundred thousand pounds in the Funds left to her by her late husband, Sir Randolph.

My aunt invited me to stay with her in Belgrave Square but I declined her hospitable invitation, as I much preferred to stay in temporary lodgings with my old friend, Sir Lionel T——, whose Saint John's Wood house was not perhaps so grand a mansion but certainly offered more privacy and far more opportunity to enjoy an occasional bout of fucking of which Sir Lionel, like myself, was very fond.

So I gratefully accepted my friend's offer of bed and board but on the strict understanding that my sojourn there would be strictly of a temporary duration. I would not insult Sir Lionel by offering him monetary recompense, so I bought him a somewhat unusual gift (of which more later) when I left his home to take up permanent lodgings.

The family was by now well dispersed. My parents had sailed the week before to the Balkans where the *pater* was involved in some tiresome diplomatic negotiations on behalf of our Government. My elder brother, Archie, was already in the United States of America engaged in a dalliance (which was later to lead to marriage) with the daughter of one Mr Barnes, a cattle rancher whose estate, so I was reliably informed, was as large as the combined counties of Berkshire and Buckinghamshire! My young sister Vera was enjoying herself in the company of her best friend, Victoria, the eldest daughter of Sir Timothy and Lady Shackleton who were taking the girls on the Grand Tour of the Italian States where, no doubt, the lecherous knight and his damsel would avail themselves of some of the Continent's more *recherché* eroticisms.

This leads me to the starting point of my new adventures in dear old London Town. I had paid a final filial duty visit to my parents before they left for Serbia. My father insisted on furnishing me with a great deal of advice and instruction (which I must regretfully admit did not meet with the approval deserved) and more to the point and to my delight and surprise handed me a new leather wallet containing twenty ten pound notes nestling comfortably inside. He added a final warning to keep out of debt and urged me to invest at least fifty pounds with Coutts so that I would always have a nest-egg to fall back upon in any emergency.

He also added that I should keep clear of loose women but that if I should find myself in need of medical advice (as he delicately framed the words) I should not hesitate to visit Dr

Dannels in Oakland Street whose discretion was assured and who had treated the intimate complaints of the highest in the land.

So there I was, ensconced in idle luxury until I took up my articles as a legal clerk. On the third evening – I remember it as if it were yesterday – we had dined at Sir Lionel's club. We were enjoying a glass of port in the lounge and my old friend was waxing eloquently on the lack of a large enough building to house the nation's pictures. At that time the Royal Academy had not yet removed to Burlington House and the National Gallery was desperately short of space.

'It is absurd that two such great rivals should have to contend for so scanty a space!' declared Sir Lionel.

'There is hardly a second-rate town on the Continent that has not a better gallery for its pictures than the moiety supposed to satisfy the wants of our myriads of visitors.

'Trafalgar Square is the best site although it is true that a painting may need more care and cleaning there than in Kensington or Brompton. But all the modern processes now employed are much less harmful than in the old days. Large pictures can be protected by glass and all the apertures can be guarded with fine gauze against dust.

'We need to enlarge the space up to Leicester Square and send the Royal Academy packing to its own place of abode!' he ended, as I nodded my head in total agreement.

As he finished his little speech, a plump red-faced gentleman passed by us. He had not noticed Sir Lionel but my friend recognised the gentleman as an old acquaintance.

'Hello, Sailor!' he called out to the gentleman who turned his head to see who had called.

'Bless my soul, Lionel, how good to see you!' responded this gentleman with obvious pleasure. 'Why I haven't seen you for months now.'

'It has certainly been a long time,' agreed Sir Lionel. 'Sailor, I would like you to meet my young friend, Andrew Scott. Scott has just left Nottsgrove Academy and is staying with me for a few days before settling down to becoming an articled clerk.

47

'Andrew, allow me to present Harold Sailor, one of the most interesting photographic artists of the decade.'

I stood up to shake hands with Mr Sailor. It was a great privilege to meet the famous photographer, whose name was certainly far from unknown to me. His artistic studies of the undraped female figures had been surreptitiously passed round the fifth form at Nottsgrove whilst I had been there.

'A glass of port?' asked Sir Lionel. 'Well, now, Sailor my dear chap. Have you been on one of your continental trips of late?'

'Yes, I returned last night from Switzerland.'

'Had you been working there, sir?' I asked.

'I most certainly was, young man. Many of my best photographs have been taken abroad. Not only are the scenic views of interest in themselves but the young ladies who pose for me are less shy than our English roses. Mind, I always insist that no plates are ever left in the country where I work. This ensures as far as possible that no photograph of a lady is ever available in her own land. This leads to far greater co-operation and the complete lack of inhibition needed to capture the true spirit of the fair sex.'

'I am sure that you are familiar with Harold's work,' smiled Sir Lionel.

'Oh, yes. Most of the lads at Nottsgrove know of his charming studies. I wish that I could take up such an enjoyable occupation,' I said to our affable new friend.

Mr Sailor returned my grin but gently rebuked me, saying that there were many perils in his business. 'I suppose you think I make love to all the women I photograph,' he commented. 'I regret to inform you that this is not the case.'

'No, there must be one in fifty who says no!' murmured Sir Lionel.

'About one in ten is more like it,' said Mr Sailor. 'However, I did enjoy a most pleasurable experience in Switzerland. Come, would you like to hear the details, though I am afraid they may make you jealous!'

'That is of no import,' rejoined Sir Lionel, and after we had ordered more port, Harold Sailor told us of his recent journey which had led to his coming back to Britain with some fresh photographic studies and a very sore prick!

'I do not know whether either of you gentlemen are familiar with the waterfalls near Schaffthausen. The Rhine is fed by the outflow from Lake Constance and the water is sparkling clear and free from silt.

'The falls are quite spectacular. At an elevation of four hundred metres above sea level, the level of the falls measures well over one hundred metres, some one hundred and thirty yards as we would measure it, between the banks of the river which drop some fifty yards to the lower level below.

'It is known locally as the *laufen* which is the German word meaning to flow. And I arrived just two weeks ago in the middle of June when the rate of flow is greatly increased by the snow melting in the Swiss Alps.

'I was staying in the nearby village of Wieslin and to my great delight, there were two extremely attractive girls in attendance at the local hostelry. Unlike so many of our compatriots, I am fluent in both French and German so the girls' rudimentary grasp of English did not prove an insurmountable barrier to social intercourse. We conducted all our conversations in German and though the girls were happier with the Swiss variant of that tongue, we had absolutely no problem in understanding each other. For the purposes of this anecdote, however, I will recount their words in English.

'Their names were Helga and Giselle. Both were nineteen years of age. Helga was the innkeeper's youngest daughter. She had two other sisters who had both married local men and they lived nearby. Giselle, who was also a Swiss, was a clever girl and had won a place to study mathematics in Zurich. Her parents owned property in the area and she had known Helga for some three or four years. Little did I know at the time, but they had both lost their virginity together and that by the same lucky boy, but that is a tale which will have to be told at another time.

'I first struck up their acquaintance whilst sitting outside the inn in the village square, enjoying a glass of beer after my morning constitutional. I was pondering on the problem of finding suitable models for my photographs when these two delicious girls came into view.

'Both were wearing dark skirts with white blouses and I must confess to staring at them with delight. Helga was slender with a marble smooth complexion with a pretty hint of pink in her face that was enhanced by the fine lines of her cheekbones. Her mouth was full and her lower lip being particularly voluptuous. An aquiline nose, neither short nor long, large chestnut eyes and an abundance of soft, dark hair completed the most pleasing nubile curves of her figure.

'Giselle was an extraordinarily beautiful wench. Her fair-skinned features were well cut with a hint of pretty freckling round her nose. Her light blue eyes sparkled in the sunlight and her tresses of blonde hair just overlay her collar, a style that well suited her, and were shaped quite close to her head with a short, parted fringe. Both were perhaps somewhat taller than average but their firm well-kept curves were to be sensuously imagined by an artist such as myself!

'I tipped my hat and we quickly struck up a friendship. On the Continent there is not nearly as much false reticence between the sexes as there is here in England. I believe that this leads to a far easier and far more enjoyable relationship for both men and women and indeed it took very little time for me to inform them of the purpose of my visit to this beautiful part of Europe.

'"You have come to photograph the waterfalls?" asked Giselle.

'"In a manner of speaking," I replied. "But my real purpose is to find beautiful women to pose for me by the waterfalls."

'"For poses plastiques?" giggled Giselle. I was shocked that this lovely girl knew of such affairs but before I could answer, Helga asked her friend just what were these things.

'"They are photographs of naked girls!" said Giselle who seemed quite at ease talking of such a delicate subject.

'"Heavens above! Is this true, Herr Sailor?" Helga enquired of me.

'"I cannot deny it," I replied boldly. "My work is known

50

throughout Europe and I photograph only the most beautiful ladies in the most refined classical poses." I suppose that this was not the truest answer I could have given but no matter, I could see that I had aroused their interest.

'Giselle looked at Helga and then turned to me and said: "Have you ever photographed two girls together?" "Only very occasionally," I told them as many women were shy about revealing their naked charms to each other.

'"We are not shy," said Giselle but I could see that Helga was somewhat more doubtful about a possible adventure.

'"I pay a very reasonable fee for the privilege of taking the photographs and all my models receive a set of free prints. In addition, I can promise faithfully that the photographic plates will be taken back home to England with me."

'I could see that the bait had almost been taken. The girls whispered between themselves and then Giselle said to me:' "We would have no objection to your taking our photographs, Herr Sailor, as to be honest with you, Helga and I both have boy friends and it is the local village carnival next month where it is a tradition that the girls give their special boys a gift. As neither Franz nor Ernst have seen us fully nude, I cannot think of a more exciting gift for them."

'"Neither can I!" I echoed happily and after telling them the fee I would pay [always a liberal amount for I only want the best for my clients] we arranged to meet in one hour's time on Neumann's Ridge, a piece of ground that stood out near the bottom of the falls so that behind the subject of the photograph a most clear and exciting view could be seen of the rushing flow of water.

'You may well imagine my joy at solving my problem so neatly. I knew that this session would yield perhaps the finest results of my career to date and I was not to be disappointed.

'I had my apparatus all set up when exactly on time these two brazen young ladies made their appearance. Fortunately, a few tourists knew about Neumann's Ridge but to forestall any interruption, I had scrawled out a warning sign about the dangers of a landslip which I placed by the clump of trees which hid the ridge from general view and we enjoyed the privacy needed for the escapade.

'"Well now," I said. "Who would like to be first?"

'As I expected, Giselle immediately volunteered. Helga stood behind me as her lovely friend went behind a tree to slip off her clothes.

'Now, in my profession, you see many, many naked women but gentlemen, I caught my breath when Giselle appeared nude from the foliage. She was a perfect specimen of celestial beauty. She brushed the blonde tresses from her face, and her superb young breasts, plump with large exquisitely formed pink aureoles and high tipped erect nipples, jounced up and down with movement. Her flat belly led down to long, long legs as sweetly shaped as any that the finest sculptor might have fashioned, the calves and ankles slender and the thighs fulsome. Between them nestled a mass of light blonde curls that frothed silkily all about her mount and I could see the shell-like lips of her cunney pouting out as I dived beneath the black cloth to adjust my camera and the fit of my trousers as my cock rose to salute this veritable goddess of desire.

'I positioned this beautiful creature in several most artistic poses but when I asked her to swing her hips to the right, she pretended not to understand me. So I went towards her and took hold of her luscious young body and moved her physically so that she stood in the manner desired.

'"Mein Gott," Giselle smiled. "You must have a big cock hiding in your trousers if that bulge is anything to judge by!"

'As you know, Sir Lionel, I do not always take too much notice when girls talk to me in polly fashion for sometimes the excitement of standing nude before a stranger unleashes the tongue, but the intention thereof can sometimes be misconstrued, as in the case of The Hon. Mrs Sarah F——.

'Anyhow, it was now my turn to pretend that I did not fully understand and I ignored her remark. But to my not unhappy surprise, the gorgeous Giselle slid her hand lasciviously between her legs, letting her fingers slide in between that exquisite muff of golden blonde hair. I could see her slipping her index finger into her now moist channel that opened up to her touch. She began dipping her fingers in and out, rubbing her thumb knuckle against her clitty in a series of movements that were driving her towards a self-induced ecstacy.

'I watched as one entranced when suddenly a rustling sound distracted me. It was caused by Helga frantically tearing off her clothes and in an instant she was locked in a naked embrace with her friend. They exchanged burning kisses as they sank to the ground and now Giselle was on the ground, spreading open her legs and giving me the most perfect view of her silky blonde muff and of the juicy cunney from which an erect little clitty now protruded.

'Helga began to kiss Giselle's breasts, licking all round in circles then sucking on the proud stiff nipples. As Giselle moaned in delight Helga got her hands on Giselle's bum cheeks and pulling her towards her, nuzzled her head in between her legs so that she could lick and tongue her friend to the utmost pleasure. I could hear Helga's wicked tongue slurping in and out of Giselle's juicy cunt and the tribade was sucking away with all her might as Giselle's body jerked up and down in excitement. 'Ohhhh!' screamed Giselle as the lovely girl achieved a glorious spend.

'"Have you come, dearest?" enquired Helga.

'"Oh, yes, that was marvellous, simply marvellous."

'"Now it is my turn!" muttered Helga, lifting her mouth from Giselle's dripping love box.

'Her lips were all shiny from Giselle's juices as she heaved herself up and stretched out on her back, her thighs spread wide, legs raised and began to massage her raven haired pussey, the left hand moving rapidly over her clitoris and two fingers of her right hand working in and out of her pussey as she panted and groaned, her hips bucking up and down, her fingers deep inside her.

"Aaaah! I am coming, I am coming!" she cried as she writhed as one demented on the ground. Then suddenly she shuddered to a climax and lay still, gasping for breath. She withdrew her fingers which were covered in her froth and I noticed the whiteness of her juices all along her sex lips.

'The sight was too much for any man to bear! In a trice I had ripped off my clothes and I threw myself on top of the sated girl, covering her sweet mouth with burning kisses. To my delight, these were returned with equal urgency and after running my hands across her large breasts, squeezing up the nipples to a grand stiffness, I trailed the fingers of my right hand down the smooth belly, probing in the wetness of her glistening black bush of pubic hair until I found the quivering quim and slid in my fingers which began to massage that hot little clitty.

'I was in no mood for preliminaries after the performance I had witnessed. I plunged my throbbing cock into her squelchy, tight cunt and Helga and I were locked together as I fucked her vigorously with long, sweeping strokes sliding my rock hard prick in and out of her sopping pussey and thrusting in hard until my balls banged against her bum.

'She whimpered gently and her inquisitive tongue went into my mouth as her body joined my rhythm and I could feel my penis going deeper and deeper inside her. I flexed it inside her and felt the vaginal muscles contract around it, milking the full length of my tool. I withdrew so only the red knob of my cock teased her cunt lips. With a moan, she threw her arms around me, pulling me down on top of her as I arched my hips forward, pulling every inch of my prick down into her very vitals. This frantic fucking could not last and all too soon my body exploded into action and I shot spasm after spasm of thick globs of spunk into her willing womb.

'I lay back exhausted but I was not to be allowed to rest! With a gay laugh, Giselle straddled her legs over me with her back to my face. Then she leaned forward and the shape of her superb young backside made me lick my lips in anticipation. I slid my hand between her legs and fingered her delicious cunney as her velvet lips kissed my cock which rose almost instantly as she began to jerk the shaft up and down in her hand, capping and uncapping the bulbous red knob which was still coated with love juice from Helga's cunt.

'Her moist tonguing brought my prick standing to full erection as she nibbled the so sensitive tip. Then she opened her mouth wide and began to suck in long, satisfying bursts, at the same time stroking my balls. I knew that I would be unable to hold back for long and I ejaculated my spunk in short sharp bursts which she swallowed greedily, continuing to suck my organ until it went limp.

'As we lay recovering our senses, Helga said: "I see you swallow all his sperm, darling. That is something I do not like to do."

'"Oh, I love sucking cocks!" cried Giselle. "It is almost as good as getting fucked. I know that some girls do not like to do so but I can suck a prick for hours although it never lasts so long! I am so proficient at sucking that the boy squirts off too quickly. I like a man like Mister Sailor who shoots a lot of spunk so at least I have something to swallow. This is most satisfying, swallowing the clean, fresh cream and of course there is no worry about a possible swollen belly afterwards!"

'"Well, I do enjoy taking a man in my mouth," said Helga seriously. "But I do not enjoy sucking him to the climax. I like him to spend inside my cunt. So I work on his cock very gently, caressing the tip with my lips and tonguing the uncovered knob. Then when I put the cock in my pussey it is as hard as iron!"

'"I think that most girls do enjoy sucking pricks," I commented. "But they need to be educated by tender and understanding partners to experience the great joys of the exercise. Similarly, there are men who have not entertained the idea of lapping the juices from a pussey. The idea of slipping a tongue between the sex lips of even the prettiest girl does not excite them."

'"How strange!" said Giselle. "Is this the case in England?"

'"I can only speak for England," I replied. "But I am sure that there is little difference between Englishmen and others."

'"I find the Germans have the thickest pricks," said Helga.

'"The Italians have the longest pegos," giggled Giselle.

'"But the French are experts in *l'arte de faire l'amour*," said Helga, a sentiment I felt duty bound as a patriot to challenge. Anyhow, all this smutty talk fired us up to new sensuous adventures.'

But alas, we were destined never to discover what Giselle actually did (though one may hazard a guess without too much difficulty!) because Mr Sailor's enthralling narrative was interrupted by Sir Lionel's old friend Anthony Osborn-Miller who came over to us waving a newspaper in a state of great agitation.

'Lionel, have you heard the terrible news? Lord Francis Douglas has been killed in a mountaineering accident!'

What a tragic coincidence that we should have been listening to an anecdote of passionate love in Switzerland, that country of mountains. For myself I have never understood the pleasures or uses of scaling precipitous rocks. And Lord Francis was a very decent man who had needlessly thrown away his gift of life for what? As we later found out, the tragic party, led by Edward Whymper, had set out to climb the Matterhorn, a feat that they successfully concluded but on the descent a rope broke and some of the party, I forget now how many lost their lives, falling from precipice to precipice onto a glacier some four thousand feet below. At least their deaths must have been mercifully quick but we were most upset to learn of these evil tidings.

Sir Lionel ordered brandies and we toasted the gallantry of the lost climbers. But as Mr Sailor commented, life must go on and he left us for an appointment with the Hon. Mrs C—— B—— who had requested his presence at an evening reception at which the Belgian Ambassador would be present and she required a photograph to be sent to the society papers.

I suggested that we visit a music hall to complete our evening's entertainment but my dear old friend had an even more pleasing idea. He was a member of the Riverhead Club, that most august and secret private house of pleasure in London to which only a select few men have been privileged to join. I accepted his invitation to join him with alacrity for I had never frequented any such place before and the thought of a splendid fuck began to make my young pego swell in my trousers.

We were given our hats and cloaks by old Crapps, the doorman, who thanked Sir Lionel profusely for the generous tip given for the menial task of calling a cab. In fact, his son, Bob, worked with his father on some weeknights and the boy

56

ran towards the nearest rank where the cabbies waited for custom.

'How is young Bob getting on at school?' enquired Sir Lionel.

'Not too bad, sir,' replied old Crapps. 'But his English teacher is always correcting his written work. His grammer is fair terrible, I'm afraid to say.'

'He must persevere!' said Sir Lionel warmly. 'Grammar teaches us how to make use of words. Anybody can, without teaching of rules and instructions, put masses of words upon paper. But to be able to choose the words which ought to be employed, and to place them where they should be – this is important. We must accept a knowledge of certain principles and these principles constitute what is called grammar.'

'Remember what I said Crapps, and tell young Bob to take heed,' said Sir Lionel as we climbed into our cab. Sir Lionel told the driver to take us to Monarch Row, a small thoroughfare which turned out to be north of Oxford Street just a short distance east of Regent Circus.

We were not kept waiting long at the door which was opened by a portly, dignified butler.

'Good evening, Sir Lionel,' he said, 'Dear me, it must be some three months since we enjoyed the pleasure of your company.'

'Thank you, Newman,' said Sir Lionel, taking out a coin from his purse. He always carried his cash in a purse, never having approved of the habit of carrying it loosely in the pockets as so many do nowadays. 'This is Mr Scott, who is my guest this evening. All his expenses are to be put on my account. May I leave that important business in your capable hands?'

'Certainly, Sir Lionel,' replied Newman. 'Is there anyone in particular you have in mind for Mr Scott? I expect you will wish to see Miss Lizzie who has only just come in and I know is free at the moment.

'Excellent!' cried Sir Lionel, 'and I think I will leave it to your good judgement as to who young Andrew should squire tonight. No expense to be spared now.'

'Then I would recommend Miss Cecily, a friend of Miss

Lizzie's who is new to this establishment. She is only nineteen and is ravishingly beautiful.'

'My goodness, I am tempted to have her myself but I will defer to my friend,' laughed Sir Lionel, 'We will retire to the drawing room, Newman. Ask the girls to meet us there and bring a magnum of champagne.'

'The house wine, sir?'

'No, no, I feel like splashing out tonight. Let's have the Veuve Clicquot '54 if there is any left. I know that old General Bell is determined to finish every bottle himself!'

Newman smiled and we entered a lushly furnished drawing room. It was an extremely large room as the dividing wall between the front and back rooms had been knocked away. In fact there were only three gentlemen, all in evening dress (as we were), conversing with three extremely attractive girls. They ignored us and Sir Lionel did not offer any greeting.

'They are a little stand-offish!' I whispered as we sat down.

'No, no, no, Andrew, it is a cardinal rule of the establishment. When entering the club you must never greet a member as many gentlemen here hardly wish their presence to be advertised in any way.'

As Newman came in with our champagne the other gentlemen got up and went out, as I later found out, to meet the ladies of their choice in the upstairs bedrooms. And as Sir Lionel grasped the neck of the bottle, Newman too left the room only for the door to open almost immediately afterwards for two very pretty young girls who swept in and greeted Sir Lionel with the warmest effusiveness.

Sir Lionel acted as master of ceremonies as he was well acquainted with one of the girls, Lizzie, a wild flame-haired wench of no more than twenty years old, quite petite with large breasts and long tresses of auburn hair, blue eyes and a saucy little snip of a nose and luscious red lips. Her friend, Cecily, was as voluptuous as Newman had hinted, a finely developed blonde girl with deep blue eyes, pouting lips and a full heaving bosom which swelled like perfect volcanos of smothered desire under the loose flowing gown of rich dark cashmere.

58

We drank a bumper of champagne and then Cecily said: 'Andrew, we have not as much time as we would wish to enjoy ourselves with you. Let us consume the rest of this delicious wine in the *salle privée*.' I readily agreed and we made our excuses to Lizzie and Sir Lionel who were engaged in conversation.

Cecily led me through to the far end of the room and, taking out a key from a pocket of her dress, opened a stout door which led into a smaller room, richly furnished and artistically draped with magnificent black and gold curtains and in the middle of which was, as I had guessed, made of silk and Cecily gently pushed me down so that I sat down on the side of the bed. She sat down next to me and pertly placed her hand on my knee.

'I do hope that you have not indulged yourself with another lady today,' she giggled, 'or indeed been guilty of playing yourself as Sir Lionel says that you have a mighty weapon and I want to receive the full benefit in my love-nest.' And before I could even draw breath to assure her that I was innocent on both counts, the cheeky young miss opened my trousers with her own delicate hands and pulled out my rapidly rising tool. She drew back the foreskin and said: 'Ah! Yes, I can see that you have been good. If the prepuce is all red then I know you have recently been in some kind of action. But this jewel is pale and I see no traces of recent excitement.'

Her directness acted as a spur and we threw off our clothes in an ecstacy of abandonment. Our lips met in a passionate kiss that shook us both by its probing, violent tonguing as we explored each other's mouths.

Then suddenly she wrenched her lips away and pulling my torso down onto the bed, she climbed up on her knees on the silken sheet, and with a quick smile suddenly her head was down between my legs and her hands were grasped around the root of my prick. She kissed the tip of my cock and then licked all around the knob, wetting it with her tongue. She brought her mouth down and her tongue ran along the length and width of it, salaciously sucking my throbbing cock, sending me into raptures of delight. She sucked away with relish, moving her pretty head in a way that the marvellous sensations ran throughout the whole length of my prick. At the same time she brought her hand gently beneath my balls, gently grazing the skin with her fingernails. Her movements were so exciting that all too soon I felt that searing wave of exquisite pleasure building up inside me and I knew that all too soon I would spend. I quivered as the girl's warm, wet lips continued to encircle my swollen penis which jerked uncontrollably as the fire flared in my loins and the white jism spurted out into her receptive mouth. She continued to suck and gobble my cock, greedily swallowing every last drop of sperm until my trusty tool was milked dry.

My blood was up and raising her head, I kissed the darling girl, sinking my tongue inside her mouth and my hand began to stroke her thigh as she in turn grasped my cock and rubbed it vigorously up and down until it was smartly erect, twitching with delight at her sensual touch. My hand stroked through her thick pubic bush as she pressed her lips even more firmy against mine, soaking up the exciting sensations that thrilled her as our melting kisses stimulated us to further exertions.

My fingers probed downwards and caressed the lips of her cunney and her body began to shake with excitement as my thumb found her clitty and I began rubbing it with a steadily increasing rhythm that had her clinging to me as tightly as she could. Now it was my turn to break off our kiss as I moved my head down to her naked breasts, tracing little circles with the tip of my tongue around the stiffening nipples.

She moaned with pleasure as she lay down on the bed, opening her legs wide as my hand ran over the soft wetness of her open crack. I raised myself above her and positioning my cock with my hand, guided the knob in between the inviting folds of her welcoming cunt. Our bodies tumbled together as I pounded down upon her, pushing in my cock until my balls banged against her bottom as she lifted her rear up to receive the full length of my prick. She moved excitedly under me as my prick jerked inside her, exploring every minute part of her tight little love box. I could see by her wriggles of delight how much she was enjoying this glorious fuck and she panted:

'Andrew, oh, my dearest, how nice, how lovely, oh, how you do make me spend, I can feel my juices gushing from me, now, my darling, do inject me with your cream!' I prolonged the pleasure for as long as possible, slowing down my thrusts and often stopping to feel the delicious throbbings of cock and cunney in their perfect conjunction but nature was not to be denied and we swam all too soon in a mutual emission, both of us being so overcome by our feelings that we almost swooned in our ecstacy.

Ah, what an engagement we had, though as Cecily had warned, time was short, but I shall never forget it, short as the fuck was, for it was one of the most enjoyable I can remember.

We dressed and went back into the members' lounge where Sir Lionel and Lizzie were waiting for us. My friend had taken Lizzie up to her room for a quick erotic frolic. I learned later that our stay at this most exclusive house had cost more than twelve pounds including the gratuities to the girls and to Newman to whom I also gave ten shillings for his excellent recommendation of Cecily. We hailed a passing cab and within ten minutes had reached St John's Wood: Collins, the butler, let us in and Sir Lionel gave him instructions to lock up and not to wake us until eight o'clock the next morning.

The next day Sir Lionel had arranged to take Lady Dorothy O—— to luncheon after attending to some matters of business in the morning. My diary showed no engagements so I resolved to see the lower classes disport themselves at the Crystal Palace where the Most Ancient Order of Foresters were holding an 'outing'.

I journeyed by train, a mode of transport I much favour, although as expected, the carriages were quite full. In spite of the increased fares, the railway was more extensively patronised than the roads and the trains were literally thronged with people. At the intermediate stations, it was impossible for would-be passengers to board my carriage. I arrived after consuming a light lunch in town and the first of the bands were already marching in the great procession. After a while I wandered around the grounds and stood by

61

the archery butts and watched some skilful attempts to win the main prize offered of twenty pounds. Unfortunately the weather turned unpleasant and I felt extremely sorry for the poor people who had looked forward so much to their summer 'treat' only for the rain to dampen their spirits. However, many refused to let the rain worry them too much, for after all they had each paid a shilling to enter the fête and most were determined to have as much as they could for their hard-earned money.

I decided to make my way to the dancing platforms where there was a great crowd and the band played lustily as couples went in and shuffled through the throng. My eye was taken by a truly stunning girl of not more than eighteen years old dressed in a fetching blue dress. She had very long dark silky hair that cascaded down over her shoulders. She was tall, just under my height (I am five feet ten and half inches tall), and possessed of a vivacious beauty, her chin being most charmingly dimpled, her lips, full and pouting, slightly open, gave just a glimpse of two rows of ivory, which appeared set in the deep, rosy flesh of her small and elegant mouth.

She was giggling with two other girls and I overheard her saying how much she would like to dance but that there were no men here that she knew who could take her round the floor. I wondered whether she had seen me stare at her and whether her words were meant for my ears. I have often wondered what happens when people believe they are being overheard. How much of what they say is truly sincere and how much is shaded by the knowledge that someone who they may or may not know is listening...

I decided to follow the maximum drummed into me at Nottsgrove by Dr White: 'You should always ask for what you want,' he would boom out to the sixth formers in discussion periods, 'and you should always ask politely. If you see a female to whom you would like to speak and there is no-one to effect an introduction, do not be bashful. Introduce yourself and gauge the reaction. If she does not wish to speak to you, then of course you must gracefully retire. But you may well find that she too would like to meet a new friend. Later, if you desire to kiss her, you must first ask permission. If you strike gold you may then ask her if she would like to take matters a stage further. Kindness and consideration will win you more cunney than rough and ill-mannered boorishness.'

In for a penny, in for a pound, I thought as I approached the sweet girl and tipping my hat, I said to her: 'Excuse me, I know we have not been formally introduced but it would give me great pleasure –'

'I'm sure it would!' laughed one of her companions, who was of a vulgar disposition.

'– to dance with you,' I said, ignoring the coarse remark.

'Well, thank you, sir. I accept your kind invitation,' she said demurely, though her dark eyes twinkled with joy. I introduced myself and she told me that her name was Rose Merkin and she worked as a governess to the young son and daughter of a Jewish family who lived in Stamford Hill in North London. Her companions were housemaids in the same establishment and I asked Rose if she was happy in her work.

'Oh yes, Mr and Mrs Greenberg are very kind and they love music. I give the girls piano lessons and I am paid extra for this service. I need the money as my papa died three years ago and though we come from a good family in Gloucestershire, my poor mother has very little as poor papa speculated unwisely in Hudson's railway stock.'

'It must be awful giving lessons to young girls thumping out scales with their thick fingers!'

'No, no. I quite enjoy it. I count myself fortunate to have found such a pleasant situation. The maids are not so happy as the family are observant in the practice of their religion which really makes for quite a lot of work for them.'

'Oh, yes, there were four Jewish fellows in my school and though not so strictly religious, they would not eat bacon or pork,' I said, clutching her waist firmly to glide her round the crowded dance floor.

'Where did you go to school, Andrew?' asked my pretty new friend.

'Nottsgrove Academy in Hertfordshire,' I answered.

'Goodness gracious, what a coincidence. My cousin Pelham has just left there. Did you know him?'

'Pelham McKenzie? But of course, he was one of my closest companions. He has joined the army, I believe?'

'Yes, that's right. The Guards, I believe. What a happy chance it is that brings us together. I am a great believer in fate, Andrew, aren't you?'

'It certainly seems fated that we should meet at the fête,' I said and we both burst out laughing at my unintended pun.

By now the two maids had found partners and I offered to take Rose out to dinner. Dame Fortune again smiled upon me as the Greenberg family were away for a few days and Rose could return at any time to the house at which only an old cook-housekeeper was in residence.

We took a train back to London and decided to dine at Sir Lionel's. In fact, my friend was not at home and had left a note saying that family matters had called him to Oxford where he would stay the night.

However, Mrs Stewart laid out a fine cold collation for us and I knew that my dear friend would hardly begrudge a bottle of claret from his ample cellar. Most of his wine came from a Mr Merton in nearby Eton Avenue who I can heartily recommend as a supplier though I have a fancy that he has since moved to Folkestone.

Be that as it may, the wine certainly fired our young limbs and after I had dismissed the servants I led Rose to the sofa and drew her to my side. I sat down with her and clasping her in my arms, covered her lips with a burning kiss. This caused her to blush and struggle somewhat to release herself from my embrace. But then she looked into my eyes and leaned forward saying: 'Andrew, you are a dear, sweet boy!' To my delight she now responded passionately as I imprinted further kisses upon her pouting lips which she opened to give my tongue free rein inside her mouth. I then slipped one hand into her bosom, feeling and moulding her firm round breasts.

I grew bolder and slipped a hand under her dress and raised her clothes to her knees. Squeezing and playing with her legs, I slid my hand further and further upwards till my palm rested along her mound. I pulled her tiny hand down onto the bulge that threatened to cause damage to the material of my trousers and she grasped my straining cock with relish. I undressed her carefully and as each article of clothing was discarded I exclaimed softly: 'How beautiful you are, Rose!' or 'Your breasts are delightful, I cannot wait to suck upon your titties,' and other words of fond endearment.

I quickly divested myself of all my garments and Rose and I stood naked in each others' arms. I gloried in her young nubile body with her large, full breasts crowned with little upright nipples and her smooth slim waist and flaring full hips which she moved sensuously as she walked towards the sofa and motioned me to sit down. I obeyed and she lay across me, her soft hand resting on my chest.

Slowly she ran her fingers across my chest, tweaking nipples and then gently, with the tenderness of a butterfly, Rose ran her tongue down my body. I writhed as she reached my navel and her silky dark hair brushed against my staunchly erect cock which was aching for attention. She smoothed her cheek against the shaft and then buried her head in my crotch. She caressed my testicles with her moist tongue and I opened my legs wider so that she could explore the whole deliciously sensitive area. Her soft hands ran over my stomach and then moved down to take my cock in both hands. She gently frigged me as she wet her tongue against her lips and then took the uncapped knob full in her mouth, sucking with gusto as my cock throbbed with pleasure at her ministrations.

But sensing that I would spend too soon, she stopped sucking and lightly placing a kiss on my knob, dived down to place a light series of little kisses up and down the stem, encompassing my hairy balls, running beyond to the oft-neglected area between prick and arse. She followed this up with sharp little licks on my swollen cock which was agonising to be placed in her cunt. But that was to happen a little later for now Rose thrust my trusty tool in and out of her mouth in a quickening rhythm, deep into her throat and out again with her pink tongue lapping the tip at the end of each stroke and soaking up the drops of thick liquid beginning to form near the 'eye' of my knob. I tried to prolong the pleasure but her expert sucking was too powerful for me to prevent the sperm boiling up inside my balls and I pumped a thick creamy emission into her mouth which she happily swallowed sucking every last drop of juice from my now semi-limp prick.

We were quite tired after the exhaustions of the day and I told Rose that she could stay over until the morning. She happily agreed to this suggestion as she would not be missed at her place of employment since the housekeeper knew that Rose had a second cousin living in Clerkenwell with whom she sometimes stayed the night on the infrequent occasions when she had two days or more away from her position.

So soon we were curled up snugly in my bed and though pleasantly drowsy, neither of us were ready for slumber yet were not quite ready for another bout of fucking so we talked of our amorous experiences and it turned out that young Pelham had been Rose's first lover.

She told me: 'I was only seventeen at the time I crossed the Rubicon though to be quite candid I was not totally innocent of the minor joys of love. I had let previous boy friends run their hands over my bare titties and I had been fired to rub a cock or two though I had never let any young sport unbutton his trousers. I would only feel the bulge through the cloth of the boy's trousers and indeed I had never seen a naked prick until that fateful day at Aunt Mary's house when I lost my maidenhead to the mighty tool of my cousin Pelham.

'What happened then was not entirely dissimilar to our experiences today – a serendipity of events that led inexorably to Pelham and I enjoying a passionate bout of fucking. His father, General McKenzie, was away on some Army manoeuvres on Salisbury Plain and Aunt Mary, my mother's sister, had planned to invite some family friends to a musical evening.

'However, as fate would have it, Aunt's best friend, one Mrs Cheadle, was stricken by an attack of laryngitis so the ladies circle decided to spend the evening at her house so she would be spared going out in the chill air of the evening.

'This meant that Pelham and I would spend the evening together at McKenzie Lodge with only the deaf old butler,

Wilshaw, for company. The other servants had been given permission to hold a party in the servants' hall and both Pelham and I knew that there was really no possibility of being disturbed.

'In no time at all we were (not for the first time) clasped in each other's arms on the sofa. I was somewhat nervous yet so excited that I made not even a show of resistance when Pelham began to feel my breasts. My dress opened down the front and in no time at all, the dear boy had my naked breasts in his hands and was rubbing my nipples up to little twin peaks of hardness. Nothing loath I began to fondle the bulge that threatened to tear the soft cloth of his trousers. Emboldened by my wanton actions, my bold cousin completely stripped me of my clothes until I was quite nude. "Ah, Rose, what a marvellous body you have," he exclaimed. "And it will be my privilege to make you a real woman!"

'I knew that the Nottsgrovian code of ethics would allow me to keep my virginity if I so desired even at this eventful stage (though I would have rubbed Pelham's prick to emission to enable the dear boy to relieve his feelings) – and the thought did indeed flash through my brain. But I decided to break through the barrier and see how much more pleasure it was to have a fine stiff cock in my cunt instead of the wooden dildo we girls used at Miss Coote's College for Young Laides in Cheltenham where I completed my formal education.

'I unbuttoned Pelham's trousers and out sprang his magnificent cock! It was diamond hard and yet when I stroked the shaft, gently rubbing up and down to cap and uncap the fiery red-headed knob, the skin possessed a quality of warm smoothness which was bliss to my touch.

'Now matters began to take their natural turn as Pelham slipped out of his clothes till he too was naked. Then, laying me on my back on the thick white ornamental rug that was set in front of the fire with two cushions placed as pillows behind my head and behind my bum for comfort, my lovely boy parted my legs and began to kiss my very wet pussey. He moved round so that his head was over my stomach and his huge, throbbing cock was very near to my mouth. I could not resist sucking his enormous prick and I gobbled the ruby head with relish and my hand jerked his foreskin up and down the shaft of his gorgeous cock.

'Meanwhile, Pelham's face was buried in my bushy mound as he rapturously licked the spendings of my tight little cunney and then, oh my, his tongue found my clitty and I twisted my legs round his head as Pelham licked and sucked furiously at the love juice that was fairly dripping down the inside of my thighs. We knew that the time had come for the *coup de grace* and Pelham wriggled free and the moment I had waited for had finally arrived!

'He leaned over me and I grasped the monster cock as I felt the knob nudge against my pussey lips. I was so juicy that I had little need to guide him so that he could enter me easily. He slipped his cock into me and I cried with joy for this what I had dreamed of for so long, the amazing feel of Pelham's prick deep, deep inside my cunt. Gently, his cock began to move in and out in slow rhythmic thrusts and oh, the delight as I felt his prick push in and withdraw, push in and withdraw and how exciting was the sound of the slurp as our juices eased the passage of his cock when suddenly Pelham arched his hips and bang! I felt his tool crash against my hymen and after a moment of agonising pain a gush of pleasure swept all over me. As I shuddered with voluptuous ardour, Pelham spurted out jets of spunk into my ensanguined cunt yet his cock remained diamond hard in my still tight sheath of love which was now so well lubricated that we enjoyed another fierce bout of ecstatic fucking. All pain was now forgotten as we revelled in the delights afforded by our bodies.

'I was hungry for more of that delicious cock even after we had spent three or four times in our delirium of love-making. But my darling Pelham begged me to be moderate and not injure my cunt by excessive fucking.'

This sensual story had worked its effect upon me and my cock was now standing stiffly erect as I pulled Rose's hand round my shaft.

'My goodness, I think you must want to fuck even more

than I!' she murmured as she lay back to receive me.

She moved against me, anxious to please, and quick and eager to return my caresses. We exchanged fiery, passionate kisses and I ran my hand along the soft wetness of her open crack. Her nipples were erect as my cock that stood out proudly and Rose manoeuvred until her full, pouting mouth covered my cock, sucking furiously until I gently moved her head away so that I could climax in her squelchy quim. I plunged my aching prick in her tight yet juicy cavern and I fucked her with long, sweeping strokes as my long, stiff cock slid in and out of her sopping cunney.

I was too tired to fuck for too long so when I felt the creamy jism boiling up inside me, I made no attempt to stem the speed of the thrusts of my throbbing prick. I let out a little gasp of warning and then I plunged my tool as far as it would go inside her willing cunt and my balls banged against her bum cheeks as the delicious girl arched her back to receive the squirts of cum that jetted out of my jerking cock. To my delight, Rose closed her eyes and stretched out her limbs in a shudder, the cunney muscles relaxing so that I knew she had experienced the greatest of pleasures that man is capable of giving. I was so pleased that she could spend without difficulty when we fucked. Some women never achieve the ultimate joy during intercourse, needing the extra stimulation of a hand or mouth on the clitty. Some take a long time and some can only orgasm infrequently but Rose was a highly sexed girl who could bring herself off simply by playing with herself.

So-called 'self-abuse' is a subject, if you, dear reader, will allow me to digress, about which I have strong views. Many English physicians hold that tossing-off produces the most dreadful mental and physical ailments. Some authorities, of whom a good representative would be Sir Lionel's friend from Islington, the singularly endowed Dr Roy Stevenson, maintain the practise can induce deafness. But I hold to the view of Professor Wankel of Vienna who ridicules this view. After all, argues the Professor, all boys play with themselves yet this has no bearing upon who reaches a ripe old age. What

69

harm can there be in cupping the hand to mimic the vagina and rub the clenched fist up and down the erect penis until ejaculation? Certainly, no-one can catch an unwanted infection by tossing-off as many ladies as well as gentlemen can testify.

For the fair sex, finger-fucking can be jolly but a better sport is to play with a godemiche. The best dildoes are shaped like cocks and Lady P—— possesses one that is basically a hollow cylinder, piston shaped that may be filled with a warm solution so that at the desired time the imitation cock can ejaculate and fulfil the woman's desire. Many girls, frightened of taking the risk of a swollen belly, will only suck their boys' pricks and not allow them to place cocks in their cunts. But there can be no harm in sucking cunney which is an art sadly neglected in this country although the French and other Continentals have no such qualms.

Most women love the sensation of a man licking and sucking their cunneys with tongue and lips. Many girls can be worked up to a frenzy by a cunning tongue darting around the cunt, nibbling the stiff little clitty which usually brings on the gush of juices as the spending is achieved.

If anyone wishes to read Professor Wankel's little book on this subject, it may be bought from John Hotten's bookshop in Piccadilly. Of course, it is not on general sale but mention of my name will suffice for a copy of the English language edition to be purchased discreetly for the sum of eight shillings and sixpence.

Forgive the digression, friendly reader, but I believe this to be a matter of some importance. Many young men and women are made ill not by their natural instincts of sexual exploration but by the bigoted attitude of certain medical buffoons who perhaps take a perverse pride in the misery caused by their puritanical pronouncements.

Let us return to my tale... Rose and I slept soundly and I was the first to wake up. She was still asleep as I quietly lifted the sheet to expose all her naked charms for the night was warm and we had both slept quite nude.

My eyes drank in the beauty of her large, firm bubbies and

I could not resist rubbing one of the little nipples to a hardness. She sighed as I did so and moved onto her back and I slid my hand along her thigh till my fingers rested in the thick moss of dark hair that overhung the entrance of her cunney. And what a cunney this was, a most ravishing affair almost beyond all description. The bushy Mount of Venus swelled up into a hillock of firm flesh, surmounted and covered with rich, mossy almost coal-black hair, straight and fine as silk. The lips were most luscious, fat, pouting beauties and on opening them, one could feel an extremely large clitoris though the orifice was narrow allowing for a most superb bout of fucking. In all my many years of experience in *l'arte de faire l'amour*, I do not think I have ever come across a notch that was lasciviously tight yet so marvellously elastic that even the most passionate thrusts could be made without damage to the thickest prick.

The spark had been kindled, the fire burned and waking up my beautiful Rose, I planted innumerable kisses on her lips, almost sucking the breath from her. She threw her arms around my neck and repaid with interest the kisses I had just given. With what fire and enthusiasm did she meet and receive the piercing thrusts of my huge hard cock! I licked and sucked her high-tipped erect nipples as I drove again and again into the furthest recesses of her willing pussey.

I began to jerk rapidly in short, convulsive movements as I exclaimed: 'Rose, my dear, I'm going to spend!'

'I'm spending too, my dearest! Ah, what bliss! Oh, heavens, quicker, quicker, Andrew! Oh my, oh my, I'm spending! I'm spending! Keep fucking me, come on now, let me feel your cream spurt into my cunt!'

'Here it is, Rose, my sweet darling!' I panted as her wriggling and the delicious contractions of her cunney brought down from me a copious emission of frothy sperm which jetted into her cunt.

We spent the morning in an orgy of fucking but then Rose had to leave for Stamford Hill and I noted her address for I very much wanted to see her again.

3

Now what was I to do for the rest of the day? The sun was shining and there was not a cloud in the sky so I decided to take myself off to Brighton for the day. I partook of a delicious luncheon at the railway terminus and by half past two o'clock I was strolling down the seafront promenade. Reader, if I were a racing man, I would certainly not have wagered that so soon after meeting dear Rose, I would be as fortunate as to find another darling girl to share my bed. But when Dame Fortune bestows her bounty, all goes well and sure enough, near Bumstead's Famous Tea Rooms, I chanced on an old friend of my brother, Algy Horrocks who had in tow not one but two beautiful young fillies.

They had obviously consumed a substantial amount of drink and alas Algy was indeed known for his fondness for the bottle. I greeted him and to my embarrassment he called back loudly: 'Why, it's young Andrew Scott! Andrew, what are you doing here? I heard you were going to be a lawyer. Or was it a liar. Oh, it's all the same I suppose. The best lawyers are liars as my dear Papa told me many years ago!'

The girls laughed merrily as he burst out singing: 'She's pert and slim and takes a swim down by the harbour wall. She's only a cobbler's daughter but she gives the boys her awl.'

'Algy, you are a clown!' shrieked the tall blonde girl whose waist was adorned with Algy's right arm.

'What a lad you are,' chimed in her dark-haired companion.

'Introduce us to your friend,' said the blonde girl.

'Certainly, my dears. Andrew, I have the honour of

presenting Grace and Mary, the jolliest girls in the whole of Sussex!'

I gave a little bow and shook hands with the two girls. Mary was the tall blonde girl and I must say that my trusty truncheon wriggled a little as I pressed her long fingers.

I readily accepted Algy's suggestion that I joined the party and we went back together to his suite of rooms he had rented at the Hotel Splendide, a private and discreet establishment run by Miss Crapps, the sister of the doorman at Sir Lionel T——'s London club.

After enjoying a bottle of champagne in the lounge, Algy led the way to his rooms and then promptly fell asleep on the sofa!

'Poor old Algy! He looks to be flat out. Shall we stay and wait until he wakes up or shall we leave him?' asked Grace.

I was not too sure as to what I should reply but was dumbfounded when Mary piped up: 'It is now getting just a little chilly with the sea breeze blowing somewhat strongly. Grace, perhaps you would like to look after dearest Algy for a time whilst Andrew and I enjoy a little fuck in the bedroom.'

'What a splendid idea. I am sure that Andrew has a large juicy cock. I quite envy you, Mary. Perhaps when you have finished you would not mind if I sucked it for a while.'

'I have no objection whatsoever although it is Andrew's cock, after all and you must obtain his permission to suck it.'

I hoarsely stammered out my appreciation of their thoughtfulness as to be sure I have always enjoyed having my prick sucked.

'Let us see the size of your cock,' said Grace, unbuttoning my trousers and pulling down my underpants. My cock was rising slowly as Mary grabbed the shaft and began to vigorously rub it to full erection as it stood stiffly waving under her ministrations like a flagpole in the wind.

Grace looked critically as Mary pulled back my foreskin exposing the swollen red knob.

'He does have a lovely cock,' said Mary.

'Yes, but I think Algy's a little bit bigger.'

'Grace, I have told you before that size is relatively

unimportant. It is the attitude of a man that should be the prime consideration. My friend Sir Edmund has a nine and a half inch cock but I far prefer Charlie K——'s instrument even though it only measures four and three quarter inches.

'Edmund had the biggest prick I have ever seen but he was a terrible lover. His overgrown cock mangled my pretty little pussey whilst Charlie's little tool was far better accommodated in my love box.

'I must admit that before he entered me I thought that fucking Charlie would be a waste of time but that was before he entered me. After Charlie had slipped in that miniature weapon I was in heaven. That little cock was like a paintbrush in the hand of a talented artist. It wriggled beautifully in my cunney and I don't think I have ever come so quickly! No, my sweetest Grace, size is not so important as quality,' she said, happily squeezing my balls.

'I still like a big thick prick,' demurred Grace.

'Oh, yes. I have nothing against thick pricks. But I do assure you that though a larger cock gives a boy confidence, it is the manner of usage that makes the difference between an enjoyable fuck and a truly magnificent one!'

'Maybe you are right, my dear Mary. Anyhow, Andrew's cock is a fine specimen so jolly good luck to you both!' said Grace gaily.

With that, Mary took hold of my rock-hard prick, gave it a couple of good rubs and then grabbed hold of it as she led the way into the small bedroom. After she had closed the door, we threw off our clothes and my strong arms entwined the saucy miss.

Our mouths met and putting my tongue in her mouth, I explored the top half between teeth and lips with a long probing kiss. My hands examined her hard little nipples and then quickly descended below over her flat belly to reach her sopping dark muff and her lower lips which were already soaking wet with anticipatory juices. Her hands too were busy, circling round my cock which already had a blob of sticky fluid at the end of the knob. She gave a last wiggle of her tongue inside my mouth and then dropping to her knees, jammed down my foreskin with her hands and began to suck greedily on my bursting prick. She clasped my bum cheeks in her hands as she sucked furiously on the throbbing pole as I jerked my hips backwards and forwards, thrusting every inch of my prick into her willing mouth. Mary was certainly an expert at sucking cock as she managed to take in the whole of my shaft without gagging until my hairy balls dangled in front of her straining lips.

My climax was soon to arrive and when I felt the rush of liquid fire boil up to ejaculation I pumped my thick jets of spunk down into her eager throat and she swallowed my creamy emission with much relish as I pulled her head closer to me as my cock, milked dry by her exquisite sucking, began to lose its stiffness.

We clambered onto the bed and laid down to rest. I thanked Mary for the marvellous sucking-off but she waved away my praise.

'Andrew, I do love sucking pricks. Indeed, I can suck for hours but unfortunately none of the men can hold back for more than five minutes. I do so enjoy caressing the uncapped tip with my lips and sucking the lubricant out. I like the taste too and I can spread it around the knob with my tongue. And when the boy begins to squirt out his spunk, oh it is so exciting as it shoots into my mouth! I cannot think of anything that tastes so fine and clean. Alternatively, I stop before ejaculation so that the boy's cock is as hard and as ready as possible before I slip it into my cunt.'

She gave me an encouraging kiss and spreading her legs open to give me a marvellous view of her curly haired bush and pouting cunney lips that protruded through the thick hair. My prick began to stiffen as she raised herself up and bent over in front of me, the shapely tender cheeks of her lovely young bum high in the air as those wicked lips again kissed my knob. She ran her pink little tongue up and down the now erect shaft and she varied this by nibbling the so-sensitive tip.

My prick was now back at its full length again and she stopped licking and lay back with her legs spread open. Now I knelt in front of Mary as I pushed her legs even further apart, trailing my hand through her cunney hair until I found her quivering clitty and I slid my fingers round it as she gasped with pure delight. My fingers massaged that hot little clitty until it was aching for my fiery red-headed cock and then I plunged my prick into her sopping cunt and began a rhythm in a frenzy of passion. Ah, her sopping little cunney was like a violin and my prick was like a bow and every stroke raised the most ravishing melody on the senses that could be imagined! This time the build-up to our mutual spending was slower as we abandoned ourselves totally, our matted hairy triangles both soaking with each other's juices as my prick slid in and out, in and out of those folds of sensuous glory. Our surging cries of joy echoed around the room as we travelled down the road to ecstasy. Then I started to tremble and began shaking like a leaf from head to toe until a huge climax flooded through my body sending thick wads of creamy jism crashing into her as she now screamed with delight as she spent just as the hot, frothy spunk drenched her womb.

We lay panting with exhaustion until she leaned down to pick up her handbag which she brought up onto the bed and began to look for something inside it.

'Do you smoke after intercourse?' she asked.

'I don't know as I have never looked!' I answered facetiously and she roared with laughter at my witty reply.

I grasped her hands and said: 'I do not care to smoke as I believe the habit to be injurious to health. Certainly, in the great cities we have enough industrial smoke and terrible fogs to choke up our lungs and I am sure that cigars and cigarettes only add to the burden carried by our poor lungs.'

'You are probably right but I do find it quite relaxing after a good bout of fucking. Perhaps a glass of wine would be better for me.'

'I quite agree with you there,' I said, taking her bag and putting it down again on the carpet. 'Like many men, and indeed women, I dislike the smell which clings to your hair and makes your breath foul.'

'Yes, I should forgo this habit. Grace has told me to stop

smoking as she is even more meticulous than I about keeping hair clean and she says that people who smoke have a terrible smell that clings to their bodies and clothes. My darling, order us a bottle of wine and I promise I shan't smoke. Make it champagne and I'll even throw away the silver case of cigarettes I have in my handbag!'

I readily agreed but persuaded her that we should first drink the bottle of claret that rested on Algy's dressing-table along with two glasses and a parcel wrapped in brown wrapping-paper. I padded over, still quite nude, to the table, opened the wine and poured out two glasses of the fine wine, a '53 Bollinger, and brought them over to the bed. I looked again at the parcel and Mary saw that my attention had been drawn to it.

'Do you want to know what is in the parcel? It's a book from Hotten's shop in Piccadilly,' she told me.

I knew that old Algy would not mind my opening the package so I went back for the package and opened it up. To my surprise I saw that it was an English translation of Professor Wankel's book on sexual intercourse and I asked Mary if she would mind if I looked through it.

'Not at all so long as I can read it with you. Or better still, read it aloud whilst I enjoy this excellent wine,' said the agreeable girl, giving my backside a friendly little slap.

I smiled and opened the book at random and the chosen page turned out to be a treatise on positions during sexual intercourse. I cleared my throat and began to read: '"The Indian book of love, the *Kama Sutra*, lists twenty major sexual positions, though Dr A. Kleiman insists that there are really only six with all others being variants.

The most common is for the man to lay on top of the prone woman with her legs either spread wide to accommodate his body. This position is made more exciting if the woman twines her legs around the man's waist as he is then able to thrust deeper into her vagina with increased sensation for both as the entire length of his penis is stimulated. This position can be even more enjoyable if the woman has

77

learned the technique of tightening her vaginal mucles, enabling her to clasp the entire length of the penis. This also has a good mental effect, giving additional 'closeness' via the leg-embrace setting it aside from the straight-forward position in which the woman simply lies prone, her legs apart and straight out and where there is therefore only a minimum of body contact.

A second position is that of rear entry with the woman on her hands and knees, her legs spread as the man enters from the rear. This can be made more pleasurable if the woman bends forward, throwing up her buttocks as high as possible. This method is frowned upon by some as being too 'animal' though anatomically it is a most natural position for sexual contact. The woman can support a man's weight more easily since she is on her hands and knees with her back and thigh muscles (the strongest in the body) working. Both of the man's hands are free to fondle and stimulate the woman's breasts, legs and buttocks and indeed can thrust his penis inside the vagina whilst at the same time fondling the clitoris to give his partner additional pleasure.

The third position is for the man to be prone and the woman on top facing him. This position is disliked by some men who feel their masculinity threatened by feminine 'domination' but others believe the position is comfortable and that it allows their women to 'serve' them.

'I see no objection to that position, Andrew,' interrupted Mary, 'I am sure that many boys prefer their girls to do the work whilst they hardly have to move a muscle.'

'I like that position occasionally,' I said.

'Yes, it's fun. There you are, Lord Muck with a beautiful girl on top of you with your cock deep inside her. She slowly moves up and down, rotating her hips, her breasts jiggling temptingly, exciting you even more than you already are. You can fondle them – go on Andrew, squeeze my titties – and then you begin to enter the spirit of the joust and begin thrusting upwards to meet her urgency. She moans, picks up the pace, bouncing up and down. Then still moving, she lowers herself, pressing her taut-nippled bubbies against your chest... aaah, that's better,' she crooned softly as she clambered up on top of me and placed my now erect prick between her cunney lips.

I'm afraid I never found out just what were the other positions favoured by Professor Wankel as we dissolved into a splendid mutual fucking session that made the bedsprings squeal. We were now quite exhausted but Grace came in with Algy who had by now slept off the after-effects of his earlier intoxication.

'I hope you don't mind if we share the bed?' enquired Grace.

'Not at all,' I replied. And Mary nodded her agreement as Grace began to undress. She was a most attractive filly with her long blonde hair and plump yet firm breasts that swelled out to beautifully formed high-pointed rosebud nipples. Her flat belly led down to a petite bush of silky light-coloured hair and as she stood naked by my side my hands automatically slid up between her legs and I felt the wetness there as she wriggled her shapely young bum.

'Fair's fair. I must fuck Grace first,' said Algy with a smile and I could not but agree with him. In any case my poor prick was *hors de combat* for the present so Mary and I simply relaxed and enjoyed watching our friends fuck.

Grace sat down on the bed and reached out to take hold of Algy's thick cock which swelled up to full erection as she began to massage the shaft, capping and uncapping the ruby headed knob. His prick looked to be thicker than mine though I fancy I had the edge on length on my old pal. Algy climbed on to the bed and lay smiling as Grace continued to toss him off. Then slowly he moved on top of the delicious young blonde girl and allowed her to guide his quivering prick into her cunt. She moved excitedly as he continued to swell and move inside her cunney. She felt Algy's lips on hers and pushed her tongue into his mouth. His slim, smooth body moved in rhythm, faster and faster until the bed was rocking furiously as Algy pounded his thick cock into her willing love-box. Grace was rolling in ecstasy, screaming for satisfaction, bouncing up and down, forcing his prick into the furthest recesses of her cunt. I could see her legs contract so that her cunney muscles could milk the cream out of that prick and she tensed as her climax approached. At the height of her passion she became a frenzied, wild madwoman, thrashing her hips against his arched body, absorbing every inch of cock inside her. Then she relaxed and went limp as Algy withdrew his extended, swollen penis, squirting hot jets of sperm all over her heaving belly.

I later found out that Grace was frightened of getting with child and would only let a man spunk into her arsehole except just before and after her monthly bleeding. In fact, Grace immensely enjoyed fucking with her regular young man and I told her that Professor Wankel has written that very frequent sexual intercourse can (but is on no account to be relied upon as a foolproof means of contraception) lead to 'sperm exhaustion' which makes conception extremely unlikely.

I read a little more from the book and when I began to read about the sensitivity of the female breasts, Grace interrupted me. I will jot down her remarks in full as I feel they may provide a valuable lesson for would-be considerate lovers, an attribute far too often lacking, I regret to say, in England which is why so many pretty English girls keep their legs crossed at home yet offer their cunnies to foreigners!

She spoke thus: 'I know that most men's pricks will stir at the sight of a pair of lovely titties. And with good reason for what else is so visible and dramatically female? So young girls worry about when their breasts will begin to grow, girls in their prime flaunt their proud beauties whenever they can and older women try desperately to prevent their bosoms sagging.

'Meanwhile, boys look for the perfect breasts, firm, youthful and pert. Certainly, all girls enjoy having their breasts caressed, kissed and sucked and handling a girl's titties with considerate care will earn a boy her deepest gratitude, even though she may be driven almost insane with pleasure! Yes, I do like being complimented about my breasts and my regular friend Adrian never fails to do this as we begin our love-making.

'I do so enjoy the way Adrian touches me. He begins by touching just the very edges of my breasts, where they just start to swell, and he moves his fingers in a big circle around the outside. He works on one at a time, gradually decreasing the size of his circle, getting closer and closer to my large pink aureoles and then finally he reaches my nipples.

'These are the most sensitive areas of course so as his hands approach I become more and more excited. I start to juice down below and begin to twist and turn as he tweaks the titties between his long, tapering fingers. Oh, the joy is quite excruciating and by this time, my nippies are erect like miniature cocks. He may pinch one now, though not too hard, and when he does this I do believe that I can feel it in my cunney. Anyway, it always makes me open my legs and then Adrian enters me and his hard cock finds my cunt already soaking with love juice as he thrusts his tool deep inside me. Whilst we are fucking he often sucks on my titties and gives them little bites. This sends thrills all over my body. Oh, I do enjoy having my boy play with my bubbies. All girls appreciate attention being paid to these fine female assets and if you boys want to please your girls, just do not forget to pay your respects in a manner I have just indicated!'

'Consideration for your partner is of paramount importance,' said Grace firmly. 'My first lover was a fine boy and he showed me every courtesy, allowing for my nervousness. Shall I tell you how I lost my virginity?'

We chorused our assent and she began: 'My story opens on the eve of my seventeenth birthday. I make no secret of the fact that I was in service with a very genteel family who lived in Kensington. The master of the house was a doctor, and the eldest son, Billy, was also just sixteen years of age. He was a very good-looking boy and I could not help but notice that I seemed to catch his eye.

'It did not take long before he found an excuse to come up into my room and we kissed and cuddled a few times until one day he began to stroke my breasts and before I hardly knew what was happening, this handsome young fellow-me-lad had unbuttoned my blouse and my naked breasts were exposed to his touch.

'He squeezed them lightly and began to play with my titties which were now as stiff as two little pricks against the palms of his hands. As if drawn there by a power over which I had no control, I dropped my hand over the huge bulge in the front of his trousers and I stroked the hard shaft I could feel throbbing violently beneath my touch.

'This episode was interrupted by footsteps from below (though fortunately we were not disturbed) but later that week we found ourselves alone in the house. Doctor Bucknall had taken the family for a walk and the other servants were busy with their work. Young Billy whispered to me that the coast was clear and we crept up to my room.

'As soon as the door was closed behind us, Billy pulled me into his arms, eagerly raining kisses on my cheeks and neck. I responded wildly and for a moment he held me away from him. "I must fuck you, Grace, you will let me won't you?" Oh, I knew I should say no but the luscious, appealing look on the dear boy's face was more than I could resist. I made no show of resistance as he pulled me back to him and crushed me against his chest as his lips hungrily sought mine.

'I was almost fainting from the excitement of the moment. I felt a queer tingling in my stomach that spread like a warmth through to my cunney. I knew what it was like to be desired and the thought made me weak with pleasure. I clung to him more tightly, pressing my full breasts against his chest, knowing I was making a decision I could never undo. But I was ready and I wanted to know what it meant to be a woman – how it felt to be taken by a man.

'"Oh, Billy," I sighed as he swept me into his arms and laid me down gently on the bed. Now even though his own young passion was at a peak, he treated me gently, slowly unbuttoning the front of my blouse until he could slip his hands to cup my straining breasts. He kissed me deeply and demandingly while he slipped off my blouse and the rest of my clothes. He then hastily shed his own clothes and for the first time I saw a naked boy. I admired the silkiness of his hair, his strong shoulders, the curvature of his chest which was as smooth and hairless as my own, the shape of his lovely arms and as he turned to put down his shoes, the suppleness of his white bottom.

'But then as he turned back my eyes fastened upon the *piece de résistance*, his massive cock, so very big for such a young boy, as erect as could be, the stiff rod up against his tummy and as he approached me I took hold of the huge uncapped knob in my hands. It throbbed as I stroked this monster and I could feel the thick veins running along its length, so thick that I could barely grasp it. A piercing, hot sensation shot up between my legs as my cunney oozed its juices and I wanted him inside me. Our two nude bodies rolled in ecstasy and I could see that great bursting cock was more than ready to enter my tiny pussey.

'I grasped it and with almost savage passion guided that thick red knob between my cunt lips and Billy gave a great thrust. I shrieked out in pain as I shuddered in exquisite agony. My dear Billy wanted to withdraw but I would not let him and told him to push on. I stretched my legs to the widest and then, aaaah! his lovely cock had pushed open the gate and now I quivered with mad pleasure as my maidenhead was fairly and squarely broken. I felt his hot kisses all over my body as Billy shuddered to a climax and I felt the mingled blood and spunk trickle down my legs. I wiped the blood off his dear prick and for the first time I took a cock into my mouth and began to lustily suck the silky, hard shaft back up to a rock hard stiffness.

'I greedily sucked in as much cock as I could and Billy slid in his shaft all the way to the back of my throat. His cock was so big it strained my jaw so I massaged the underside with my tongue, moving my head up and down as Billy jerked and suddenly went rigid. His cock spurted jets of hot, sticky fluid which I swallowed and swallowed until every drop of juice had been milked from that gorgeous prick.

'I kissed his lips again and again! You may imagine that we continued to fuck until the dear boy had no more strength in his body. Three times he came inside me and three times I sucked him back to erection and twice I sucked and swallowed the sperm from his lovely cock.'

'The moral of my tale is this: first love may be idyllic or it can be a disaster. This depends on circumstances and on the chosen partner and of course to a very great extent upon ourselves. Naive, shy and a little bewildered by the event taking place, we can easily spoil what can be a most marvellous situation. I was indeed fortunate to find a young man who possessed a fine cock but who also took the trouble to understand my needs and made our first sexual union one that we may both remember fondly.'

This lascivious tale set us all in the mood for a further bout of fucking and I have always remembered that day in Brighton. It taught me that though all animals copulate, only man is capable of expanding a physical need into an act of love and this ability sets us apart from the lower species. We need not listen to those who wish to take away the joy of this natural drive and to defy nature. Apes perform sexual intercourse in under ten seconds with the male needing only some ten thrusts of the phallus to complete the act. Is this the standard to which we should aspire? Eight seconds and ten thrusts?

Such revelations stirred us to renewed vigour. My member stood like an ivory shaft of love, while Algy had a fancy to take Grace's bum hole. The dear girl bent over me and began to suck my cock up to its fullest length, tickling my balls with her busy hands and sticking out her fine white skinned arse cheeks ready for Algy to board her. Nothing loath, he lubricated his prick with cold cream and spread a little cream between Grace's bum cheeks. Then in a trice he was behind her, his hard cock quite eight inches long, battering against the tight dark nether hole of his love.

He positioned his prick so cleverly to the mark that he almost immediately completed his insertion up to the roots of the hair and was revelling in the delicious sensations and pressures to which Grace's arse was treating him.

She continued to suck my swelling cock but mumbled: 'Beautiful, beautiful! Go, go quick. Spend! Ah, Aaaah!!!' and Algy fucked her bottom with renewed fury in a perfect frenzy of lust as she wiggled her bum to extract the greatest pleasure from his exertions. My blood was up and soon the spunk boiled up in my balls and I shot thick wads of creamy spend into Grace's mouth as she sucked and smacked her lips with gusto as Algy jetted his streams of white sperm into her arsehole, spending so exhaustingly that he must have fallen backwards had he not clung to Grace's neck.

We finished our fucking with some more champagne and Algy led us into singing some bawdy songs some of which were not totally devoit of wit. I can remember but one which the girls particularly enjoyed singing:

My Jamie is a lover gay
    He is so very funny.
When last we met to sport and play
    He took me by the cunney.
Then drawing out his sturdy prick
    Right in my hand he placed it,
And said 'twould be a jolly trick
    If in my mouth I'd taste it.

I kissed its bright and rosy head
    And then began to suck it;
He felt about my cunt and said
    He wanted now to fuck it.
Down on the bed he laid me,
With bursting balls, and prick's round head,
    Love's sweetest debt he paid me.

Let maidens of a tim'rous mind
    Refuse what most they're wanting,
Since we for fucking were designed
    We surely should be granting.
So when your lover feels your cunt,
    Do not be coy, nor grieve him;
But spread your legs and heave your bum,
    For fucking is like heaven.

Thus we passed a most delightful afternoon, refreshing ourselves from time to time, for the worship of Venus and Priapus requires continual stimulation by the most invigorating of delicacies.

85

4

I journeyed back to Victoria by the fast train and arrived at
the bustling terminus at around half past six o'clock. An
unfortunate incident occured whilst I was waiting in the
orderly queue for a cab to take me to Sir Lionel T——'s club.
A smartly dressed young woman asked me if I could oblige
her with change of a sovereign as she wished to reward a
railway attendant for his services in moving her baggage.
Whilst I was fumbling in my purse for the necessary coins, she
stumbled towards me as if she had been pushed from behind
and the coins from my purse went spinning on the ground.
Another young lady, who at the time I assumed to be her
maidservant, helped me pick up my money but it was only
afterwards when I went to pay the cabbie that I discovered
that my purse was lighter by at least three pounds and that a
beautiful silk handkerchief given to me on my birthday by Dr
White's niece Belinda had been audaciously removed from
my pocket.

Luckily I had enough cash left to pay off the cab though no
doubt old Crapps would have stumped up on my behalf. I
told our genial doorman of what had happened and he
advised me not to bother to inform the police. 'It happens all
the time, sir,' he said with a resigned smile. 'My son, young
Bob, was out with Cecilia, his young lady, a couple of months
back and they were passing Charing Cross Station on their
way to catch an omnibus back home.

'They decided to enjoy a cup of tea first in the station
restaurant when two respectable looking women came up
and engaged them in conversation about the next train to
Sevenoaks. Blow me down if one of them tried to pick
Cecilia's pocket!

'As you can appreciate, sir, ladies' pockets are somewhat deep in the dress and an expert pickpocket can take out a purse without too much difficulty. Cecilia screamed when she felt a strange hand in her dress, but the women ran off before Bob could summon assistance. So you must keep your eyes open in old London town, sir, to be sure.'

I felt I should report the incident, for these women would undoubtedly prey on travellers until they were caught, but I am ashamed to say that I was so exhausted after the afternoon's bout of fucking that I ate a quiet dinner alone and left the club in the carriage of Lord Davis, whose son Colin and I were both members of Nottsgrove's cricket team. As ever when travelling through the capital, I was struck by the dense crowd of people who throng the West End streets. Perhaps above all I was struck by the gaiety of Regent Street and the Haymarket.

It is not only the architectural splendour of these aristocratic streets but the brilliant illumination of the shops, cafes, Turkish divans that impresses, and night-houses as well – and of course the troops of elegantly dressed courtesans, rustling in silks and satins promenading along these superb streets among the throngs of persons of every order, from the ragged crossing-sweeper to the high-bred gentleman of fashion and scion of nobility.

I espied an especially pretty young girl, who could not have been more than eighteen years of age, dressed in an elegant black silk cloak. She had a pert little face and I called out to the driver to stop for a moment. She told me her name was Katie and that for the sum of three pounds she would spend the night with me. As I had enjoyed myself that very afternoon, it was greed rather than need that made me accept her offer – I was struck by her gentle voice and genteel manner – and she climbed into the carriage with me and stroked my cock as we made our way to St John's Wood.

When we arrived at Sir Lionel T——'s house I gave Kate her money, as I was in truth slightly ashamed at having to pay for the *amour* and I wished to forget the sordid monetary transaction as soon as possible. Fortunately, Sir Lionel had telegraphed to say that he would not be home until the next morning and the under-butler, Dennis, was the soul of discretion. I took Kate directly to my room and without any hesitation she began to disrobe.

Ah, she was indeed a saucy little Venus with breasts as white as snow, capped by nut-brown nipples which were already jutting out proudly in anticipation of an impending fuck. The crisp triangle of curls looked more inviting to my hungry lips than a plate of the rarest, most expensive delicacies from the finest of French chefs. I tore off my clothes and laid Kate down on my bed and she pulled my face towards her and sank her naughty little tongue into my mouth. Everything was happening so fast that I just lay down there soaking up the sensations of her kiss. I stroked her pussey bush with my thumb and let my fingers caress the lips of her already damp cunney. Her body began to vibrate as my thumb found her clitty and I began rubbing it with a steadily increasing rhythm that had her clinging to me as tightly as she could. Now her hand was grasped round my rampant cock and she began to rub my shaft in time with my teasing of her clitty.

I gently removed her hand as I did not want to spend too quickly and lowering my face I nuzzled between her legs and after sneezing a trifle as a mass of thick curls tickled my nose, my tongue was soon twirling and I sucked away at that delicious little slit as Kate's body jerked up and down, making it more exciting as my face rubbed against her thick, curly bush. 'Ooooh!' she screamed as I worked my tongue until my jaw ached as, heaving violently, the lovely girl reached the pinnacle of delight. She was more than ready for my cock but the toil of tonguing had left it in a state of only semi-erection.

'Let me first suck your cock before you put it in my cunt,' said Kate brightly as she slid down the bed. Feeling the warm grasp of her lips around my tool, I arched my back in ecstasy and in a trice my prick was back to its former rampant stiffness. I felt my cock slide further in as Kate sucked lustily and in order not to spend in her mouth I gently relinquished the alluring caress and the understanding girl smiled and cast herself on her back, legs wide apart.

88

'Come now, Andrew, put that gorgeous cock where it belongs!' she said sweetly. Nothing loath, my cock waggling with excitement, I clambered upon her without delay. I positioned my cock between her cunney lips and delighted in the exquisite pleasure as my knob parted the lips and I slowly but firmly inserted my throbbing tool inside her juicy cunt. I moved but a little to enjoy the grip of the velvety walls of her slit as she began to move her hips sinuously, finding that she could work her cunt up and down my prick with ease as I began to pump up and down and my balls smacked a fine dance against her bottom with every thrust. I pounded to and fro, my hands clasping her full, round bum cheeks as I felt the spunk boiling in my balls. By great effort I managed to delay the exquisite moment as the silky walls of Kate's cunt continued to sleek back and forth along my delighted cock.

But now I could wait no longer and with a mighty groan I flooded her cunt with a torrent of sperm as jets of frothy white spunk poured out of my prick, completely filling her cunney and trickling down her inner thighs.

Gad, that was a fuck to remember and I later wrote down her address so that if I ever needed her services again I could contact her. In fact, I also gave her the address of the Riverhead Club for she was quite a refined genteel girl (her father was a bankrupt politician in a small Dorset town and she had come to London to seek her fortune) and had no need to walk the streets for her daily bread. At the Club she would probably find a gentleman to care for her and set her up in a nice little apartment. And indeed that is what soon came to pass, as old Johnny Clarke of the 47th Lancers took a shine to Kate and kept her in some style for several years.

After I instructed Giles the coachman to take Kate home I enjoyed a good night's sleep. Sir Lionel returned in the morning in quite a distressed condition. I asked my old friend what was the matter and he told me that his coach had been attacked by a hooligan mob about a mile from Guildford in Surrey.

'Andrew,' said Sir Lionel, 'I saw happenings that would have disgraced a fair in the wildest districts of Ireland. There must have been a local celebration of some sort for everybody who happened to pass through a little village named Stockmanlands on the Guildford and Portsmouth high road had to run the gauntlet of a shower of stones from some two hundred roughs and vagabonds.

'The miscreants lined the roads on both sides, entrapping the unwary travellers between them and set about harassing any individual who stopped to remonstrate. Why, I almost had the coat torn off my back and two persons who tried to avoid the danger by taking a side-road by the river-side were pursued by the mob and forced into the water.'

My old friend was genuinely upset by his experience and so, soon after he had refreshed himself with a large brandy and soda, he decided to retire to the library and compose a letter to *The Times*. The brandy had mellowed his mood, for as he was going out of the room he said: 'Andrew, please do me a small favour. You know that good-looking young wench Charlotte who I have employed as a parlourmaid? Well, she is apparently unwell, according to Cook. Would you be so kind as to look in on her and if she really is ill, summon Dr Hall. However, my own belief is that she is malingering.'

Naturally I agreed to oblige my friend and so I climbed up to the attic where her bedroom was situated and knocked on the door.

'Who is there?' she called out.

'It's Andrew Scott. May I come in? Sir Lionel has sent me to see how you are.'

'Oh do come in,' she replied and I opened the door.

Charlotte was sitting up in bed wearing nothing but a pink cotton nightgown which emphasised the swell of her large breasts. The material was so thin that I could well see the points of her nipples sticking out underneath their flimsy covering.

She was an extraordinarily pretty girl – no, she was more than that, she was quite beautiful. She possessed uncommonly large hazel eyes and she wore her shining dark brown hair quite long, gathered with graceful looseness at the back of her head. Her pink nightdress set off the translucent pink and white of her skin and she looked at me in a bold, inviting manner that made me blush. It was if she knew what was racing through my mind as she licked her lips and said: 'I am feeling very much better today, thank you. I think Sir Lionel has forgotten than I was suffering from the monthly problem and he kindly told me to take today off. In fact, I am now fully recovered so if there is any work to be done, I will gladly get dressed.'

'Oh, no, Charlotte,' I said. 'A promise is a promise and Sir Lionel is a man of his word.'

'I am glad to hear so. I shall stay in my room for the time being. I do hope that you are not too busy. Perhaps you would like to stay and we can talk awhile. I have so few visitors for as you know, I come from Coventry and know no-one in London.'

Well, there it was: it needed very little to read between the lines. It is true that we had passed the time of day and our eyes had locked together in a knowing kind of fashion. As the Bard of Avon so rightly commented, young limbs and lechery are inseparable and within a short space of time I was throwing off my clothes and jumping into the narrow bed with this delightful creature.

Our bodies were touching from head to toe as we kissed with great ardour, our tongues probing and sliding into each other's mouths. I stroked her lovely breasts and caressed her hard little nippies through the soft material of her nightgown. Then I gathered up the garment so I could fondle her legs, stroking the silkiness of the naked warm flesh of her thighs. Then I encountered the sticky wetness between her legs as she began to moan with pleasure as I ran my fingers through her silky mound.

We continued to kiss and she ran the tip of her tongue over my lips. I felt her hand grasp my pulsating cock and a feeling of sheer, exquisite pleasure flooded through me as she massaged gently, the tender, sensitive tips of her stroking fingers gently slipping the soft flaccid foreskin up and down over the uncapped polished dome.

I glided my own hand into her eager cunt, sensing the

91

sexual juices welling up inside her, my fingers slipping in and out in unhurried rhythm as her body moved slightly forwards and backwards. She broke off our kiss to look greedily downwards at my iron-hard stiff prick and whispered: 'Oh my, that lovely cock looks good enough to eat!'

Twisting herself round so that my fingers remained embodied in her juicy pussey as she straddled me with her luscious bum cheeks almost touching my lips she bent down and began to gobble my thick rod, sucking the dome into her mouth and then sucking in another inch or two of the shaft, licking and salivating my throbbing cock with her naughty little tongue. She cradled my balls in her hands as she continued to suck my cock with evident pleasure.

But I wanted to feel my hard prick inside her pussey so I eased her off me and she lay down on her back, my hand still between her legs and my hand liberally covered with cunt-juice. I slowly eased my cock into her lovely, tight, beautiful little cunney as she opened her thighs to their fullest extent. She held her own legs wide apart with her hands as mine reached under her to grip her delicious bum. Her hips arched towards me as if trying to entice every inch of prick as far as possible inside her.

Indeed, Charlotte was an uninhibited lover and I was concerned that her gasps and moans of delight might awaken Sir Lionel in the library two floors below. As I thrust hard in and out of her as we fucked each other wildly, her cunney making little squelching sounds as her pussey muscles squeezed my cock tightly. After a very few minutes I felt the spunk boiling up inside me. As I surged up to the climax, the trembling girl gave a loud scream, gripping her legs like a vice over my back as I pumped squirt after squirt of frothy white sperm inside her waiting cunt. I shuddered with each jerk of my knob until after some six or seven thrusts, my prick was milked dry.

We continued to fuck for another two hours or so, clinging to each other in repeated storms of passion. But it was now nearly time for luncheon and Charlotte asked me to leave word in the servants' hall that she would come downstairs for her meal in about fifteen minutes. We exchanged a brief farewell kiss and I promised Charlotte that I would fuck her again later that evening.

My face was no doubt flushed with all this exertion and I noticed a smile playing around Sir Lionel's lips as we sat down to luncheon.

'What amuses you?' I enquired somewhat acidly.

'Oh, nothing, my dear old chap, nothing at all.'

'Well then, pray let me enjoy the jest!'

And at this riposte Sir Lionel could not restrain a hearty guffaw.

'Oh very good, Andrew. We should not keep any secrets from each other.' His eyes were streaming from laughter. 'When you began to fuck Charlotte – come, sir, you cannot deny it – Molly, the young under parlourmaid was in here to take away the morning newspapers. But she and I were both aware of what was happening above our heads.

'For a start, Charlotte's bedsprings are terribly creaky and even more to the point, when she reaches the apex, she screams out without inhibition. It was really most entertaining and the sounds made both Molly and myself feel extremely randy. So much so, that I just could not resist smacking her delicious little rump as she bent down to pick up the newspapers. But instead of chiding me and running out of the room, she simply sighed and, throwing down the papers rushed into my arms. We kissed with a mad abandoned passion and to my great joy she unbuttoned my trousers and grabbed hold of my naked prick which jerked within her grasp as she moved her clever fingers along the length of it, bringing the droplets of salt liquid running onto her hand.

'Our blood was up and it would have taken an earthquake to prevent us taking the road to happiness. In a trice our clothes were off, Molly was on her back on the couch with her legs apart and I was licking and sucking her gorgeous cunny. Her nipples stood out like little walnuts as I flicked them against my palms and chewed on her darling rosebud clitty until she cried out for me to board her.

'I raised myself above her and in one quick movement slid my yearning cock swiftly home amidst the folds of sensuous glory. I pounded to and fro, drawing her up and down with me. My hands were clasped forcefully behind her back as the surging cries of fulfilment echoed around the room as we reached the state of ecstasy. I thrust again and again in and out of her slippery tunnel.

'She grabbed my hand and pressed it to her right breast. It was warm and resilient and as we continued to fuck I squeezed it which added to the excitement as she began to contract her vaginal mucles, gripping my cock shaft in an exquisite way. "Oh, oh, I am going to spend!" Molly gasped, her hips writhing and rolling, her cunt tightening ever more squeezing my cock to fresh transports of delight.

'A great shudder shook her entire frame. "I'm spending I'm spending!" she cried out. I myself was on the verge, trying to hold back but now I too began to shoot thick wads of creamy white spunk, ramming my cock deep inside her, holding it there as I spurted endlessly whilst her movements slowed under me.

'We lay panting with exhaustion, covered in perspiration. At last she stirred and my now limp prick slipped out of her. She was still game for more fun and ten minutes ago that mop of blonde hair was between my legs, and that luscious pair of lips was greedily slurping over the top of my prick which was soon as stiff as a poker under her gentle ministrations. With one hand she cupped my balls, and the other gently played around the base of my shaft as she sucked away lustily on my prick until I spunked a tremendous emission of froth into her throat which she swallowed with great enjoyment.'

'I am delighted that Charlotte and I led the way for you and Molly,' I said with genuine feeling.

Of course we spent the rest of the day enjoying ourselves. Both Molly and Charlotte were somewhat shy and neither would take up the invitation to partake of a *ménage à quatre*. However, being gentlemen and ever mindful that we were both British and Old Nottsgrovians to boot, we did not of course insist.

As a matter of interest, both these young dollymops (the

94

slang term for young girls who bestowed their favours without asking for money – The Editor) went on to better themselves quite handsomely. Just a few moments after our joust, Charlotte met and within a month married the scion of an old Scottish family who settled three thousand pounds a year upon her. The family were horrified that Chesney McG—— had married beneath him and questioning his sanity, tried to obtain a writ of *de lunatico inquirendo*. However, to his credit, Sir Lionel arranged for Dr Jonathan L— to give evidence on the young couple's behalf and the writ was thrown out. I have kept up my acquaintance with Charlotte though naturally I have never fucked her since her marriage.

By the greatest of good fortune, Molly met an admirer at the Cremorne Gardens in Chelsea for at first sight a wealthy young American became enamoured. And so now Molly is mistress of a fine estate in New Hampshire, where, coincidentally, she became friends with Charlotte's older sister who was working there as a companion to an invalid lady. Ever generous hearted, Molly soon found a good-looking young buck for the girl and they are now blissfully engaged in conubial life in a small town nearby.

If only nature could always provide such neat signposts down to the roads of happiness! For what a narrow divide there lurks between misery and joy, between the sublime and the ridiculous! They are often so nearly related that it is difficult to class them separately. One step above the sublime makes the ridiculous; and one step above the ridiculous makes the sublime again!

That evening, after we had both enjoyed good, long sessions of fucking with our delightful new lovers, Sir Lionel was forced to take temporary leave of us. He had promised to take Major Bookers to a private magic lantern performance arranged by Henry Sailor. 'King Solomon In All His Glory' would be illustrated by Sailor's own photographs. This meant that we were one prick short when after partaking of a light meal and a bumper of champagne, Charlotte, Molly and my goodself found ourselves lying all quite nude on Sir Lionel's large bed.

Molly was lying on her back, her large breasts crowned by those inviting pink rosebud nipples. She giggled as I bent down to lick them up to erection. At the same time, Charlotte put her hands round my waist and stretched down to enclose my stiffening cock with her right hand. She commenced to toss me off quite vigorously but I had no desire to spend too quickly and I gently removed her hand from my now rampant stiff prick. With my left hand flicking Molly's titties, I turned and put my right arm round Charlotte and drew her close to me. Our mouths met in a fiery French kiss that shook us both by its violent tonguing as we explored each other's mouths. I wrenched my lips away, gasping for breath and moved my head down to lick the smooth white skin of her breasts and I darted my tongue over the hard, pert tittie standing up for me like a little soldier at attention.

Molly now raised herself and began to gobble my throbbing prick, kissing and sucking my red-knobbed tool which twitched and bucked in delight as her moist pink tongue travelled up and down the length of my shaft. I gently moved Molly's head from my cock and thought quickly as to how best give these two delightful girls what they wanted. But they knew better than I and it was Charlotte who whispered 'You first, my dear' to Molly who lay back on the bed with her legs wide open to await me. Charlotte took hold of my meaty cock and guided it firmly between Molly's swollen cunney lips, edging the fiery red knob in and out of her friend's juicy cunt.

'Oooh, that feels good!' Molly cried out. 'But I want more cock! Plunge into me, dear Andrew as hard as you can!'

Nothing loath, I pushed down as hard as I could, burying my cock in her warm, tight-fitting little love box and we began to fuck in hard sweeping strokes. What joy, what exquisite joy I experienced, sliding my cock in and out of that wet and willing pussey. We bounced up and down on the bouyant mattress with the force of our love-making as Molly squealed: 'Yes... yes, I am spending... yes, yes, I spend... aah, aah, what happiness!'

For a moment I thought she had cried 'What a penis!' but

quickly realised my error. I still managed to pound away, my cock driving in and out of the wet, tender folds of her hot cunney. 'My turn, my turn, Molly before he spends,' cried Charlotte.

'Quickly then!' I panted as I could feel the sperm about to burst through from my balls. I pulled my pulsating prick away from Molly's cunt. Charlotte pushed me to one side and on her hands and knees took up position where I had been only she lowered her pretty head to kiss and suck Molly's dripping pussey lips and I could see her pink little tongue slipping in and out of her friend's quim. 'Oh, oh, OH!' screamed Molly as Charlotte found Molly's clitty and began to kiss and roll it around her tongue.

Meanwhile, I positioned myself behind Charlotte whose beautifully rounded arse cheeks were moving in rhythm as she sucked happily away on Molly's clitty. Again, the dear girl took the lead for Charlotte pulled back her right arm to reach for my sturdy cock and directed the vermilion head in between the glorious cheeks of her bum. She let go to continue to play with Molly's titties, but I needed no further encouragement. I wetted my knob with a little champagne from the almost empty bottle that lay beside us and worked my cock between those luscious bum cheeks until I found the tight-looking wrinkled little brown hole that lay between them. I attacked my target with vigour but not too quickly as I had no wish to hurt the dear girl. So I fucked her bum hole slowly and I could tell by the wriggling of her arse how much she was enjoying it while my hands were kept busy frigging her cunt in front.

I continued to fuck her bum until my own body could not be denied. We screamed loudly in a frenzy of emission, Charlotte swooning with delight as I fell exhausted upon her. We soon recovered and engaged in *l'arte de faire l'amour*, pressing our lips together in a threesome kiss, wiggling our tongues around in each other's mouths in a most sensuous, uninhibited fashion.

But I must admit that a woman is far better equipped than a man for a *menage à trois*. With one man and two women, one partner can sit on his prick whilst the other sits on his face so that he can suck her pussey. Women can continue to fuck for longer than us as well. After we have spent, we need a period, however short, for recuperation but a woman can continue for a good while until she gets tired and sore. Who says that they are the weaker sex?

5

I realised that I could not stay for too much longer in St John's Wood. For though Charlotte, Molly and I both enjoyed our marvellous bouts of fucking, one should never mess on one's own doorstep, as the common vernacular has it. So it was fortuitous that my Godfather, Colonel Reginald M——, happened to be passing through town on one of his infrequent visits to our capital city. He was on some obscure government committee looking into the pollution of our rivers by industry and, by great good fortune, the London Club where he was staying was the same as Sir Lionel's. Old Crapps knew of the relationship between my Godfather and myself and told the old gentleman that I was at present staying at the home of the genial baronet.

My Godfather was somewhat concerned that I should be roaming around town in what he correctly considered to be a fast set. He was even more concerned that I might be ensnared into an unfortunate marriage. Therefore he sent a message to me suggesting that we met at the Club as soon as was convenient.

We met about a week after my first fuck with Charlotte and after exchanging pleasantries, my Godfather commented that I looked rather wan. Well, I could hardly explain to him just why I was so damnably tired. Young Charlotte was almost insatiable and we were spending at least three or sometimes four hours a day fucking like a couple possessed. I just do not know how such a slightly-built girl came to enjoy such a robust constitution for she was always ready for more when I was at the point of almost total exhaustion. I muttered something about eating some lobster that had not agreed with my digestion but my Godfather dismissed this admitted falsehood with a wave of the hand.

It happened that my Godfather, long married and settled in the utmost respectability in the pleasant Derbyshire spa town of Buxton, had taken me on one side when we had last met for what he called a man-to-man talk. He made it clear to me that in his youth he had been something of a young blade about town.

'Marriage, my boy,' he had said to me, 'marriage is an excellent and most proper institution and I pray that you may, when your time comes, have as satisfying and comfortable a relationship as that granted to me with my own dear wife...'

Here I should interject to say that whilst I have the highest affection and regard for my Godfather, I would be the first to accept that he is of a wordy nature and somewhat overgiven to holding forth at great length and often in sentences of great complexity. Both as a pillar of his local business community and as father of a family of seven, he has grown accustomed to being listened to in a respectful silence. I knew however that he has always been a man of generosity and that if I heard him out, it could well be that I would hear something to my advantage.

In this belief I was soon to be confirmed. After much clutching at his lapels and marching and countermarching across the drawing-room carpet, he made it clear that he had himself, before marriage, enjoyed what he described as 'The Fleshpots of the Metropolis' and that he considered it only right and proper for any young man similarly, before settling into the responsibilities of career and marriage, to enjoy some years of freedom and the pursuit of enjoyment. Furthermore, it transpired that he, as my Godfather, considered it both his duty and pleasure to assist me in this most understandable of endeavours.

Now came the practical part of his discourse. He, knowing that the pursuit of pleasure in London could be a damnably expensive undertaking, proposed to make me for the space of three years an Allowance sufficient to enable me to take lodgings which if not of a luxurious character, would be at least of a decent standard of comfort. I would need, he said, a place where I could with discretion entertain friends including it might be those of the opposite sex, but where I would be looked after and my domestic needs catered for.

My mind, which had wandered somewhat during his peroration, and my imagination, which had commenced playing upon the word Fleshpot, remembering the succulent, moist receptacle of the delicious Charlotte into which I had plunged myself with such eagerness and at such length but a few hours before, snapped back to present attention when he set out his generous offer.

It further transpired that not only was he prepared to pay my lodging expenses, but that he knew of an establishment that would be well suited to my needs. Situated in Sussex Gardens in that district north of the Park known as Bayswater, it was convenient for the West End, for Belgravia and for most of the main line railway termini. The house was owned by a most understanding woman, Mrs P—, who, being a widow, her husband having after some years service in the Indian Survey died consequent on contracting a debilitating fever whilst on tour in the Deccan, was forced to supplement her pension by letting out part of her house as a set of rooms suitable for the needs of a young gentleman about town.

My Godfather intimated to me that Mrs P— was an old friend. Indeed I was given to understand that they had first met during his own youthful enjoyment of the fleshpots of London and that they had stayed in some sort of communication with each other during the years when she was in India and he of course in Buxton. The impression was further given that my Godfather's wife and family knew nothing of Mrs P— and that there were certain sorts of dear friendship that were best protected by discretion. I, as a young man, would presently come to appreciate the part that discretion played in such affairs...

And so it happened that on a fine autumn morning I hailed a

101

cab and set out on a voyage of discovery to Bayswater. They say that in the spring a young man's fancy turns, but I can state with some authority that the season makes little difference to my fancy.

After provincial life the streets of London seemed positively awash with feminine delights. My attention was constantly caught, here by a well-turned ankle and there by a well-filled bodice. Full lips and saucy glances were everywhere. I passed into a reverie of heated concupiscence, so much so indeed that Mr Pego rose stiffly to attention as I sat back in the Hansom. When we came to a halt before a tall town house of a type that I later found to be typical of the area, I found it difficult to stand fully upright without a most unseemly and revealing bulge in my trousers.

The cabby glanced at me somewhat impertinently as I paid him off. I stood on the pavement hoping that my lust-inflamed member would have the grace to lie down, but I was further discomfitted by a pair of what I took to be serving girls who looked down at the seat of my straining embarrassment and giggled the one to the other before turning down the area steps of the house next door to my objective.

However embarrassment is a prime remedy for lust and subsiding quickly to a condition of propriety, I walked up the steps and rang the bell.

The maid, a pretty little thing who I judged to be of no more than seventeen years, showed me into the morning room where I was soon joined by Mrs P—. A dark-haired, handsome and high-complexioned woman, she was quite without any trace of that jaundiced look that one sees so often on the skin of those who have spent many years in the East. Quickly she put me at my ease, offering me a glass of madeira and letting me know that she entertained the fondest memories of my Godfather from whom she had recently heard and so had known of my recent arrival in Town. It so happened that her last lodger had departed a few weeks ago, having passed his Examination and been accepted into the Indian Civil Service.

I was shown the rooms which, without being over-luxurious, were decently enough appointed. It was indeed a most satisfactory situation. I would have every privacy, yet my meals would be prepared for me and my laundry and other domestic necessities would be included in the very fair terms. It was accepted that I could entertain friends. As Mrs P— said with a smiling sideways glance, 'Whilst I would ask you to be reasonable in the demands that you make on the servants – cook would not take kindly to a sudden demand for dinner for seven – a light supper *à deux* or even a nourishing breakfast for an overnight guest would be well within the bounds of what is proper.'

I understood that apart from Mrs P— herself, the household consisted of her two daughters. One, after studying at Lambeth School of Art, was employed in the pottery studio of Messrs Doulton in their riverfront manufactury while the second was training to be a nurse at the nearly adjacent St Mary's Hospital.

I looked forward to meeting the two young ladies, for it was quickly agreed that I should move in at once. As I left, the same fair-haired little maid was informed that I would be occupying the rooms and that everything was to be put in order for me. Emily, for that was her name, bobbed a demure little curtsy to me and said softly that she hoped I would find everything to my satisfaction.

Later that afternoon I had my things, such as they were, packed up and sent round. Then after taking my leave of Sir Lionel, I myself repaired to my new home. That evening I was invited to dine with the family, Mrs P— explaining that her daughters would want to become acquainted with what she described as 'the new man in the house.'

As to what we actually ate, I have no clear recollection. I have to admit that I spent the whole meal in such a state of sexual arousal that all other considerations were driven clean from my mind. Mrs P— as I have already said was of that dark-haired, heated complexion that as later experience has repeatedly born out denotes a woman hot for fucking. Her daughters, Hannah and Becky, were of their mother's complexion but with the dew of youth upon them. Both of course had their hair up and were most properly dressed, yet in both there was that delicious sense that such propriety and such formality were but barely controlled. Here a tendril of dark, lustrous hair would charmingly escape its coiffure, only to be negligently pushed back into place. Here a button would be but half done up while there a bodice with difficulty restrained what promised to be a gloriously lush yet firm bosom. In my mind's eye I could see breasts springing free of their imprisonment with their large brown nipples rising eagerly to my tongue.

As I sat, Becky on one side and Hannah on the other, whichever way I turned I saw lips and eyes, the delicious outlines of breasts and hips. Of what we conversed I was barely conscious. All I know is that whenever a mouth was opened, whether to admit some morsel of food or to utter some observation or question, I would see the small even white teeth and the full red lips and imagine those teeth gently nibbling the length of my now huge and pulsing cock, and those lips closing round the purple, straining head of my love staff.

So suffused was I with my raging need to fuck these ripe creatures that I must have appeared a stammering idiot, hardly able to complete a sentence. Mrs P— asked me much about Nottsgrove and the good Dr White with whom I discovered she had had some correspondence and of whose educational principles she said she was well informed and much approving. As I struggled to tell her also of the attention to correct grammar and the proper grounding in the Classics that, along with its distinctive ethical and moral standards, the school instilled in its pupils, there was a brief interruption.

Mrs P— had to pause and turn to answer some question that the maid had raised. This, it seemed, concerned a misfortune that had overtaken the pudding in the kitchen. As she was preoccupied with coping with this domestic crisis, Hannah, or was it Becky, so confused was I in my lust, turned to me and said in a delightfully low voice yet with an absolutely calm gaze into my eyes, 'Is it true that all Nottsgrovians have truly enormous pricks?'

At this the other gave a wicked little laugh while I was quite unable to speak. I could feel my eyes bulging and the blood rushing like a great tide to my already throbbing, monstrous member. Suddenly Becky, or was it Hannah, so confused was I, knocked over a full glass of wine which flooded across the table and poured down into my lap. As I looked down in horror at my straining, inundated crotch, Becky, or was it Hannah, gave a little cry of concern and anguish.

'Oh, look what I've done. You are all stained. Emily, quickly, fetch a cloth. Mr Scott is quite soaked through.'

With that she picked up her napkin, wetted it with her tongue and dabbed it down on to my now painfully bulging trousers. As her hand closed on the tight cloth she rubbed her palm across the enveloped head of Mr Pego and said, 'We will have to take you in hand, Mr Scott.'

This last was too much. With something of a groan I doubled up, inadvertently trapping her hand between my thighs, just as her mother, looking across to us as though nothing untoward was happening, said, 'You must excuse me for a minute. It seems cook is in the midst of some sort of upheaval in the kitchen and the Spotted Dick is quite spoiled.' With that she rose and said, 'I hope Hannah and Becky can keep you suitably amused for a little while. If there is to be no pudding, then we shall find some dessert.'

As soon as she was out of the room, Hannah, or was it Becky, said, 'Andrew, we are being most unfair and are teasing you most unmercifully.'

'But,' said the other, 'enough of this playing. I am most ready for fucking.'

'I also,' said her sister. 'But we have only a few moments before mother returns. The fucking will come later but for the instant all we can to is to make you more comfortable.'

With this I was unbuttoned, as urgently playful hands reached inside my trousers from both sides to bring out my immense swollen cock which immediately leaped up so that its whole pulsating length with its already weeping head was exposed, standing proud above the dining table.

Both girls drew in their breath and looked at each other.

'Truly that is one of the most magnificent fucking machines that I have ever seen,' said one.

'We are going to be very lucky to have such a pleasure staff around the house,' said the other. 'But that must wait.'

As if planned two faces were lowered in unison towards my lap and two tongues licked out to stroke my member, one from the right side, one from the left. Two hands, one from the left side and one from the right, reached out to delve inside my gaping trousers and take my aching balls in hand. Gently they squeezed while their questing lips met at the moist head of my gigantic erection. Tongue touched tongue and both tongues jostled to poke at the open eye of my prick. With a tidal rush the hot spunk burst from my cock, jetting into mouths, over lips and into the air. Hands stroked and milked the great spasms of cum. Nails scratched lightly along the blue, distended vein as I spent myself in a shuddering ecstasy of relief.

Each in turn, my spunk still sticky on her lips, kissed me open-mouthed, thrusting her tongue to meet my tongue. 'See,' said one, 'we may tease a little but we are not so unkind as to leave you without *any* satisfaction. But now Mama will shortly return and you are not properly dressed for the remainder of dinner.

'We shall explain that after your misfortune with the wine you have retired in order to effect a change of clothes,' said the other. 'But when you are returned, now that we have helped you, we would ask of you that for the remainder of dinner you make some attempt at conversation. There is much in London and in the world that is interesting to discuss. In return we shall not tease you further.'

'Rather,' said the other, 'we can promise you that there will be much that you can do for us before the evening is complete.'

With this, she seized my hand and guided it under her skirt and up along her thigh, pushing the petticoat aside until I rested on her already deliciously wet cunt.

'Now we can both look forward to a most thorough fucking tonight.'

Already I could feel my love shaft stirring to life once more but, with a quick kiss to its head, my prick was bundled back inside my clothing and I was bundled out of the room with a cry of 'Don't be long now!'

'But you must be long later,' said the other with a quick giggle.

As I repaired somewhat hastily and in some discomfort to my rooms, brushing past the maid Emily who was carrying a scuttle full of coal towards the drawing room, I was conscious of my stained and not wholly proper appearance. There at the bedside I found another maid whom I had not previously seen. 'Mary, Sir,' she said, dropping a curtsy, 'the Mistress told me to make your room ready. There is a hot water bottle already in the bed.' Then her gaze happened upon my wine-and-cum darkened trousers. 'Oh, Sir, you have met with some misfortune at the dinner table. I shall at once bring hot water.' 'Mary,' I said. 'Mary,' fixing her name in my mind for in truth, even in my hurried and embarrassed state, I could not but notice that here was another pretty young creature who, even in the severity and plainness of her servant's dress, held out the promise of pleasure for some lusty young man, 'I must change and quickly return to the table.'

As she withdrew, I speedily found another pair of trousers and thankfully dropped my soiled pair to the ground. My virile member was still swollen and engorged, and indeed showing every sign of springing so rigidly to attention once more that I realised that it would be with difficulty that I would be able to force it back into a decent state of subservience inside my trousers.

Seizing hold of the ewer of water that stood with a basin on the wash stand, I doused my throbbing ardour with handfuls of cold water. Shuddering with relief, I watched as my prick shrank down to a more manageable and docile state. By the time Mary returned with hot water, I was altogether in command of myself again. After some industrious sponging and towelling I was ready to dress once more and face the delightful attentions of my landlady and her two daughters.

When I returned to the dining room, Mrs P— was already back in her place at the head of the table. 'I am sorry about your mishap, Mr Scott,' she said. 'I have alas to report that the kitchen mishap was not so easily remedied and the Spotted Dick is quite beyond recovery.' 'But,' said Hannah, or was it Becky, 'we have some passion fruit for dessert.' As she said this both she and her sister turned such wide-eyed gazes upon me, and upon in particular the seat of my earlier difficulties, that I sat down abruptly in my place lest some stirring of my dormant member should renew my embarrassment.

'I am not acquainted with the passion fruit, Ma'am,' I said.

'It is not a normal part of the English cuisine,' said my hostess, 'but you will recall that I and my family have spent may years in the East. You are not acquainted with the exotic cultures of those parts, I assume?'

'Indeed not,' I replied, 'even London is quite new and exciting to me.'

'Well, Mr Scott, then you do indeed have much to look forward to. However, one word of warning. We have in this household certain understandings and certain rules that are not those of our neighbours or of what is sometimes called Polite Society. There is a frankness of word and even of action that is not to be taken as general. I must admit to a little subterfuge earlier when I was questioning you about the ethics and moral precepts instilled in you by Dr White at Nottsgrove. I am indeed well acquainted with his philosophy and approve of it most thoroughly. I was interested to see that you had so well absorbed his teaching that you were in turn, able to describe it to me with conviction. Dr White and I have indeed had considerable correspondence in the recent past. The name of Mr Richard Burton is no doubt familiar to you as an explorer and sojorner in strange places?'

I intimated that this was indeed so and she went on to tell me that she and Dr White, who had an extensive interest in matters exotic and a library well stocked with certain Eastern arcana, had long been encouraging Mr Burton – who she had first met many years before when he was a subaltern in a Regiment of the Bombay Native Infantry – to translate certain Works of Oriental technique, including something she described as being a wholly delightful and thoughtful treatise on the art of love called the *Kama Sutra of Vatsyayana.*

'You are aware of Ovid's *Ars Amatoria,*' said my hostess. 'No doubt, like many a schoolboy, you read it in a group in the dormitory with many a giggle and guffaw.'

'Not at all,' I replied. 'It was always Dr White's belief that such things should be openly studied for he said that it was great literature and dealt with a subject that should be spoken of frankly and enjoyed without pretence or hypocrisy.'

'It is indeed refreshing to be told that the good Doctor is so open and holds so fast to his own philosophy. You have been well taught Andrew, for I think that we are enough acquainted for me to so call you. If you hold fast to his precepts, then you should have no difficulty in understanding those conventions that rule in this household.'

Interesting though the conversation was and pleased as I was to realise that I had entered into a very unusual family indeed, I had become increasingly distracted in the last few moments, not so much by the intoxicating promise of Hannah and Becky, for there I had the delicious glow of certainty that within the evening the three of us would be joined in that most fulfilling of healthy pursuits, sexual congress, but rather by an intermittent and ever loudening squealing that seemed to come from below stairs. Eventually the cries became so intense that Mrs P— could no longer pretend that nothing was amiss, whilst both Hannah and Becky were unashamedly shaking with merriment.

'I can't think what that girl is up to,' my hostess said.

'Oh, Mama,' cried out Becky, 'after all your little lectures on openness and so forth. You know, and I and my sister both know that that is the sound of Mary. That is our pretty maid Mary, fucking and being fucked.'

'Well, my dears, with Andrew being only recently made a member of the household, I must admit to a certain reticence in description –'

'Mary,' said Hannah, 'is a screamer. As you are doubtless aware Andrew, there are amongst women, those who moan, who sigh, who catch their breath, those who laugh, some who are quite silent. And then there are some, a few, who scream. It is not done to shock or to tease. It can not be helped.'

At this juncture the door opened to admit Emily who deftly and efficiently brought in one decanter of port and one of brandy, together with glasses. Mrs P— looked at me and said, 'One house convention is that, since we are three women who delight in conversation and in the exchange of ideas and since there is no man at our head, we do not withdraw while any gentlemen present settle down with cigars and brandy. You are most welcome to smoke but first I suggest you help yourself to the port before passing the decanter on to me.'

At this point, just as Emily decorously slipped out of the room, the screams of downstairs delight reached a new peak of intensity.

'Nonetheless, I must speak to that girl,' said Mrs P—.

'You can hardly do that now, Mama,' said Becky. 'Mary is a good girl. She is honest and industrious and neither insubordinate nor impudent, but at the moment we all know that she is quite incapable of paying attention to you or anyone else. She is on her back with her legs drawn up to her shoulders whilst her cunny is crammed full of Tom the Tool who is battering at the very entrance to her womb.'

'And,' said her sister, 'his balls will be banging against her pussey lips –'

'Really, my dear,' said her mother, 'I do not think you should call that nice young man Tom the Tool. He has a perfectly good name.'

'Oh Mama,' said Hannah, 'of course he is a perfectly nice young man. And he is very good for Mary. He fucks her most thoroughly and most regularly. He is nice, he is polite and clean. But I do not think that there is much more to him than that. Cecily Arbuthnot says that he is a most willing and efficient outdoor servant, good with the horses, reliable on errands –'

'And he has an absolutely enormous prick,' interrupted her sister.

110

'Really dear, how can you possibly know?' asked her mother with a touch of impatience.

'Because I asked Mary,' said her daughter unashamedly. 'She said that it is the biggest thing she had ever seen since she left the country and came to London to seek a position.'

'Well she certainly seems to have found a position all right.'

'A well-filled position, I would say by the sound of it.'

'Girls! girls!' cried their mother, then turned to me. 'Tom is Mary's follower. She is allowed to entertain him in the evenings as her duties permit and during her time off. As you will gather, I am most broadminded and do not think it any business of mine what the servants do, although I like to know that they are not being made unhappy. This Tom is a straightforward young man –'

'And straightforward in his fucking and strong. Mary says that he can make her come again and again,' said Becky.

'If only she wasn't so *noisy*,' said her mother. 'She knows that she is not supposed to disturb the household, particularly when we are at dinner and most particularly when we have guests. I must have a word with her.'

She rang for Emily and told her that Mary was to present herself in the dining room in an hour. 'That will give her time to recover and restore herself to a state of some decorum,' she said. 'Tell her that I am not angry but that we have to reach some understanding.'

'We were entertaining the Dean of Ormskirk once,' said Hannah. 'He and his wife stayed overnight and after they had retired to bed, Mary had a most juicy, screaming fuck. The Dean thought someone was being murdered and rushed out in his night shirt, picking up a poker and went as he thought to her aid. Mary was on all fours in the laundry room, while Tom the Tool was banging away, his hands clutching at her titties and his huge cock thrusting deep into her cunny, when the door burst open and there stood the Dean, night light in one hand, poker in the other. Tom the Tool backed out with terror but Mary was too far gone and was shrieking 'Fuck me, fuck me, fuck me Tom. I'm coming, I'm coming,' while Tom was going.

The Dean, being somewhat confused, and thinking on the

instant that he was confronted by a mortally wounded woman, commenced administering the Last Rites as he knelt by her. Mary, quite overcome by the waves of her orgasm that were now convulsing her, clutched the Dean by the nightshirt, her thighs gripping him round the waist and rubbing her engorged nipples against his chest whilst still crying out 'Oh, fuck, Oh fuck.' The Dean, discovering as he later said, that the flesh was weak – by which he meant that part at least of it had become rather strong – found himself grappling with a completely strange woman on a stone flagged floor, surrounded by piles of laundry. Mary was thrusting against his now rubbed-and-ready clerical staff, utterly oblivious that it was a Man of the Cloth who in her frenzy of coming she was near to fucking.'

'My God!' I exclaimed, choking with laughter but also much aware that the sound of the dark-haired Mary and the picture that was being painted by the mine-for-the-fucking Hannah had caused a moistening ramrod to re-erect itself in my lap. 'What was the outcome?'

'I was disturbed by the commotion,' said Mrs P——, 'and knowing by what that sound was occasioned, descended hastily to the basement. I was just in time to rescue the Dean from the inadvertent commission of the Sin of Adultery. Mary, poor thing, had a weeping fit, believing that she was about to be dismissed instantly without a Character. It was after that that I had a good talk with her and exacted a promise, not of continence for that would be a sore deprivation for her, but of Common Sense. She knows that when there are visitors in the house, she is to be discreet. That is why I am not well pleased with her tonight. I know that no great harm is done and I know that if you are to lodge with us, you will have to become used to Mary. Nonetheless, it was silly of her, not yet being properly aware of your status in the household, to allow young Tom to provoke her into such an outcry. We do, as I have said, have certain rules in the house. They are there not for the mere sake of the exercise of authority, nor in the service of some moral code that frowns on all enjoyment and believes that abstinence and denial of the urgings of the flesh are virtues to be striven for. It is rather that we have to live one with another, in a state of co-operative self-discipline, hoping always to avoid discomfitting others by our actions. But I fear that I am becoming somewhat prolix and didactic.'

'It is the port, Mama,' said one daughter. For all the while the decanter had been circulating between the four of us.

'You will not be too harsh on the girl,' I said. 'She was most solicitous earlier in attending to my needs when I had to repair the consequences of my slight accident at the table.'

'No. It is generous of you to worry on her behalf. I shall not punish her but will remind her of her promise to exercise some self control. I shall go and talk to her shortly and then, if you will excuse me, I have some notes that I promised to write up for Mr Burton, concerning certain practices that I encountered among the Temple Dancers of the Ganges Valley. I shall leave you to be entertained by my daughters and hope to see you in the morning. Breakfast is a movable feast. You may take it either in your own rooms or *en famille*.'

With that, she bade me Good Night and then quite unexpectedly, put her arms around me and kissed me on the forehead. 'I have a feeling that you will fit easily into this household, My Dear,' she murmured. And with that, she was gone.

'I can think of at least one place in the household into which you will be most welcome to fit,' said Becky, a flush rising to her cheek and her full lips parting in a most enticing smile.

'I also, feel ready to accommodate you with some ease,' said her sister.

'I stand ready and eager to be of service,' I replied.

'But,' said Becky, 'there is a problem. Splendid though your love staff is, it is but one. But here are two cunts, each of which demands to be first served. Sister, we must cut the cards to see who shall be first impaled and ridden into ecstasy.'

With that, she rang the bell and when pretty Emily answered, called for a pack of cards. Emily, a fair haired, almost frightened wisp of a creature, hurried off and soon returned, bearing the cards on a salver. 'There is no need to wait up further, Emily,' said Hannah. 'We will attend to Mr Andrew's wants. Mary has made his room ready, has she not?'

'Indeed yes, Miss Hannah,' said Emily, and was gone.

'Now Andrew,' said Becky, 'Hannah and I will cut the cards and the first to turn up a Black Queen will claim her prize.'

'But first,' said Hannah, 'I insist that the prize be put on view for it will add greatly to the excitement of the game.' With that she commenced to unbutton me.

'But,' I protested, 'surely I also should have *my* prizes displayed before me for whilst I have earlier, for a most tantalising moment, felt one of the two love nests that await me, I have as yet seen neither. Nor have I seen one, let alone a pair of the delicious titties that I know also lie in hiding for me, yet I have spent the whole evening in a veritable haze of imagination.'

'That is a most fair request,' said Becky, beginning to unlace and unbutton her clothing. Hannah also, whilst she completed the release of my straining cock, then began to unloose her garments.

Suddenly first one and then a second pair of the most glorious breasts spilled out into full view. How right I had been in my imagining for all were delightfully flushed and each proudly dark nipple was already rising and engorged.

'An anointment and a libation is called for,' said Becky merrily as she leaned over me, her ripe fruit proffered teasingly before me. Straight away she dipped her fingers into her brandy glass and rubbed the smooth but fiery liquor over her splendidly firm-fleshed titties. At once Hannah followed suit.

'Now Andrew, you must lick clean your prize,' said Becky.

I reached out to take first one and then the other titty into my mouth. Sucking and grazing on this bountiful harvest, my mouth moved from one to the other, drawing the brandy-soaked nipples into me, my tongue rolling each darling bud and my teeth nipping gently at each swollen aureole.

Meanwhile, Hannah, having freed my distended prick from the last of its encumbering clothing, was clutching it between her juicy breasts and rubbing its purple head in the brandy and sweat-soaked valley that ran between them.

Becky drew me to my feet, my trousers and undergarments slipping to the carpet, and as she swiftly unbuttoned my shirt, I felt Hannah slip round behind me, rubbing her breasts against my back as she helped her sister ease my shirt off my shoulders. Then as she lifted her skirt to her waist, I felt the succulent dampness of her bush as she twined one leg round mine and rubbed herself like a cat up and down against my thigh. Reaching behind me, my hands closed on the twin globes of her bottom and I pulled her hard against me, the jut of her pussey scratching deliciously against me.

Now Becky, pulling away from my questing mouth, also lifted her skirts to stand, switching her hips like a Spanish dancer, flaunting the dark luxurience of her pubic forest. Firmly she took my hand and introduced it into that dark warmth. My fingers touched cunt lips that parted and slicked a sudden wetness over my enquiring finger tips.

'Wait, wait,' said Becky breathlessly. 'Here are two cunts, each slippery and wide open to you. We must hurry and cut the cards and settle the order of precedence for I am already wet and ready for your entry.'

So saying, both dropped down on hands and knees and started to cut the pack while I fondled their pretty arses.

'Seven of Hearts,' cried out Hannah.

'Four of Spades.'

'King of Spades.'

'Ten of diamonds.'

My prick, fatly throbbing, the head blood-purpled, its eye milkily runny, was aching with the need to spend and spend the spunk that at any moment would start to force its way up from my burdened, throbbing balls. As Becky and Hannah played out their game, the heat rose from them and I sensed their cunts, flared and juicy with anticipation.

'Four of Clubs.'

'Queen! Queen of Spades!'

Becky, moaning almost with excitement, turned over on to her back, drew her legs apart and upwards and cried out 'Fuck me! Fuck me!'

'Darling Becky, he is coming at you now,' said Hannah. 'Fuck her, Andrew. Fuck her!' Gasping, I plunged myself into her. The heat and wetness of her drew me up and in, in. Her legs spread wider as her head rolled from side to side. Her sister, crouching at her head, still holding her arms down, commenced to kiss her, mouth to mouth, their heads twisting and turning, each in ecstasy.

Suddenly a convulsion lifted Becky's hips and arse clean off the ground as she gripped my cock like a vice.

'Quick, quick, Oh quick! I'm coming,' she cried as I felt the hot spunk surging through my prick to spurt again and again into her soon-saturated cunt. Now she matched me and more than matched me in the uncontrollable urgency of her spending. The thick juice, her juice, my juice, mingled and spurted down our thighs. Now she clung to me with a sobbing desperation, her breasts crushed against me while her sister clung to the two of us, her mouth seeking and sucking as she shared in our coming.

The last spasms of cum jetted into my darling's filled cunt. Panting, she wound her arms round me.

'Stay inside me,' she cried. 'Let me feel you in me.'

We lay, all entwined, our bodies slippery with sweat, our love juices leaking out and soaking into the carpet.

'Messy, messy,' Becky murmured in my ear. 'We're messing the carpet. Stay in me. Let me feel you go soft. Mary will clean the carpet in the morning. Mary will clean it all up. Cunt juice. Cock juice. Woman juice. Man juice. Love juice. Mary knows about love juice.'

She was beginning to giggle almost hysterically. 'I fuck, you fuck, Mary fucks. We all fuck. Oh, fuck, fuck, fuck. What's the Latin for fucking? We're doing the grammar of fucking.'

I felt a great fondness for this wild creature who had abandoned herself so utterly to me and to fucking. I lay, completely spent, my whole body like lead, collapsed upon

116

her. I remembered that someone, back in those Nottsgrove days that seemed an age ago, had said to me that a gentleman always takes his weight on his elbows. Just for a moment I tried to raise my body, my elbows digging into the rug. A Kelim rug. Strange how I recalled then my darling's mother telling me about the oriental carpets that they had brought back on the P & O boat from India. For a moment I wondered whether some Indian temple dancer had ever fucked on that same rug.

Would Mrs P—'s friend, Mr Burton, ever complete his translation of the *Kama Sutra*? My mind drifted until Becky murmured something and pulled herself to me as I felt myself finally go limp. As she twitched her hips, I slipped out of her. Half asleep in her exhaustion, she reached for my prick.

'All gone. All gone,' she whispered like a child, her lips as though unconsciously sucking at my nipples.

Suddenly I shivered as a chill passed over my body. Becky too started and shivered. I could hear the ticking of the Grandfather clock that stood in the corner. I lifted my head. The fire was burning low in the grate. Hannah was sitting cross-legged a few feet away, a little smile on her face, sketching industriously. As she saw that I was watching her, she held up her drawing for me to see.

There, half-completed, was a most detailed likeness in pencil of my now detumescent member. I looked at it with interest.

'Hannah,' I said, 'that is a very true portrait of my present state. If in a little while I can re-erect myself, will you attempt a further drawing from Life?'

'Certainly,' she answered. 'Indeed I think that it is almost revival time.' With that she poured a little brandy into a glass.

Then she cupped the glass between her naked thighs, drew her index finger along her already wet cunt lips and placed it in the liquid. Now she switched and twitched her hips to warm the vital spirit with her heat while the promise of her cum mingled with the liquor. Raising her hips, she offered up the glass to me. Lowering my head, I lapped thirstily like a cat at the flesh-warmed brandy.

Becky too sat up, pulling her clothes about her and hugging

her arms round her pretty, still love-swollen titties. As we all three shared the brandy, she said to me, 'Andrew, I must tell you about my sister.'

'We have already met,' I said, with a poor attempt at humour.

'Andrew, there are two things you must know about her. She is a most talented artist and she loves to fuck. Don't you, Hannah, dear?'

'It is indeed true that I love to have a pencil in my hand and a prick in my cunt,' said Hannah.

'Have you considered accommodating both things at once?' asked Becky.

I could see that they were playing a game, both with me and with each other.

'I have indeed considered it and have tried it in the past but find that I am often quite put off my stroke,' answered Hannah, still scribbling industriously away. 'I am putting the finishing touches to this evening's sketch,' she said.

She was now down on all fours, wielding her pencil with great seriousness as one may see a young child, intently licking the point and concentrating utterly on completing her drawing. As I leaned over her the better to see her work, she raised herself slightly and rubbed against me, the cleft of her bum pressing against my still-limp cock.

At that touch a renewed charge of energy seemed to course the length of my sorely tried member. The soft caress of her secret hair gently brought Mr Pego back to life. Turning her head, she looked sideways up at me and smiled most teasingly, her tongue darting out to lick her lips. Again she raised her delicious cheeks to butt and rub against me. I ran my tongue lightly down the ridge of her spine and then gently pulled apart her bum cheeks, massaging the delicious flesh with the palms of my hands.

With a purring little giggle, she ducked her head and lifted her bum still higher, rather as a tumbler at the circus commences a forward roll. Now her most private parts were most public and most parted. As my tongue flickered first around the rim of her back passage and then along the secret

118

pathway between back passage and front entrance, I slid under her.

Now she sucked my quite revived member into her mouth, taking in its entire ramrod length and letting it slide easily down over her tongue to her throat just as a sword swallower will without gagging take in a lethal weapon. By now my face was quite buried in her damply dense bush, my tongue tracking through her enveloping jungle to seek out first her cunt lips, already opened and welcoming to my intrusion, and next her clitoris, engorged and swollen like an answer to my own erect staff.

As my tongue rubbed over the head of her yearning clit and delved deeper into the swamp of her cunt, she within an instant began to writhe and shudder. Still holding my bloated prick in her mouth, she started to moan as her hips bucked and pumped ever faster. Then in moments her whole body convulsed and the waves of her orgasm surged through her. Hot love juice filled my mouth as I struggled to hold her in the repeated surges of her passion.

Soon, trembling and sweat-soaked, she subsided on to me, every muscle relaxed, her whole body softened and inert. Gently, slowly, slowly, she released my still charged cock from her mouth and slid from me to lie cuddled at my side. I lay still and she also for some few moments until her hand reached out to cradle my balls. Shivering slightly, she kissed me lightly on the tip of my still upstanding prick, hugged me and said, 'And now I want to feel the whole length of your cock slide slowly into my cunt.'

So saying, she lifted herself, straddled me and lowered herself on to me. I could see my straining prick inch by inch disappear into her open-mouthed pussey. She settled, wriggled as though to seal our union. Then, sitting bolt upright, she arched her back so that her magnificent titties jutted out above me. Putting both hands behind her neck, she shook her head, tossing her dark hair and looking down at me with an air of sly triumph. Then, reaching down and taking her weight on her hands, she kissed me on the lips as she lifted herself so that she was once again clear of my erect but

119

unmoving cock.

Again she lowered herself, pausing so that her cunt lips could brush the very tip of my prick before slipping her luscious wetness down the full length of my shaft. Again she paused before lifting herself once more. This time she did not quite pull clear before slipping down. Again, and again, she settled into a slow regular rhythm.

I rose to meet her slippery descent, thrusting up, but she firmly rested her weight on me and said with a secret smile of pure lust, 'No, no, you must be patient.' The control she was exercising over the urgent desires of her own body and of mine was focussing all her senses and now mine also, our whole beings, on that one area of absolute, concentrated pleasure. Yet there is a point where pleasure and pain become one. My whole cock had become so sensitive to the slow rhythmic slip and slide that I swear I almost flinched at the touch. So swollen was my member that I could feel the blood pulsing, beating, beating in it, along it, through it.

Then I felt that first stir, that first movement as my spunk began to force its way up my distended shaft. As though she sensed this, she ceased all movement, her cunt half way down my prick, and broke the spell of my concentration by reaching down once more to kiss me. Twice more she arrested my coming and then lowered herself once more to fully engulf me. But now she began to move with shorter, faster thrusts and I began to respond. Her mouth was open and she was gasping and moaning. Both of us were at the very brink of ecstasy as the pace increased to near-frenzy.

Suddenly the muscles of her cunt tightened about me in a long rippling seizure that ran from the root to the very tip of my prick. Three times more this clutching spasm travelled the length of my staff as though she was milking me of my juice. Then she relaxed and at once the spunk burst out of me, forcing its way, hot and seething, into every recess and cranny of her cunt. Gush after gush jetted along my shaft, spurting uncontrollably up, up, deep into her.

In a near-delirium I realised that I was crying out 'Yes! Yes! Yes!' and thrusting up so hard that she was clinging to me like a rider on a bucking horse whilst she ground her pussey against me as she surrendered at last to her own orgasm. Her teeth were biting into my shoulder as she choked back her cries. Her breasts were crushed against me and my fingers were digging deep into the flesh of her bum, pulling her on to me. Our cum juices were leaking out of her to flood over our bellies and thighs.

As we slowly subsided I reached down into our mingled wetness and rubbed it over her body, over her succulent titties. She did likewise and in moments we were completely oiled and stickied with our cum and our sweat. Panting and near exhaustion, we lay entwined in an intimate muddle of flesh upon flesh, limb entwined with limb. A warm wave of spent fatigue washed over me and I do not know how long we lay there, barely conscious.

6

A little later, suffused with a damp lethargy, we lay, the three
of us, before the fire, our bodies touching in a delicious post-
fuck intimacy, wrapped in a littered nest of long-discarded
clothing and rugs. Cradled between breasts and thighs,
balloon glasses of brandy warmed and were passed, one to
another. Sipping slowly, sometimes one licking the spirit
from the lips of another, sometimes sharing glasses, we
sleepily talked. I watched as Hannah put the last touches to
the drawing of my now quiescent cock. As she finished, she
touched her lips to the sketch and passed it to me as she bent
to kiss first the original of her study and then my lips.

'Show Andrew some others of your sketches,' said Becky,
with a knowing smile.

Hannah, a happy little chuckle in her throat, produced a
portfolio of some twenty or thirty sketches. Most were boldly
precise anatomies of those parts of the human body that
convention decrees should be kept hidden. Here in exquisite
detail were pricks and cunts and titties and bums. All had
seemingly been drawn from life. With a twitch of delighted
recognition, I saw before me all those parts of her sister that I
had so recently enjoyed. Here also were mirror images of her
own lovely cunt and her own dark-nippled breasts. There
were pictures also of parts belonging to people that I did not
recognise as well as conjunctions and couplings of parts. Here
was a spirited likeness of Becky cradling a male member to
her breast, a lightly drawn sketch of Becky again, taking a
cock into her mouth. Here was detailed a rigid member
plunging into a densely bushed cunt.

'Becky?' I asked, on seeing this.

'Or Hannah?' queried Becky.

'Truth to tell, I cannot be sure,' I replied.

'Well, Andrew, either my drawing is not a good one, or you, who have so recently enjoyed both our cunts, have not paid either of us the close attention we might hope,' said Hannah. 'See, here are both the originals before you. Pray give us the courtesy of an inspection.'

With that each girl smilingly spread out her legs to display their dark-haired treasure caves to me.

'Now, Sir, if you are still undecided,' said Hannah, 'we will both have to press our claims upon you in the future.'

'In fact,' said Becky, 'I for one will not be satisfied until you are so practised that you can distinguish blindfold which cunt is which.'

Without wishing to cause any offence, I replied, 'It may be that I will prove a slow pupil but I do promise that, until I have learned my lesson, I shall be most prompt in attending any revision that you shall present to me.'

'You will, I promise, be well and repeatedly schooled,' said Hannah.

'I look forward to my testing,' I replied, fondling their dark and lush fannies, 'but in the meantime, let us return to the portfolio. There are features and faces here of which I am quite ignorant.'

As I leafed through the drawings I came upon two where recognition stirred. One was of a girl with her skirts thrown up and her naked bum thrust out towards the beholder in such a fashion that, between the spread legs, one could see her bush and indeed her cunt lips already slightly parted as if in eager anticipation of some thrusting entry. There was a general familiarity of outline and figure although I knew that I had never actually seen the naked parts so lovingly detailed and spread out before me on the page. Could it be the maid Mary, I wondered? Mary whom I had seen only briefly in my room when I had been preoccupied with my dining table misfortune but from whom I had heard so memorably a while later.

'Mary?' I asked.

'Oh, no, we cannot tell you,' said Hannah. 'It would not be right to divulge any names, for all these drawings are for private pleasure only. Supposing, Andrew, I was to circulate the likeness of your cock. You might well not want it bandied about amongst gatherings of strangers, or passed from hand to hand amongst your acquaintance.

'However if you should ever discover, or better still enjoy, the original of what you see before you, then we would confirm your discovery. But we will demand a most detailed account of how you came by your evidence as well as a proper description of the event. Until that time our lips are sealed and you must think of it only as The Unknown Cunt. The only clue I shall give you is that, should you uncover it and be invited to enter it, you will find it a most capacious and welcoming tunnel of love.'

One further drawing I did recognise and with great certainty. Here was the pretty but thin little maid Emily. It was a likeness of her face, a touch of sadness in her eyes, her blonde hair curled about her cheeks and a shy but happy smile upon her lips as she kissed the tip of a male member that she had carefully cradled in her hands. Here was a sensitive, almost loving sketch that would long linger in my memory with its suggestions both of vulnerability and of a half-ashamed boldness. I knew that I must not ask yet felt sure that there was a story lying behind that pencil portrait.

But as I passed on to the rest of the drawings I realised that apart from these often tantalising sketches from life, Hannah had created a series of what I can only describe as fantasy scenes. All were wildly imaginative and often splendidly witty as well.

Here was a landscape, a sketch of the celebrated Ancient Monument of Stonehenge. However every upright stone, as well as those leaning and lying on the ground, had been replaced with the likeness of a gigantic male organ, sprouting and bursting up from the ground.

Here was a representation of a bowl of sweetmeats except that every one was a bum in fondant or a titty in chocolate. Next was what I can only describe as a cunt's-eye-view. It was as though one was staring out of the widened cleft and regarding the bloated head of an enormous prick that was bearing down on its target. Finally there were several rough but happily suggestive drawings of musicians – except that in every case their instruments had been replaced with others of a decidedly unmusical nature. A woman played upon a greatly elongated prick as though it were a flute; another, seated, had between her knees a giant cock that she bowed like a double bass while a tympanist clashed two proudly nippled cymbals over his head.

'Is not my sister a remarkable artist?' asked Becky.

'Why, yes,' I replied. 'And like all true artists she sees more than the ordinary mortal's eye.'

'I set down my imaginings,' said Hannah.

'It would seem that your imagination tends always towards one subject,' I said.

'Andrew, you really must not be so solemn,' she replied. 'Surely, when you walk down the street and you see and even brush against women of all ages and classes, does not your imagination sometimes wander as you wish your hands could?'

'I admit to the charge,' I said.

'And what do you see, in your mind's eye?'

'Cunts,' I said. 'I see cunts everywhere and all about me: prim, virgin cunts, loose-lipped bushy cunts, recently-satisfied, sleepy cunts, hungry, questing cunts, brown-haired pussies, black-haired pussies, golden-haired, young, scarcely-furred pussies, mature, greatly experienced pussies, very private cunts reserved for one member only and open-to-all-comers cunts.'

'Well, Andrew, such eloquence! You see now how the imagination can be stirred,' said Hannah. 'So I am not unusual in what I see. Only possibly more honest in setting it down.'

'And more talented,' I added.

'You are most generous and gallant,' she said.

'No,' I said, 'just honest in my admiration. If only I had such abilities. Surely you could earn great sums with such artistic skills?'

'I do not think that I could openly display my imagination

125

in the galleries,' she said with a little giggle. 'I would most certainly be brought up before the magistrates and my imagination would be shut up in some House of Correction.'

'To put your pussey behind bars would indeed be a great pity,' I said.

At this she giggled again and seized hold of paper and pencil to begin sketching furiously away. Curious, I looked over her shoulder but she pushed me away.

'No, you must wait until it is finished,' she said. 'But now, Sister, you must be my model pussey.'

Becky at once lay back, opened her legs and raised her knees to put on display her lovely cunt.

'Tomorrow,' she said, interrupting my lingering and lip-licking inspection of her prettily posed pussey, 'maybe you shall see my sister's sketches for her pottery. Some are based on Indian sculptures and some on Ancient Greek and Roman Reliefs. Do you know anything of pottery and its techniques?'

'No,' I said, 'but if it is a medium for your sister's imagination, than I am most ready to be informed. But, you, Becky, what outlet do you have for your imagination? Do you also draw or paint, or perhaps you play upon some musical instrument?'

'I have certain skills upon the organ,' Becky replied with a most provocative chuckle, 'but I have never really enjoyed the arts and crafts thought proper for young girls. When at school, we were taught needlecraft and forced to embroider a sampler. All the other girls in my class painstakingly produced efforts with such maxims as "Bless This House" or "God Save the Queen" but I regret to say that I disgraced myself.'

'Your sampler said what?' I asked.

'It did not *say* anything,' answered Becky, now engaged in holding her cunt lips well apart at the request of her sister. 'But it did depict, as far as I could imagine it for I was very young and quite inexperienced at that time, a male member standing handsomely upright and executed all in pink stitching. Our needlework mistress was altogether shocked. She of course had to pretend not to recognise what the subject was while all the other girls gathered round and asked her such questions as "Miss Pratt, what is that funny thing that Becky has embroidered?" or "Are they really like that, Miss Pratt?" for that was her name.'

'What happened?' I asked.

'Mama was most annoyed that I had been so silly. But after that I was not put to needlework again. I have written a few poems and have tried my hand at essays but what I would really like to do is to write a novel. I read much. Mama has always encouraged us both in this. Even on Sundays, from an early age, we were allowed to read such as Mr Dickens. Mama mentioned at dinner that her friend Mr Burton was engaged on certain translations from the Persian and from the Indian languages. It is an endeavour that I would like to help in. I do not have the scholarly knowledge that Mr Burton and some of his circle have but such works as *The Perfumed Garden* and the *Thousand And One Nights* are greatly interesting to me. You also might be persuaded by their philosophy. Now that you have come to live in our house, there are many things that we might show you.'

At this moment Hannah sat up, looked at her sketch and held it out to her sister. Both laughed and she passed it to me. It was inscribed *To Andrew, Who Gave Me the Idea* and under that the legend *Pussies Behind Bars*. There was a most hilarious depiction of several pussies, some lightly sketched, but one in the centre finished in great detail, all pushed up against the bars of some prison cell, their lips open and the hair of their luxuriant bushes poking between the bars as the words 'Let Miaout' emerged from the open-throated beauty in the centre.

I took the cartoon sketch and, gently parting Becky's legs, kissed her lips lightly.

'Hannah, I will always keep this as a memento of a most delightful evening,' I assured her.

By now it was very late, and we were all three silly and sleepy with fucking and fatigue and brandy. We started to gather up our scattered clothing. I for one knew that what I yearned for most of all was some hours of deep, untroubled

127

sleep, knowing that any dreams that might come would be happy.

'Tonight we shall sleep in our own beds,' said Becky. 'Mary or Emily will bring hot water in the morning. You may of course have breakfast in your own room, or you may join us. Any time after half past eight there will be both hot and cold dishes on the side in the dining room. Good night Andrew. This has been a most pleasant evening.'

Yawning sleepily, she for an instant lightly cupped my balls in her hand, kissed my member, picked up an armful of clothing and walked slowly out of the room and upstairs. I watched the delicious cheeks of her bum twitch with her hips as she disappeared. Then Hannah, having gathered my things into a bundle, thrust them into my arms, similarly kissed me and said, 'Off you go, Andrew, I will put out the lights and follow as soon as you are safely up the stairs. We do not want you blundering about in the dark, especially dressed as you are.' With this she pressed her hand against my arse, the middle finger rubbing gently into the cleavage and pushed me firmly towards the door.

My bed was a most welcoming sight. The stone hot-water bedwarmer, manufactured I noticed by that same Messrs Doulton who were the employers of the succulent Hannah, ensured that after my enforced cold-water wash, I was quickly lulled into a most comfortable drowsiness. As I sank into unconsciousness, I remember looking back on the events of a quite memorable day. I had made the acquaintance of a most congenial family. I had found a place to lodge and indeed for some part of me I had found at least two places to lodge. My new life in London held out every promise for the future. With this thought, I speedily fell into a deep sleep for in truth I was quite exhausted by the events of the day.

Yet the much needed restorative of a night's unbroken sleep was not to be. At some time well before dawn, when all was still utterly dark and still, I awoke. A cold draft of air had stirred me into something approaching wakefulness. I sensed that it came from my now opened bedroom door. I half heard a creak as it was closed again and then sensed some presence near me. I reached out to strike a light for the candle in its holder by my bed but a small hand closed over mine and held it away from the box of vestas. Then a finger was placed on my lips, as though enjoining silence. As I sat up, somewhat bemused by this turn of events, a slender, completely unclothed body slipped in under the sheets to lie beside me. The delicious scent of warm woman's flesh was about me. Already my questing hands had told me that this was neither Becky or Hannah. My fingers encountered a slight, girlish figure. I stroked a small featured face, soft, silky curls of hair. The shoulders and arms were delicate and indeed bony in a most appealing manner. The breasts, for my voyage of downward discovery had now taken me so far, were small, not much more than can be found on a man. But the nipples were, both in proportion and absolutely, unusually long. As I stroked one and teased it under the ball of my thumb, it stiffened delightfully. I could hear the excited beat of a heart in that fragile body. Still a small hand was placed over my mouth as a signal that I was to say nothing. Nor was any word spoken by my silent visitor.

My hand now circling lower, I explored a flat belly, the hip bones prominent on either side. Below, covered in a most delicate tangle of pubic hair, her mount rose up, flesh padded but firm. Gently my finger touched and probed still lower. Her legs however were tight closed. Whoever this sweet night visitor was, she was not yet ready quite to open herself up to me.

We stayed almost still for some minutes. Her head was cradled into my shoulder and I felt the warmth of her breath on my chest. She was trembling and clinging to me. Slowly I circled my hand on her mount, feeling the soft rub of her pussey hair. My fingers slid down towards her secret cleft and her legs parted but only a little. In my fatigued state, I had wondered if this was but a happy dream. As yet but half aroused, I parted her hair and my finger touched her cunt lips. Again her legs opened a little more and she caught her breath, nay choked almost. Suddenly she clutched me tighter still and shuddered from head to toe. She seized my questing hand in hers and forced it downwards. Her thighs drew wide apart and she guided my fingers into her cunt. As my fingers dipped into her hot wetness, I discovered with an arousing excitement that I was fingering the widest, most gaping cunt that I had ever entered. That such a slight, small boned creature should reveal this great soft-fleshed opening was an amazement to me.

Now, still clasping my hand, she made it the instrument of her pleasure, rubbing her clit, which like her nipples was of such an unusual length that, as I was subsequently to discover, when aroused it protruded beyond her lips. Now I squeezed it between two of the three fingers that were stretching her wider yet. Now my fingers were being drawn deeper so that her lips rubbed against my knuckles. As she drove me on with increasing urgency, I frigged her faster and faster. Her breathing shortened into a panting as though she was desperate for air. Then, opening so wide that I thought she would tear herself apart, she plunged my hand into her and I felt the tremor of her coming rise up from deep inside her like a series of subterranean waves that welled to the surface with uncontrollable force. Surge after surge shuddered through her and all the while she clung to me as if in fear at her own body's reactions. Then, as the spasms lessened, her pussey began to close and as my fingers paddled in her copious juices, I was slowly guided out.

Still not speaking, she lay quiet, her heartbeat slowing, her breathing now soft and regular. Then my hand was released as her hand reached out to grasp my by now fully aroused prick. With finger and thumb she circled its base and then slowly drew her fingers up along the whole extension. For a moment she paused as though she was considering what she had encountered. Then, hidden wholly by the sheets, she turned and twisted downwards and I felt her mouth close over the flushed head of my member.

As both hands and mouth caressed and stroked and nibbled at my prick. I recalled suddenly the sketch by Hannah of the little maid Emily and knew at once that this was my visitor. I almost spoke her name out loud as the endearing little creature played and sucked me to coming point but such had been the deliberation with which she had urged me into silence that I stayed quiet. I ran my fingers through the tight curls of her hair and stroked the nape of her neck as her mouth, opened and wet as her cunt had been before, drove me on. Suddenly my cum was jetting into her mouth as she swallowed and sucked and swallowed once more. Soon she was milking the last drops of spunk from me before releasing me from her mouth. She rubbed her face over my still swollen parts, like a cat rubbing against its owner.

We clung to each other, she cradled against my chest and I sank utterly spent, into a blissful, undreaming sleep.

Some hours later I surfaced from my exhausted sleep. I sensed rather than saw the first light of dawn. All was quiet. Half-waking, half-dreaming, my hand reached out to explore a still warm, still damp space in the bed beside me. My night visitor had gone. Not quite sure whether I had not in fact dreamed the whole strange episode, I shivered in the now chilly air of my bedroom, pulled the covers tightly around me and drifted back into more much needed sleep.

In the morning as I awoke from a magnificent dream in which I was fucking the delicious Hannah, or was it Becky, I was aware both that I had a huge morning erection and that in every probability, during the course of the day my dream would come true. This was quite the most pleasant way in which to commence a new day. My mood was further improved when the maid Mary knocked and brought in my hot water. After Emily I began to wonder whether I might also be able to gain access to Mary and perhaps cause another such outpouring of vocal ecstasy as I had heard the previous evening.

Mary however was conducting herself with the quiet deference of one who knew her place so I resolved upon complete discretion concerning any wakening ambition that I might have to fuck her. I recognised also that I should in all propriety ask carefully of my landlady before entering into any further intercourse with her staff.

It was in fact lucky that I had so resolved for when after breakfast I discreetly mentioned to Becky that I had had a strange night visitation, she at once took me on one side.

'Emily?' she asked.

'By deduction, although I neither saw her nor had any conversation with her.' Becky then asked such questions concerning the events that had transpired in my bed that I quickly realised that such occurrences were a familiar part of life in the household. She then went out to have some words with her mother and shortly afterwards Mrs P— herself came in, sat down at the table with me and explained certain things.

'Andrew,' she said, 'firstly I must speak generally. Household servants and women in particular are very vulnerable and open to abuse. A girl knows that she can be dismissed by her employer at any time and also that if she is turned away without a reference she will then be unable to obtain another position in any decent household.

'It can easily happen that a young girl, her parents and family being most often many miles away in the country and depending on her employer not only for her wages but for her board and lodgings, can have great advantage taken of her. She may be grossly overworked and utterly hemmed in with rules and demands. She may also become the victim and the object of the lusts of perhaps the son of the family or even indeed of the head of the household himself.

'Many serving girls have for instance been forced to become the subject of a son's first sexual experience. She may be seduced, forcibly entered, treated as some piece of sexual property, played with, passed from hand to hand and then let drop. I hope that not many families treat their servants so but it does happen.

'It is for this reason that I am quite adamant that no servant in this house will ever be mistreated in such a way. Doubtless whilst you were at school the phrase *In loco parentis* was mentioned. Well, I also feel that I have duties that verge on the parental where my staff are concerned. If I found that anyone staying under my roof had forced himself on one of the maids he would be ordered from the house at once and for all time.

132

'I do however know well that women as well as men have desires and appetites. Hence the maids are allowed their followers as,' she said with a somewhat rueful smile, 'you heard plainly last night. In addition if any servant chooses to form an attachment with a guest or with whoever is lodging here, then I have no objection providing only that the smooth running of the household is not too much disrupted. But it must be for the girl to make the first approach.

'Now Becky has told me of your night caller. That was of course Emily. She is a strange girl and one who has been badly hurt in the past in just the way that I have alluded to. It was your predecessor, young Robin, now gone to India, who first encountered her and was the instrument of her introduction into the household.'

Here Becky took up the story. 'It was some two years ago that Robin was invited to dine at a friend's house. I believe that they had been at school together. In any case he found that the company consisted of some six or seven young men; one on leave from his Regiment, one a student at the Inns of Court and so on. After a dinner at which much wine was consumed and after the senior members of the household had retired to bed, the talk turned to matters of fucking. After some exchange of stories and much boasting of women conquered and maidenheads taken, one of the young men began to question the host about the availability of the maids. Emily, who had been waiting on them that evening, was sent for and the teasing began.

'"Emily," asked one of the party, "is it true that you are still a virgin?" Robin recalled that Emily stayed silent but was clearly somewhat embarrassed by such intimate questioning.

'"Tell us plainly Emily," went on the same young man, "has your tight little quim ever been entered by such as this?"

'So saying he revealed his erect member and as she turned her head away, another of the company said, "I wager that little Emily fucks." He also then unbuttoned himself and produced his prick with a flourish, saying, "Perhaps this is more to your taste?"

'Two others followed suit, although Robin remembered that one was already so pickled in liquor that his offering lay

133

quite limp in his lap.

'"Come, Emily," said one. "Here is a very cornucopia of cocks. Which are you going to select?"

'Emily, who had become more and more distressed and was trying to evade the attentions of the hands that were reaching out to engage her, suddenly, and to her everlasting credit, became angry and replied bravely, "Sir, you have no right to ask such questions. It is not your business." Then, as a chorus of jeers broke out, she said, "I do fuck but I would not fuck with any of you here. It is not fair to proposition me so."

'With that she burst into tears, fled the room and refused to answer the summons of the bell.

'"That girl is insolent," said one.

'"Not a good sport," said a second.

'"Personally, if it were my household," said the third, "I would have her dismissed."

"But fucked first," said the first, with a leer.

Robin, who had become quite incensed by the turn of events, left the room and went below stairs, where he found Emily still in floods of tears. She flinched away when she saw him but, keeping his distance, he assured her that if she found her present position intolerable she could present herself at my mother's house, for we were at that time short of a maid. He told her that my mother would be told of what had gone on and that he knew that, should she enter service with us, she would never again be so rudely bullied. After a while, Emily recovered somewhat and indeed thanked him for his kindness. He then left, resolving not to dine again at his friend's house.

'Two days later, without warning, a weeping Emily appeared at the house. She had again been abused by the son or by his friends. Mama took her in and arrangements were made for her to be employed here.

'I do not know the whole story of Emily's life,' said Hannah, 'but I believe that she has not found much happiness before now. We all therefore treat her with tenderness, for she is a sweet natured and hard working little creature.'

'I am glad, Andrew, that you have had the courtesy and

consideration to tell me what has happened,' said Mrs P—. 'Not only is there no question of blame, but should Emily offer herself to you again, then I believe that it would be quite correct for you to accept what is offered.'

With this, she left the room.

'Now that Mama has gone,' said Becky, 'I can speak more plainly to you about Emily and her habits. Now that she is settled and at ease with us, it has become plain that she can be an eager participant in sexual pursuits. She does not often fuck, but she loves to explore and be explored. She has, as you will have discovered, a most capacious cunt. Both Hannah and I have often played and frigged with it, as she has with ours. You will recall that drawing of Hannah's where Emily was sucking and handling a cock? That was Robin. He quickly became intimate with her. As soon as she realised that he would not press her in any way – not that this demanded any great effort of continence on his part, for he had free range of my parts and Hannah's also – she showed her pleasure in many matters sexual. She doubtless misses him still, for she is of an affectionate nature. It is good that she trusted you enough to creep into you last night. Whether she will be a regular visitor I cannot say. But I hope for your sake that she may. Her body is most pleasurable and her parts most sensitive.'

It was some time later that morning when I was writing some letters, including a note to my Godfather, informing him that I was now settled in at Mrs P—'s and thanking him for his introduction to a house and a family who had been marvellously warm in their welcome, that Mrs P— came in.

It was clear that she was, if not actually agitated, then at least somewhat exercised in her mind.

'Andrew,' she said, 'I have a favour to ask of you. But first I do beseech you not to acquiesce in my request if it is in any way inconvenient. I say this because I do not know what plans you may have for the next two days.'

Intrigued, I reassured her that I would be quite open with her but that I did not at present have any obligations or

135

appointments in the near future. In truth, although I did not mention this to her, I had found so much of interest *within* this delightfully bohemian establishment, that I had not found it necessary to go *out* of the house or to look for entertainment elsewhere. Indeed as I considered the pleasures of the household, my prick began to stir in anticipation of the presence that evening of Becky and Hannah, as well as the intriguing possibility of some further intercourse with Emily.

'Andrew,' continued Mrs P—, 'I have this morning received a letter with some troublesome news. No one has met with an accident or fallen ill,' she said hastily, seeing a look of concern on my face, 'but there has been a slightly unfortunate incident. I have a niece, who is also my ward for her parents were the unhappy victims of a Tribal Outrage on the North West Frontier where my brother was stationed as a Political Agent among some of the more dissident tribes. My niece has been at school, an Academy for Young Ladies it styles itself, on the edge of the Mendip Hills in Somerset.

'She has been always of a rather wilful temperament and although a thoroughly charming and high spirited girl, has not found it easy, or even possible, to accede to the discipline of school life. I have been asked by the school to take her away. It seems that she is a disruptive influence on what the letter calls "the genteel atmosphere of the establishment." In short Rosalind, for that is her name, has been Expelled. We are to remove her at once. I do not know what her latest offence is for the headmistress, being always a discreet woman, has refrained from giving any details other than to say that Rosie's behaviour has been "shocking in the extreme." Someone must therefore travel down to the Country and bring Rosie back here. I do not quite know what we will do with her but for the moment she must stay here. I myself would much prefer not to go down to the school. I am much occupied with some literary work on behalf of Mr Burton of whom you have heard so much. Neither Becky nor Hannah are likely to be acceptable as chaperones by the school.'

'But surely,' I asked for I could see what was about to be asked of me, 'I am even less so?'

'Indeed yes, Andrew,' said Mrs P—. 'If you were to turn up at the school gates and announce that you had come to take Rosie away, the headmistress would certainly not allow her to be put in your charge. The school has always taken its duties of moral and spiritual guardianship to the girls most seriously – slightly too seriously for my taste. But still I shall not have to concern myself on that score any more.

'No, Andrew, I am about to ask you to go down to the West Country, but to Bristol only. A good friend of mine, Colonel Moore, has been in Town for the last few days but is now returning to the bosom of home and wife in Bristol. He will travel down by train tomorrow and I hope that you will agree to accompany him.

'The plan is that you will stay with them for one night or possibly two. Colonel and Mrs Moore will then present themselves at the school the day after tomorrow and collect the disgraced Rosie. They will return to Bristol and Rosie will then be placed in your charge for the journey back to Paddington. Will you do this for me?'

'Most certainly,' I answered.

'Now I am trusting you, Andrew. I have subjected you to something of a moral lecture this morning. I do not intend to deliver a second. These things are tedious. You are intelligent enough to understand what I expect of people, in particular of young men. Rosie is seventeen and can be a forward little minx. She is of an age where youthful impetuosity might lead her into adventures that could hurt her. You are to behave with responsibility while you are escorting her.'

It was quickly agreed that I would play my part in the transport of Rosie. Mrs P— would arrange with Colonel Moore a time when we should meet at Paddington and I would make clear to the maids those things that I would need for my sojourn. I understood that no formal clothes need be taken. The Moores placed no great stress on formality and in any case Rosie was not likely to be in a position to dress for dinner.

Mrs P— then disappeared in order to make all arrangements and I returned to my letter writing.

A while later Becky came in, kissed me warmly, somewhat tantalisingly fondled Mr Pego for a moment and announced that she would shortly be leaving to attend her friend's At Home. I was informed that her mother would be out that evening and also that it was cook's night off. A cold collation would be set out for our evening sustenance and I would be welcome to share the evening with Becky and Hannah, who would return from her art pottery studio around five o'clock.

I spent the rest of the day, after a light lunch, in a pleasantly lazy fashion. I had every hope that renewed calls would be made on my energies that evening. Indeed at one point I sank into a very pleasant reverie from which I was startled by the discovery that I had a healthy erection and that Emily was standing by me. As I sat up, she blushed a little, gave me a sweetly naughty smile and left the room.

It was late afternoon when Becky returned from her At Home. I heard her entry but did not see her for I had returned to my rooms, my letter writing completed, in order to make a start on the daily Journal of Events that I had decided to keep. However I had found that all attempts to write were proceeding but fitfully as my mind was on the immediate future rather than on the recent past.

I descended to the drawing room, found it empty and passed on to the dining room whence I could hear Becky's voice. She had a flushed and satisfied look to her as she made arrangements of a domestic nature with Mary.

As I entered she looked up and said, 'Andrew, I have a most interesting tale to tell but it must wait until my sister is here.'

It was then that I heard a cab draw up at the front door. There was some hustle and bustle in the hall before the door flew open and Hannah rushed in in a positive whirl of activity. Hat, coat and gloves were being pulled off and impatiently thrust upon the waiting Mary. Somewhat dishevelled and with an eager look on her face she advanced into the room. I looked up, stood politely and said, 'I trust you have had a satisfactory day at your place of employment?'

138

'Very,' she said, 'but now I am a mass of appetites. I need feeding and I need fucking and neither desire can wait upon the other.'

So saying she fell upon the cold collation that was spread out on the sideboard and seized a lamb cutlet. Holding it between finger and thumb, she took a great bite of the lean meat. Then brushing a fleck of seasoning from her lips, she said to me, 'There is no reason why both my appetites should not be satisfied at the same time. Andrew, I must call upon the services of your trusty member this instant.'

She reached down, unbuttoned me and flipped Mr Pego out into the light of day. Shocked by the suddenness of her proposition and its immediate execution, my member did indeed raise its head but could not at once gather full strength.

'Ah, the cold evening air,' said Hannah. 'Do not worry. See, here is a warm place into which he can burrow.'

With this, she revealed herself in a hasty flurry of skirts and underthings.

'Becky, dear,' she said, turning to her sister, 'I am about to be most delightfully immobilised. Can you bring over a good selection of the cold meats, and maybe a big slice of game pie, a baked potato possibly and a large glass of claret. Two large glasses. And another for Andrew here. He needs building up.'

While thus organising her sister she had seated herself on my lap, thrust the lamb cutlet into my mouth in order to free her hands, laid hold of my now swelling member and guided it swiftly and completely into her eager quim.

Retrieving the cutlet, she commenced to chew her way through it, tearing at it with her teeth. Meanwhile she was beginning to ride me, moving up and down my cock which, recovering now from its surprise, was properly able to play its ordained role in the affair. As the warm juices began to flow, I sucked her fingers clean to allow her to gulp down a glass of wine, pause for breath and then take up a huge slice of pie. As she neatly broke off a piece and stuffed it into my mouth, I could feel that she was fast fucking herself towards a state of fulfilment. I swear I could feel the lips of her cunt sucking hungrily at my fully charged firing piece.

As she swallowed the last morsel of pie crust, she said with a broad and satisfied smile, 'Andrew, you must forgive my breach of manners for I know that a young lady should never fuck with her mouth full.'

'You are quite forgiven,' I said. Then, as I felt the first tightening of her cunt muscles about my member, I added, 'Although I hope that you will also remember what your Nanny must have told you, that every mouthful should be chewed at least twenty times before it is swallowed.'

'No time for that, Andrew,' she cried out, 'for I am coming.' With that her fucking reached a crescendo of excitement and, as she sucked her breath in, I felt the first waves of her orgasm shudder through her body as she twisted and rode on my prick. Gasping and clutching at me, all slippery with her coming, she cried out 'Fuck me! Fuck me! Fuck!' Then she bit her lip as though to force herself into silence. Seconds later her last spasms coursed their way through her wracked body and I felt her thighs open wide and her cunt slacken. She relaxed and lay still for a moment, securely impaled on my still-rigid prick.

A minute later and she reached out for an apple and bit crisply into it before raising herself from me to stand straddled over me and pulling her clothing down into a state of more public decency.

'Now I feel somewhat recovered from the deprivations of the day,' she said. 'Indeed I am now more or less capable of rational conversation and a display of the nicer social graces.'

'But Sister,' said Becky, who so far had been first handmaiden and then quiet onlooker in respect of Hannah's homecoming. 'You are leaving poor Andrew still awaiting relief from the appetites that you have woken in him.'

With this she crouched down beside me, taking my boldly upright member in her hands, and said, 'Andrew, this is to be a somewhat informal evening. Would you please unpin my hair.'

So saying, she bent her head and with her tongue licking and teasing most assiduously, took my length in her soft mouth. As I busied myself with releasing the glorious dark cascade of her hair, as it spilled over her shoulders, she sucked thirstily at my cock while reaching down to the very root of my desire to delicately finger my swollen testicles. Then she nibbled daintily at the purple straining head of my prick as Hannah interrupted.

'Becky, dear, pray remember Andrew's insistence that every mouthful be well chewed before it is swallowed.'

I felt the provoking vibrations of Becky's laughter as her mouth closed once again firmly over my prick and she pursued her insistent way down its shaft. Then as I pressed her head down onto me, I felt the first hot waves of spunk flood along my member to burst out again and again into her greedily receiving mouth. Swallowing and sucking, she speedily drained me of my resources. Squeezing the last few milky drops of my cum from the head of my prick, she carefully took my now happy but wilting member in the palm of her hand and watched with a look of gleeful interest as it inched its way back down to its sleeping state.

Then she deftly tucked it back inside my trousers, saying, 'I think it is time he was put to bed for a little while. Though I hope that later in the evening he will be able to get up again.'

'For that relief, much thanks,' I murmured. 'But what about you? Your sister has a satisfied cunt. I have a satisfied prick. But I hope that I may shortly be able to provide once more that service that you so charmingly demanded of me last night.'

'That is most thoughtful of you, Andrew, and I hope that it may be so, but for the moment, I must confess that my need is not so urgent. For unlike my sister I have been able to achieve some fulfilment during the day.'

For an instant I felt a twinge of jealousy. I knew that this was not a noble emotion and said nothing but Becky must have seen some little flicker of my feelings in my face.

'Andrew,' she said, taking my face in her hands, 'I do believe that you are jealous! Oh, such a solemn face.' Then she pulled away from me, to lean against the table. 'I must talk seriously to you for a moment. Andrew, you must not become possessive. Tomorrow I know that you are to depart to Bristol at Mama's behest and you will be away for two nights. I do not know what adventures may befall you whilst you are in the West Country but I believe that fucking is not unknown in those parts. It could be that you will find some country love nest that is pleased to welcome you inside for a rural ride. Should this happen you do not need to conceal it from me. I shall not be upset. So it is with me. See, I have something to show you.'

With that she drew her legs apart and revealed her dark bush to me. Then she took my hand and placed it underneath her so that her cunt lips brushed gently against my palm.

'That, Andrew, as you well know, is my cunt and last night you placed your prick in it and we had the most delicious fuck. It would please me very much if this evening we could do the same. But first you must understand that yours was not the last prick in my cunt. This afternoon I attended my cousin's At Home and there made some new acquaintances as well as meeting several old friends.'

With this reassurance that I still had the *entrée* to Becky's cunny, and indeed the promise that I should be there again that evening, my disquiet and jealousy were replaced by a curiosity and a nascent excitement.

'Are you to tell me of this adventure?' I asked. 'Although of course I do not ask you to reveal the man's name.'

'Man?' said Becky. 'Men, rather.'

'What,' I said, looking at the warm and accommodating cunt that I held in hand. I could imagine a strange prick sliding in. Two pricks in hungry succession perhaps. 'You have had a full day. Two fucks in one afternoon,' I ventured.

'Five,' she said.

'Five!' I must have looked somewhat dumbstruck.

'Well,' she said. 'It was a very unusual afternoon.'

'And you will tell me about it?' I asked, being now aware that my growing excitement was becoming apparent.

'Yes, Andrew dear. And Hannah?'

'I am also all agog to hear of your adventures,' said Hannah, 'for between Andrew's entry last night and this much needed fucking of a few minutes ago, mine has been a day filled only with work. So you see, Andrew, that this has been a quite continent cunt.'

So saying, she patted herself and smiled sweetly. 'Now, Sister, when are we to hear of your encounters?'

'Later, Sister. I shall tell all with every detail that may be demanded.'

'And when will that be?' I asked.

'Later when we are fucking,' said Becky. 'When I talk about fucking it makes me want to fuck. So why should we not do both things at once? But now we must change for I have been in my day dress for quite long enough and besides I need a good hot bath for I am still somewhat sticky with the afternoon's procedings.'

She rang for the maid but when pretty Emily answered, she said with some surprise: 'Emily? I thought it was your evening off? Is not Mary there?'

Emily, who had looked at me with a shy smile as though she was half-acknowledging her night visit to me, replied as though she was anxious she might be rebuked. Mary, she explained, was indeed on duty but her friend Tom had called round unexpectedly to say that he had to accompany his master to the Country for a few days, so that he and Mary would be apart for that time. 'So,' said Emily, 'I said I would take care of her duties for a little while. I hope that you are not annoyed with me, Miss Becky? Miss Hannah?'

'Not at all, Emily,' said Becky. 'That was a generous offer, I suppose that they intend to have a fond farewell fuck?'

'I'm sure I couldn't say, Miss Becky,' said Emily primly.

'Oh, come, if I may speak metaphorically,' Becky said as she glanced across at me. 'We shall all know shortly enough if they are fucking.'

With that Emily was dispatched to draw Becky her much needed bath. Hannah also was to bath and change so I retired to my rooms likewise to prepare myself for the evening.

However I realised that with both Becky, Hannah and myself demanding hot water for our ablutions and Mary being quite unable to service our needs, poor Emily was going

143

to be quite rushed off her feet. I decided therefore to descend to the kitchen in order to fetch up my own hot water. So it was that as I went below stairs, I saw through the kitchen door a most fetching domestic scene.

Mary was about to entertain the fully extended length of Tom the Tool, for so I immediately understood him to be if only by the much spoken-of size of his member. It was indeed a most remarkable achievement. As I gazed with a certain incredulity at it, I recalled cock-measuring sessions in the changing rooms at Nottsgrove. There we had made good use of the mathematics and algebra that Dr White had insisted on as part of the curriculum for all boys.

By careful measurement of the length and diameter of each competing cock and then using the formula $\pi r^2 l$, where r is the radius and l the length of the cylinder, we had been able to calculate the cubic size of each entrant. Nottsgrovians, probably as a consequence of the healthily balanced if not always acceptable nature of the school food, were for the most part well-developed specimens of manhood and I recalled having seen many a sizeable organ paraded for our inspection. But this tremendous Thing that was even now being manoeuvered into position opposite Mary's waiting portals, was for both length and thickness, so much larger than anything I had previously seen, that had it been entered for Nottsgrove's most coveted if unofficial award, the *Victor Pudendum*, would surely have won the trophy outright and ended the competition for all time. By no stretch of the imagination, could one anticipate anything to surpass such a record holder.

Here I hope I may be permitted a small digression, for I also recalled the time when by a judicious replacement of some part of the Chairman of the Governors' speech on the occasion of the school's annual Prize Giving, the *Victor Pudendum* had actually been awarded before the entire body of the school there assembled, together with the parents, governors and those assorted worthies who always occupy the dais on such formal occasions.

I can to this day recall the sonorous voice of the Chairman,

144

Dr the Revd Miles Platting, DD, PhD, Master Elect of some minor College at Oxford, and a man of great self-importance, as he read out:

'And this year's winner of the *Victor Pudendum* for the largest genitalia in the Sixth form is Percy FitzNicely whose whopper was at least two inches...'

Here his voice had trailed away into an outraged silence as he realised what it was that he was reading out, whilst among the audience those who had retained sufficient consciousness to actually listen to the peroration began to show signs of open-mouthed astonishment together with, from several parts of the School Hall, guffaws of laughter desperately cut short as parent or boy struggled to recover some semblance of gravity.

Three days later two boys were very publicly expelled by Dr White and the wrath of the Governors assuaged. Those of us in the upper forms who had come to know our Headmaster well were quietly given to understand that both boys had already assured futures, chiefly by inheritance, so that no real damage had been done to their prospects. We knew also that Dr White had had such difficulty in retaining a straight face as he sat among the assembled dignitaries that he had suffered from indigestion for some two days afterwards.

But to return to the scene that was unfolding itself before my amazed eyes. Tom's mighty tool was primed and ready. As I studied its daunting size I wondered how many women would be able to take in such a huge engine. Emily, as I had discovered from last night's manual exploration, was surprisingly well equipped enough to accept it, but was surely too frail to withstand the fearful battering that such a prick must inflict. But Mary, from both Hannah's and Becky's account as well as from Hannah's sketch and the evidence of my own ears, had the capacity not just to cope with but positively to enjoy its monstrous attentions.

Indeed even as I watched, quite transfixed by the sight, she lay back and with both hands commenced guiding him into her. Soon, with a first resounded cry of delight, she had completed feeding his entire length into her bushy cave. Then she pulled him tight in, locking her legs round his waist and raising herself to effect a secure union. As he seized hold of her joyfully offered titties, the fucking commenced. Then knowing that I had to, if not interrupt their coupling, at least trespass on their conjunction as I went about the business of fetching and carrying my bath water, I entered the kitchen.

Mary saw me and ceased in her thrusting. I apologised for my presence and suggested that they should continue. Tom who had looked somewhat embarrassed took heart and recommended his pumping.

Five trips I made between kitchen and my rooms. As I scurried up and down the stairs, Tom and Mary rapidly became quite insensible to my comings and goings. Mary's cries of delight rose to first one climax and then a second and a third. Tom's great machine was ramming into her time and time again while she clung to him, greedily holding him into her capacious and quite crammed cunt. As I completed my last trip and retired at last for my bath, he was still battering away with his giant prick and she seemed altogether abandoned to her repeated comings.

With her screams of delight still ringing in my ears, indeed half-deafened by her cries, I was about to regain my rooms when another sound impinged upon my consciousness. From a part-opened door came the murmur of feminine enjoyment. Overcome with curiosity I looked in.

Becky was bathing herself with the assistance of Emily who was also quite naked and kneeling by her mistress's bath. Her lovely little titties which before I had handled but never seen were brushing against the edge. The succulent long nipples were flicking lightly against Becky's body as she soaped and massaged her mistress's superb titties. With a soothing thoroughness her skilful hands soaped and sponged the length of Becky's body. Sometimes as Becky also lathered and fondled her own body, their hands met and caressed each other.

I saw Becky reach out and take one of Emily's nipples daintily in her fingers, rubbing it lazily as it rose and hardened to her touch.

'See Emily,' she said, 'how I am soaping your titty. Soon you will have not just the prettiest but the cleanest titties in all London.'

Emily said nothing but looked first at her own body and then at her mistress's with such a look of shy delight that a surge of pure cunt-hunger ran through me and I nearly came on the spot.

As Becky sat up and turned towards Emily, their breasts touched. Then, each holding out her own hard-nippled titties, they began to rub them slowly against each other. Next each grasped the other round the neck and they bent towards each other to kiss with an excited affection. Each was paying a fascinated, intimate attention to the other's body. So different yet so arousing was each in all its intimate detail that I wondered for a moment at the Providence that had provided such a delightful variety, such a profligacy of bums and cunts, of bushes and nipples, so that none is ever quite like any other and new discoveries lie always ahead. I thought also that though until this time I had always bathed unaided, I would then and there make a vow to seek help in the future.

As I stood there unobserved playing the part of the philosopher, Emily, who had resumed her ministrations, reached gently down to Becky's bush. I saw her hands commence to fondle and curl the dense hair as she raised a fine lather. But next as her fingers slipped further down to rub against the coral lips of her mistress's half-submerged treasure cave, Becky held her hand fast for a minute.

'No, Emily, that part I will handle for myself. I am still a trifle sore from the exertions of this afternoon and must be gentle with myself if I am not to risk spoiling the enjoyment of the evening.'

As Emily made a little pout of disappointment, she went on, 'Do not be too upset, Emily, for you know that my fingers and my tongue ache for the sweetness of your cunt just as much as I know yours do for mine. We do not now have the time for such pleasures but they are merely postponed for a little while.'

After a little careful attention to her secret parts Becky allowed herself to be sluiced down in fresh water and then

147

stood upright in the bath, displaying for a moment the full voluptuous length of her magnificent body. At once however Emily swathed her in a freshly laundered bath towel and began to vigorously rub her dry. I watched as the delicious flesh of arms, shoulders, breasts was briskly dried and revealed in all its rosy freshness.

Quickly but quietly I retreated to my own rooms to undertake my own ablutions. Such was my state of rigid arousal that I welcomed the fact that my once-hot bath was by now quite tepid. The touch of cool water was desperately needed to reduce my manhood to a more manageable condition. By dint of careful concentration on the matter in hand and by paying no attention to the promptings of my imagination I was eventually able to complete my toilet and ready myself for the evening's social intercourse.

7

A short while later the sound of the dinner gong being energetically beaten warned me that the time had come to descend, refreshed and prepared to play my proper part in the diversion that lay ahead.

Hannah it was, I soon discovered, who had so impatiently summoned us to the dining room for she alone was waiting as I entered.

'I have been dressed and down and waiting for you all for ages,' she said to me.

'Mary has finished her fucking. Emily and my sister have no doubt been enjoying their bathtime intimacy. As to what you have been doing, Andrew, I can only guess. But in the meantime I have been waiting here quite alone and without distraction.'

I kissed her firmly, feeling her lips part and her tongue flick briefly against mine.

'I am sorry that you have been left so unattended,' I said.

'Do you promise to pay me some close attention shortly?' she demanded, 'For I am in receptive mood and look forward to inviting in our guests.'

'Guests?' I asked. 'We are to be joined by others?'

'Why yes,' she replied. 'Were you not told. That was most remiss of us. We are indeed entertaining. We have just heard that some old and dear friends are in Town and will be calling shortly.'

'I know only that Becky had promised to tell us of her experiences of the afternoon,' I said.

'So she doubtless yet will,' said Hannah. 'But now we can anticipate something further in the way of entertainment.'

A few moments later Becky herself came in, fresh and glowing from her preparations.

'Mary has finished her fucking with Tom the Tool,' she reported. 'He has withdrawn. Emily is once more going about her chores and our guests should arrive at any minute. And Andrew is also ready to rise to the occasion and take part in the evening's events. I have told him that guests are expected.'

'But while we wait, are you now going to tell us of your afternoon's fucking?' I asked.

'Not yet,' said Becky. 'As I have said, when I talk about fucking I prefer to actually fuck at the same time if that is at all possible. So we must await the completion of our company. I quite refuse to start without them. It is not considered polite to be in mid-fuck when one's guests arrive. Although I do remember dear Mama telling us of the occasion when she was shown into the morning room of a lady of her acquaintance, only to find her bent double over an occasional table while what Mama took to be a manservant rammed himself into his mistress from behind. Mama said that she was most impressed by her friend's ability to keep up a flow of chit chat and social gossip whilst being most comprehensively rogered.'

'How did your Mother cope with this somewhat unusual situation?' I asked.

'Why,' said Becky, 'by taking her cue from her hostess and engaging in the small talk as though nothing out of the ordinary was taking place.'

'And what happened?' I asked.

'Nothing very remarkable. The manservant banged backwards and forwards. The lady of the house reached behind her from time to time to make sure he kept his fucking under control – Mama said that he seemed a bit erratic and not well co-ordinated in his efforts – until he let out a couple of gasps and began to come. "In *me*, James. Not all over the carpet," his mistress ordered at this point. He obediently emptied himself into her spreadeagled quim and withdrew in due course. "I do like my mid-morning fuck," said my mother's hostess. "Together with a glass of maderia and a decent-sized slice of seed cake, it quite sets me up for the rigours of the domestic day." Then she just smoothed down her somewhat disordered skirts and carried on as though nothing out of the ordinary had occurred.'

'A charming tale,' I said, not altogether sure whether Becky might not have just made the story up on the spur of the moment. 'But tell me, exactly who is coming?'

'All of us I hope,' said Hannah with a quick smile of anticipation.

At that very moment there was a ringing at the front door and after a short pause two young men and a tall, slim red-haired girl were shown in. There was a flurry and squeal of pleasure as Becky and Hannah greeted the new arrivals and then I was pulled forward by the hand to be introduced.

'Andrew,' said Becky, 'these are our dear friends Ian and Donald Ferguson and their cousin Catherine.'

As we shook hands I noticed first the healthy, fresh-complexioned faces of the two men. Then I noticed their healthy, fresh-complexioned knees, for both were in full Highland evening dress. Catherine, who had a cool elegance about her, was also dressed in what I took to be the Highland fashion. I particularly noted a very attractive silver- mounted Cairngorm brooch at her throat. With her dark Titian hair and pale fine-boned features, she had an amused and intelligent air that I found most attractive but also a little daunting. I tried to imagine her writhing and moaning on some engorged prick – my own perhaps – but could not quite conjure up the picture. I wondered what the evening held in store.

The two brothers, I was given to understand, were fleetingly in London, having travelled down from their home near Inverness to attend certain matters of business.

'We were this evening to have attended a Scottish Ball in Mayfair,' explained Ian, 'but suspecting that the company would be somewhat tedious, we decided rather to call on old friends. Hence our arrival at such short notice. We are indeed happy that you were able to receive us.'

'Scottish dancing,' said Donald, 'can be a most pleasant

way of passing an evening. But it is an entertainment frequently indulged in at home. During our sadly infrequent visits to London there are other more Metropolitan pleasures that we would prefer to take part in. Pleasures that are not so readily available where one is known to the entire County and where the repressive hand of the Ministers of Religion lies heavily on all society.'

'Fancy not being able to fuck when you feel like it,' said Becky with a look of wide-eyed concern.

Ian gulped and continued, 'Having made the acquaintance of the Misses P— about a year and a half ago when they were visiting some near neighbours in Drumnadrochit close by Loch Ness, we have endeavoured to maintain our friendship whenever we are in Town. I am happy to say that we have been made most welcome on several occasions and have been greeted with open arms.'

'Cunts,' said Becky.

'What?' I queried.

'Open cunts. We greeted them with open cunts. Let us speak plainly. Andrew, you see displayed before you two fine Caledonian cocks, both doubtless bursting with vigour for they thrive in the healthy open air life of their native countryside.'

'We were delighted at our very first meeting,' said Hannah, 'to discover exactly what it is that the men of Scotland have under their kilts. But it does seem to us a great pity that growing up as they do strong and healthy, hanging free yet protected from the inclement elements under their tents of tartan, they should be put to so little use.'

'But now,' said Becky, 'I know that you have not properly dined. Mama is away and it is cook's night off but, as you can see, there are plenty of cold dishes set out on the side. We have wine and brandy in quantities.'

'And even,' interjected Hannah, 'some whisky. As soon as we heard that you would be with us this evening, we had a search made in the cellar.'

'So please, everyone,' continued Becky, 'do not wait to be asked, but help yourselves as you need it to both food and drink.'

152

'My sister has a tale to tell,' said Hannah, 'and she has kept us waiting until both time and place are right to divulge all.'

'Let us delay a little more,' said Becky, 'until we have satisfied at least one of our appetites in part. I shall then ask you all to sit down while I tell all. After that Hannah and I have a game in mind in which we hope you will all take part.'

'And Cousin Catherine?'

'Oh! how silly and how rude of us,' said Hannah. 'In the excitement, we had clean forgotten that you have never met.'

'Catherine,' said Becky, 'may I introduce you to Mr Andrew Scott. His Godfather is an old friend of Mama's and he is presently lodging with us. He has already proved to be a most lively successor to dear Robin whose departure for the colonies you must surely regret as much as does this household.'

'Andrew, this is Miss Catherine Ferguson, second cousin to Ian and Donald and also our good friend.'

'I moved to London some months ago, Mr Scott,' said the elegant Catherine. 'I came to keep house for my brother who is unmarried and has just taken up the post of Lecturer in Persian and Sanskrit Studies at the University.'

'Kate's brother is a very worthy person,' said Hannah, 'but is always somewhat buried in his studies so Kate has to look to her friends for much of her entertainment.'

I was still uncertain about how to approach this handsome but seemingly reserved creature. It was quite clear that the two brothers were open and friendly young men who fitted happily into the society of the house. Both were at ease, and had clearly enjoyed access to Becky and Hannah in the past, but Catherine was as yet something of a mystery. I hoped that the puzzle might be unravelled in the course of the evening, for with the prospect of a tale to be told by Becky, a mystery to be revealed and the promise of some good fucking later on, the evening showed every sign of being both full and enjoyable.

It was nearly an hour later after much amiable chatter about such Highland pursuits as Tossing the Caber – during which the brothers, while attempting to demonstrate with their hands the size of the object concerned, had caused Mary the maid to laugh out loud, somewhat to her embarrassment – when Becky clapped her hands and ordered the men present to sit down on a row of chairs that had been lined up with a quite military precision. We were commanded to pay close attention as she embarked on her account of that afternoon's events.

'I was,' began Becky, 'as some of you know, this afternoon present at my friend Charlotte's At Home. There was quite a crowd of young people and we had been promised some musical entertainment at the hands of her cousin who studies the pianoforte at the Conservatory in Paris. He it was who, along with Charlotte, introduced us to a musical game that they say is quite the fashion amongst a certain set in La Belle France.

'The gentlemen were lined up and seated as you are,' she continued. Then she approached Donald. As he politely made to get up, she ordered him to be seated again, stood over him and then briskly flipped his kilt back to reveal his substantial Celtic member. As she took it in hand, it obediently stirred to her touch.

'Donald,' she said, 'I must call on your help, for I feel a growing need not just to describe but to demonstrate this game. But first I must be comfortable.'

With that, and by dint of some careful stroking and priming, she brought Donald's piece up to the fully cocked position. Then she plunged her hand beneath her skirts to similarly make ready and lubricate the source of her own passions before lowering herself carefully but easily on to his straining cock.

'Now Donald,' she said, 'you must sit still for I have a tale to tell you of a very musical ride. Now that I am mounted I shall by stages proceed from the trot to the canter and then to the gallop before embarking on my point-to-point circuit.'

'Let us hope that the going remains firm for you,' I interposed.

'I am certainly at my best in such conditions,' said Becky, 'although I go well in sticky conditions also. Let us hope however that it does not become too soft on top for then even

154

I might fail to come to the finishing post.'

While this exchange had been taking place Donald, who had become rather flushed with the excitement of Becky's slippery descent, had valiantly remained almost motionless as bidden – although some sign of strain was beginning to show in his face. Realising that she could not expect him to remain under starter's orders indefinitely, Becky hurriedly continued her story.

'As I recall, there were some seven gentlemen present that took part in the game and some five ladies. The latter lined up in front of the seated gentlemen and Charlotte's cousin seated himself at the piano and commenced to play a selection of Mr Liszt's more flamboyant pieces. Each gentleman was revealed, just as you were, dear Donald. The ladies, hoisting their skirts, displayed themselves to their row of fine upright partners and proceeded down the line, each lightly brushing her pussey against each straining member in turn. Suddenly the music stopped and each lady lowered herself, just as I did with you Donald, on to the member that confronted her. Once securely seated, each began vigorously to raise and lower herself, the gentlemen remaining unmovingly at attention. As soon as the music recommenced, each cunt was lifted and the parade continued. Again the music stopped and again five juicy pusseys were lowered.'

'So that, if I recall the number aright, at each pause there were two unsatisfied pricks?' I said.

'You have a head for arithmetic,' said Becky.

'Pray how did the game continue then?' I asked.

'At about the fourth or fifth pause, the first of the pricks dropped out,' said Becky.

'Dropped out?' asked Ian.

'One of the young men, whom I had not previously met, unable to control his emotions after having been enveloped by such a succession of hungry pusseys, came most splendidly. I was in fact the happy recipient of his spending and I quite milked him dry. He, being now crestfallen, withdrew from the game and so we continued. The next to fall by the wayside quite disgraced himself by coming between

155

enthronements. Charlotte was most scornful as he jetted his cum straight up into the air and let it splash on his neighbour.'

'How did matters proceed once you had less members than pusseys?' I enquired.

'Why, it became a game of musical chairs,' said Becky. 'As the music stopped, there was a great scramble for a prick and the loser had to stand aside. Then another member discharged prematurely and another pussey was counted out. So it continued until only Charlotte and myself were left standing and one most regimental prick was left sitting, and standing, so to speak.'

· 'Who won?' I asked.

'Why me,' said Becky. 'I cheated.'

'How?' I asked.

'I refused to move,' said Becky. 'I was by then so juicily aroused and the feel of this enduring member so luscious in me that there and then I fucked us both into a state of satisfaction.'

'Did not Charlotte object when you had so rudely seized the prize?' I asked.

'I believe she might, but she was at that moment taken from behind by one of the members who had earlier dropped out but was now once more ready to take part. The whole party then fell to fucking and frigging.'

'While Charlotte's cousin continued at the pianoforte no doubt?'

'While Charlotte's cousin dismounted from his stool and advanced upon us, revealing such a tuning fork that I for one fell upon it with great delight. As a musical entertainment, I can recommend it without reserve.'

As Becky had continued with her description of this most intriguing parlour game, she had begun to ease herself with a regular yet increasing rhythm up and down the ram rod of Donald's prick. As she went further into details of her musical ride, so he seemed to penetrate further into the depths of her tunnel of love. She began to emphasise the lowerings and upliftings on the parade of pricks by plunging more deeply and more breathlessly down onto her charged

156

mount. Donald too was beginning to thrust and drive into her. As she reached the climax of her story, so she commenced the climax of her fuck.

Soon there was the delicious sight of Becky riding almost completely out of control as she rubbed her swollen clit along the top of Donald's slippery, distended member. As she suddenly cried out I could sense the tremors of her coming sweeping through her body. Donald too was calling out what I took to be some Gaelic oath as he jetted his Highland Cream into her.

Hannah and I had been watching in a state of contagious excitement. At one stage Hannah seized my hand and guided it up into her warm furry pussey, rubbing it back and forth in her agitation as though unconscious almost of what she was doing.

Ian at this juncture announced that he would show us a true Scottish Sword Dance if he could but get his claymore out of its scabbard. He then produced his straining member with a flourish whilst beginning to exhibit some nimble footwork. He leaped up and down, pointing his toes and his weapon as he raised his arms, letting out whoops and yells while he demonstrated what he later claimed was called Bonnie Prince Charlie's Jig-a-Jig.

Only the enigmatic Catherine stood aside from this scene of animation with a self-absorbed little smile on her face.

When Becky and Donald were quite spent they fortified themselves with a glass of nourishing port and lay quietly for a few minutes. Then Becky raised herself up on her elbow and said, 'So that is the story of my afternoon's delight, but now, Sister, it is time we all joined in and played the Blindfold Game.'

Hannah at once clapped her hands with glee and said 'Oh yes, for Andrew here has never I suspect played such a jolly game.'

'What is it?' I enquired.

'As a child, Andrew, you must have played Hunt the Thimble?' said Hannah.

'Why, yes,' I replied.

157

'Well now you are a bigger boy, you have to hunt something a little larger.'

'Much larger in some cases,' said Becky with a little laugh.

Hannah slipped out of the room but returned instantly with a black silk bandanna which she waved about her.

'Now,' said Becky, 'we must ask the gentlemen to draw lots to see who is first to be blindfolded.'

As the night before, cards were produced and Donald, Ian and myself cut to see who would first draw the Black Queen. Not knowing what the game would entail but trusting from experience that it would be an intriguing one, I was more than happy to be the first to turn up a Black Queen.

'Now Andrew,' said Becky, 'you must go out of the room with my sister who will blindfold you. You must then wait outside the door until you are called in.'

So it was that I was led outside by Hannah. Just before she bandaged up my eyes, she unbuttoned her bodice to reveal her splendid, large nippled titties. As I kissed them and licked the nipples into twin peaks of swollen promise, she said, 'Just before you enter the world of darkness, I thought you'd like to have something pleasurable to remember.'

With that I was blindfolded firmly and deftly.

'Now, no cheating,' she said. 'My sister and I have played this game many times before and we will quite certainly know if you are trying to peek out from under your bandage.'

I reached out towards her in my sudden darkness and she took pity on me, grasping my wrists and pressing my eager hands against her warm, yielding breasts. I played with her for a few delicious moments until the summons came from inside the room. Gently she disengaged my questing hands and after a little pause, escorted me in and led me to what seemed to be the centre of the room. Then she slipped away and I was left in darkness and silence.

Then I heard some rustling and suppressed giggling and a voice said, 'We call this game *Touch and Tell*. You will be spun round a few times and then you must find your treasure.'

'What will that be?' I asked.

'Why that you must work out for yourself. That is why the

158

game is called *Touch and Tell*. But we will give you a clue.'

With that I heard a loud purring noise while a voice I recognised as Becky's said 'Miaou' and broke down in snorts of laughter.

'We will all be standing quite still and you must find us, identify what is to hand and say to whom it belongs,' said Becky.

Unseen hands turned me round and I had quite lost my sense of direction. Then I was released. I felt about me but encountered nothing. I moved two or three cautious paces forward until I bumped against the sideboard. Carefully I felt my way along its edge, found that I was grasping empty space once more, moved again, nearly fell over a chair but gaining confidence that I knew where the furniture was, began to feel along walls and into corners with increasing freedom.

Suddenly my outstretched fingers brushed against soft fabric and I felt the warmth of a body. Gently I explored, tracing the outline of the woman's body that I knew was before me. Then my fingers touched bare flesh. Thighs I knelt down and felt the taper of thigh to calf. I quickly realised my unknown catch was standing with her legs a little apart. I ran my hands slowly up inside her thighs until my hand brushed against a splendid bush. I rubbed my fingers against her yielding warmth. In a moment I felt a slick of wetness and lips opened to admit my enquiring fingers.

'I am happy to say that I know what this is,' I said. 'It is a most moist and succulent quim.'

'Well done,' said a Scottish male voice from what I judged to be the other side of the room. 'But can you tell us whose?'

The familiar eagerness and pouting plumpness of the part I was now fingering to open-mouthed excitement told me that this was a place where I had been before. But was it Hannah or Becky? Not wishing to offend either by an incorrect identification, I decided to employ the other senses. As I nuzzled into that gloriously dense thicket of pussey hair, still blindfold, I was deliciously enveloped by the scent of sex-warmed honey pot. Now as I flicked my tongue out to play upon the parted lips, to find and lick into erect life an enticing

159

clit, as my tongue then plunged into a soft and juice-eased cunt, I could taste the freshness of an awakened but as yet unsatisfied pussey.

'Hannah,' I said, half muffled by the unseen nest of delight into which I was delving.

'Right you are,' said the same Highland voice. 'But you must keep your blindfold on. For your prize, you must identify a second buried treasure,' said Hannah.

'This is most cruel,' I said, 'for I am in a state of some discomfort.' As I spoke I could feel my prick throbbing and my balls aching with the need to discharge myself into that ready cunt before me.

'No,' said Hannah, pulling away from me. 'You cannot receive your reward just yet. But as you quest on, Andrew, I must tell you that you have so aroused me with your attentions that I can wait no longer. Ian,' she went on, 'it is some months since I last felt your splendid Cock o' the North force its way over my border and invade my lush Southern pastures. See, the way lies open before you. I am wide and hungry for your fucking.'

At that I had to listen, sight unseen, to the tantalising sounds of their eager intercourse. I swear I could hear every detail, every suck and slip as his great prick was thrust into her juicy cunt. In my imagination I could see his engorged member rammed home up to the hilt, time and time again. Their gasping and half-cries so close to me drove me to a condition of such frustration that I could barely restrain myself from tearing off my blindfold. Yet somehow, by an act of self-control I would have thought beyond me, I desisted.

Hannah was crying out 'I'm coming! I'm coming! More! Oh God, More!' and I knew from her sobs of ecstasy and his violent, triumphant gasps that they were coming together, his spunk and her cum mixing and swamping their parts in one glorious tide of passion.

Their cries subsided but I did not.

Bent nearly double in my need to contain my burning erection, I resumed my urgent voyage of exploration, groping my way round the room, bruising myself unexpectedly in a

160

collision with what felt like an upright chair and '~en stumbling and measuring my full length over an over-stuffed pouffe.

From quite close at hand came Hannah's contentedly just-fucked tones. 'Oh Andrew, do be careful. Stop scrambling about so. There are cunts warm and waiting for you but you must not bump into them like so much furniture.'

I calmed down and forced myself to stop still for a moment. Then slowly, slowly I recommenced my blindfold search. Soon I sensed another form in front of me. My nostrils twitched at the scent of warm, clean female flesh. Mr Pego twitched also, assuming a state of such complete rigidity that I was sure that any accidental bump would cause him to snap clean in two.

My fingers twitching also as though with the palsy in my trembling need to find my prize and bury myself in it, I hastily felt my way up this living statue. Then in a somewhat ungentlemanly hurry I sought out and started to handle this second pussey.

What I had encountered was I knew, even in my rush, a pussey I had not previously entered. So, as this was not Becky it must be the aloof Catherine whose unexpectedly large and thickly forested quim was now easily opening before the inquisition of my fingers. I was a trifle surprised to find such a splendid broadness of hip and such well-formed thighs. This hand-warming Burning Bush into which I was now delving deep was quite out of character as judged by her distant expression and manner. Once again I marvelled at the delightful surprises that women hid beneath their fully clothed and public appearances.

'Catherine!' I exclaimed triumphantly. 'Now may I take my blindfold off and relieve myself of a burden I swear I cannot support for a moment longer?'

'No Andrew,' said Hannah. 'You must do it in the dark. I am sure you will find it not only possible but an exciting night time exercise.'

Without more ado I released my engorged prick from its trousered bondage. As it sprang erect into the sight of all but me, I heard delighted gasps from two other parts of the room.

'Oh, I am quite jealous,' cried out Becky. 'Later, Andrew, I am determined that I too shall feel that monster coming deep inside me.'

'Me too,' came Hannah's voice. 'That is truly a thing to treasure.'

Meanwhile my immediate port of call stayed silent but welcoming. Seizing her by the hips, I thrust my prick deep into her more than ready cunt. Even in my abrupt haste, I was easily accommodated. Then, solely aware of my own near-desperate needs, I fucked her in a frenzy of to-ing and fro-ing until in a matter of seconds only it seemed, I felt the first wave of cum bursting upwards like a hot geyser and jetting out into the wetly welcoming cunt in which I was enveloped. Wave succeeded wave as I felt it discharge far into the capacious cave. Then, as my urgency was all too soon spent and the last drops of my passion flowed hesitently out of my still engaged prick, I cried, 'Catherine, oh, Catherine, I have come far too soon. I could not hold myself back for even a moment longer. I am sorry but I promise to do better next time.'

Still she said nothing, but Hannah's voice came. 'Do not worry Andrew. We all know that you have been previously provoked to near bursting point. But now you can remove your bandage.'

At that I speedily tore off my blindfold to find myself, blinking in the sudden light and standing, my trousers round my ankles, still fully embedded not in Catherine but in pretty Mary the maid who was standing with the hem of her dress stuffed in her mouth and her magnificent pubic forest pressed into me.

Delighted peals of laughter rang out as Becky, Hannah, Ian and Donald guffawed at my utter surprise.

'Well done, Mary,' said Becky, 'I was so afraid that you would cry out and spoil our game.'

'Thank you, Ma'am,' said Mary, 'but see, the hem of my dress is bitten almost clean through. Had Mr Andrew delayed his coming for a moment or two more I should have been quite unable to keep quiet. Sir,' she said to me, 'if I may be so bold, that is a very fine prick that you have placed in my safe keeping.'

'Thank you, Mary,' I said, beginning to recover from my shock. 'I am only sorry that I have not been able to adequately substitute for your friend Thomas.'

By now Mr Pego was rapidly withdrawing into his shell, so to speak, and as I slipped out of Mary's still welcoming but not yet satisfied cunt, I said, 'I hope to be able to continue what I have started but first there must be an interval.'

'With Mary's permission,' said Donald, 'I would immediately volunteer to step in and try to fill the breach that you have opened up.'

'You may count on me also,' said Ian. 'I will shortly be more than ready to help this maiden in distress.'

'If you don't mind, Mr Andrew,' said Mary, 'I am very open and need very much to continue at once what has already begun. If you wish later to come into me again, I shall be happy to be at your service.'

With that, still holding her skirts above her waist, she bobbed a little curtsy as with a quick pang of regret, I let her generous cunt pass out of my hands and Donald took her, embraced her, fondled her and led her to the *chaise-longue*.

'Lie down, Mary and I promise you'll feel a thing,' he said and with that revealed his massive Scottish member.

Within minutes, as Ian urged his brother on with whoops and cries of 'Here's to the Act of Union' and suchlike North of the Border witticisms, Donald had driven Mary to her first squeal of pleasure. As her wails of abandoned ecstasy rose louder and louder, all conversation was quite drowned out. Like a contagion, the heat of her fucking spread round the room. Ian was grabbed hold of by Becky and pulled away from his cheerleading war dance. I saw her bend over and invite him into her from behind whilst Hannah began to frig herself. Donald was thrusting himself powerfully into Mary's wide opened cunt as she twisted and turned upon his great harpoon. Her shrieks of delight climbed to a pitch of almost unbearable intensity and it passed across my mind that the

163

crystalware on the sideboard might be in danger of a sudden shattering.

The hunger of their coupling was beginning to transmit itself to my crestfallen cock. As it began to waken into new life, Catherine, till now an elegant onlooker, came to me, put her arms around me and whispered in my ear.

'Andrew, I know that you must think me quite reserved but I feel that now is the time for the reserve to be brought into play.'

With that she kissed me firmly and lingeringly on the mouth. 'I am no ice maiden,' she said. 'In fact I am becoming a rather damp maiden.' Then, with deliberate care, she began to divest me of all my clothes, folding them neatly in a pile on a chair. When I was quite naked she led me over to the fire and looked me up and down. She ran her hands lightly over my body, cupping my balls in her cool hands. Then she stepped back and started to unbutton herself.

'Andrew, there are hooks and eyes that need your attention,' she said as she turned and raised her arms.

Bending to my task and with a care equal to her own, I undressed her as deftly as my eager fingers would allow. Soon two piles of clothing lay beside one another and she was as starkly naked as I. Imitating her control, I held her at arms length and looked at her slim cool body. I explored and caressed her, feeling her elegant neck and then her smooth shoulders. As she again raised her arms my fingers wandered over the soft flesh of her arms. Next came a delicious change of texture as I encountered the silkiness of her unshaven underarm hair. Again I moved in to feel her ribs and then the full yielding flesh of her neatly proportioned breasts.

Brushing the back of my hand against her nipples I felt and saw them begin to swell and stand proud. Onwards and downwards I pursued my exploration. A slim waist, the outward curve of her hips. Her hipbones cupped neatly into my palms as I paused and held her for a moment. Then, as I started to trace out the slight curve of her stomach and my fingers met for the first time the soft down of her pubic hair, she put her arms round my neck, pulled me to her, kissed me again and slowly rubbed the length of her body against mine.

She looked me straight in the eyes and a little smile parted her lips. Her hands were now firmly wandering down the sides of my ribs and then pressing and rubbing my back. I was fondling the firm fleshed cheeks of her bum. Mr Pego had by now fully recovered from his previous excursion and was ready for another outing but I was still a little worried.

I knew that this mysterious creature was quietly ready and even determined to fuck and be fucked. Yet I could not put it from my mind that only a few minutes ago I had cried out her name and plunged myself in a quite abandoned fashion into what I believed and claimed to be her cunt, and that, heedless of any of the social graces, I had then unceremoniously flooded that cunt with my cum. When, my blindfold being snatched off, I had realised that I was in another cunt completely, I could not help but feel that some apology was in order, both to Catherine and to Mary.

Mary, however, had clearly been greatly enjoying both the joke and my urgent fucking. In any case within seconds of Donald's Loch Ness Monster rearing its great head at the entrance to her Great Glen, she had been utterly incapable even of hearing any apology from me. But Catherine was a different matter. I doubted that there was any entry in any book of etiquette that gave instruction on what to do or say when you have confused one cunt with another. It was clear by her approach to me that she was not in truth at all put out but yet I was still uneasy.

She must have sensed that I was hanging back and worried for she started to rub and massage the cheeks of my arse. Then she looked me straight in the eyes, kissed me firmly and at the same moment slipped a finger deep into my back passage.

I gasped with the shock and Mr Pego immediately responded with a convulsive forward leap so that he was butting blindly at her still hidden cleft. Reaching down, she took me in hand and guided me up against her slightly parted cunt lips. I felt the silky dryness of her bush give way to the damp promise of her entry. Rubbing herself against me, she

165

continued to ply my member against her ever-opening slit.

Now she slowly lifted one leg and with a dancer's grace and balance, hooked it round my waist. My prick, guiding hands no longer needed, at once slipped easily half way into her cunt. As I pressed myself deeper into her she carefully, slowly linked her hands behind my neck and swayed back to look at me at arms length.

'Fucking can be like ballet as well as like wrestling, Andrew. No-holds-barred and dancers' holds both have their places. Now, you must lift me.'

So saying, she pulled herself to me and raised her other leg. As her legs locked round my waist she impaled herself completely on my member. Clinging to me, she bit and nuzzled at my neck and I felt a flutter of sheer pleasure run through her. We paused. I clasped her to me and we paused again for a moment of delicious but quite controlled stillness. Then she gave a little sigh and wriggled as though to seat herself quite firmly around me. Next, as I held her by the waist, she again swayed back but this time let go of me so that her body was arched back and her arms hanging loosely, her fingers trailing on the carpet.

Then as I supported my delicious burden, she slowly pulled her body back up to me. I felt all the muscles in her back ripple under my hands as she repeated the movement two or three times more. But next, as she clung to me again, she lifted herself slightly, taking her weight now on her arms and pressing down on my shoulders. With her legs still locked round my waist, she started to slip in an almost teasing way along my prick. I felt the butterfly pressure of her clitoris as it rubbed its way out and back the length of my hugely swollen prick. Now I felt her clit itself swell and press more firmly against my slippery shaft. Her juices were now flowing freely. All her body was warm and damp with her exertions. She began to rotate her hips and she seemed to widen about me in her mounting excitement. But still that amazing muscular control was there and she slowed down once more, again clung close for a second and then whispered to me,

'Hold me very tight and then turn half round.'

Carefully I did as she said. We had turned so that we could both see what was going on in the rest of the room. It was indeed a strange and abandoned sight. Kate and I were the only two who had any pretence of control left. The scene could only compare with some part of one of those orgies of classical times that I had seen in certain of my old headmaster's books of engravings that he kept locked up in the bookcase of his study.

Donald was on his back, measuring his full length on that very same Kelim rug on which I had first entered the delicious Becky the previous evening. In truth it would be more accurate to say that Mary was measuring his full length for she was astride him, her strong thighs clutching him as she rode herself to yet another orgasmic eruption. This time, however, her cries were at least partly stifled by the great distended length of Ian's Highland erection which was thrust into her mouth while she grasped him round the waist and pulled him into her by the cheeks of his arse. He of course was standing, straddled over his brother so that Mary could take in her double portion of Scottish gamecock at both head and tail.

Meanwhile Hannah had bared her splendid bush and lowered herself so that Donald could lick and suck at her open-mouthed quim. Donald indeed was almost enveloped in cunt with both Mary's and Hannah's proud pussies settled on him and each demanding simultaneous service. I saw his tongue rubbing and flicking against Hannah's eager clit before plunging deep into her hot and juicy orifice. She was writhing and crying out in her need to come while Emily, who had entered on to the scene while my attentions were fully engaged by Catherine and her carefully choreographed *pas de deux* was caressing and massaging her mistress's voluptuous bared breasts, lovingly squeezing and rubbing her erect nipples as Hannah clung to her and parted her thighs wider and wider yet so that Donald's thrusting tongue could delve ever deeper into her cunt.

But what of Becky? She alone was not joined in this great chain of cunts and cocks and mouths and bums that heaved and twisted before our enraptured eyes.

Becky was not indeed actually *joined* to any part of the chain but she was certainly joining in and was in contact with many parts. By now stark naked – and possibly also a little intoxicated with the wine and the fucking – she was moving amongst the delicious, ever moving tangle of humanity, laughingly annointing them all with generous quantities of liquor and food.

I saw her dribbling brandy over her sister's twisting body and then rubbing it in like some astringent lotion so that Hannah's skin gleamed and shone in the reflected firelight. I saw her feeding peeled segments of orange into Ian's mouth before embracing him and kissing him open-mouthed. I saw her licking spilled wine and cum from Donald's sorely-tried body. She wriggled and turned, pressing and rubbing herself against the conjunctions and connections that were all about her.

But now she looked up and saw Kate and I standing, linked, watching the contortions and permutations of the rest of the company. As I still held Kate, impaled and slippery on my member, Becky detached herself from her culinary efforts and came towards us.

Standing before us, definitely, I realised, a little drunk, she made a coy little pretence of covering her mouth-watering nakedness. One hand was placed decorously over her dark pubic forest, but yet I could not help but notice that her little finger was teasing and tickling her clit. With her other hand she made a completely ineffective attempt to cover up her superb bosom. Then she essayed a look of great solemnity, gazing at us with a wide-eyed seriousness, opened her mouth to speak but instead gave an accidental hiccup.

'Oh, dear,' she said, her hand covering her mouth so that now her luscious titties were completely revealed once more, 'Oh, dear, I seem to have become completely separated from all my clothes. Andrew and Catherine, I hope you can overlook a certain lack of formality in our entertaining.' Again she gave a little hiccup and giggled.

Catherine, as I held her tightly on her throne of pleasure,

reached out an elegant arm and rested it on Becky's shoulder. 'Becky,' she said, 'Andrew and I are entertaining each other quite happily.'

'Good,' said Becky, 'as your hostess, or one of your hostesses, I would not wish you to lack for anything. Anything you want, you have only to ask.'

With this she gave a rather flamboyant wave as though offering the entire treasure trove of fleshly delights to us. Then she staggered and had to clutch at us to keep her balance. This had the effect of putting me off my balance. For an instant I struggled to keep my footing but with the impaled Catherine now clutching for support at Becky and Becky now trying to emulate Catherine's earlier demonstration of one-legged balance and failing miserably, the outcome was inevitable.

With excited squeals from Becky we all tumbled over in a flurry of arms, legs and bodies. No damage was done but Catherine slipped off my supportive prick as we fell. Becky who was now laughing and hiccuping uncontrollably, saw what had happened.

'Andrew,' she said, 'you've come out of Catherine. You must go back in this very minute, do you hear me!'

With that she seized my cock, noticed that in the stress of events it had lost some fraction of its former ramrod hardness, held it for a moment and said in a governessy tone of voice: 'Andrew, this will never do. I see I shall have to lick you into shape.'

So saying she lowered her head and drew the empurpled head of my cock into her mouth. After two or three passes with her tongue and a judicious squeeze or two of my balls, I was once more fully erect.

'That's better,' she said. 'Catherine, I believe that everything is in working order again. Now, I want to see you two joined together again. And if any man tries to put you asunder, at least before you've had a thoroughly satisfactory fuck, I shall be very cross indeed.'

With this, she glared round the room as though to repel all comers. In fact of course, the others were still so intent and so

169

entwined in their fucking that there was not the slightest chance of any interruption.

As Catherine, who was also beginning to laugh uncontrollably at this turn of events, kissed and rubbed her face against Becky's outstanding titties, she also reached out and took my achingly stiff prick from Becky's hand. For a moment I felt like a baton being passed from hand to hand in the old school cross-country relay race.

I was firmly re-introduced to Catherine's cunt as she pulled me in from behind. Now there was no more of the former balletic graces and control as she backed on to me to ensure I was at once fully engaged. As we coupled on all fours and as I began to thrust myself ever faster into Kate, Becky was nuzzling at my bum, her tongue licking deliciously at the rim of my back passage. Then suddenly she had gone. I saw her crawling across the room, struggling through the octopus-like wrestling that was now spreading across the carpet as positions were changed and changed again. For a moment I saw Donald's bum, or was it Ian's, raised up before he drove down again into the uplifted cunt of Hannah.

Becky was now reaching up to grab from the table either a bowl of fruit or another decanter of wine. Whatever her intended prize, she failed in her efforts for at that precise moment she was seized from behind and pulled down into the melee. Clutching at the table in her surprise, she managed to dislodge not only a generous display of fresh fruit but a large blancmange that had stood quivering on a silver salver.

Ripe pears, oranges and soft skinned peaches tumbled and rolled across the floor. The blancmange landed with a cold slap on the bare stomach of either Ian or Donald. Whichever it was, let out a bellow of surprise which was cut short as Becky dived on top of him, squeezing the chilly substance so that it spurted for all the world like cornflour-stiffened cum over arms, legs, breasts, thighs and bums.

While all this was going on, Kate and I had persevered with our fucking so that now we were both nearing our climax. I felt her begin to shiver and moan under me. Deep down at the root of my staff I felt the first wave of my spunk begin to force its way up my prick. No longer trying to hold back, I let it jet out into her. As it flooded out and into her, her own coming was triggered. Panting and pumping, we rolled over, clutching hold of each other as the violence of our joint spending wracked our bodies.

Moments later and we were wrapped round each other, Kate moaning and crying a little. As she nestled against me, my prick still in her, she murmured in my ear, 'Don't be alarmed Andrew. I always cry when I have been well fucked. I love it so much. I think I go sad at the thought that it might never happen again. I am not miserable. That was lovely.'

'Don't worry,' I said. 'I hope very much that it will happen again. I certainly will do everything in my power to make sure it does.'

With that she gave a small sniff, bit me suddenly and wriggled her lovely little titties against my chest. 'Come again soon, as they say,' she said. But our intimacy was all at once interrupted by the return of Becky.

'Andrew! Catherine!' she cried, 'I have had a misfortune. See, I am all sticky.' She was indeed quite covered with fruit juice, blancmange and wine.

'Waste not, want not, as Mama says. It is all good nourishing food. I think that I need to be licked clean and dry. You should start here.' With this, she thrust out her lovely titties. 'And then work your way down.'

'This is indeed a mouthwatering invitation, Becky,' I said. 'I'm sure that there is enough for two. Miss Catherine, would you care to join me in some light refreshment?'

'Why, yes,' she answered demurely, 'that is very kind of you. It is so important to eat regularly and I am sure that the company will be most congenial.'

As I began to lick and nibble at Becky's titties, Catherine started to do likewise. 'Presentation is so important in matters of food,' said Becky, cupping one ripe breast in her hand and offering it to my hungry mouth. 'How lucky that I have a pair so that you can have one each.'

The taste of fresh fruit mingled with what I now realised was brandy is a culinary delight in itself. When it is served up

171

on the fragrant warm flesh of a woman's body, when one can feel an engorged nipple rising and hardening even as one's tongue and lips are seeking out and sucking in the sweetness and tang of distilled grape and peach juice, then one is transported to a veritable heaven of sensual pleasures. Catherine must also have had similar thoughts for as she ran her soft mouth along the swell and contour of Becky's titty she lifted her head for a moment to look at me.

'Nectar and ambrosia', she said.

'The food of the Gods',' I agreed.

'Better than school dinners,' said Becky, joining in.

'And much better served,' I added, remembering the somewhat spartan furnishing of Nottsgrove's Dining Hall and the often chipped, institutional-white crockery from which we had had to eat.

As we pursued our lip-licking way down Becky's body, she wriggled happily as our tongues rasped and licked over her bare flesh.

'There is, I think, some of cook's lemon-flavoured blancmange in my navel,' she said.

'I did notice your accident at the table,' I answered.

'I'd have thought you'd have been too intent on your fucking to notice such a small domestic incident,' said Becky.

'The results were somewhat spectacular,' answered Catherine. 'And personally I always fuck with my eyes open.'

'Blancmange?' I asked Catherine, offering Becky's succulent little navel up to her.

'That is most kind,' she answered, smiling gravely at me.

As she lowered her head and poked her tongue deep into Becky's navel, Becky giggled and wriggled.

'That tickles,' she said, lying back and throwing herself from side to side in a vain attempt to escape Kate's inquisitive tongue. As her knees rose and her thighs parted I saw spread out before me another enticing sight.

'I believe I see a taste bud,' I said and opened her legs yet further. Quickly I continued my downward expedition, my mouth and tongue grazing at her dark brandy-soaked forest before dipping into the now openly revealed cleft. As my

172

tongue teased and probed at her swollen lips, forcing its way into the warm wetness of her cunt, her giggling turned to rising moans of excitement. Catherine, I was aware, was now caressing and massaging Becky's body from neck to pubic bush while I plied her with my tongue, inhaling the heady perfume of her aroused sex.

As her moans and cries rose to a crescendo, I realised also that Emily had joined us and was hugging her and kissing her insistently. By now, with the three of us attending to her, Becky's whole body seemed to be one exquisitely sensitive instrument of passion. Every part of her was alive with the ecstasy of sex. She was crying out as her love juices flowed and her whole body flushed. As we held her and fondled her, as her cunt gaped and her hips thrashed wildly she gave out a great long shuddering howl of pleasure and surrendered herself wholly to her coming.

I believe we all felt that that last overwhelming orgasm of Becky's marked not just her climax but the climax of the evening. Ian, Donald, Hannah and Mary had disentangled themselves. We were all happily spent with frolicking and fucking. Emily and Mary were told firmly that all clearing up was to be left for the morning. Huddled and half-drunk with fatigue, wine and sex, we sat and talked for a while. Practicalities arose. Catherine had to get back to her brother's establishment. Ian and Donald would be staying there also and so would escort her home. I was ordered to get a good night's sleep since Colonel Moore would be arriving in the morning and I must be ready for my journey to the West Country and my encounter with the errant Rosalind. Mrs P— arrived back shortly after eleven, put her head round the door, tactfully failed to notice the considerable mess and considerable undress of some of the party, greeted the Scottish contingent warmly and then bid us goodnight.

And so my second evening at my new lodgings drew to a close. I liked London, I decided. I wondered whether I would like Bristol. I also knew that on my return to the Metropolis after my short sojourn in Somerset, I could look forward to more adventures among the splendid array of quims that I had come upon so luckily. Wearily, slowly, I went up to bed eager to envelope myself in the Arms of Morpheus. That night I slept alone and uninterrupted.

8

The next morning, after an early breakfast, Colonel Moore arrived. He was an elderly person of a military bearing. Mrs P— had greeted him warmly and it was clear that they were indeed old friends. After they had talked privately for a while they came in to the drawing room. I was introduced as his travelling companion to Bristol.

'Andrew, Colonel Moore knows all about the problem. He has met Rosalind before.'

'She can be something of a handful,' opined the good Colonel, 'but I think that between us we can have her safely delivered to you.'

Mrs P— wished us Godspeed, a cab was procured and shortly afterwards we were on our way to Paddington Station in order to catch the quarter to twelve train. 'Called the *Flying Dutchman*,' said the Colonel. 'Takes about two and a half hours which is about as good as one can get these days.'

I had already decided that the Colonel was going to be an affable and entertaining companion. He had a fund of anecdotes and strange tales of life in the Colonies. We quickly found our First Class seats and settled in to the compartment. Luckily, as the train drew out it became apparent that we had the compartment to ourselves. I describe this as lucky since it allowed us to talk freely.

No sooner were we properly under way when the Colonel lit up a cheroot and produced his hip flask.

'Brandy?' he said, passing me the flask. 'Settles the stomach. Keep us going until we get to Swindon where we can get something to eat, if you can put up with ten minutes of

175

bedlam in the Refreshment Rooms. Now, tell me, Andrew, have you ever fucked on a train?'

'What?' I asked, dumbfounded.

'No, I can see you haven't,' he said. 'Well take my advice. Try it. Some of the best fucks of my life have been on trains. Tried it once on top of an elephant in India, but that's another story. Yes, railway rogering. Excellent sport. And the beauty of it is that it's so easily done.' Seeing that I was looking at him with surprise, he went on, 'Something to do with the speed and the motion. Women love it. Always have, ever since they invented railways. Ever read the *Journals of Fanny Kemble?* The actress? She writes of the thrill of speeding along at over thirty miles per hour and standing up with her bonnet off, drinking in the air. All sorts of stuff about feeling she was flying.

'That was when she travelled on the Liverpool and Manchester and she was quite right about the excitement of it all. I was there. People remember the accident that befell Mr Huskisson that day. First passenger to be killed on the railway. What they don't know is that the first railway fucking took place on the same occasion. I know. I was doing it. At the very moment that poor Huskisson was struck down by the *Rocket*, I was penetrating a most luscious wet pussey. You could have your own private carriage attached in those days. Of course the wretched third class passengers were jammed into open trucks. Soon as it came on to rain they'd get drenched to the skin. Play your cards right. Invite a couple of ripe, damp beauties into your carriage. Help them take off their wet things. Offer to warm them up. Pull the curtains to for the sake of maidenly modesty and in no time you'd have an eager, grateful woman impaled on your member. Never failed.'

'Never?' I asked, not quite believing his story.

'Well, not always. But you'd be surprised how often it did work. It's best tried on the express services. Gives you time between stops. Wife and I consummated our marriage on the Scotch express, non-stop between Euston and Crewe. I came at Tring, my wife came at Rugby and we both managed it

176

together passing through Tamworth. Remember it to this day. Though I'd be grateful if you don't mention it to Mrs Moore when you meet. She's a paragon of virtue and much respected in Bristol Society these days.

By now I was in a state of open amusement at his stories. I decided to prompt him into further accounts of his past.

'What about the occasion on the elephant?' I asked.

'Kashmir,' he said. 'We were out on a tiger shoot, bobbing along in this *howdah* on the beast's back, the *mahout* perched up on its shoulders. I was accompanied by a very game little widow woman I'd met up at Darjeering. We had to be discreet, what with the bearers and guides. But we managed it. She'd already been investigating my equipment with her hand under the travelling rug and I eased her over so that she could sit on my lap. She opened her thighs and I felt my erect member slide in to her. Then she half raised herself to have a better sight of where we were going and then sank back on to me. We could feel the steady motion of the powerful beast beneath us and in no time I knew I was about to come. Then, just as the first spurt forced its way up and into her, a huge tiger sprang at us from the trees.'

'What happened then?' I asked, determined to keep him spinning his inventive yarns.

'Shot it. Single-handed since I had to use the other hand to keep the widow in place. Magnificent creature, the tiger. Fully grown male. I had it skinned and presented the hide to the widow. She kept it hidden in a closet and only used to bring it out when I came up to see her at the Hill Station. We'd have a burning hot curry together and then we'd fuck on the tiger skin. But Andrew, I mustn't bore you with an old man's memories.'

'Oh no, Sir, I am quite enthralled by your accounts. I find fucking a fine sport but I know that there are many things that I have not yet done and many places where I have not yet been.'

'Do not dismiss what I say as mere travellers' tales. Look about you next time you are in the presence of women on a train or on the platform. You will see a brightness of eye, a

177

flushed complexion, a slight breathlessness as they regard the snorting beast that is transporting them. Dammit! your locomotive is the very symbol of sex. Ever seen the painting by that Turner chappie? Called *Rain, Steam and Speed*. Violent storm, steam and thunder clouds, glare of flame from the engine. Now I ask you, what's the painting all about? Not a careful delineation of meterological conditions. No, it's all about excitement and fucking. On railways. Mark my words, Andrew, there are openings for many an amorous adventure when you're safely locked into your compartment and the countryside is speeding past.'

He fell silent and I could see the light of reminiscence in his eye.

'You probably don't recall the Great Staplehurst Disaster? Too young. It was back in the Sixties. Sixty-five if my memory serves me. Never was too good with dates.'

'I think I do remember my father and mother talking about it.' I answered. 'Did not the train run off a bridge of some sort that was under repair? On the Dover line, between Tonbridge and Ashford in the middle of the Kentish Weald? Mr Charles Dickens was a passenger was he not? I'm sure there was a drawing of the accident in the *Illustrated London News*? Don't tell me, Sir, that you were an eye witness to the tragedy?'

'Indeed yes,' the Colonel replied. 'I had only moments before coupled up to a Continental Passenger, a Frenchwoman whom I had got to know a good many years before at the Great Exhibition in Hyde Park. In fact she always used to call me, or part of me, her Great Exhibit. She had a way of solemnly unleashing my member and saying "One of Zee Triumphs of Victorian Engineering" before sinking on to it with a happy squeal of *joie de vivre*, as the French say. And quite a squealer she was, but not quite in the same class as one of the maids where you're lodging.'

'Mary,' I said.

'Ah! Come across her already have you? Tremendous set of lungs on her. Talk about making the welkin ring! The Frenchwoman wasn't in that class but still pretty noisy.

178

Actually had her for the first time *in* the Crystal Palace. She was on top of me and working herself up to a climax, yelling her head off and I was looking up at that great glass roof, thinking "Hope she doesn't bring that lot down on us."'

'But all was well?' I asked.

'Oh, yes. Fine. Except a pigeon dropped dead on her.'

'Not struck down by her cries of passion, surely?' I said, trying not to laugh.

'Oh, no! Pure coincidence, no doubt,' answered the Colonel. 'Though sound waves can have the oddest effects. Came across that often enough in the Army.'

'But what about the train crash at Mablethorpe?' I asked, anxious to return to the story in hand.

'Staplehurst,' he said. 'Yes, well, there I was with the Frenchwoman deliciously wrapped round me. I was escorting her back to Dover in order to catch the Channel Packet back to Calais. She'd been staying with me and the wife for a couple of weeks. We were living in Blackheath at the time as I was stationed at Woolwich. Nothing underhand about the business, y'know. Wife knew all about it. Matter of fact, we all three used to sleep in the same bed when Marie-Claire, that was her name, came to stay. Not that we slept all that much. Very demanding women, both of them. Used to fuck all the time. Wife was very taken with the Military Life. I'd come back from my Regimental Duties at the barracks. Field Artillery we were. Wife would demand that I showed them the drill for bringing a six-pounder into action. Marie-Claire would be leaping up and down saying things like "Mon Dieu, what a magnificent firing piece. I 'ope eet will be pointing in my direction when it ees discharged." The wife meanwhile would be going in for a bit of spit-and-polish. Wonderful soft mouth she's got. Like a Labrador. Anyway,'

'The train crash,' I interjected.

'What?'

'You are getting side-tracked, Colonel Moore,' I said. The Frenchwoman had just wrapped herself round your Military Equipment, when?'

'When there was this terrific crash. I felt the earth move. In fact the whole carriage moved. We were tipped on end, thrown from one side of the compartment to the other. I remember the doors bursting open. There was splintered wood everywhere and a terrible banging and crashing. People were screaming. The Frenchwoman was screaming. Everyone else was calling out "Help me! Help me!" but The Frenchwoman was calling out "Fuck me! Fuck me!" Then the entire carriage seemed to disintegrate and the next thing I knew, we were half way down an embankment or something, both bare-arsed as baboons in a mass of stinging nettles. The Frenchwoman,'

'Marie-Claire,' I said.

'That was her. Marie-Claire, who was always a very copious comer, was far too far gone in her coming, if you see what I mean, to stop. Luckily everything else was such chaos and distress that I don't think anyone really noticed what we were doing. I discovered then that cum is very good for nettle stings. Much better than dock leaves. After we'd uncoupled, we smeared each other's bums with our juices and I don't think either of us felt any pain at all.'

'So what is the moral of the story?' I asked.

'No moral whatsoever, young man. Just one example of the tight spots you can get into when you travel by train.'

'And some sticky situations,' I answered, quite wittily I thought.

'So,' he said, 'mark my words. Railway fucking. A splendid activity.'

As he said this the train drew slowly to a halt. Looking out of the window I could see nothing but fields and a small herd of grazing cows.

'Middle of nowhere,' said the Colonel. 'Signals, I suppose. Though we can't be far from Swindon now.'

Just then a London-bound train also drew to a halt on the opposite track.

'Don't make it too obvious,' said the Colonel, 'but have a look at what's going on opposite us.'

Trying not to turn my head, I peered sideways to look at the compartment facing us.

Two voluptuously endowed creatures had been surprised in what they must have assumed was to have been an uninterrupted, non-stop, Swindon-to-Paddington excursion into the delights of Lesbos. Neither I would calculate could have been more than twenty years of age. Each was flaunting her large and well-formed titties.

'Reminds me of the hills above Darjeeling,' said the Colonel who was beginning to chew thoughtfully at the silver-headed top of his stick.

One was in the act of fondling the glowing cheeks of her friend's bum while the latter was frigging herself with what appeared to be a large dildo, fashioned in the exact likeness of a gigantic male member.

The one with the dildo inserted was far too preoccupied with her frenzied activity to notice that their train had drawn to a stop and that they were now overlooked not only by the two of us but presumably by the passengers in the compartments adjacent to ours.

The second, however, had realised that they were no longer alone. For a moment she desisted from her intimate embracing of her friend, looked across at our train and for an instant made as though to hide her well-displayed charms. Then she caught my eye and a blush crept across her cheeks.

Distracted from the Colonel's stories by this quite unexpected addition to the Wiltshire landscape, Mr Pego at once rose to a commanding height. Miss Saucy opposite had apparently realised that to be overlooked by complete strangers whom one will never see again, may be an occasion for a teasing display rather than maidenly modesty. She gave a wicked smile and cupped her great titties in her hands, offering them to her audience across the track.

'Splendid, splendid!' cried the Colonel. 'Andrew, do you know Semaphore?'

'What?' I said, only half-hearing. My attention was rigidly drawn to the fleshly delights that were facing me.

'Time to make a signal in return,' said the Colonel. 'Show her your flag staff. Get it out and give her an answering wave.'

So saying he pointed with this stick at the now positively

181

Alpine bulge in my trousers. For a moment more I hesitated.

'Go on, boy. Got to seize life's opportunities with both hands,' he urged.

At that I released my questing quim-seeker. It sprang at once upward into the view of the lovely temptress opposite. It is of course possible that mine was not the only answering flourish that she was receiving from our side. She certainly responded to our appreciation for now she held her titties so close to the window of her compartment that her huge nipples brushed and stiffened against the glass. Next she began to trace little circles across the pane as she simultaneously squeezed and manipulated her breasts.

By now I had risen from my seat in excitement and was likewise displaying the full length of my response while the Colonel was banging his stick on the floor and barking out military commands such as 'Take Aim,' 'Present Arms,' 'Up Guards and At 'em', along with instructions not to fire until I could see the white of her eye, whatever that meant.

Now a most enticing double act ensued, for her companion, carefully setting aside her dildo, pulled her friend's skirts up and back so that her great black haired pussey was revealed to its avid audience. Fingers were inserted and the cunt lips pulled apart while a finger and thumb gently pinched and caressed a fine fat clit into public prominence.

Through the mahogany walls of our compartment we could now plainly hear on the one side, cries of outrage and from the other, cheers of encouragement. I began to handle my giant erection as though offering it in return to the nameless beauty that pouted at me from the other track. She, her tongue licking hungrily at her lips, was now switching and gyrating her hips, still thrusting her titties against the window as her friend stroked and fingered her with ever increasing rapidity.

Suddenly our engine gave out a crowing whistle, my engine spurted out the first of its load of cum, the train lurched into motion once more and I, caught off balance by the sudden motion, stumbled and banged myself quite painfully against

182

the door. As we drew slowly away from the splendidly staged scene that had so wholly captured our attention, both girls in one final flamboyant gesture of farewell, turned and displayed their bared bums, pulling the cheeks apart so that for an instant we could see what the Colonel called The Eye of the Needle. Two needles.

'Just imagine threading yourself into those openings,' he said. 'Railways and fucking. Hope you'll believe me now.'

I for my part said nothing as I busied myself with restoring myself to some semblance of public decency. Now the outskirts of the great railway town of Swindon began to pass before us and by the time that I had subsided into good order we were slowing to our scheduled ten-minute halt. We descended from our carriage to make our way to the First Class Refreshment Rooms. There was on all sides a great hustle and bustle, much shunting and banging of trucks and carriages, much steaming and snorting of locomotives. From Mr Brunel's busy railway works and from the locomotive sheds, came the huffing and puffing, the smoke and steam, of innumerable Iron Horses. On the station itself crowds of passengers mingled and jostled, some looking quite lost, some intent and organised. Footwarmers and refreshment hampers were loaded and unloaded. Porters manhandled trunks and valises as uniformed railway officials glared importantly at watches, waved flags and blew whistles.

I should have been quite lost in the hurly burly and general commotion but Colonel Moore, who clearly knew his way around the station, took charge and marched with military bearing along the platform while I followed in his wake. Soon we were safely inside the Refreshment Rooms and ensconced at a table, doing justice to a light repast that, along with two bottles of stout, had been ordered and provided with quite amazing speed by the pretty and willing girls who presided at the elegant and well-stocked counters. I was quite overwhelmed by the variety of food and drink, from sandwiches and Banbury cakes to basins of hot soup or cold fowls, from humble tea to aristocratic champagne or iced lemonade, all served with a kind of *heigh presto* rapidity. But I had barely time to appreciate the splendid dimensions and the elaborate *trompe d'oeil* decoration before Colonel Moore was demanding my attention and introducing me to a tall, delightful woman whose discreet mode of dress did nothing to disguise her lushly attractive figure.

'Andrew,' he said, 'this pretty creature is Tess. Tess, this is a young friend of mine, Mr Andrew Scott. I have been telling him of the pleasures that can attend travel by the railway. Now, Andrew, we do not have time for you to get better acquainted with Tess for our train is about to depart but suffice it to say that she is one of those pleasures. Tess, should Andrew here at some time in the future find it necessary to change trains at Swindon or delay his onward journey for an hour or so, I hope that you will extend him every courtesy.'

'Just as long as he extends himself towards me,' said Tess with a most lascivious smile. 'If I am not visible, then you may ask for me at the Chief Cashier's Office. It is most likely that they will know my whereabouts.'

'Particularly in winter, when you may become somewhat chilled in your travels,' said the Colonel, 'you will find Tess most adept at warming you and sending you on your way with your circulation much restored. She may even be persuaded to accompany you for a ride down the line.'

'Footwarmers,' said Tess, 'are all well and good. But there are other parts that need to be kept well-warmed. I am told that frost-damaged organs can drop off and such a happening would never do. The Railway Company prides itself on its attention to the creature comforts of at least its First Class passengers. Of course the service I offer to a few select persons such as the Colonel is quite unofficial but I believe it to be a valuable adjunct to the more openly advertised facilities of the Company.'

'I can see that you are indeed a most public-spirited person, Tess,' I answered.

'You are most kind,' she said. 'I have also to admit,' and here she lowered her voice, 'that I have a cunt that yearns to be fucked and that if this does not happen at least twice in the day, then I become quite upset and restless.'

At this, my prick immediately rose to readiness.

'I am sorry, Andrew,' said the Colonel, noting my condition, 'but we cannot delay.'

'Mrs Moore is expecting our arrival at Temple Meads on time. We have to arrange the collecting of the errant Rosalind from her school so for the moment your interest in Tess must remain unfulfilled.'

With that I was again dragged along in his wake as we hurried back to the platform and clambered into our compartment once more. I can report that nothing more of any note took place on the remainder of our journey. The Colonel dozed for some of the time while I looked at the passing scenery.

At Bristol, where we arrived some ten minutes late much to the disgust of the Colonel, we quickly obtained a cab and were transported to Clifton, where resided the good Colonel and his lady. I quickly apprehended that Clifton was a most pleasant place, situated on the height of a precipitous cliff, overlooking the Gorge through which flowed the River Avon with its busy traffic of shipping. Large and imposing houses attested to the wealth of the City which seemed to be dominated by a number of very fine churches.

The Colonel, who I gathered had if not converted at least become most interested in the Buddhist Religion while out East, was not very informed or informative concerning such places of worship.

'My wife,' he said, 'attends some church or other most Sundays. She does not press me to accompany her, which suits me well for I am more interested in the beliefs of the Orient. I have indeed certain works of Persian scholarship that you might like to peruse if we have time.'

I informed him that Mrs P— had told me of her interests also in such matters and had told me of her friend Mr Burton.

'Good man,' said the Colonel. 'There are several of us who encourage him in his endeavours of translation. However, I would be grateful if you would be guarded in your allusions to such matters in the presence of Mrs Moore. Since we have settled in Bristol she has embraced respectability with all the fervour of a convert.'

He then proceded to tell me of an unfortunate incident

when his wife, returning early from Evensong through a passing feeling of faintness, had discovered him surrounded by his books of Eastern Art, trying, as he said, 'to recreate in the flesh a delightful but somewhat complex depiction of the Garden of Heavenly Pleasures according to a Zoroastrian text.'

'What was actually happening?' I asked.

'I had prevailed upon some ten or twelve young people to aid me in my scholarly pursuit. Dear Hannah, who was staying with us, was helping me. Have you yet seen her pottery?' he asked me. 'Although it is created in the Doulton Studio, the pieces of which I am speaking are private commissions. The technique is I believe called *'s-graffiato*. Figures are scratched through a surface glaze before it is fired so that an underlying pigment shows through. That at any rate is the essence of the process I believe. The results are a decorative *tour de force*.'

'But what are the designs actually of?' I asked. Once again I could see that one story was leading to another and since I knew we must be nearing our destination, I was anxious to find out exactly what it was that the Colonel had been up to when surprised by the early return of his wife.

'Figures,' he said. 'Human figures, both male and female, dancing round and round in circles. Figures linked to one another in an endless daisy chain of fucking.'

'And it was this endless daisy chain of fucking that you were trying to recreate in the flesh while your wife was at her devotions?' I said. 'I can well imagine that such a scene would be a little upsetting, especially if she was feeling unwell.'

'I think,' said the Colonel, 'that it was not on her own behalf but on that of the Churchwarden that she was disturbed.'

'The Churchwarden!' I exclaimed.

'Yes,' he said. 'He had very kindly offered to escort my wife home when she became ill in the church.'

'He also was upset to stumble upon such a scene?' I asked.

'Not noticeably,' said the Colonel. 'In fact he took it very well. He muttered something about the natural exuberance of youth and seemed more than prepared to stay while I explained what was going on. My wife however hurried him out of the room, thrust him back into the cab, apologised profusely and then returned to quite put a damper on the goings-on. All the young people, with the exception of Hannah, were driven out of the house.'

'Still without clothes?' I asked.

'Oh, no. They were given a few moments of respite before the exodus,' he answered. 'Such lively and willing young people. Friends mostly of Hannah. Those girls of Mrs P— have the amiable characteristic of knowing so many people in so many parts of the country who aren't ashamed to display the naked human form. But alas such open mindedness accords ill with the prevailing temper of the times.'

'I agree,' I said. 'My headmaster, the good Dr White, lamented often and loudly upon the hypocrisy of the Age. Although it must be said that in any age, even the most open, a wife might be forgiven for being disturbed by the discovery of her husband surrounded by such cavorting and fucking.'

'In fact,' he answered, 'there was comparatively little fucking going on. It is, as we proved that afternoon, really very hard to caper and fuck at the same time. It was certainly quite impossible to caper at any speed. The effect was more that of a slow shuffle. Hannah said that she had long suspected a degree of artistic licence on the part of the original illustrators whilst I had argued for a greater degree of flexibility on the part of the trained Eastern temple dancer. Nonetheless it was a worthwhile attempt and very much in the interests of scholarship.'

'Mrs Moore was, I imagine, quite mollified when the matter was explained to her?'

'Not altogether,' answered the Colonel. 'Hannah had to be told to pursue her more advanced artistic reconstructions elsewhere but in our house. She herself is, I'm glad to say, quite *persona grata*. My wife is a forgiving woman, merely rather more concerned with appearances than I or indeed your landlady.'

Shortly afterwards we arrived *chez* Moore and I was taken

in to meet the Colonel's long-suffering wife.

Their house was quite large and quite stuffed with ornaments and furniture that reflected the years they had spent out East. In the Library, which contained several locked cabinets, were the fruits of the Colonel's collecting: rare editions and volumes of lithographs that all bore witness to his deep and learned interest in Eastern and Middle Eastern erotica. Assuming that I would be interested, he promised to show me some of the gems of his collection after dinner.

In the meantime after a late, light lunch plans were made for the fetching of the errant Rosalind from her school. The Colonel and Mrs Moore would go down to Shepton Mallet, the nearest station to the school, the next morning.

'Not a difficult journey,' said Mrs Moore. 'We go to Bath and then change on to the Somerset and Dorset line. The school is, I gather, out on the Wells road and we can hire some conveyance to take us from the station.'

'Meanwhile, Andrew,' said the Colonel, 'you'll have to amuse yourself during the day. You have the run of the library, of course, and you can always go off and explore the delights of Bristol.'

'The fleshpots?' I queried, remembering my Godfather's expression.

'I'm afraid you'd need some introductions,' said the Colonel, understanding at once that I was alluding to the less public pleasures that might be available in such a City. 'Alas there really isn't the time so you'll have to content yourself with the quieter pleasures of reading and walking.'

'I'm certain Andrew will welcome a short breathing space after all the racketting around that he must get up to in London,' said Mrs Moore. 'Or you might like to accompany us as far as Bath, where you could sample the curative waters and take tea in the Pump Room.'

'Lot of nonsense,' said the Colonel. 'Nothing that he needs curing of at his age. You'd be better off widening your knowledge of Eastern cultures in the Library.'

'I am indeed most interested in the subject,' I answered. 'From the descriptions both of yourself and of Mrs P—, I am sure that there is much I could learn from such studies.'

'Very well,' said Mrs Moore, 'although I would also commend to you the virtues of a good, healthy walk. Stuffed up in that Library, peering at all those old books and drawings, you could end up going blind.'

In the event, the remainder of the afternoon and the evening passed quietly. After dinner the Colonel and I did indeed retire to peruse his collection. I was particularly taken by a portfolio of sketches made in a Turkish harem. These, the Colonel explained, had been made by an early traveller in Arabia who had gained entry to the establishment in the guise of a eunuch. Before being discovered and as a result actually becoming a eunuch, he had observed in intimate detail the rituals and enjoyments of the inhabitants of the harem for several weeks on end.

Here, all drawn with an arousing wealth of detail, was such a proliferation of pussies, such a massing of mammaries, so many women doing so many things to so many other women that I was quite overwhelmed with hunger. However there was to be no outlet for my pent-up frustration. Colonel Moore's endless stream of reminiscence had dried up under the influence of fatigue and possibly for fear of interruption by Mrs Moore who was bustling about making arrangements for the morrow. The whole household retired quite early for bed. I had no night visitors and fell asleep wondering what Rosie the naughty schoolgirl would be like. My own schooldays now seemed so far behind that I found it hard to believe that we would have much in common. No doubt she would either be subdued and shamed by her expulsion or else she would prattle on endlessly about this school rule and that school rule and how beastly and unfair Miss X and Miss Y had been.

I consoled myself with the thought that the day after tomorrow I would be back in Sussex Gardens and there waiting for me would be Becky and Hannah, Emily and Mary and possibly further visits from the graceful Catherine. Meanwhile I would make the best of my monk-like existence and practise the virtue of continence.

9

The next day did indeed pass for the most part in the quiet
pursuits of reading and the perusal of Colonel Moore's
volumes of Eastern engravings, except that around midday I
fucked the cook.

The Moores had left around mid-morning on their mission
to the Mendips. They expected to be back at some time after
four o'clock. Not knowing what arrangements had been
made for my lunch, I went down in to the kitchen to discover
that today was obviously baking day. Cook who was a large
woman, big-bosomed and broad of hip, was energetically
kneading and rolling great quantities of dough. Bread was
being made and pies and tartlets and what I took to be drop
scones. Cook, with flour up to her elbows and with smudges
of flour on her face where she had pushed back a stray wisp of
hair from her eyes, was leaning forward, flushed and
breathing heavily from her efforts. She looked up as I came in
to the kitchen and smiled in greeting.

'Just a minute. It's Mr Andrew isn't it? You'll be thinking
about a bite to eat, I'll be bound. Let me finish rolling this
pastry out and then I'll see what I can do.'

There was such a clean, warm smell about the place, such a
mouthwatering atmosphere of fresh bread and warm woman
as she went happily about her work that without thinking I
went and put my arms round her from behind and gave her a
friendly cuddle. She looked over her shoulder at me, still
wielding her rolling pin and as she dusted it with flour to stop
it sticking, said, 'A big growing boy like you'll have a healthy
appetite. Mrs Moore and the Colonel like their guests to leave
satisfied.'

By now, what with her evident friendliness and the rhythm of her body under my hands as she to-d and fro-d with her rolling pin, I was becoming unexpectedly excited. Mr Pego rose and she in turn felt him as he pressed against her substantial but firm-cheeked bottom.

'Now Mr Andrew, I can feel what you're up to,' she said. 'You young gentlemen are all the same. Some of the old'uns as well. I've got a little way to go yet with this so you must either hang on for a bit or come into me from behind.'

At this I started to bunch her skirts up at the back in order to lay bare her lovely big arse, but in so doing I accidently pushed her against the kitchen table.

'Now stop it,' she said. 'You're getting me all messed up. There's flour and dough all over my dress.'

'I'm sorry,' I said.

'Don't fret,' she said. 'For the moment, you just use your fingers on me and get me nice and ready. Soon as this is done with, we can do it properly.'

So saying she parted her legs and allowed me to slip my hand through from behind. My fingers at once felt their way through a fine forest of quim hair and found their objective. A big, healthy cunt opened at my touch and accepted my fingers. Then she closed her legs, trapping me inside her and as I started to probe and fondle her, she began to slowly bump and grind with her hips.

She looked back at me again. 'That's nice, nice and steady. I'll soon be ready. We can leave the dough to rise for a bit. You get yourself all ready as well. Better you get your cock out for yourself. I've got pastry all over my hands.'

I did as I was bid and with some eagerness for by now my member was swollen and throbbing in its eagerness to penetrate her. Moments later she'd finished her work. She turned and held up her flour-covered hands to me. I realised that it was up to me to lift her skirts and underthings so that she was exposed to me. At this juncture she saw my prick for the first time.

'He's as fat and big as he felt,' she said. 'Just the thing to give my pudding bowl a good stir round.'

191

Then she took my kitchen implement in her hands. 'Sorry,' she said, 'I've got flour all over him. Never mind, let's feel him inside of me.'

There and then she lay down on the stone flags and pulled me on top of her. I entered easily for we were both already well greased with our juices. I slid my full length deep in to her and as her legs spread wide and welcoming began to fuck her. She was as ready and willing as I and as I thrust into her faster and faster, she lifted and thrust back again. I could feel my spunk beginning to churn its way up my hugely distended prick. For a moment I held it back but then realised she also was beginning to tremble with the onset of her coming. As I relaxed and felt the first spurt of my cum flood into her warm and welcoming cunt, so I felt also her own answering contractions and shudders as she came, basting my cock in her cum. Again and again, I rammed myself in to her, filling her with my cream. We reached our happy climax together, clutching and moaning in each other's arms. Then, as we subsided and lay in an exhausted huddle, she raised her head and looked at me.

'That was nice. Much better than a toad in the hole at any rate.'

'Better than a jam roly poly,' I answered.

'Banger and mash!'

'Spotted Dick!'

'Stop it, Mr Andrew,' she said. 'Now you let me up. I've still got work to do. And besides, I've got a cold bum from this floor.'

'I'll rub some warmth back into it,' I offered.

'You can do that but I want you out of my kitchen.'

'Tempt me with food,' I said. 'I'm feeling a bit peckish.'

So saying, I helped her up and started to massage and knead the flesh of her buttocks.

'Better?' I said.

'Better,' she answered. Then she turned and slapped a lump of dough on the end of my prick. 'Now you take him away before I start thinking about making a Beef Wellington of him.'

Feeling cheerfully satisfied from my unexpected fuck, I

asked if there was any other way in which I could help her but was firmly told to leave her to get on with things in her own way. I went back upstairs, a large bowl of soup with dumplings appeared soon afterwards and I ate and relaxed. I even had a nap for a short while. The rest of the afternoon passed in a state of pleasant inertia as the hour neared when I could expect the return of my host, Mrs Moore and Rosie the Reluctant School Girl.

It was in fact rather later than I had anticipated that I heard a cab draw up outside and I realised that the Mendip expedition had returned. I went out into the hallway to greet them.

'Hello, Andrew,' said Colonel Moore. 'God, what a journey we've had. Missed the damn train at Bath on the way back. Rain been pouring down half the day. Nothing but mud and damp cows. Too long out East I'm afraid to appreciate the beauties of the English countryside.'

'Stop chattering on,' said his wife to him. Then she looked back. 'Come along Rosalind! Stop fussing over your belongings. The cabby will bring them in.' She pulled the errant Rosalind in. 'Andrew, this is Rosalind. Rosalind, Andrew.'

Rosie was not at all what I had expected. Petite, she had masses of light brown hair that tumbled carelessly about her face. She had a pretty, pretty face, round cheeked and round eyed with a determined little chin. She was smiling and her eyes were alight with mischief and excitement. Hatless, she had drops of rain in her hair. She was dressed however in a particularly unbecoming school uniform.

'I've escaped. I've escaped,' she said. 'How wonderful to be out of that place. Dear Mrs Moore, you've no idea how grateful I am that you've helped me out of that School. I want to forget about it at once and completely. Everything that reminds me of it has got to go. Starting with these awful, awful clothes.'

With that she started to pull off her admittedly hideous school clothes, throwing them with wild abandon around the hallway.

'Rosie! Stop this at once!' cried Mrs Moore. 'Rosie!'

But it was to no avail. While the Colonel paid off the cabby and shut him firmly out in the street, Rosie had now stripped down to her chemise and was twirling and dancing about the place.

'Rosie! Behave yourself,' said Mrs Moore. 'Whatever will Andrew think! This is no way for a nicely brought-up young lady to behave!'

'I'm not a nicely brought-up young lady,' said Rosie. 'I'm a very badly brought-up young lady. The school said so. I'm so happy to be free!'

'Edward,' said Mrs Moore to her husband, 'Do something at once. This child is quite beyond my control.'

I could not help but notice, however, that the Colonel seemed much less disturbed by the turn of events than his wife. Indeed I noticed an appreciative glance directed at Rosie as she pranced around. Truth to tell, Rosie in her underthings was a very fetching sight, quite the animated bundle of fun. I realised at once that whatever problems she posed, at least I was not going to be stuck with some sulky child on the trip back to London.

'I'm sorry, Mrs Moore,' she said, rushing over and hugging her now flustered hostess, 'I didn't mean to shock you. See, I'll pick everything up and take it to my room.'

As I watched, still a little bemused by the suddenness of her arrival and the unconventionality of her behaviour, she turned to me, twitching her hips most provocatively. She then clasped her hands together at her bosom with a teasing gesture of modesty, lowered her eyes demurely and said, 'I am glad that you are to be in charge of me tomorrow, Andrew. I do promise to behave myself properly. You need have no fear that I shall show you up in public.' And with this declaration of ringing insincerity, she allowed herself to be led upstairs by Mrs Moore.

'Quite a handful, that girl,' said the Colonel. 'Quite a delicious handful,' he added. 'Andrew, you will have to have your wits about you tomorrow – and remember also that she is in your trust. Just make sure you deliver her safe and sound to her Guardian.'

'I'm sure I'll do my best, Sir,' I said. 'She seemed a cheerful little creature.'

'Cheerful!' expostulated the Colonel. 'She's been driving us half mad all day! It's because of her we missed our connection at Bath. She'd managed to attract the attention of a Dissenting Minister in the train. A Congregationalist, I believe he turned out to be. She'd spotted a bull in a field by the line who was in the act of servicing a cow. She so pestered him with questions as to what the two creatures were doing that when we arrived in Bath, the fellow insisted on taking me on one side and having the impertinence to lecture me on the ways of Satan and the need for children to be well disciplined. By the time I could get away, our train had gone. Yet I don't think she's particularly bad. In fact she can be a quite charming little thing. I've got some sympathy with her over the matter of those school clothes.'

'She certainly looked better with them off than on,' I suggested.

Colonel Moore looked at me sharply. 'Quite. That is why you must remember that she is in your care until you hand her over to Mrs P—.'

A little later Mrs Moore came down and said that Rosie was, in her opinion, overtired and that after a good hot bath she was to have supper taken up to her on a tray and then to have an early night.

'She does have rather more luggage than I had expected and it has not been properly packed,' she added. 'I can understand that the school was eager to get rid of her but nonetheless they should have sent her off in better order. Since she positively refuses to wear any of her school things any more, there's a good deal of ironing and pressing to be done tonight if she is to have anything in a fit state to wear on the journey tomorrow. It's lucky that she does have some of her own stuff. As there is so much to be done, Andrew, I hope that you will excuse me after dinner. I shall have to leave my husband to look after you while I sort everything out. I do hope that you will come and visit us again in the future when I can spend more time entertaining. Perhaps you could come down with one of the girls. Both Becky and Hannah are always more than welcome here.'

'Such charming girls,' said the Colonel.

'And talented too,' added his wife.

'Ever seen Hannah's drawings from life?' asked the Colonel.

'Edward!' Mrs Moore said warningly. 'Enough of that. But now, if you'll excuse me, I must go about my duties.'

So saying, she went upstairs again, coming down only to join us for a rather hurried dinner. Rosie, it seemed, was indeed tired after the stress of the day and would not be coming down even to say Goodnight.

So it was that the Colonel and I retired after dinner to his study where he could light up one of his small but pungent cheroots.

'Dutch,' he said. 'Tobacco comes from their East Indian colonies. Got the taste for them when we were in Malaya for a while.'

He poured me a brandy and we stretched our legs out in front of the fire.

'Colonel Moore,' I said, 'I am highly intrigued by Rosie. I know that it is none of my business but exactly what did she do that finally caused the school to ask her to leave – and, moreover, to insist that she be taken away immediately?'

He chuckled, thought for a moment and then said: 'Andrew, I will tell you in the strictest confidence. It is after all up to Rosalind and her Guardian to decide what and to whom they should divulge news of the events at the school. However, Rosalind was found outside the school's bounds and at a place where the girls were expressly forbidden to go. Also, she was not alone.'

'Not alone?' I asked.

'She was in the company of a former art master.'

'A retired teacher,' I said.

'Not exactly retired,' said my host. 'Well, not in the sense of his having reached a natural retiring age. He was in fact dismissed some two terms ago.'

'For what?' I asked.

'For gross moral turpitude,' said the Colonel.

'Gross, I understand. Moral also. But turpitude is a concept which I have never fully understood,' I replied.

'The dictionery describes it as Vileness, Depravity and suchlike qualities. However, the offence of the former art master was in my estimation not quite as dramatically awful as that. However I accept that it was beyond the range of permissable behaviour in such a school.

'Williams, for that is his name, has it seems long been working on a rather unusual physiological scheme. You are aware no doubt that the fingerprints of every human being are unique to that person. You may also have heard of the science, or some would call it pseudo-science, of phrenology?'

'It is something to do with feeling the bumps on a person's head and telling their fortune from them,' I answered.

'Not quite,' he said. 'It actually assigns the various mental and emotional faculties to different parts of the head. A phrenologist, as I understand it, would by the observation, measurement and indeed the tracing of the bumps on a person's head be able to build up a picture of the mental characteristics of that person, could in fact classify them: "This is very much a so-and-so sort of person; this is a classic example of such-and-such a type." And on this basis, knowing the balance in that person of the various mental abilities, he might be able to predict that such a person would behave in such a way or would be best suited to such a course of action.

'But I ramble. Forgive me. It is a claimed prerogative of old age. The point is that the classification of human beings, rather as Mr Darwin has classified the animals under his theory of Evolution, the precise delineation of characteristics, whether mental or physical, is an activity that appeals strongly to the scientific mind. The study of fingerprints of course shows both that each of us is unique and also that, because a large collection of prints exhibits certain sets of characteristics, of likenesses if you will, we can also be marked down on some great chart of human types. This collecting of data and then the marshalling of it into some great elaborated scheme with ingenious rules and precise patterns has always been with us. You are aware no doubt of the medieval Doctrine of the Humours?'

'Colonel Moore, pardon my impatience but what exactly was Rosie doing with the late art master?'

'He was photographing her,' said my host as he pulled himself together and returned from his philosophising to the matter in hand.

'Photographing?' I asked. 'Not painting or sketching?'

'No, photographing. It seems that he had also become an enthusiast for the science of photography and has a great collection of equipment which he transports about the country. He is well known for asking all sorts of conditions of people to pose for him.'

'So Rosie was posing?' I said.

'He was pointing his camera at her bum,' said the Colonel, beginning to chuckle. 'Rosie was bending down and had bared her buttocks to him. He was taking a picture of her from an intimately short distance.'

'And was that all?'

'I believe so, at least on this occasion. You see, Williams has developed a theory that human beings can be classified by the shape of their bums although each bum is also unique. To this end he has been assiduously photographing bums for some three or four years now. He has it appears amassed a substantial collection of pictures of the bum. A veritable gallery of *derrières*. Two rooms of his house are filled with them.'

'How do you know all this?' I asked.

'Rosalind has told me some of it and there are also people in the neighbourhood who have seen, strictly by private invitation, some part of his collection. I have made it my business to ask of certain of my acquaintances and they can swear that it is a truly remarkable display.'

'So there are bums of all sorts and ages? Men's and womens?'

'At the moment? No. All the photographs are of young girls' bottoms. Although I gather that he intends to widen his range at some time in the future. But at the moment, he says, he has laid his hands on such a rich treasury of young female

198

bums that it takes up all his spare time.'

'Is this why he was dismissed from the school?'

'Indeed yes. It was discovered that he had been regularly photographing the virgin bums of the school. Not only were there many girls' portraits but he had also arranged some quite large scale group pictures. I have myself seen one of these and a quite distinctive piece of work it was. Some twenty girls were displaying themselves in a parody of a school photograph in three tiers; one row standing on the floor, the next on a bench and the uppermost on a table. Each, with the suppleness of youth has not only bared her firm little bottom, but has then bent down to look back through her parted legs at the camera. It is a wonder that he persuaded them all to stay still for long enough but I gather he was well liked among the pupils.'

Here a certain gleam came into his eye and he sighed as he refilled his glass.

'And he has continued this singular activity since he was dismissed?' I asked.

'Why yes, although with some difficulty. Rosalind has been very useful to him. It appears that she has introduced him to a goodly number of her friends and goes so far as to actually organise times and places when he can pursue his hobby. She claims that it is an honour to help advance the cause of science in this way and that he is a great man.'

'And you believe this also?'

'I believe he is a man who likes photographing girls' bottoms. It is an appealing hobby. And if he intends to publish a well-illustrated book explaining his theories, I would be happy to buy it and evaluate the evidence for myself. Mine is the true scientific spirit of scepticism. Besides, I believe that Rosalind has gained something from her friendship with this man. She has become most interested in photography and with his patient help has become more than ordinarily proficient in the skill. Williams has in fact made her a present of some of his older but quite serviceable equipment. You will have noticed that her trunk was rather heavy?'

'I had noticed that the cabby appeared to have ruptured

some vital organ when he lifted it,' I said.

'Take care that you do not leave a trail of damaged porters and cabmen behind you as you return to London,' he said. 'Unless Rosie is intending to build up a photographic library of ruptured male parts, that is.'

'I am certain that, if not now, then in the near future she will come to appreciate that such organs are more pleasureable in proper working order,' I said.

Our conversation was interrupted by a commotion overhead. There was a crash and a female cry of alarm. The Colonel and I dashed up the stairs. The door to Rosie's bedroom was open and Mrs Moore was already there. We heard her exclaim 'Oh! My poor dear, I should have warned you that it was cracked.'

As we entered we were arrested by a strange sight. Mrs Moore was wringing her hands and uttering cries of anxiety. Rosie was sitting on the floor among the remains of a chamber pot. She was laughing uproariously. Mrs Moore saw us and in a great fluster, hurried us out of the room.

'What has happened? demanded the Colonel.

'Our guest has met with a small accident,' replied Mrs Moore. 'Delicacy does not allow me to explain further.'

'I was about to take a piss when the chamber pot shattered beneath me. I am not much hurt,' called out the irrepressible Rosie through the doorway. 'But I find myself in a quite ridiculous position. Please, will someone help me to my feet?'

We both gallantly responded to her plea. As the Colonel took her hands in his and pulled her gently to her feet, I could not help noticing, even in the midst of this medical emergency, that Rosie's bottom was indeed rosy. It was in fact the neatest, tightest little bum that I had ever seen. Her delicious cheeks almost clung together while below their plump smoothness, I could see the exciting shadow of light brown hair.

But returning to the business in hand, I started to collect the shards of willow pattern potty. Mrs Moore in the meantime had seen that Rosie's bottom was in fact a little cut in one or two places.

'I must fetch some soothing ointment for you,' she said. 'My dear, you must be brave. I shall return in an instant.'

With that she was gone while Colonel Moore and myself tried to calm the still-laughing Rosie. 'Please,' she giggled, 'I have only a badly hurt dignity. It was a great shock, but apart from some smarting about my bottom, I am quite uninjured.'

Mrs Moore returned with the maid, a bowl of warm water, a flannel, a bottle of some astringent lotion and a small pot of cold cream.

'Now, dear,' said Mrs Moore, 'Betty and I can tend your injuries.'

'I am certain Andrew would be prepared to rub some cream into my poor bottom,' said Rosie with a pert but inviting look in my direction.

'Certainly not!' exclaimed my hostess. 'I want both you men out of this room this instant. We must have some decorum in these matters. Rosalind, you are not to be so forward.'

With that we were driven from the room and repaired downstairs where, as Colonel Moore said, 'We both need a stiff nightcap in order to recover from the distressing scene we have just witnessed.'

We talked a little more and the Colonel reminisced about arses he had known and about encounters on railway trains but quite soon we decided to call it a day and retired, he to Mrs Moore and I to my room where I fell asleep thinking of Rosie's smart little posterior and wondering what more I might see of her when I had escorted her back to Sussex Gardens.

Next morning Mrs Moore, whom it was quite clear made all the day-to-day arrangements in the household, suggested that Rosie and I should leave for London after an early lunch.

'There is a train soon after one o'clock,' she said, 'which will get you in at Paddington a little after five. In the meantime Rosalind and you might like to spend the morning getting better acquainted. She has had a much-needed good night's sleep and will be joining us presently for breakfast.'

Indeed it was just a few minutes later when Rosie entered

There was a lightness to her step and a brightness in her eye that suggested that she was well rested and completely recovered from the trials and tribulations of the preceding day.

'Just think,' she said as she seated herself at the table, 'No more school. I am a free woman!'

'My dear,' said Mrs Moore, 'you are certainly not yet a woman and I suspect that you are not yet free of school. Your Guardian, Mrs P—, will doubtless be seeking another establishment to which you can be sent to complete your education. But in the meantime, since Andrew here has so kindly volunteered to escort you up to London, I suggest you repay him at least in part by showing him some of the sights of Bristol and Clifton. It is a clear morning and a healthy walk would be a good idea before the two of you are shut up together in a stuffy railway carriage.'

'Why yes, Ma'am,' she answered, 'there are indeed things that I would enjoy showing Andrew and I am sure that both of us will be glad to undertake some healthy exercise together. I shall show him the *camera obscura* on Clifton Downs.' Then turning to me she said, 'Do you know what a *camera obscura* is, Andrew?'

'I have heard that you have developed an interest in photography,' I answered. 'While I admit to complete ignorance in that field I am most happy to be taught all that you know.'

'The *camera obscura*,' said Rosie, 'is rather fun. It is a building, not just a camera. It is darkened and through a lens above the roof the entire scene round and about is reflected downwards and shown greatly magnified on a large round table. It is like being able to share a telescope so that you can point out things of interest to each other. We shall set out across the Downs as soon as we have finished breakfast.'

So it was that an hour or so later, with Rosie eagerly pulling me along, we paid our small fee and entered the *camera obscura*. It was indeed a most entertaining sight. Walking round the slightly dished table, we could see all the surrounding greenery as well as the fashionable houses of

Clifton. There were several other people there and in the semi-darkness I heard a sudden murmur and an outraged voice say 'Avert your eyes, my dear. Children, you are to go round to the other side at once, do you hear me.' Dimly I could discern a *paterfamilias* with his most respectably turned-out wife and their three children. One of the children had seen something in the magnified image.

'But Father,' the child was saying, 'What is it that they are doing behind that shrubbery and why is the gentleman lying on top of the lady?'

'Go at once to the other side,' thundered the father. 'If you are disobedient you will be well thrashed when we are home.'

Rosie, who had of course heard all this, then nudged me firmly in the side in the darkness and set off round the table to the spot now being hastily evacuated by the family. I followed her round and soon saw what had caused all the commotion.

A couple, believing themselves well hidden behind a substantial privet hedge and not knowing of the large man-made eye that was the lens looking down on them from the conical roof of the building, were engaged in what seemed at this distance to be a most energetic fuck. I could see a voluptuous pair of titties spilling out of an unloosed bodice. His quite bald head was nuzzling and sucking greedily at her splendidly fleshy orbs as she pressed him to her, forcing him down into her yielding bosom. As the sun caught his tanned pate turning this way and that amongst the milky whiteness of the proffered breasts, I saw his mouth sucking thirstily at now one and now a second engorged nipple.

Next she raised her well-made thighs and clasped him around the waist in a vice-like grip. His buttocks were pumping up and down as he thrust repeatedly into her. Rosie, who was leaning forward, utterly engrossed in the scene unfolding before our eyes, sensed that I was standing behind her and all of a sudden pressed herself backwards against my already excited crotch. Even through the layers of her clothing I could feel her tight little bum rubbing against my fast-stiffening member. With a little giggle she began to rotate her cheeks in time with the thrusting of the unknown couple on whom we were spying.

By now the family was being hustled out of the building by the outraged father as he denounced the immorality of the age and threatened to find a policeman to arrest the couple, whose now quite abandoned fucking was clearly reaching its climax.

'Rosie, I am not convinced that you should be watching this exhibition,' I said.

'If it is unsuitable for me, then it must be equally unsuitable for you,' answered Rosie in a whisper. 'Look, I think he's coming.'

Sure enough the rise and fall of his arse had increased to a frenzied pace and I saw the woman's hips lifting clear of the grass as she forced him even deeper into her. Now they were so clenched together that I swear I could feel the sudden tightening of their bodies as his cum spurted and welled up from his swollen testicles.

'I think he is discharging his obligations,' said Rosie, reaching back a hand to tweak my painfully distended member. 'Her cunt is being quite flooded with his juice.'

'Rosie,' I said, 'that is no way for a young lady to talk. And will you please let me go for I fear some kind of accident if you do not.'

By now the anonymous couple had completed their climax and, as we watched, subsided into a quivering stillness. Then as he slid from her, I saw him produce what was doubtless a handkerchief. With this he proceeded to mop first his and then her private parts. She sat up and leaned forward to take his now quiescent prick in her hand. Bending over she kissed it gently and tucked it back briskly into his trousers before buttoning him up. He in turn lowered his head between her still gaping thighs and kissed her briefly before pulling her skirts down over her knees. Both got up and brushed themselves down.

'Grass does so stain one's clothes,' murmured Rosie as she pressed herself against me. 'Andrew, I am sorry that I have so provoked you but I was thoroughly caught up in the encounter we have just seen. I must make amends and help

204

relieve you of your discomfort.' With that she deftly reached in to me and fished out my straining cock and rapidly squeezed and rubbed me to the point where the first spurts of cum forced their away along my throbbing prick.

'Careful!' I gasped and she at once seized hold of the enpurpled head of my manhood and pointed me out over the table with its view of Clifton. As she aimed me, my spunk jetted out in repeated splashes across the landscape.

'Look,' she said, 'You have quite spoiled the view.'

'Rosie, I am supposed to be in charge of you. Suppose someone was to come in. Whatever would they think?'

'They would think nothing because they would see nothing, at least not until their eyes had grown accustomed to the darkness,' said Rosie in a very practical way. 'But in any case, now that I have eased your problem, I will ease your conscience.'

With that I was put back in my place as Rosie adjusted my clothing and said, 'Now you are in a fit and proper condition to appear once more in public.'

With this we left the *Camera Obscura* and set out for home.

'And did you find it an interesting place to visit?' asked Mrs Moore when we were returned.

'Quite remarkable,' I replied.

'Always something intriguing to see there,' added Colonel Moore. 'I once saw a couple behind the bushes.'

'Edward!' exclaimed his wife warningly. 'I do not think that these nice young people want to hear your stories, besides, they have a train to catch. Now you go and get yourselves ready and my husband will see that you get to the station on time. There is a light lunch ready for you and cook has packed a small basket of food for you in case you get hungry on the journey.'

With that we were all sent off briskly to attend to our packing.

Later, after a light repast, our Goodbyes were made. Both Rosie and I were warmly kissed by Mrs Moore and, along with the Colonel, chivvied into a waiting cab. At Temple

Meads Station the Colonel purchased tickets and found the London train.

Settled into our compartment after ensuring that Rosie's trunk had been safely stowed in the luggage van, it seemed once more we would have no fellow passengers. But just as we were about to pull out of Temple Meads station, a somewhat flustered clergyman scrambled in.

'Excuse me, Sir,' he asked worriedly, 'but can you confirm that this is the Bath train?'

'Yes, indeed,' I answered. 'We shall arrive in some twenty minutes or so.'

'I have a most difficult task awaiting me,' he hurried fussily on. 'I have to take over the pastoral care of two congregations. A most regrettable incident has temporarily left both St Wilgefortis and St Mungo without incumbents. Until new appointments can be made the Cure of Souls in both parishes will have to be undertaken by this humble Servant of the Lord.'

'What happened?' I asked.

The Man of the Cloth looked uneasily at Rosie and said in a somewhat *sotto voce* fashion, 'I would not like to embarrass your charming travelling companion.'

Rosie, who had assumed a most demure countenance, blushed prettily and said, 'Sir, matters of clerical preferment or misadventure are quite beyond my experience. I have only been exposed to the attentions of our School Chaplain, the Reverend Thomas Paddlebottom.'

'Good God! Old Spanker,' our companion said, but then as though discomfitted by his sudden ejaculation, fell silent.

'Oh, you also know him by that nickname,' said Rosie with a rather knowing little smile.

'Just a joke based on his name, you understand. We were at Cambridge together,' he replied hurriedly.

'He is a most firm disciplinarian,' said Rosie. 'I am afraid that I fell short of his expectations in matters of scriptural knowledge on several occasions and had to be a little chastised at his hands.'

I could see that our companion was becoming noticeably

flushed as the conversation continued.

'I am certain, Rosie,' I said, 'that the Reverend Gentleman does not want to hear of your backsliding in matters religious.'

'Oh, on the contrary,' he said, 'I am always delighted to hear of events concerning a fellow cleric, especially one who was something of a friend.'

'I can assure you, Sir, that your friend has been most regular in his endeavours to keep us up to the mark. Indeed he has left his mark on his flock in many ways.'

Our companion was now becoming perceptibly excited at the news of his old friend.

'I hope,' I said, 'that your duties at Bath will not prove too onorous.'

'It will indeed be a demanding task. I fear that both congregations will be in a somewhat distracted state of mind,' he said.

'I believe I remember now what occurred,' said Rosie. 'Was there not some mention of the incidents in the newspaper?'

'Young lady, I am alarmed to hear that you have access to the public prints when you are in attendance at your educational establishment.'

'Oh, no, the newspaper is strictly forbidden,' said Rosie, 'but I saw by chance a copy in the Vestry of the School Chapel when I was being lightly chastised for my failure to correctly set in order the Journeys of St Paul. I do believe also that I heard some blow-by-blow account of the incident from our Art Master.'

'Most unfortunate. Most unfortunate,' said our companion. 'I am sure it will all prove to have been a terrible mistake. Appearances, as I am sure we can all agree, can only too often deceive.'

'But,' said Rosie, 'the discovery of two Men of the Cloth, both thoroughly unfrocked and in the company of no less than seventeen pupils of the Convent of the Immaculate Conception and Our Lady in Bath, all splashing and cavorting about in the Tepid Swimming Bath, is difficult to reconcile with the usual duties of a parson.'

'My understanding is that they were engaged in a rehearsal of the convent's Advent play. A drama of a highly uplifting and moral nature portraying certain events from Scripture,' said our companion in a not altogether convincing fashion.

'Yet, I was given to understand that each of the gentlemen was surprised in hot pursuit of his charges, crying out that here was a litter of naughty pussies who must be soundly smacked,' said Rosie.

It seemed that the temporary Curate of St Wilgefortis and St Mungo was coming close to an apoplectic seizure as Rosie continued remorselessly. 'Sir, I do not in any way seek to blame the Reverend Gentlemen. I know that I too have in the past been a naughty pussey and I know that naughty pussies must be well punished. Indeed I still bear the marks of such a chastisement.'

With that she stood up, only to bend down before the highly agitated cleric. Then as a nerve commenced to twitch uncontrollably in his cheek, she suddenly straightened up again.

'Alas,' she said, 'I see that we are just now coming into Bath Station where you must get off so I shall not have time to show you the evidence that I have been recently corrected. This is a great shame for I must further confess that I know that I have behaved in a greatly forward fashion towards you Sir, and should you have considered that I deserved punishment, I would have readily submitted to your disciplinary hand. But as it is we have quite run out of time.'

At this moment we came to a halt as a porter commenced to cry out 'Alight here for Bath Spa. Change for Bradford-on-Avon, Trowbridge and all stations to Westbury!' The good Parson was so overcome by Rosie's remarks that he grabbed his suitcase and fled from the train quite doubled up in his struggle to conceal the giant erection that bulged through his clerical garb.

'Rosie,' I said in the sternest manner I could summon up, for in truth I was close to choking in my laughter, 'That was most unfair. You have teased that unfortunate clergyman without mercy. He will not find it easy to fully concentrate on his pastoral duties at St Wilgefortis or indeed at St Mungo.'

208

'I am truly sorry,' said Rosie. 'You would now lik to chastise me I suppose?'

'No,' I said, 'I am not interested in such activities.'

To be truthful. I would gladly have been presented with another showing of Rosie's delicious bum but knew that the instrument that I would wish to use on it, although to hand, was one not of correction but of insertion.

Then as the train drew away and we had once more our privacy, Rosie said, 'Andrew, I have studied the timetable of our journey with some care. Before our next stop at Chippenham we have just twenty-eight minutes in which to fuck.'

'What!' I exclaimed.

'But between Chippenham and Swindon we have a full three-quarters of an hour followed by a ten-minute refreshment stop. It is then another forty-four minutes to Didcot. From there to Reading is twenty-seven minutes. Reading to Maidenhead is a short twenty minutes and finally from there to our terminus at Paddington is another three-quarters of an hour.

'I should most like to be fucked between Chippenham and Swindon for not only is there enough time but we can start quite soon. It is now but some nineteen minutes before we come to our starting point and I am already becoming quite damp in anticipation. I would not like to wait until Didcot, whilst Maidenhead would be far too late.'

Even by the standards of boldness I was coming to expect from Rosie, this was most brazen behaviour. I must have looked both shocked and, truth to tell, greatly excited by her proposal for she added, 'You should not be so amazed, Andrew, I know that Colonel Moore has introduced you to the idea of fucking on trains. Is this not a lucky opportunity to indulge in what he has so persuasively described?'

'Is there not a possible hitch in your scheme?' I asked for I was still half mindful that Rosie had been put in my trust by her Guardian. 'We are alone now but who can tell whether another passenger or passengers may not invade our privacy at Chippenham?'

'Indeed that is a possibility,' said Rosie, 'and the later we leave it, the more that problem of unwanted company increases. Let us settle for a Chippenham-to-Swindon fuck. I am sure we can keep other passengers out for one stop at least. I shall feign an illness which you must describe as of a possibly infectious nature to anyone attempting to enter out compartment.'

By now I was completely won over by Rosie's arguments and her persistence.

'Well,' I said, 'it seems you have quite made up your mind in this matter.'

'You are to be my first Great Western Fuck,' said Rosie. 'Now, we have only a few minutes before we arrive at Chippenham. I shall assume the disposition of an unwell traveller and start also to make myself ready for your prick.'

With this she assumed a reclining and languid position in one corner and drew up her skirts to display her sweetly brown-haired pussey. She began to run her fingers through her curly bush, then rubbed her delightful mound before slipping her fingers between her opening thighs and brushing the tips along her crack.

'See, Andrew, I am becoming all wet and eager,' she said as her fingers delved and caressed.

I was myself fully charged and Mr Pego was standing rigidly to attention as the train drew into Chippenham and we commenced our charade.

It happened, though, that our playacting ability was but little put to the test for of the few passengers waiting to board our train, one only made as though to enter our compartment. A middle-aged woman of a governessy appearance, she quickly chose not to enter when Rosie gave a little moan and said 'Andrew, I am afraid that I may be coming down with the mumps. See, I am all swollen up.'

Then as the train pulled out Rosie said 'We have exactly forty-five minutes for fucking. See, you also are quite swollen.'

With that she reached out to release my straining member and take it in both hands.

'Andrew,' she said, 'I know that you must think me most

forward and wanton but I am not so experienced as I may pretend. I have only been fucked by four or five pricks and you may find me a little tight. I must also tell you that in all other parts I am still a virgin although I hope that this condition may be remedied in the near future. So please enter me with care. I am so looking forward to feeling your prick passing into my tunnel but I do not wish its portal to be damaged so that I cannot receive you should you seek a second entry.'

As for a moment she looked quite solemn, so I in turn remembered my responsibilities towards Rosie. I might even then have hesitated but she, sensing perhaps what was going through my mind, leaned forward and licked the tip of my staff. As her tongue brought me once more to attention she said: 'Andrew I am counselling care, not delay. See, I am ready and some three minutes of our allowance has already passed by.'

With that she spread herself wide and I carefully placed the swollen head of my prick at the very entrance to her cunny. Then, as she opened herself up before me, I eased my way in slowly, slowly.

'Oh! Andrew, that is lovely. Come further into me.'

Hers was indeed a tight little cunt, but a very warm and willing one. Inch by inch I worked my way in. Her neat little clit was rubbing enticingly against my cock as I wormed further and yet further into her. Soon she had accepted my entire length and I paused for a moment, feeling the clinging tightness of her.

'Fucking is such fine sport,' she said. 'I do believe that I would like to spend the rest of my life with a prick in me. Surely this is not wrong.'

With that she gave a little sigh of excitement and began to slide gently backwards and forwards upon my staff. As we proceeded with our slow but determined movements she offered up her lovely rounded titties for my inspection. As I sucked eagerly at them I realised that Rosie was indeed all rounded: round cheeked, round faced, roundly outstanding titties, a seductively round bum. Even her stomach, though not fat, was nicely round. 'Quite a handful,' the Colonel had called her but in fact she was handful after handful, and all delightful. Everything about her seemed to fit neatly and pertly in the palm of one's hand.

With these thoughts, my hands now cupping her bare shoulders as I kissed her warm little mouth, we continued the regular back and forth of our fucking. There was nothing of desperation about Rosie. She fucked with the complete concentration of one to whom this was a new interest which claimed the whole of her attention in all its details. I was more than happy to take things thus slowly. She was hot and now quite slippery around me. The curly brown hair of her youthful bush was damp beneath me as we rubbed together.

I could see the rise and fall of her titties as she began to breathe more and more deeply. Her eyes were wide open and she was fast losing herself in the sheer delight of her fucking. By now although her cunt was still tight around me, we were so well lubricated that I was slipping easily and faster up and down the length of her tunnel. All too soon I could feel the first stirring of the first wave of my coming. I knew that I must control myself for Rosie was too young and too inexperienced to have learned those tricks of delay or acceleration that her elder sisters in sex have acquired.

Deliberately I slowed down and reduced the depth of my thrusting. She looked at me with a questioning anxiety.

'Oh, Andrew! Don't stop. Don't stop. This is so wonderful!'

'I'm not,' I said. 'But I do not want to come too soon. There is plenty of time and Swindon is a long way away as yet.'

'Oh, thank you. It feels so good.'

Now I discovered the trick of feeling the rhythm of the train as we clicked over the joins between the rails. With such an even pace I was able to relax and prolong our fucking. I doubt if Mr Brunel had such things in mind when he constructed his Broad Gauge line, but it was a most easy yet compelling rhythm. Safe for the moment from any worry about a premature end to our coupling, I found that I could enjoy Rosie and enjoy also the feel of Rosie enjoying herself. We were not adventurous in our positions. She lay back along the railway upholstery and I lay on top of her. Her titties rubbed firmly against my chest and sometimes we kissed. Yet all the time and in time with the train, we moved with an even intensity. It was quite simply the longest and most continuous fuck that I had ever experienced.

Of course all good things must come to an end and come we did at the end. Again there was nothing over dramatic about it. Rosie quite suddenly quickened her pace and as I responded, no longer needing to exert any control, she gave a half cry, half gasp, almost as though she was catching her breath and as she clutched at me, her fingers digging into my back, I felt the first quick spasms of her orgasm. I now let go and let the flood of my coming pump into her, filling her as she gripped me.

'Oooh! I can feel your cum. It's lovely. It's running over me. Andrew, I am so satisfied! I will be so quiet and good for the rest of the journey. I shall be like a little church mouse.'

Ours was not the only rhythm that had changed. As the train rattled and swerved across points and junctions, I realised that Swindon was at hand. Carefully I withdrew.

'Quick, give my titties a squeeze before we make ourselves respectable,' she said.

With one last lingering fondling of tit and bum, I let her go. She then, practical soul, produced a hand towel from her luggage and we made ourselves clean and decent, putting all our clothing in order so that as we slowed and stopped at the platform, I was sitting opposite her and she was looking with demure interest at the people waiting to get on. At the last second however she leaned towards me and said, 'That was the nicest forty-five minutes of fucking I've ever had.'

Since we had the usual ten-minute wait at Swindon while they changed engines, I suggested that we dismount and stretch our legs. We neither of us needed anything to eat or drink but a breath of fresh air, even if it was mostly steam and smoke, would be a good idea. However as we stood there, surrounded by the rush of passengers getting on and off, the fretting over luggage and the tipping of porters, who should I

213

see but the Colonel's friend Tess. She was with a well-dressed man with the reddish complexion and sturdy clothes of a countryman. She clung to his arm as they walked down the platform. He was obviously looking for his seat on our train. She also saw me but with a gesture of her eyes, made me realise that I should not accost her. Then, as her companion disentangled himself from her in order to issue some directives to a porter who was wheeling along quite a barrow load of cases, she caught my arm for an instant.

'Why, it's Colonel Moore's friend, Mr Andrew, isn't it? I can't stop to talk now as I am accompanying this gentleman on the train as far as Reading. It is a matter of business I suppose you could say. You too are on the London train then?'

'Yes,' I said. 'Tess, this is Rosie, my travelling companion. She also knows the Colonel well.'

'Does she also...?' Tess asked quietly.

'Yes,' I answered.

'And have you?' asked Tess.

'Yes,' I replied. 'Between Chippenham and here. The whole way, more or less.'

'You're talking about railway fucking aren't you,' said Rosie bluntly, obviously having caught the gist of our low and hurried conversation.

'Tess here has to go now with her gentleman friend. They're going as far as Reading,' I said to Rosie.

'Are you then returning directly to Swindon?' asked Rosie.

'I usually would,' said Tess, 'although my ticket is a through one to Paddington, just in case.'

'Andrew, quickly, could we invite Tess to travel with us for the last part of our journey if she would like it. We have friends in common and she might like to relax with us. Her gentleman friend has something of a bad-tempered look to him.'

'Yes,' I said. 'Tess, I leave it to you but you would be welcome to join us at Reading if you choose.'

'Thank you both,' said Tess. 'That is kind of you. I may well take you up on your invitation. Now I must go.'

With that, she turned away. Her companion, who had been engrossed in an altercation with a porter who had apparently not stowed the luggage quite as he wished, now opened the compartment door next to our own and clambered in, calling out to Tess in a peremptory fashion, 'Come along, girl. Let's get settled.'

Tess half averted her head, gave a little grimace of distaste and climbed in after him, pulling the door to behind her.

Rosie looked at me. 'Not a nice man,' she said. 'Why does Tess choose to go with him?'

I who had earlier realised that Tess was the travelling equivalent of a Lady of the Night – a Lady of the Line perhaps – realised that I would have to explain to Rosie that it was not so much a matter of choice as of professional necessity. As we again had the compartment to ourselves, somewhat to my surprise, I was able to embark on my deduction and my explanation as we settled again in our seats.

Rosie was not at all shocked but was full of sympathy for Tess.

'How awful it must be not to be able to choose,' she said. Then she continued, 'Didcot is the next stop. It is forty-five minutes precisely according to the timetable but if the station clock was right, we started off again three minutes late. They must be planning to fuck between these stations as Didcot to Reading is much shorter and also there are likely to be passengers from Oxford getting on at Didcot.'

'You seem to know the Great Western timetable by heart,' I said.

'I used to read it at school,' said Rosie. 'I used to plan my escape almost every evening, I hated it so much.'

'Not every evening, surely,' I said. 'What about the times when you were assisting Mr Williams in his photographic project?'

'So Colonel Moore has told you what transpired,' said Rosie. 'Well surely it was no great crime. I now know lots about photography. I even met his great friend Mr Fox Talbot at Laycock, Wilts. I didn't mind having my bum recorded for posterity.'

215

'A Posterior for posterity,' I murmured.

'That's a terrible joke,' said Rosie, 'and apart from his Art, he was a nice man and he really only ever fucked the bigger girls and not even all that many of them.'

'You were amongst that number?' I asked.

'Yes,' she said. 'But I had to ask him first. It was in the train. He'd been photographing another in the series he called "Landscapes with Bums" and said that his equipment would get all spoiled by the wet. That was my second time and I caught a bit of a chill afterwards.'

The train meanwhile had gathered pace and we were speeding through the countryside. Both of us were now a little tired but cheerful after our activities.

'Andrew,' said Rosie musingly, 'Do you like my bottom?'

'What I've seen of it,' I replied. 'It's a most enticing specimen.'

'It would be nice if you would give it some attention,' she said. So saying she stretched out on her stomach and pulled her clothes up so that her rosy bum was exposed to my gaze. As I reached over to squeeze and fondle her bared cheeks she gave a contented sigh.

'That's nice,' she said, as my fingers played with her tight little arse and gently probed her cleft. Then she paused as a new thought struck her, 'Andrew, just think. On the other side of this quite thin partition your friend Tess and the bad-tempered man are in all probability in mid-fuck. Doesn't that seem strange? His prick and her cunt only inches away from us, hidden away behind where we're sitting.' Then her mood of curiousity changed abruptly, 'I do hope she's all right. He really didn't seem a very nice man.'

'Well, we'll find out pretty soon,' I said. 'As you so rightly said, it'll probably be all be over by Didcot and then if she wants to, she can come and join us after he gets out at Reading.'

Rosie relaxed and I carried on quietly feeling her pretty bum as the train sped along, Wiltshire turning to Oxfordshire and the distant line of the Downs slipping past the window.

Didcot came and with it a small fuss. An elderly couple

who had made as though to get in to the next-door compartment while confirming with a porter that this was indeed the Reading train suddenly halted half way through their embarkation and changed course, scrambling in to ours instead. Both were flushed and clearly put out by something that they had seen or some remark that had been passed by the next-door people, that is to say Tess and her companion. Rosie, not wanting their company any more than I, at once tried to put them off, saying to me, 'Andrew, I'm just about to be very, very sick!'

The unwanted couple, still muttering and agitated, very understandably looked even more alarmed at this. However Rosie's playacting was too late as the train was already being whistled away and any attempt they might have made to transfer to yet another compartment was stillborn. They sat down, exuding concern while Rosie, now acting out of sheer naughtiness, gave a series of unnervingly convincing gulps before crying out: 'I'm afraid it is the shrimps. I said that they did not taste right.'

Then she got up and rushed over to the window, opened it and leaned out as though gasping for fresh air. This manoeuvre caused her *derrière*, albeit now decently covered of course, to jut out provocatively right under the very nose of the elderly gentleman. Since I was sitting opposite him, conversation could only be achieved by one or the other of us half-raising himself in order to see over this delightful, but to him at least, embarrassing projection.

'I am sorry that my cousin is not feeling very well,' I said, realising that something had to be said but hoping that Rosie was soon going to abandon this charade.

'Andrew,' said Rosie, looking back over her shoulder, 'I think I've got something stuck in my throat. Can you pat me on the back and see if that will dislodge it?'

I rose to do this, taking at the same time the opportunity to whisper to her that she should stop misbehaving at once. Her response to this was to give first one and then another abrupt hiccup. Her whole body shook with the violence of her invented attack and her bottom was twitching up and down

217

with each spasm. All at once the elderly gentleman leaped to his feet and brought his hand down in a stinging slap on her rear. Rosie was completely taken aback, let out a yelp of pain and surprise, bumped her head on the top of the open window frame and pulled back into the compartment.

'Sudden shock,' said the elderly gentleman. 'Best thing in the world to stop the hiccups.'

Rosie paused and then quite deliberately gave another little 'Hic!'

By now I'd decided to take a hand in the whole business and myself gave her a second substantial smack on the bottom just as the elderly gentleman repeated his earlier resounding effort.

I had an uneasy presentiment that the game could get quite out of hand. But at this juncture the elderly gentleman's wife acted. She had been eyeing her husband's activities with a look of stony-faced disapproval. She now rummaged through her bag, produced a small bottle, uncorked it and quickly thrust it up against Rosie's nose. Rosie gasped and spluttered as tears filled her eyes.

'*Sal volatile*,' said the woman. 'Brings them to when they've fainted and stops them in their tracks when they're getting over-excited.'

I had the feeling that a bluff had been called. Rosie, her eyes streaming, was now sniffing into a handkerchief and the elderly gentleman who had been more than ready to carry on with his shock treatment had now subsided into his seat with a look of disappointment on his face.

'Thank you,' I said. 'It certainly seems to have done the trick.' Then I handed my own more substantial handkerchief over to Rosie. 'Now Cousin! Dry your eyes on this. You might also like to remove the large smut that has been deposited on the end of your nose. If you sit down quietly we shall be in Reading in a minute or two and we can leave the train there if you are still feeling unwell.'

As I had hoped, my reminder that we should soon be in Reading where Tess might be joining us had the desired effect of keeping Rosie quiet for the rest of the way. When a few minutes later we came into Reading station, Rosie, saying that she would stretch her legs, got out along with the elderly couple. I saw her look into the next compartment just as Tess's companion descended, luggage in hand, and strode off, apparently without any word of Goodbye to Tess. There was some brief conversation and then Tess, looking rather tired and a mite distressed, followed Rosie back in to our compartment. We shut the door firmly to discourage any fellow travellers.

'Maidenhead next,' said Rosie as we pulled out.

'Hardly,' said Tess with a wry smile.

'Now Tess,' said Rosie, 'Tell us all about it. A blow by blow account if you please.'

'Stop ordering people about, Rosie,' I said. 'Let Tess have a rest if she wants.'

'Sorry,' said Rosie. 'You are all right, aren't you, Tess?'

'A bit weary and a bit sore, too,' answered Tess.

'Tess,' I said, 'if you want to unburden yourself of your story I shall be the soul of discretion. I was educated in this estimable habit by my old Headmaster, Dr White.'

'Not Dr White, the Headmaster of Nottsgrove Academy?' exclaimed Tess.

'Why, yes,' I answered. 'You have heard of him then?'

'More than that, I have actually encountered him in the flesh, in the line of duty, so to speak.'

'In the line of duty?' I queried.

'On the Midland Railway, on a train from Derby to St Pancras. He got on at Harpenden and got in as we pulled out of St Albans. He himself pulled out as we passed Cricklewood. He was I recall a big man but solicitous of my comfort. I understood that he was going up to Town in order to attend a gathering of Headmasters. But now I am being indiscreet.'

'Do not worry,' I said. 'Is it not a small world. Both this young lady's Guardian with whom I lodge and our mutual friend Colonel Moore have encountered Dr White.'

'Then I feel I can speak freely,' said Tess.

'And I of course am far too young to understand such matters,' chipped in Rosie.

'Rosie, stop it!' I said. 'I believe that Tess may need

sympathy so do not be so pert.' I turned to Tess. 'Rosie was in fact most concerned about your well-being earlier.'

'That is all right,' said Tess. 'I do not have any remarkable story to tell. As you will have worked out, I have spent the journey between Swindon and Reading in intimate congress with a man I did not previously know and who I do not particularly wish to see again. I am not damaged but I was handled carelessly and thoughtlessly.'

'Oh, Tess!' said Rosie contritely. 'You are not hurt, are you?'

At this Tess got up and pulled her clothes up to display her naked pussey.

'Bruised,' she said, 'back and front.'

'Back *and* front,' repeated Rosie. 'Tess, I am as yet if not completely untouched certainly unpenetrated in the nether regions. Is it not then an enjoyable experience?'

'It can indeed be, my dear,' said Tess, 'but it must be done with care, especially the first few times. I have a certain amount of experience in these matters but even now if the entry is too abrupt then it can be a hurtful encounter.'

'And he has hurt you before as well as behind?' I asked.

'It was not a comfortable ride,' replied Tess.

Apart from my genuine concern at Tess's predicament, I was also I must confess most taken and most distracted by the alluring display of bush and cunny that was staring me in the face. I reached forward to gently stroke and investigate Tess's private parts. But as my hand touched her flesh she winced and her hand closed over mine.

'Be careful, Andrew, I am bruised here, and here, and sore also.'

By now she was aware that along with my sympathy, I had also developed an erect interest in the idea of entering into her, if not now then at least at some time in the near future.

'Andrew,' she said, 'I suspect from the evidence of that rather large bulge in your britches that you have a problem that I can still help you with even though some avenues of exploration are temporarily closed. Maidenhead is almost upon us. If we three are not invaded by an outsider then I will

220

do what I can for you immediately afterwards.'

We were indeed uninterrupted by any other passengers during the very short stop at Maidenhead and as soon as we were moving away again Rosie piped up:

'Tess, I would like to help in the handling of Andrew's problem. We had the most delicious and lingering fuck earlier on the journey and I would like to make him an offering of any other part of me that he might enjoy.'

Tess smiled at her. 'Rosie, that is a kind thought. I think we might play follow my leader this time.'

With that she swiftly leaned over and unbuttoned me. Mr Pego leaped out into the light of day.

'What a fine plump fellow,' said Tess. 'I shall enjoy this.'

'Isn't he,' said Rosie. 'I know that I do not have much experience but that is quite one of the most handsome cocks that I have entertained.'

Tess now commenced to lick and tongue-probe the great flushed head of my prick. Then, with a practised hand, she cupped my balls in the palm of her hand and gently raised me up so that she could gradually envelop me in her mouth. Her lips pressed and sucked at the naked shaft. Her teeth nibbled teasingly at me as she lowered her head, feeding my entire length into her mouth. Sucking back and forth along my now throbbing prick, she soon brought me to a state of utter rock-hard delight. Windsor Castle passed unnoticed on the horizon as Tess tongued and licked me to a point of near explosion. Then, still holding me in her hand, she quietly withdrew from my member.

'Rosie,' she said. 'Do you wish to take your turn?'

'Oh, please!' said Rosie, 'although this is the first time that I have taken a man's prick into my mouth.'

'Gently,' said Tess. 'Take it as far into your mouth as you wish. You do not have to choke yourself. And no biting!'

Rosie quickly lowered her head and applied her lips to my Tess-wet prick. Whilst she lacked Tess's experience, she was eager to learn and clearly enjoying her schooling.

'That's it,' said Tess, as she urged Rosie to caress and suck at my prick. 'Perhaps I should have been a schoolma'am.'

'Even at Nottsgrove,' I said, 'such lessons were not a formal part of the curriculum.' I kissed her, our tongues touching and pressing as Rosie continued her Priapic devotions in my lap. Tess reached down and with her finger and thumb commenced encouraging my now near-bursting cock deep into Rosie's throat. Rosie responded gallantly, sucking away as though her life depended on it.

'Gently, gently,' said Tess. 'Rosie, Andrew is about to come. Do you wish to finish him off or shall I?'

Rosie looked up and almost spluttered as she tried to reply whilst my shaft was still driven deep between her lips. Then she pulled away as Tess knelt down beside her.

'You do it, Tess. I am so grateful that you have initiated me into this art but as yet I am unskilled compared to you. Let me watch as Andrew comes into your mouth.'

Tess kissed her briefly and then took me in again. She had indeed judged my state correctly for in moments my cum was jetting uncontrollably upwards in answer to her smooth-tongued ministrations. As her lips closed firmly round the base of my cock she began remorselessly to suck every last drop of cream from me. Again and again she swallowed down my offering whilst Rosie, looking on with wide open eyes, began to rub and finger her pussey.

Tess kept me in her mouth as I relaxed and my now flaccid but still fattened member lay along her tongue. Then she pulled back and said to Rosie, 'There is one last delicious drop for you and then we must wrap him up neatly and put him back in his place.'

Rosie delicately licked me clean, licked her lips and said appreciatively, 'Next time I shall do this all on my own. Thank you, Tess, for sharing it with me.'

I was tucked up safely and the two of them sat down on either side of me, their heads nestling against me.

'Just a few minutes more and we shall arrive at our destination,' said Rosie. 'Tess, I hope that this will be *au revoir* and not Goodbye.'

'I hope so too,' I said. 'Tess, when you are next in Town you would be a very welcome visitor to Sussex Gardens. I have *carte blanche* to entertain friends at my lodgings and I believe that you would be welcomed by the entire household.'

'That is a kind invitation,' she said. 'I do indeed pass through London on occasions and would be more than happy to be taken in.'

'I hope that you in fact will take *me* in,' I responded.

'I believe I should be able to accommodate you,' said Tess.

'Old Oak Common,' said Rosie. 'See, there is Wormwood Scrubs to our right.'

A few minutes afterwards we drew slowly into Paddington. As we got off I realised that I had to oversee the transfer of Rosie's heavy trunk to a cab. A porter was summoned and with much struggling and heaving we and the luggage were loaded into our conveyance. Tess waved us away. So ended a railway journey so packed with incident that I was quite exhausted with my travelling adventures.

Back at Sussex Gardens, Rosie and I were warmly greeted by Mrs P—. Rosie was taken up to her room while I went into the dining room in search of a restorative glass or two of brandy.

Becky who was already at home welcomed me warmly.

'You look somewhat fatigued from the rigours of your visit to the West Country,' she said. 'Tell me, was it an enjoyable expedition?'

'Indeed it was,' I answered. 'I shall tell you all about it if you so wish after dinner.'

'You had a good time a-fucking?' she asked.

'Yes,' I replied, 'and saw and heard and felt a goodly number of novel things.'

'Mama tells me that Rosie has developed an interest in photography,' said Becky.

'Perhaps we will be able to prevail on her to set up her equipment and record us for posterity.'

'It would be a great pleasure to pose with you and with Hannah,' I said.

'I have in mind a series of pictures, a sort of frieze of fucking,' she answered.

'We must discuss this further over dinner,' I said, 'but now I

223

must go and change. Before I do though, I have missed you all. Would you just let me have a glimpse of the future please Becky?'

Without saying a word but with an enticing smile, she slowly lifted her skirts and stood before me, her wonderful pussey displayed to me.

'My cunt is ready for you,' she said. 'Hannah's also. I know as well that Emily has missed you, as has Mary, although Tom the Tool is back in attendance so she is being taken good care of.'

'Rosie,' I said, 'as long as she is staying here, will prove to be a very pleasant addition to our number. She is eager to seize hold of all new experience with both hands.'

'We will all welcome her,' said Becky. 'Oh! I forgot, this *billet doux* arrived for you. I understand that it is from Catherine.'

I opened the sealed note. *Dear Andrew, I very much hope that we will be able to fuck again in the very near future. Even as I write this I can feel my pussey dampening with anticipation, Catherine.*

'Well?' said Becky.

'An invitation to fuck,' I replied.

'We have a full programme ahead of us,' said Becky.

I quickly buried my face in her warm bush.

'Kiss me on the lips,' she said, 'and then we must get ready for dinner.'

'I am indeed hungry,' I said. 'And afterwards, who knows, there may be more games to play.'

[To be continued]

BOOK 3

career ... happily ... in the ... West End of London which was
... of trade produce in the West End of London Society. One of his
... ... naval Arthur Somerset, an equerry of The Prince

Preface

Since the rediscovery of *The Oyster* in the mid 1980s, there has been much speculation as to just who were the authors of this infamous Victorian underground magazine.

In her preface to *Oyster 1*, Professor Antoinette Hillman-Strauss suggested that the unknown 'Sir Andrew Scott', whose autobiographical novel *A Fond Recollection Of Youthful Days* – concluded here – made up the contents of *Oyster 1* and *Oyster 2*, was probably a journalist on one of the fledgling popular publications being produced for the more literate public of the 1880s.

And indeed sexologist Oliver Panther, in his introduction to *Oyster 2*, names the late Victorian pulp-fiction writer Gerald Burdett (who was known to have written for *The Ram*, a similar illicit journal in the same vein as *The Pearl* and *The Oyster*) as our possible scribe, though Dr Terence Cooney speculates that the work may be that of more than one scribbler.

However, there is no problem in identifying one writer in this third book of material culled from the pages of *The Oyster*, a journal that flourished throughout the 1880s, only to disappear without trace during the next decade.

Doctor Edward Parsifal (1840–1928) enjoyed a controversial medical career. During his heyday in the 1880s, he headed a most profitable practice in the West End of London which was patronised by many members of London Society. One of his patients was Lord Arthur Somerset, an equerry of The Prince of Wales, who was forced to flee to France during the Cleveland Street scandal in 1888 when Scotland Yard finally acted against the owner of a brothel for upper class homosexuals. In all probability, the Lord S—— mentioned in the latter half of the script is indeed the disgraced Lord Arthur who lived a lonely life in Northern France until his death some

5

thirty years later.

By the end of the 1880s, Doctor Parsifal had amassed a considerable fortune. He lived in style in a fine country mansion in rural North Finchley (as it was then), though as we note from his book, he kept a London apartment for his many assignations.

In the end, his voracious sexual appetites led to his downfall when, at the ripe age of forty-six, he was named co-respondent in a divorce petition involving the pretty Mrs Denise Wright, the twenty-three-year-old wife of a wealthy businessman who had consulted our hero about some 'nervous complaint'. As we can see from his memoir, this lady was just one of many to fall for the charms of the handsome doctor who was indeed fortunate to escape the strictures of the General Medical Council.

In fact, Teddy Parsifal gave up medicine after the case and he then became an extremely wealthy gentleman of leisure. Already possessing a healthy bank account, he dabbled successfully in the Stock Exchange under the guidance of his old friends Rufus Isaacs and Sir Ronnie Dunn and, indeed, his estate was worth more than £750,000 when he died just sixty years ago in December, 1928.

What possessed Teddy Parsifal to reveal his intimate secrets to the readers of *The Oyster*? The script was written immediately after the well-publicised divorce case which he knew would effectively end his medical career, so perhaps he wrote his apologia in a simple spirit of careless bravado.

It must have distressed his wife, the Society belle Lady Sarah Andrews, though their union survived all his amorous encounters. Indeed, to Lady Sarah, her handsome rogue was a model husband and father to the family. And indeed, according to his eldest son, Adrian, the blissfully happy Lady Sarah never suspected Teddy of the slightest infidelity and knew nothing of the robust secret life enjoyed by the naughty doctor until his eightieth year.

This third selection of material from *The Oyster* is concluded with an episode of Sir Andrew Scott's autobiography *A Memoir of Youthful Days* which was first published in *The Pearl* (*The Pearl III*, New English Library, 1984) and continued in *The Oyster* (*The Oyster 1* and *The Oyster 2*, New English

6

Library, 1987). The unknown author (for 'Andrew Scott' is a pseudonym) writes with gusto and occasionally with a stylish wit which has led some authorities to wonder whether the young Oscar Wilde might have contributed to the manuscript. Both he and Lord Alfred Douglas were known to be aficionados of underground magazines such as *The Pearl* and *The Oyster* that surfaced during the 1880s but which sank without trace after Wilde's trial in the early 1890s.

Happily, a set of *The Oyster* dating from 1887 was recently discovered in the locked drawing cabinet inside a large Derbyshire country house. This has afforded us the opportunity to relive the exciting, amorous lives of Doctor Teddy Parsifal and 'Sir Andrew Scott' – tales that show a completely different side to Victorian manners and mores, so very different from the starched picture usually used to portray these fascinating years.

Graham Grafton
Manchester
November, 1988

7

The sublime and the ridiculous are often so nearly related that it is difficult to class them separately. One step above the sublime makes the ridiculous; and one step above the ridiculous makes the sublime again.

Thomas Paine
(1737–1809)

The Private and Unexpurgated Memoirs of a Medical Gentleman in Great Britain and the New World

Author's Introduction

Dear reader, I earnestly hope you derive pleasure from this set of memoirs culled from my memories of many glorious years spent in perfecting *l'art de faire l'amour*.

Many readers of this distinguished journal are members of Society, so my name will not be unknown to them. After all, Doctor Edward Marmaduke DuCane Parsifal, Member of the Royal College of Physicians, Fellow of the Royal College of Surgeons and Sometime Visiting Professor at the Universities of Washington and Bombay, is a name with whom the very highest in the land have been well acquainted. Not that I am one to stand upon ceremony, you understand. I far prefer the simple soubriquet of Doctor Teddy than any other mode of address.

I hope to entertain you with the recall of some of the bizarre, intimate incidents of my younger days, already recorded in a secret journal, but which the editor of *The Oyster*, whose name must never be mentioned for fear of police informants, and my dear old friends Doctor Jonathan Arkley and Sir Clive Freedman, have persuaded me are worthy of a wider readership amongst the cognoscenti.

So the time has come to share my most exciting experiences of a personal nature, and I must warn readers of a delicate disposition that, unfashionable though it be in this age of euphemism, I insist on calling a spade a spade and refuse to mince words for the benefit of mealy-mouthed hypocrites who wish to bowdlerise our good old-fashioned Anglo-Saxon

11

vulgarities. I doubt, however, that there are many such personages amongst the readership of this robust journal!

So settle down and enjoy my jottings, and may I take this opportunity of wishing you all, ladies and gentlemen, a Happy New Year of licking and lapping, sucking and fucking in 1887.

> Doctor Teddy Parsifal
> Ford Manor
> Sussex, December 1886

My Early Days

As my old friend Lady Pokingham has written, the natural instinct of the ancients was that copulation was the direct and most acceptable form of worship they could offer to their deities.

I am convinced that there cannot be any great sin in giving way to natural desires and enjoying to the utmost those delicious sensations with which the Creator has endowed us.

So no apology will be forthcoming for the unashamed voluptuousness of this memoir and without further ado, let me begin my narrative.

My earliest years were spent in Canada and India as my Papa was attached to the Diplomatic Service. I shall not bore you with the details but until the age of ten I had hardly lived in this sceptred isle of Albion more than six months or so. But on my eleventh birthday I was sent to school in England where my elder brother, Cecil (more of him will appear later in this tale), was already a student, though we returned home to Mama and Papa in the holidays wherever they happened to be living at the time.

Even at this tender age I evinced a taste for the fair sex and I will never forget our governess, Mrs Radlett, who proudly displayed what appeared to my young eyes an enormous pair of breasts in the tightest of bodices, creating a cleavage that caused many a visitor to make excuses to visit the nursery, the avowed purpose being to see the youngsters, but in reality to see Mrs Radlett bending forward. I recall that in Toronto (Mrs Radlett travelled with us wherever Papa was sent on command of the government) one visitor, Doctor Dunn, always managed to drop his handkerchief or some other trifle so that Mrs Radlett bent down to retrieve it. I realise now that the good doctor was not as clumsy as he seemed!

13

I recall that often at night, Mrs Radlett would undress in front of Cecil and myself and as those magnificent breasts cascaded from their cramped confines, she would sigh with relief and gently massage them to restore lost circulation. If we had been good boys that day, our kind governess would allow us each to massage a breast for her. We enjoyed this small chore as did Mrs Radlett, who whimpered with pleasure as we performed the task with vigour. She asked us to roll her stalky red titties on the palms of our hands and after a minute or so she would breathe more rapidly, squeeze her thighs together and emit a strange grunt and shudder all over in what to us was a rather alarming fashion. She would then thank Cecil and I for our labours, asking us to promise not to tell anyone of our little game.

On one occasion I recall passing by Mrs Radlett's bedroom and the door was slightly ajar. I peeped round and saw our governess naked on the bed, completely oblivious to the world, making those strange noises of pleasure she emitted whilst Cecil and I were rubbing her teats. But this time, she was engaged in self-gratification of her own. So massive were her titties that she had been able to place one erect nipple in her mouth and she was busy sucking it to great effect. This breast was supported by one hand whilst the other was plunged inside the hairy black bush of hair between her legs, and I looked on with interest as she plunged her fingers in and out of this mound. I watched, mesmerised by this act as again she squeezed her thighs and with a little scream, shuddered violently and then lay back exhausted, withdrawing her hand from her mossy growth, a hand that I noticed was strangely moist (had she wet herself, I wondered in my innocence) which she wiped across her great breasts, smearing them with what, of course, was her cunney juice.

This strange experience led to my first footsteps across the Rubicon to complete sexual happiness. For whilst I had been gawping at this handsome naked woman, my little cock had begun to swell inside my trousers. I unbuttoned my trousers and felt for the stiff little shaft inside my underpants, enjoying a sensation of a somewhat uncomfortable pleasure.

This feeling was further heightened when Mrs Radlett heaved herself off the bed and I saw the massively hairy black bush of hair between her legs. She picked up a small towel and rubbed it between her legs, threw it down onto the bed and then sauntered into her bathroom to soak in her tub. When she closed the door behind her I sneaked into the room, my cock still as hard as a rock, picked up the towel and instantly caught the aroma of her most intimate parts. This aroma was to haunt me for the rest of my life and prove to be an instant stimulant for sexual arousal.

I pulled the towel down to my cock which was pulsating with excitement. I rubbed the shaft furiously whereupon a glistening of white fluid appeared on the tip, and as the surge of pleasure coursed through my body, I felt a jet of liquid squirt out – fortunately it soaked into the towel or I would have been forced to make a confession as to how Mrs Radlett's carpet came to be stained! I was both alarmed and excited at this happening. Luckily my dear Papa had decided that it was time for my sexual education to begin, so (as he had done with my brothers) he had left by my bedside only weeks before a copy of *Human Procreation Explained For Boys and Girls* by the celebrated Doctor Roy Stevenson, the well known authority on sexuality.

So fortunately, unlike so many of my unhappy contemporaries, I had no great fear of guilt about tossing off. As Sir Andrew Scott has rightly pointed out in previous editions of *The Oyster*, several misguided physicians hold that wanking can produce the most dreadful physical and mental ailments. But I hold to the view of Doctor Stevenson who ridicules this view. After all, he argues, all boys play with themselves and this practice has no bearing upon the ability to reach a ripe old age. What harm can there be in self-stimulation of the prick – or, come to that, the cunney? Certainly, no-one ever caught an unwanted infection through tossing off, and no lady ever suffered an unwanted swollen belly through finger fucking.

But to return to my narrative – I sneaked back into my own room still clutching the towel, locked the door and threw off all my clothes. I wrapped the still-damp towel around my semi-erect cock and within seconds it stood upright again amidst the tiny first sprouts of pubic hair. Carefully, I rolled back the foreskin from the swollen red dome and manipulated the shaft up and down in my cupped hand, unwittingly mimicking the sliding of the prick through the cunney lips into the juicy love-channel of the cunt. I closed my eyes and in my imagination saw again Mrs Radlett's enormous naked titties and I thought how wonderful it would be to place my prick between them. At that age of course, it takes only the merest stimulation to spend, and all too soon I felt the boiling of the spunk in my tight little balls and the frothy jet of white spunk fairly flew out the top of my cock in a miniature white fountain. I gasped with delight as my first real spend cascaded out of my pulsating prick.

I mopped up as best I could the spunk from the eiderdown and placed the damp towel in the dirty linen basket.

After that first encounter with some of the more intimate parts of the female body, life became somewhat more mundane. The next interesting extract from my private diary comes when I was at a more advanced age of sexual awareness – fourteen. By now I was fully aware of the pubertal happenings that my body had undergone. I had grown quite tall for a chap of my age. In fact, I was the tallest in my class and also the most well developed. I had a facial growth that necessitated regular shaving as well as the beginnings of some bodily hair growth. Pubic hair grew in a tight knot above my male member. This was also seemingly well grown for, after games, my friends would all look on in amazement at not only the length but the thickness of it. Modestly comparing it with my closer friends (as one does at that age), I would judge it to be at least twice as thick as theirs and nearly half as long again.

I was educated up to the age of seventeen at Cockshall Manor in Arundel, under the excellent tutorship of Professor James Bagshott-Coleman. At the end of one particular term of schooling, I returned home after the final, rousing game of footer between the two top houses. Being a big chap, I was the captain of my house and led the team to victory. I thus returned home rather dirty, streaked with the mud and sweat of a good, hard-fought game. I came back with my school report sealed in the ominous brown envelope, conveying either a good summer, being treated well by Papa, or a miserable one spent swatting at the subjects in which I was least good. Thank goodness my report was a good one. Papa was pleased that I had done well in the classics and in sport, winning the junior Victor Ludorum that year as best all round sports chap. Thus praised, I went off to have a soak in a well-deserved bath that

Alice the upstairs maid had drawn for me. Papa told me to join the rest of the family on the lawn for tea when I had bathed and changed.

After my luxurious soak in a steaming bath, I dried myself off in front of the mirror, feeling very pleased with myself and really looking forward to a super fun summer break. As I dried myself, I lightly stroked my member, which instantly caused it to spring to life, it almost having a will of its own. I found that it would grow and swell very rapidly to its stiff proud self at the slightest stimulation. As I have intimated before, it had developed into a weapon of inordinate size and when proudly erect was measured by my closest friend, Terence, to be nearly one foot in length. Its thickness was at least twice that of my nearest rival.

As I was standing there admiring myself, I saw in the mirror that the young maid Alice was standing to one side of me at the doorway, staring at my body. I hurriedly grabbed a towel to cover myself, when she came into the room and quickly locked the door. I was so shocked at her doing this that I dropped my towel, exposing my slowly shrinking member.

'Oh, young master Teddy, you *are* well developed are you not? A good boy like you with your school report and such an enormous cock deserves a treat.' So saying, she came over to where I was standing next to the mirror, knelt down in front of me and proceeded to take my penis in her warm, soft hands. It immediately began to swell to its fullest extent, needing little or no encouragement to do so. Alice cupped my ball-sack with one hand and gently squeezed them, whilst running her other hand up and down the shaft of my tool. The feeling I experienced was one of the utmost delight, far better than the feeling I got when playing with myself. I uttered a little groan as the feeling built up in my balls. 'Do you like that, Master Teddy?' whispered Alice. All I could do was to nod my head as I was far too excited to reply coherently.

'Well, if you like that, young master, see what you think of this.' With that she leant right forward and to my amazement took my now throbbing prick and proceeded to put it into her hot wet mouth. The feeling was unbelievable. Her darting tongue moved to and fro along the shaft of my by now aching cock. As she licked the tip of it, I felt my balls begin to swell and

17

fill with come. I thrust frenziedly into her hot mouth, almost choking her. I knew I was close to shooting my cum in her mouth even though she had been sucking me for barely thirty seconds. Alice also felt my urgency, for she sucked good and hard, at the same time squeezing my balls hard. The exquisite pain of her hard squeezing, together with her darting tongue, caused a rush of spunk up the channel of my pulsating shaft which exploded into her mouth as it jerked and emptied my balls of steaming hot spunk. I could not believe the sensation as she drank my cum. My balls contracted as she squeezed the last drop out. I must have really shot a great load of cum, for even though Alice greedily swallowed my juice she could not contend with the gush I produced. My spunk seemed to fill her mouth and gushed out the sides, down her chin and onto her cleavage. After finally sucking every drop of juice, she gently kissed my still rock hard member, wiped the cum off her chest and sucked her fingers clean.

'My, you have got the biggest tool I have ever seen for a lad of your age,' said Alice. 'And I have never known anyone to spunk like that. I can normally swallow it all, but you were drowning me with it.'

I stood there, dazed, as she tidied herself and lifted up her skirt. 'Goodness. I'm soaking wet here,' she said as she pulled her knickers down to reveal a wet patch on them. At the sight of the dark patch of pubic hair adorning her private parts, my semi-limp rod instantly hardened again, bringing back distant memories of my governess. As it leapt back to hardness, Alice looked up in amazement.

'Are you ready again?' she asked. 'You have only just shot your load! Well, if that's the case, young master, we can't go wasting such a lovely erection, can we? I was going to save the pleasure of you fucking my cunt 'til another day. But seeing as my cunt is so wet and ready, we will introduce you to the delights of a soaking wet fanny. This is your first time with a woman, isn't it?'

I replied that that was indeed the case. She quickly slipped off her now considerably wet drawers and tucked them in her pocket. As she bent down I noticed her pert young breasts spill over the top of her maid's blouse. I reached forward and cupped one in my hand. It felt so soft and tender. I brushed the pinky-brown nipple and felt it harden beneath by fingers. Alice gasped a little, stood up and took both ripe pears out. She took my hand and guided it to her now sopping wet juice-box. At the same time, she forced my head to her breasts and with no encouragement I greedily sucked her now erect nipples.

This was my first experience of actually touching the previously hidden areas of a woman's body. The feeling of a pert nipple in my mouth, together with the wetness of Alice's quim made me groan with delight and I realised that I would soon spunk again. Alice, being the experienced girl she was, aware of the build-up of spunk in my balls and the imminent explosion, quickly extricated herself from me and lay on the bed with her legs wide open, allowing me to see for the first time in my life the pink portal to heaven. Alice noted my interest in her cut so obligingly spread her cunt lips widely with her finger, revealing the very depth of the hole from which I could see her love-juice slowly dribble. As soon as I saw this my knob began to throb. Alice, seeing the closeness of my state of coming, beckoned me over. With expert hands she guided my rod to the entrance of her cunney. Thus placed, I needed no other encouragement than Alice whispering, 'Go on, big boy, fuck my juice-box like you have always dreamed of.' With that I plunged my now dribbling great cock deep into her beckoning cunt. It felt like nothing I had ever experienced before. I instinctively rammed my cock hard into her, whilst she wrapped her legs around me holding me firmly inside her. I shafted in and out, in rhythm with the ever quickening thrusts of her hips. Suddenly, I could feel her love-box begin to tighten. 'Oh fuck me hard Teddy,' she gasped, 'I'm coming.' As she said that, I could feel a surge build up inside her. The contraction of her wet pussey was enough to cause my balls to explode and, as she shuddered in ecstasy, my hot sticky cream poured into her, mingling with the soaking wetness of her juices. I pumped and pumped until my balls were totally voided. The feeling of my first sexual dalliance was a rare one. I lay back bewildered and spent. Alice looked over to me and said: 'Master Teddy, there you are, a treat for doing so well at school. But my, aren't you well endowed. You're as big as ever I've had and without doubt the thickest. I could feel you fill up my cunny and I can normally take them with room to spare! With a cock like that, young master, you will keep many a young girl happy and sore.'

With that, she quickly tidied herself up, but did not put back on her wet knickers. She checked herself in the mirror, tidied her dark locks, ran to the door, looked back and threw her panties to me.

'There,' she said, 'a prize for your first time. Your father did not get a pair the first time he fucked me, so you really are going to be good.' With that amazing remark, she left me holding her sopping panties and looking at my father in a new light.

So, dear reader, you are now privy to my first encounter with the fair sex. I was but a young stripling of just fourteen years of age at the time, and since then I must have fucked at least four hundred women, but the memory of that glorious initiation into the delights of sexual intercourse remains as bright as if it happened but yesterday.

However, let us return to my story. That last remark uttered by Alice, casual though it may have been for her, came as a total shock to me. Could she be telling the truth about Papa? I had always looked up to my father with total respect and awe as befitted a young man of my upbringing. I asked Alice repeatedly to enlarge upon her words, but the little minx refused to say anything further on this subject which, for the time, had to remain a closed book.

I still found it difficult to conceive that my Pater, a regular churchgoer and pillar of the local community, could have succombed to Alice's ministrations. And yet, I decided finally to take Alice's word that Papa had been dipping his wick, and I was forced to look upon Papa in a new and somewhat more critical light!

I saw Alice daily as she continued to perform the services of an upstairs maid, but regretfully I must admit that nothing of a titivating nature occurred until the end of the summer vacation. Unless, of course, one took into account the provocative looks she would often give me, gazing directly between my legs and licking her lips in a most lascivious way. This led to almost instant erections and often I would leave my room, meet Alice on the landing and then dash back inside my room, lock the door, hastily unbutton my trousers and take solace in a frenzied tossing-off. Just the merest thought of her pert titties and juicy cunt sent my right hand shooting down to my throbbing shaft, but this regular masturbatory activity was but a poor substitute for the richness of a real fuck.

Nevertheless, those summer months were quite the most eventful I had ever experienced and I recall those days with gladness. I was most fortunate to have a close friend, Terence Browner, living close by (many of you will remember his later exploits with the 69th Lancers on the North West Frontier) and we remained close friends for many years. General Browner (as of course he is now entitled to be addressed) still lives in Delhi and we correspond on a regular basis. He was a great cocksman and I am sure he will relish the retelling of some of our joint escapades together when we were but lads.

Our summer hideaway was a disused farmhouse and assorted outbuildings. Well, disused is perhaps too strong an adjective. The land had been farmed by a tenant of Lord Friary who had decamped suddenly to the New World in search of wealth during the California gold rush of '49. No-one had taken up the tenancy and the place had remained vacant. Terry and I had played many a childish game there but at the end of this fateful summer, we played games of a more adult kind!

One of the most memorable and highly enjoyable days occurred when Terence and I believed ourselves to be alone in the house. We were sitting in the lounge discussing, as I recollect, the chances of my ever being able to fuck Alice again and also – a very important matter to Terence – whether she might accommodate my best friend who was extremely anxious to lose his unwanted virginity.

'Are you certain that you are ready for such an experience?' I said earnestly. 'After all, you are three months younger than me and anyhow, very few boys of our age can have had the opportunity to enjoy a good fuck.'

'I'm as ready as I ever will be,' said Terence indignantly. 'Why, my cock is almost as big as yours, Teddy, even though you probably have the thickest prick of all the third formers.'

'That's awfully kind of you,' I replied modestly. 'However, you and young Bob Cripps must come joint second behind me.'

'Do you really think so? It's surprising that Bob has a sizeable cock as he is the shortest chap in the whole year.'

'Oh, yes, without a doubt. Indeed, I have often thought that it is highly inappropriate for that new prefect Davis to call Bob a little prick.'

'Ha! Ha! Ha! That's a good one. Anyhow, Teddy, where is that curious book you promised me?'

'It's a book of photographs by Harold Sailor. I heard Pater talk about this man to his friend Colonel Golthorpe. It seems that he has a special shop in Piccadilly where people can buy something Pater called "gallant literature". Anyhow, I heard the Colonel ask Pater to keep this book for him until he returned from India.'

'Gosh, let's have a look at it,' said Terence eagerly, his eyes sparkling with animation. 'I should wonderfully like to look at it.'

'Here it is, Terence, only I hope it won't excite you too much. You can look it over by yourself as I read the newspaper,' I said, placing it in his eager grasp.

He sat close to me in an easy lounging chair, and I watched him carefully over the top of the newspaper as he turned over the pages and gloated over the beautiful plates. There was a superb collection in there, which I had already seen, of coloured plates of boys and girls in the nude, both singly and together, and towards the end of the book, some of the photographs showed a fine young couple enjoying a good bout of fucking.

I could see Terence's cock harden in his trousers until it was quite stiff and rampant.

'Well, well,' I said, laying my hand on his bursting prick. 'What a tosser yours has grown up to since I gave you that book. We must compare our cocks as I think that yours must be almost as big as mine.'

'I told you I am ready for my first fuck,' he said with a laugh. 'Yes, do let's see which prick is the biggest,' and opening his trousers, he pulled out his fine red-headed cock, which stood in all its manly glory, stiff and hard as marble, with the hot blood making it warm to my touch. He then helped me pull out my own thick stiff truncheon, frigging it up to its fullest measure.

We proceeded to handle each other in an ecstacy of delight, which ended with us tossing each other off and aiming each other's jets of frothy white spunk into the fireplace.

'Ah well,' sighed Terence. 'I enjoyed that but I am sure it it not as satisfying as the real thing.'

I was about to make a soothing reply when we were both startled by what sounded like an ornament crashing to the ground just outside in the hall.

'What was that?' asked Terence.

'I don't know but let's find out!' I replied grimly, and arming myself with a poker from the fireplace, I rushed to the door.

I had no need of the poker, dear reader, for the noise in the hall had been made by Charlotte, the seventeen-year-old parlourmaid who had been doing some menial task in the scullery and had crept upstairs when she heard our voices as she too thought that the house was unoccupied except for her. But when she had heard us talk and saw us play with ourselves, she stayed to view more closely as she had never seen a naked stiff cock before and the sight of not just one but two had fascinated her!

Unfortunately, in her attempt to steal away unnoticed, she had bumped into a small vase on a mantelshelf which had fallen down and shattered on the parquet floor.

'You won't tell on me, Master Teddy, will you? Please don't tell or I'll lose my job', she begged me.

'I don't know about that', I said severely. 'It's a pretty serious matter.'

'I'll do anything you want', she said with imploring eyes.

'Anything at all?' said Terence quickly. 'How about letting us fuck you?'

'Now, now,' I said reprovingly, 'that's not fair. As it says in Doctor Stevenson's book, a man must never blackmail or cheat his way into a girl's bed.'

'Oh, you are kind, Master Teddy. I am a virgin and I've never even let a boy slip his fingers in my cunney,' cried the pretty girl.

'Goodness, you must have had a boy friend', said Terence.

'Not really, Master Terry. I have never had the pleasure of having male arms around me except Mister Baigue the butler who always pinches my bum when I walk past him.'

'Don't you ever feel you want to be fucked, Charlotte?' I asked.

'Of course I do, Master Teddy. We girls like to imagine lustful matters just the same as you boys', she said. 'Why, don't you think we can enjoy ourselves in sole fashion just like you do?'

'Girls can spend by themselves?' said Terence in amazement.

'Of course they can', laughed Charlotte who was now quite at ease. 'Shall I tell you how I do it?'

'Yes, please', we chorused and I added that this recounting of her secret pleasures would constitute a sufficient punishment for breaking the vase and that I would not peach on her to my parents.

'Well,' Charlotte began, 'I like to start after I have had a bath. I then stand in front of the bathroom mirror, slowly drying myself with a towel. On a summer morning, if the sun is shining like today, a gleam of light beams in making my body shine with a golden glow. Still looking in the mirror I let my gaze run down to my dark, thick pussey hair that curls round my crack. I then slowly rub my clitty and that makes me feel good all over.

'Then I scuttle into my bedroom and pick up a hand mirror and the dildo that I have taken from Alice's room. She is unaware that I know of its existence. I then place the mirror on the floor between my legs and, by crouching down, I have a lovely view of my cunt lips. I then separate my pussey lips and I can see to the very depths of my now damp, tight cunt. Then I push two or three fingers up to get my juices flowing and as soon as my cunney is dripping wet, I pick up the dildo and slowly rub it up and down my slit, rubbing my little clitty until it throbs and tingles.

'After a few moments, I push the dildo between my pussey lips and then gently take it out – at first slowly and then faster and faster and deeper and deeper until wooosh! My body is enveloped in a beautiful, most wonderful ecstasy as my cunney explodes and my love juices flow unabated. Afterwards, I lick my creamy cum from the dildo which also sends shudders of pleasure throughout my entire frame. This all takes about ten minutes and leaves me feeling drained but I feel sprightly and rejuvenated quite soon afterwards.'

This racy narrative excited both Terence and myself so much that our cocks were fairly bursting out of our breeches and we were forced to unbutton ourselves to be comfortable.

Charlotte blushed when she saw our two stiff cocks standing

stiffly to attention, but she said shyly: 'Would you like me to rub these for you? I've never done this before, but I've seen Alice and her friend Pelham, the Vicar's coachman, together and Alice rubs and even sucks his prick. I'll have a go, if you like.'

We readily gave our assent and her delicate little hands were soon grasping two eager thick pricks. Terence was so excited that he spent almost immediately Charlotte squeezed his shaft, but I lasted a little longer before I too jetted gushes of hot spunk onto the rug.

'Damn, how are we going to get the sperm stains out of the rug?' wailed Terence and I must confess that the problem had me most concerned.

Fortunately, Charlotte had the answer. 'Don't worry, boys, I know how to clean the rug so well that no-one will ever know that you spunked onto it. I'll rub in some of Doctor Watkins' cough medicine!'

'A cough medicine, that's odd,' I said.

'Yes, but it works wonders. Alice showed me how to take the sperm and cunney juice stains out of her sheets after a good bout of fucking with young Pelham,' said Charlotte with an infectious little giggle.

'Mama gave me some of that stuff when I had a cough last year,' said Terence. 'I'll never ever swallow another mouthful!'

'Oh, I wouldn't worry, Master Terence. Old Giddens the gardener puts some on his roses – and they won a prize at the village fête last week.'

We collapsed with laughter. Charlotte unbuttoned her blouse and showed us her curvey breasts. Plump and white they were, tipped by rose-red little stalks that I tweaked and rubbed against my palms. Alas, we were interrupted by the noise of a carriage drawing up outside for otherwise I am sure that Charlotte and Terence would both have crossed the Rubicon that morning, but as matters stood, both had to wait a little longer before ridding themselves of their virginity.

I was to see both Charlotte and Alice regularly over the next few days. I was certain that they had confessed of their sexual exploits with Terence and myself though nothing took place of a sensuous nature until the beginning of the following week, despite some provocative lip-smacking by Alice when she passed by me in the house. This often caused my cock to swell straight up and made my cheeks crimson with embarrassment. After all, at fourteen years of age, how was I to know the delights that a young stiff prick could afford a lustful young lass like Alice?

So, for a week, I sat in my bedroom, tossing myself off as I daydreamed of Charlotte's pert breasts and Alice's juicy cunney. But after the riches of genuine fucking, self-stimulation was but a poor substitute.

Matters came to a head after I decided to send Alice a love-letter. I first thought of writing some verses myself but truth to tell, I am no poet. Terence offered some verses which I copied down:

> How oft I've sworn to Alice dear,
>   The world no sight can show,
> To match her locks, her lips divine,
>   Her bosom's hills of snow.
> But oh! I find myself forsworn,
>   Two lips I have beheld;
> Still lovelier, on this happy morn,
>   A mount that those excell'd!
> Her bosom boasts no swell so fair
>   No tints that these eclipse;
> Her head has no such suburn hair,
>   Nor such enchanting lips!
> Yes, I've beheld the mossy mount,
>   Where all the graces centre;
> I've seen the rosy nectar'd cunt,
>   Where he she fucks will enter!

'Terence, you are a genius!' I said warmly. 'If this works, I shall entreat Alice to let you fuck her as well.'

'That's kind of you, old boy,' said Terence. 'Let's see if it works. Gad, though, what about fucking both Alice and Charlotte together in a whoresome foursome!'

What a splendid idea. I thought as I sat down and composed a covering letter to go with the poem. I wrote:

Dear Alice,
    I dedicate this piece of verse to you. It is sent with my

heartfelt thanks to you for initiating me into the mysteries and joys of coition. I think long and hard about that glorious romp and since then my desire for you has been ever heightened. Do let us enjoy ourselves again before I go back to school.

With gratitude and affection,

Teddy Parsifal

After checking that the coast was clear, I placed the note and verse in an envelope which I slid under the door of her room later that day. My parents and I dined at our friends, Lord Gordon and Lady McChesney, so I had no opportunity to see Alice until after breakfast the next day.

I was sitting in the study reading what appeared to be a geography textbook (but I had pages from *The Pearl* pasted inside the volume!) when Alice suddenly breezed in, ostensibly to dust the room. As she dusted she came close to me and whispered that she loved my letter but that she could not read very well and so Charlotte had read my poem to her! I must have looked somewhat shocked for she added that Charlotte could be trusted implicitly and indeed would not be averse to taking part in a little romp that afternoon – especially if 'that handsome young Master Terence would come along'.

We arranged to meet at two o'clock, in the old barn that stood, disused for some years, in Farmer Phillips' field, adjacent to our own grounds. I knew that Terence was more than keen to take part in a most wondrous and joyful new experience. How time stood still as we impatiently counted the very minutes until two thirty!

At two thirty four Terence said gloomily: 'I bet they won't come. She was having you on, Teddy. They have made monkeys of us both.'

'What sort of monkeys, Master Terry?' broke in a female voice from the entrance. It was Charlotte who asked the question, and to our delight we saw that she was not alone. Alice was with her, carrying a couple of blankets across her arms.

'You *are* monkeys,' chided Alice. 'Did you really think that I

27

would tease you about such a serious matter as fucking? Shame on you both.'

We apologised profusely and we helped Alice spread the two blankets on the ground.

'Oh damnation, I've forgotten the pillows,' said Alice. 'I'll have to go back to the house and get them.'

'Don't worry on our account,' said Terence, but Alice insisted that we needed pillows 'for our heads and our bums' and that it was foolish to spoil the ship for a ha'porth of tar.

'Charlotte can begin the game,' she said, as she turned to trudge back to the house. 'I just hope you two young sparks won't spunk off too much whilst I'm gone. I'm looking to a good fuck just as much as you are!'

To put Charlotte at ease, I decided to take no part in the introductory fondling and petting. After all, I knew that the sweet girl's desire was to make love to Terence, so I resolved to be the gentleman, though my own prick began to swell in my breeches as the young pair moved towards each other as if drawn by a giant, invisible magnet.

Terence clasped the trembling young girl in his arms and they exchanged a most passionate kiss as they sank down upon the blanket. Terence's nervous fingers fumbled with Charlotte's blouse so the clever girl quickly stripped off all her clothes and she lay back so that both Terence and myself could have full view of her naked charms.

Gad, Charlotte was a beauty! Her bare breasts rose and fell and the firm swell of those succulent young globes was such that my hand automatically went to my prick which I hastily let out of my trousers before any damage was done to myself or the trouser material! What lovely titties they were, well separated, each looking a little away from each other and tapering in well proportioned curves until they came to two crimson points. Those taut nipples acted as magical magnets to Terence's hands which squeezed and moulded those succulent spheres, the very first time that those deliciously hard and pouting stalks had ever been felt by his eager fingers.

She then slid her hands to the front of his trousers and deftly unbuttoned him as my best friend wrenched off his belt. As he pulled off his shirt, she pulled down his drawers and her hands grasped his swollen shaft, jerking up and down, faster and faster until seconds later the white love juice gushed out of his purple helmet like a miniature fountain.

This exciting sight was too much for me to view and I pulled off my clothes and knelt in front of Charlotte, pushing my rampant, hard cock in front of her face. Her blood was up and she licked her lips before flicking out her pink little tongue to tease the uncovered mushroom head of my prick. Emboldened, she now opened her lips wide and encircled my cock as I instinctively moved forward to push my yearning prick even further into her mouth. Her magic tongue circled my knob end, savouring the juices, and her teeth scraped the tender flesh as she drew me in between those luscious lips, sucking slowly from base to top again and again, delighting me to experience new heights of unbelievable pleasure.

She stroked her tongue up and down along the underside of my bursting cock, making it ache with excitement as it throbbed with ever increasing urgency. Then she cupped my balls in her hand, gently stroking them as she slowly sucked my prick even deeper inside her mouth. She squeezed her free hand under the base of my shaft, sucking me harder and harder until I felt my balls hardening and I shouted that my climax was imminent.

'I'm going to spend, Charlotte!' I cried out, trying to take out my cock from the sweet prison of her warm, wet mouth.

But she was enjoying the taste of my prick in her mouth so much that she grasped the cheeks of my bottom, moving me backwards and forwards until with a final throb, I spunked a hot stream of sperm into Charlotte's willing mouth. She swallowed my copious emission and licked all round the head of my cock to take up the last drains of love juice.

'M'mmmm, that was delicious, Master Teddy. I've often thought about what it must be like to suck a cock and Alice has told me how delightful it can be – especially as there is no chance of a swollen belly afterwards.'

She lay back and her soft, white belly was bared to our eyes and exposed to our lascivious gaze, hidden in a luxuriant growth of curly black hair, was her superbly chiselled crack with its large pouting lips which she parted with her fingers to reveal a gleaming little clitty.

'Come on now, Master Teddy,' she said. 'I've sucked you off

29

so how about repaying the compliment? Or perhaps Master Terence would like to have a try.'

I looked up to see if Terry would take up the invitation but my priapic partner shook his head. He was, as he later confessed, frightened to accept Charlotte's kind offer, as he was unsure as to exactly what was required of him.

I must swiftly digress here to note how poorly Englishmen perform in this particular amatory art. All the Continentals, especially the French and Italians, suck a lady's pussey with far more aplomb than the sons of Albion. Whilst this is a technique that could hardly ever find its way onto a syllabus of a learned institution – except perhaps at Nottsgrove Academy, where my old friend Doctor Simon White now presides [see *The Oyster 1*, Editor] – it is an art that needs to be practised far more widely and with far greater skill than at present.

'Show me how to eat pussey,' whispered Terence. And to his immense delight, I instructed him although my experience was to say the least limited to reading Doctor Roy Stevenson's fascinating manual on *les affaires d'amour*.

I let my tongue travel down the length of her velvety body, lingering briefly at her belly button before sliding down to her thighs.

I was still in a kneeling position when I parted the curly thatch of dark hair to reveal her damp, inviting slit. As I worked my face down into the cleft between her thighs, I could not help but notice how appealing her pussey looked and how delicate was the faint aroma that drifted towards my nose.

By this time, I was now down on my stomach, between her legs, with one hand under her gorgeous bottom to provide a little elevation and the other reaching around her thigh so that I was able to spread her pussey lips with my thumb and middle finger. I placed my lips over her swollen clitty and sucked it into my mouth, where the tip of my tongue began to explore it from all directions. I could feel it grow larger as her legs wiggled and twitched up and down along the side of my body. More by luck than judgement, if truth be told, I found the base of her clitty, and began to twirl my tongue around it. As I flicked it up and down rapidly, she became very excited and I discovered that the faster I vibrated my tongue, the more of a reaction I wrenched out of her, a valuable lesson to both Terence and myself and one that we never forgot in our many muff-diving expeditions in later life.

Meanwhile we had not noticed that Alice had returned with the pillows and, in a mock serious voice, she said: 'I see that you have begun the game without waiting for me! Well, boys, I think I'd like to wait a while as far as you two are concerned because I want your cocks to be as big as possible when I give you both something to think about!

'Meanwhile, Charlotte and I will give you a little exhibition that will show you that despite what you may have been told, we girls can enjoy ourselves even when there are no pricks around. Shall we do that, Charlotte?'

The younger girl nodded her assent and Alice began to undress. First she unbuttoned the little mother of pearl buttons on her tightly stretched blouse revealing her large breasts with their quivering hard nipples that were soon exposed in their glorious nakedness. Then she slipped off her shoes and stockings and as she rolled down her skirt, we saw that she was wearing no underwear. I saw Terence's cock rise as she bared her delicious bum cheeks in front of him. I was equally excited by her titties and the thatch of blonde hair that barely covered her prominent pussey lips, which she stroked lasciviously, saying to Charlotte: 'You've been a naughty girl, Charlotte. You know what happens to naughty girls, don't you?'

'Yes, Alice,' said Charlotte meekly, rolling her lovely naked body over towards Alice and finishing on her belly, exposing her luscious bum-cheeks to us all. To my surprise, Alice began to smack Charlotte's beautiful bottom, lightly but quickly as Charlotte cried out: 'Oooh! Ooooh! Alice! Mercy, mercy! No more, I beg of you, please, enough now, finish me off, please finish me off!' as she winced and wriggled as her skin turned from milk white to a rosy pink.

'All in good time,' said Alice, continuing her chastisement of Charlotte's bum. 'You deserve this and besides, I love to see your lovely arse change colour. It should always be this fine shade of pink and I just adore the way your cheeks jiggle as I slap them!'

But in the end she relented and I passed Alice a pillow so that Charlotte could lie back with her tingling bum resting on something softer than the mossy ground. Alice knelt between

Charlotte's legs and my cock stiffened perceptively as she began to slowly lick the inside of the young girl's thighs with sensuous, unhurried movements. Charlotte was now totally aroused as she pulled Alice's face downwards, ramming it between her long legs. Charlotte lay back with her legs high in the air as Alice muzzled and slurped the love-juice that was now pouring from Charlotte's cunney.

'Oh, Alice, you are the best clitty sucker in the world!' cried Charlotte. 'You make me wild with desire. Can you feel my love juice squirting all over your face. AAAH!'

The lovely girl screamed out with delight as Alice slipped a hand behind her and began to frig her arse as she continued to lick and lap at her dripping cunt. I sat back looking on with rapturous attention as the two tribades moved into a *soixante neuf* position, each tonguing the other's cunt, licking, lapping each other's quims. I could see Alice's juices dribbling like honey from her parted pussey lips as Charlotte flicked gently with her wet darting tongue at Alice's erect little pink clitty. Clutching my now rock-hard prick, I moved round to see Alice give Charlotte's furry bush a thorough tonguing, soaking her curly hairs with sweet saliva and working her tongue deeper and deeper into her soaking snatch.

Alice saw me and grabbed my cock and before going down again on Charlotte cried out: 'Oh, Charlotte, look, I'm tossing off Master Teddy's thick prick. He's going to empty his balls any second now, I can feel it! I can feel his juices beginning to flow. Finish yourself off, Master Teddy, I must see to Charlotte!'

She let go of my cock but I needed no urging to take over where she had left off. I rubbed my shaft up and down, covering and uncovering my glistening red knob and as the girls jerked in a mad frenzy against each other, panting and biting, then screaming with excitement as their orgasms came jointly as they shuddered to their mutual climax. At the same time I thrust my hips together and spurted my jets of frothy white spunk over Alice's face as she shrieked in delight, rubbing it all over her face and breasts. When the juices finally stopped cascading out, she milked my still throbbing cock of all its jism by sucking the very last few drops from the knob. And not to be outdone, Charlotte was sucking hard on Terence's cock as he stood over her until with a squeal of joy she took his prick out of her mouth and let her titties be drenched with the jets of spunk that squirted out of his mushroom-domed knob.

'There you are,' said Alice. 'That's a lesson they don't teach you at school, and I hope you enjoyed it.'

'What's that, Alice?' I panted.

'Well, you saw Charlotte and I lick each other's cunneys and frig each other's arses. And the lesson is that only women really know where those special areas of pussey exist, those that drive us wild with excitement. We know just where to lick and suck and probe. Mind, I still enjoy a good thick cock up my cunt more than anything else, truth be told.

'You do seem to be able to spunk deliciously, Master Teddy. I wonder if after a little rest we can all fuck together to finish off the afternoon's entertainment?'

As far as Terence and I were concerned the question was unnecessary! We were ready in almost a trice. Gad! In those days I could fuck all day and night and be ready with a stiff cock the next morning. And if I only knew as much about fucking then as I do today. Good Heavens, I can hardly bear to think about it. Still, as my old friend Oscar Wilde said to me quite recently: 'Youth is wasted on the young!'

It took little time before we were ready and waiting for a whoresome foursome. Terence started the ball rolling by covering Charlotte's mouth with a burning kiss and the lovely girl responded by reaching out for his stiffening prick, holding it firmly yet gently between her long, tapering fingers.

'Go on, Master Terence, giver her a good fucking!' cried out Alice as Charlotte moaned with pleasure as my friend slid a hand between her legs, feeling her hairy crack, rousing her to new bouts of passion. As they rolled together on the blanket Terence tenderly opened her tender pussey lips, sliding his fingers into that dainty slit that was already moistening to a delicious wetness. He continued to frig her with one, two and then three fingers as she took hold of his cock with both hands and wriggling across him bent forward to receive the uncapped red knob between her eager lips. She sucked at the mushroomed head, her soft tongue rolling over and over, slipping her hands now underneath to cup his tight little ballsack.

She rolled on to her back, eyes closed, mouth open. She was ready to be fucked – and Terence too was ready, as he positioned himself on top of her – while Alice took hold of his bursting cock and placed it between lips that opened wide to receive it. Terence thrust forward, sending his shaft deep inside her willing cunt. Charlotte cried out as she felt his prick fully inside her. She wrapped her legs around his waist as she bucked to and fro with her buttocks coming off the blanket as she gyrated faster and faster. Charlotte began to grunt, her breathing heavy and strained as her movements quickened and suddenly she was like a wild animal as he pounded to and fro and the surging cries of fulfilment echoed throughout the old barn as Charlotte began to milk the thick cock thrusting in and out of her soft, wet cunt.

'Ah, Terreeeee!, push harder, again, and again, there!' she screamed in ecstacy as they came together. She arched her hips, forcing Terence to withdraw. Alice grabbed his swollen red prick to squirt his hot jets of spunk across Charlotte's belly as the young couple sank down into the reverie that follows the opening of the gates of the reservoir of love.

My own cock was again as stiff as a poker as Alice whispered: 'Just lie back, Master Teddy, just lie back and leave the rest to me.'

I did as I was told and Alice gently stroked the underside of my cock, allowing her fingers to trace a path around and underneath my balls which made my whole body tingle with gratification. After a while she closed her hand round the throbbing shaft and suddenly her tousled mane of blonde hair was between my legs as she sucked lustily upon my rampant cock.

'Oooh! Oooh! I'm going to spend, Alice, I'm going to spend!' I cried out desperately.

Immediately she ceased her sucking and struggled up, standing over me, legs apart like some divine female Colossus. Her teeth flashed in a lustful smile, her eyes twinkled as she slowly lowered herself upon me. She rubbed her cunney over the tip of my red-headed shaft and then expertly slid herself right down on me, my prick sliding straight between her pussey lips and into her moist cunney at the first attempt. I felt her muscles contract and relax as she rocked up and down my shaft. I flexed myself to thrust into that exquisite silky wetness as she pumped her tight little bum cheeks furiously up and down, digging her fingernails into my flesh as she held on to my body. Each voluptuous shove was accompanied by a wail of ecstacy as I grabbed her large breasts and brought my head up to suck and lap on those rosy nipples.

We both began the final ride to our climax and I felt her cunney grip my cock even harder as we entered the last moments. She shivered and trembled as she reached the haven first, pulling me in as tightly as possible until, with a final push upwards, I too began to spend, spurting my hot love juice into her willing cunt. Alice gurgled with joy as the frothy white cream flooded into her and I felt her shudder as she drained me of every last drop of jism.

The four of us lay panting with exhaustion for a while and then we developed a superb fucking chain with Charlotte on her knees, leaning forward to gobble my cock and Terence pushing his cock into her from behind whilst he frigged Alice's cunt as the dear girl exchanged passionate kisses with me while I fondled her crimson nipples that were as hard as two miniature little pricks to my touch.

To end with, the girls lay down and played with each other's pussies, each rubbing and fingering the other while Terence and I knelt down to have our cocks sucked, mine by Charlotte and Terence's by Alice.

As my old friend Sir Andrew Scott has written, first love can be idyllic – or disastrous. Which it will be depends much on the partners concerned and to a very great extent upon our own selves. Terence and I were naive and perhaps bewildered by our experiences but there can be no doubt how fortunate we were to make our first journeys down the highways of love with such willing, loving girls who were willing to cater to our every desires. The old country law says that one's first experience should be in an open field, at night, under the stars. Maybe so, but our romp in the old barn, which was also Terence's introduction to fucking, certainly did us a power of good. We learned much from our joust, not least the need to experiment until one finds the best way to please both oneself and one's partner. This was a maxim I have never forgotten and have always urged the lucky young men just about to begin their first rides on the roundabouts of love-joys.

Later that evening I found myself alone with Alice, as Charlotte had been given the evening off – and as you can guess, dear reader, she and Terence spent the evening down nearby Lovers' Lane sucking and fucking until his cock and her cunney were just too sore to continue!

Not that Alice and I were doing anything very different up in my bedroom! We had enjoyed a grand session of fucking and we were lying sated on my bed, with Alice toying with my cock in her hand.

'Have you taken part in a great deal of fucking?' I asked Alice somewhat artlessly.

'Not as much as I would like, Master Teddy, but that's because I'm careful in choosing the days. I'd rather go without or use a dildo than rely on you boys to take your cocks out just before you're about to spend.

'I was always careful about letting a cock up my pussey – even the very first time, when I wanted it so badly,' she added.

'Oh, you must tell me all about that,' I said eagerly.

'Well, if you really want to know, Master Teddy, I lost my virginity working in my last situation.'

'Do tell me about it, Alice,' I begged. 'I'm sure that will make my cock swell up again. After all, I've only come twice and Mama said they would be returning late tonight. I want to fuck you at least twice more before they come back.'

'My, could you really? I've been looking at that book by Doctor Roy Stevenson that your Papa gave you and he says that too much fucking is as bad as too little.'

'Oh, never mind all that!' I exclaimed. 'Tell me about the first time you fucked.'

She smiled and said: 'Well, all right, I will tell you all about it. I was working as a kitchen maid in a big house in North London. My employer was a publisher and he often brought home books for the servants to read. Well, one afternoon, I was walking down Holywell Street and I thought I would look into one of the bookshops there. I noticed there were several shops selling prints but I did not know that this was a notorious centre for smutty books. After all, I was just a simple country girl of sixteen years of age. I couldn't help noticing that some of the prints displayed outside Toby Watson's bookshop looked rather rude. Of course, I did not know that the prints that had caught my eye were classic sketches by the great caricaturist Thomas Rowlandson.

'Suddenly a man's voice behind me said: "Do you like the work of Rowlandson? There are prudes who would wish to ban his drawings but I think the man was a great artist, don't you?"

'I blushed and turned round to see who was speaking to me. He turned out to be a good-looking man in his late twenties or early thirties, smartly but not richly dressed. We struck up a conversation but I could tell that from the way he was staring at my white frilly blouse that he was attracted to me – as I was, it must be confessed, to him.

'We engaged in conversation for about five minutes and then he offered to take me to a public house for a drink. I liked him even more when he did not demur after I said that I would prefer a nice cup of tea. So he took me to Bourne's Coffee House in Gray's Inn Road and we chatted away animatedly over tea and cakes. He told me that his name was Kenneth Kenhall-Watkins and that he worked as a salesman for a big London publisher. And what a coincidence! He worked for Goulthorpes, the company for whom my employer, Professor Pelham, was the chief editor.

'He lodged nearby in John Street and I needed little encouragement to agree to see the etchings he had purchased the previous week which were, of course, in his rooms.

'So very soon afterwards, I found myself sitting on a couch in Kenneth's room, looking at a book of very saucy prints. There was one particular print that I shall always remember as it sent shivers of lust throughout my body. Indeed, it makes me randy now just thinking about it.

'The scene was of a richly decorated bedroom and upon the bed lay a ravishingly beautiful young girl in a state of deshabille. She lay with her eyes closed, her petticoat and shift thrown up, her thighs wide apart, revealing to my burning gaze a rounded white belly, the bottom part of which was covered by a generous growth of jet black hair; and from between the locks that grew over the mount above a delicious-looking little crack, I could perceive two rosy lips slightly gaping open, from which oozed traces of whitish-looking foam. Next to the girl was standing a handsome young man, totally naked, whose huge erect prick was being lovingly grasped by the reclining girl whose mouth was open, teasingly near the uncapped knob and ready to perform sweet suction upon this lucky youth's stiff cock.

'You may well guess what happened very after that, Master Teddy! I hardly noticed the dashing rogue raise my petticoats and inserting his hand between my legs, letting it rest on the golden covering of blonde hair that covered my delicate little crack.

'With the other he dexterously undid the top two buttons of my blouse to view better the firm swell of my breasts. I was unsure as to how best to react – but for better or worse I was given little time to think about it as he suddenly pressed his face close to mine and kissed me passionately upon the lips.

'In spite of my surprise, I felt a rush of excitement surge through my veins. There was something about Kenneth's kiss that made it impossible not to respond. His hand slipped down to close gently over my breast as his other began to stroke my dampening pussey thorugh the thin cotton material of my drawers.

'Everything was now happening so fast that my memory is but a fond blur. I do remember though that I didn't try to resist him although being a gentleman, Kenneth later assured me, he would have acceeded to my wishes if I had wished to break away from his embrace.

'Be that as it may, his hand reached the top of my legs as I pressed my lips more firmly against his, he now stroking my pussey harder with his thumb, his fingers probing and caressing the lips of my cunney. Then I felt my whole body vibrate with excitement as his thumb found my clitty! He began rubbing it with a steadily increasing pace that had me swooning with delight. Ah, at that moment, I must confess, I knew for certain that I would be glad and willing to let him do anything he wished with me.

'Kenneth now let go of my breast and began to undo the buttons at the back of my blouse. Then he slipped it off me completely and ran his hands over my naked breasts, tracing circles around the stiffening nipples with the tips of his fingers. Then he bent his head down and took one of my erect teats in his mouth, and the wet friction of his tongue made me gasp with bliss as he sucked firm and deep.

'Now I culd feel him tugging at my drawers and I lifted my bum off the seat automatically to assist him as he pulled them down. I was feeling incredibly aroused and when Kenneth took hold of my hand and planted it firmly between his legs, I knew I just had to be fucked by this sweet man. My whole body panted for him! My breasts seemed to be swelling as if they would burst and the little red cherry-tipped nipples were as hard as peas and tickling me! And as for my cunt, oh, such a throbbing as went on in it as I had never felt before.

'"Now, Alice,' he said tenderly. "I do so want to fuck you. Would you like that, my darling?"

'"Very much so!" I replied quietly and with that Kenneth swiftly undressed and I gazed with longing at his thick, stiff cock which stood up so proudly, attended above by a fine swatch of thick black hair and underneath by the velvety wrinkled ballsbag. I might never have been fucked before but I had seen a few cocks before then, from the time I played "Doctors and Nurses" with Dudley Lovell, my cousin, at his fourteenth birthday party, to the extraordinarily thick but battered-looking prick belonging to Taylor, the Scottish butler at the house where I worked, whom I saw fucking the cook and the youngest pantrymaid one after the other on the kitchen table just a few weeks before. Fortunately I had been warned to keep away from this man who was well-known for his propensity to stick his enormous truncheon up any skirt given half a chance.

'But Kenneth looked so handsome without a stitch of clothing on him. He looked so powerful, so lithe! His shoulders were as broad as mine were narrow and his deep and manly chest, coverd lightly with dark hair contrasted so well with my graceful, swelling bosoms. He stretched me out on the big couch and knelt alongside me, kissing my titties and belly and running his hand up and down my thighs.

'My excitement grew even more stronger as I lovingly clutched his head, moaning my approval as he pressed his lips down onto my bushy mound. He worked his tongue up and around my clitty, sucking and lapping my soaking pussey as I ground my slit against his mouth. He was an excellent pussey-eater, one moment gently nibbling my cunney lips and the next sucking on clitty until I just could not wait any longer for his cock to nestle down between my legs.

'"Please, please fuck me, Kenneth!" I implored.

'"But I want to make sure you wish to lose your hymen," he muttered, not leaving his stimulation of my pussey for more than a moment.

'"I lost that by fingerfucking years ago," I said. "I want your cock, though, to be the first to enter my slit especially as it's a good time of the month to let you come inside me."

'"I don't want to play Vatican roulette," said Kenneth. "But 'pon my soul, you are such a beautiful girl, I don't think my cock would ever forgive me if I did not place him in your dear little pussey."

'Kenneth needed no further urging as he climbed over me and I eagerly lifted my hips to welcome his thrusting prick that slid easily between the lips of my pussey. His cock was thick and long, as I said, and I squirmed in sheer ecstasy as for the first time I experienced the joy of a throbbing, hot cock pump in and out of my love-channel. I was in heaven having waited so long for this moment to arrive. Kenneth was an expert at fucking, or *l'art de faire l'amour*, in a salute to the French whom he insisted made their love-making far more fun than in our stuffy old country.

'Still, his prick was a perfect fit for my nest. I remember the way he played with my breasts as my titties bounced back and forth in rhythm to his thrusts. My pussey was soaking with love juices but it was still tight and I loved the way – how shall I put it – well, how my pussey lips and clitty appeared to move to and fro, sending me into a delicious spend as Kenneth thrust and thrust again as he clasped me to him and in a convulsive thrill he pumped a luscious flood of creamy spunk into my womb!

'There, Master Teddy! That's how I lost my virginity. Did you find that an exciting story?'

'Your tale certainly has made me feel randy again, Alice,' I replied. 'Why, look at my cock! It's swelling up again beautifully.'

'So it is, Master Teddy! My, you are lucky to have such a big cock. It's even fatter than my last friend's tool and his was quite enormous. His name was Trevor Williams, an assistant in John Hotten's special bookshop in Piccadilly and I think he must have enlarged his tool by playing with it all day while reading all those naughty books!'*

[EDITOR'S NOTE: The bookshop to which Alice refers was well known to the cognoscenti of erotic literature one hundred years ago. The owner, John Camden Hotten, enjoyed a tremendous reputation as a publisher and distributor of banned books, magazines and photographs. Among those known to have frequented the shop which was situated near the junction of Piccadilly and Albemarle Street were the Prince of Wales's equerry, Lord Arthur Somerset, H. Spencer Ashbee, Sir Lionel Trapes, the noted war correspondent George Augustus Sala, and the Cambridge Univeristy don, Professor Norman Blakeley.]

As we lay back on the bed, I felt her warm hand encircle my throbbing cock. She turned onto her back and whispered to me to stroke her. My hand glided smoothly over her white skin, brushing lightly over her breasts, her hard, erect nipples and then down over her stomach. When I reached her pussey, she opened her legs for me. My fingers slipped over the moist lips of her cunt and when I found her clitty, her hand tightened around my shaft.

She said: 'Oh, Teddy, lie down beside me with your head towards my feet. Do you know how to taste a girl?'

'Not really, Alice.'

'Just lick me,' she instructed. 'Slide your tongue slowly over my cunney lips. Once you do it you will see how naturally it comes to you.'

And she was right! Once I had got a taste of her creamy cunt, my tongue seemed to develop a life of its own, whipping back and forth, up and down, boring deep inside her tender love channel. I felt her tongue flick over my knob, down the shaft and over my balls and then reversing the route back to the top. Dear Alice, few girls know how to suck cock better than she!

With one gulp, she slipped the remainder of my shaft in the wet warmth of her mouth and lying on our sides, we sucked away at each other until she spent, grinding her soppy pussey against my face. Suddenly, she backed away from me and my cock slipped out of her mouth. She raised her knees up, legs wide apart and told me to put my trusty tool inside her.

Nothing loath, I leaned forward, pressing into her until my entire shaft was buried in her snatch. She cried with delight as I pumped away, pressing to meet my thrusts to make certain that every inch of cock was inside her juicy pussey. Naturally, it took only a short time before I felt myself ready to climax and I shot great globs of white frothy sperm inside the lovely girl's cunt.

We lay panting after this lustful emission but later that afternoon she showed me the joys of tit-fucking and how to squirt my spunk over her breasts. Alice taught me many of the secrets of sexual pleasures that summer. She was patient and loving and every woman I've made love to since has benefitted from her kind tutelage. I am glad to say that Alice married a young teacher and emigrated to Australia where they now live, happily in considerable prosperity near the town of Melbourne.

This summer of my fifteenth year was truly a memorable time. For I must now pass on quickly to an event that occured just two or three days after my glorious joust with Alice.

We were enjoying a quiet breakfast when my father suddenly broke off from reading *The Times* to say: 'Ada, boys, listen to me. There is a most interesting item in the newspaper this morning.'

'What is it, Father?' enquired Cecil, who I should mention was now seventeen and a lordly sixth former at Cockshall Manor Academy.

'Do you remember that Swedish gentleman, Mr Karl Andersson* [*Editor's note: Mr Parsifal must have been referring to the distinguished Scandinavian explorer Karl Johann Andersson, who was rated as only second to Livingstone. He died while trying to reach the source of the Cunene river]? You will doubtless have recalled that we met him at Sir Douglas Walker's reception in aid of the West London Home for Unmarried Fathers. Well, he has written a letter to *The Times* from East Africa about his experiences with elephants. You will be fascinated by what he has to say.'

'Who cares a shit about that boring old fart?' muttered Cecil under his breath. Fortunately Father did not quite catch what was said and registered his disapproval only by a glare.

'Oh, do read the letter to us,' said Mother placatingly, though I am sure that she had no real desire to listen to my Father. Actually, I was rather interested, not having met the

42

gentleman concerned and I had just finished reading an exciting adventure about explorers in the Dark Continent.

'Very well, my dear,' said Father. 'Pay attention, boys. The letter begins: "I address you now from the wilds of unexplored country about a hundred and fifty miles from Nairobi. During my travels I encountered a very considerable number of elephants but unfortunately chiefly cows with their young which are both dangerous and unprofitable. I have had some perilous adventures with these animals and have been taught some severe lessons which I am not likely ever to forget. If I have not obtained a great deal of ivory I have gained a great deal of experience and some interesting insights into the natural history of the African elephant.

'"Nothing gives a person a better idea of the elephants' stupendous powers than a day's walk through one of their favourite haunts. There may be seen whole tracts of forest laid prostrate and such trees sometimes! The trees, which for the main part are of a brittle nature, are usually broken off short by the beasts; but when they meet with a tree that seems to them too tough to snap at once, up it goes, root and all.

'"The other day, after many hours of fatiguing tracking, I was closing with a very large troop of elephants, consisting chiefly of females, when to my left I suddenly espied another troop of what I took to be males. I at once left the first troop to attack the second. I stalked unperceived to within twenty-five paces of the herd when to my annoyance, I discovered that they were also mostly cows and calves. There were however, a couple of fine bulls among them, one evidently acting as paterfamilias to the herd. This beast's position was unfavourable and I was waiting for him to present a better mark when to my astonishment they all made off.

'"As they were disappearing into the brushwood I fired at one of the hindermost – a male, as I imagined. In an instant the herd wheeled about, and with a terrific rush came crashing through the bushes nearly in a direct line towards me. But after running for about sixty or seventy paces they stopped short, evidently annoyed at not finding the enemy.

'"I felt very much inclined to take to my heels, but a moment's reflection convinced me that safety lay only in keeping close; and it was as well I did so for in a few moments

43

the paterfamilias made an oblique rush through the jungle with such force as to actually send a whole tree that he had uprooted in his headlong course spinning in the air. A huge branch remained fixed to one of his tusks. His head he carried aloft, his huge ears were spread to the full, while with his trunk he sniffed the air impatiently. In this position, and when within less than a dozen paces of me he remained, I should say, for about half a minute. I think it was the most striking and thrilling sporting scene that I ever saw . . .

'"I have shot many giraffes, gnus, hartebeests besides elephants but I make a point of not destroying unless absolutely in want of meat to feed either my party or the hundreds of poor devils constantly following my track."'

'Well, that sounds very exciting, doesn't it, lads?' said Father, folding the newspaper and putting it down on the table.

'I don't like the idea of killing for sport,' I said.

'Neither do I,' said Cecil. 'I am glad that Mr Andersson only shot those poor animals for food and not simply wantonly as do so many hunters.'

'I am in agreement with you, boys,' said Mother. 'Your sentiments certainly do you proud.'

'Yes, I would not disagree with that,' said Father. 'Anyhow, the reason that I read that passage to you is that Jumbo the elephant is at the London Zoological Gardens in Regent's Park just now and I thought that we would take a train up to town and see him. Would you like to go?'

What a splendid treat lay in store, I thought, as Cecil and I chorused our assent. But Mother declined the invitation as she was due to take tea that afternoon with the squire's wife, Lady Le Baique, and felt it would be impolite to cancel the arrangement at such short notice.

'But you three men must go!' said Mother kindly. 'I will go another time and anyhow, your Papa and I saw Jumbo last year when we went up to town for Lord Bourne's Autumn Ball.'

'Very well, my dear, I will call young Owen to take us to the railway station so as we can catch the noon train. It so happens that I want to see my old friend Sir Lionel Trapes who lives nearby in St John's Wood so I shall be able, if you will forgive the perhaps inappropriate colloquialism, to kill two birds with one stone.'

We travelled up to town on the good old London, Brighton and South Coast Railway and the train pulled into Victoria Station within a minute of its scheduled time of arrival. We disembarked and strode up the station platform to the cab rank. We were waiting in a fairly long queue when Father suddenly snapped his fingers and grimaced.

'Boys, I have just remembered that I promised to undertake a chore for Sir Lionel which will necessitate my leaving you to visit the Zoo by yourselves,' said Father.

'I promised to pick up a book for him, some learned text or other that has been ordered especially for him from the Continent. The bookseller promised it would be ready for collection today so I wrote to my friend and said that I would collect it and save him a journey or the cost of postage.

'So here are two sovereigns, Cecil. You and Teddy can take a cab directly to the Zoo. I think it best if you meet me at Sir Lionel's this afternoon. In case you have forgotten his address, here is his card. Be there by five o'clock. I will have to see Jumbo another time. And perhaps I will be able to take your mother with me,' he concluded.

The day was turning into a great adventure indeed. We waited with Father for our separate cabs and he warned us of the dangers of pickpockets who lurk round railway stations and any large gathering of people.

'You can sometimes tell the thieves by an unrest about them, for they seldom journey on a train,' explained Father. 'They hang around the ticket offices or queues like this. When they see people engaged in conversation they go up to them and plant themselves by their side while the others cover their movements. Then one might pretend to bump into the victim and extract his wallet, for these thieves have very quick fingers. So be warned, and keep an eye out for your money and your pocket-watch.'

With those words, Father climbed into a cab and fortunately a second cab soon appeared and Cecil and I were off to the Zoo.

'I say, Cecil, what sort of book is Father getting for Sir Lionel?'

'Something he'd never let us see, like French postcards or a copy of the *Cremorne*!' said Cecil. 'Did you know that Sir Lionel's nephew is in my form at school? And from what young Daley tells me, old Sir Lionel's a bit of a sportsman. He belongs to the Jim-Jam Club in Great Windmill Street. Now that's run by Major Ferguson, whose nephew is also in the Lower Sixth at Cockshall Manor. And Scott Ferguson told the prefects that all the London swells go there to fuck, if you know what that means.'

'Of course I know what that means!' I cried indignantly. 'Why, I've already fucked two girls myself this summer.'

'Gosh, have you really? One of them must be Alice. No, no, no, you must not tell me, Teddy, for a gentleman never ever reveals the names of girls he has fucked unless he has caught a dose of clap from them. And then, in that case, it is his bounden duty to inform his friends. Still, good luck to you, little brother. I didn't think you could even manage a cockstand yet,' smiled Cecil. 'However, I don't suppose you would be interested in having a fuck at a rather special private club I know. After all, I'm sure you would much prefer to see the animals at the Zoo.'

'Don't tease me, Cecil,' I said. 'You know bloody well that I would give up my house cricket colours for the chance of another fuck. But Father has always warned us against loose women. Won't we be risking catching some awful pox?'

'Father is quite right. You must never pick up a woman in the street. But the girls at the private clubs cater exclusively for gentlemen and they are checked every so often for any problems. Don't worry, Teddy, your cock and balls are quite safe at Maison Alfred's.'

'Well, I'm game if you really mean it. But how about lucre? We've only got Father's two sovereigns between us and we'll want some tea and then we'll need another cab to be at Sir Lionel's by five o'clock, won't we?'

'No problem, young brother. I've five pounds here that Father's cousin, Doctor Arkley, gave me for coming first in the Public Schools' cross-country race last April. I can't think of a better use for the cash than to spend it on two lovely girls, a slap up spread and a magnum of bubbly, can you?'

Cecil instructed the driver to change his route though, as it happens, Maison Alfred's was not all that far away from the Zoological Gardens, being situated at the north end of

Marylebone High Street.

The club was in a private house and Cecil gave five sharp raps on the door with the heavy brass lion's head knocker.

'That's a signal known only to club members,' he told me.

The door was opened by a rather stout maitre d'hotel, who asked Cecil for his membership card which he fished out of his waistcoat pocket.

'I'll sign in my brother,' said Cecil breezily.

'I regret that the minimum age for entry is sixteen, Mr Parsifal,' intoned the attendant.

'Well, young Teddy's sixteen, Soames.'

'He looks far younger, sir. We would require proof of his age. Have either of you any such proof?'

'How about this?' said Cecil, slipping a sovereign into the man's hand.

'That will do nicely,' said Soames happily. 'May I recommend the Chelsea Room on the first floor. Polly and Sophie are awaiting custom.'

'Excellent, excellent. Send up a cold collation with a magnum of fizz in as soon as possible. Look, Soames, I'll leave five pounds here, that should cover it and leave a fair old tip for you, right?'

'You're very generous, Mister Parsifal,' murmured the servant as Cecil led the way up to our salon. He tapped on the door and opened it. I peered from behind him and saw an exquisitely furnished room that had a small table near the windows which overlooked Marylebone High Street and two couches drawn up near the fireplace though naturally at the height of a warm summer's day, the fires had not yet been lit.

And sitting on one of the couches were two of the prettiest girls I have ever seen in my life. One was slender and of medium height of no more than at most eighteen years of age with a merry little face which was sheer perfection. Her chin was charmingly dimpled, her lips, full and pouting, slightly open, gave just a glimpse of two rows of ivory that appeared set in the deep rosy flesh of her small and elegant mouth. Her nose was of the Roman cast, her eyes a sparkling lustrous dark brown and her forehead was middling high, setting off a mop of brown, shiny hair.

She wore an emerald green dress, low-cut with a long wide

skirt, nipped in at the waist and her nipples were only barely concealed by the fabric for her corset thrust forward her pert young breasts and my eyes were immediately riveted upon those white alabaster beauties.

The other exquisite creature was red-headed, her hair drawn back in a bun which she was in the act of loosening when Cecil opened the door. Her skin was white and of a clarity that it seemed illumined from within. She was wearing a cream coloured outfit, the jacket of which, being fashioned tightly to her torso and waist, allowed me to see the perfect development of her fully-rounded breasts while her lower limbs were clad in a long, pleated skirt. Her features were finely shaped, the best features being a *retroussé* nose and sparkling light blue eyes.

'Well, do you like what you see or do you want to send us back to the shop?' said the divine-looking redhead.

'No, no, not at all. It's just that my young brother and I have been struck dumb by this exciting sight of two luscious lovelies such as yourselves,' stammered out Cecil.

'How kind of you to say so,' chipped in the brunette. 'In that case we had better introduce ourselves. I am Sophie and this is my sister Polly.'

'Heavens, two brothers and two sisters together, how exciting!' said Cecil.

'Ha, ha, ha! Yes, well actually Sophie is only my half sister but I love her very much!' cried Polly.

'I'm sure you do,' rejoined my brother. 'Anyhow, I am Cecil Parsifal and this is Teddy, my young rogue of a full brother. At least, to the best of my knowledge he is my full brother although I must confess that Nature has been kinder to him than me as I hear from a variety of sources that he possesses the biggest prick in Cockshall Manor!'

'My, he's rather young, isn't he? How old are you, Teddy?' asked Polly.

'Old enough!' I replied. 'I'm sixteen years old next week.'

I believe that the girls saw through my unblushing lie but they smiled and said nothing more about my age. I think they both fancied a fuck with a young teenaged boy after having to deal with older men who frankly often had trouble keeping it up.

'I've made all the arrangements with Soames,' said Cecil,

who was obviously eager to get on with the action. 'He'll have a cold collation and some bubbly up here soon.'

'Oh, he won't be here for at least an hour,' said Sophie. 'It's very hot in here, boys, why don't we take off some clothes and let the pleasant warm air get to our bodies.'

We needed no further bidding but perhaps it was the first time Cecil and I had undressed together for many years, we were both somewhat inhibited and I found to my surprise that unusually, my cock stayed flapping down between my legs. I stole a glance at Cecil and saw that he too was at half-mast, his knob being only partially uncovered by his foreskin.

'Those look like sizeable weapons once they are primed,' laughed Polly.

'Yes, you're right. What can we do to stiffen their cocks?' Sophie pondered. 'I know, let's tan their hides!'

'What a good idea, Sophie,' chirped Polly. 'Now, who is going to be first. You are the older, Cecil so let us begin. Bend down, sir and touch your toes.'

Quite nude, my brother did as he was told, opening his legs slightly so we had fair view of his hanging balls. Sophie passed a hand lightly across his bare bum cheeks and then she nodded and they immediately began to smack Cecil's arse with their palms. As one girl smacked his bum, the other began to undress so by the time Cecil's bum was rosy coloured from their sweet slapping, both the girls were stark naked.

'There, you naughty boy. How dare you come to us with a limp prick?'

'Such an impudent boy! There, take that, and that, and that!'

I craned my head forward and observed a very perceptible rising in his cock which had swelled up and soon stood out up against his belly in a rampant state of erection. I had not even noticed that my own prick had also stiffened up to its fullest height and was also standing high majestically against my flat belly.

'They're both ready now,' cried Polly. 'Now, Cecil, your poor bum took a beating so you can fuck first!'

And with that she grabbed hold of Cecil and after a cheerful preliminary embrace the lovely girl stretched herself out on the luxuriously thick carpet. She was absolutely beautiful with extremely large breasts topped by equally well proportioned aureoles and nipples. Her mound was covered with a profusion of rich reddish hair and the glowing chink between the slips of her cunney looked highly inviting.

Cecil took a deep breath, blew out his cheeks as he expelled the air from his lungs and took his rock-hard cock in his hand. As he knelt down he drew back the foreskin, making his purple knob bound and swell.

Polly heaved herself up and she too knelt forward, pushing out the chubby cheeks of her bum to afford me a truly excellent view of both her cunt and her arsehole. This excited me no end and it was all I could do to restrain myself from frigging off there and then.

She grasped Cecil's cock with both hands and slowly began first to lick my lucky brother's knob and then, after giving the shaft a good rub, taking almost the whole length in her mouth until it must have surely been touching the back of her throat. Then she began to suck noisily on Cecil's bursting prick, moving her head to and fro so that his shaft moved smoothly back and forth though always a part was engulfed between Polly's pouting lips. Meanwhile, she played with his balls, gently squeezing them until she felt that Cecil was near the peak of pleasure.

Now she took his throbbing member out of her mouth and, still keeping tight hold of his shaft, gently whispered to him to lie down on his back. Cecil obeyed without demur and lay flat on the carpet, his rampant cock sticking up as firmly as a flagpole under the gorgeous Polly's expert handling.

The delicious girl rose up, and still keeping my brother's prick in her hand, turned her peachy bum cheeks to his belly and calmly proceeded to sit firmly on his cock, straddled over his lap in a position that I was later to learn enabled her to enjoy the very last fraction of a cock length in her heated cunney. They stayed almost motionless for a few moments as in a tableau vivant, enjoying the mutual sensations of repletion and possession so delightful to each of the players of the glorious game.

Then they commenced those soul-stirring movements that led inexorably to a grande finale of frenzy. One could almost feel their muscles contract and relax as she rocked up and down on Cecil's cock.

As their orgasm approached, Polly drove down hard with a delighted squeal, spearing herself on Cecil's bursting prick which was glistening wet from her cunt juice. The pair then melted into a torrent of mutual spendings as they came together with great cries and Cecil shot a great gushing stream of spunk into her womb.

Now it was my turn to join in this erotic frolic. Sophie and I were now both stark naked and the gorgeous girl embraced me passionately as we stood belly to belly, with only my thick, hard cock being squeezed delightfully between our tummies.

'What a monster,' laughed Sophie lasciviously. 'My goodness, Teddy, you have a gigantic prick for such a young fellow. I do believe it is even bigger than that of Peter Stockman, that young theology student who fucked me so divinely last Thursday.'

'Do you think so?' said Polly with interest. 'Well, let us see if he can use it as well as Peter who you said was the best fuck you have enjoyed since you had the Bishop of Finchley.'

I inclined the willing wench backwards upon the soft carpet and we lay at full length, side by side, both of us eager as possible for the game; my head was buried between Sophie's loving thighs, with which she pressed me most amorously, as I inserted my tongue into her inviting little crack, making her gasp with passion. She sucked my stiff prick, handling and kissing my balls till I spent in her mouth as her tongue washed my knob. She sucked down my copious emission whilst I repaid her loving attentions to the best of my ability with my own active tongue.

I rolled over this delicious minx, spreading her legs wide as she grasped my cock to feed it to her juicy pussey. She rolled back my foreskin and kissed the shiny dome as she guided my knob to the lips of her hot pussey and slowly, thrillingly, I inched my shaft inside her willing cunney as it sucked in my throbbing prick. I fucked her with long, smooth strokes and we laughed merrily as I hovered above her, supporting myself on my arms. My balls slapped in slow cadence on her buttocks and thighs as I moved down, up and down again, increasing the pace as I thrust with a new intensity, cheered on by Cecil and Polly who were greatly impressed, and I apologise if I do sound boastful of my prowess in *l'art de faire l'amour*.

As I approached the heights, I changed the tempo to one of swift, short jabs as she rotated her bum cheeks as I pulsed in and out of her squelchy pussey. We climaxed together as my cock squirted out jets of spunk that mingled exquisitely with her own stream of cunney juice. Now she had tasted me Sophie wanted more, so she rubbed up my cock to a second fine erection and I took her doggy fashion, gripping her hips as I thrust my rampant tool deep into her cunt from behind, my balls jiggling against her firm and nicely rounded bum cheeks. I fucked away energetically just as if I had never spent just minutes before, as the throbbing and contracting of her inner cunney muscles on my enraptured prick spurred me to further efforts until with a hoarse cry I pumped a second stream of sperm into her willing womb. I fell on top of the sweet girl and we sank down exhausted entwined in each other's arms to enjoy the lovely lethargy that comes after a fine bout of fucking.

None of us had noticed that whilst we had been fucking, Soames had entered the room and set up a table upon which he had placed a selection of cold meats, fruits, and a magnum of champagne in an ice-bucket.

(I understand that the contract for the club's ice was so valuable that the tradesman concerned, a Mr Tong, slipped Soames a five pound note the first Friday of every month but that is neither here nor there).

We were so warm from our games that we stayed quite naked as we ate and drank our way through the informal little luncheon. It transpired that both the girls were well educated young ladies and had entered their work not so much from want as from sheer enjoyment of the business involved and Cecil and I enjoyed a very interesting conversation with them as we sipped our nice champagne.

We sat idly around talking of this and that when Sophie said: 'I must say that I really enjoyed my lunchtime fuck. You boys are in the first flush of youth and eager to please your girls.

'But you would really be amazed at the ignorance and sheer, utter selfishness which Polly, myself and all the working girls at Maison Alfred and other private clubs encounter daily.

'Now I know you gentlemen are paying for your pleasures but if, for example, some customer actually took the trouble to ask if there was a particular mode of fucking I preferred, I would be so grateful that I would be able to give him that little bit extra – that certain *je ne sais quoi* that stands between a good fuck and a great one,' she added warmly.

'I must agree with every word you say,' said Polly. 'I know that different men have different preferences and indeed their performances are governed by both physical and mental factors.

'And yes, many only want to fuck in one specific fashion. But I must add that I have no objection, and nor I am sure have you to giving relief to those men whose own upbringing (let alone that of their wives) mean that they cannot enjoy the full flavour of the fruits of the marital bed. I mean, incredible though it may seem to liberated girls like us, many women recoil with distaste at the very notion of sucking a prick! Is that not quite astonishing?'

'They just cannot know what they are missing?' chimed in Sophie.

'Perhaps it is as well, my dear, or you would both be out of business,' said Cecil and we all laughed heartily at his quick-minded wit.

'Ah, I would wager a day's pay that your Papa has a copy of Doctor Roy Stevenson's manual in his library,' said Polly, her eyes twinkling with merriment. 'I recall the passage where the good doctor lays down the rule that between lovers there should be no rules.'

'You would win your wager, Polly,' said Cecil. 'However, I was actually thinking of what Doctor Stevenson says about rear entry.'

'Oh, about how some folk believe it is not quite genteel to poke in your prick from behind?' smiled Sophie. 'Why, I enjoy that position immensely. How some people can believe that the manner in which most mammals copulate is somehow unnatural is almost past my comprehension. I also enjoy the sensation of a lovely smooth cock entering my pussey from behind. I believe this position allows an extra inch or two of the shaft to enter the cunney and that it always a bonus.'

'Indeed it is,' mused Polly. 'And I do believe that it allows the knob of the cock to touch the clitty which is even nicer! Why, just feeling a knob against my clitty and cunney lips brings me off in a trice.'

'Let us put into practice what we have been talking about,' said Cecil, massaging his cock up to a fine state of stiffness.

'Very well, Cecil dear. But do have patience as I would like to have young Teddy fuck me from the rear,' said Polly, looking with interest at my youthful prick which was rising majestically upwards as she was speaking until it stood upright in all its glory, the rich red ruby dome uncapped as it throbbed out its need for a juicy quim in which to bury itself.

Sophie took hold of my cock as Polly leaned over the arm of the couch, spreading her legs a little and raising her bum so that both her arsehole and cunt were waiting for my arrival.

'Would you like this colossal cock up your bum, darling?' enquired Sophie, with characteristic eloquence.

'No, not now, but thank you so much for asking, my sweet. But please put Teddy's prick in my cunney, there's a dear, as I have a great fancy for it just now. I want to feel his hot cock nudge between my bum-cheeks until his knob touches my cunt lips.'

The lovely girl grasped my cock firmly and soon the red head of Cupid's battering ram was brought to the charge. Sophie opened the lips of Polly's cunt and placed my cock just on the edges, whispering to me: 'Push on, push on, Polly has a marvellously tight little pussey! And she really wants to feel every inch of your big cock inside her!'

I moved my hips in rhythm so that with each plunge forward, an extra inch of my shaft was embedded in Polly's sopping cunney. We enjoyed a most pleasurable fuck, moving slowly at first till her rapid motions spurred me to faster plunges, her deliciously tight pussey holding me like a warm, silken hand. Her juices lubricated her cunney walls so that soon my shaft was sliding in and out with ease though I was able to feel my foreskin drawn backwards and forwards with every shove.

'Ah! You dear boy, push on! Come now, Teddy, empty your balls!' she screamed in ecstasy as we came together though I was too tongue-tied to be profuse in my terms of endearment. As we lay still after it was over, her tight little pussey seemed to hold and continually squeeze my delighted cock by its contractions and throbbings and it was only a few minutes before we ran another thrilling course in this most voluptuous way imaginable.

By this time Sophie was down on her knees lustily sucking on Cecil's stiff prick. He had his hands on her head as she sucked greedily on his shaft, caressing his large balls with one hand and frigging herself with the other, the fingers vigorously sliding in and out of her hairy cunt.

She changed course after a minute or two and clasped my brother's buttocks and squeezed him close up to her mouth till his balls slapped against her chin.

Cecil shouted: 'My God! I'm going to spend! Suck me harder! Oh yes, that's it! I can feel my cream coming! I'm going to shoot my spunk!'

And with short convulsive jerks of his dimpled bum, he shot wads of spunk into Sophie's willing mouth. She swallowed his copious emission joyfully, smacking her lips as she milked Cecil's prick of the last frothy drops of spunk as he quivered with convulsions of delight, sinking to his knees to join her as they wrapped their arms around each other and sealed their joy with a passionate kiss.

We stayed a while longer to enjoy the pleasure of the company of these two delightful girls. We had strength for a final round of fucking before we pulled on our clothes and made ready to go.

For time was now pressing as we had to meet Father at Sir Lionel Trapes' imposing town-house off Avenue Road in St John's Wood and we had promised to be there by five o'clock. So we made our farewells and Sophie slipped me a piece of paper with her home address written on it saying that she had enjoyed our fucking so much that I would be a most welcome guest in her West Hampstead apartment at any time and that the fucking would be free of charge.

'Quite a compliment,' said Cecil with a wry chuckle as we climbed into the cab that the thoughtful Soames had called for us.

'Do you think she means it?' I said.

'Perhaps yes, perhaps no. After all, she has to earn her daily bread so she cannot be expected to let you fuck her for nothing. If she were a milliner, for example, she would hardly be expected to give away her hats!'

'Well, I am sure that she would be generous to her friends.'

'And in no time she would be out of business, for once you

start giving something away nobody else will pay for it,' said my cynical brother.

I shrugged my shoulders and smiled as Cecil took out an afternoon newspaper he had picked up from the hallway table at Maison Alfred.

'This is very interesting, Teddy,' he said. 'Look, you are thinking of taking up medicine, aren't you? Now here is a most interesting news item about a Mancunian consultant, a Professor McChesney, who says that smiling is good for you.'

'Well, it doesn't need a consultant to state the obvious, Cecil, does it?'

'No, no, there's more to it than that. Professor McChesney maintains that when we smile we push our facial muscles against bones, we temporarily divert the blood flow from the brain to the face. This may influence brain temperature and stimulate the production of endorphins, the body's own natural pain killers.'

'So smilng is good for you not just because it makes you feel better but it is actually beneficial regarding body chemistry?'

'Precisely, Teddy. I think I will ask Father if we can come up to town next week to hear Professor McChesney lecture at the Aeolian Hall.'

'Is he speaking about smiling?'

'Indirectly perhaps,' said Cecil. 'The lecture is entitled "On Natural Relief of Piles". No doubt anyone who is relieved will smile quite broadly afterwards!'

The roads were quite busy as many people had decided to spend the very pleasant afternoon taking the air in Regents Park. Inside the park, the air was strangely still and I was reminded of the lovely words of Goethe we had been diligently studying at Cockshall Manor under the stern guidance of Herr Grossputz. I can still recite much of Goethe's verse from memory. Despite the prejudice against a sometimes gutteral tongue, I believe that German can sometimes sound as melodic as the Latin languages.

Anyway, the words that came into my mind are from Wanderers Nachtlied:

> Uber allen Gipfein
> Ist Ruh,

In allen Wipfeln
Spurest du
Kaum einen Hauch;
Die Vogelein schweigen im Walde.
Warte nur, balde
Ruhest du auch.

I will translate for those of my readers unfamiliar with German:

O'er all the hill-tops
Is quiet now,
In all the tree-tops
Hearest thou
Hardly a breath;
The birds are asleep in the trees:
Wait; soon like these
Thou too shall rest.

But I was rudely awakened from my reveries by my brother who suddenly grabbed hold of my right knee and hissed: 'Hell's bells, Teddy! See what I've found!'

'What is it?' I asked a little irritably. 'Have you left something behind at the Club?'

'No, no, no. It's what I've picked up there, young fellow-me-lad.'

'Not a sore prick or worse,' I suggested facetiously.

'Not that either,' rejoined Cecil. 'But I did pick up something at Maison Alfred all right. Look, Teddy, you see this newspaper that I took from the hall table. Well, I didn't actually ask Soames if I could take it as he was busy hailing a cab for us. Anyhow, I decided that the gentleman who had purchased the paper would hardly miss it and in any case he would in all probability want to buy a later edition.

'But the chap who left it out in the hall has left a letter inside the paper and it's pretty hot stuff, I can tell you. Would you like to read it? It's addressed to a Miss Kitty Easthouse from – My God, Teddy! It's from our Uncle Arthur!!!'

Our Uncle Arthur was a respected lawyer who had only recently been appointed one of Her Majesty's judges in the

High Court. What was Uncle Arthur doing at Maison Alfred – as if we didn't know!

'Be sure your sin will find you out, Reverend Shackleton would say,' said Cecil. 'Funny though, I thought that Uncle Arthur was only keen on polo especially as Aunt Philothea has a figure roughly approximate to a pony's backside.'

'Well, he wasn't about to play a chukka at Maison Alfred.' I commented. 'The old devil! Mind, it might be useful to tackle him about it if we ever find ourselves in trouble with the law! Anyway, let me read it.'

With a guffaw Cecil passed over the closely written sheets. 'What a twerp to keep such an intimate letter inside your newspaper.'

'He has simply put it there prior to posting it,' I said.

'I know,' said Cecil. 'Let's post it for him!'

'That is very kind of you.'

'Not really, Teddy, as I aim to compose a rather interesting post-script.'

'What on earth do you mean?'

'Wait, we're almost at Sir Lionel's. I'll tell you about my plan as soon as possible.'

Cecil paid off the cab and we knocked on the door of Sir Lionel's rather grand house which was situated off Avenue Road at the North end of Regent's Park. His butler, Denis, answered the door and informed us that we were expected. He showed us into a beautifully decorated drawing room. We did not have to wait long before Sir Lionel and Father came in from the library. After exchanging greetings, Father told us that we were to be given an extra treat.

'I am going home now and must leave shortly to catch the six o'clock train. But Sir Lionel has generously suggested that you two boys might like to stay over in London tonight. He has tickets for the theatre which he cannot use and rather than let his box be empty, he is offering it to you.'

'How kind of you, Sir Lionel. Teddy and I would like to thank you for your hospitality.'

'Not at all, not at all,' said the genial baronet. 'It so happens that some of your clothes are still here from your previous visit last Spring, when your dear Mama took you both to the Italian Opera. The only slight inconvenience will be that you will have to share a bedroom as my two spare rooms are being redecorated and the smell of the paint which was applied today is really quite overpowering. You'll both be far better off sharing a room – so long as neither of you snores!'

'It is good of you, Lionel,' said my Father. 'You are so fond of the theatre that I am surprised that you would miss seeing the great Charles Irving play Macbeth.'

A great pity, I thought, that Sir Lionel did not patronise the music halls which at this time were just beginning in their present form, but as we were studying this play at school I knew that seeing it acted would help me pass my summer examinations *cum laude*.

'Well, yes, ordinarily I would most certainly attend the performance,' said Sir Lionel. 'But I have been asked to go to a lecture by Jonathan Arkley. It seems that the whole of Society is under the spell of one Professor McChesney from Manchester who is supposed to be an expert on self-healing.

'Arkley is sure that the fellow is a charlatan and plans to stand up during question time and expose him. That should be quite fun so I don't expect the evening to be all as dull as it sounds and I can see Irving tomorrow night with Lord Bracknell who is always glad to escape one of his wife's ghastly dinner parties. Lord Bracknell is a good example to show you boys why I never married.'

'McChesney will be piles of laughs!' muttered Cecil and I only just managed to keep a straight face.

After Father left, Denis showed us to our room. Fortunately, we both had full evening dress hanging in the wardrobe so we could go to the Lyceum properly turned out. At our request Denis prepared a hot bath and Sir Lionel popped his head round the door to tell us that he had written a note to the Secretary of his Club to enable us to eat there afterwards, for his cook was unwell and that we would do far better at the Savile. His carriage too was at our disposal as he would be travelling to the Aeolian Hall with Doctor Arkley.

'Here's a five-pound note for use in an emergency, plus your return railway tickets for tomorrow. I'm dining at the Travellers with Doctor Arkley who will be here any minute as we have some previous business to finish before leaving for Professor McChesney's lecture.'

We wished each other a pleasant evening and after luxuriating in a hot tub and dressing myself up to the nines I felt like a real man about town.

Cecil and I were sipping whisky and sodas in Sir Lionel's drawing room when Cecil produced Uncle Arthur's letter.

'You'll have a good laugh reading this, Teddy,' he said, passing the letter to me.

I have kept the letter (throughout my life I have been an inveterate collector of ephemera) and so I can reproduce it in its entirety. Here it is:

My Darling Kitty,

How my mouth yearns for another kiss of your succulent cunney lips! The last time I buried my face in your hairy bush was so delightful that I can hardly wait for the next time! I dream of you constantly and sometimes fancy that I am back on your bed with your lovely naked bottom sitting on my face so that I can kiss and suck your pussey!

At other times in my dreams you catch hold of my cock and rub it up to a fine erection, saying sweetly: 'I refuse to let you go, Mr Pego, unless you promise to fuck me!'

You cannot wonder at these dreams, sweetheart, for they are only repetitions of the facts of the day!

Give my love to your beautiful cunt which I hope will be conjoined with my prick very, very soon.

From your own ever devoted admirer,

Arthur

'Good grief, what on earth shall we do about Uncle Arthur?' I exclaimed.

'Well, I don't suggest we should peach on him to Aunt Philothea,' said Cecil warmly. 'After all, I would imagine that she only opens her legs once a month if he's lucky. Although with her looks he probably doesn't want any more fucking than that – at least, with her.

'However, the silly clot deserves to be taught a lesson for his carelessness. After all, he has not only compromised himself but also Kitty Easthouse. Now where do I know that name? I

60

am sure it rings a bell somewhere in my memory. Anyhow, I have an idea for a jolly jape. I'm going to write another letter to Miss Easthouse and I'll get old Pemberfield, Sir Lionel's coachman, to deliver them both in the same envelope – look, Uncle has written her address down on his letter. My, what a coincidence, she lives only three minutes walk away in St John's Wood High Street.'

'What are you going to write?' I asked, my curiosity being aroused to the highest pitch.

'Come over to the desk and simply watch me write the letter,' rejoined my brother, who was to show me, not for the first time, that he possessed a most creative imagination, for this is what he wrote:

Dearest Kitty,

I quite forgot to mention that my two young nephews, Cecil and Teddy Parsifal will be in London today (Wednesday, June 17th). Teddy had just celebrated his fifteenth birthday and I cannot think of a finer present for the young scamp than to become acquainted with your lovely pussey! His brother Cecil, although only seventeen, is, I am reliably informed by our mutual friend the Rev. Robert Bacon, extraordinarily fond of fucking and indeed is quite expert in *l'art de faire l'amour*. I believe his special delight is having his tool sucked and I know how much he will enjoy thrusting his young cock between your lips to be milked by your ever eager tongue and mouth. My own prick is rising just by thinking about such a naughty scenario!

As you well know, jealousy is not among my mortal sins, so you have my full permission to fuck both the boys. I would suggest that to begin with you should let Cecil fuck you from behind whilst Teddy eats your juicy pussey. But I am quite happy to leave the details to you.

I would always expect to spend at least fifty guineas on young Teddy's birthday present so if you are agreeable I will send you a cheque for that amount. They are staying the night in town with that old reprobate Sir Lionel Trapes whose penis must one day fall off if there is any justice in the world – the rogue rogered my dear lady wife only last

61

Thursday – but I must admit that Lionel would never peach to the boys' Papa so my birthday present would remain a secret.

The lads are going to the theatre tonight. They could be with you at around eleven o'clock. Send a note back to them via Pemberfield, Sir Lionel's coachman and they will attend you at that time.

My love as always,

Arthur

P.S. I have dictated this letter to Miss Formby of the Jim Jam Club who is kindly acting as my personal secretary whilst my own factotum Mr Nettleton is away in India supervising my business interests in the Punjab.

'You are not really going to send that letter, Cecil?' I gasped.

'Just watch me!' said Cecil merrily, ringing the bell for the butler.

'Ah, Denis,' said Cecil as the old butler came in. 'I want this letter to be sent round as soon as possible. And would you please ask Pemberfield to wait as there will be an immediate reply.'

'Very good, sir,' said Denis. 'I will see to the matter straight away.'

'Good fellow that,' said Cecil as Denis left the room. 'He knows the secrets of at least half of London Society. But he will never reveal what he knows. Last month I heard Sir Lionel tell Father that some brash young journalist tried to bribe Denis to spill the beans about Lord Alfred Douglas and his telegraph boys.

'And even though Denis even knows the vintage of the bottle of port Lady Pence attempted to stick up Lord Euston's bottom, not a word passed his lips. Oh, he is the very soul of discretion and we can roll in at two in the morning without any trouble. Mind, I'll slip him a sov. for having to stay up so late.'

'You are pretty certain that Kitty Easthouse will agree to the terms?' I asked.

'I would swear a thousand pounds on it,' said Cecil with

great confidence. 'Why the very thought of it makes my prick really swell up!'

I looked across and saw the bulge in my brother's breeches and he undid his buttons to let out his rampant red-headed cock, caressing it in his hand until it stood in all its manly glory, stiff and hard as marble with the hot blood looking ready to burst from his distended veins.

'Put it away, Cecil,' I hissed. 'Suppose one of the servants came in.'

'I wouldn't mind,' said Cecil, happily stroking his shaft. 'Indeed young Millie the parlourmaid could do a far better job than I on my cock! Whoops, I'm going to come, Teddy!'

Always a considerate fellow, Cecil moved to the fireplace in order to steer the jets of spunk that shot out from his cock into the empty grate.

'I wonder if sperm is inflammable,' he said thoughtfully, buttoning up his flies.

'It may surprise you but I've never attempted to set light to mine,' I said with heavy sarcasm.

'All right, all right,' said Cecil with his usual good humour. 'Look, I'm quite respectable now. Let's have a whisky and soda whilst we wait for Pemberfield to return.'

Neither of us have ever been great imbibers of spirits although Dr Arkley has always assured me that an occasional nip of Scotch is truly beneficial to one's continuing good health. However, we enjoyed our little drink and read the newspapers until in just only an hour or even a little less, old Pemberfield returned.

Fortunately, I had not taken up my elder brother's wager for indeed, Miss Easthouse had readily consented to meet us at her house after the theatre. What a night beckoned us onwards! Truly, this would be an evening to remember!

Indeed, after Cecil had torn open the pink envelope in which Kitty Easthouse had couched her reply, I could scarcely contain my excitement. And this was further heightened when Cecil passed over to me Kitty's response to 'Uncle Arthur's' invitation.

It read as follows:

'Dear Cecil and Teddy,

I have received a lovely letter from your dear Uncle Arthur asking me to provide a very special birthday treat for young Teddy – and I agree absolutely with your thoughtful uncle that it would be wrong for Cecil to miss out on some saucy sport as from what he tells me, Cecil has a taste for the delights of love.

I look forward to meeting you both then, at eleven o'clock at my house. To get you both in the mood, perhaps you would like to know how I first met your sweet Uncle. It so happened that I was caught in a sudden shower of rain some six weeks ago whilst taking a stroll through Regent's Park. Your uncle was also passing the afternoon listening to the military band but he had wisely brought an umbrella along with him. He walked briskly over to the tree under which I was attempting to take shelter and said: 'Madam, please allow me to offer you the protection of my umbrella as the branches of this beech are proving inadequate to the task of protecting your beautiful dress.'

Well, such gallantry deserved a reward for I have always believed that manners maketh the man and no man however wealthy or good-looking could hope to win my heart (or my cunt) if he behaved in a boorish fashion.

Anyhow, he asked me to dine with him at Fine's Chop House that evening and I accepted his invitation. We drank champagne throughout the evening and this is a drink that always puts me in the mood. Our conversation over dinner was animated and I must confess that a large part of my attention was concentrated on my new beau and what I'd like to do with him.

You will soon know how it is when you are sexually attracted to someone – there is a real energy that magnetically connects you both and the plain truth of the matter was that all I wanted to do was to lunge across the table, kiss him long and wet and get my hands down around his thick, delicious cock and ravish him completely.

We exchanged heated glances across the table and I knew that Arthur was just as randy as I was! I was wearing a black evening dress with a low neckline and I calculated that if I leaned forward in a certain way he would be given a clear view of my ripe breasts. Just the thought of this had my titties standing erect and longing to be loved and sucked.

It was all too much to bear so I slipped off my shoes and moved a silk-clad foot up between his legs. Under the cover of the linen tablecloth I was able to feel the meaty bulge between his legs and soon I was stroking the stiff length of his shaft with my foot. He began grinding his groin against me in desire but above the table was all calm as I softly declined the waiter's offer to refill my glass with some more bubbly. Arthur too looked stoical and except for the odd steamy glance when he thought no-one was looking, he never let on that his prick was threatening to burst out of the confines of his trousers.

As perhaps you know, Arthur has a great sense of humour and before I knew it, he too had slipped off a shoe and I felt his foot insinuate itself between my legs. I was so aroused as his toes rubbed around my crotch that my silky knickers were soon wet with my juices.

We could hardly wait to finish our meal and it was even more difficult to contain ourselves in the cab. But we managed to restrain ourselves until we were back in Arthur's London *pied a terre* in Welbeck Mews. No sooner had we walked into his front room than we began to tear off our clothes. Arthur has a fine physique and I admired his thick prick which was swelling by the second. I stood there trembling with excitement in the middle of his living room in just my silken knickers and stockings held up by my frilly garters.

He took me in his arms and we kissed passionately. His cologne smelled beautifully and I adored the sensation of his abundant chest hair tickling my nipples. He put his hands around my bottom and presented his cock into my belly. I didn't touch it at first as I had no desire to appear a wanton but as he took my hand and wrapped my fingers around the throbbing shaft, I gently peeled back his foreskin whilst his fingertips slid their way into my now juicy pussey.

"Egad! What a lovely little filly you are, Kitty! I must have you here and now," said Arthur softly. "Come into the bedroom and I am going to take you from behind. You will enjoy it, I promise you."

Somewhat nervously I followed him into the bedroom and watched with interest as he smeared pomade on his burgeoning cock. Dear Arthur motioned me to stand by the side of the bed and then placed my left knee on the quilt. I leaned forward looking a little apprehensively over my shoulder as Arthur smoothed his hands over my buttocks and then pulled them apart as I felt his gorgeous knob jiggling between my now dripping cunney lips.

He slowly slid his rampant pole into my juicy cunt and then withdrew all but an inch before slowly sliding it in again. He increased the tempo as he felt my excitement rising until with a grunt he slammed the entire length of his thick shaft inside me so that his black mossy grove of pubic hair brushed sensuously against my bum. Oh, how exciting it all was! In no time at all I was bucking and writhing like a crazed beast and I shouted out "Fuck me! Fuck me, darling Arthur!" in sheer unadulterated lust!

Arthur too was now past the point of any return – "I am going to spunk into you, Kitty!" he shouted. "Here it comes!" – and with a delighted yell he pumped his jets of love juice just as I too reached the dazzling heights of a magnificent spend. What a fantastic fuck this was – and it was the first time I had been fucked "doggie style" (if you will pardon the popular description of the act). But as Arthur explained to me later, despite the mendacious warnings from the pulpits and elsewhere, a fuck from behind is often extremely pleasing for the woman as it enables her clitty to be more stimulated than when a shaft enters the cunt from the front.

Enough now, for all these lewd memories are making me eager for immediate relief and I must wait until eleven o'clock when I hope that both of you will be able to satisfy my voracious sensual desires. If either of you can perform even half as well as your Uncle, I shall not have waited in vain!

Kitty Easthouse

Cecil breathed heavily as I passed the letter back to him.

'Well, young Teddy, no tossing off for you tonight!' he exclaimed. 'You will enjoy a grand fuck with Kitty and I. Let's first have a bite of supper and then on to the theatre.

'But do not drink too much for you remember what the Porter in Macbeth says of the effects of drink to Macduff: "Lechery, sir, it provokes and unprovokes; it provokes the desire, but it takes away the performance: therefore much drink may be said to be an equivocator with lechery: it makes him and it mars him; it sets him on and it takes him off; it persuades him and disheartens him; makes him stand to, and not stand to; in conclusion, equivocates him in a sleep, and giving him the life, leaves him."'

Although I well realise that those reading my memoirs in *The Oyster* (long may it flourish!) are perhaps more interested in my exploits *in flagrante delicto*, I am sure there are many, in a minority, perhaps, who will readily forgive my noting down in some detail now my remembrances of that magnificent production of the Scottish play staged at the Lyceum by the company lead by Mr Irving.

Cecil and I sat transfixed by the power of his performance and the quality of the entertainment. In the foyer beforehand we listened to the rumours on the cost of the production – on the costumes and on the scenery. Sir Arthur Sullivan's music was known only to a select few; people whispered of a golden dinner service for the banqueting scene; the three witches were to be such as never been before beheld.

We were not to be disappointed; Mr Irving is a tragedian of the finest rank. In the latter part of the play especially, he rose in awesome power as the toils gather round Macbeth. All through the scenes up to the final struggle nothing could well be better than Mr Irving's picture of the man. His courage is undaunted and he will fight against any odds until he finds on Macduff's avowal that he was from his mother's womb 'untimely torn' that the weird sisters have paltered him in a double sense. Then his arm falls powerless, he reels like one smitten with disease, he seeks to avoid the encounter until, stung by Macduff's taunts, the old courage flashes up – 'before my body I throw my warlike shield' – and the noblest part of him is his death.

Miss Ellen Terry's presence as Lady Macbeth added an extra lustre to this admirable *coup de theatre*. Our senses were spellbound as that enchanting being in gorgeous robes reads her husband's letter and determines that nothing can come between the new Thane of Cawdor and the throne of Scotland. Yet soon afterwards we suspend our disbelief that this glorious looking woman is capable of calling upon the spirits to unsex her and fill her with the direst cruelties, a woman capable of urging her consort onwards to deeds of unspeakable horror.

One last word on this magnificent spectacle. The scene in which the weird sisters appear for the final time is admirably managed. The cauldron-work and the procession of grisly kings, even the witches disappear; and Sir Arthur Sullivan's lovely music breaks upon the audience as the gloom and darkness of witchcraft melt into space whilst a glorious dawn is greeted by white-robed spirits who sing 'Come away, come away.' – a surpassingly beautiful scene as gradually the sky changes from rosy dawn to noontide light, the curtain falls on a picture which precipitates Mr Irving's appearance. And as Cecil and I heard Sir Richard Segal say afterwards, this Lyceum *Macbeth* was about the grandest revival that, in this age of theatrical art, the present generation has seen. Mr Irving, Miss Terry and the entire company well deserved all the praise and honours lavished upon them by the critics.

Now I return to my narrative proper and again crave the indulgence of those readers uninterested in the theatre (of which I myself have always been extremely fond) but they have naught to fear for there are many further stories, all true, of my own and several other people's intimate affairs.

And so, as Pepys nightly commented, to bed. But what a bedroom frolic my brother Cecil and I enjoyed with Kitty Easthouse, one of the most enthusiastic girls with whom I have ever cavorted.

Beforehand, Cecil and I had little knowledge of her expertise in *l'art de fair l'amour* although her spectacularly rude letter to us boded well for the hours ahead.

We were shown into Kitty's opulently furnished drawing room by a silver haired old butler and after just a few moments, an enchanting creature entered the room – no wonder my Uncle Arthur had offered to shield her from the rain regardless as to whether his own clothes would be left without protection from however hard a downpour!

Kitty could not have been more than twenty-eight years of age (I found out later that in fact she was only twenty-five) and she looked ravishing in an emerald green dress cut low in the front which accentuated her exquisitely large, well-proportioned breasts. Kitty was head-turningly pretty, being of dark complexion with large, languid hazel eyes. Her full lips were a succulent shade of red, earlier moistened by a sip or two of claret and when she smiled a welcome to us she showed pearl white teeth which sparkled through even the muted electric light of her tastefully fashioned home.

'Hello boys,' she said in a soft sensual voice, 'you must be Cecil being the taller and this is obviously young Teddy of whom I have heard so much from your Uncle Arthur.'

For some moments Cecil and I stood transfixed by the beauty of this delicious girl. Kitty smiled at our shyness and said: 'Come now, you two, there is no need to be bashful. Sit down on this couch and let us see if you two are really chips off the old block as Uncle Arthur has intimated to me.'

We did as we were bid and she sat between us, her hands touching each of our thighs in turn. 'You know,' she murmured, 'my breasts are so sensitive. Why, I can spend just by having my titties played with. Would you two nice boys like to see that?'

We nodded our assent and Kitty unbuttoned the French silk blouse that Uncle Arthur had purchased for her at Madame Adrienne's famous Mayfair establishment. She shrugged the garment from her shoulders and (for as we were to discover very soon she was wearing no underclothes that evening) her splendidly round succulent breasts were naked to our delighted view.

Kitty's fingers deftly unbuttoned our trousers and our two naked stiff cocks were soon in her sweet grasp. I thought that I would spunk just by drinking in the beauty of Kitty's beautiful breasts which were as big as those I had seen in the picture book of *poses plastiques* one of the boys in school had smuggled in from Paris last term. Her brown nipples were as hard as little rocks, sticking out at least a whole inch in length. Following the dear girl's directions, I held one tittie and Cecil held the other and we squeezed and rubbed them as she wriggled and squirmed with pleasure, holding on to our cocks all the while as

69

her whole frame shook with the pleasures of her climax.

So quickly had she climaxed that neither Cecil nor myself had squirted our sperm and I watched as Kitty let go my cock and slid to the carpet, holding on to Cecil's cock which she placed between her magnificent breasts, squeezing them together so that my brother was treated to a most delicious tittie-fuck. 'Now then Teddy, kiss my pussey!' she cried out so I knelt down behind Cecil and as I put my head under her dress Kitty wrapped her legs around my neck. I buried my face in her silky thatch of black pubic hair. I kissed her salivating pussey lips and began licking her slit with long, lascivious swipes. Her vermilion pussey lips parted and between them I felt with my tongue for her stiff little clitty which I rolled around in my mouth.

'Oooh! Oooh! Ahh! Ahh! AHH!' cried Kitty. 'Suck harder Teddy, suck harder and make me come!'

I sucked and slurped with great ardour, rolling my tongue round and round, lapping up the sweet love juices which were now flowing freely from Kitty's juicy cunt. She began to spend as her hips bucked violently, her back rippled and then from her cunney spurted a fine creamy emission that flooded my mouth with a milky essence which I greedily lapped up until Kitty shuddered into limpness as the delicious crisis slowly melted away.

Cecil's cock was still being massaged between those hugh globes and Kitty pulled his bum cheeks forward so that he was sitting astride her as she slipped his throbbing shaft between her red painted lips and gave my brother a most delightful sucking off. Her mouth worked up and down, licking the length of his prick, taking playful little licks at the uncapped knob with her little tongue. When she felt Cecil was about to spend, her hands gripped the base of his cock and pumped up and down as she sucked his balls but quickly transferred her mouth back to his cock to milk his prick of every last drop of milky froth.

Somehow I had just managed to refrain from handling my own cock although the temptation to toss myself off was almost overpowering. My reward was now to come as Cecil moved off Kitty who quickly tugged her dress over her shoulders and now quite nude she turned round and climbed on top of me, straddling my cock with her still wet, juicy slit.

Treating me to a long ride, she·fucked me slowly, taking in every inch I had to offer, sitting flat on my crotch, moving back and forth as my cock prepared to pump spouts of spunk inside her eager cunney.

I grabbed her hips and began to fuck her from underneath, working my cock into a frenzy. I could no longer wait to spend and that is exactly what I did after a few deep thrusts. Kitty moaned with pleasure as the sperm boiled up in my balls and shot out of my shaft into her warm, inviting pussey. Even after my abundant drenching of her womb, Kitty continued to move up and down on my now deflating cock, hoping to milk more spunk out of my twitching tool.

Cecil stood up and padded across to the table and opened a bottle of Bollinger '72 (Kitty knew the difference between good and indifferent champagne) and after she had refreshed herself she said: 'I don't think it fair that only Teddy should have the pleasure of fucking my cunt. I'm quite ready for another joust if you two are feeling up to it. Let us go into the bedroom and continue our sport in there. Teddy, perhaps you would kindly bring another bottle of champagne and our glasses – there is a tray just behind you. Cecil, you come with me.' She grasped my brother by his cock and led him not unwillingly to the bedroom as I did as I was told and followed them into the room.

We now removed our remaining clothes and I sat on a chair as Kitty pulled Cecil close to her and said: 'My darling boy! Tell me how you are going to fuck me!'

From an early age Cecil was always the most articulate member of the family and with only a momentary pause as he slipped his hands around her back to caress the plump cheeks of her warm bottom, he murmured: 'You wish to know how I am going to fuck you, Kitty? Well, I shall first mount you and then I shall decide which way we shall take our pleasure. But first I shall lie upon your belly and insert my thick, long cock slowly in your deliciously inviting little snatch. Then, by moving my rod in and out of your juicy cranny we shall be jointly intoxicated with delight and each shall expel our liquid pleasures – you upon my cock and balls and I by the velvety clinging of your slit.'

'Oh, that's well said, Cecil my dear boy,' she breathed, 'so please let me feel the actions to follow those lovely words and

71

fuck the arse off me!'

How splendid the two lovers looked as Kitty slowly ran her tongue down my brother's slim body. Cecil's prick began to rise again almost with the tenderness of a butterfly's flight as Kitty's mouth reached his naval. He writhed in delicious agony as her silky dark hair brushed against his now throbbing member which ached for further attention. She brushed his cock with her cheek and caressed his heavy, hanging balls with her warm, wet lips.

It appeared to me that Cecil's testicles were appreciably larger than mine, but then I recalled the good Doctor Stevenson's book which assured its readers that there was not the slightest medical connection between the size of the testes and their spunk-producing function.

But I digress – Kitty's smooth hands smoothed over Cecil's slender frame, sending him into fresh raptures of delight. Then, moving quickly, sliding herself on top of him, hungrily searching for his lips, they kissed passionately, moving their thighs together until their pubic muffs rubbed roughly against each other. Cecil's stiff cock probed the entrance to the exquisite little crack, throbbing with a powerful intensity until Kitty eased her hips, grunting with delight as the swollen knob forced its way between her pussey lips, massaging her clitty until Cecil arched his own frame upwards, plunging his trusty tool inside her wetness.

I could not bear to stand motionless any longer as Kitty shouted: 'Oh, Cecil, keep sliding that lovely cock in and out! What a marvellous young lover you are! More, more, more!'

My own right hand simply flew to my own proudly erect prick and I quickly frigged myself off. Wave after wave of pleasure engulfed me as I pumped spurt after spurt of my hot, sticky cream over the entwined lovers, who oblivious to my coating of the pair with jism, were still jerking in new paroxyms, panting and biting,then screaming, with excitement as the summit of the mountain of love was finally scaled and they sank back, sated, on the soft sheets.

I joined the happy couple and Kitty laughed, saying: 'Let us see if Teddy's young cock and balls are in top working order!' And without giving me further time to recover my senses, the lewd girl commenced immediately to play with my prick which she hugged, pressing it to her large breasts, squeezing it between them, pressing it against her cheeks, gently rubbing it with her hands and taking the uncapped head between her lips, softly biting it and tickling it with the end of her tongue. Then she suddenly thrust the whole shaft into her mouth and by her exquisite palating and sucking, proudly erected the monster till her little lips could hardly clasp it.

Cecil was lying on his back, his cock again now stiff as a flagpole and Kitty gently eased herself upon it and began to pump herself forwards and backwards.

'Ah, Teddy,' she gasped, easing my cock from her mouth, 'will you give me the double pleasure of fucking my bottom whilst I ride Cecil? Go behind me and wet your cock with some pomade, which you will find in that little pink jar on the side table. Then come back and slowly shove your gorgeous cock up my bum.

Ever obedient, I did what was gently requested and knelt behind Kitty who thrust herself forwards as far as possible and raised her beautiful bum cheeks so that I was given full view of her little wrinkled arse-hole that beckoned me in so invitingly. I took hold of my cock in my hand and carefully positioned my knob between her bottom cheeks, which I grasped and opened wide the crack in between so that her bum-hole was fully opened to my impending attack. Then I pushed forward and despite my initial worry that I might injure the dear girl, I shoved slowly and steadily until it felt impossible to reach any further.

Kitty writhed and twisted so much that she could hardly keep Cecil's cock inside her but soon I could feel my prick rubbing against his with only the thin divisional membrane between them. It was all so exciting that we both spent quickly, our joint spunking deluging both cunt and arse, spurting the frothy jism over each other's balls at every thrust.

Cecil was now *hors de combat* and was forced to retire but Kitty saw that my cock still seemed to have a twitch of life about it.

'Are you still able to continue, Teddy?' Kitty asked me, with a roguish twinkle in her eye.

'I believe I can enjoy one further ride on the roundabout of love,' I proudly answered. And without further ado, I sank to my knees in front of her lusciously juicy cunney. Like nipples, like clitty, say the Hussars, and Kitty proved the truth of the adage, her stiff little clitty gleaming long and erect through the bush of her mossy black pubic grove.

I let my tongue travel the length of Kitty's velvety smooth body, lingering briefly at her belly button before sliding down to her thighs. I was still in a kneeling position when I parted her soft, lightly scented pubic hair with my fingertips to reveal her swollen clitty. As I worked my face into the cleft between her thighs, I could not help but notice how clean and appealing her pussey looked after its coating of love juices.

I placed my lips over her clitoris and sucked it into my mouth where the tip of my tongue began to explore it from all directions and I could feel it growing even larger as her legs wriggled and twitched up and down along the sides of my body.

But just as I was about to proceed further I heard a door open and a girl's voice cry out: 'Kitty! What an earth do you think you're doing?'

'I am having my cunney sucked, my dear Rosemary, what do you think I am doing, playing cricket?' said Kitty coldly, angry that her enjoyment was being interrupted.

Of course, the surprise led me to wrench my lips away from the succulent morsel upon which I was chewing so nicely and I looked up to see a pretty red-haired girl looking across the room at us with ill-concealed irritation.

'Just what are these men doing in our bedroom?' said this petite sprite with some sharpness.

'Our bedroom?' repeated Cecil, raising his eyebrows.

'Yes, our bedroom, if you must know,' she said. 'Pray leave us immediately, gentlemen, you have no further business here.'

'Oh, I think that is rather for me to decide,' drawled Kitty. 'Rosemary, may I introduce Cecil and Teddy Parsifal to you – and gentlemen, let me introduce Miss Rosemary Sharpe-Somerset who resides with me when she is staying in London.

'Rosemary, you will enjoy fucking these two boys – Cecil is an accomplished lover and young Teddy here has the most extraordinary staying power for one of such tender years.'

So here was a potentially most embarrassing situation. I had no real experience of tribades and Rosemary's preference for her own sex in matters of *l'amour* was for me a strange affair.

Meanwhile Rosemary began to berate Kitty for welcoming boys into her bed. 'Fucking remains a means of making a woman inferior!' she trumpeted. 'All that pushing and thrusting simply represents the male acting out his supposed domination of us, the inferior sex.

'Historically, women have always had their sexuality controlled. For most of us the opportunity to define our own wants and desires does not exist. We who reject men are forced to keep our secret as such thoughts are taboo and we must find our pleasures where we can. Now you are betraying the cause!'

'Oh, come now, that's going a bit far!' protested Cecil.

'Indeed it is,' cried Kitty, a flush of anger now clearly visible on her face. 'I fully believe in the freedom of adults to do anything they like to each in bed as long as both consent and, as Mrs. Campbell says, they don't do it in the street and frighten the horses. But I enjoy having a strong, thick prick up my cunney just as much as a dildoe or even your wicked little fingers, so there!'

'Oooh! You cat!' squealed Rosemary and forgetting, perhaps, that Cecil and I were there, she sat down on the bed and stripped off her clothes in amazingly quick time. She possessed a boyish figure, with small but nicely rounded breasts and both her cherry-red nipples were like erect little stalks. She may have been small but she was strong for, before you could say Jack Robinson, she had turned Kitty on to her tummy and exposed her generous bum cheeks to our delighted gaze. Rosemary then began to smack Kitty's beautiful bum, lightly at first but then harder and in rapid succession until the poor girl cried out: 'Oh! Oh! Oh, no more, Rosie, I beg of you. No, no, no, no more. Ow! Ow! OW! Ooooh!' as she wriggled and winced as her skin turned from milk white to bright pink.

'Quiet now, Kitty!' snapped Rosemary. 'You have been a very naughty girl and all naughty girls get slapped. Besides I just adore to see your bum change colour. It should always have that pinkish tinge and anyway I love the way your bottom cheeks jiggle as I slap them!'

By now, both Cecil's cock and my own were rock-hard as we watched this stimulating exhibition. In no time Cecil was on his knees next to Kitty who, despite her tingling bum, eagerly clamped her full red lips around Cecil's cock and began sucking his prick with unashamed gusto.

'Come here, you wretched boy!' Rosemary called out to me, without missing one beat of her rhythm as she continued to slap Kitty's bum. 'I suppose I must give you the same treatment for as a good Socialist I believe in fair shares for all!'

I needed no second invitation as I jumped on the bed to complete the quartet. Mercifully for Kitty's bum, Rosemary ceased her spanking and circled her hands around my pulsating prick which already had a blob of milky spunk on the knob. She jammed down my foreskin and bending low, lashed her tongue round my pole thudding away like a steamhammer. I could see that Kitty's ministrations with her mouth had already brought Cecil to the point of climax and Kitty greedily milked his cock of spunk as she sucked up noisily every drain of love-juice.

Now Kitty raised herself on her hands and knees and lowering her pretty head began to kiss Rosemary's mossy ginger bush which I could see was already damp with excitement. Her pink tongue slipped effortlessly in and out of her friend's cunt.

Now I pulled my prick out of Rosemary's mouth and positioned myself behind Kitty whose rounded bottom cheeks were moving in fine rhythm as she sucked contentedly on Rosemary's pussey. The darling girl then reached out behind her and took hold of my throbbing cock and directed its purple domed knob to the glorious cheeks of her bum and to the tight-looking wrinkled brown hole that lay between them.

Cecil thoughtfully plastered my prick with the pomade as I attacked the fortress with vigour. 'Aaah! Not so deep, my dear Teddy, not so deep! Oh, pray, enough – Oh! Oh! Ah, yes, you're there!' she shrieked.

I rested a moment or two and then began slowly to pull in and out as I fucked her arse-hole. I could tell by the wriggling of her plump bum that she was enjoying it as much as I was and she took my hands to her front so that I could frig her cunt as all the while she licked and lapped at Rosemary's pussey which was now expelling a veritable flood of love-juice.

Rosemary's wriggling about and the delicious contractions of her bum-hole brought down a copious discharge of the nectar of love.

'Oh, heavens!' she exclaimed. 'Ah! what pleasure I feel rushing into me! How hot it is and – yes, now I come too; it is running from me. My God! What delight! Ah, what lus – lus – luscious pleasure!'

She almost swooned away in delight for as I was fucking her bum and frigging her clitty at the same time, she was procured of the exquisite double pleasure.

So you see, dear reader, both Kitty and Rosemary were capable of extracting pleasure from intimate relations with both genders, an ability which I must confess I do not share, keeping my bed strictly reserved for members of the female sex.

We were now totally exhausted and so we refreshed ourselves with some more champagne. It was now so late that we sent word that we would not be returning to Sir Lionel's until after breakfast. I was concerned that Father would hear of our escapade but Cecil said: 'Don't worry, Teddy, Sir Lionel is a man of the world and won't preach – and I don't think that Uncle Arthur will say anything when he finds out because if he says anything, he'll have to do an awful lot of explaining to Aunt Ada!'

I talked at some length with Rosemary, who was studying political economy at the nearby Bedford College. Although her father was the possessor of a vast hereditary estate in Cumberland, Rosemary had become an ardent Socialist. I had no great interest in politics (our family were to a man supporters of Mr Gladstone and of course a distant cousin, Oliver Parsifal, has been for many years the Liberal MP for a Cornish constituency) but I was curious to know what had attracted this rich young girl to sit at the feet of Burns, O'Driscoll and Mann.

Rosemary explained: 'We have witnessed during this century an unparalleled sudden increase in our powers of production, resulting in huge accumulations of wealth. But only the owners of capital have benefitted, while for the great numbers there has been an increase only in misery and insecurity. Unskilled labourers are falling into destitution and even the best-paid artisans labour under the permanent menace of being thrown out of work in consequence of some of the continuous and unavoidable fluctuations of industry and caprices of capital.

'The chasm between the modern millionaire who squanders

all in a vain, gorgeous luxury and the pauper reduced to a mere existence is growing more and more. The working classes will no longer endure this unfair division of society and in proportion, as all classes take a 'more lively part in public affairs, their longing for equality will rightly become stronger and their demands for reform become louder and louder until they can be ignored no more.

'The worker is entitled to claim his share in the wealth that he creates – not only in management of production but the additional well-being in the higher enjoyments of science and art. These claims conform with my natural feelings of justice and they find support in a daily growing minority amongst the privileged classes themselves.

'Socialism has thus become *the* idea of the nineteenth century and neither coercion nor pseudo-reforms can stop its further growth!'

This was quite a speech and we sat silently contemplating her words, which frankly made little sense to me, until Cecil broke the serious mood that had descended upon us by saying: 'Well, if Socialism means fair shares for all, then I am all in favour! Especially if it means a fair share of pussey!' he roared, tossing back a bumper of champagne and presenting the company with a capital stiff-stander.

But Kitty, between whose bum cheeks he had placed his prick, wriggled across to Rosemary saying: 'Oh, darling, you are such an orator. Let us celebrate your discourse with some love-making.'

And the two girls dissolved into a passionate embrace, kissing rapturously and thrusting their tongues into each other's mouths. Rosemary clasped Kitty firmly by the buttocks whilst with two fingers of her right hand frigged the girl's bottom and pussey at the same time. She then laid Kitty down, kissing her lips gently whilst softly rubbing her huge breasts until the nipples stiffened into hard little cherry bullets. Then she stroked Kitty's pussey as the girl opened her legs wide giving a glorious view of the paraphenalia of love. She had a quite splendid mount covered with glossy black hair; the serrated lips of her cunt slightly parted from which projected quite three inches I am sure, a stiff fleshy clitoris as big as a thumb. Rosemary opened the lips with her fingers then bending her head down, passed her tongue lasciviously around the sensitive parts, taking that lovely clitty in her mouth, rolling her tongue around it and playfully biting it with her little teeth.

It was exciting to watch and all too exciting for Kitty who cried: 'Oh! Oh! You make me come, darling!' as she spent profusely all over Rosemary's mouth and chin.

'Now it is my turn to repay the delicious pleasure I owe you,' sighed Kitty as she sat up and pulled Rosemary down beside her, kissing her rapturously and with her fingers, opening the pussey lips hidden in Rosemary's ginger bush and rolling on top of her, directing her stiff clitty into Rosemary's crack, closing the lips upon it with her hand in a novel yet delightful conjunction. Without separating for a moment, the girls writhed and rubbed against each other, swimming in a veritable sea of lubricity until they both reached the acme of pleasure and sank back exhausted, their arms wrapped tightly round each other.

Cecil and I looked on in no little bewilderment. How were these girls introduced to all-girl sexual encounters? wondered my brother.

'I will tell you,' said Kitty. 'Like many women, I do not believe in picking up any strange man just for the sake of carnal desire, although just like you or any other man, I am in regular need of good satisfying orgasms.

'Then one day last summer in the *Morning Telegraph* I read a small advertisement that said: "Woman to Woman: A selective group of attractive ladies wish to meet others to join their circle. Write to Lady SL for full details."

'I wondered whether this was one of the select private clubs that I knew existed in London where ladies meet to relieve each other's sexual tension. I had heard how they fondle breasts, suck pussies and use dildoes on each other to achieve the peaks of pleasure and I found the idea somewhat fascinating. After all, it was better than sitting at home alone, playing with yourself!

'So I wrote to "Lady SL" (who turned out to be none other than Susannah Loomlane, whose sister Brenda was an old schoolfriend of mine back home in Hertfordshire and she invited me immediately to a meeting at her grand house in Lots Road, Chelsea.

'For the sake of the family fortunes, which had been badly depleted by some most unwise speculation by her Papa, Susannah had married a dour Edinburgh gentleman some years her senior, one Geoffrey Hurton, who spent more time in the Highlands tracking down antiquarian books for his library than in his own bedchamber. Considering that Susannah was a most attractive lady in her middle twenties, I think I can say without fear of contradiction that not only was Sir Geoffrey a very great bookworm but an exceedingly foolish old fart!

'You must remember that at this time I was totally unaware of the joys of tribadism. Anyhow, I went round to Lots Road and Susannah showed me round her large home. A most interesting feature was a small cabin that had been erected in the garden. She told me that this is where her circle met regularly and I thought to myself that this seemed a small edifice for a ladies' meeting.

'But after I accepted her invitation to go inside, things became clearer. The floor of the cabin had been partially scooped out and a tiled bath – or perhaps a miniature swimming pool would best describe it – had been laid. It was fully plumbed with both hot and cold water and splashing around in the pool were two beautiful naked girls of about my own age, nineteen, whom Susannah introduced to me as Nancy and Alexandra.

'Do join us, Rosie,' said Nancy, shaking long blonde tresses of her away from her pretty face. 'Take off your clothes and jump in with us. The water is deliciously warm.'

'What a splendid idea,' said Susannah.' I have to entertain the artist Mr Lawrence Judd-Hughes for a while as I have to negotiate a fee for him to paint the charming views from our country home near Tunbridge Wells. But I am sure that Nancy and Alex will deputise most effectively as hostess whilst I am away.'

'I was somewhat shy at first but eventually I was persuaded to disrobe and I stepped gingerly into the pool. Actually, Nancy had been telling nothing but the truth, for the water was indeed nicely warm and we splashed around gaily. Then, as I rested momentarily at the side of the pool, Alex began to rub my crotch with the palm of her hand. The sensation was frankly delicious and I relaxed totally. Soon, I found myself being seduced by the two harpies. On one side Nancy was caressing my breasts and tweaking my nipples to full erection whilst Alex ran her hands between my legs, playing with my clitty.

'It was very erotic, especially as Nancy began whispering what she would like to do to me. She was rubbing my breasts and kissing my titties whilst at the same time murmuring about all the sensual things she wanted to do to me – like how she wanted to stick her tongue up my cunt and rub her face all around my hot, wet crotch and suck my clitty till I spent!

'I was so fired up by her words that I took her hand and placed it next to Alex's between my legs. Her fingers became alive as she started diddling me. Then Alexandra said: 'You cannot eat pussey under water.' So we all got out of the huge tub, dried ourselves and went into an adjacent little room which was just big enough to accommodate a large double bed upon which had been laid the most luxurious silken sheets.

'I was gently laid down on the bed and Alexandra began to stroke the insides of my thighs, opening my legs to accommodate Nancy who began to lick and lap at my wet pussey, sending me into spasms of desire and wanting desperately to be fucked. The little minx was licking along the insides of my labia, not putting her tongue inside me. I told her how hot she was making me and how I could feel an orgasm coming on. I told her to finish me off by fucking me with her tongue but then I heard Alex's voice saying: 'It's all right, Rosie, dear, I'll do that for you.'

'I opened my eyes and saw that the sweet girl had strapped on a belt round her waist which at the front had attached a black wooden affair shaped exactly like a giant cock, complete with carefully fashioned balls. This was the first time I had seen a didlo although of course I had read about these affairs in Doctor Roy Stevenson's famous manual – ah, I see you are acquainted with this excellent tome of which I believe no fewer than one million copies have been subscribed all over the world – so I was unsure as to what to expect.

'Anyhow, I spread-eagled my legs as Alexandra climbed on top of me, giving me a passionate kiss on the lips as she reached down and inserted the head of this wooden cock between my pussey lips. It certainly had the desired effect! I wrapped my legs around her waist and locked my ankles together. Then she leaned forwards and the dildo began to slide into my sopping cunney and I gasped with pleasure, urging her on. It took only a little while to get the rythm right but once I did, I discovered that the dildo gave me great joy. Every time she thrust forwards it rubbed against my clitty and at the end of each thrust, when the dildo was in as far as it could go, it would rub into my deepest recesses and send sparks through my entire body.

'It only took a few minutes before I spent, my cunney disgorging a flood of love juice and Alexandra spent too, so fucking me that we both managed to finish off together. We had so much fun that afternoon, especially when Susannah returned to join in the games, that I have almost gone off fucking with men, and especially since I began to share my bed with Kitty.'

'Have you ever strapped on a dildo?' Cecil asked Kitty.

'Yes, quite often, although Rosie and I take turns to play the masculine role,' she replied. 'Something happens to me when I put one on. I feel powerful for suddenly I have a cock mounted between my legs and I can thrust it into another girl and give her an orgasm just like a man whilst I can enjoy one too!

'It's difficult to describe how this feels but the last thing I want to do is try to replace men. I still feel that there is nothing like sucking a good stiff cock and then fucking it!

'But playing around with other girls makes me randy. I remember one day last week Rosie and I were sitting on the bed, our legs spread apart and our fingers buried in each other's pussies when your Uncle Arthur walked in. I was almost ready to come and I wasn't about to let Rosemary stop what she was doing so I unbuttoned his trousers, took out his prick and sucked him off. Then when he had recovered he fucked us both.

'I enjoy threesomes of any computation of the sexes. I believe that threesomes offer the most intimacy. When there are three persons, you feel like you are sharing something very special. We don't have to worry about embarrassing ourselves and my, we can have such fun' she added.

Perhaps it was just as well that we had no further time to explore this newly proposed avenue of pleasure. For, as you may well imagine, dear reader, Cecil and I were by now completely *hors de combat*. I do not believe that either of us, after all the priapic exercises I have already described, could have managed another cockstand even at the appearance of Lily Langtry, Gwendolen Bracknell or even Jenny Everleigh who is reputed to have been fucked by both Lord Robert Cripps and Major General David Haines after a wild country house party in Cheshire.

However, we left our ladies with the fondest salutations and the sworn promise to return to see them on our next visit to London. Whether Uncle Arthur would have approved is another story but as my wise older brother Cecil succinctly commented when I ventured to bring up this point: 'Uncle Arthur can go and fuck himself.'

We were forced to catch a slow train back home as workmen were carrying out maintenance work to the railway tracks near Egham. It was a bright morning and I noticed a group of chattering magpies in a high treetop where they were fluffing up their feathers and fanning their long tails.

'Why are magpies supposedly unlucky, according to superstition?' I asked Cecil. I knew he was a one for such clever brain-teasers.

My brother smiled and replied: 'Well, Teddy, the story goes that when Noah summoned the animals to enter the Ark, the magpies stayed outside to jabber maliciously at the drowning world. Another tale goes that they were further cursed with black and white plumage for refusing to go into full mourning with other birds at the Crucifixion.

'Some twerps actually doff their hats, spit towards the birds and say: 'Devil, devil, I defy thee. Two magpies, incidentally are supposed to be lucky, but all should be saluted by bowing and spitting. Mind, if you believe such nonsense, you deserve to have your arse kicked to the middle of next week!'

I laughed but noted his explanation. Even at this early age, I was already interested in folk-lore. [*Dr Parsifal was a contributor to Lore and Language in the West Midlands 1750–1880 edited by Professor Kenneth Watkins published by Singer and Le Baigue in 1890 – Editor*].

By the time we reached our station, we were feeling somewhat randy and as Cecil had surreptitiously purchased a copy of *The Pearl* from a newsvendor at Victoria, we had divided the publication into two sections and had each taken a portion to read.

'Damn me, but it's amazing how quickly one recovers from a good spell of fucking!' commented Cecil, stroking the bulge between his legs. 'After reading this randy stuff, I could really do some girl a favour!'

'Me too, 'I said. 'Mind, we are lucky that we have such big pricks. There's that fat fellow Ivor What's-his-name in the fourth form whose cock can only measure a couple of inches on the dangle though I've never seen it ready for action.'

'Don't fall into a trap here,' advised Cecil. 'Other fellows tools will often appear to be bigger than your own. This is simply because you are looking at theirs from an angle whereas you see your own cock only by looking straight down on it which is why it always will appear to be larger when viewed in a mirror.

'And as for young Ivor, his prick will probably grow as he gets older. Our bodies all mature at different rates. Anyhow, size is unimportant except I suppose that there are quite a number of girls who get excited at the sight of a really big juicy cock. Many others, however, I am told are far more aroused by a manly chest or the slim flanks of an athlete.'

But remember that there are times when small is beautiful! For example I can quote from the poet Alexander Pope who you may know was a man of very small stature. I think I can remember the very words he wrote to a lady who had dared to mock his size:

'You know where you did despise
(T'other day) my little Eyes,
Little Legs, and little Thighs,
And some things, of little Size,
    You know where.
You, tis true, have fine black eyes,
Taper Legs and tempting Thighs,
Yet what more than we all prize
Is a Thing of little Size,
    You know where.'

So it's not the size that counts, it's what you actually do with the equipment provided,' finished my brother.

84

Well, as chance would have it, a message was waiting for us at home from our dear parents who had been called to the bedside of my mother's aged Uncle Frederick in Brighton. As Uncle Frederick was reckoned to be worth at least a cool quarter of a million, my parents (along with other nephews and nieces) had cancelled all arrangements to journey to Brighton post-haste. Well, the old gentleman had no children – at least, none the right side of the blanket, and there were no bastards of which we knew.

Cecil and I were commanded to change into sombre clothing and join our parents forthwith. They were staying with Colonel and Mrs Bedwell, who were old friends since before Cecil and I were born. When the Colonel retired from the Army, he bought a splendid country mansion very close to Preston Park. Cecil was extremely friendly with the Bedwell's youngest son Richard, a cheery young man who was of a similar age and, as I was about to find out, a chap with similar and quite singular tastes!

Indeed, when we arrived at Bedwell Manor, we were ushered in by the butler to the billiard room where Richard was waiting to greet us.

'Hello, chaps,' he said warmly. 'How smashing to see you again. How are you keeping Cecil, old boy? Hasn't fallen off, has it? No? Well, that's a relief I'm sure and, good heavens, is this young Teddy? Christ, I would never have recognised you. You've got hairs on your chest by now, I suppose and elsewhere if you're anything like your brother!

'Dunn will take your things upstairs. We have the house to ourselves as my folks have gone with your parents to see your Great Uncle Frederick who I am sorry to say is probably on his way out this time which is quite a sad business really.

'My parents were friendly with him, you know, and I thought he was an interesting old cove. He was quite healthy until he got sozzled at a *soirée* Lady Fransmann arranged for that young Scottish poet Douglas Walker, the *protégé* of Oscar Wilde whom London Society seems to have taken to its heart.

'So an over indulgence in wine has caused his downfall,' said Cecil.

'Well, indirectly, yes,' Robert continued, 'though he could always knock back a bottle of bubbly without any problems.

What happened was that he was walking home from Lady Fransmann whose house was only down the road when he slipped upon some very fresh evidence of horses and feeling somewhat tired, he decided to sleep under the stars. Alas, he caught a chill which has settled on his chest and the quacks hold out little hope of recovery. They've even brought down Doctor Jonathan Arkley from Harley Street but it looks all up with the old boy.'

'What a deuced shame.' I said. 'How old is Great Uncle Frederick?'

'He was ninety two last month,' answered Cecil. 'So he has had a good innings. But what a way to go – slipping in a pile of horse-shit!'

'Well, he was too pissed to have smelled it,' said Robert and I'm afraid we rather inappropriately burst into peals of laugher.

Still, as the Eastern sage Mustafa Pharte says, when old words die out on the tongue, new melodies break forth from the heart.

Needless to say, our new melodies centred around l'amour and after a light luncheon, we sat in Richard's private room where he regaled us with an account of his latest conquest. I should add that he was a good-looking young man approaching eighteen years of age and many girls of all walks of life lost their hearts (and often their cherries) to the handsome boy.

As we settled down to our post-luncheon liqueurs(both Cecil and I chose brandy whilst Richard sipped at a port), our host told us of his encounter the previous night with Augusta, the pretty young daughter of Sir Clive and Lady Bonney who lived nearby.

'We had attended Colonel Burbeck's ball,' said Richard, 'and Augusta had pencilled me in for several dances. She really is an attractive young miss and she looked quite ravishing in a low-cut dark blue ball gown that accentuated rather than hid her full, snowy white breasts. She is almost as tall as I am and as we danced we found out that we shared the same birthday. 'Maybe people who were conceived at a certain time share similar characteristics' she smiled as I held her tightly in my arms. I was trying to ease her back from my erection at the time for although we had known each other for some time we were hardly bosom friends and as a gentleman I had no desire to embarrass the girl who, for all I knew, might still be a virgin.

'But as I tried to wriggle free, to my surprise, the gorgeous girl pressed herself even harder against me and softly whispered: 'My, my, my, Richard, that's quite a bulge I can feel down below. Is that all your cock or have you pushed some padding down there to make it feel bigger?'

'Certainly not,' I replied, 'But I am astounded to hear you talk so freely of such matters, Augusta, I really am.'

'But you are not sorry, are you, Richard?' she twinkled, squeezing my cock with her hand as we waltzed our way into a secluded corner. 'If you have had enough dancing, shall we take the air outside? It is so warm this evening, is it not?'

'As you may well imagine, I hardly needed a second invitation and with alacrity piloted her through the crowds and we stepped out on the patio and then walked down the path towards the little gardener's shed where to my amazement a key was in the lock and Augusta motioned me inside. 'I borrow the key from old Newman, the head gardener, for five shillings and no questions asked,' she whispered. 'And I have spent another ten shillings getting my maid Elizabeth to clean out the shed and lay down a nice mattress on the floor. Several of the girls clubbed together to buy the mattress and we take it with us to all the dances around the country. We take it in turns to use it although if it is one's turn and there is no boy worth fucking, then a postponement is permitted. The Hon. Celia Nutworthy is secretary of our little circle and she keeps our accounts.'

'What a splendid idea,' I exclaimed. 'Yes, and as you are the boy I have chosen tonight, I am sure that you will not mind reimbursing us for the cost of bribing the servants and other incidental expenses,' said Augusta.

'I readily agreed to pay up and my offer of a guinea was deemed acceptable by Augusta who pulled me to her ample charms. We sank down onto the soft mattress and kissed and embraced with ardour. I peeled open the buttons on her dress and her large breasts poured out of their cups and I gently caressed the saucer-sized nipples which rose to rosy little bullets under my touch.

'We undressed each other without difficulty as the

moonlight flooded into the shed through the large window. I gasped with delight as I ran my hands over her white globes and flat belly. Then I let a hand run through the silky dark hair of her bush and I could feel the dampness as I rubbed my knuckles over her moistening crack.

'She reached out and stroked my throbbing cock which was now as hard as rock. She pulled down my foreskin and ran her fingers over my knob. Then bending over me, she kissed and licked my pubic hair as I lay back to enjoy what was to come. She started to move her face slowly, feeling my hard prick against her soft cheek. She took strands of her long dark hair and made a web round my shaft that was by now almost bursting as it stood stiff as a flagpole as she parted her lips and sucked up my knob into the inviting warmth of her mouth. Then, taking my shaft in her hand, she bobbed her head up and down so that I was fucking her mouth in a most delightful manner. She sucked me off so beautifully that all too soon I could feel the sperm rushing up from my balls. I could not hold back as with a cry I pumped a stream of hot spunk into her mouth. Augusta sucked up and swallowed every last drop, milking my prick until it wilted under the sweet urgency it had encountered.

'What a truly magnificent fuck!' ejaculated Cecil trying hard to keep a note of envy straying into his voice.

'It was certainly extremely pleasurable,' said Richard. 'In fact, I would go as far as to say that Augusta is amongst the best three ladies I have ever fucked. She was really quite insatiable that night and just thinking about the way that her love sheath throbbed around my tool makes me very randy!'

'What a grand night of passion,' I sighed.

'Oh, but that isn't the end of the story,' laughed Richard. 'We were lying there a little exhausted after our romp, feeling a little drowsy for the makeshift bed the girls had provided was quite marvellous, with its snow white sheets and fluffy pillows that cushioned up beautifully. Anyway, I had not thought to bolt the door and for a moment I was horrified to hear footsteps outside. I lifted my head from the pillow to see the door open and I could just make out the shape of a feminine form in the moonlit shadows.

'Augusta too had been woken from our reverie and she

called out: "Who's there?" "It's only me, Penelope Hunt," said the intruder.

'"Oh, Penny, thank goodness, I thought it might have been a stranger," said Augusta with audible relief. "Penny, I think you have met Richard Bedwell, haven't you?"

'I had indeed been introduced to Penny, a tall, most striking blonde girl earlier that evening. Her Great-Uncle was Henry Hunt, the famous Radical orator who had been present at the dreadful Peterloo massacre in Manchester when the cavalry had been ordered to disperse a crowd.

'"This looks very interesting," said Penny, pulling away the thin sheet to expose our nude bodies to her enquiring gaze. "Very interesting indeed. Is this a game that only two can play or may I join in to make a threesome?"

'"I don't mind if Augusta has no objection", I said and, to my delight, Augusta smiled and indicated with a wave of her hand that Penny should join us on the bed. "Stand up Richard, and help Penny take off her clothes," ordered Augusta.

'I stood up and Penny turned round to allow me to unhook the catch at the nape of her neck. I helped pull the dress down and to my astonishment, immediately perceived that this beautiful young girl was wearing not a stitch of underwear. I marvelled as I felt her heavy breasts which were naked to my loving touch. We kissed fervently with our tongues deep in each other's mouths but I soon wrenched my lips away, moving my head down as I dropped to my knees, kissing her extra-ordinarily thick blonde pussey hair whilst my hands went upwards to squeeze the rich full breasts, tweaking the pert little nipples that were standing up high to my ministrations.

'My cock was now rising up to its full majestic height and Penny sank down besides Augusta to carry out a close inspection of my prick. Augusta was now bending over in front of me, the shapely, tender cheeks of her lovely young arse slap up almost against my mouth as her hands ran up and down the length of my shaft, slipping back my foreskin to uncover the red mushroomed dome as Penny began to lick and lap the tip of my hot thrusting tool.

'I soon learned that Penny's speciality was sucking rather than fucking although I would have awarded the girl at least a beta plus for the latter exercise. But her sucking certainly deserved an alpha and I was in the very seventh heaven of delight as her moist, pink tongue travelled up and down my excited cock. Augusta however was not to be denied and she began to kiss and suck my balls as my shaft slipped in and out between Penny's generously proportioned lips.

'What more could a chap desire in this world? There I was with two delicious damsels sucking me off with my left hand cupped round one girls's breasts and the other sliding in and out of the other's juicy crack.

'"May I be the first to be fucked?" gasped Penny, taking her lips away from my cock for a brief moment. She flipped over on to her back where she lay with her legs spread open and with her fingers parting her cunney lips that stood out in the midst of that hairy blonde minge. Augusta leaned over to squeeze Penny's nipples with wild thrilling pinches that brought the little cherries up to peak hardness. And it was the unselfish Augusta who took hold of my thick cock and guided it in between Penny's inviting cunney lips. I plunged my prick into her warm cavern and soon Penny and I were locked into a superb rhythm of long, sweeping strokes as my trusty truncheon slurped its way noisily in and out of her sopping cunt.

'I spurted my spunk to delicious effect but I sank back on the pillow absolutely shattered – after all, before all this fucking we had wined and dined quite sumptuously. But the two girls were still feeling randy so they turned to each other for further stimulation.

'Augusta began the proceedings by running her fingers through Penny's thatch of silky blonde public hair. She ran her hand along the length of her slit allowing it to come to rest at the base of Penny's clitty. She then grasped the trembling girl's bum cheeks, one in each hand, and gently kissed her dampening pussey, her mouth gently pressing against the soft, yielding fleshy lips, probing her utmost parameters of desire with her clever little tongue.

'Soon they were entwined in a *soixante-neuf*, Augusta's head buried between Penny's legs whilst the blonde girl's busy fingers were nipping and pinching Augusta's own finely developed clitty that stood out like a miniature cock from between her pussey lips. Penny then pulled her pussey to her own lips and nuzzled them round the curly bush that surrounded her cunt. The two tribades wriggled and cooed with delight as Penny produced an India-rubber dildo which she had hidden underneath the mattress and with a giggle passed it to me. I took hold of the dildo which was well crafted to the dimensions and shape of a good-sized prick and pressed it between Augusta's wet cunney lips. I must confess that I found the thrusting of the dildo in and out of her sopping cunney very exciting although I was just too tired to raise a decent cockstand.

'Now Augusta began to moan wildly, twisting and turning as I plunged the dildo in and out of her insatiable cunt. Penny too was madly excited and swooped her head down to my cock to suck it up to an almost full erection, with one hand on my swelling shaft and the other between her own legs as she frigged herself to an orgasm.

'Now meanwhile dear Augusta had wriggled over on her tummy and stuck her firm bum cheeks up in the air, slightly parting her legs so I could see her juices dribbling like honey from her cunt, for her pussey was by now creaming with pleasure. I looked at the wrinkled little bum hole that winked at me from between her arse-cheeks and as my cock was now standing fully at attention, I gently eased Penny's head away and getting up on my knees I slipped the head of my cock in and out of the puckered little rosette. "No, no, don't fuck my bottom," cried Augusta, "I would far rather that you dipped your cock into my cunt, I need it there so badly."

'How could I refuse such a request? I gave my cock a few rubs until it was rock-hard and, holding my red-headed weapon in my hand, I made Augusta stoop forward, as I plunged my cock into her wet welcoming crack from behind, my balls fairly bouncing against her bum.

'"Aaah! Aaaah! What a fine fucker you are, Richard, that's right, push harder now, further in, further in! Empty your balls, sir! That's it, that's it!"

'Her arse responded to every shove as I drove home until, excited to new raging peaks of lust by my lusty cock, the poor girl fainted as the maddened thrusts and contractions of her cunt sucked the sperm from my shaft. The sweet friction of her cunney lips against the head of my prick made every nerve thrill with that exquisite, unique pleasure. Happily, she soon recovered from the temporary delirium into which her senses had been plunged and she lay with her eyes beaming, her lips apart with the tip of her rosy tongue slightly protruding between two rows of the whitest pearly teeth – the very picture of sated voluptuousness!'"

'What a fantastic experience!' I said wistfully. 'I should very much like to meet those girls!'

'Would you, young Teddy?' said Richard with a smile playing about his lips. 'Well, how do you feel about it, Cecil?'

'Not without me being there,' rejoined my brother. 'You have made me so randy by telling me of your *nuit d'amour* that I think my cock will burst if I don't let it out.' And with that, he unbuttoned his fly and took out his swollen cock and began gently frigging his shaft.

'Quite a tosser you have there,' said Richard. 'But don't spoil your appetite because the lovely Augusta will be with us in less than half an hour!'

'Is that really so?' I exclaimed, feeling my own prick rise up in excitement.

'Yes, indeed, Teddy. So put your cock away, Cecil, you'll need to be in tip-top condition to satisfy Augusta.'

With difficulty, Cecil complied, stuffing his stiff cock back inside his trousers.

Richard continued: 'Oh, yes, Augusta knows all about what to expect, although I had to tell her that you, Teddy, were a little younger and I did not know if you had even fucked your first girl yet.'

'He is very advanced for his years,' grunted Cecil, 'and his cock is almost as big as yours and mine. Well, not as huge as yours Richard, but then you were the captain of the school's Thick Prick club last year. I forget which girl told me that she thought your cock reminded her of a cricket bat but it's well known that you are magnificently endowed and your story shows that you are certainly in no need of tuition in how to use your marvellous equipment. Not even Doctor Stevenson could teach you anything about *l'art de faire l'amour*.'

'Thank you very much,' said Richard modestly. 'Anyhow, Augusta is so looking forward to meeting you both. She told me later that night that wherever possible she loves to fuck three boys at the same time. This can present some practical problems but she tells me that she feels absolutely sated with a prick in her mouth whilst cocks are entering her arse-hole and cunney. Almost immediately, she experiences a huge spend, especially if the boys squeeze and caress her body with tender, loving care.

'She also likes sharing a man as she did with Penny and myself,' he added.

'What does she prefer in that case?' asked Cecil.

'Oh, simply divide the boy into two halves, so to speak. She sits on his cock whilst the other sits on his face and has her cunney sucked and then they change places *ad infinitum*. As Augusta says, a girl is far better equipped for a *ménage à trois* than a boy. For once he has spunked, it takes a while before he recovers but a girl can go on and on for quite a while until she tires or gets sore. So, as Augusta says, who says that women are the weaker sex?'

But before my question could be answered, Dunn the butler opened the door to announce that we had a visitor.

'Oh, is it the beautiful Miss Augusta, Dunn?' enquired Richard. 'She is a trifle early but no matter at all.'

'I fear not, sir,' replied the old retainer. 'It is a strange gentleman, or rather I should say a person who insists on seeing you.'

'A strange person? Whatever do you mean – did he give you his name?'

'Yes, sir. He also gave me his card and told me that he is known to you.'

How curious, I thought to myself as Dunn passed over the card and I peered over to read the ornate inscription: 'Hymie Singh Goldberg – Artists Agent.'

'That's a curious name,' I commented.

'He's a curious fellow,' grinned Richard. 'Hymie's mother was a Sikh but his Dad was the famous Issy Goldberg who was running a clothing emporium in Delhi during the Mutiny. He saved the lives of Lt. Colonel Wilson and his family by wrapping rolls of cloth round them when the mob was howling for blood and searching the shops for Europeans.'

'But didn't they want to lynch Issy?'

'They would have done but he was giving free bagels and lox

to any customer who purchased items to the value of five annas or more even on sale goods. There was already a queue and rather than have to wait before pillaging and looting the store the mob went on to the next district. By the time they returned, the Army had moved in so Issy, his store and the Wilson family were all saved.'

'That sounds an incredible tale,' said Cecil doubtfully.

'It's true, I assure you,' said Richard. 'Issy married a beautiful Sikh girl who changed her religion to his and they decided to move back to London a few years later and I believe that Hymie was born in Whitechapel.'

'How unlike the home life of our own dear Queen,' I said.

'Hymie is an art dealer,' said Richard. 'I expect he has some amazing bargains at never to be repeated prices to show me. He's quite a character so let's see what he has to offer.

'Dunn! Show the gentleman in.'

Dunn looked a mite peeved but did as he was told and retired momentarily to announce our visitor. 'Mr Hymie Singh Goldberg to see you, Mr Richard.'

Hymie came bustling in with a clutch of unframed paintings under his arm. He was a short, quite handsome man of coffee-coloured hue and he wore a deep red turban although his clothes were of a European cut.

'Ah, Hymie, how nice to see you again. These gentlemen are my house guests and I am sure they would be delighted to see the amazing world of art you have brought to sell me at extraordinarily inflated prices,' said Richard.

'Very droll, Mr Richard, very droll. I earn so little on any painting you buy it's hardly worth while making the journey. If it weren't for the fact that my old Auntie Hetty lives in Brighton I wouldn't bother, and that's a fact.'

'But now you're here you'll let me see what you have acquired. Is there anything worthwhile?'

'Anything worthwhile, he asks! Mr Richard, have I got some paintings for you! Look, here are four superb classical studies of heroines of Greek mythology. I should warn you and the other young gentlemen that the figures are undraped so if the sight of a nude girl offends, I won't take them out of the wrappers.'

'No, no, no that's quite all right,' said Cecil.

'Very well, gentlemen – here is the little collection. Now being young men of culture, you will know that without doubt the greatest single influence on Western civilisation has been the legacy of Ancient Greece. There is no corner of Art that is not founded firmly in that period and many people are well versed in the heroes of Greek mythology.

'But what about the women? We all know of Ulysses, Zeus and Hercules but what about the female counterparts? This young artist I am representing is himself a Greek who has turned his artistic talent to painting after some years making urns which was frankly not a profitable line.'

'Why, how much does a Grecian urn cost?' I asked.

'Round about two pounds or so. But that's not the point. This artist, Nedis Mousaka, has had the benefit of having those gorgeous dark-eyed Greek maidens pose for him. They have enabled him to capture the writhing golden forms of those Titans of old. Look, I'll show you what I've got.'

He unwrapped the pictures and spread the four paintings on a wall.

'Look, gentlemen, the first is a portrayal of the beautiful Andromeda, fairest daughter of Cassiopeia, the second of scheming Aphrodite, the goddess born of the sea, the goddess of sexual love, you should pardon the expression, and who was most widely worshipped of all the immortals. Then there's Maria, the mistress of Zeus, the fairest daughter of Atlas, if I am not mistaken, whilst the last is a depiction of the magnificent Nike, the mighty goddess of victory and Zeus's personal favourite.

'Now I ask you gentlemen, aren't these paintings stunning? Look at the detail, the depiction of the nude female form drawn with such power and eloquence!'

'They *are* rather good, Hymie,' said Richard, 'and if you could only provide one or more of those delicious girls to grace my bed tonight, I'd buy the lot.'

'Oh, you will have your little joke, sir. But at the price I'm asking, they must be a marvellous investment.'

We looked more closely at the paintings which were, truth to tell, rather good with the naked girls posing most sensually with complete abandon showing their breasts, bums and cunneys quite freely.

'I must say I like the look of Andromeda,' said Cecil. This painting showed the back of a girl, her hair flowing in the wind with firm, globular buttocks that fairly ached to be grabbed!

[To be continued]

Introduction to Part Two

This witty, amusing vignette was penned by Dr Jonathan Arkley, one of the leading lights of the South Hampstead set in the last twenty years or so of the nineteenth century.

It first appeared in *The Oyster* of November, 1893 just over a year before Oscar Wilde's 'The Importance of being Ernest' was first staged. I mention this because Arkley's characters – Gwendolen, Cecily, Algernon etc – all have the same names as characters in Wilde's masterpiece and it confirms that Wilde must have discussed his play with the good doctor who was known by many members of top London Society (including Lord Arthur Somerset, Sir Andrew Stuck and other well known men about town) as a consultant who might be able to cure any sexually transmitted diseases. Syphillis was rife at this time and the need for safe sex was as urgent then as it is now for the disease was as incurable as AIDS is today.

Arkley was himself somewhat of a roué, seducing many of the ladies who visited his consulting rooms in Welbeck Street. In her secret diary, Lady Danielle Freedman wrote in 1889 of 'the handsome Doctor Jonathan's charm which soon led me to his bed... I just hope that his enormous prick has not been inserted into too many ladies though I know for sure that Mrs Faine and Rosanne Oaklands have both been in his bed – probably together!'

Besides his interest in erotica, Arkley possessed a fine collection of early nineteenth century art and he was the author of two papers on abdominal pain that appeared in the *New England Journal of Medicine* in 1898 (Arkley's long-suffering wife was American and the family moved to New York in 1896

97

although they paid several visits back to Britain before the beginning of World War One).

Godfrey Goldhill

Axminster, December 1988

Sketches from Life
In which two Young Ladies enter the World of the Artist

(from *The Oyster*, November, 1893)

'Today is a very special anniversary,' said Gwendolen. 'It is two years to the very day since my first fuck.'

'Oh, how delicious,' I murmured.

'It is also,' she went on, 'the second anniversary of my second fuck, and my third.'

'Gracious,' I said. 'That sounds very exciting but also somewhat complicated.'

'Not really, Cecily,' she said. 'One day. Three fucks. All one after the other.'

'You certainly started with a bang!' I said.

'Don't be coarse,' said Gwendolen, 'or I shan't tell you all about them.'

'Oh, that would be so cruel,' I answered, 'for you know how I have always loved to talk of such things. You simply must tell me every last detail. See, I am already quite beside myself with excitement.'

With that, I squeezed my thighs together, trapping Gwendolen's hand as it teased and petted my pussey.

I should explain that we were sitting together on the top of a London omnibus. As luck would have it, we were all alone except for the driver up at the front who was far too busy guiding the horses through the traffic that seemed to come at us from all sides to have time to pay the slightest attention to what two fashionably attired young ladies might be doing snuggled together on the back seat.

I had met Gwendolen by chance two days before at a private

dance arranged by my aunt. At once we had flown into each other's arms with great squeals of recognition and joy for whilst we had been at school together, we had not seen each other for two full years or more. I, the older by a year, remembered Gwendolen as the sweetest little minx I had ever shared a bed with. Indeed, during the last year at Miss Bradshaw's Academy for Young Ladies we had truly been the most intimate of friends. But, alas, she had been forced to stay on for one further year to complete her education whilst I, heartily glad to escape from the damp glooms of Somerset, had been living in Town with my dear aunt.

So upon that chance meeting, we had rapidly made plans to see each other again and to exchange confidences for we both had much to tell and many adventures to recount. So thus it was, on this fine day in late Spring, we were journeying along the Bayswater Road with the intention of attending a private viewing of paintings by my cousin Algernon.

As soon as we were discreetly settled and it had become apparent that we were alone, Gwendolen's roving hands made it clear that she wished to resume that same loving closeness that had marked our last year together at Miss Bradshaw's Academy. Pleased though I was to receive her attentions, truth to tell, I was also a little alarmed at her disregard for any proprieties.

'Suppose someone should see us,' I had asked anxiously as I first felt her fingers begin to unbutton and burrow their way into my clothing.

'Do not worry, Cecily,' she had answered. 'Here, I have had the foresight to bring with me a good-sized travelling rug. We can tuck this round our legs and laps and anyone who notices us will simply think that we are taking sensible precautions against the chills and breezes attendant on top-deck open-air travel.'

With that, she wrapped us up firmly with a plaid rug (featuring as I recall the pattern of the Black Watch tartan) which neatly concealed the hand that now began to slip into my underclothing, sliding through the opening of my drawers and gently stroking the curls of my pussey hair. I turned my head and kissed her warmly as she for a moment, lowered her head so that it was pressed against the swell of my right breast.

'How I wish I could set your pretty titties free here and now,' she said. 'Oh, to see them spill out of your bodice. Those lovely, big titties that have given me such pleasure in the past. Oh, I do so wish I could kiss them and squeeze them and nibble at those delightful little cherries this very moment!'

'I would indeed love to feel your mouth sucking at my nipples.' I answered as a flush of desire warmed me and I could feel my nipples swelling and standing up in response to her urgings. 'But that must wait for later. Meanwhile...'

And I eased my thighs apart and felt her fingers seeking and then finding the already damp entrance to my secret cave. Suddenly she touched upon my eager clitty. I must have jumped at the thrill that shot though my whole body as Gwendolen giggled and continued to rub it firmly.

'Now, now Cecily, try to be still for we must be discreet as you so rightly said. Besides, I have so much to tell you. Let us sit here, hand-in-glove, so to speak while I begin, for as I said before, today is a very special anniversary...'

'It all started in the washplace outside our dormitory,' she began.

Here I must explain that at Miss Bradshaw's Academy for Young Ladies (situated near Petherton in the Quantock Hills), the headmistress had been particularly concerned that her charges should not be tempted into committing what she regarded as the Sin of Vanity. Consequently, she had arranged that there should be no mirrors above the washbasins where we might have been tempted into spending valuable time in such frivolities such as arranging our hair or admiring our fresh, youthful complexions. All that was needed, Miss Bradshaw had decided, were a few pier-glasses at the doorways so that we could ensure that we were neat and tidy before going out of doors.

To this day I can remember the rows of basins with chocolate brown shiny tiles behind them and the small windows which were set so high up that we could not see out of them without climbing up on the basins. Add just three baths in cubicles and a set of lockers where we kept our washing materials and our nighties and you have some idea of the spartan, indeed almost prison-like surroundings that Miss Bradshaw considered suitable for her girls.

101

'Oh, Gwendolen, we did have such fun, though, didn't we, all girls together,' I said, as I recalled those times of illicit evening pleasures.

It will be readily understood, I am sure, that being all of the same sex, shut up in a large and gloomy establishment in the heart of Somerset without a single member of the male species to be found anywhere on the premises, with the exception only of the old school chaplain, we explored amongst ourselves, so to speak for our pleasures. It was hardly surprising that there were many friendships of the most emotional kind flourishing amongst the young ladies and it will be further understood that within such an establishment there were many formal school rules laid down by the Headmistress and other unofficial rules created by the pupils, not written of course, but obeyed with much more care and to the very letter, far more so in fact than the official ones. Thus, only girls who were in the upper form could walk across a particular strip of grass outside the main boarding house. Senior girls were allowed to wear a plain ribbon in their straw boaters. Junior girls had to avoid looking into the prefects' day room and disobedience meant being shut up in a dark little cupboard. Such customs seem to grow up in all schools and many of them when looked on later in life appear to be very silly indeed.

However, at least in my boarding house, we did enjoy obeying one most delightful and entertaining rule. As I have said, there were no mirrors behind the washbasins in the big room where, morning and evening, we performed our ablutions. I have already touched upon the fact that, amongst two hundred and seventy girls, deprived of any contact whatsoever with the opposite sex and subject to the most repressive regime where such matters are concerned, many very intimate friendships grew up. Such passions and crushes abounded freely and many were the sighs of unrequited love and great was the gossip and whispered rumour about so-and-so and such-and-such. Many too were the intense conversations conducted quietly in corners or on staircases and many were the sly touches, the gentle pressures of hands on hands that ached for an answering response. Many an arm was slipped casually around a slim waist in the expectation of a quick smile and an equally swift hip-to-hip rub as a signal that other and greater intimacies might be enjoyed in the near future.

Yet in all these hopeful approaches and longing caresses there was as well the fear and the pain of possible rejection. Oh, the shame and embarrassment when the pretty object of one's utmost desires brushed away the half-hearted embrace or worse still, laughed and tossed her head in a gesture of scorn. And then the mortification of knowing that soon you would be the victim of giggling tales told in the dormitory or the subject of scornful notes passed between desks during lessons. Indeed, I have always maintained that one's most private pain becoming the subject of ribald public comment is without doubt one of the most humiliating things that can happen to a human being.

So, in order to lessen the chances of such unfortunate and painful occurences, a convention – one that in my experience was always complied with – had grown up at the school. If the object of one's desire was bending down at a washbasin having her before-lights-out wash, it was accepted as permissable to approach her from behind and, without a word being said, to touch and to stroke her. A finger could be gently run down her spine or the hands were allowed to cup themselves over her hips. If these advances were not checked, one might then slowly run one's pussey against the swelling cheeks of her bum.

She in turn was honour bound neither to cry out nor turn round to see who it was who had thus approached her. She could then respond, either by silently accepting or rejecting her unknown would-be friend. She might, for instance, remain quite still and make it clear that she did not welcome a continuation of this encounter. She could, if need be, gently reach back and remove the clasping hand and relieve a too insistent pressure. There are many subtle ways by which one can quietly yet firmly refuse an unwelcome attention and women are far more expert than men in expressing this unspoken language.

However, since we were for the most part a high-spirited and healthy collection of girls, it happened more often than not that this same silent language was employed to accept and even to urge on such welcome, delicate contact. In this case, still without a word being spoken or a head being turned, a simple

103

touch could be followed by a loving, exploratory caress. How many times, whilst busily splashing myself with water or carefully soaping my face and neck, have I sensed a warm presence behind me and felt the delicate touch of soft, unknown hands running the length of my body and massaging my flesh through the thin cotton of my nightdress. Ah, and then to press and nestle against the smoothness of the unseen adventurer, to wait in thrilling anticipation for those same hands to reach round and cup one's breasts, squeezing and rubbing the titties until one's nipples rose proudly erect with swelling excitement.

Then there might come the hoped-for pressure of one's mystery partner's hairy bush being pressed against one's bottom, of hands playing with the cheeks of one's bum. How lovely too if on the other hand one were the instigator of the approach, to feel a quiver of delight course through the welcoming body of the beautiful girl, to feel the first parting of the thighs, to see her shyly raise her bum as a sign that the road ahead was clear. Then would come the magic moment when the nightdress was raised up past the hips and the rosy delights of her arse were laid bare, first for an admiring gaze and then to be kissed, stroked and perhaps lightly slapped.

Truly, there are few more pleasurable things in life for me than to feel a hand slip between my thighs, to quiver with pleasure as the long tapering fingers begin to caress my pussey, to feel an enquiring finger seek out and rub my clitty and to be laid out on my back, with my legs apart and have a head wrapped between my legs with my partner's questing tongue probing delicately round my notch, licking and lapping at my pussey.

My first experiences than occured at Miss Bradshaw's Academy – many was the time that I cradled my head on my arms against the cold rim of the basin, shuddering with anticipation as unseen hands playfully but persuasively prised open the yielding lips of my cunney. Oh, the delight as a finger slid its way into the dampening warmth of my cunt! How often have I been driven to the full ecstacy of spending, yet never turning round as the first heaving surges of pleasure have coursed through my frame and the sticky flow of love juice has soaked my curly, thick bush.

It was not unknown, I well recall, on venturing into the washplace, to find such a loving scene as I have described being enacted before one's very eyes. Then, I must confess, I too would become greatly excited and want most urgently to join in. I remember being both the recipient and the instigator of such a multiple occasion. The first time it was I who was enjoying a most complete frigging from behind when I became aware that other hands had joined in the game, that the two fingers that were delving deep within me actually belonged to two different adventurers, and that other hands were fondling my titties.

Here I must digress and admit, nay state openly, without false modesty, that my titties are not only large and most delightfully firm, but they are most exquisitely sensitive. I can be driven almost to the delirium of my coming just by their being squeezed and nibbled upon. In turn, I have often rubbed them against another's bottom and felt them swell and throb with pleasure.

I was in fact once engaged in such a activity with the prettiest little new girl in our class when I was approached from behind by a third. Obeying the rules – for I am of course fully in favour of obeying both the laws and the customs of the land as long as they seem reasonable to me – I in turn didn't turn but continued to busy myself with the pretty little newcomer whose darling little bottom was by now opening up under the careful probing of my tongue. At the same time I also felt hands reaching out to finger my pussey hair and within minutes I was playing piggy-in-the-middle as part of a wriggling threesome.

But I digress at too great length. Suffice it to say that when Gwendolen mentioned the dormitory wash place, many, many memories came flooding back to me and I had high hopes of any story that began in such a setting.

'It was an evening towards the end of the Summer Term' continued Gwendolen. 'I was, I suppose day-dreaming – or rather night-dreaming for I was looking forward to an after-lights-out assignation with someone who had recently become a very dear friend. As I slowly attended to my toilette I became aware both of a hastily suppressed giggle and of a presence behind me. Shivering slightly with excitement I waited for that first tender touch. Unseen hands clasped me firmly around the waist and I wriggled backwards at once to give me assent for anything that might follow. Surprisingly quickly the hands were withdrawn and I felt my nightie being pushed up so that I knew that I was fully exposed to sight and touch. The same hands then urged me on to spread my legs, which I did most happily. Here was the first real surprise for the unseen hands were altogether more roughened and stronger than any I had previously encountered. As one finger at once found my little clit and rubbed it to a state of upstanding excitement, another finger had most expertly penetrated by cunt lips and was exploring me in a most forthright but delightful way.

A great warmth spread over my whole body and I sighed contentedly as I felt that familiar slow wetness begin to infuse my pussey.

Suddenly the hands were withdrawn and I felt the close heat of a body pressed up against me. Then ... Oh, Cecily ... Something quite amazing happened. This ... this Thing was thrust between my legs and straightaway plunged into my quim. For a moment I was quite unable to understand what was happening. Here was something quite new in my experience. Before I had a chance to consider or to do anything to sort out this puzzle, this great Thing had burrowed its way right up to its very hilt in me. Then, as it drew back, almost to the entrance to my cunt, it was thrust in again. It seemed to harden still more inside me until I was completely filled with its swollen length. Yet such was my own ever-widening instinctive response that it caused me no pain although there was no doubt in my mind that nothing so large and so forceful had ever penetrated me before.

By now all curiosity and all thought had been driven from my mind by its insistent thrusting and I surrendered myself completely to an ever mounting ecstasy. Moaning and even biting my wrist to stop myself crying out with the sheer pleasure of what was being done to me, I felt wave after wave of excitement pass through my body. My whole being, the whole world even, seemed to be concentrated in the heat of my pussey. Without knowing what I was doing, I was gripping and releasing this great pleasure instrument with internal muscles that I had not till then known I possessed as it slid ever more rapidly up and down the length of my cunt.

Then all of a sudden there was a momentary pause before a

renewed, frantic pressure as it discharged itself right in the furthest recesses of my tunnel of love. Again and again I felt a great spurting and what felt like a very torrent of juice was flooded into me.

Rapidly this delicious spurting slowed down and before I could do anything to stop it, this great engine of delight had been withdrawn. As the lips of my cunt closed I could feel the warm flow of our mingled juices running down the inside of my thighs.'

'Oh, Gwendolen', I said. 'I am so affected by your story. Please help me a little before you go on.'

With that dear Gwendolen did indeed pause in her account and with her skilful, soft fingers, opened out my own cunt and eased and teased my own clit into a most fatly happy state. Then as I snuggled up against her, I said, 'That's lovely. Please Gwendolen, go on with your story, but please also keep your hand exactly where it is now.'

'I can feel how happy you are,' she said. 'Truly you have always been the most warmly welcoming pussey of my acquaintance.'

'Then,' she went on, 'I was so overcome and still so filled with a hunger for more that I broke the rules. Panting, my hair all damp and dishevelled with the heat of the encounter, I partly turned round, having at the same time to half support myself. There in front of me was something never previously seen in a dormitory washroom in all the history of Miss Bradshaw's Academy for Young Ladies. A man. A naked man. He had a quite sun-burned body. He had wild, curling hair, a ring in one ear and strange designs tattooed on his arms and chest. But the most remarkable feature and one to which my eye was at once drawn, was this great Thing that jutted out between his legs. That very Thing with which he had just invaded my body and caused me what I knew without thinking to have been the most exciting time of my life so far.'

'Your first cock!' I exclaimed, rather too loudly in the circumstances.

'Sssh!' said Gwendolen. 'That is not a proper word for a young lady of good breeding to cry out in such a carrying way.'

'I am sorry,' I replied, as I realised that I had been so intent on her story, accompanied as it was by the steady caressing of her fingers in my pussey, that I had quite forgotten myself. Luckily the driver did not appear to have heard anything unusual coming from the back of his omnibus (although Gwendolen afterwards announced that she had seen one of the horses prick up his ears and raise his tail in surprise. However I do not quite believe this myself as I know that dearest Gwendolen cannot always resist the temptation to embroider a story in the retelling.)

'Do go on . . .'

'My first cock,' said Gwendolen. 'And I know now that it was a pretty handsome specimen. Anyway, as I leaned there, wondering where this sudden forbidden visitor had come from, I became aware of two other things. The first was that four of my dearest friends were with him, their eyes shining with delight and excitement at what they had just seen.'

'Your first fuck!' I exclaimed.

'My first fuck indeed,' Gwendolen replied.

'And what was the other thing you noticed?' I asked.

'That although I had been brought to the very brink of coming, I had not yet been driven over the edge. My titties were all swollen and I could see my nipples pushing out under my nightie. My legs were trembling and I could feel blood surging through all my body whilst my private parts were throbbing with an urgency I had never felt before. But as I rested against the basin, I spread my legs as though to let some cooling air in to calm the heat and the wetness of my pussey. Without thinking I fingered myself, opening myself up to my audience. Seeing my distress, two of my friends came to my aid. One, Mary quickly knelt down and, burying her face in my bush, began to lick my swollen clit. But the other, Meg . . .'

'I remember her,' I said. 'A tall Scottish girl . . .'

'Who as you might have heard, later behaved in a most immoral fashion whilst on the passage to India where her father was stationed,' said Gwendolen. 'According to her account, no less than seven young officers from one of the Mounted Regiments passed her portals, and all accomplished whilst steaming the length of the Suez Canal.'

'However, Meg . . .' I prompted her.

'Meg first kissed me with open-mouthed eagerness and then brought forward the strange man. Placing one hand under his still large but now limp pleasure staff, she urged me first to lick its purple end, and then inch by inch, slowly, take it into my mouth. As my lips gently slipped further and further down its length, I felt it stir in my mouth. Understanding at once what was taking place, I sucked and pulled at it with my lips. Meg meanwhile had slipped her hands beneath his balls and was very carefully squeezing them.

Before I had time properly to realise that sucking a man's cock can be a very great pleasure in its own right, he had so stiffened and enlarged that I felt in some danger of choking. At once he withdrew and as my two friends eased me down on to the floor and as I spread my legs apart, drawing my knees up so that my entire pussey was forced into full view, he entered me once again with his now glistening and re-erected member.

Cecily, I have since then seen some of the classic Indian texts on lovemaking and have studied the positions. All I can say is that I have never needed to be taught. Fucking, I now realise, comes easily to me. As if I had been doing this all my life, I raised my legs and grasped him round the waist, drawing him fully into me. There I held him for a while, savouring the delicious feeling of my cunt absolutely filled with his prick. Then, releasing my grip somewhat, I let him recommence that to-ing and fro-ing that previously he had done from behind. This time I had the added pleasure of being able to watch that great tool thrust deep into me and then slide back in order to repeat its effort.

By now my body was responding as if by instinct and I was thrusting to meet him time and time again. This time he was much much, more controlled in his fucking and as he slid back and forth like a great piston, I began to lose control once more. Then it was that I broke the second rule. I did not mean to but I could no longer stay silent. I hardly knew what I was crying out but the others later recalled that I had been shouting out "More! More! For God's Sake! Fuck me! Fuck me!" My head was twisting from side to side and I had pulled my nightdress right up over my tits. I was rubbing them, squeezing them almost to the point of pain as I felt my legs split apart as though I was trying to suck the whole of him inside me. Then my back arched and I realised in one wonderful instant that I will never ever forget, that for the first time in my life I was coming with a man inside me.'

By now I was again so excited by Gwendolen's story that I could feel an answering wetness begin to flood down me.

'Gwendolen, quick, hold on to me tight. I think I'm coming as well. No, no! That's it. I need a second finger in me. Go on. Tell me some more.'

'Well,' said Gwendolen, only a little put off her stride by my interruption, 'Suffice it to say that I came and I came and I came. It seemed as though my coming would never end. When at last he also came for the second time I was so carried away by our fucking that I bit him quite badly and scratched him all over his back. Luckily he can't have felt a thing – although later the others said they had to dab some antiseptic lotion over him. I may say that afterwards I found that he also seemed to have bitten me, for one of my nipples was very sore.

But at the time all I can remember is that I seemed to dissolve into a some sort of sticky blancmange. I swear my eyes went out of focus and all I could see was a haze. I was so drained and so happy that I would have just stayed there on the floor for ever, feeling the last waves of my coming wash over me. Then Meg and Mary and the others took charge and they lifted me up gently and put me in a warm bath. They washed me all over with great thoroughness, paying particular attention to my much exercised private parts. They were also good enough thoroughly to sponge down the strange man, who all the time had said nothing, before they led him away.

'What happened next?' I asked. By now I also had calmed down and was happily content to leave Gwendolen's hand resting gently on my more satisfied pussey.

'They dried me off and led me back to bed. Where I slept dreamlessly and deeply until the bell rang at seven o'clock the next morning. I remember half getting up and than half wondering if it had all been a dream. I sat there on the edge of my bed feeling strange and very different somehow. I think Meg must have noticed my odd expression for she came over to me and said "You weren't dreaming. You had your first fuck last night. And your second, and your third."

"Three?" I asked. "It all seems so muddled but are you *sure* there were three?"

110

"Definitely," she said. "One from the back. One from the front – when we had to hold you down, you were throwing yourself about so. And one with you on top, after we'd got you all clean again and towelled you down. You stood up, your eyes all glazed, dropped the bath towel we'd wrapped round you for decency's sake, wound your arms round him and almost forced him over. You were sitting on him, riding him as though you'd been doing this sort of thing all your life and at intervals you'd lean forward so that your tits brushed against him and he was sucking them and biting them while you wriggled and yelled as he impaled you on his great tool."'

'Do you know,' said Gwendolen, 'from that day to this, I simply can't remember that third time. If it really happened I must have been quite out of my mind with fucking.'

'Well it's not a bad way to go,' I said. 'But maybe Meg was exaggerating. After all, some of her stories do sound a little suspect.'

'Like seven army officers between Port Said and Suez?'

'It certainly sounds like military service on a grand scale. Three or four? Now that I can imagine. But anyway, it's a lovely story. Did you ever find out who the man was and how he came to be there? And did you get to fuck him again?'

'It was all Melissa's idea,' said Gwendolen.

I remembered Melissa. A tall well-built girl. Full of energy and mad-cap ideas, she was definitely a character. Terribly untidy and somewhat scatter-brained, she was the despair of Mrs Bradshaw and the staff. Brought up on a farm, and with a knowing eye, she had a most unladylike knowledge and interest in the less polite activities of the animals. I remember clearly an incident when we were both only just arrived at the school. There was a rather fussy little man who in those early days used to come in twice a week in order to teach music. One day he brought in his small and rather fussy little dog. Of course we all gathered round to stroke and pet the little creature. When it suddenly started yapping and then made as if to snap at one of the girls, he snatched it up.

'Bobo's a touch on the nervous side,' he twittered agitatedly. 'A highly strung little dog.'

'She's not a dog,' said Melissa. 'She's a bitch. Look, she's got

111

nipples.' Poor Mr Fotheringay was very shocked at her plain speaking and when Melissa made things worse by going on 'All females have nipples. They're for babies to suck milk from. Young ladies have nipples too,' he became speechless and stopped the lesson there and then.

Later Miss Bartholomew, the Deputy Headmistress, sent for her and she was told in no uncertain terms that she was never, never to use such language again in the school. Her parents were to be told of her misbehaviour. She was to apologise to Mr Fotheringay, who had had a severe nervous attack after the incident and she was to lose all sorts of privileges for the rest of term.

We all thought that this was absolutely beastly of Miss Bartholomew who was such a stick-like creature that in her case it was more than possible that she in fact did not have any nipples. She certainly had no visible bosom.

Anyway, Melissa had gone from bad to worse in the eyes of the Mistresses and had got better and better in the opinions of all her friends. Of course in the midst of all our passions and night-time friendships, one subject above all was the great topic of excited conversation. Men. As I have said, apart from the school chaplain, The Rev. Mr Paddlebottom, and occasional visits from Mr Fotheringay, we never saw one at close quarters on the school premises. We were terribly ignorant about Men and in particular about what Men did to Young Ladies.

Melissa inevitably was the one who told us all, when we all were in our first term. 'They have this Thing,' she told her wide-eyed audience in the dorm. 'And they have to put it in girls' wee holes so that they can have babies.'

Naturally there was a chorus of disbelief from most of us. Apart from a vague idea that having a baby involved help from a clergyman, since babies were only born after a proper Church wedding, there was a school of thought that they came out of the belly button but mostly we were just ignorant and terribly shocked.

'Ugh!' said a squat girl called Hermione, 'That sounds horrid. I certainly wouldn't want a man's Thing pushed into *my* wee-hole. I can think of nothing worse.'

At this there was quite a babble of agreement but I noticed, here and there, a number of girls with thoughtful looks on their faces who didn't join in the general outcry. I was somewhat relieved because the idea of a man's Thing one day reaching up inside me seemed a proposition not to be dismissed out of hand and one to be considered carefully for the future.

The fact was that I had already made certain discoveries about my-still dormant pussey. A little gentle exploration with my own fingers had awakened feelings of pleasure and excitement. Nor, as I realised later that evening, was I alone in my discoveries. After Melissa's lecture on the Facts of Life had ended and lights were out, I voiced my thoughts on the subject of men's Things to my friend Thomasina. She at once confided that she also had engendered feelings of a quite thrilling nature in and around her hidden parts by a process of quiet self-exploration. Emboldened by our whispered conversation, I quietly did a round of the dormitory, asking a carefully picked selection of girls whether they also had any sympathy with my ideas. Quite soon seven or eight of us were sharing confessions. We all agreed that if at any time in the future, a man's Thing were to be presented to us, we would at least greet the proposition with an open mind.

In the meantime several of us agreed that if we could get such pleasure at our own hands, maybe the touch of other hands would be as nice or even better. In no time at all, amid hastily hushed giggles, a mass exploration was going on. In the darkness, unseen hands were reaching out. Demurely pressed-together knees were being eased apart and careful journeys of adventure were being made into unseen places. Of course we were still too young to understand the peaks of ecstasy that lay ahead but we had made a start.

So Melissa had entered my life and Gwendolen's early. Her night time lectures and quite explicit explanations had been our introduction to sexual matters. Now it seemed that, like the good teacher she was later to become, she had not only awakened our juvenile interests in the subject, but had set my friend her final examination – and one that she had passed with flying colours. In short, she had arranged her first fuck. But how? Where had the man, with his splendid Thing, come from? What had happened to him?

Melissa, it seemed, had finally tired of listening to the moanings and complaints about the great lack of Men during

113

the dormitory conversations. There was Adam the school gardener. But he was reputed to have been employed by Miss Bradshaw not for his expertise in horticultural matters but because he was safe where Young Ladies were concerned. This followed an incident in the Crimea War when he had been damaged by a Russian musket shot in those parts that are the seat of the male passions. The only other man to be found within the convent-like confines of the school, Mr Fotheringay having retired to a sanitorium, was as I have said, the chaplain, Mr Paddlebottom.

He however had always restricted his attentions to the backsides of his pupils. 'Spanker' as he was called, was in the habit of indulging in regular chastisements of those of his flock who had failed to come up to his expectations where biblical knowledge was concerned. All of us had at some time or other felt his rod upon our bottom but he had never displayed any interest in our other parts. So many a maiden's prayers had gone unanswered and no man's Thing had ever raised its head within either school or pupils.

How we had bemoaned our fate. How eagerly we had chattered and dreamed about men and their Things. We made up stories and hoped that one day we would find such a combination within the school grounds. But our citadel was well guarded and its multitude of young pussies quite unapproachable. I remembered clearly those endless after-dark speculations, those moist sighs and breathless fantasies. But I digress.

Melissa, as Gwendolen recounted, had become impatient and decided that something must be done to fill certain long felt wants.

'There is a gipsy encampment on the common,' she had announced one night. Blank stares had greeted this piece of news. 'Gipsies,' she had continued, 'are well known, in lore if not in fact, for their habit of kidnapping babies and small children. Is it not time that the tables were turned? I have a splendid scheme. We will capture a gipsy.'

'Why?' several of her audience had chorused.

'Why?' she had answered. 'So that we can make use of him.'

'How,' those same voices asked.

'We will bring him back here and use him for our pleasure.'

114

At this there was a great hubbub of questions and objections.

'Listen' she went on. 'I have thought this out with great care. We can smuggle him into the school and keep him in the attic where all our trunks are stored. No-one ever goes in there until the end of term. I have talked to one of the village girls who works in the kitchens. She is very taken with the idea and has promised to put on one side sufficient food for us to sneak in to him.'

'But surely he will be able to escape,' Meg asked. 'We cannot mount a guard on him.'

'But will he *want* to escape?' replied Melissa. 'School food may not be enough temptation but school pussies will surely be. I am quite convinced that he will be more than ready to endure his confinement when he realises that he is to be presented with a succulent diet of unblemished fruit, ripe for the plucking.'

'It would never work,' one or two of her enthralled audience had objected, albeit wistfully.

'It could,' she answered. 'We will have to be very careful. Above all, no-one must breath a word of what is to happen. So first we must all swear on our Honour – or rather our hoped-for Dishonour – not to say anything, not even a hint, to anyone.' By now all were becoming quite wrapped up in her plan, and quickly agreed to become sworn sisters in secrecy.

There is not time to recount every detail of the plot but suffice it to say that Melissa's already well-thought-out scheme was seized upon by two of the girls whose fathers were both in the Army. Between them they had listened far too many times over the parental dinner table to accounts of military expeditions for them not to understand the necessity of good forward planning.

The key to the scheme lay in the hands of Bess, the kitchen maid who had already promised to keep back enough food for their inviting guest. Unlike the Young Ladies, she was no stranger to men and their Things.

'I'm sure I'm not much of a one for reading,' she had confided in Melissa, 'nor for either of the other two Rs, but the Three Fs are another matter. Feeling, Frolicking and Fucking are an education in themselves.' She eagerly volunteered to be their accomplice. Melissa and four of the stronger girls had slipped out into the school grounds after dark. Waiting for them was Bess. She had led them down the lane and then to the edge of the common where there was a barn, half-filled with hay.

'I think I can get him to follow me in here with no trouble at all,' she had said. 'He' was a tall gipsy in the prime of life that she had already spotted while hanging round the camp.

'And as soon as he's in here, we grab him?' said one of Melissa's press gang.

'Not if you please, Miss,' said Bess. 'Beg pardon, but I would like to be repayed for my services.'

'Of course,' Melissa had answered. 'I am sure that I can cajole a little money out of Papa when I go home...'

'Oh No, Miss! I didn't mean anything like that,' Bess had answered. 'All I know is that if I can get him excited enough to follow me in here, then I will be excited enough to want to offer him what he's after.'

'First fuck!' exclaimed Melissa.

'First fuck,' agreed Bess. 'That is only fair is it not?'

'Indeed, yes,' said Melissa. 'It was quite thoughtless of me not to have made the offer.'

'Besides,' went on Bess. 'He will be easier to capture when he is all spent. I may not have the benefits of an expensive education but kitchen work makes a girl strong in the arm and in the thighs. I can promise to quite drain him of any fighting spirit for a while.'

'So we should hide behind these bales and watch for our opportunity,' said Melissa.

'If you would, Miss. Although it is quite dark in here, I am sure that you will be able to see enough, and hear, to know when the right moment has arrived.'

They had watched from the barn as Bess had gone down to the gipsy encampment. By the light of a fire they had seen her silhouetted by the gate. They could not hear what was going on but presently they saw a tall man leave the fire, where no doubt the gipsies were engaged in roasting a hedgehog or some game poached from the neighbouring estate, and walk over to her. They had heard an enticing laugh from Bess, a murmur of conversation and then she had turned back towards the barn and the ambush that waited within. As she approached, leading him by the hand, they had all hastily retired into the dark recesses of the barn.

With a giggle, she had thrown herself down on the straw and raised her skirts to him. They saw a quick flash of naked flesh as her legs were spread in welcome. They saw him unbuckle and unbutton himself before first sinking to his knees before her and then covering her with his body. In the half-darkness, they could make out that Bess and the gipsy were clasping each other, locked in passionate kisses. Then he raised himself up and for a moment they saw his great swollen cock. Two of the party, this being their first sight of such an instrument of delight, gasped out in amazement and excitement. The gipsy, even in the throes of his pleasure, had looked up at the sound.

'That old barn owl,' Bess had said with great presence of mind. 'There is a nest up in the roof.'

Not needing much reassurance, the gipsy had fallen to his work. Bess's thighs, the black shadow of her pussey deep between them, had seized him round the waist and she had drawn his engorged prick deep inside her. Quite beside themselves with envy, the school party had watched as the two of them coupled and wrestled on the straw.

'There was such a thrusting and a panting,' Melissa had reported, 'that it seemed some great threshing machine was at work.' Bess had been crying out and wriggling her bottom as though to clamp him forever in her. But he had continued to drive his way up and down her lover's lane as it opened up before him between the dense thickets of her pussey. Then she wrestled him, still embedded in her, over on to his back and began to ride him ever faster and faster. He responded like a thoroughbred, his prick rising to meet her downward thrusts.

'I shall never ride side-saddle again,' someone had whispered in Melissa's ear as they crouched in the darkness.

Then, as Bess and the gipsy reached their climax, straw and chaff rising in a cloud around them, he bucked and moaned and the watchers sensed the cream churning and spurting up along his great member. Bess, like any good milkmaid, accepted every drop in her waiting receptacle, clutching at him and urging him on. Clamping his head in her hands, she pressed her open mouth against his as though she was trying to eat him, while his cum flooded into her and shudders of pleasure ran through both their bodies.

Then, as their movements grew less frenzied, the watchers had to pull themselves together and remember there was work to be done. The gipsy gave one last pumping heave. Bess collapsed down on him and they lay locked together for a moment or two. The ambushers crept forward, not quite certain whether now was the time to pounce. As they hesitated, Bess raised herself up, paused, and then sat back on her heels, letting his still fat but limp prick slip out of her. Bending forward, she cupped his balls between her hands, sucked hungrily at the tip of his juice-wet cock and sat back again. She raised her arms and beckoned them forward.

In a nervous scurry, Melissa and her friends scrambled across the straw and gripped and pinioned their quarry's arms and legs. Exhausted though he was, he began to struggle, looking round wildly at his attackers. Bess at once threw herself back on top of him, kissed him and whispered urgently in his ear.

'Lie still now, dear,' she had said. 'No harm is going to come to you. But there is something these friends of mine want you to do for them.'

Quickly she explained what the plan was, how he was to be secreted in the school attic for no more than three days, how she personally would make sure he had three square meals a day. 'Food prepared with my own hands,' she said, giving his cock a friendly but firm squeeze. 'Better food than you'll get round that old camp fire of yours.'

After having had to live on the school food for a number of years, there was not one of the girls who considered this possible, but a small lie was needed in the circumstances. Then, as the nature of the duties he would be called upon to perform became clear to him, at the thought of all the virgin pussey, the unawakened clits and the hitherto unpenetrated passages waiting for him, he stopped any pretence of struggle and surrendered to his fate.

So he was brought back to the school, smuggled in through a back door and led up stairs. Bess tiptoed up from the servants quarters with a big bowl of soup and several thick slices of bread. These he wolfed down like a man who hadn't eaten for days on end.

'Fucking makes you hungry,' explained Bess. 'And you've got to feed him up and keep him in condition. Anyway, I like him.' She turned to him. 'That was a fine country fuck, she said. 'Now you must trust these young ladies. There is a lot you can do for them. Besides, some of them are very well connected in these parts. I've no doubt that if you or your family are ever caught with the odd pheasant that you have poached, one or other of them will be able to have a quiet word with her father, invent some story of a small favour owed, a lost brooch returned, and nothing more will be said. The gipsy, who was not stupid, realised that he was being offered a free harvest of fucking followed by the free run of the game coverts of the area. He accepted this unusual turn of affairs with a good grace. Because we were all well brought up young ladies, it was arranged that he should be bathed and made quite clean before we would receive him. Bess meanwhile promised him that a message would be taken by her down to the camp to say that they were not to worry at his absence and that he would be returning to them in a day or so.

'But were you not a party to this plot?' I asked Gwendolen.

'Alas no,' she replied. 'I had had the misfortune to be confined to the school sanitorium with a slight chill for a couple of days, so knew nothing of it.'

'But they let you into the secret,' I said.

'They let the secret into me,' corrected Gwendolen. 'Both Melissa and Thomasina had absolutely insisted that, since had I been well, I would without doubt have played a leading role in our adventure, I should be given the opportunity to enjoy a Romany Ride.'

'That was very good of them' I said. 'But how long did you keep him for in the end?'

'Three nights in all,' said Gwendolen. 'On the third night, about dawn, we released him back into the wild.'

'And nothing was ever discovered?'

'Not really.'

'What do you mean, "Not really"?' I asked.

'Well, there was one tiny incident . . .' said Gwendolen. 'Do you remember Miss Brightwell?'

'The young temporary art teacher,' I said.

'Yes,' said Gwendolen. 'Well, she happened upon Bess

119

creeping up the back staircase that led from the kitchens to the attics. Bess had a bowl of nourishing stew under a cloth. Thinking that some sort of forbidden night-time feast was taking place in the dormitory, she had followed silently behind her. She found the gipsy, John Smith was his name, in the lumber room, giving some private tuition to two of the girls. A lesson had just finished. Meg was lying back, recovering from a most searching examination of her inner parts, while Deirdre . . .'

'That thin girl with a most active tongue,' I said.

'The same,' said Gwendolen. 'She was using the same active tongue in order to lick our tutor back into sufficient life for him to perform his duties all over again. She was most assiduously sucking and teasing his cock back to its standing position when Miss Brightwell appeared at the door.'

'How terrible,' I said. 'What did she do?'

'She was a jolly good sport,' replied Gwendolen. 'Everyone, of course had stopped what they were doing except Meg who was too far gone in her post-fuck daze to notice anything. She just lay there, stroking her exhausted quim while Miss Brightwell looked about her and the said "John Smith, I believe." The gipsy turned and said "Rachel!"'

'Goodness me,' I said.

'It turned out that they had met some months previously when she was engaged in a series of circus sketches on Blackheath in south London. That of course was immediately prior to her having taken up a temporary position at Miss Bradshaw's. I later saw some of her drawings. They are most exotic. Trapeze artists and acrobats are flexible beyond the imaginings of us ordinary mortals. Such contortions and such fucking and all in positions that I swear would be quite impossible without grave risk of permanent injury to someone untrained. One of the artists, wearing only a little spangled costume, had her legs locked round the back of her own neck and had then craned forward so that her face was but a few inches from this immense cock that was plunging deep into her gaping quim.'

'Gracious!' I said, 'What a coincidence.'

'Furthermore,' Gwendolen went on, 'it appeared that she

had not restricted her activities to just recording such details. She had several times enjoyed a thorough fucking at the hands, or rather the prick, of John the Gipsy. Although these instances she had not of course been able to record in pencil or watercolour.'

'What happened then?' I asked.

'She very sportingly said that she would not report anything that she had seen just so long as she took the next turn. Miss Minge – for that was John the Gipsy's nickname for her – quickly slipped off her rather artistic and loose fitting dress and stood before us in a delightfully unashamed nakedness. She was so slim and pretty that my heart went out to her. Her breasts were quite small but she had the longest, most provoking nipples that I have ever seen.'

'Like nipples, like clitty,' I murmured.

'Indeed, yes,' said Gwendolen. 'John's gipsy tongue almost at once had all three protuberances flushed and charged. The contrast between them and her slim, white body was tantalising in the extreme. When she drew in her breath, all her ribs stood out and her hipbones framed the plumpness of her curly haired mound. They fucked standing up, very quietly and very deliberately. We were all spell-bound and I realised that the human body can indeed be a work of art in itself. Bess was standing there open-mouthed, quite forgetting the bowl of stew which was growing cold in her hands. Only when Miss Brightwell came with a little choking cry, did she remember where she was. I think we were all in something of a trance. John the Gipsy, who had been very controlled in his fucking, held on to her as she quivered and shook with her coming. He stayed in her until she had ground to a halt, supporting her until she had regained her composure.'

'One of nature's Gentlemen,' I said.

'Far more of a gentleman than some others much better born that I have entertained,' agreed Gwendolen. 'He was Consideration personified.'

'I have been secretly reading the works of Mr Engels and Mr Marx,' I said. 'And I have developed a great sympathy for the lot of the working classes.'

'And there was a lot to this member of the working classes,'

Gwendolen responded quickly. 'I may not understand the economic sciences, but I am full of admiration for the hard Labour he performed that night and the next. Of course we looked after him with care for none of us knew when we would be able to lay hands on another such rod, pole or perch.'

I smiled at her reference to our mathematics lessons.

'Or Rod, Staff and Comforter,' I riposted in what I thought a clever little allusion to Mr Paddlebottom's scripture classes.

Gwendolen looked puzzled for a moment and furrowed her dainty brow. I squeezed her hand affectionately with my thighs.

'But do go on,' I said.

'There is not much more to tell,' she said. 'Miss Brightwell returned to her room with a warning not to make any noise. "Since," as she said, "I know that your evening is not yet ended. You have my assurance both that John will be able to stand up to further exertions in a short while and that I will report nothing of what I have seen, and felt, this evening."'

She then made a firm agreement with John the Gipsy for her to come down to his encampment one night after he had been returned and commence to put together a portfolio of drawings of Romany life.

After she had withdrawn the fucking recommenced. Thomasina, who had been waiting patiently for her turn, was next. Then Meg. Melissa and I had to console ourselves, each with the other, while the rest moaned and gasped in sequence upon the floor. We had to place a firm hand over Deirdre's mouth at one juncture for it was clear that she was about to scream out in her delight. But the danger was averted and we composed ourselves, knowing that we were the first to be served the next night when our efforts were resumed.'

'So he lasted the course?' I asked.

'Towards the end of the third night he became a bit weak at the knees,' said Gwendolen. 'But as I now realise, he held out most manfully to the very end.'

So if today is the anniversary of your first three fucks, tomorrow...'

'Is the anniversary of my fourth and fifth,' Gwendolen agreed. 'And the very last, just before we had to take him back to his caravan, was most extraordinary. I actually slid down the bannisters on to his eager prick.'

'No splinters in the bum?' I asked.

'We had smeared the surface carefully with a soothing cream. It was the smoothest of descents and the easiest of entrances. I realised then that fucking would be my chief delight for the future.'

At that moment we heard the sound of another passenger clambering up to the top deck of the omnibus. Of course, being two well brought-up young ladies, we did not do anything so immodest as to turn to look at the new arrival. Indeed we both hoped that he – for it was a he as I could see from the corner of my eye – would move up to the front so that our happy intimacy, and our conversation, could not be intruded upon and we could continue to exchange information. However it was not be to be.

'Gwendolen!' exclaimed the newcomer. 'What a splendid surprise.'

Gwendolen looked round.

'George!' she answered. I too looked round at this juncture. Standing before us was a young man who I had never seen before in my life. I barely had time to register that he was dressed as though for a funeral, when he half raised his hat in greeting and extended a hand.

Here a problem arose. Gwendolin instinctively sought to half rise in response and to hold out *her* hand. Unfortunately her right hand was still beneath the travelling rug, burrowed into my underclothing and caressing my nicely damp pussey. Gwendolin though barely hesitated. Deftly she withdrew her hand from my private pleasure place and held it out to the stranger who claimed acquaintance. He took it between his own and bent to kiss it, whilst steadying himself against the end of the seat in front in order to preserve his balance since the omnibus was once more swaying and jolting through the ever heavier traffic, the driver flicking his whip and muttering uncomplimentary things about the competing drivers and cabbies. (Indeed I distinctly heard him call in question the parentage of one tradesman's van driver.)

The young gentleman warmly placed his lips upon the backs

of her fingers, lingered for a moment and then looked her steadily in the eyes, at the same time allowing himself a small smile.

'No gloves,' he said. 'And on such a cool afternoon.' Gwendolen looked a little embarrassed at his remark, particularly when he lowered his lips to her hand once more and rather boldly licked her fingertips.

'But one hardly needs gloves when one has a warm muff to hand,' he continued with a wicked little chuckle.

Then, before I had had the time to consider how I should react to his sudden turn of affairs, Gwendolen hurried to make an introduction that set my mind quite at rest concerning the propriety of the conversation.

'Cecily, this is my dear friend Mr George Russell-Lupin. Not only is he a very close friend whom I have known now for many, many months, but he has a truly gallant prick which is most prompt to stand up for any lady, no matter what the situation.

'One likes to be of service . . . ,' he responded.

'George, this is my dear, dear former schoolfriend Cecily, with whom I am resuming acquaintance after a most painful separation of two whole years. We were indeed bosom companions and I very much hope that we shall shortly be able to resume that relationship. However this is not of course a sufficiently private place for that purpose.'

Mr Russell-Lupin, or George as I had already determined to call him for I have long been opposed to over-formality in social intercourse, looked at me with a wicked gleam in his eye, then darted out his tongue to lightly touch Gwendolen's fingers again.

'Cecily,' he said, 'I look forward to holding your hand in greeting. But in the meantime, here is an unusual and enticing state of affairs. Although I have not yet touched you, I have had the priviledge of tasting you. The sensation is wholly delightful.'

'This, Sir, is a situation that I have never seen dealt with in the books of etiquette and I am somewhat covered with embarrassment.'

'Just as dear Gwendolen's hand is somewhat covered with your cum,' he answered. 'You must have both been deep in conversation when I intruded upon your privacy. Should I now withdraw and seat myself towards the front of the bus so that you can resume your intercourse.'

'No,' said Gwendolen. 'Don't be silly. We had just come to a natural pause in our conversation. Cecily also had just come, but that's by-the-by. It was all my doing for I had been recounting the events of a most important day in my life.'

'Of course,' he responded. 'It is your anniversary. Your first fuck!'

'Cecily', said Gwendolen, 'I must explain that George has already heard the story of my first fuck.'

'And her second? And her third .. ?' I murmured.

'Cecily,' said Gwendolen, 'you will gather that George is already *aù fait* with every last detail of that memorable day. Indeed he was present on the first anniversary.

Not to put too fine a point on it, George was thoroughly embedded in me when I first told him the story. In spite of showing great self restraint during the account, his final reaction was the same as yours.'

'I came,' said George, 'But only after one of the longest and finest fucks of my life.'

'When George was young,' said Gwendolen, 'he was well tutored in certain Eastern arts of Love by his Nanny.'

'His Nanny!' I exclaimed.

'The family were out East. The Nanny was passed on to them by a family who were returning to England. She had the highest references. She also turned out to have spent the formative years of her life in a harem and had there learnt many of the exotic practices that are such an exciting part of Eastern tradition and culture.'

'By the time I was fourteen,' George explained, 'I could, with the aid of some strenuous mental exercises, remain erect and fully inserted for ten or more minutes. By the time I was sixteen, I had got it up to twenty minutes.'

'Got it up *for* twenty minutes, surely?' I responded. 'Is it not unusual to still have a nanny when one is sixteen, even in India.'

'Indeed, yes,' he asnwered. 'But my parents were more than happy that their, may I say it, occasionally unruly son, had been so well taken in hand. When not engaged in his Regimental duties, my father was altogether taken up in his polo and my mother was quite taken up in an illicit liason with the Adjutant.'

'Which came to an abrupt end,' interjected Gwendolen, 'when she was accidently revealed astride the Adjutant, stark naked except that she was wearing his boots, his Sam Brown belt and flourishing his riding crop.'

'As you can see,' went on George, 'my parents led a full life and were more than satisfied when it became clear that I was growing up to healthy manhood with little effort on their part.'

'So the nanny stayed,' I said.

'Indeed, yes,' he answered. 'And I quickly realised that the reason her previous employers had retained her services long past the time when most nannies have to pass on to another charge, must be connected with her very special abilities in the training of British manhood in the arts of the Orient.'

'And British womanhood, I gather,' said Gwendolen.

'I have to explain,' said George, 'that after the unfortunate public exposure of her affair with the adjutant, my mother took to her bedroom in shame for several days. Nanny, being of a kind and thoughtful disposition, spent many hours comforting her as she lay in her darkened room. She personally made sure that light meals were delivered to her. She shoo'd all the other servants away – and also my father who had been so upset when word reached him of the scandal that he fell off his polo pony and was accidentally struck on the head by the mallet of an over-enthusiastic brother officer. Mother, in the meantime, aided by the skilled ministrations of Nanny, quickly discovered a new interest in life. So enthusiastic did she become in the erotic arts of the East that she quite soon set off in disguise, with only Nanny to accompany her, on a tour of some of the more explicit Indian temple sculptures.

'You may have seen,' said Gwendolen, 'a privately printed monograph of restricted circulation entitled *An Introduction to the Eastern Art of Fucking*, by a Lady Much Experienced in Those Parts. There was a somewhat dog-eared copy in circulation in the Senior Dorm in your last year.'

'That was George's mother!' I exclaimed. 'I have long wished to meet the author, if only to encourage her to publish a sequel.'

126

'So there are two members of George's family who have much to thank his nanny for,' said Gwendolen.

'And may I enquire if her services extended as far as your father?' I asked.

'Alas, No,' said George. 'Remaining true to what he considered the finest traditions of the British Empire, he continued to be what is vulgarly called a 'two-minute man' and was quite soon afterwards invalided out of the army with a nasty dose of something he picked up in an Officers Only establishment in Calcutta. He retired to Ireland to breed horses and was sadly trampled to death by a mount of a nervous disposition while thrashing about in the straw of a horse box with a young girl from the village.'

'How terrible,' I said. 'Was the girl all right?'

'Bruised only,' said George. 'The family of course took pity on her – she could hardly remain in the village – and brought her over to London where she is still in service in my aunt's establishment. She recovered fully from her injuries and quickly resumed a most energetic life of fucking. I have in fact been honoured in turn to introduce her to those Eastern practices that I had learned at the hands of my nanny.'

'What a complicated family history you have,' I said. 'I am sure I should never be able to remember quite who did what and with whom.'

'Do not worry,' said Gwendolen. 'You are not about to be examined on the subject.' She must have seen the quick look of disappointment that passed across my face. 'At least not in the schoolroom sense of the word,' she went on hurriedly. 'I am sure a physical examination in the subject could be arranged.'

'An oral one too?' I asked, with a little shiver of daring.

'It would be my pleasure,' said George.

'It would be *all* our pleasures,' said Gwendolen firmly. 'George,' she went on, 'One thing I must tell you – I hope I do not embarrass you, Cecily dear – is that Cecily has a pair of the biggest, most delicious titties of anyone I know. I am almost beside myself in my desire to see them once more, and to feel them responding to my touch.'

'Oh, and your tongue too, Gwendolen dear,' I burst out. 'To feel myself being stroked and sucked into ecstasy. And then to rub them all over your own lovely titties while our fingers begin to explore each other's most secret parts. But I must not continue with these imaginings. I am becoming all wet with the thought of such an encounter.'

'We must indeed all sit quietly,' said George. 'Already I feel a bulging reminder that this is a public place and proper public behaviour is called for.' With this he sat down in the seat in front of us and began to adjust his tie and cuffs.

'But later we will all fuck,' said Gwendolen, quietly.

We began to make small talk as the top deck filled up. George asked where we were going. I explained about the Private Viewing of my cousin Algernon's paintings. George, who had been going to visit his tailor somewhere off St James', decided that instead he would accompany us if that was acceptable to the two of us. We of course quickly agreed and apart from the promising warmth of Gwendolen's body as we sat squeezed together in our seat, the rest of the journey passed without incident.

The gallery was but a short walk from the omnibus route, in one of that maze of little streets behind Bond Street. *En route* I referred glancingly to the fact that George was dressed as though on the way to a funeral. In fact it turned out that he was on the way back from a short memorial service.

'Someone close to you?' I asked.

'A family friend,' he answered. 'She had been my great aunt's companion for some years. A paragon of Good Works, always prattling on about the Deserving Poor and Visiting the Sick. Most days she went out with a servant and a bowl of nourishing soup – a rather thin and watery brew. Personally I can think of nothing worse when ill than being forcibly visited by Miss Windermere and having a quantity of undrinkable soup thrust upon me. I believe that many in the parish felt that way. But whenever anyone who came within her definition of Deserving took to their bed, you can be sure that within hours there would be a loud knock on the door and in would traipse Miss Windermere, a bunch of religious tracts in her hand and the servant struggling behind with the gruel.

There was no avoiding your fate. Miss Windermere had the most remarkable Intelligence system. The first whisper of sickness and she would swing into action. She was without doubt the most feared woman for miles around.'

'How did she die?' I asked.

'Blown up,' George answered.

'Blown up?' I exclaimed. 'Surely an unusual fate for a spinster of advanced years.'

'The outrage was quite accidental. It seems that the latest of her bed-bound victims was an elderly lady who had worked as a governess in St Petersburg many years ago and still had friends in Russia. It was the nephew of one of these friends who was inadvertently responsible for Miss Windermere's demise. An anarchist student from Minsk, he had entered this country in order to effect the assassination of some visiting Russian General who was also a relative of the Tsar.

Whilst staying with the former governess, he had been engaged in the construction of two bombs which he intended to lob at the General while he was riding in the Park. The explosives were cunningly hidden in the chamber pot that was under the governess's bed. When Miss Windermere was standing over her, asking after her spiritual welfare, she knocked over a candle that was beside the bed – the room being darkened in order to sooth the governess's headache.

The candle, in falling, set fire to a rug by the bed. In a trice this had in turn ignited the fuse and the chamber pot exploded. Miss Windermere was cut down by a hail of china splinters.

The governess however was luckier. Her bed took the main force of the explosion and collapsed on the burning remnants, largely extinguishing them. The governess, a woman of initiative and good in an emergency, quickly put out the still smoldering rug by peeing on it. She was unscathed and the servant only slightly hurt, chiefly by the scalding hot soup which was flung all over her, but Miss Windermere was already beyond the help of all but the clergy.'

'What happened to the anarchist?' I asked.

'He fled to London and I understand that Scotland Yard are searching for him all over the East End.'

'Why the East End?' I queried.

'That is where all good anarchists gather. They sit in cafés and discuss politics in loud and quarrelsome voices. The police know that, so that is where they will be looking for him.'

'So if he is a wise anarchist, he will be staying in a completely different part of London?'

'If he has any sense, yes,' he answered.

'And the memorial service?'

'A very tedious affair. After a lifetime of Good Works it was inevitable that her passing would be attended by representatives of every Charity, Mission to the Heathen and Society for Promoting This and That in the country. Pew upon pew of worthy citizens, pious expressions and a long sermon in which the Canon expressed his belief that Miss Windermere is already busy in Heaven, no doubt pursuing off-colour Angels, Saints and Martyrs with bowls of soup. I think we can expect a mass emigration from Heaven in the near future.'

'Goodness,' I said. 'What a sad tale. I do hope the anarchist is not lurking somewhere in the vicinity.'

'I did see a most furtive little man, wearing a long black cloak on the omnibus,' interposed Gwendolen at this juncture. 'He was carrying a large Gladstone bag.'

'Did you see where he alighted?' asked George.

'Oh dear! I do believe that it was at the same place that we disembarked,' said Gwendolen. 'He must be following us.'

'Unless any of us has connections with the Russian Royal Family we are unlikely to be the target of his dark plot,' said George.

'I did once have a night of passion with a Hungarian Count,' volunteered Gwendolen. 'Well, two.'

'Two nights or two Hungarian Counts,' I asked.

'Two Hungarians,' said Gwendolen. 'The Count and his Countess.'

'How advanced of you,' I said. 'And how exciting.'

'It was more strange than exciting,' replied Gwendolen. 'The Count occupied his time almost entirely by sniffing my more intimate garments and wrapping them round his body. While he then spent himself rolling around on the floor, the Countess – who had commenced by disrobing me with great care – then proceeded to chastise me with her stick, before engaging me in a positive orgy of Sapphic delights.'

'Gracious me,' I responded.

'Cecily, I learned that night that there is much that an older woman can teach a young and innocent girl.'

'Innocent. Oh Gwendolen! that is not an epithet with which I would reproach you. I, of all people know the very day on which you lost your Innocence.'

'You debauched me,' said Gwendolen.

'That is not a pretty word,' I replied crossly.

'Yours were the first hands that were ever laid on my virginal body. But, dear Cecily, I am only teasing. It was the most delicious initiation into the mysteries of love. To this day I can remember the delicate play of your fingers on my pussey. You were most gentle – and most thorough.'

At this turn of the conversation, I once more felt a familiar warmth spreading through my body. I snuggled up against Gwendolen as we walked and then reached out to draw George into our comfortable companionship.

'Is it true what Gwendolen says about your titties?' he asked, his arm linked in mine.

'Modesty forbids me to sing my own praises,' I replied. 'But they are I consider two of my finest features.'

'I look forward to feasting my eyes on them,' he continued.

'Cecily will be better pleased if you feast more than your eyes on them,' said Gwendolen. 'I have always found that Cecily most appreciates some nibbling. Not to mention a sharp nip or two when she is well advanced in her enjoyment.'

'Please stop it,' I implored them. 'Such talk is causing me positively to swell with anticipation. My nipples are rubbing most painfully against my bodice.'

'I also am swelling with anticipation,' answered George. 'We must put off all such thoughts and deeds for the near future. Where is the gallery?'

'Just around the next corner,' I said. 'I hope this will not be too stuffy an occasion. But you should enjoy my cousin's paintings. They are held in some quarters to be rather advanced.'

With that, we arrived and when he had handed over our coats and Gwendolen's tartan travelling rug, we passed into an already crowded salon. But here I must explain a little about my Cousin Algernon.

Cousin Algernon had the unusual claim to fame of having been found as a baby in a handbag in the Left Luggage Office on Brighton Station. After such a Bohemian start to life, it was I suppose inevitable that he became an artist when he grew up.

131

Of course like all proper artists, he led a properly scandalous life, chiefly with his model Babette, a voluptuous creature who came originally from Northamptonshire and who cooked well.

Actually the fact that she came from Northamptonshire – Kettering to be precise – was not generally known. Nor was the fact that her real name was Edith. Instead like all proper artists models, it was understood that she was a *Parisienne* and had been either a seamstress or a *midinette* before a struggling and penniless artist had discovered her and transferred her to his *atelier* to grace both canvas and bed. Babette was, as I have suggested, a big woman. In fact she was huge. Cousin Algernon, himself a big man and an altogether larger-than-life character with a commendable appetite for all the good things in life, delighted in painting Babette.

Most frequently he depicted her in Classic guise. Babette, wearing little except some carefully placed, vaguely Grecian draperies or wisps of white muslin, displayed herself in a variety of mythic poses. Here she was taking part in the *Bath of Psyche*. Here she was *Diana Surprised by Actaeon*. Most frequently she was a nymph or some such, being ravished by Zeus, or on occasion by what seemed like the entire Pantheon of Greek Gods, in any number of disguises: a Swan, a Bull, a Stallion – and in one memorable instance what appeared to be a Parrot, although Cousin Algernon insisted that it was an Eagle. He did later also admit that it was one of his less successful works.

Babette was also the central figure in a completely different series of paintings. Working in what he described as his French Interior Realist mode, Cousin Algernon showed her, this time without any trace of clothing whatsoever, as a washerwoman or scrubbing floors, laying a fire or at some other domestic task.

Whether it is the habit of French servants to perform their duties stark naked I do not know, but the paintings clearly made a considerable impression in London. In truth these vigorous oils of big Babette, for instance, leaning over a tub full of suds, her huge forearms and magnificent bosom highlighted by the painter's art, were not unpleasing, if occasionally verging on the laughable. The views of Babette scrubbing were for the most part seen from behind. The great spheres of her buttocks rose like a double moon to fill the scene. Every roll of fat was lovingly rendered and she seemed to glow with what I gather is called 'rude health.'

His latest masterpiece, *Babette at the Mangle* had quite a crowd of admirers around it. Cousin Algernon had managed to give the impression of a woman panting and heaving with her exertions, her breasts swaying and shaking as she turned the mangle while her skin glowed and there was the sheen of perspiration on her body.

I noticed that the preponderance of the people at the viewing were men, and men of a middle aged and generally prosperous men. I was told by an elderly man, who claimed some knowledge of things artistic, that Cousin Algernon had successfully created a small fashion among the *cognoscenti* for such scenes of domestic undress. A number of fellow artists, all living and working nearby in north London, had followed his lead. Known in the art world as the Crouch End School, they had a growing and enthusiastic band of collectors quite clamouring of their works.

Of course, my informant confided in me, many of the academic critics poured scorn on the Crouch End School. Mr Ruskin had described Cousin Algernon's work as 'A battery of buttocks, thrust into the Public's face' while the Academy steadfastly refused to hang his pictures. Nonetheless, as someone who dabbled in dealing, he could vouch for the fact that a surprising number of the more flamboyant *Views of Babette*, as he called them, could be seen discreetly displayed in many of the most reputable gentlemen's clubs.

'Indeed,' said my aesthetic informant, 'if one could but see through the grey facades of Pall Mall, I fancy we would be regaled with the mouth-watering sight of Babette's mountainous buttocks flaunted cheek to cheek, so to say, along almost the full length of the street.'

Be that as it may, many of the priviledged viewers at the gallery, as they gazed intently at every detail of Babette's anatomy, were showing those powers of concentration and stamina, that must have accounted for their undoubted success in business and public affairs. I noticed also that for many there was an improving moral lesson to be gained from a close perusal of the paintings.

'Ah! The dignity of Honest Toil' announced one gentleman

as he raised his *pince-nez* to his eyes, the better to scrutinise the spread of Honest Toil's thighs.

'Application and Dedication in all Endeavours, Domestic as well as Professional', agreed another.

'An Example to the Labouring Classes,' said a third, who later confided in me that an earlier work by Cousin Algernon hung in his study. '*Babette Preparing Vegetables*, it is called. So exemplary do I consider his work that on occasion I call in my housekeeper or cook after dinner so that they also can gaze upon it in my company and reflect on its moral worth.'

One senior clerical gentleman, suffering what I was later given to understand was hay fever, had to be led away, his eyes watering and his chest heaving after standing as if transfixed in front of *The Rape of the Sabine Women* in which Babette appeared in no less than twenty seven poses.

'Such flesh tones,' he had started muttering, 'And such flesh! And so much of it!' Then, as he began to stammer and had to reach out for some support, I, recognising him as a Man of the Cloth – he was in fact the Rural Dean of N———d assumed that he was in the throes of some transcendental experience. Gwendolen, who has a sharp eye for such things, claimed rather that he had become dangerously over-excited by the proximity of no less than twenty seven naked Babettes on one canvas and that he had in fact come in his trousers.

'Look on my Mighty Works and Despair' proclaimed a tall, cadaverous man as he traced out the outline of Babette's great pendulous breasts with his walking stick. 'How bounteous is Nature. See where the twin globes of her bosom seem to loom like planets in the celestial firmament of her flesh. Truly a sight to make one humble before one's Creator. All things' he went on, 'Wide and Wonderful, all Creatures great and tall . . .'

I was afterwards informed that the tall gentleman was a hymn writer of some distinction and regularly attended such showings as this. He claimed to be able to detect the Hand of the Lord in the most unlikely places.

After a while most of the people began to drift off and quite soon, apart from the three of us, there was only a small knot of some half a dozen or so gentlemen. Cousin Algernon suggested that we all withdraw to a smaller room that opened off one end of the gallery. He then came over to have a word with us, announcing that Babette herself was about to make an appearance.

'In the flesh?' I asked.

'Not immediately,' he answered, with a quick smile. 'But if you would like to stay on with your friends, I am sure you could be accommodated.'

'Some entertainment is afoot?' asked Gwendolen.

'In a matter of speaking,' he answered. 'Several of the gentlemen gathered here belong to a private club. They dabble in oils in a strictly amateur way. Since they are also collectors and valuable customers, I have arranged that they be given the opportunity to sketch Babette from Life.'

'What an enticing idea,' said Gwendolen. 'But will we not be something of an embarrassment?'

'I suggest that you all act as my assistants. You can help with the arrangement of certain properties, take Babette's robe from her when the moment comes to reveal all. That sort of thing.'

'This sounds great fun,' said Gwendolen. 'But I promise we will behave ourselves and do nothing to prejudice your commercial interests.'

We were ushered through to the smaller room. Various items of a domestic nature were heaped in one corner. They included scrubbing brushes, a mop, a portable washtub, a couple of flat irons and a neatly folded pile of linen. It was obvious that Babette would be able to display herself in any number of household chores.

'What's that?' asked George, indicating a stout wooden pole with a cross piece at one end and a round piece at the other with five short legs.

'A poss stick,' said Cousin Algernon. 'It is used to stir up the washing in a tub when it is soaking in the hot water.'

'I am afraid that George, like so many men, has never paid proper attention to the domestic duties that have to be performed in any household,' said Gwendolen.

'I used to venture into the servants area at home when I was much younger,' said George, 'But I was firmly excluded after my mother found me helping one of the maids to adjust her clothing. There was also the small matter that she was holding my youthful prick in her hands and licking the tip in a most attentive fashion.'

135

'I assume from that that you have led an active life,' said Cousin Algernon. 'A man after my own heart. But for the present, could you give me a hand in setting out a nice derangement of objects. Our amateur painters can then make the decision as to which pose they would wish Babette to adopt.'

At this moment Babette herself swept into the room. Truly a magnificent creature, she was wearing a regal purple robe which entirely swathed the bountiful promise of her body but yet which hinted at the well-fleshed splendours it concealed. We were quickly introduced and she embraced us all warmly but briefly.

'Cecily, I have heard all about you from Algernon,' she said. 'Do either of your friends have any knowledge of the world of the artist?'

'I have a distant cousin who is employed as a designer of pottery at Messrs Doulton's establishment,' said Gwendolen.

'But she does not have to appear in a state of undress?' asked Babette.

'Not at her place of work,' answered Gwendolen, 'Although on more private occasions she is frequently quite eager to reveal herself in a state of nature.'

'Perhaps I might be introduced to this cousin,' I interjected. 'She has the sound of a person of sympathetic disposition.'

'You will have much in common,' said Gwendolen. 'Fucking and being fucked is her chief delight. What a quartet we will make.'

'Quartet?' I queried.

'She has a sister of similar tastes. Their mother is also a woman with refreshingly unconventional ideas. They now also have staying with them Rosalind Murphy. You may remember her. She was a year behind us at school.'

'Rosie!' I exclaimed. 'Rosie with the rosy bottom. What fun it will be to meet her again.'

'Enough of this chatter,' said Cousin Algernon. 'Our would-be painters will be making their entry shortly.'

With this we fell to sorting out the pile of domestic articles. George and Cousin Algernon pulled the mangle into place and a woman appeared with pails of warm water with which the washtub was filled. In a trice the stage had been set for

Babette's performance.

Our amateur artists were led in. For a moment they fell silent in awe and anticipation at the sight of Babette. She, as yet fully clothed, moved among them, exchanging greetings as they were introduced. Ranging from the middle-aged to the elderly, one and all appeared to be respectable and sober representatives of the professional and upper commercial classes. Two, I vaguely recognised as men of some importance in Public Affairs. Two others were of military bearing and a third, of Gallic appearance, had the ribbon of the *Légion d'Honneur* in his lapel.

'Gentlemen, I am honoured to welcome you to our Private Master Class in painting from Life,' said Cousin Algernon. Let us now prepare ourselves.' Easels, paints, palettes and canvases were produced. There was a intent bustle of activity. Babette advanced on them with an armful of smocks.

'To avoid any splashes,' she said. 'Painting is an enjoyable but messy exercise.'

She passed among them, removing coats, slipping the smocks over them, buttoning them or tieing them briskly at the back. Many of the gentlemen were clearly quite excited at the touch of her hands. One who in turn attempted to place his hand on her splendid rump, had it firmly removed but all was done with a half-smile on her face and a twinkle in her eye so that not only was no offence caused, but a teasing air of promise caused the gentleman to become somewhat purple with pleasure anticipated.

'Gentlemen,' said Cousin Algernon, 'Madame Babette will now take up the first pose of the evening. However, the choice is yours. Would you have her at the tub, at the mangle, or possibly on all fours in her imposing imitation of a servant engaged in scrubbing?'

A veritable babble of competing voices was raised.

'The mangle,' cried one.

'No, no, for myself, I would prefer to see her leaning over the wash,' said another.

Two others were adamant that they could only do justice to their subject if she was crouched down. Yet one was all for her presenting her bottom to the class whilst the other, somewhat confused about domestic positions, I considered, wished to see

137

her on her back.

'As though she has had a slight mishap on a slippery floor,' he explained somewhat unconvincingly.

Cousin Algernon let the argument rage for some minutes until it quickly became apparent that no one faction was in the ascendancy.

'Gentlemen,' he said, raising his voice to cut through the uproar. 'Since I can see that agreement is not be to easily reached, I have an alternative idea.' With that he clicked his fingers and a small but sturdy kitchen table was conjured up, along with a rolling pin and a large quantity of dough.

'May I present *Madame Babette Kneading Dough*!'

With the flourish of an experienced actress, Babette marched across to the table and in one flamboyant motion, shed her purple gown.

A gasp of admiration rose up from the assembled gentlemen artists, for underneath she was utterly and hugely naked. With an exquisite sense of timing, she leant over the table and seized the soft, pliant mound of dough. As she forced her hands into it, squeezing it back and forth, then shaping it and thumping it flat again, her breasts swung between her arms, her belly rubbed against the table and her tremendous buttocks jiggled up and down with the effort of her labours.

Her audience stared at her open mouthed, hardly moving, so transfixed were they by this vast vision of nakedness. From the back of the assembly there came a stifled groan.

Several were visibly shaking with suppressed artistic inspiration.

Then first one and then a second, pulling themselves together, took up their brushes and squeezed paint on to their palettes. Next there was a scraping of easels and stools as a number of them began to move into their preferred positions. I noticed that he who had been loudly in favour of the kneeling-seen-from-behind pose rapidly moved into the appropriate line-of-sight. I also noticed that he stationed himself within no more than an arms length of the twin subjects of his delight as they rose and fell in their majestic rhythm.

'Alas, I grow increasingly short-sighted,' he said hurriedly in order to justify his close proximity to Babette's bottom.

'A more convincing excuse if only he were wearing an eye

glass or spectacles,' whispered Gwendolen, nudging me gently. The three of us were now standing quietly against the wall as this amazing *tableau vivant* unfolded itself before our fascinated eyes.

Now the gentlemen fell to their painting with a quiet but splashy intensity. Brushes charged with full loads of paint were slapped and smeared on canvases. By the sweeping motions of their paint strokes I could understand that the great curves of Babette's body were being energetically, if none too skilfully, transferred to canvas. Cousin Algernon, in his role of teacher, moved from one to another, advising and encouraging. Here he deftly showed one how to mix a convincing flesh tone. There he demonstrated how to achieve the fullness of texture demanded by the subject.

Meanwhile Babette plunged and swung and thrust and kneaded. At one point the self-declared short-sighted gentleman crouched down on the floor peering intently up between her massive thighs.

'So difficult to catch the play of light and shade low down,' he muttered, with even less conviction this time.

'Ah, yes, a close scrutiny of his subject is a sign of a true artist,' replied Cousin Algernon. 'But you would not wish to impede the view of your fellow artists I believe.'

A little reluctantly, the myopic enthusiast withdrew, understanding that a polite reprimand had been given. Then Babette paused in her labours.

'Please, gentleman. A moment's rest for Madame Babette,' said Cousin Algernon.

A subdued ripple of disappointment ran round the room but this was instantly replaced by a collective sigh of pleasure as Babette stood upright and then slowly stretched herself. All eyes were on her as she displayed the full splendour of her body. Paint dribbled unattended from wavering brushes. Several of the gentlemen sat down with shudders of emotion, some almost bent double as if in pain. Trousers were hastily adjusted and first one and then another hurriedly left the room in order to answer an urgent call of nature.

Babette turned to our direction, her lush pussey hair standing out proudly against her flesh, and winked very slightly at us. I smiled back but swiftly resumed my most demure countenance. George stepped forward and handed her her robe which she put on with an easy but most provoking twitch of her shoulders.

'A short break for refreshment before we resume our artistic endeavours?' suggested Cousin Algernon as a decanter and glasses made their appearance.

After ten minutes or so, Cousin Algernon called upon his class to resume their places.

'Another three quarters of a hour will be enough,' he said to us quietly. 'I find that my more mature students can only stand a couple of hours. Such is the intensity of the artistic experience that for the most part they will be quite drained and more than ready to adjourn quietly to their clubs or their homes.'

So the second half of the art lesson passed. Babette, clearly a woman of considerable stamina, ploughed her swaying, quivering way through a second mountain of dough. As she sprinkled flour on hands and board to prevent the mixture sticking, smears of flour and dough transferred themselves to her face, her forearms and even to the Himalayan mounds of her bosom.

As first a lump of dough clung from one dark plum-like nipple and then as a sifting of flour settled on her luxuriant bush, so the brush work of the amateur artists became more and more wild and erratic. As though in sympathetic response, flecks and gobbets of pigment landed on smocks and faces. Whilst some were working themselves up to a positive frenzy of strokes and dabs, so others began to grow slack and exhausted. Eyes began to glaze over and brushes wilted in trembling hands. Soon several members were standing open-mouthed, sucking air into their labouring lungs like athletes at the end of a long foot race.

Babette herself began to move slower and slower, though still driving and pummeling the dough. Beads of perspiration stood out on her forehead and trickled down her heaving flanks. As she breathed ever more deeply her chest expanded and contracted and her enormous breasts undulated, rising and falling in a surging tide of flesh. Her well-planted legs flexed and trembled while her short-sighted posterior attendant, knees buckling, lowered himself on to his stool and sat there gasping for air like a landed trout.

'Time, gentlemen, please,' said Cousin Algernon. 'I feel we have accomplished enough for one evening.'

There was a half-hearted groan of disappointment but fatigue had indeed caught up with the best part of them.

'I hope though that you will all come again,' he continued. 'I suggest we reconvene in two weeks time at the same hour. I propose to join you in attempting to do justice to *Babette Kneading Dough*. If I am satisfied with my own work, I might, when it is completed, put it up for auction, restricting the bidding to those here present.'

This scheme was enthusiastically welcomed. The class began to filter out to the cloakroom in order to wash and generally make themselves presentable enough to face the outside world. Babette clutched her robe round her once more. She favoured the assembly with a sympathetic but slightly roguish smile as she stalked out to her dressing room. A few last lingering glances were directed at the generous hemispheres of her buttocks as they disappeared, like a double eclipse, behind the enveloping draperies of the curtain. Then the *amateurs de la peinture* bid their goodbyes and ambled out into the early evening air.

'You must all stay while everything is tidied away,' said Cousin Algernon. 'Babette will be rejoining us in a few minutes, as soon as she is refreshed and clothed once more. I have a couple of bottles of claret and some whisky also. We must all take a little wine in order to celebrate what I believe to have been a highly successful event.'

We fell to drinking and light conversation. Presently Babette reappeared. A glass or two restored her to full vigour and animation. We plied her with questions about the rigours of life as an artist's model.

'It can indeed be tiring at times,' she said. 'But that is generally the way with work, is it not? Yet I find that there is great satisfaction to be gained from it so long of course as one does not mind appearing unclothed before members of the opposite sex. For my part, I must confess that I have always had a certain yearning to appear upon the stage, in the theatrical limelight.'

'Do not artist's models usually pose motionless,' I asked. 'I know that, clothed or unclothed, I should find it impossible to keep still in one position for more than a moment or two. Would one not suffer terribly from aches and cramps?'

'Holding a pose for any length of time is indeed a demanding discipline,' she agreed. 'It is one that can be learned quite easily, but I confess that I do infinitely prefer your Cousin's moving presentations. If I am an actress *manqué*, then Algernon is an actor-manager *manqué* and an accomplished Master of Ceremonies as well.'

'I see that there are attractions to the job,' I answered thoughtfully. Babette looked at me with an appraising gleam in her eye.

'Do not take this amiss, Cecily, but I think that you may well have the makings of a model. I suspect that under that modest but quite charming dress there is concealed a fine display sufficient to hold the attention of the most discerning audience. Might I be allowed to...?'

'Oh, no!' I said, as natural modesty vied with a little tingle of excitement, 'No, I don't think I possibly could...'

'Madame Babette,' interrupted Gwendolen. 'Although it is two years since I saw Cecily, my memories of her are such that I can indeed confirm you in your beliefs. Cecily unclothed is a sight for the connoisseur's eye. Cecily, we are all friends here. I do implore you to allow us the pleasure of seeing your lovely titties. If Madame Babette will give you some instruction in the art of posing...?'

'Why, yes indeed,' she answered. 'I would be delighted to be confirmed in my belief that you have a most fetching figure.'

'Mouth-watering,' said Gwendolen. 'Oh Cecily, how excited I am. Two long years since I last feasted my eyes on your titties. You do not know how often I have dreamed of them and longed to nestle against them once more.'

'Dear, sweet Gwendolen,' I said. 'What a wonderful speech. How can I possibly refuse you.'

'I should perhaps withdraw from the room,' said George. 'I would not like to intrude upon such an intimate scene.'

'I also,' said Cousin Algernon, although with a marked hesitation.

'No,' said Gwendolen. 'Cecily, it would be too cruel to deny them a first sight of your bountiful charms.' She turned to them. 'All Cecily's body is a sight for sore eyes. She has the nicest, best-shaped bottom that I have ever clapped hands on. Her waist is adorable and I swear her pussey is the warmest, most welcoming pussey in the whole wide world.'

'Gwendolen,' I said, 'You go too far.'

'Oh! don't be cross,' she answered. 'I am so looking forward to an unveiling.'

'Well, I said, a little shocked and confused with the daring of such a plan but beginning to tremble with the excitement of it all. 'You will have to help me.'

Gwendolen eagerly hugged me. She buried her face in the nape of my neck and then before I had time to protest any further, I felt her fingers dextrously begin their work at the buttons of my dress. There came the sudden breath of cool air upon my now exposed back. I crossed my arms protectively over my bosom with a quick pang of shyness. Light hands played for an instant along my bare flesh and then my dress was pushed forward over my shoulders.

As I stood there, huddled and uncertain, Babette strode across to me, lifted my chin and looked me straight in the face.

'Not like that, Cecily,' she said. 'Keep your head up. You should be proud, not shamefaced. You are about to present your audience with a show for which they should be privileged and grateful.'

Emboldened, I did as she said. I straightened my back and stretched out my arms. George and Cousin Algernon unbuttoned my cuffs and Gwendolen pushed my dress and chemise off my shoulders so that it descended and gathered in a rustle of silk at my waist. I turned and presented my bared breasts to Gwendolen for her approval. Then, hands on hips, I deliberately twisted slowly round to the rest of my audience.

'Cecily,' said Gwendolen. 'How lovely they are. Surely they are even larger and more delectable than I had remembered. You have grown a little since I last saw you.'

'Such succulent fruit,' said Couson Algernon with an expansive gesture. 'Oh that a man might suck sweet nectar from those ripe nipples.'

I recalled that Cousin Algernon had always tended to the florid in his manner of speech. George meanwhile was quite tongue tied. Babette, her hands on mine, held me at arm's length and gazed with professional approval at me.

143

'You are a delight, my dear,' she said.

'Such beauties belong to the world,' Cousin Algernon went on. 'You are Aphrodite and Bathsheba and Lakshmi, all rolled into one.'

'Lakshmi,' said Gwendolen, 'is surely the Indian goddess with *eight* breasts. I think you are getting a little carried away.'

'Now turn round again. Slowly, slowly,' said Babette. 'Remember you are on stage.'

Quite overcome by the attention, all shyness was forgotten as I felt my nipples begin to stiffen and my breasts to swell with excitement. Arching my back, my hands clasped behind my neck, I held myself out to my enthralled audience. Then a sudden thought came into my mind. What if Miss Bradshaw were to see me now. Would she not fall in a swoon to the ground? I burst out laughing and, cupping my breasts in my hands, advanced on Gwendolen.

'If I am still pleasing to you, pray show me with your soft mouth that you are as loving and eager for me as I am for you.'

I smiled, the picture of a shocked Miss Bradshaw beside herself at such unladylike behaviour looming large in my mind's eye. Gwendolen, as though she could read my thoughts, smiled back.

'Schooldays,' I said.

'Schooldays,' she replied.

Forgetting my other admirers, I enfolded her in a warm embrace. As she responded, I kissed her. Gwendolen kissed me in return. Our tongues touched and probed. A familiar glow of expectation warmed me and my titties seemed to throb with anticipation. Each nipple rose, engorged and hungry for love. A little mew of pleasure escaped my lips. Breathing more heavily, I pressed her to my half-naked body and whispered to her.

'Gwendolen, I am becoming very damp in another place.'

Then as her hands slyly cupped my breasts, I bit her ear, trying to stifle the gasp of sheer pleasure that welled up inside me.

Gwendolén, with her well-remembered skills with tongue and hands was rapidly bringing me to a first climax of ecstasy. I know that my whole body was flushed and my breasts aching

144

with the need for relief. Gwendolen was now becoming quite rough in her fondling and massaging. My hands on hers, I pressed them hard against me, spreading out her fingers so that they encompassed the twin orbs of my breasts. She squeezed and stroked and then suddenly pinched each erect peak. She steadily increased the pressure until I cried out. Pain and pleasure mingled. My heart was beating as though it would burst.

All at once I was aware of a sudden wetness between my legs and I closed my eyes, lost and drowning in the flood of sensual delight that swept over me. As I clung to her, she disengaged herself and moved her hands down to my waist. She eased me round to face and display myself to my audience.

'Cecily,' she said, 'Truly you are God's gift to all those lucky enough to behold you.'

The others were enraptured. Cousin Algernon and George were both standing, open mouthed. Great bulges betrayed their manhoods, each thrustingly erect and eager to be released from its bondage. Babette was smiling her approval.

'This is such pleasure,' said Cousin Algernon, 'What can we possibly do to repay you for this lovely display?'

'I think I'd like . . .,' I replied faintly, 'I want . . . I want very much to be fucked. Now! Fuck me now, please.'

My legs felt suddenly weak and I half leaned against Gwendolen. She held me tenderly and led me over to a table. Realising what was to come, I eased myself up and on to it, lying back and raising my knees so that my cunney was opened out before my audience. Gwendolen came round to my front and eased her hands under the cheeks of my bum as I raised it towards her sweet face.

She buried herself in my bush before sliding out her tongue and finding my clit. Licking and sucking delicately at it, she brought me in an instant to the very verge of coming. Then she withdrew her lips and tongue and ran one finger down the length of my cunt lips.

'See, the parting of the ways,' she said.

As I groaned, she looked round the room. 'George, Algernon, which one will be the first to volunteer to fill this aching need?'

Fumbling and overcome by the urgency of the summons, they responded. First Cousin Agernon's and then George's prick sprang out into full view. Each was rigid with the desire to thrust its way forward into the dark depths of my cavern. Yet courtesy was not forgotten.

'George, it is for you to make the first entrance,' said Cousin Algernon.

'No, I am an outsider here,' replied George gallantly. 'Surely you would wish to keep it within the family.'

'I insist,' answered Cousin Algernon. 'Besides, I know that dear Babette will take me in hand if needs be.'

Without waiting for further urging, George stepped forward.

'Cecily,' he said, 'I am at your service.'

'Fuck me!' I panted in reply. 'Fuck me! No more talking.'

Then, as I watched, he placed the tip of his immense prick at the gateway of my desire. At the first pressure of that swollen, empurpled head, I opened wide and reached forward to cradle his balls in my hands. I held them for an instant, feeling their heavy weight and sensing the spunk that was already beginning to force its way up his prick. Impatiently I pulled him straight into me so that the entire length of him slid its way up and up to the very hilt. I gripped him fast and then released him.

Needing no further urging, he commenced to thrust backwards and forwards, up and down the gaping depths of my cunt. A fever of excitement ran through my body and I became senseless with the joy of fucking. Vaguely I was aware that I was crying out, quite abandoned to my longed-for fate. Steadily the tempo of our coupling increased. We thrust against each other, all our strengths concentrated in the intensity of our fucking. Hunger fed upon hunger in mounting need.

Suddenly I felt the first long drawn-out shudder of my coming sweep over me. At the same moment he cried out and the first surge of his spunk shot out of his prick, jetting into the innermost recesses of my cunt. His cream flooded into me, mingling with the love juice that flowed in me, soaking the already moist forest of my fanny.

Gripping him with my thighs, I forced him still deeper into me.

'More! More!' I heard myself cry out, desperate to prolong the moment of our fulfillment. Gamely he drove on. I swear that never had such copious quantities of cum deluged me, overflowing and running down into the crevice of my bum so that I began to slip and slide in a veritable pool of our juices.

All good things must come to an end, as my governess had often said to me, and George's Thing had indeed come to my end – and his. One last spasm wracked our bodies and I was borne down by the full weight of his body, as he fell exhausted on me. I felt his distended prick relax inside me and we clung together, panting with our exertions. We lay still for a little while and then I pushed him from me in order to bend forward and lick the last milky drops of his cum from the tip of his now-softening prick. I ran my hands over his balls and rubbed them in the stickiness of his manly forest. I held him lightly by the wrists and drew his hands down to my wet cunney. He rubbed and fondled me until I raised his fingers to my lips. Sucking and swallowing, I licked him clean. Taking his cue, he similarly first kissed and then sucked my fingers.

Then, as I smiled up at him, he was pushed to one side and Gwendolen was crouching between my opened thighs, nuzzling and lapping at my wetness.

'Darling Gwendolen,' I murmured weakly, 'What a wonderful *bonne bouche* after such a feast of fucking.'

Contentment and a delicious fatigue suffused my body.

'Like a cat that has stolen the cream,' I heard Cousin Algernon say.

'Not stolen, but offered,' said Babette, with a little laugh.

'Oh dear!' I said, remembering where I was. 'You must all think me very forward.'

'Backward *and* forward!' said Cousin Algernon. 'Backward and forward. A most energetic and enthralling display. What a subject to be immortalised on canvas.'

'Certainly not,' I said, sitting up in alarm and pulling my dress down over my knees. 'If you dare...'

'Only my little joke,' said Cousin Algernon. 'I have long reached the years of discretion.'

'The very idea!'

Smoothing my skirt I stood up, glaring haughtily at him and then realising that my stance was less than impressive, since I was still naked to the waist. Angrily I reached down to drag my dress up over my bosom.

Gwendolen came forward, hugged me and calmed me. Next she deftly covered my embarrassment, slipping my arms back into my sleeves and buttoning me up at the back. For a quick instant she reached inside my dress to fondle and caress my titties before they were finally hidden from view. We kissed gently and she pushed a stray lock of my hair back into place.

'There, there,' she said. 'Cousin Algernon was only teasing. You must remember that he has just had a very teasing time himself.'

As Babette solicitously linked her arm in Cousin Algernon's and whispered something in his ear, Gwendolen released me and went across to poor George who was standing there looking somewhat crestfallen, unmindful of the fact that his trousers were still lying in a crumpled heap on the floor.

'George,' she said, 'You have played your part manfully. Now we must all get dressed and ready to go home but I do hope that you will in turn entertain me with that same part in the very near future.'

As she helped him into his trousers, tucking his now pliable prick back inside and making all secure, she kissed him also with friendly affection. He brightened up, glad that the little spat had passed.

'Thank you, Miss Cecily,' he said gravely. 'That was the most magnificent fuck that I have enjoyed in a very long time.'

'Next time, I hope that we can enjoy it for an even longer time,' I said with a quick smile so that he could see that I was no longer annoyed. 'I was quite beside myself with the need to fuck.'

'So endeth the art lesson,' Cousin Algernon. 'We must finish the decanter.'

So saying he poured out the last of the claret. 'A toast,' he said as we raised our glasses, 'To the Muse of Painting.'

'And of Fucking,' said Gwendolen.

'I don't believe there is one,' said Cousin Algernon.'

'Gwendolen's grasp of the Classics is not so secure as her grasp of anatomy,' I replied.

'Never mind. Let us drink to the missing Muse,' said George.

148

'To practical matters,' I said. 'I am in need of a bath and a change of clothes. George, would you escort me home in a cab. I had not intended my exposure to the world of the artist to be so prolonged or so complete. I have to dine with my Great Aunt Tabitha tonight where we will doubtless talk of her scheme to establish a Home for Aged Horses.'

Hurriedly I made arrangements to call on Gwendolen the following afternoon. Babette bade us Goodbye.

'I had not intended your first lesson in posing to be so active,' she said, 'but you are cordially welcome to return, possibly to Algernon's studio, in the near future, when we might continue your course of instruction. Gwendolen, I hope that you will accompany your friend, and George also.'

'I believe that I am developing a taste for such things,' I responded.

We kissed all round and George and I went out into the evening.

THE END

Introduction to Part Three

Since the first publication of extracts from the *Oyster*, there has been a certain amount of interest as to the real identity of 'Sir Andrew Scott', for unlike Doctor Parsifal, 'Scott' hides behind a pseudonym. In her Introduction to *The Oyster 1* (New English Library, 1985), Antoinette Hillman-Strauss speculated that the writer of these memoirs was one of the writers eking out a living on one of the burgeoning group of popular magazines that catered for the newly literate mass-market. Further research by Farquhar Platting and Huish Hampton brought in the names of Gerald Burdett and Oswald Holland, authors of the spectacularly rude Victorian underground novel, *The Adventures of a Ram*, as being possibly responsible for this witty, light-hearted romp.

But it now seems that 'Sir Andrew Scott' was none other than our old friend Sir Lionel Trapes (1826-1908) who appears both in *Oyster* and in other similar magazines. Trapes was a high-ranking Treasury official and a wealthy man in his own right, having inherited close on a quarter of a million pounds from his father, the third baronet in the line.

Sir Lionel was a member of the fashionable South Hampstead set amongst whose members were H Spencer Ashbee ('Pisanus Fraxi') and the notorious Doctor Jonathan Arkley whose own extraordinary story will hopefully one day be written. Both these gentlemen were indefatigable collectors of erotica and Doctor Arkley, a fashionable medical man in Harley Street just over one hundred years ago, was known to have organised orgies for the very highest in the land. So limited – and exclusive – was the circulation of the *Oyster* that the use of real names became something of an indulgence, a curious private joke.

It is interesting to compare Sir Lionel's deft writing with his staid little book on the Kentish water colourist Lawrence Judd-Hughes which he published privately in 1896. Judd-Hughes name of course, is mentioned briefly in the present volume – an illustration of the playfulness of an author writing not for the general public but for a close, private world of which he was so enthusiastic a member. Further research is in progress which will, it is hoped, shed light on the identities of some of the other characters in these writings: it seems highly likely that many are based on intimates of the author(s).

Jack Axelrod
Newcastle-Under-Lyme
November, 1988

A Further Episode in the Sentimental and Erotic Education of Mr Andrew Scott

For new readers, the story so far:

The young Mr Andrew Scott, his schooldays at Nottsgrove Academy now behind him, has moved to London and is in lodgings in Bayswater. The house is owned by a widow, Mrs P——, a longtime friend both of Andrew's Godfather and also, as it transpires, of his old Headmaster, Dr White.

Mrs P—— is a woman of refreshingly progressive views in matters sexual, believing such activities to be both natural and healthy and to be indulged in without shame with but the one *caveat*: that both parties should be equally willing. Her views have been long matured through her experiences in India where her acquaintance has included Mr Richard Burton, later to find notoriety as the translater of such Eastern classics as *The Perfumed Garden* and the *Kama Sutra*.

Also resident in the house are Mrs P——s two daughters, Becky and Hannah; the first follows the vocation of nursing, the latter is a skilled artist and designer employed at Messrs Doulton's Lambeth manufactory. The household is completed by two maids, Mary and Emily.

The detailed description of Andrew's ups and downs, his ins and outs in this most liberal of establishments has been set down in previous issues of the *Oyster*. It remains only to add that, as our story continues, Andrew has returned that very afternoon from a trip to the West Country, whence he has escorted Mrs P——'s Ward, Rosie who has been peremptorily expelled from her school for offences against the school rules involving her friendship with the Art Master and her growing interest in the skills of photography.

Now read on:

Dinner that evening displayed Mrs P——s household apparently in more conventional guise. Mrs P—— presided at the head of the table. Both Hannah and Becky were present and correct. Rosie, who had been installed in one of the two guest bedrooms, had been formally introduced to the household and now took her place with a display of maidenly decorum that would have been entirely convincing to any outsider who had not before been exposed to her wayward nature.

I was at once eagerly pressed on all sides to describe everything that had taken place on my trip to Bristol. For my part I was of course careful *not* to describe all that had gone on. I was only too aware that while Rosie had been placed in my care by Mrs P——, I had at certain points discharged my duties in a way that might have seen lax or even improper by conventional standards. Thus I glossed over a great deal of what had transpired on the railway journey, in particular omitting the fact that Rosie and I had enjoyed a First Class Great Western fuck all the way from Chippenham to Swindon [see *The Oyster vol. 2*] and mentioning only, with approval, the efficiency and punctuality of the Railway Company.

Rosie for her part was reticent to the point of near silence concerning the events that had led to her summary expulsion from her Academy for Young Ladies in Somerset. Nonetheless the soup course passed pleasantly enough, although without any great incident. When this had been cleared away, a fine roast joint was brought in and placed before me to carve. (Mrs P—— was quite firm in her view that, as the only man present, I should undertake this traditional male chore).

As I rose, carving knife and fork in hand, and made the first incision in the mouthwatering piece of beef in front of me, I was suddenly grabbed from under the table round the ankle by what I judged to be a small but determined hand. Startled, I looked down but could see nothing since the table's edge and the overhanging table-cloth concealed all.

Saying nothing, but glancing rapidly round the table to confirm that all the family were indeed in their places and that both the maids Emily and Mary were visibly going about their duties, I manfully carried on carving while the unseen hand began to stroke and explore first my ankle and then the lower part of my calf.

With what I felt was a praiseworthy determination to abide by the standards of polite society, I managed to carry on with my task while at the same time continuing a light conversation as though nothing untoward was going on. Meanwhile of course my mind was racing. Was this some typically high-spirited lark by either or both of the daughters? Discreetly I looked about me. Both Hannah and Becky were already beginning to eat with their usual gusto. I could detect nothing evasive or furtive about their expressions, no sideways glances in my direction or suppressed giggles. Mrs P—— and Rosie were engrossed in an animated conversation on the merits, or lack of them, of life in the country. All was innocence and order except for the wandering hand under the table.

Then as I sat down, took up knife and fork and savoured a first delicious mouthful, the hand all at once moved lightly but speedily up my leg, along my thigh and reached into my lap. There it rested for a moment but before I had had time to do more than register and then hide my renewed surprise, it moved again.

Burrowing beneath my table napkin, it felt for, found and squeezed the till-then dormant length of my virile member. Mr Pego at once responded, quite against my wishes at that moment, and began to extend into life.

'Tell me, Andrew,' said Mrs P——, recalling my now wildly distracted attention with a jolt to the above-table world of propriety and social graces, 'Did Colonel and Mrs Moore have the opportunity to show you the sights of Bristol?'

Determined not to allow the increasingly strange turn of events get out of hand, so to speak, I swallowed and managed manfully to carry on a polite yet, I hoped, animated conversation. Mentioning my expedition to Clifton in the company of Rosie (but drawing a discreet veil over what had happened in the darkness of the *camera obscura* on the Downs [see *The Oyster vol. 2*] I expounded on the architectural and topographical merits of the city, gave my impression of the lively hustle and bustle in the streets that betokened its commercial vitality and embarked on what I pride myself was a not-uninteresting and well-informed dissertation on the Bristol origins of the phrase 'paying on the nail'.

Mrs P—— showed every sign of interest as I continued to inform her of the present state and past history of our premier south-western seaport. As she plied me with questions I was thankful that the good Dr White, my Headmaster at Nottsgrove Academy, had insisted that a working knowledge of Geography and the Commercial World should be instilled into his boys.

But behind my mask of calm, I was becoming more and more agitated. The hidden hand had now unbuttoned me, had reached in and exposed Mr Pego. A shrinking embarrassment at my predicament struggled with a swelling excitement as my prick was teased and stroked into life. Soon it was standing erect and throbbing. I leaned forward, seized by the disconcerting thought that the by now fat and dampening tip of my member might actually come poking up into sight above the table.

Desperately I carried on, trying to do justice to the meal before me and to keep my conversational end up. I was uncomfortably aware that the strain of appearing normal was causing me to clench my teeth at each new caress and I could feel beads of perspiration forming on my brow.

Deliberately drawing a deep breath and making a great effort to relax, I had just impaled and forked a large Brussels sprout, raising it towards my mouth, when the unseen hand struck or rather stroked again. Firm fingers wrapped themselves round the now near rigid shaft of my prick, forcing it down. There was a bumping and a boring between my thighs and the unseen hand was joined by an unseen mouth. Deliciously soft lips first kissed lightly and then opened to admit my pulsating cock. Inch by inch, I was sucked in while a probing tongue began to lick its way down the underside of my shaft and towards the very root of my straining manhood.

Convulsively I bit into the still steaming hot sprout, just as my invisible attachment nipped sharply at the open-eyed head of my engorged organ. I gasped as my teeth jarred painfully on the prongs of my fork and the soft inside of my mouth was scalded by boiling hot sprout. Again I gulped and tried to swallow my mouthful as at that very moment I became aware of the first rising spasm of my cum beginning to force its way up and along my distended shaft.

At once a slippery wet tongue was damped firmly down on the already weeping eye of my prick, bottling up the hot tidal gush of spunk that was now moving upwards.

For an instant I could feel a bursting pressure as my love juice was damned up. Just as a gardener will place his thumb over a watering hose in order to produce a more powerful jet, so my hidden succubus was engineering a veritable gusher of cum. Ecstasy and agony were mixed and I choked on my barely-chewed and burning Brussels sprout.

'Oh, dear', said Hannah. 'Something must have gone down the wrong way.'

With that she got to her feet and came round behind me to pat me on the back. As I coughed, my eyes watering and my throat on fire, I was unstoppered down below and a great geyser of cum shot uncontrollably, but safely, Thank God, into a now greedily welcoming mouth.

Hannah was now banging me heartily on the back as I doubled up, spluttering and drawing in great gulps of air while I was hungrily sucked and swallowed to an unforgettable climax. Shudders ran through my whole body. Mrs P—— looked at me with evident concern. Rosie and both maids all had the same idea and poured out glasses of water, pushing them or carrying them over to me. Wracked with pain and illicit pleasure, I waved my hands as though to say 'Just leave me alone. I'll be all right in a minute.' The last spasms of both my coming and my choking were coursing their way through my whole body. There was a momentary pause and I shuddered again as I felt at one and the same time the first blissful relief of being able once more to breathe freely along with the slow relaxing wave of sheer satisfaction at my relief down below.

As I mopped my brow, Hannah ran her fingers round the inside of my collar, helping me to breathe but also allowing herself the opportunity unobtrusively to rub her splendid titties against my back. My composure was rapidly being restored and I could feel myself being licked and tidied into quiescence. The last few drops of sticky cum were expertly sucked from the now withdrawing head of my prick. Fresh air helped to reduce my member back to more managable proportions and a more pliable condition. Hannah, with a last little squeeze to the nape of my neck, went back to her place. I was conscious of the very lightest of kisses to the very tip of Mr Pego before he was tucked away and I was made as decent down below as I was now composed above.

General conversation resumed although I now played a lesser part in the dinner table chit chat. I was tired, suddenly ravenous and had the best part of my roast beef, Yorkshire pudding and three vegetables still in front of me. As I ate I half-listened to Rosie who had now embarked on a description of the rigours of boarding-school life and a general denounciation of the educational system as it had affected her. I was left wondering Who? Who? I had looked down as unobtrusively as possible and had seen, nestling between my thighs, the top of a golden curled head as it lifted away from my still gaping flies but no recognition had dawned. Although the mystery presence had withdrawn, I knew that she was still there, hidden but close. I half-expected to feel her touch once more at any minute.

Tentatively I stretched out first one leg and then the other, feeling cautiously around me as best I could, hoping that I would be able to locate the golden-haired stranger. But nothing. Although all my other appetites were either well satisfied or well on the way, my curiosity was not just aroused but aflame.

Stretching a little too far under the table, I accidently half-nudged, half-kicked Becky who was sitting at my right. She at once responded in kind and then half-turned towards me, running her tongue lingeringly over her upper lip in an unmistakable gesture of promise. Just for a moment she fingered the upper button of her bodice and looked me straight in the eye before turning back to take her part in the great debate on education that Rosie seemed to have provoked.

The main course was succeeded by a tasty pudding. The maids went deftly about their business. Mrs P—— reminisced about Colonel Moore and the interesting times they had spent together in the Orient. The question as to who exactly was hidden under the dining table was of course unanswered. Coffee was served. Then Mrs P—— rose and excused herself.

'I have some reading to do,' she said. 'I will have to leave you young people to entertain one another.'

As the door closed behind her, I could contain my curiosity no more. Speedily I bent down to look under the table. But quick as I was, my anonymous explorer had been quicker still. As I peered underneath I saw the swish and flutter of the cloth at the far end of the table as an escape was made. Hastily I withdrew my head. Too quickly, as it turned out. I caught the top of my head a nasty crack on the polished mahogany, let out a sharp cry of pain and then set there in my chair, nursing my injured head in my hands while my eyes filled with tears once more.

Becky and Hannah were at my side in an instant.

'Oh, poor Andrew,' said Becky. 'What on earth is the matter with you this evening? First you choke on a vegetable and now you have banged your head.'

She pressed my damaged head to her delightful bosom. Then, running her fingers through my hair, she announced that a nasty little lump was raising itself on my forehead. Under the delicious pressure of her ministrations, I was aware that a rather larger lump was pushing against the tight cloth of my trousers.

'Becky', I said, my face still buried in her embrace, 'Something very odd happened earlier in the meal. I was about to carve the joint when I was approached from under the table...'

'How strange,' said Becky, 'But do go on.'

As I recounted the odd events, Hannah and Rosie gathered round me, concern growing on their faces.

'An hallucination,' said Hannah firmly. 'If it is possible to eat and talk and dream at the same time, then you have just managed it.'

'No!' I said. 'It really did happen. See, I was sitting forward, like so...' I recreated the scene, looking round the assembled company earnestly.

'When I felt a small hand, a feminine hand, reach out and grasp me by the ankle...'

160

At that moment a small, feminine hand really did reach out and grasp me by the ankle. I leaped to my feet in surprise. Three alarmed faces looked into mine.

'Not another hallucination?' said Hannah.

'I . . . I don't know,' I spluttered wildly. The unseen hand was now tugging peremptorily at my trousers. I sat down again with a bump. Hannah and Becky reached forward and seized me by the hands.

'Calm down Andrew,' said Becky, gripping me hard round the wrist. 'Rosie, pour him out a glass of water.'

Held as in twin vices as I was, I could not free myself. The unseen hand then reinserted itself into the seat of my passions, unbuttoned me all over again, released Mr Pego who sprang out once more. A soft, unseen mouth was clamped hungrily over the straining head of my prick and I felt a first greedy sucking.

'It's happening all over again,' I cried out, pulling at their hands to get free.

'What?' said Becky as she and Hannah resolutely resisted my struggles.

'There's someone under the table,' I said.

'Nonsense! You're imagining things. Now hold still and Rosie will massage the back of your neck,' said Becky.

'I am not,' I said while I strained to see downwards. 'I am being sucked off under the table by a complete stranger!'

'Such language!' said Becky. 'That is not a polite expression to use before three young ladies.'

'But it is true!' I yelled out despairingly.

The warm, loving mouth was now softly moving further and further up the distended length of my prick. Once again an eager tongue was licking delicately at the very tip of my member.

'Close your eyes,' said Becky. 'Take a deep breath. Rosie, sponge his forehead. Andrew is clearly suffering the most terrible pangs.'

Now I felt a gentle tickling as an unseen hand began to play lightly over my aching balls. I squeezed my eyes shut and wondered if I was going mad.

I must have groaned out loud for suddenly Hannah burst out laughing.

'We have teased him too much,' she said. All three released me and I rocked back on my chair, desperate to uncover what was going on.

There, nestling between my thighs was the same golden head that I had glimpsed earlier in the meal. Then, with one quick little nip, the mouth was withdrawn and the sweetest, most adorable little face was turned up to look me full in the eyes.

Starting backwards, I over-balanced on my chair. Flailing my arms I fell over. Rosie and Hannah jumped forward and just caught me before I measured my full length on the carpet. Pushing the chair upright, they allowed me to leap to my feet. Crouched before me a complete stranger. I barely had the time to register that this was a quite delectable creature, when she rose to her feet, smoothing down her dress and holding out her hand.

'Andrew,' said Becky, 'This is Gwendolen Bunbury. A cousin.'

'The Honourable Gwendolen Bunbury, to be precise,' said Hannah. 'Had you been looking out of the window at the right time on your journey from Bristol, you would have seen on the horizon the distant outline of her family seat in Berkshire.'

'Miss Bunbury,' I said, struggling to regain my composure but uncomfortably aware that the decorum of the occasion was marred by the fact that Mr Pego was sticking out of my trousers and was drawn up rigidly to attention and in full view.

'Mr Scott,' she replied, 'It is a great pleasure ...'

With that, she dropped a greatly exaggerated curtsy and once more took the tip of my member in her mouth.'

'Do you come from these parts?' she said, looking up at me.

By now Hannah, Becky and Rosie were all in uncontrollable fits of laughter. Tears were flowing down their cheeks and they were holding on to each other, almost helpless in their mirth.

'This is your Welcome Home present,' said Hannah. 'Gwendolen is in Town after a long sojourn in the country and Becky and I thought that the two of you should meet. You in turn are Gwendolen's Welcome to London present.'

'But presents,' said Rosie, 'That I hope we can all share in.'

'It was Hannah's idea in fact,' said Becky. 'She thought that it would relieve the possible tedium of the dinner-table conversation. You are inclined, Andrew, to hold forth somewhat and we guessed that we might be subjected to a dissertation on the history and economy of Bristol. Poor Mama did very well in plying you with the right questions. You should have seen your face when Gwendolen started her ministrations on you. You went all flushed and for a moment I thought you were quite going to lose the thread of your argument.'

'This has all been very unfair,' I said.

'Do you not like having your cock licked into action by a young lady?' she said.

'Especially one as pretty as Gwendolen here.'

'Of course I do,' I expostulated. 'But not while I'm eating roast beef and three vegetables. And trying to carry on a normal conversation.'

'Think of poor Gwendolen,' answered Becky. 'At least you got something to eat. She must be positively starved.'

'I did in fact have a little to eat,' said Gwendolen. She licked her lips. 'And very satisfying it was.' She grasped my prick firmly in her hand. 'But I confess I am still a little hungry.'

'Very nicely said,' replied Becky. 'But we have saved some food for you. Andrew is not the only one who must keep his strength up!

She rang and Emily the maid came in.

'Emily, can you fetch something for my cousin to eat,' she said.

Emily bobbed a curtsy but then clapped her hand to her mouth. She went very pink and I realised that my member was still exposed.

'I'm sorry,' I said. 'I had quite forgotten...'

'Which, I suspect, is more than Emily has,' said Becky. 'We all here have the clearest, fondest memories of him. But for the moment, I suggest you put him away or you might catch a cold.'

'Here, let me,' said Hannah, as I began to fumble with my fly. 'You're all fingers and thumbs.'

'I am a little flustered, I must confess,' I said with relief as she busied herself. Soon all was proper again and as Gwendolen ate, the others explained in greater detail all the connections between them. Rosie could remember her very well at school although Gwendolen had been as she explained, 'One of the big girls.'

'How I envied you,' she said. 'You and Cecily . . . Cecily . . .'

'Cardew,' said Gwendolen. 'My dearest friend in the whole school.'

'All the younger girls had such a crush on the two of you. We used to loiter, quite against school rules, in the corridors, hoping that you would notice us.'

'You *were* noticed, Rosie,' said Gwendolen. 'And I am very, very happy to see you again. But I understand that you have recently left Miss Bradshaw's under something of a cloud. and rumour has it that there was an incident involving the Art Master.'

So the whole story of Rosie's sudden departure came out. When she got to the point where she was revealing her new interest in photography, I saw Becky and Hannah exchange meaningful glances. By now I knew them well enough to realise that an idea had crossed both their minds and that they would soon be hatching another of their plots.

'A group photograph,' said Becky after a moment's thought. 'Since you have a whole trunk full of photographic equipment up in your room, we must get everything cleared away just as soon as Gwendolen has finished eating.'

'What about the exposure,' I chipped in, rather cleverly I considered.

'Your jokes get worse and worse,' said Hannah. 'But you do have a point. Rosie have you the technical knowledge to do justice to your subject? We want two group studies. One with and one without.'

'One with and one without what?' I asked.

'With clothes and without clothes.' she answered. 'One that can be openly displayed and sent round to all our relatives. And one that will be kept private, restricted only to those of us here. And maybe sent privately to one or two carefully picked friends.'

'I have a better idea,' said Becky. 'It will take some time for Rosie to set up her equipment. I shall send an urgent message by cab to Catherine, asking her to come round immediately if she can. She might even be able to find the Scottish contingent.'

'Ian and Donald,' I said. 'It would be splendid if they could join in the fun. And I had the most warm, loving note from

Kate on my return this afternoon.' [See *The Oyster vol.2*]

So it was decided. A note was written and despatched. Rosie summoned me to help her unpack. Gwendolen volunteered to come with us. She squeezed my arm affectionately as we went upstairs.

'I hope you are not angry with me,' she said. 'I hope that when the photography is finished we can get down to the serious business of fucking. I have seen enough of you to know that I should like that very much.'

How could I refuse such an enticing offer? I hugged her to me.

'I'd like that very much as well,' I answered.

Rosie, who was a step or two ahead of us, turned.

'What about me?' she said sweetly. 'Can I join in?'

'Of course, Rosie dear,' said Gwendolen. 'This will be quite an old school reunion.'

That first photographic adventure was unlike anything that I had previously experienced. I had before been into a studio on two or three occasions. Formal portraits of my family had been taken. I had featured, two or three rows back, in a school photograph. I was accustomed to the slow deliberate proceedings as the photographer ordered his subjects, arranged his backgrounds, then buried his head under a black cloth. I knew how to pose motionless, staring at the camera. But to sit or stand, leaning on a classically styled pillar was one thing. To hold oneself immobile with one's virile member poking unmoving at the tender entrance to a generously spread cunney is a different matter.

Rosie was a paragon of brisk efficiency. As we helped her place the camera on its tripod, as she squinted though the viewing window, ordering us to close up or rearrange our groupings, she gave us a short explanation of the technicalities and the history of the craft.

We started with one or two more ordinary exposures, fully clothed. Catherine and the Fergusons brothers had not yet arrived although we had received a message that all three would present later on. Meanwhile Rosie was getting a little bored with the unrelieved decency of the proceedings.

'Andrew,' she said all of a sudden, 'I would like you to sit between Hannah and Becky. Gwendolen, would you sit on the carpet at their feet.' She looked carefully at us. 'Not very interesting. I have an idea. Andrew, would you take off all your clothes!'

'Just me?' I said.

'Just you for the moment,' she replied.

'This seems somewhat unfair,' I said.

'Hannah, Becky!' she called. 'Andrew is beng stuffy about this. I think you should help him out of his things.'

Before I could protest any further, hands were reaching out. Gwendolen had untied my shoelaces and slipped my shoes and then socks off my feet while jacket, waistcoat, shirt and vest were peeled and pulled off me. Rosie stepped forward and appropriated to herself the job of removing my trousers. As Mr Pego was all at once exposed to public view, I was suddenly somewhat bashful. I crossed my hands in front of him.

Gwendolen reached up from the floor and gently placed her hands on mine.

'Don't deny us the finest sight of the evening,' she said as she slowly pulled my wrists apart. Just as she did so, I felt a finger from behind. Whether it was Becky or Hannah I could not tell. As the cheeks of my bottom were parted, the finger was slipped gently but firmly into my back passage. With a jump, Mr Pego shot upright. Gwendolen and Rosie both gave a little cheer.

'Quick, sit down!' ordered Rosie. The rest of you, get into position.'

Hannah sat to my right. Becky to my left. Gwendolen arranged herself cross-legged at my feet.

'Gwendolen! He's beginning to flag,' said Rosie.

Gwendolen turned and stuck out her tongue, letting it play on the tip of my cock. It responded immediately. Then she traced out the line of the blue vein along the top until her hand came to rest at its root. She gave a short squeeze.

'That's it,' said Rosie. 'Cup your hand under his balls. Now, keep very still everyone.'

There was a flash of burning powder. The light seemed to fill the room. I heard the shutter click. Everyone held their breath while Gwendolen held my throbbing prick.

'Wonderful,' said Rosie. 'Now I want everything reversed.

166

Andrew, back into your clothes. Girls, off with yours'!'

Grumbling, I struggled back into my clothes. Mr Pego was by now most unwilling to lie down again and as I tried to force him back inside my trousers, the other three began to undress. At this Mr Pego became even more unwilling to bend to my will. Meanwhile before my enthralled eyes first Hannah's and then Becky's luscious titties were bared. Next their lovely rounded bottoms were revealed. Lastly I saw with rising excitement their dark and densely furred pussies. By now I was getting quite distressed with my unrelieved need to slip my prick into one of those welcoming quims.

'Andrew,' said Becky, 'I have a slight tickle. Here,' she said, taking my hand and placing it on her bush.

I felt its warmth and then the sudden yielding of her cunt lips as that first slick of wetness lubricated my finger.

'Just a little rub,' she said. 'And a little more.' She sighed.

'Not yet' said Rosie like some school ma'am. 'That comes later!'

Gwendolen, who had once again closed her hand gently over the engorged length of my cock, paused.

'What about you, Rosie dear?' she said. 'I am certain it would put us all more at ease if you were to appear in the same state of Nature.'

Hannah at once went across to help her before she could demur. Gwendolen had in the meantime handed me over to Hannah while she also began to divest herself of all her clothing.

Quivering, my hand still engaged with Becky's quim, I saw the full golden beauty of Gwendolen brought to light. What a mouth-watering contrast was there. The dark swelling mounds of Becky's and Hannah's pussies were contrasted with the fair silky down of Gwendolen's. Rosie's girlish, brown-haired beauty that I had examined so memorably on the train to Paddington was bared in turn. I was surrounded by the most welcoming but varied array of cunneys that any man could imagine even in his wildest dreams.

But Rosie was a hard taskmaster. I was forced back into my clothes and made to sit upright between the now naked Hannah and Becky. Looking down at Gwendolen I could see

167

past the golden curls of her hair to her quite outstanding titties and then down again to the half-hidden promise of her pubic treasure.

Rosie, naked also, retired behind her camera. 'Smile', she said. We all smiled except I suspect my smile was more like a grimace as I held myself desperately in check, aware of the warmth rising from the eager bodies that surrounded me.

Then, just as Rosie bent to her camera, there was a soft knock at the door and Emily slipped in. She paused at the unusual display that met her startled eyes, then pulling herself together said 'Miss Catherine Ferguson and her Cousins have called.'

At once there was a bustle of activity. Hannah and Becky rose to meet their guests. Rosie, a little uncertain of herself now that strangers were arriving, contrived to hide most of herself behind her photographic equipment. Gwendolen stayed exactly where she was, cross-legged on the floor.

Catherine, elegant as ever, swept into the room, closely followed by Ian and Donald. With a social poise that I could only admire, she did not hesitate in her stride but embraced first the naked Hannah and then Becky warmly. Without blinking an eyelid, she then turned and gravely offered me her hand.

'I am happy to see you again so soon, Andrew,' she said. 'I hope you got my note.'

'Indeed yes,' I replied. 'It was waiting for me on my return from the West Country.'

Ian and Donald has been less successful at concealing their amazement at being so ushered into a room full of the most delicious bevy of undressed feminine beauty. They stopped dead in their tracks. They gulped in unison. Their eyes quite started from their heads. Then as Becky and Hannah went across to embrace them also, broad grins broke out on their faces. As each was hugged to a naked bosom, I saw both Becky and Hannah, as if each could read the other's thoughts, reach out a discreet hand and reach under their kilts. Both were drawn forward.

'Gwendolen, Rosie. May I introduce you to three very dear friends. Miss Catherine Ferguson and Mr Ian and Mr Donald Ferguson.'

Rosie, shyly came forward. Gwendolen rose with a lithe

grace from her seated position. Ian and Donald gasped at this sudden vision of golden haired loveliness.

'I am delighted to ... to ...' stammered Donald.

'To be at my service?' asked Gwendolen with a tantalising smile.

'Yes ... Yes ... To be ...' stuttered Donald.

'I hope you can both recover your composure sufficiently to join in the fucking that is about to take place,' said Becky. 'But first, Rosie here is going to take all our photographs. Oh,' she went on, 'How rude of me. Rosie, there is no need to hide yourself away like that. I hope that you are going to take a full part in the events of the evening.'

Rosie allowed herself to be led forward and introduced.

'I hope that before long all our parts will be full,' said Hannah. 'I can see already that your Highland Things are showing a considerable interest in what is spread before them.'

I realised that mine was not the only cock that was bursting with life and a straining desire to find its way into one or more of the inviting treasure caves that surrounded us.

Ian and Donald rapidly tore off their kilts, sporrans and bonnets. As their erect pricks sprang into general view, Becky took one in each hand.

'The staff of life,' she said. 'Two staffs to be accurate.'

Rosie laughed, quite put at her ease by Becky's merry conceit. Catherine clung to me and whispered in my ear.'

'Let us be different,' she said. 'For a few moments let us remain fully dressed. At least until the photography is over. Then, Andrew, I want you to undress me. Slowly. I want to savour for a moment or two longer the thought that your prick will soon be sliding deep into me.'

Now it was my turn to gulp and try to keep myself under control. I tried manfully to think of anything other than the welcoming hunger of the cunt that I knew awaited me under that cool exterior.

'A slow fuck. A little time taken. That is what I need. But a very thorough fuck. A whole evening of fucking. Under all this clothing, she went on, I am already quite moist with expectation.'

I looked round the room. Gwendolen, very sweetly, was stroking Rosie and reassuring her.

'You're trembling a little,' she said.

'Oh, Gwendolen,' Rosie replied. 'I am indeed. This is very forward of me. When one is fresh from the schoolroom, it is so exciting to see not one but three such lovely big Things displayed before one.'

Gwendolen took Rosie's hand and placed it on her own blonde haired pussey. Then she drew a delicate finger along the cleft of Rosie's brown haired cunney.

'See,' she said, 'We are both the same. Both wet with the thought of what is to come.'

Rosie kissed her gratefully.

'How nice you are,' she said. 'I know that I am going to enjoy this.'

Suddenly there was an abrupt shriek of delight. I looked round. Two of our party had not been able to wait until the photography was over. Becky was bent forward while behind her Ian had sunk his shaft right up to the hilt in her generously displayed cunt.

'That's it,' she cried out. 'I want it right in. I want to feel all of it right up inside me. I need to be fucked fast. Now.'

Ian needed no urging. Spreading her legs even wider open with his thumbs, he plunged again, and again into her. She staggered under the impact of his mighty thrusting but still cried out for more. Ian rose manfully to the occasion, driving her on and on until she was beside herself with ecstacy. Surely Becky and her sister must be unrivalled in their sheer prick-hunger!

Hannah meanwhile was standing before Donald, squeezing and offering her magnificent breasts to him. Naked but for his argyle socks and sturdy brogues, he gasped in amazement.

As he bent to suck hungrily at her dark, swollen nipples, she clutched him by the cheeks of his bum and commenced to rub herself against him. Rosie, for her part, was now staring unashamedly at the activity. As she stood there, Gwendolen had crouched down before her and I saw her tongue bury itself deep in Rosie's young quim. Rosie began to tremble quite uncontrollably, instinctively opening herself up to Gwendolen's mouth.

Becky's first coming was upon her. She was kneeling down on all fours, her bum raised, perspiration covering the flush that was spreading over her whole body. God knows what

Gaelic oaths were being forced from Ian as she cried out and great shudders of desire shook her. Then her cries reached a crescendo of pleasure and the first fuck of the evening reached its climax.

But now Catherine regained my attention. With an insistent hand on my prick, she led me over to a corner of the room.

Enough of this watching,' she said. 'The time has come for us to begin that slow fuck that I need.'

Another memorable evening in Mrs P——' establishment was well under way.

[To be continued]

A Letter to the Editor of The Oyster from Lady Louise Kitely-Brown

15th June, 1891

Sir,

I am sure your esteemed readers will be fascinated to know of a most interesting and enjoyable experiment in which I took part last week with my good friends Doctor Jonathan Arkley and the Honourable Noreen Ravenswhite.

Both Noreen and I are twenty one years of age and though not entirely unschooled in *l'art de faire l'amour* we are neither of us as sophisticated in such matters as the good doctor who is of course somewhat older and who is known to you and many members of Society as one of the great fuckers of our times.

We had dined at Jonathan's house and fired by the warmth of the glorious summer evening and the fine champagne we had quaffed in abundance, it was perhaps not entirely surprising that we found ourselves in Jonathan's large bed. We were all quite naked and enjoying a delicious threeway kiss; pressing our lips together and wriggling our tongues around in each other's mouths.

Jonathan then turned to me and said: 'Louise, my dear, I have the strongest fancy to see you kiss Noreen's pussey. Would you humour me and go down upon her. Noreen will have no objection, will you my sweet?'

'Far from it,' laughed the pretty girl, 'I do so enjoy having my cunt sucked off that I don't care who does it. Indeed, in my experience, girls know how to tickle my clitty far more effectively than boys!'

I was more than willing to oblige especially after Noreen's agreement. It felt a little strange at first as although I had been in bed with other girls before, we had never made love together in the presence of a man. But I did enjoy the thought of making

173

love to this cheeky young girl who lay in her proud naked glory at my side. She was certainly a beauty with large snowy bosoms, well separated, each looking a little away from the other, each perfectly proportioned and tapering in perfect curves until they came to two rosebud points. Her belly, smooth, broad and dimpled in the centre with a sweet little button, was like a perfect plain of whiteness which appeared the more dazzling from the thick growth of dark black hair which curled in rich locks in the triangle between her legs.

Jonathan quickly pressed my head down onto Noreen's gloriously large breasts and the lovely girl sighed with delight as I moved my tongue from one bubbie to the other, twirling my tongue around her erect little red nipples.

At first she lay passively but then with a cry she put her arms round me, holding her soft body to me as I continued my nibbling and sucking of her titties which were by now like little red stalks as I teased and suckled them up to new heights. Now I let my tongue travel the length of her velvety body, lingering briefly at her belly button before sliding down to her thighs. Her skin was so soft and smelled so clean that this was a real pleasure and I felt my own motte beginning to dampen.

The gorgeous girl whimpered as I pulled her long white legs apart and nuzzled my full lips around her curly dark bush. My own hands clamped around her firm bum cheeks as my tongue flashed unerringly around the damp pubic hair and her pussey seemed to open wide as she lifted her bottom which enabled me to slip my tongue through the pink lips, licking between the groves of her clitty in long thrusting strokes. With a groan of ecstacy, I lost myself in her delicious cunt, licking and lapping the sweet juices of her honey pot.

'Ah, that is heavenly!' she gasped. 'More! More! Oh, Louise my darling, you are making me spend!' My tongue was now revelling in her sopping muff, out of which her clitty was now protruding between the pouting lips. I took her clitty in my mouth, rolling my tongue all round it as Noreen quivered all over and began jerking her body all over the bed. It was hard for me to keep my tongue on her clitty as her legs tightened around my head. Then she arched her back and with a second all over shudder she screamed: 'Oh! Oh! Oh! There, there, suck my juices, Louise, oh, that's just divine!' I worked my tongue until my jaw ached sucking up her love juice as the lovely girl again heaved violently and managed to achieve a tremendous orgasm.

Noreen sank back exhausted but my blood was up and I was delighted to see that our little tribadistic encounter had excited Jonathan whose sinewy, stiff cock was now rock-hard. He frigged himself up to a gigantic erection but I had no intention of letting him waste his spunk by himself. I moved his hands away and took this monster cock in my own hands, peeling back the foreskin and running my tongue in the sensitive groove under the red, mushroom knob.

Jonathan groaned with pleasure as I leaned forward and took the dome shaped helmet between my lips, jamming down his foreskin and lashing my tongue around the rigid shaft. Then I sucked hard, taking at least half his shaft into my mouth until I could take no more. I sucked firmly, sliding my lips up and down the rock-hard shaft, gulping noisily as the head of his grand prick slid along the roof of my mouth to the back of my throat.

His cock was now throbbing furiously and I knew that soon he would be spending. I continued to gobble the pulsating tool as the rogue cupped my breasts in his hands, deftly flicking my titties with his fingernails. I began to give him sharp little licks on his swollen rod followed by a series of quick kisses up and down the stem, encompassing his hairy balls, thrusting his cock in and out of my mouth with a quickening rhythm, deep into my throat and then out again with my pink little tongue licking at the tip at the end of each stroke, lapping up the drops of creamy white fluid that were beginning to ooze out of the tiny eye at the top of his knob.

As soon as I felt he was on the verge of spending, I made ready to swallow his love juice. Jonathan thrust upwards and his cock shuddered violently between my lips and then in one long spasm he emptied his balls, first a few early shoots and then woosh! My mouth was filled with juicy, foam as his cock gushed almost uncontrollably as I held it lightly between my teeth. I let the sweet juices run down my throat as I washed his now spongy knob with my tongue and then, very gradually, I allowed the wet shaft to slide free.

Now it was Jonathan's turn to sink back gracefully next to

Noreen — but still here was I, instigator of their bliss still unsatisfied myself! This was quite unfair and I had no hestitation in telling them so!

'We are well rebuked,' cried Noreen, 'and you certainly deserve a beautiful fuck, Louise. Now, how shall it be, by cock or by tongue? The choice is yours.'

'Perhaps by both,' I replied gaily, 'although I would not want either of my dear friends to think me greedy.'

My two dear friends insisted that I deserved the fullest attention. Jonathan disengaged himself and stood by the side of the bed, allowing me to admire his magnificent nakedness, his wide chest, his flat belly and his enormous cock that stood up so excitingly from its thickest of pubic hair. Yet how could I neglect the sweet Noreen who lay stretched out besides me, her hands jiggling her firm, uptilted breasts in such an exciting fashion?

I lay down beside her and leaning over, kissed her upright little nipples, flicking them up to a fine state of erection as I lay on top of her. Gently, the dear girl caressed my buttocks and pushed me onto my back as she now took over as mistress of the revels.

I spread my legs as Noreen bent down in front of me and began kissing my pussey. Instinctively, I opened my legs to make my wet, swollen cunney lips more accessible and Noreen paused for a moment to savour the musky aroma before quickly kissing my pink pussey lips which were aching to be opened by her questing tongue. Lovingly, she began to eat me, forcing her tongue deep into my juicy love-channel, sliding up and down my crack until I screamed with pleasure as she found my engorged clitty. I tried hard to keep still so that Noreen could suck my clitty but she had a difficulty staying with me as I rubbed myself off to a delicious spend against her mouth.

Now it was my turn to take a more positive role so we changed positions. Now it was Noreen flat on her back with her head still clamped between my legs, eagerly lapping up my cunt-juice as I returned the compliment, placing my knees either side of her beautiful breasts and leaning forward to nuzzle my own head between her legs. This left me sitting on Noreen's face which enabled her to continue pushing her pretty face deep into my crotch, kissing and sucking until I could feel the moisture fairly dripping down the inside of my thighs. Naughty, but nice!

Doctor Jonathan was so taken by this action that he positioned himself behind me and after anointing his huge tool with pomade positioned his cock between my bum cheeks. I raised my backside in the air, opening my legs slightly so that he could guide the tip of his cock into my bum-hole. At first I felt some discomfort as his cock penetrated my bum-hole but then it felt quite delicious as he started pumping into me with swinging thrusts and my arse arched up and down to receive his delicious rod. We rolled about happily, the three of us, we two girls sucking each other's cunts and Jonathan fucking my bottom so stylishly. I could feel his build-up coming as his big balls slapped against the back of my legs. As his climax juddered to boiling-point, I felt the throb of liquid fire rage inside me with every throb of that divine cock as his creamy froth spurted inside me just as my saturated clitty sent jets of spend into Noreen's wet mouth.

We continued our threesome for some time aftcrwards. Noreen and I sucked off our mutual man. We both nibbled and licked at his stiff, pulsating cock but I could not contain myself with an hors d'oevres so I brought his mushroomed knob to my salivating lips and tongued the dome, tasting his salty juices. I then grabbed his shaft with both hands and hungrily stuffed it into my mouth as far as I could. He pumped further and further down my throat until I felt that he was again ready to spend and whilst I have no objection whatsover to swallowing spunk, I had a fancy for Jonathan to fuck my cunney.

I pulled his prick from out of my mouth but it was now too late. The juices were oozing from out of the tip which I lapped up instantly and then the first creamy jet of sperm came hurtling out of his prick. The first jet hit me on the right cheek but I hastily sucked on the jerking shaft, enabling me to gobble up as best I could the jets of frothy white spunk. As his spurting knob rested on my tongue, I swallowed quickly to keep pace with him. Then, as his spend passed its peak, I took his whole cock back into my mouth and sucked for all I was worth to extract the very last drops of love-juice from his twitching prick.

We lay silent for a spell and I declare that we would have

been happy to stay together all night but Noreen and I could not afford the chance of being discovered with the good doctor in the morning so reluctantly, we decided to take our farewells at about half past midnight.

Before we left, however, Johnny made us all some coffee and Noreen brought up a most interesting matter into the conversation which I feel is well worth relating here.

'My good friend Caroline Seale has a problem, Jonathan,' said Noreen, 'I think you have met her at one of Sir Andrew Stuck's parties. She is a very pretty girl and not averse to a little nookie.'

'You are being too kind,' I murmured somewhat unkindly, 'It is well known around Chelsea that she fucks like the proverbial rattlesnake as our American cousins are wont to say.'

'A curious analogy,' mused Jonathan, 'for as far as I know, the rattlesnake has a somewhat quiet sexual life.'

'Never mind all that,' said Noreen with some impatience, 'The simple fact of the matter is that she is conducting a discreet little affair with Sir Andrew whilst his other *amorata*, Mrs John Paterson-Thyme, is out of town.

'Her problem is that Sir Andrew enjoys oral sexual activity and Caroline is unschooled in the art. Furthermore, despite his urgent pressing of the matter, she has confided in me that she relay does not want to learn the art of *fellatio*. Surprising though it may sound to either of you, she recoils at the idea of taking a cock in her mouth. Yet she longs to please him and make him happy but the thought of pleasing him in this way is to her, well, horrid. So we have an impasse, Jonathan. What do you suggest? Or indeed, Louise, perhaps you have an answer to this dreadful situation.'

'A lot of her problem is probably based on ignorance,' said Jonathan, stroking his chin.

'You would be surprised how many girls are kept unaware of the pleasures of sucking a thick prick or having their pussies licked out – or if such ideas are even obliquely mentioned, they wuld be banished by friends in whom they have confided. Why, one girl who came to me with a not dissimilar problem even thought such activity was illegal!

'My own opinion is, as you know, that when two people love

178

each other, almost nothing they do in private should be considered wrong or harmful. As my old friend Mrs Patrick Campbell has said: "All I ask is that they do not do it in the street and frighten the horses."

'But any activity that for whatever reason is repugnant to one partner could become physically or psychologically harmful and no-one should be pressured to perform bedroom antics that make them feel uneasy.

'Yes, I do remember Caroline who seemed like a very nice girl to me. I am sure that she longs to give Andrew sexual bliss but if she just cannot bring herself to suck his prick then alas, both must simply find more compatible sexual partners. There's no magic cure, I'm afraid, Noreen, though you might like to tell Caroline that she should at least try her hand, or rather her tongue I should say, for I believe you should try everything once!'

'She will take your advice, I think,' said Noreen, 'for I know how much she values your opinion. Meanwhile, let me pay you a medical fee in kind!'

She kneeled down in front of Jonathan and opened his robe, taking his shaft in her hands. His hands pressed down upon her head as if he wanted to force her head into his crotch but he didn't need to do so as she was more than willing. She licked the pubic hair that encompassed his stiffening cock and heavy balls and then she began to move her face slowly, enjoying to the full the sensation of feeling his cock hard and erect against her soft cheek. Now Noreen made strands of her hair and made a web round the shaft, stroking it slowly, feeling it throb and grow even harder as she touched him.

Noreen moved her head across the red helmet of the handsome young doctor's knob and kissed the top which was already oozing·drops of moisture. Then her tongue encircled his knob, savouring the juices as she drew him in between her rich, generous lips, sucking lustily as Jonathan instinctively began to push forwards and backwards as her warm hands played with his hairy, hanging balls.

She sucked happily away at her lollipop and Jonathan bucked wildly as his huge cock slurped in and out of her hungry mouth. He gasped: 'I'm spending, I'm spending, I cannot hold it!' and Noreen began to swallow in anticipation. She was proved to be right as Jonathan sent spurts of white frothy cum crashing into her throat. She sucked and nibbled greedily, milking his trembling cock of every last drop of love-juice.

'Ah, Jonathan, I do enjoy sucking a nice thick cock like yours,' Noreen said with a smile. 'Caroline may not enjoy it but I could happily suck your cock for hours. It never lasts that long of course and like all you men you squirt off in just a few minutes.'

'I've heard it said that General Aspis, the Belgian Chargé d'Affaires can keep going for half an hour,' I interrupted.

'That's probably just a rumour,' said Noreen. 'Anyhow, I just adore sucking and swallowing for nothing tastes so clean and fine. And there is the additional benefit of knowing that I can enjoy myself without getting in the family way!'

'So very true,' added Doctor Jonathan, 'but I hope you and Louise realise that whatever tricks you get up to in bed, the essential core of enjoyment lies in choosing an understanding and tender partner.'

With these wise words ringing in ours ears, we went home. Although Noreen was staying the rest of the night with me, we were back well after the time we had promised my Uncle Stanley. Fortunately, he had gone to sleep and Baigue the butler was not averse at telling the occasional white lie to my Uncle for the not unreasonable price of half a sovereign so Noreen and I went unpunished for our escapade. Hastening to our beds, completely worn out by our interesting little sexual experiments, we fell into a delicious sleep from which it was almost eleven o'clock before we awoke.

A final thought, Sir, before I end this letter; all animals copulate but only the human species is capable of extending a physical need into an act of love. This ability to combine sex with passion sets us aside from other animals though it is surely an unfortunate fact that far too few people recognise and develop this unique talent with which we are all blessed.

I am, Sir,
Your obedient servant,

Louise Kitely-Brown
Allum House
26 Piccadilly
London, W.

180

Preface

This final extract from The Oyster dates from July 1894 – not long after the Prince of Wales was involved in a somewhat sordid affair at a country house weekend where one of the guests was accused of cheating at cards. The Prince's involvement (and his threatened exposure as an adulterer in a separate juicy piece of scandal) did little to enhance his reputation.

We now know that in all probability the novelette (serialised in the magazine throughout 1894) was written by Phillipa Lintern, the wife of a wealthy London printer whose factory churned out the popular 'French postcards' during the 1880s and 1890s.

The narrator of the yarn is 'Estelle Bicklah', a young music hall artiste whose current amour is an aristocratic Army Officer, Captain Woode who takes her to a weekend shoot on the Scottish Moors. Most of the action is confined to the mansion and to her delight, Estelle learns that one of the guests at the party is the Prince of Wales.

Taylor Cuthbertson
Falkirk
December, 1988

I well recall the evening that I was first fucked by the Prince of Wales. I was chatting with my old friend Captain Marcus Woode about the events of the previous night when Lord Montmorency bustled up.

'Come on, you two,' he cried, looking anxiously at his watch. 'I've been looking everywhere for you! The Prince will be here very shortly, and we must be ready to welcome him. Everyone else is assembled in the Great Hall.'

Relieved that I was beginning to feel a little more like myself again, I did as I was bade. Shortly afterwards, almost exactly on the stroke of twelve, I found myself in the exalted presence of Royalty for the first time in my life.

To say that I was honoured would be an understatement. I, whose own life not so very long ago had been such a very quiet one, was almost overwhelmed by the occasion! As I curtseyed before His Royal Highness – Lady Montmorency had given us instruction on the correct mode of behaviour in the Prince's company – I felt faint with nervous trembling. But Lizzie – who as the daughter of a Lord is much more familiar with the high and mighty than I am – said afterwards that I was splendid, and acted impeccably, and that at the luncheon which almost immediately followed the presentation the Prince had asked his hostess to tell him more about me, as he was particularly struck even on so short an acquaintance by my beauty, and courtesy, and pleasant disposition, so much so that I blushed quite hotly and told her that she must be making it all up, for who would be so bold as to say such things about a little orphan-girl such as myself. But it was all true, she insisted most forcefully.

We decided among ourselves that for the duration of the Prince's stay there must be no repetition of the wild debauchery which had so far been the way of things at Montmorency Castle. At all times we were in danger of discovery – a fact which nonetheless added a certain spice to proceedings – but were word to be let out that such goings-on had taken place in the presence of Royalty, then our disgrace would be swift and final. Marcus would be certain to be stripped of his command, and reduced to the ranks. Thirkettle would lose the title he confidently expected would be his in the next Honours list; the Count and Countess of Courtstrete would very probably be forced to quit Society forever, and go and live abroad; while Lizzie and her parents – though they themselves were entirely innocent of any blame – would never live down the opprobrium that would be heaped on their heads, and the ruin of the name of one of the greatest families in the land.   That afternoon the gentlemen accompanied the Prince to the butts which had been specially prepared for the Royal party, while we busied ourselves in innocent pleasures at the castle. Marcus told me at table that evening that the Prince was a capital fellow; an excellent shot, to be sure, and the owner of as fine a pair of guns as any he had ever set eyes on either in military or civilian life, but also a most companionable fellow – very ready to hand round his hip-flask, incidentally, and a fund of good stories. Now that the ice had been broken I was able to talk to him with a little less stiffness and nervousness than before, and found as we spoke for a few minutes by the fire in the Great Hall that evening that he had a ready wit and good ear for what other people had to say to him – an attribute which, I am sorry to say, is not always to be found among those whom fortune has chosen to elevate to life's higher stations. Though of scarcely more than middle height, he was quite a handsome man in my book, with lively eyes and an easy smile.

'And you are looking forward to the ball tomorrow evening, Miss Bicklah?' he asked me.

'Oh, yes indeed, your Highness. It is the social highlight of the week, and I am sure everyone is greatly honoured by your presence here.'

'You are too kind, dear girl. I do enjoy dancing a great deal, I must confess. Perhaps you would do me the honour of allowing me to mark your dance-card when it is available? They say I am the devil at the *mazurka*.'

My heart almost stopped beating.

'Why, I would be honoured, your Highness,' I managed to stammer at length.

'Good! Then it is fixed then – we will dance the *mazurka* together. Montmorency has engaged the services of the finest musicians in all of Scotland for the evening. I suggested he do so, because after a fortnight at Balmoral one might possibly have heard the "Gay Gordons" once too often. Strictly between you and I, the sound of pipes is guaranteed to set my teeth on edge. Had Montmorency had nothing but pipers and fiddlers on hand I think I might well have made my excuses and left for London as soon as my train could be made available.'

Even on so trivial a matter, I was sincerely flattered to be taken into the Prince's confidence. I was even more delighted that I should have taken the liberty, once I knew that there would a grand ball at the end of my stay in Scotland, of having a spectacular ruffled gown in black *crêpe de chine* run up for me by Lizzie's superb dressmaker, Madamoiselle Thérèse, and to have the not inconsiderable fees for her work charged to Lizzie's own account. Worn with my very finest jewellery, I was sure that this was precisely the right outfit in which to make an impression on the Prince. What a pity that he would not be able to see the divine set of undergarments which Madamoiselle Thérèse had made up specially to go with the dress. Though white has for so long been popular, these were exclusively in black, a fantasia of silk and lace that, when I first tried the garments on and saw my reflection in the glass, seemed the very epitome of womanly loveliness. Ah well, I reflected, if the Prince would not see them I was sure Tom or Marcus or whoever would be delighted to help me out of them when the time came.

On my best behaviour, though not without a certain longing, I retired to bed a tad before eleven that evening. Truth to tell, my head still rang a little from the night before, and I was glad of an uninterrupted night's sleep. My pussey, too, had felt a little sore and inflamed – especially as a result of the double stretching I had received when spitted on the Count's prick and enculed in rear by Tom. A night's abstinence would enable my body to make a full recovery, ready for the adventure of the morrow.

By all accounts, the shooting went extremely well in the morning. The Prince was sure there were more birds than he had ever seen before on the Montmorency estate, and certainly none plumper. Lord Montmorency's careful husbandry had obviously had the desired effect.

Before the sun was too high in the sky – Tom Feather told me that the deep shadows cast by the noonday sun were to be abhorred by every photographer, since out of doors they quite obscured the features when a hat was worn – a splendid series of photographs was taken, first of the Prince in the company of his Lordship and some of the more distinguished guests in the party, then of all the guns grouped together, with the morning's 'bag' before them, and finally of the entire party, ladies included, lined up on the great terrace outside the library.

After that, it being such a fine day, with nary a cloud in the sky, a wonderful luncheon was enjoyed at tables set out on the lawns of Montmorency Castle. I spent the afternoon with Lizzie and Miriam – we were all on first-name terms now – and we discussed the latest fashions, and the season's taste in hats, and the best new plays in London, and all the little tittle-tattle which makes intercourse between ladies so delightful.

With so many birds there for the asking, the Prince was keen to be out with guns and dogs again in the afternoon, a wish with which the gentlemen readily concurred. A high-tea in the traditional Scottish style was taken at five by those who wished to avail themselves of it – a buffet supper was to be served at the ball – and what a delightful repast it turned out to be. The species of kippered fish known, I believe, as an 'Arbroath smokie' was perfection in itself, as were the quail's eggs and the almost limitless range of cakes and other delicacies with which we were tempted. As for myself, I am afraid, I succumbed all too readily, and it was only the fear that I might so fill my stomach that I would be unable to squeeze into my new black ball gown that stopped me making an utter pig of myself.

By seven I was in my bath and by eight, freshly talcumed and scented, with my hair already dressed, I was stepping into my new black undergarments for the first time.

'My goodness me, Estelle, you look a picture,' exclaimed Lizzie, who was sitting on the edge of the bed in her underthings. 'I think, if I were a man, I would ask you to keep them on while I made love to you. I'm sure I never saw a lady attired in such a provocative way.'

'You can thank your Madamoiselle Thérèse for that,' I replied, flattered by her kind words. 'And perhaps I will keep

185

them on, at least for a little while.'

'It does seem to delight the gentlemen so, does it not? Harry insists that I keep my stockings and garters on when we are in bed together, and I am always happy to oblige.'

At half-past eight we all stood in line as the Prince, with Lady Montmorency on his arm, led the way into the ballroom. The band struck up the anthem, and then Lord Montmorency made a brief speech. Then, at last, the great event was under way.

My first partner, for the waltz, was Marcus, who looked most dashing in his full dress uniform. Then, for the polka, it was the turn of Tom Feather. Next came General Yardley of the clacking teeth and after that Lord Montmorency himself twirled me around the floor for a turn or two, during which I was quite convinced that his hand was deliberately placed a good deal lower on my back than is normal for a dancing partner, especially as he contrived to squeeze my bum a few times as we glided along. But he is a dear old boy nevertheless, and as generous a host as one could ever hope to be entertained by.

A vigorous fox-trot followed, in which I was partnered by the Count. So energetically did he dance, that I was quite glad to regain my seat afterwards, and to refresh myself with a water-ice from the buffet. The Count sat beside me, and applauded the musicians loudly as they played a selection of popular overtures.

'Montmorency must certainly have some influence in musical circles,' he whispered in my ear, 'for some of the Empire's finest musicians are in this ballroom tonight. See, there is Goulthorpe, the oboe player, and Cripps, playing the fiddle, and is that not the great Mr Webb himself performing on the piccolo? How strange it is, that man with so huge a physique should be able to coax such marvellous sounds from so tiny an instrument. I am sure that at times he must almost lose it in that great beard of his, and yet they say that he has no peer in Europe.'

I drank some more champagne, and listened to the band, and began to feel most delightfully happy. The convivial atmosphere evidently communicated itself to everyone in the room, for even when Marcus – who is not, I am sorry to say, the most graceful of dancers – had the misfortune to propel me directly into the path of the Prince and the Countess of Courtstrete, the Prince was most insistent that it was himself who was at fault, and that he had two left feet to be sure – even though I knew him to be as elegant on the dance-floor as is a swallow in flight – and that he hoped Marcus and I would forgive him for his appalling clumsiness.

'It is the *mazurka* soon, is it not, Miss Bicklah?' he said as we waited for the beat. 'I have not forgotten your promise.'

Round and round we went, and then there was champagne, and more dancing, and I am sure I never knew so delightful an evening. By the by I stepped out on to the terrace – it had become quite warm inside the ballroom, and I was glad to feel the cooling air on my face. I stood there breathing in great draughts of God's sweet wine when the Count came up to me once more.

'How absolutely ravishing you look tonight, my dear. I am sure I never saw you looking quite so beautiful.'

'You flatter me, Count. I was only going to say how gorgeous the Countess looks herself. She and the Prince made a fine picture as they danced the polka together.'

'They are old friends, Estelle, and have known each other many years. Once, in fact, before we were married, they were closer friends still, if you see my meaning. But what I wish to say to you now is this' – and he dropped his voice a little.

'Although we have already agreed that there should be an embargo on our amatory exploits for the duration of the Prince's visit, his Highness has discreetly suggested that, were a select group of us to desire to carry on after the ball is over in a little private entertainment of our own, he might even be favourably disposed towards joining us. Would you care to be among our private party?'

A voluptuous thrill of excitement coursed through me like burning brandy.

'Of course I would,' I breathed. 'It would be an honour indeed.'

'Good. Then I will no doubt speak to you later.'

Just then the waltz came to an end, and I realised it was time for me to dance the *mazurka* with the Prince. I dashed back inside, and found him waiting for me by the dais.

'Miss Bicklah!' he cried, his arms extended wide in greeting. 'Or may I call you Estelle now?' he murmured as we took the floor (I had not the nerve to address him by *his* Christian name!)

The band immediately struck up the tune in triple time, and we were away! Oh! how we danced! The Prince was everything I had dreamed of as a partner, leading me this way and that, holding me with a light but firm grip, until I felt myself to be mere butter in his hands. On and on the tune went, and my happiness knew no bounds. The other guests stood back to admire us as we swept by, and I even heard a smattering of applause as we executed a particularly intricate turn with perfect grace.

'You dance divinely,' I found myself murmuring in his ear, and then momentarily rebuked myself for what might seem excessive familiarity.

But he seemed entirely nonplussed, and held me closer, and whispered compliments so delightfully unexpected that my whole heart melted. As I abandoned myself to his arms I could clearly feel his prick pressed firmly against me, in a manner that suggested the gesture was hardly accidental. As we rejoined our friends when the music was finally over, I had already accepted his invitation to join his private party later.

The rest of the ball passed in a flurry of delightful anticipation. What kind of entertainment could be in store? I was almost beside myself with expectation, but when the Prince partnered me again for the *schottische* he gave no further hint.

A little after midnight a select group assembled in the Prince's private chambers: the Prince, the Count and Countess, the Thirkettles, Miranda Welsh, Lizzie, Marcus, Tom Feather and myself. I had not previously visited these rooms before; they were, so Lizzie told me, reserved for the exclusive use of Lord Montmorency's most exalted guests. In luxury and elegance they far outstripped any accommodations I had ever seen before: beneath twinkling chandeliers of pure crystal the walls were hung with the finest paintings, and the floors were draped with exotic rugs of Oriental manufacture.

Champagne quickly loosened our tongues and made us forget any inhibitions we may have had concerning our situation. Nevertheless, I was more than a little taken aback when I saw the Prince and the Countess disappear into the royal bedchamber together.

'I see your wife and the Prince seem to enjoy each other's company,' I observed to the Count.

'Of course they do! He's fucked her with my blessing countless times. At the very least, it puts me in good favour with the Palace.'

'Don't you mind, Count? Are you not taking your loyalty to the Crown a little too far.'

The Count laughed.

'Not a bit of it!' he exclaimed. 'Why should I mind? A woman like Miriam needs a spot of excitement to keep her in trim. Besides, the Prince knows a thing or two about satisfying a woman. He's probably got his prick in her already – he's not one to mess around – and a fine one it is too, as Miriam never ceases to tell me. Perhaps he will consent to let me watch them fuck one day.'

'Why do you think we're all here?' I asked in all innocence.

'Because the Prince likes his pick of the pretty ladies, my dear. Goodness me! That was quick! Here's Miriam now.'

Visibly purring like a contented cat, the Countess emerged from the royal bedchamber and rejoined her husband. The Prince emerged shortly afterwards.

'Ladies and gentlemen!' he called, clapping his hands together. 'As my old friends will know, a visit to Montmorency Castle is never complete without our rounding off the evening with a small, intimate gathering such as this. This year I am delighted to say that we have a novel entertainment. Mr Tom Feather, whose acquaintance I am delighted to have made during the course of my brief stay at the castle, has some splendid lantern-slides to show us which I am sure we will all enjoy enormously. If you would make yourselves comfortable, Mr Feather will let us see some choice examples of his art.'

The room was dimmed, and the beam of a lantern speared the darkness. An evening of lantern-slides? How unusual, I thought. However, my curiosity soon turned to amazement when the first slide was projected on to the wall. There was the glen by the castle, and there was I, as naked as the day I was born, with my bosom and cunney shamelessly exposed to the camera. The darkness hid my blushes, but I need not have feared for my modesty for it was followed by an image of Lizzie and Miriam licking the Count's cock.

'Capital! Capital!' cried the Prince, who was evidently delighted with what he saw. Miriam, I noticed, was sitting on his lap, with her hand inside his shirt.

Next, Tom showed a sequence of pictures showing Marcus and Effie fucking, of which I had seen prints earlier in the day.

'Is that your girl, Woode?' called the Prince. 'She's a fine one, isn't she? She's a goer, all right, I'll wager! Does she enjoy a cock in her pussey?'

'She certainly does, Your Majesty,' replied Marcus, sounding slightly embarrassed.

'Don't bother with that "Your Majesty" business here, old boy! That's just for public consumption. We're all chums here, aren't we, what? My goodness, look at the size of those titties.'

I now knew what kind of an evening we were in for. The Count took my hand and placed it on his cock, and I played with it through his trousers as we watched the sequence of slides. When the lights came up at the end, the Prince and the Countess were to be seen kissing passionately, without any inhibition.

This seemed to act as encouragement to the rest of us. Soon the air was filled with soft sighs. Angelica Thirkettle quickly undressed both Marcus and herself and in a trice they were fucking with gusto on the floor in front of us. Lizzie and Angelica's husband were similarly engaged elsewhere, while Miranda Welsh showed her gratitude to Tom by kneeling down in front of him and lustily sucking his sinewy cock in tribute to his talents.

Not wanting to be left out, I arose up and divested myself of my ball-gown. Immediately all eyes were drawn to me as I stood there in my black underthings, which had been so lovingly crafted by Madame Thérèse that they seemed to accentuate rather than hide my womanly attributes. In a trice the Count and Tom, both naked, were at my side, and I could feel their stiff pricks pressed against me through the black silk and lace of my chemise.

The Prince, too, paused in what he was doing – licking Miriam's cunt, by the look of things – to admire me in a way that I found particularly gratifying. Fixing him with a soft and wanton stare, I slowly divested myself of my finery until I stood there naked but for my black stockings and a wasp-waisted corset of similar hue.

'Here, Estelle!' called Marcus. 'Come and sit on my prick.'

He was laid down on the floor, quite naked, with his member standing up proudly as though in salute to our guest of honour. I squatted over him and made him lick my cunt while I took his prick in my mouth. Then, changing positions, I was just on the verge of impaling myself on his cock when a lewd idea struck me.

'Put it up my bum, Marcus,' I whispered. It was not easy, with Marcus lying flat, but eventually the insertion was achieved. Marcus's great prick filled my rear passage most delightfully but I was still not satisfied.

Tom and Miranda were next to us and I took hold of Tom's prick while Miranda leaned over me and licked my titties, her delightful pink-tipped nipples brushing against me as she did so. I found that by stretching slightly I could also frig Mr Thirkettle at the same time – three pricks at once, but still my apetite for *recherché* eroticisms was not satisfied!

While Lizzie, Miriam and Angelica amused themselves with the former's splendid ivory-shafted dildo I bade the Count straddle over me and I licked his balls and his prick stem until he was driven almost insane with desire. I could see that the Prince was watching me intently as I took the Count's cock deep into my mouth and sucked hard on its purple tip.

'My God!' cried the Prince, unable to contain his lust any longer. Tearing at his clothes and throwing them heedlessly down about him, I was at last rewarded by the sight of a member of the highest family in the land – nay, even in the world! – as naked as the day he was born. Miriam was certainly right about the royal cock: it was among the biggest I had ever seen, so long and thick that I wondered if I could take it up me even if I did not already have Marcus's splendid prick in my arse!

I parted my stocking-clad legs as wide as I could before the Prince. In a flash he was upon me, and that great royal tool was at last within me. With the light of pure lust in my eyes I frigged two cocks and sucked on a third, but my senses were all attuned to what was in my cunt. How the Prince pumped into me, and how the walls of my pussey seemed to part to allow him entry! In a delirium of lust I sucked even harder on the Count's prick, and pressed my bum wantonly against Marcus as he fucked me from beneath.

The air was filled with bawdy oaths and cries of lust and longing, and I sensed that my spending was upon me. And even as I came, again and again, in a great tidal wave of pleasure I could feel the Prince's spunk shoot into me, and Marcus come boiling forth into my bum, and two more jets of spunk shoot out on to my tits even as the Count's prick seemed to shudder and convulse and deluge my mouth with spendings, which I greedily sucked down until I felt I would choke with happiness.

And afterwards, when the others had retired to their separate bedchambers, the Prince and I spent the whole night together, and enjoyed every conceivable kind of eroticism, many of them so novel to me that when I awoke in the morning it seemed they were but a dream were it not for the photograph which was placed by the bedside.

It had been taken by Lizzie – to whom Tom had entrusted the alchemical secrets of his the photographer's art – and the two of them had evidently been up half the night with their bottles of solution to have it ready for the Prince when he departed in the morning. In full and graphic detail, it showed the remarkable climax to our evening's enjoyment – all the more noteworthy, since Lizzie seemed to have captured the exact moment when all six of us – the Prince, the Count, Tom, Marcus, Thirkettle and myself – spent simultaneously in a crescendo of passion. I placed the print in its gilded frame back on the table by my bedside in the royal chamber. And as I lay back on pillows of the purest goose-feather my hand stole down under the bedclothes towards the still-sleeping royal phallus, which would shortly receive as delightfully rude an awakening as any it had hitherto enjoyed ...

[To be continued]